DAUGHTER OF TIME
TRILOGY

DAUGHTER OF TIME TRILOGY

10th Anniversary Rewrite

Reader, Writer, Maker

EREC STEBBINS

This book is a work of fiction. Any references to historical events, real people, or real locales are used fictitiously. Other names, characters, places, and incidents are the product of the author's imagination, and any resemblance to actual events or locales or persons, living or dead, is entirely coincidental.

To SG

Contents

It has now been ten years since the original publication of my *Daughter of Time* trilogy. Of all my writings, this series is the most important to me in nearly every aspect of a novel that might matter: plot, ideas, themes, characters, and writing. Unlike my thrillers, which were written strongly to match what I understood of the expectations of the genre, I had allowed myself a lot more creative license with *Reader*, *Writer*, and *Maker* (especially *Maker*).

In this edition, I have undertaken a rewrite based on approaches I developed with my thrillers over the years. This approach tightens text considerably, and would often trim 10% of a book's words without altering a scene. Producing text that was leaner and more driving seemed to fit the thriller genre's expectations, but I was hesitant to apply it to the *Daughter of Time* series as I felt I might lose some of that wilder creativity by taking this editing machete to the project.

In the end, I created a hybrid method where I went through the many procedural steps in "trimming the fat" I'd used previously, but in the process of rewriting also allowed myself to let my imagination run more freely. I was able to remove twenty-five thousand words from the series (10%) and even add an additional chapter.

I hope readers enjoy this new edition, whether encountering the story for the first time or returning to it after many years for a fresh perspective.

Erec Stebbins

December, 2025

Reader

Daughter of Time, Book 1

Time is the fire in which we burn.
—Delmore Schwartz

Prologue

Who sees the future? I am conscious of being only an individual strug-
gling weakly against the stream of time.

Ludwig Boltzmann

Demons defiled my dream at dusk.

Misted light saturated the afternoon. A breeze caressed the grass of our backyard and sprinkled the strong smells of the plowed earth. Squinting into the sun's glare, I skipped across the lawn to the edge of our cornfields. My short legs stumbled, my fingers stretched toward a tall shadow in the brilliance before me. I was five years old.

The sun shimmered as my father's frame refracted its radiance, and the shadow shifted to his familiar form. I leapt into his outstretched arms, squealing. His soiled hands gripped and swung me, his auburn hair dancing. I giggled as I stared into his gray eyes.

He tossed me skyward. The ground receded, half grass-green, half rich red from the overturned soil. The cyan surrounded me in a strange stasis as my upward momentum eased. Gravity grasped my stomach and yanked me back to Earth and his arms, a thrill of adrenaline like fire in my limbs. Several times he launched me, and I went farther and laughed harder each time. Higher and higher I soared. The blue turned black surrounding a sphere painted with continents and seas. Bright stars lanced through a thinning atmosphere.

For a moment, I floated, thrown so high I flirted with the field of force tethering me to our motherworld. The stars tugged, beckoning, luring me with a frosted intensity. My naive senses recoiled. Giddiness sharpened to anxiety. Something was wrong. Something unclean stalked the diamond-pricked blackness. Something searching... *for me*.

Earth reasserted her will. Air rushed and howled in my ears. I darted through clouds and frothing air currents. To the edge of my vision, a patchwork of squares and rectangles replaced the colorful sphere. These expanded and resolved into the familiar patterns of my family's farm. Twirling downward, I watched my father from above, waiting with arms overhead and hands held high. Was I going too fast, falling without aid from the edges of space? Could he possibly slow my momentum, catch me before I plunged like some fiery meteor into the dirt?

But he did. With an embrace, he cradled me in his arms, extra momentum diverted into a dizzying rotation. I spun in circles with bubbling giggles. He wound to a stop and set me on the ground, my head a wreck and woozy, my legs wobbly.

He beamed down at me, tousled my hair, and chuckled. "The sky is yours, Ambra Dawn. The world won't hold you."

He filled his phrases with love, yet they clotted in my heart, an ominous echo of what was to come. Mirroring my deep fears, his face clouded. He focused behind me, rising from a stoop and scowling toward our house. My eyes followed him upward, and I turned to track his gaze.

My mother planted her feet outside the back door that exited our kitchen. Her strawberry hair produced a waterfall in the wind. She stood still. *Terribly still*. Her face was stone-frozen, anxiety and fear etched in every line. She raised one arm at ninety degrees to her body, an arrow indicating the front of the house. She pointed, unmoving, a directional sign demanding obedience.

My awareness rushed forward, braking beside her face. For one sharp breath, I paused. I followed her arm from the bright light of the day into the dim house, and out again by the front door to the falling dusk.

Three black cars with tinted windows thrust headlight beams in my face. A troop of hulking men in suits spewed from them with hateful faces. My child's body morphed to a preteen of eleven years while they brushed me aside. The shadows herded my parents into the house. I trailed behind, ignored and unwanted. A poisonous foreboding sickened me as I stumbled inside. The men's dark clothes chilled like the emptiness of space encountered moments before.

Moments? Or was it years? *Separations of time. The way of dreams.* For me, the way of life.

They invaded our kitchen. The smaller men engaged my parents. The larger ones stalked like suspicious soldiers about the house and out by their cars.

My mother's words shivered with anxiety, shrill notes in her Irish brogue scraping the stillness of the room. "I don't understand. We don't know who you are. We can't just be handin' her over to you!"

"Mrs. Dawn," rasped the smallest man. The voice raised bumps on my skin. "We are a singular governmental division. We develop unique technologies for the military. One of these is a special laser. Army doctors have shown it kills cancer cells. We can promise a full cure, without major side effects. No one else can. But this is top-secret technology. We cannot share this with you or anyone else—not even your doctors. Her treatment must remain secret."

He took off his dark glasses, his face angled toward my parents and away from me. "A doctor in the Omaha unit is a friend of mine. He was direct with me—she won't live past next year with current treatments. We are your last hope."

Tears dotted my mother's cheeks.

My father set his jaw. "Now, you look here," he growled. "You've got no cause to be speaking like that and upsetting my wife. This is all irregular. Government or not, it ain't my way to trust shadows. If what you're saying's true, we'll work with you. But we got to know more."

"But, Frank, you *heard* him," my mom began.

"Never you mind what he said. I don't like this talk. This is our Ambra." He glared at the man. "She's our world."

I dropped the wooden toy. A hand-carved mini-globe with the continents embossed on the surface. It struck the hard floor with a crack and rolled out of the kitchen to the living room. My heart constricted. *The Earth. I didn't want to lose it!*

The small man across from my mother turned.

I screamed.

I couldn't help it. At eleven, it was overwhelming. That demon face—I had seen it before. *In other dreams.* Dreams churning inside dreams.

His face was a splinter of a forgotten vision. It rushed back through me like nails in my veins. Flashes of future memories whipped my mind—pain, fear, loneliness, and horror. Each shard a facet of the mask worn by this fiend from hell, grinning back at me.

I ran. I jumped from my seat and dashed like I'd never in my life. Behind me, the voices of my parents faded. Instead, the harsh barks of his soldiers blasted like gunshots.

"Get her!"

Horrible screams. *My parents?* I couldn't stop running. A predator pursued unseen in the void behind. Its breath stank. Its fangs glinted, nearing, gaining ground. Claws extended to grapple my back and legs.

I sprinted and my chest pounded, ready to burst. I raced over the manicured green of our backyard and into the thick forest of corn. The stalks slapped my face, arms, and across my neck. I wheezed like some dying thing.

Where was I going? I didn't know. *Away.* I had to get away.

"On the other side of the cornfields!" something shouted in my mind.

Safety! Through the fields, to the road, find a car, someone to help, protect me from pursuing monsters. *Please.* I was close! My panting whistled like a windstorm.

A bright light flashed. A sharp pain. On my back, I gasped for air. A dark shape towered and eclipsed the moon. Warm liquid spurted from my nose as I choked. A mountain pressed me to the earth.

The figure loomed, shrouding all light. In the shadow of his body, I saw that demon face again, smirking downward, mocking me with laughter.

"We've hunted you a long time, little girl. Don't think you can escape. Don't ever *dream* you can escape from us."

I couldn't speak. Fear, pain, and nausea dragged me like a lodestone. The world spun and shrank to a speck as darkness seeped inward. In a moment, all was black.

The same dream. Experienced countless nights. The past reincarnated. Aching scars reopened. My deepest grief, relived.

But this time, the *darkness* faltered.

In that absolute black, I heard voices. *Your* voices. Millions of them. A tsunami rising, a chorus calling across the ever-changing fabric of time. And in a drowsing state, moments before waking, when inspiration meets the practicality of day, my eyes *opened*.

The answer crystallized within my mind.

Part I

A child's life is like a piece of paper
on which every person leaves a mark.

Chinese proverb

To those of us who believe in physics, this separation between past, present, and future is only an illusion, if a stubborn one.

Albert Einstein

Nothing is as it seems or as it might be.

Stay with me for a while, hear my story, and you'll understand. Understand your sweeping ignorance—of yourself, your loved ones, our enslaved world. Your naive ideas of truth. Maybe then, you'll come to terms with how critical you are to what might someday become.

On the cover of this book, you're reading an author's name. He believes this story is full of his ideas, born from his own mind. It's not. *I* am writing it *through* him. In his delusion, it's all part of a clever plot he's stitched together, down to this very sentence saying he *isn't* writing it. Instead, it is the effort of my mind reaching out, back through what you call time. I inspire him, shape his thoughts, convince him of this reality.

Sound crazy? It is. I know it is. And *I'm* the one doing it. But it is also *true*. A terrible truth that will grow and grow with my words until it all but overwhelms.

I don't enjoy this, playing puppet master with this citizen of your time. But our need is hopelessly desperate. We have lost more than you can imagine. Nothing remains but ashes in the cold of space.

I've done worse. This is dangerous, both for his mind and my own. Already, I have failed many times to send my message. Wayward efforts wrecked the receiving minds, driving them to madness. At other times, what has come out of the author is a story so warped by his own imaginings that my message is garbled. Your libraries hold some of these disasters. I pray this, my last effort, will not fail.

You must understand so much before you can accept the message. Strange things. Horrible things. Things that can't possibly be true but are. Understanding, you can find the faith to take the final step.

You will need to break free from your shallow and misguided conceptions of time. This may be the greatest stumbling block. Isolated, time is a crushing monolith. A glacier pressing forward with a godlike, unstoppable force, flattening history. Time freezes the past. It is untouchable and unchangeable. And what will happen, the future, is imprisoned by the now.

Can you hear the universe laughing at such childish ideas?

The first dogma to release is that time is alone. *Space* and time go together, feed off one another, in grand loops and dances, changing both. I know this, I *live* this, because this unceasing dance performs in my mind's eye like a rainbow in the mist.

You must surrender the distortion that the past is set and the future immaterial. *Spacetime* is an ever-existing clay trapped inside the great bubble we call the cosmos. Like clay, it can be shaped, changing past, present, and future. Always with rules. But not yet with rules any creature has come to fully understand.

These are empty abstractions, colorless phrases teaching little and distorting much of the living experience. I hope you will understand more as you hear my story.

It is because of these truths I can reach you now, and only because of them that I need to. You see, as much as the future can reach back into the past, the *past* can reach *forward* into the future. And in our time of need, we need you of our recent past. You have a part to play in righting a terrible wrong, saving billions of lives, and reversing humanity's horrific fate. Somehow in these pages, I must convince you of this. May I be forgiven if I can't.

My parents called me Ambra Dawn, and I am a Reader. And while I tell you my story, it is not mine alone. It belongs to all of us.

Chapter 2

*It seemed that our family had been on this land for thousands of
years; that we had sprung from the earth, born of its flesh like a tree or
a flower, deep-rooted, not by our feet, but by our hearts.*

Thea Halo, *Not Even My Name*

I was born beside the yellow-green cornfields of Nebraska.

My father was one of the last independent farmers in the
Midwest. The great agribusiness corporations of the twenty-
first century had eaten most. He was tall and lanky, in his mid-forties
when I lost him. Of Scottish heritage, his fair skin reddened but
refused to tan in the long summer seasons. He had crisp gray eyes and
large hands that held me like a small ear of corn. And, just like the
dream, he loved to toss me into the air, laughing with a thousand
lines creasing his face.

Remembering him now, I see he was beautiful.

Unstudied and little learned, he had a real gift for predicting the
weather. A more accurate forecaster than the best meteorological

models, which saved more than one harvest. It was a stark sign of the terrible genetics that would combine to produce me.

My mother was also beautiful. From a Celtic background too—an Irishwoman new to the United States. She *found* my father more than she met him, a destiny she orchestrated. You'd find her a stereotype out of a book of fables—a classic lady of the Green Isle. Pale and redheaded, fiery in spirit and with her tongue.

The recessive genes just keep adding up.

More than my father, she *forecast*, but beyond weather and into many areas of life. In the Dark Ages, fire and a stake might have been her fate for witchcraft. But my mother was a devout Catholic. Her abilities were all too natural. They sprang from a soft spot of unusual tissue and blood vessels buried deep within her brain. An odd but harmless clump of cells dismissed by medical science as an insignificant cyst. Pain would teach me the truth about these matters soon enough.

Two years after they married, I was born.

I got my mother's red hair and green eyes. Both parents' skin mixed in me to the palest white possible outside albinism. The real kicker? A combination of genes producing a tumor in my brain in the same place as my mother's small psychic cyst. We'll get back to that soon, because without the tumor, none of what I am going to tell you would have happened.

In the beginning, I was just a normal farm girl. Well, maybe *normal* isn't the right word. I was *definitely* a farm girl, though. With my first steps, I was playing with the animals, rolling in hay, and happiest with the earth under my bare feet.

How cruel is the irony when I think back on what has happened to me. What I would give now to see the sky again. To feel the earth underneath, or to run the plowed soil through my hands. To believe it was still there, that it existed *somewhere*. That would be enough, more than I would ask for after this terrible journey.

But normal, no. I can't say I was ever normal. Normal means

perceiving and reacting to life like most people. Resembling their behavior. Being treated in a like manner. One after the other, I lost all these things.

First to go was seeing things like others. A perpendicular perspective always colored my experience. My mother noticed. She knew something was different about me, eyeing me like an artifact from another world. She loved me, don't misunderstand. But she recognized an *otherness* about me that even a mother's love couldn't comprehend. Her own sixth sense would not be denied.

In a way, that was good. I didn't worry about surprising her or letting her down. I don't think my dad understood, not even when they came to "cure" me. Which was good in its way, since his love never had to get through any walls and always reached me.

But the first time I realized I was a freak was when my dog died.

As a child, I experienced many wild and strange dreams. After I described a few to friends and my parents, I learned by their reactions to leave them inside my own head. Crucified unicorns. Cables crawling out of my eyes. Monsters with blades cutting into my arms and legs and skull. Drowning in an infinite avalanche of ghosts—that kind of thing. But I had learned the difference between reality and dream. Or so I thought.

One night, I dreamed our sheepdog died. He dashed in a thunderstorm, barking at the deep subsonic throb driving some dogs crazy. In a flash of lightning, he seized and fell over. In the dream, I could see through him to the clot in his heart, and I watched a glow dim in his brain. I woke shaking and chilled but said nothing to anyone. Another nightmare to lock away and forget.

When distant relatives visited, my dad would always drone about the weather. Then he'd tell the Flat Joke. "Well, it's very flat out here this time of year."

Nebraska is *really* flat. The storms approach for hours. Three weeks after my dream, a tempest marched from the west. A horizon-spanning wave of gray mountains pushed across the plains. I shook, not because I'm afraid of storms, but because I was afraid of *this* storm. Because I'd seen it before.

The sun darkened. The rain poured like electrified syrup. I froze as a horror film replayed my dog barking, running, and falling over dead in the grass. This time, I couldn't see through him. But I knew. I knew what was inside.

And I knew I was a freak.

When your perception of reality diverges from that of others, you become divergent. I had eyes no one else did. They experienced visions in time. Not intuitions, not a vague sense of doom or excitement—*revelations*. They began in dreams but soon trespassed into the waking day.

In my childhood, visions of the future were a minority. For a Reader, it's a lot easier to see into the past. More and more, both kinds of visions intruded into my awareness. They disturbed my days and nights, walling me away from society. When you have seen your own birth, watched your mother scream in agony as she pushed you into the world like some deformed lump of lasagna, it changes you. When you can't tell anyone these things, this private prison warps your consciousness. You form your own thoughts. *Different* thoughts. Thoughts imprinting your psyche through unique molds.

And that is when you lose the ability to think in a normal manner.

By the time I was ten, I was one odd little girl. I couldn't relate to the kids at school or to any adults. Not with the endless parade of premonitions. Not with the divergent perspectives they brought. They were phantoms, always shadowing me. Playing reels behind my eyes, movies only I could watch. Boring. Interesting. Dreadful. Events I knew were real, or I feared would be real someday.

I became ostracized by my peers. My teachers couldn't reach me. My parents were distraught. They needed to fix me.

And so, the evaluations began. Meetings with social workers. Examinations by psychologists. Doctors. And, at last, the neurologists. Brain scans.

Finally, something concrete, something physiologically wrong with me that they could lean on. Something to explain all the weirdness and problems.

And something that brought me to the attention of those dark forces really controlling the fate of our world.

Chapter 3

Behind the ostensible government sits enthroned an invisible government owing no allegiance and acknowledging no responsibility to the people.

Theodore Roosevelt

If I could give you any one piece of advice to help you in your time, I would say turn off your TV and internet. Throw your phone into a river. *Never* look at it again. Take your video game console and controllers—build a bonfire. Don't go online again.

I'm completely serious. What I know and what you don't, is that all our digital technology was not the product of our tremendous cleverness. No, it was a gift, *from above*. Or rather, a drug, a poison—electromagnetic narcotics for controlling clueless human herds. To *Them*, you're all just a gene pool with potential. Tech keeps you docile and reproducing in ignorance. Meanwhile, the greatest show on Earth called *human culture* plays out. One giant sham.

Some of you recognize it—you with still slumbering Reader gifts. It throbs deep in your bones. Some of you outcasts, on the streets or in the mountains or institutions. You knew all along much more of the truth than our comfortable and successful swarms. You've tasted that sharp sense of betrayal, the jagged lie plunged into your psyche. The gasping certainty swimming in your thoughts that things *don't fit*.

Well, they don't. I'll explain more as we go. Meanwhile, grab a book, go stare at the stars. *Think*. You're a junkie, strapped into a pleasure tube—a pig ready for the slaughter, or worse. Don't let them control your mind one more day.

Advice from a former slave. Take it or leave it.

My journey of bondage was about to begin. The brain scans defied wishful thinking. At eleven years old, I understood. Beyond the medial reports, I had my half-glimpsed dreams.

At first, Reading the future can be like that. It's more *remembering the future* than seeing it. Have you woken from a dream, details bleeding from your mind, staring dumbfounded at the remaining, colorless outlines? That's a vision of a time to come.

Most of them, anyway. Sometimes, like a horrid nightmare, the experience will overwhelm you. And like a nightmare, these *prophecies* will break your stable state of consciousness. Prescience provides a psychic slap to the brain, branding the details into your awareness. But those were rare in my early years. Mostly, I experienced half-remembered fragments I could never reconstruct.

The visions of my own future were foggy. I struggled to retain the murky memories of my coming illness, of the soon-to-be nurtured tumor in my head. The doctors were amazed I could still see.

The mass was the size of a golf ball—quaint to me now. It grew in the back of my brain between what the neurologists call the occipital and parietal lobes. These are big slabs of flesh doing different things. The occipital lobe, at the *back* of your head, processes visual information from your eyes (which are at the *front* of your head— God works in mysterious ways, believe me). The parietal lobe does a lot of things, like sensing where you are, navigating, working with numbers, moving objects.

The tumor was expanding towards the occipital lobe like some elliptical missile, crashing into all those cells processing information from my eyes. The doctors couldn't understand why I wasn't blind already. My parents looked sick listening to all of this. I was half-scared, half-remembering some blurry future where all this awful stuff wasn't nearly the worst that was going to happen to me.

"It appears to be a fast-growing tumor," one doctor said. "Many children's tumors grow quickly, the cells dividing like the rest of the growing body, but worse. This is very serious, and very difficult to cure. We recommend you send her to specialists. We can't treat her here."

So began the quest for oncologists across the country. Nebraska has great medical facilities in Omaha, but they referred me to Memorial Sloan Kettering Cancer Center. My parents were on the phone for hours with doctors and relatives in New York. We'd all see enough medical offices to last a lifetime. And week by week, the brain scans showed the thing inside my head kept getting bigger. We prepared for a long trip to the East Coast.

Then one day, just like the dream, without any kind of warning, three black cars with tinted windows arrived at our farm. Out of these black beetles rushed the men of the nightmare I relive over and over again. They barged into our home. They tried to convince my parents to release me into their "care." And when my parents would not, they took me by force.

When I woke from the blackness, I was dragged from the car by one of the burly men in a suit. He threw me over his shoulder, grunting as he carted me towards a long, metallic, one-story building. In my foggy state of mind, it seemed so unimportant, so featureless and unreal. But it would be my prison for many years to come.

A place from which, as the man had promised, I would not escape.

Chapter 4

Madam, I have come from a country where people are hanged if they talk.

Leonhard Euler

Trapped in their prison, before they sold me into slavery, I grasped in my heart I would never escape. Beyond freedom, I entertained no hope of living long. The things they did to me, the agony of each hour, convinced me I had gone to hell. Or hell on Earth, and my time here would be the final years of torture leading to my death.

I possessed none of the critical knowledge I would later piece together. Their purposes lacked meaning. The damage they inflicted was random and obscene. Pure torment without any goal except to tear down my person, to shred all faith from the soul of a young child.

Unconscious on the ground in the cornfields my dad had planted himself—that was my last day in Nebraska. That dark evening was my final glimpse of my parents. I never returned. Now, returning is impossible.

I didn't know what had happened to my mother and father. You might assume ignorance of their fate would have been a curse. It is also a curse to know the exact fate of those you love when that fate is evil. The past is not hidden from me. It wasn't a year before I experienced a vision of their murder, the cruelty of the men who visited my house, how they disposed of their bodies without respect.

I'll spare you details. But I wasn't spared. I suspected the truth, but the endless visions denied me the grace to hope or doubt. By the time I was twelve, I knew I was alone and in the hands of monsters.

My eyesight had started to go, but I was way beyond expecting my captors to care. As you'll see, it was quite the opposite; they wanted me blind. And they always got what they wanted.

During my first year, as my vision faded, I was introduced to my new "home." My new way of life. I learned for the first time how to live in constant fear. When I displeased them, they beat or starved me for the slightest infraction of their regulations. Again and again, they inflicted strategic suffering, until they bent and broke me into the shape they required.

I became a giant exposed nerve, terrified of their cruel police sticks and electric wires. The farm girl was unmade. Her former threads were stitched into that of a caged creature, responsive to their commands. A well-trained animal.

Their rules were both simple and strange. There were the practical, if harsh, rules about living. Where to stand and sleep and eat. How to behave, how to answer questions and obey.

Speak out of turn to another child and the stick might smash. Out of your bed in the middle of the night? Because you needed to stretch, or pee, or think, or something? The cameras would record it. The next day, they might plug you into the wires, fire raging through you. Not so far as to cause permanent damage. They didn't want to devalue their product. But it was more than enough for their purposes.

The other rules were the scariest. None of the children could understand them. Nothing frightens a child more than incomprehensible demands and punishment for failure.

Many days, the techs paraded us from our rooms and force-marched us down long corridors soaked in fluorescent radiation. We'd stop at glass-encased laboratories with rows of electronic equipment. They'd sit us there, dropping headgear that sprouted a hundred wires over our heads. Opaque glass masked our vision in the helmets. Noise-canceling tech blocked sound from reaching our ears. All sounds except the commands of the experimenters. They would ask us to describe what we saw, to find our way through labyrinths our eyes couldn't see. When we couldn't, they were displeased.

My heart weeps for my twelve-year-old self, sitting alone with a giant steampunk cap on my head, surrounded by people who killed my parents, who beat and tortured me, and who asked me to see the universe in a way I did not understand.

It was far darker for the less gifted children. Day after day, they stumbled and failed to progress. Day after day, the devils hurt them.

It became clear I was special. Before they realized my improvement, I saw *something* when other stimulus vanished. More and more, I found my way through the trials they erected for me, although I couldn't grasp the purpose. As my eyesight deteriorated—the sensory deprivation did little to take away what was almost gone—I developed a conscious new sense. Patterns, substance, *something* took shape in a place I couldn't name, and I gained the power to succeed. And success was all that mattered. This hell had mangled me, broken my will. Luxuries, like purpose, didn't matter. Meaning was irrelevant. Only that the pain stopped.

Soon, I was all the rage with the people in white coats. How they fawned over me and smiled, happy with their little animal performing so well. They isolated me further from the other children. They subjected me to special experiments. Around this time, the operations began.

Meeting Ricky before they started the series of surgeries saved me.

Ricky was the one kid able to smile in this sterile place of cold lights and metal corridors. Silly and fat, a few years older than me, and an obsessed Red Sox fan who could name every player and team statistic since 1908, Ricky became my only friend. The others were too hurt, too traumatized, and too afraid to share with anyone. Like shocked lab rats, they huddled to themselves.

Ricky braved beatings. He kept his spirit through the torment. And on occasion, he made me smile. Doesn't sound like much, but in the depths of hell, a smile is a miracle.

Once, I dared whisper to him in rations line. I asked him how he had the courage to dare the things he did.

He smirked. "My old man," he mumbled in his strong Boston tones, "beat me worse than this many nights, after he'd been drinking." He leaned close to me, glancing over his shoulders, looking into my eyes, eyes seeing him as a blur now. "These whitecoats, they're mean jerks and all, but they ain't nothing compared to a good drunk."

He straightened as a whitecoat walked by, staring ahead. As she passed, I couldn't help risking more words.

"Ricky, why are we here? What do they want from us?" It was the first time I had asked anything since I arrived.

He shook his head. "They won't tell, and we ain't gonna find out. What's important is not them, but *us*. What *we* want, why *we're* here. If we make it all about them, well—" he nodded toward the other kids, "—we'll end up like them. Find your reason, Ambra. Hold to it. Don't let them be your reason, or take yours away."

Too many damn words. Two whitecoats grabbed Ricky and dragged him out of line. To another beating. They gave me, their star pupil, a disapproving glare. I couldn't stop a tear from running down the side of one cheek. *My fault*. Like so much to come. My fault.

At the time, I didn't understand his meaning. But his words stayed with me, circling in my mind. Months later, when I drowned in despair, they landed somewhere deep inside. They planted themselves, growing into a sapling. Inch by inch, root by branch, the seed became a great oak tree. With muscled roots and colossal arms and ten thousand leaves blowing in the wind of my soul. His words inspired me to find my reason, any reason. They saved me.

It wasn't long before they took Ricky away. He knew it was coming. "I can't make heads or tails of these tests," he hissed to me after a helmet session. "They won't be keeping me." He sounded sad but not defeated. I always remember that tone in his voice. He was going to lose everything. But he was not going to surrender.

Our time together wasn't long. We spoke brief paragraphs. I never knew the details of his face. But I will never forget him.

Months and years of having monsters cut on you, carve up your skull and brain, and for such a terrible purpose—I was near surrender, my soul broken. But despite their violations, I found my way. I found my reason.

Deep into the past I retreated, and out of the past I stumbled into my future.

Chapter 5

True knowledge comes only through suffering.

Elizabeth Barrett Browning

He was younger than the other whitecoats, with a sparse beard and longish black hair. At least that's how I remembered him from the earlier times he'd worked with me. Now, he was a featureless blur, and I knew him by his voice.

The excitement was too much for him. He bubbled over with words he should not have spoken.

"You're special, Ambra," he said as he yanked the helmet off my head. "We've never seen a child like you before. You've mastered all the navigation drills, succeeding in ways we don't even understand. And the other things you're doing...what *are* you doing in there?"

When they ask you a question, you have to answer.

"I don't know, sir."

He stared at me for a quiet moment. "No. You probably don't." He sighed and turned away from me. "We haven't had a visit in several years. Soon they'll come back, and we'll lose you." He sounded genuinely distressed. Not for me, to be sure, but for losing his prize guinea pig.

A thought brightened his tone. "But next week, a new phase in your training will begin. Next week is your first surgery!" he said, expecting me to understand the import of the statement.

My expression disappointed.

"You know what the surgeries are for, don't you?"

I was still naive enough to remember the original lies these criminals gave my parents before they murdered them.

"No. Maybe...for my tumor?"

His voice rose. "Yes, Ambra. Very good. For your tumor." Talking to me like I was three years old.

"They will take it out, finally? It's getting hard to see."

Silence. My stomach dropped. In my small hope, I had spoken out of turn. Worse, had I said something bad? They hadn't beaten or shocked me for a long time. The thought of either made me sweat.

He spoke, his tone melancholy. "Yes, we've noticed your visual impairment. It's not unexpected." He set the helmet down with a thud on the counter. "Come, our time is finished here. I won't see you for a few weeks, not until after your recovery. Over the coming months, we'll see how you progress."

That was the first hint of what they were planning for me. It was also my first realization that my trials were part of something larger than this place. *Who* would come soon? What was navigation? And why was what I was experiencing and responding to in their tests so important to them?

I had little time to learn more. The morning came and nurses whisked me into a prep room. They shaved me bald, drew on my burning scalp with markers, and plopped me onto a gurney. Other blurred figures wheeled me into an operating room. Bright bulbs burned my eyes, and the shapes of surgeons congregated above me. A needle pricked my arm, and a bag of liquid fed drops into my veins.

The room shrunk to a point. I was on the outside of the universe.

The lights and shapes rushed back to fill the room. "Wow," I heard myself say.

Away the doctors fled, and I gazed from infinity, the universe infinitesimal, my body a giant balloon. I plunged into black, darkness broken by a disorienting flash of pain and dizziness. My wild trip landed with a turbulent return to consciousness, lying in a bed, the room spinning.

My arm still had a tube dug into it. My head felt twice its normal size. *Still a balloon.* I reached to touch it, my fingers pressing against a large and swollen thing wrapped in bandages. Sitting at my side was a blurry shape, the voice recognizable. It was my talkative scientist friend. *Dr. Talkative.*

"You're awake. Good. That's *good*. The operation was a success. Aren't you happy?"

My throat hurt. I gargled a few phrases. "The tumor's gone? Why can't I see better?"

His clothes rustled as he shifted in the chair beside me. "No, Ambra. The tumor is still there. It will *always* be there, growing larger. We've created space for it to continue expanding."

The words hammered me into the bed, pinning my arms and legs.

"This will enhance further development of the unusual mass. The back and top portion of your skull have been opened up considerably."

The room was losing oxygen. I panted.

"The tissue proliferation will accelerate, so much pressure and hindrance removed."

"Please." My skull. Open. Under the bandages on my head, the thing was growing. *Growing growing growing growing.*

He chuckled, air blowing over my face as he turned toward me. "Don't make a face! You have a section of new skull, composite material in place with a greater circumference. It will have to be replaced, of course, as the tumor spreads. Further enlargement will be aided by the enhanced blood supply."

Excitement discharged extra horrors from his mouth. His breath tasted foul.

"The surgeons are very talented. They routed vessels from the occipital lobe over to the tumor. To better nourish it. This will accelerate the loss of vision, but that cannot be helped at this point."

A hand gripped mine, another patting it.

"*All* that matters is the tumor. Your *gifts* come from it, Ambra. It's your spacetime eye!" he chirped, laughing. "God, you're going to be a star!"

He dropped my arm and stood, walking out of the room. My limbs were still lead, too heavy to lift. I fought off hyperventilation as the monitors beeped in protest. Sweat soaked my neck.

Alone and nauseous, I whimpered from the bed, a twisted mockery of a girl.

And sure enough, a month later, I was blind.

Chapter 6

I myself am time inexhaustible, and I the creator whose faces are in all directions. I am death who seizes all, and the source of what is to be.

Bhagavad Gita

My dad used to say every cloud has a silver lining.

How much silver do you get for being stricken with a giant, literally head-splitting tumor that destroys your sight, a fake skull with grafted skin to cover the extra surface area of your head that will never grow a hair, leaving you looking like the hate-child of a bulbous-headed alien and a middle-aged man?

Extraordinary powers. *Check.* A central role in a galactic power struggle between good and evil. *Check.* Extraterrestrial friends who became my new family. *Yes.*

But all that was still to come. At the time, I got Ricky's Red Sox cap.

How did he do it? It shouldn't have been possible with all the security and paranoia of this place. But he managed to smuggle his hat into this facility. He kept it hidden from the whitecoats. And when his time came, he hid it in my room, stuffing it inside the metal tube serving as one of the legs of my bed.

I was lucky to find it. Or it was inevitable. My sight disintegrating, I used my hands and feet to explore my environment. I had to relearn how to walk, and my room served as a training ground. I took the first steps there, feeling the walls, furniture, and floor. My skin became a radar of its own. The air spoke as it changed directions and taste, telling me if a door was open or if some object sliced the atmosphere with its shape. As my sight died, my other senses were growing—including my *other* sense, but I'll get to that later.

Weeks of recovery followed my surgery. Whitecoats transferred me from medical back to my cage. Healing, I had lots of time to do nothing. The cameras didn't much care anymore what I did. One day, stumbling around in my deepening blindness, I found the cap. Ricky had wrapped it in laces, rolled and mashed so it would never recover its intended form again. But it was his hat, all right. I knew from the smell. The "World Series Champions" embossed on the side didn't hurt my deduction, either.

Wearing the cap in this prison was my first step away from the pit of madness opening at my feet. My head was already too swollen for it, and this was just operation number one. I didn't care. I unsnapped the back and yanked it over the raw wounds. The grafted skin burned, and my skull throbbed, but I wore it anyway.

Silver lining? It covered the hideous addition to my body, giving me an almost normal appearance. My hair would grow in over time from the part of the scalp that still had roots. The hat hid the rest. From a distance, if you didn't look *too* closely, I might just look like an unremarkable redhead sporting a baseball cap.

I took to wearing it all the time. At first, the whitecoats sounded disturbed by my new fashion sense. But then—*a miracle!* Since I was their budding superstar, I got special privileges. They let me wear it without further comment. I guess they wanted to keep me happy, keep me performing.

The other thing that saved me was retreating into the past. Not psychologically, where I retreat into *my* memories to hide (even if a lot of hiding occurred). I mean *everyone's* past, including my own.

As I learned later, a Reader's power grows and matures fastest in adolescence. I was right in the middle of that, my whole body changing. It might have been something I could have obsessed about if I'd had the luxury. All the other cruelty shoved puberty far to the side. But at the same time I impressed them more and more in their little examination room, other things were happening to me. I was changing in ways they didn't realize.

One of the first changes was my growing power to enter the past. I still had future visions, but what captivated me, what gleamed in high-resolution detail, what I began to be able to *control*, were my visions of what *had* happened. Or, as I like to think of it now, what might *have had* happened. Like I said—past and future, both are fluid.

In the dark and pointless hours in my cell, I traveled on long and grand adventures. Journeys to happenings of recent—and sometimes not so recent—history. Initially, I explored emotional touchstones. My childhood, my parents' lives, important world events. As I learned to control my path through time, I extended my explorations farther.

The practicality of Reading what had been, how it could impact my present and future, did not dawn on me until much later. Embarrassing I didn't think of it earlier, but I was thirteen. And I was *really* screwed up.

This developing ability allowed me to compensate for something tormenting me—my lack of education. Many children would be glad to be free of school. Not me. Years passed with an entire sea of human knowledge denied. My captors had not only made my life hell, but they also locked me from all the light of humanity. No books, music, or art. No new ideas or experiences to foster growth. They crippled me, left me ignorant and powerless. Sometimes I panicked, performing math problems in my head or reciting lines from poems I'd read. *Desperate.*

Silver lining? My starvation for knowledge synergized with my growing tumor powers. I realized that, in the past, I had access to everything our species had achieved. *So, I went looking for it.* I launched myself into those visions, extending them, improving their clarity. I mastered the technique to maintain my attention on a specific segment of history.

A phantom lurking in the shadows, I eavesdropped on humanity. Obvious places to linger were schools and libraries. But really, the entire world was open. Did I want to learn about great art? I could study at the Louvre. Advanced calculus? I could sit at the feet of Newton (not time well spent, let me tell you). I experienced the thrill of exploring oceans and mountains. I rode in zero-g above the Earth with astronauts.

As the blackness clouded the rest of my life, the visions continued to shine in opposition. Through them, I could still see, see as vividly at times as I had with my eyes. I was blind, but in a strange way, I was not.

It wasn't always *easy* to find these elements of the past. When the visions first came, I did not control when or what I encountered, although they tended to involve things close to me. As I honed my skills over the years, I could dance through older landscapes, flipping pages in some ethereal tome. I achieved a bizarre education no human being had experienced, but one I would have traded in a second to be back on my farm with my parents again.

The obsession with the past consumed me, and I allowed it to block visions of what was to come. Amazingly stupid, considering how useful knowing the future might have been. More baffling, I never sought out the history of this grotesque dungeon. I never examined the histories of its people, what and who they were, why they were acting as they did. How much could I have learned to help me cope, to escape my bonds? I can't justify my inability to realize the significance of what I ignored.

I can say this. I had sunk into a black hole of hopelessness, and through journeys into the past I had found light. It saved me, carried me through the experiments, the surgeries, the inhumanity of the place. I needed this different world too much. I guess a part of me ignored things closer at hand, however *useful* they might have been. The rest was more useful. It kept me sane in an insane life.

A silver lining.

Chapter 7

Most gods throw dice, but Fate plays chess, and you don't find out till too late that he's been playing with two queens all along.

Terry Pratchett, *Interesting Times*

They were all happy, happy techies in the glassy room.

The giant helmet came off and the usual lab clamor disrupted its imposed silence. Chugging ventilation. Machinery humming. Computer tones. I focused on the faster flits of motion of the team working with me. Their breathless motions, quick footfalls, and vocal lilts praised my performance. I was their local Olympic athlete, acing their silly mind games.

The trials were becoming easier and easier. Boredom weighed on me, while their excitement grew. Early on, it was such relief pleasing them. I looked forward to each new session. I craved the attention, their encouragement, the anticipated equipment readouts when I'd finished. How quickly it all changed, thinking back on it.

Some mysteries were yielding their secrets. This device they placed on my head stimulated the universe of my visions. Strap me in, turn it on, and I could "see" *things* created in front of me. Imagine a magic laser-disco ball, but, of course, nothing like that. A toddler gawks at the disco ball, awestruck. A child smiles and plays with it for a few minutes. Several times a week as a young teen? Well, its secrets were gone.

By my fifteenth birthday, I'd endured six surgeries. The ripening tumor was a squashed softball in my brain. Ricky's hat refused to balance on my distended skull. At least my hair could grow long again (on the sides). I vowed to myself never to cut it—in the dream place where I had such control over my life.

My whitecoat entourage had grown to a team of ten, headed by Dr. Talkative. He loved to share the latest measurements of my malignancy. He'd update me on its slowing growth. He'd outline in pleased tones how it was stabilizing within my brain.

As if I were a *willing* part of this. Like I was *thrilled* about being twisted into some grotesque monster, inch by brain-bulging inch.

The pack of them bragged about my achievements in the lab. They wanted their own trophies for what I'd accomplished. I learned that whatever it was they were doing, they didn't understand much about it. They could set it up, read the output, and conclude whether I was succeeding or not. But they understood nothing else. They buzzed around in their white coats, important and full of themselves. Twisting knobs. Pushing buttons. Recording data. But they were just clueless. People using a microwave with no idea what it's all about inside.

They were also ignorant about what I was seeing, blind to how simple it was all becoming. Underneath the helmet, my developing sense glimpsed a greater universe. One they could not perceive or imagine. As for my visions, past or future, they hadn't a clue.

The devils had cooked up this freak, but they couldn't fathom what they had made.

As I outgrew their disco ball, I aced all the tests. They became repetitive. Dull. Near the end, I could perform in the background, while I daydreamed or explored the past. That was the case on the day the news came.

The team was bubbling with joy from my latest *bored out of my mind* performance. Dr. Talkative rolled into the room like a storm cloud. The hairs on my arm pricked at the tension in his voice and movements. I smelled anxiety in his sweat. The others saw it in his face. I bet it looked bad.

"I have some unfortunate information," he overstated the obvious. He glanced at the monitor. "Fantastic work today, Ambra." He sighed. "You've outgrown us."

He placed his clipboard down with a clack and stepped back into the middle of the room to address his staff. "And like all children when they grow up, you must move on."

I heard groans and the awkward shifts of uncomfortable people. High-pitched notes squawked from a tech. "They can't come now! She's just showing us her potential!"

A baritone carped, "They won't care about what she can do, what she could become. They'll strap her into a navslav ship, and she'll waste away her life like the rest of them!"

Interesting. While it wasn't exactly comforting to hear I was doomed to a lifetime of servitude, the outburst opened my eyes, so to speak. Startled me for the first time since I had come to this place. To watch them fall from the top of the food chain—it was priceless! *The fear in their voices.* Who were these mysterious *They* who were coming and over whom they had no power? The whitecoats were my local nonbenevolent deities. It was discombobulating, but liberating, to see them shake.

"That's enough, all of you! It doesn't matter what we think or want." He paused. His next tones were a dirge. "As you know, we have, in our enthusiasm...*tampered* with their property. I believe it was a step in the right direction for science, for the potential that lies within the human race. But *They* may be displeased. I don't have to remind you how serious the punishment can be for infractions."

Silence fell for a long moment. My heart thudded against my ribs.

"Nevertheless, as your group leader, I will take full responsibility for these actions. I pray you will maintain your appropriate demeanor when our visitors arrive tomorrow."

"Tomorrow?" someone gasped in disbelief.

"Yes. For some reason, we didn't receive their communication from the Belt. They are entering orbit as we speak. We are to prepare the children for transport in the morning."

Chapter 8

Once upon a time, Zhuangzi was dreaming that he was a butterfly dancing and flying about, joyous and free. He had forgotten that he was Zhuangzi. Then he awoke and felt himself solid and sure. But he didn't know anymore if he was Zhuangzi who had dreamed he was a butterfly, or, a butterfly dreaming that he was Zhuangzi.

Zhuang Zhou

In orbit?

What in the world did this mean? In my weird journey through the annals of human knowledge, visitation from aliens didn't earn much respect. Like believing in ghosts. Sociology argued such claims were the current incarnations of demons or angels. "They are a projection of our well-documented, overly active imagination contextualized to the modern mythology," as one lecturer put it. Harvard professor, I think. Respected astronomers pointed out many clear problems with extraterrestrial arrivals. The distances between the closest stars required centuries of transit. Hyperspace and warp-speed were conceits of science-fiction authors to enable their narratives.

How ironic my future doomed me to hyperspace travel of a very real sort. A future where I'd navigate for aliens that couldn't possibly be visiting us. It was a sad case of solid thinking being wrong and loony thinking being right. Well, I can tell you—life isn't fair.

It took me a while to fall asleep that night and my sleep was disturbed. In the early hours of the morning, a powerful vision shook my consciousness. I stood in a cavernous chamber carved from strange and unearthly material. The walls and ceiling resembled marble mixed with the dirt of a termite mound. Odd patterns and unusual color mixtures decorated the floors. Huge moss-green pillars sprouted like trees. Thick vines of stone erupted from the ground, climbing to the dome-like enclosure, supporting it in a hundred places.

Rows of these columns converged on a colossal dais. On an ornate chair squatted a monstrous form, insectile, inhuman. Other beasts dragged a young man to the platform, their hard-shelled forms buffeting his soft flesh. Bloodied and bruised, his face tense with pain, he glared toward the raised throne. Chills shook me as I realized mangled human bodies hung from the walls as macabre decorations.

The creature on the throne oriented a set of three eyestalks on what might have been a head toward the man. A coarse sound filled the room as it spoke in a hideous mockery of language. Awkward, translated by some device, the grating dialogue rattled the wide space in deep frequencies. The bone and artificial material in my skull vibrated.

"Human Reader—you have lost the time. If you and we cooperate, you to be able to rescue your people. If you do not, these deaths here only a mild beginning will seem."

The young man slumped, yet a fire burned in his eyes. He clenched his jaw, and I remembered what he would say. *Madness.* I could not let him. I wanted to beg him to stop the slaughter I'd witnessed around that throne. Stop the pain lurking behind those metallic, insectile tones. Stop the terrible destiny rising to choke me like a poisonous fog.

He cried out. "You can do with me as you wish, but another approaches. She will bring your end. You cannot hide—she sees all. I feel her. Beside me. She watches even now!"

The experience overwhelmed me, and I lost the threads of the vision. I sat on my bed, cradling my knees. Tears poured down my face, and I fell asleep crying like a little child.

I woke to the sound of my door scraping open. Rapid footsteps clattered toward me.

"Ambra, you have to dress, now. You must come with me *immediately*."

It was one of the women, an aide on the experimental team. Her voice dripped with fear.

Chapter 9

In the ordinary theory of relativity, every line that can describe the motion of a material point, i.e., every line consisting only of time-like elements, is necessarily non-closed. An analogous statement cannot be claimed for the theory developed here. Therefore a priori a point motion is conceivable, for which the four-dimensional path of the point would be an almost closed one. In this case one and the same material point could be present in an arbitrarily small spacetime region in several seemingly mutually independent exemplars. This runs counter to my physical imagination most vividly.

Albert Einstein

The room was dank and yellow.

Dank because the staff had raised the humidity to some absurd level. Moisture trickled from anything it could condense on. Window glass. The metallic walls. A dark-green material like none I'd seen composing the bulk of the funky spacesuit in front of me.

Yellow because the lights in the room were filtered. Another effort to comfort Squidy as he (she? it?) swam in the sea of whatever liquid was inside the suit—water? Or why the humidity?

Squidy couldn't have been more of an alien if it tried. Either that or some mutant octopus outfitted by the US government. A sack mockingly reminiscent of a head flapped from the top of it. It was a dark brownish-green, oblong, and squishy like an octopus's head, but often invaginated. Deflating hot-air balloons popped into my mind. A random patchwork of protruding lumps suggested eyes of some sort. Long whiskers running off the head-sack gave Squidy the look of a cactus that had forgotten to shave for a few days. Octopusesque arms lacked suckers but sprouted thin dexterous tendrils at the end. These "fingers" manipulated objects floating in the suit.

Okay, you are likely asking yourself, "*How does she know all this? She's blind.*"

It was impossible, but as I saw these things, it did not surprise me. The stress of this encounter shoved my brain into survival mode. My panicking neurons integrated my new Reader sense into my mind's general scheme of decoding reality. Later, aboard the navships, I pieced together what had happened. Turns out the ability to see into the past has a practical application to the life of the blind.

So bear with me for now and trust me when I tell you, my visual descriptions of the event are accurate.

Dr. Talkative vibrated like a taut string, his face the aftermath of salmonella poisoning. The female aide led me beside him to a dripping, metallic chair in the middle of the room.

What nightmare was this?

I recoiled, my heartbeat sharp and quick, but she pushed me forward. Harsh straps hung from the seat for my arms, legs, and head. Their metal reflected the jaundiced light. I blinked, sweat pooling on my eyebrows.

She pressed me into the device and clamped the restraints over my wrists. My breathing labored when she locked my ankles. My body shook when they placed the silver band around my head. She snapped it tight, and my neck jerked backward like someone yanked my hair. I couldn't move my head. I couldn't move anything. They could do anything to me, and I was powerless to stop what might be coming.

"I'm sorry," she whispered, her voice shaking. She scampered away. The door to the chamber closed with a loud clank.

"Try to relax, Ambra," began Dr. Talkative. "You are property of the Navigation Conglomerate. A representative of the Sortax is here to examine you. You will speak when spoken to and obey all its requests. Your life and your future depend on its assessment of you today."

Squidy took over. There wasn't any doubt it had been in charge the entire time, of course.

It spoke. The sound shook me further. The artificial voice of a translator carried a tone and quality I had heard hours earlier in my dream. The voices of the insect throne room barked from a device a few feet before me. Images of mutilated corpses flashed through my awareness.

"They are that, which they changed?" it rang out.

Adrenaline raced through me as I parsed the question.

Dr. Talkative bailed me out. "He's asking about the surgeries. He means our operations with your tumor, Ambra."

"Yes, I guess, I am."

"They are that, which were not authorized."

I didn't respond, assuming it was a statement and not a question. Dr. Talkative squirmed. Squidy floated about, jerking its appendages every second or two.

"They will serve in navslav the ships and supervised. They with value, exchanged for with the Dram."

A small glowing object drifted into the path of several tendrils inside the suit. The tentacle holding the device reached out toward me.

Brightness. Fire. *Agony.* My mind burst.

I shrieked, howled, slobbered all over myself, and tore a chunk from my cheek. Truly, I had never experienced pain. Not the surgeries, not the beatings or electric shocks, nothing prepared me for that flame. You don't have my tumor, my sixth sense. I can't explain it to you.

A light thousands of times too strong for your eyes? Flooding all your experience, tied to two red-hot iron knives? Drive them together into your sockets, sear your optic nerve, and cook your brain?

No. That's not half of it. In an instant, my unique window to the universe transformed from gift to curse. It became the raw skin over which a terrible acid burned. Every muscle in my body convulsed. I projectile-vomited across the room, coating my visitor and Dr. Talkative in the process.

As the pain ceased, the world dissolved, and the next thing I knew, the sad woman hovered over me, calling my name. She wiped my mouth clean and removed a needle from my arm, her face blanched to match my own. Sweat beaded on her forehead.

"Ambra, talk to me. Are you okay?"

"Mom. I want my mom."

The woman blinked away tears. "I'm sorry. She's not here. Please, you need to wake up, *now. They* need to question you more. *They* can't wait for you to get any better." Anger tinged her tone.

She brushed another cold, damp cloth over my face. I tried to focus, to bring my concentration back from the pit of hell still burning around the edge of my consciousness. My mind was winter sap sliding down rough bark. It staggered forward. The dank room resolved. Two forms in front of me distinguished themselves. One horrible, from a nightmare. The other the man who had mutilated and deformed me, changing me into something powerful but also terribly vulnerable.

"Ambra," started Dr. Talkative. "We are sorry for that…disruption. You were being scanned with a device designed to probe your powers of perception. Only it is calibrated for a normal Reader. You are not a normal Reader. The signal was too strong," he stammered, shaking his head. Later, when examined by the doctors of the Resistance, I would learn I had almost died that day.

"Enough," clanged out the voice translator. "We again scan."

"No...please..." I begged them.

I would have done anything at that moment to prevent them from scanning me again. Given them anything. Promised anything, said anything. I would have debased myself with all my heart. It would not have mattered what—jump off a cliff to my death? Sure. A thousand times easier than being scanned.

"Ambra, it's okay. We've lowered the signal strength considerably. It will be safe now. You must be conscious for the examination. Let us know if you are in pain."

"The pain do not constitute," it injected.

"She may be valuable to the Dram," Dr. Talkative noted.

"They may be," it concluded.

It raised the device toward me again. I tensed, and while the experience was painful, I tolerated it. Despite the discomfort, it was interesting to some abstract part of my awareness. *The patterns!* This was the advanced version of the disco ball. Disco Ball 2.0. The structure and substructure. It was like nothing I'd experienced from the headsets. When it ended, images of dancing shapes in multiple dimensions burned as afterimages in my tumor, staying with me for days.

"Not authorized," it sounded out as the visions faded. "They are for the navships."

"No! She is more than that! You can't fry her mind and expect to get a meaningful scan!"

The creature turned its earthsuit-encased form toward Dr. Talkative. The scientist shrank like a shadow at noon.

"Not authorized," it spit, lumbering to a door at the other end of the room.

As it left me and the doctor alone, relief washed over me like a cooling rain. A relief in the presence of a man who had carved me into the freak I was. Relief because, however traumatized we both were, whatever he had done to me and whatever had been done to him over the years, we were human. Until you have encountered the alien, the truly alien and not simply strange, you will never understand the deep comfort the nearness of another human being brings. Even your tormentor.

I shivered, wet and stinking in my stained clothes, still strapped into the metal chair and unable to move. Every piece of my body ached.

Dr. Talkative looked at me and closed his eyes. His hand reached out and pressed a button on a controller hanging from a string around his neck. Water droplets maintained a slow rhythm, plopping against the floor as they fell. The door behind me squeaked and footsteps clacked through his defeated tones.

"You'll leave tonight with the other children."

Chapter 10

Time has no specific character of being. In relativity theory the temporal relation is like far and near in space. I do not believe in the objectivity of time. The concept of Now never occurs in science itself, and science is supposed to be concerned with the objective.

Kurt Gödel

I'm sure it must be exhilarating for kids to leave home for camp. Journeying away from the parents who have always cared for them. Living with strangers, new rules, dangers, and opportunities. Or going to college, stepping out for the first time as an adult, exciting although you might have a safety net most of the time to fall back on. *Adventure!*

To hell with adventure. I was scared. Terrified, actually. Just a few years before, I had lost a beautiful life—a nice home with parents I loved and who loved and cared for me. I spied on the past and witnessed their murder. The villains who had destroyed my family moved on to torturing and deforming me. Where was I captive, but in hell?

But this terrible place transformed. Now it was a haven, a refuge compared to the infinite dark and alien waiting above. These creatures would take me and some untold number of kids with them like trained animals. Rip us away from our home planet and from any sense of security or the familiar.

How could I cope? I would see many an Earth child *not* cope, their body degrading, their mind fracturing. Hordes wasting away or exploding in lunacy. And *They* removed the sick efficiently.

I sat in my room, wearing the long and featureless robe handed to me. My hands tensed in my lap, cold, twisted over one another. I had no belongings, no mementos of family, no toys, no evidence of a life of any kind. The one artifact was the Red Sox hat, perched on my bulbous crown, and I didn't know if it would survive what was coming. I gazed, unseeing, over my bare room as the minutes crawled by, one unit of time shuffling after the other. Waiting.

The door swung open, and I jumped. It was Dr. Talkative, which was unusual, as he had never visited my room. He was alone, which was also unusual, since his staff and team always followed him or lurked nearby. The door closed with a click. Metal screeched as he dragged a chair across the stone floor toward me. With a sigh and disturbance in the air, he sat down.

"Ambra. We don't have much time. *They* will call soon for the children, and we must deliver you to the docking chamber."

He shifted his weight, and the seat squeaked. I waited for him to say whatever he was there to say.

"It's unfortunate what happened during your examination. Years of hard work destroyed! All because that clumsy Sortax representative would not listen to me. I *know* you are capable of so much more."

Tears dropped down my cheeks. After everything, after all they had done to me, despite the sense of strength and rebellion I'd gained the last few years—it all evaporated. I crumbled into a small ball. Nothing existed but the desperate guilt of a wayward child.

"I'm sorry," I whimpered. "I really tried." Sobs shook my shoulders, breaths choked as I fought to hold the shame inside.

The strangest thing happened. My abuser rose and sat next to me. He placed his arm around my back. I couldn't help but stiffen.

"Ambra, listen to me," he said as I stifled my sounds. "Humanity is in a terrible place. There is so much you don't know."

His voice turned guttural. He licked his lips.

"*Cattle*. We're nothing more than bipedal cattle to these aliens. Dumb masses dancing. Ignorant. Stupid. And the rest of us? We're the worst."

He shuddered beside me, his arm a claw tightening across my torso. His speech dropped an octave.

"I'm sorry for what I've done to you. Years ago, before *They* took me, I would have been ashamed of it. Perhaps I am inside, still. Because I chose what I thought was the easy way. Became their willing slave. To succeed in this sick system—it was all that mattered." He inhaled. "*Don't you make this mistake.*"

The arm jerked away, and he grasped my shoulders, turning me toward him.

"I'm going to tell you something no one else knows, something important. For the human race. Something I've buried, denied, rationalized away for years."

What was I to say to that? Nothing made sense. Nobody was sane.

"Please, just listen and remember. You can't process right now. I know that. But you will, later."

He dropped his hands to the bed. His voice became a whisper, tones strange and inflected. It was like hearing scripture.

"Many years ago, when I first came to this place, still working as a tech with the new children, there was a young boy. Not much older than you are now. He was preparing to ship out, just as you are tonight. I'd given him his last series of shots like you got earlier. I was about to walk away when he spoke to me. He was a very gifted child.

Second only to you, Ambra, in what he could do with the spacetime matrices. He stared at me with his deep-brown eyes—I'll never forget. His eyes or the words that came out of his mouth.

"*Doctor, a young girl will come. She is the sunrise. She will see with truth into the darkest night. She is our hope, the savior of this world in its coming trial. You will recognize her by her signs, and you will understand after you have sinned against her. Before the end, you must give her my message: Daughter of Time, you must wake. Fear not to gaze forward and walk the terrible path set before you. We are waiting.*'"

He paused and cleared his throat, his phrases cracking.

"These were his last words the day I handed him off to a life of slavery. I shrugged them off, thought them mad ravings, pushed them out of my mind. Then you came and my ambition blinded me to everything except your astounding gift. I did not hear his voice. Or *would* not hear it. Even as the prophecy returned this year to haunt my dreams." He shivered. "Now, I can't stop hearing them."

He cupped my head in his hands. I assumed he was also staring into my eyes to make an impression. Of course, I could see nothing.

"I want to say those words again. *Daughter of Time, you must wake. Fear not to gaze forward and walk the terrible path set before you.* Ambra, he meant *you*. He was a powerful Reader, and he forecast your coming. He *found* you in the fields of time. Listen to him. I can't undo what I've done, but I can do penance. Don't be afraid. *Survive.* It may be you are important beyond the hopes of humanity."

He exhaled, stood, and walked to the door. "My actions have doomed me. They will make an example of my tampering. My final hours, my last minutes, I've spent giving this message to you."

Scurrying feet and raised voices grew from the hallway. Intermixed, I heard the chilling echoes of the voice translators. *They* were coming for us.

"Forgive what I have done and remember his words."

The door opened and slammed, the air pressure slapping my face. The swelling sounds outside spiked in intensity, an avalanche rushing my door.

I was going mad.

Chapter 11

A journey of a thousand miles started with a first step.

老子 Lǎozǐ (Lao Tzu)

When you first *see* as a Reader, you have no framework, nothing to connect with the singular sensations you develop. Your brain works the weird information into all its preexisting neurological patterns—images, ideas, emotions. Dreams are an arena to wrestle with these experiences as your subconscious decodes the strange data.

Soon after this, the new universe leaks into your waking mind. Visions become the product of this confusion. That's as far as most have gotten in human history—seers, prophets, lunatics. A supplementary sense organ in a minority of the population, stunted in its maturation. Granting a distinct sight but stealing sanity.

The irony? In all other things, we humans are the idiots of the Milky Way. We are the least evolved intelligence, life-forms others consider backward and primitive. Beyond Earth, we're worms enabled by the aid of more advanced creatures.

In this universe, where we have so little to offer, our one value is in prescience. Our odd talent rivals, and often exceeds, the gifts of species far more developed in every other way. An accident of evolution making us the idiot savants of spacetime.

They harvested us through human farmers. Centers like mine in Nebraska selected those with potential. They handed us to fiends, who carted us across the galaxy. For breeding programs. Cloning attempts.

And, most of all, for the navships. Scattered about star systems and nebulae, entombed in oppressive and harsh prisons, humans serve the space-faring needs of many creatures that are otherwise disrespectful, contemptuous of our very existence and presence among them. We are a necessary evil.

With me, their pet humans got carried away, and before they realized, my captors had created an anomaly. A monster for all involved, human and *other*. Because, while I am certainly monstrous to my fellow Earthlings, my gift is a terrible threat to the galactic hegemony of the Dram—of them, you will hear more soon.

In me, the Reader organ is beyond developed. It has become my dominant sense, unfathomable even to the most powerful Readers of any species. I no longer can see the light of day, but I can see the energy of tomorrow and yesterday. I don't possess the words to paint for you the visions I experience. But I can say it isn't different in spirit from what I saw with my eyes: beauty, horror, and everywhere, *existence*.

As the ship plowed through the Earth's atmosphere, I was still, as far as my potential, very much asleep. A sleep that was, as I tried to explain, more psychological than anything else. I wasn't ready to accept what I was becoming or to grasp the power my unique insight offered to me. I would take that journey one clumsy step at a time. But that time approached. The last words of the captured Reader lodged in my mind, buried like a bomb waiting to shake the galaxy.

I suppose a trip into space should be described with inspiring images. Breaking through the atmosphere! Encountering the first blackness and stars or the sunrise over the edge of the Earth. But mine was no pleasure cruise. For the children onboard, our hosts served claustrophobic chambers, turbulence, and near asphyxiation.

From the facility in the Midwest, they marched us down a long corridor into a vast hangar under the night sky. *Outside.* I hadn't been outside the gray walls of that glorified cage for years. The freshness of the air was a miracle. In the expanse of heaven above, the beautiful Milky Way glimmered. I gasped as wind walked along my skin again. The children stumbled forward with me to an existence where they would lose all that was familiar and loved.

The chamber rivaled a sports stadium. In the middle was a spaceship. Knowing more about these things now, I can say it was a surface transport, designed to ferry cargo planet-side from a starship. But at that moment, it was the first time I had seen anything like it, and it was overwhelming. The behemoth was as big as a tanker, shaped like a cross between a flying saucer and the space shuttle.

Doors to the building sealed shut behind us, the adults locked within. The earthsuited Sortax remained. A hundred children trembled before the monsters, their ark, and the fate awaiting above.

We crept quietly in our thin robes, fog escaping our lips in the winter chill. Several sobbed, and one or two broke down and refused to enter. The Sortax extended a dark rod towards the child, screams echoing. The awful translators ordered the crumpled shapes to move forward in line. After such pain, each did.

Inside the craft, it became clear how alien we were. The vessel was designed, of course, for its crew, the sea-dwelling Sortax visiting land with their many arms in water-filled suits. Liquid occupied most of the inner chambers. I marvel now at the compensation the Sortax must have used to offset the weight. There were airlocks ("waterlocks"?) of a kind for the natives (*Them*), that we bypassed without engaging. A short tunnel led to our holding pen. Once all the children had entered, our new masters sealed us off from the rest of the ship.

Sealed off from the rest of the ship.

That summarizes the interactions of humans with the diverse aliens that we encountered. Compatible environments were rare. Some species depended on liquid medium like the Sortax. Others required various gaseous environments. Often these gases were toxic or otherwise incompatible with our survival.

One ironic exception turned out to be the Dram, the Romans of our galaxy themselves, their planet located on the other side of the Milky Way. They evolved in an atmosphere with a similar oxygen and nitrogen content to Earth. The other were the Xix. They needed a small modification to an Earth-like atmosphere, which they achieved through a device worn around their necks in our presence. Well, if you could describe the Xix as having necks.

In most ships I was on, our captors walled us off in our own climate-controlled cells. *Controlled* was always a loose term. Conditions just slightly better than unsuitable for human survival were the norm. That was my impression when we entered our chamber on the Sortax ship, although I now realize their efforts exceeded those of many.

At the time, once the doors closed and we were at the mercy of their atmospheric system, it was oppressive. The air was acidic, burning our throats and eyes. It stank in an undefinable manner to our senses—alien and sickening. We sweltered in the noxious climate.

A single human waited inside. Her skin was gray, with cyan veins running like vines across her face and bare arms. Her hair was patchy and her eyes empty of expression. She motioned to the makeshift seats and straps, demonstrating their use without a word, placing herself within the restraints.

The rest of us gawked but moved to copy her motions as the walls rumbled. I'd just finished deciphering the buckles when the ship lurched into the sky. Several children, who were not prepared, flew to their deaths or serious injury. It made no sense. If they wanted us, why treat us like this and risk our lives? Some sort of demented natural selection for the best slaves? Or simply that they had a lot of meat they could grind through from Earth?

The ride to the starship was short. After a jarring docking (I bet such dockings weren't so bad for Sortax floating in water) and a long wait (likely for the Sortax to leave the ship and to pump out the liquid for our exit), our hatch opened. We peered through the space to see what awaited us.

Standing in the doorway were two Earthlings. Male, they wore thick, worn robes with strange markings across the back. They were perhaps in their twenties, although they looked older, drawn and poisoned like the woman who had ridden with us. As I was to learn, living under alien care was harsh. Lifespan was shorter than on Earth. Most of us did not live beyond forty years, and by the time we hit our thirties, we looked sixty.

Our silent stewardess limped past us to form a group of three adults. A moment of relief swept through the children. *Adults!* One of the men spoke, strangling that hope.

"No words," he barked. "You will do as you are told and prepare to serve the Sortax. This is a training vessel, and you will be instructed in guiding the navships to the Orb portals. Nothing else matters to your existence. If you cannot perform, you will be discarded. You are to report to us or other human shepherds. Under no circumstances are you to attempt any contact with non-human residents of any ship. Follow us to your quarters."

The three turned, and retreated from the portal, leaving us stunned and empty. One by one, we stood and stretched our sore bodies, bounced by the trip through Earth's atmosphere. We drifted through the doorway to our new life.

Part II

I am become Time, the destroyer of worlds.

Bhagavad Gita

Chapter 12

To delve into the deepest mysteries of nature and discover the under-lying truth has been denied us, but with the right imagination, a hypothesis may explain many phenomena.

Leonhard Euler

So my new life began. A life of military constraints, claustrophobic imprisonment, and protracted training periods. The most painful? The horrible separation from my homeworld and everything familiar.

Chronobiology failed us. In space, without night or day, without anything to mark time, existence staggered. Our circadian clock misfired. How much time since our abduction? How long had the navigation sessions lasted? The orderliness we took for granted and depended on vanished, and with it, all sense of normalcy. It paralyzed the psyche. Losing connections to Earth, its rhythms, its air, its life, many lost their sanity. The Sortax removed these victims, and they were never seen again.

It might have been the same with me. My being is tied to the soil and the seasons. In the metallic and sterile labs, I'd suffered for the disconnect from the land. You should remember, I'm a farmer's daughter. In the void, it was so much more terrible. But I had developed a unique relation to time and space. I saved myself again by exploring the past, finding echoes of Earth in visions.

Those who continued, in whatever ways we could, were kept busy adapting to the harsh conditions. We learned to swallow the disgusting material they dispensed to us as food. Function in the toxic air. Sleep on the cold metal shelves. Disregard privacy and cleanliness in an environment not designed to comfort human sensibilities.

Above all, we learned to pilot along the Strings that spread from the Orbs.

Through our training, we gleaned some kernel of explanation, the reason our Earth masters had taken us from our families. They had tortured us, trained us, tested us, honed our *other sense*, all to mold Readers into high-tech beasts of burden. Humanity's children bore the weight of an entire galactic civilization. Without us, interstellar travel would grind to a halt. Trade would wither. Star systems would starve. Our suffering, our terrible losses, it was all for the benefit of a culture that excluded and exploited us.

The first surprise came when the new headgear dropped over our eyes. Disco Ball 10.0. A laser lightshow labyrinth. Confusion and fear struck the other kids. But for me, I woke to a bright, sunlit city I had glimpsed only by moonlight.

Whatever these upgraded helmets did, they channeled the "stuff" of my vision. They brightened it with great contrast. Still limited to a certain color, so to speak, in a single dimension. It was beautiful in its way and yet tempted me with greater vistas to come. But within the monochromatic hues lay a skill we had to master, on penalty of death.

First came the simulations. A repetitive drill we experienced a hundred times. From a disembodied perspective, I would see myself approaching a complex sphere of light.

To call a real Orb a sphere is a criminal distortion. The word reflects the biased view of humans and aliens who cannot perceive the entity in fullness. Inside an Orb were endless layers entering independent dimensions beyond those we can discern. My mind's other sense could see in those hidden directions. The substructure dove deep into spacetime. The Orbs were more like infinite webs whose projection in three-space was a humble sphere. The simulations captured faint shadows. When we approached a true Orb, its beauty astounded me.

Our training was not focused on the Orbs themselves, but on the tendrils, the glowing Strings that spread from them. The Strings extending from an Orb traveled in many dimensions and were pregnant with possibilities. The sims reflected those limited to the visual directions. It was along those lines we were to direct the point of view (the ship in reality), when the time came to steer in earnest.

We spent weeks guiding little simulated spaceships onto the projections. One after the other in an endless parade. The galactic economy depended on this skill. The Strings served as shortcuts connecting any two Orbs. They cut the travel time between stars from eons to hours. I didn't understand how this happened or why these Orbs existed where they did. For the present, what mattered was perfecting the ability to help our masters navigate.

The aliens possessed the technology to exploit the Strings but not the capacity to peer into the spacetime matrices and plot a course. The starships required Readers for this. Readers came from many of the worlds connected by the Orbs. Or, increasingly, and far more cheaply, from the primitive world of Earth. Earthlings were bountiful in Reader potential and powerless to defend themselves from the superior technological development of the creatures depending on our singular talent.

I adapted to the tasks without problem. My unique organ granted me advantages no other human or extraterrestrial possessed. Unlike the labs in my previous prison, my mastery did not bring me advancement or attention. It went unnoticed. This ate at me until I realized it was not individual humans guiding the navships, but the *collective*. Our average effort was being used by the aliens to guide the ship to the appropriate String. I guess it made sense. Individuals make mistakes. But averaged over the whole, the outliers, the errors, disappeared. The aim was true.

It was accurate, but slow, inefficient. Frustration set in as I participated. I was always sure how to direct the craft, but the group movement was stumbling molasses, bypassing the fastest routes through spacetime. But I was one of a horde, and no one understood my potential.

The Orbs distracted me from my frustrations. Soon they occupied all my attention. *So much complexity!* Far more interesting and inspiring than hitching rides on Strings. The sim Orbs displayed little of this. But as we progressed, we made more frequent approaches to the Orb in orbit between the asteroid belt and Jupiter.

Our Orb was resplendent, *incandescent* compared to the other objects in space. Our bright sun, a ball of radiant energy in the electromagnetic spectrum, was a dim and dull object in comparison. The Orb, no larger than a major Earth city in observable dimensions, shrouded a terrible and extended beauty. Within it a pregnant cosmic potential throbbed that longed to be reached, explored, and tapped.

I focused more on the Orbs than the purpose they had set for us. These close approaches were an opportunity, not to navigate, but to study, to peer behind the veil. I dove into that project. In the Orbs, I imagined pathways, like trails in the woods, locked off by fortified gates of light. Roads to the past, the future, *elsewhere*. Was there a latch on the gate? I looked. More and more I looked.

Until one of the group leaders called me aside.

"Your scores have dropped. You must raise them or face elimination."

So they monitored the individual performances in the horde.

"What are the Orbs?" I dared to ask.

"They are a mystery. We do not approach them. We use the

spacetime distortions they propagate to travel through hyperspace between them. Stick to your lessons, or you will face elimination."

He lumbered away like a robot, and I knew he meant what he said. As hard as it was, I tore my attention from the Orbs and back to the assigned task. Our initial group of over one hundred now counted less than twenty. Attrition from madness, illness, and poor performance took its toll. But performance improved. The paths to the dynamic tendrils, while not optimal, cut a lean route through spacetime.

As we approached the Earth-Orb for the last time, the Sortax instructed us to guide to a particular String. As we did, a power surge rattled through the walls. We held our course and neared the String. The spacecraft entered its flow.

How did this appear to the human eye? Unremarkable, I would guess. Vision responds to such a limited band of electromagnetic radiation. The Orb and Strings would be plain and dim, the starship suspended in the emptiness of space. The craft would accelerate, vanishing to a point as it exited perceptible dimensions. Odd, no doubt, but bland.

My "eyes" transfigured the process. In the bright and glowing stream of the String, radiance diffused through all materials and structures. A churning river of luminescence bubbled like rocky rapids. The glow mesmerized me, put me in a trance.

Time Turbines engaged in a gleaming swirl, whirling us down a cosmic bathtub drain. A strange sensation tugged my innards and turned my body inside out. My mind drowned in showers of complex patterns of resplendence and twilight.

Infinity erupted and strobed over me. We plunged through hyperspace toward a distant world.

Chapter 13

It is unnatural in a large field to have only one shaft of wheat, and in the infinite Universe only one living world.

Metrodorus of Chios, 4th century BC

I should explain how it was I became able to "see" surrounding events. My descriptions to come all depend on this ability I tapped into on Earth during my first meeting with the Sortax. Our inaugural hyperspace journey was to their homeworld, and over Sortax seas, this skill reawakened. This time, I recognized what I was doing and began to control it.

The potential to visit the past, providing me with education and refuge, offered something else immediate and practical—the power to form images of my environment. My mind weaved my sixth sense into visual metaphors from memories of my lost sight.

These are what *visions* are for a Reader, the blending of our unique sensory impressions with imagination. It's a painting to help us understand the incomprehensible. Perhaps if we had developed the ability to Read as infants, we could do without a substitute. We would "see" in this new way just as we see with our eyes or smell with our noses. We wouldn't need to frame the experience with another sense. But our abilities activate near puberty, when much of our brain is set and less plastic than it once was.

Initially, I used this power to make discoveries I could not have known any other way. The further from my own background, the harder it was to "see," as if strange subjects were at a greater distance. Naturally, many of my greatest interests were very far away. "Seeing" the details of the unfamiliar required great concentration, and I had to practice discerning histories at such distances in any useful manner.

The significance of events near in time, those things easy to perceive, I had failed to comprehend. I'd ignored them. Why? I considered them obvious, and early on part of the world I was seeking to escape emotionally.

Then the Sortax came to Earth. In the panic and dread of the deeply alien, my survival instincts focused my awareness. My other sight concentrated on moments of the immediate past and close to me physically. Reading the proximal present is hardly different from *seeing* the present. As a bonus, I had the flexibility to see beyond the limits of eyesight. Spacetime allowed me to explore with wider vision.

And so it was and became again as we descended through the turbulent atmosphere of the Sortax homeworld. My mind converged on the imminent present, and at last, I understood what I was doing. This ability freed me from blindness and granted me an exceptional sight. It was also the launching point for the next steps of my development—the exploration of the near future and the much harder and powerful search for major events to come.

Once through the clouds, the vastness of the planet inundated me. Three times the size of Earth, the globe's expanse glinted with a sheen from purple water. A descending orbit traversing two-thirds of the circumference of the world and no sign of land. Not a small island or ice cap. There would be nothing to "land" on. These aliens lived beneath the waves, and under them we would be going.

The starship arced and made a swift dive toward the violet seas. Impact with the surface jarred my teeth. The howling atmospheric sounds ended, replaced with a churning liquid outside the walls of the vessel. Our chairs shuddered. Metal pinged and groaned as we plunged deeper into their endless ocean. How could creatures like us of fragile flesh, bone, and gas survive at the depth and pressures of their underwater cities?

After what crawled like hours, the ship, now more a submarine, stopped descending, slowed, and the metallic clang of docking rang. The terrified breathing of those nearby hissed in the air. Once again, we were alone and powerless, heading into the unknown. But this time, I was less afraid. What could be worse than what had happened to us so far?

A question reserved for the dangerously naive.

The door to our chamber opened, and our human shepherds gestured to follow. The Sortax must have exited through another location, one designed for their underwater lifestyle. Our exit was under atmosphere, and we were not given any suits to put on. The ship had docked with a corridor leading deep into the recesses of a submerged city.

We stumbled down the tunnel and through many sculptured chambers in unexpected Earth-like conditions. The construction was immaculate. Beautiful in some disturbing manner. I tried to wrap my head around why these aliens had gone to so much trouble for their captive humans. All for us. How naive I was.

"Into the examination room," barked one of the shepherds, as he pointed to a large room to our right.

The architecture inside was unlike anything a human mind could have concocted. The walls and supports undulated as they curved toward the domed ceilings. The material was a metal blend with stone never seen on Earth. It glowed a pale green. Illumination diffused from a moss-like ingredient embedded in all surfaces. The floor was of a similar substance. It was slippery and several children fell.

As we entered the chamber, we had our introduction to the Dram. Tall, insectile soldiers glared, their hateful images matching those from my earlier vision. Standing at attention beside large pieces of machinery, they toted adorned cylinders. Despite the alien composition, the devices telegraphed weaponry. Less militarized bugs, marked with indecipherable symbols on their thorax-like regions, crouched, adjusting elements of the equipment.

One by one, the towering creatures led us to these clusters. They stripped us and shoved us onto a square region in the center of the apparatus. Immobilized, they poked and prodded us in every orifice. They tore skin, hair, blood, saliva, and mucus samples from our bodies. Techs pushed gadgets over different parts of our anatomy. All the while, we lay helpless and terrified as the enormous insects appeared ready to dissect us on the spot.

As they removed my clothes, I did not resist them. But I held on to the one thing that mattered to me—the Red Sox hat. I balled it in my fists, clenching them, willing to suffer whatever might come if they tried to take it away. Lucky for me, they didn't focus on the crushed clothing in my palm. They were too busy removing all possible dignity from the rest of me.

In all the turmoil, I was unable to recognize a startling fact—the bugs were breathing the same air we were. They were comfortable at our pressures and temperatures. If I had noticed, I would have pieced together that these chambers were not for us at all. Only the clinging vestiges of naivety allowed me to believe such an absurdity. No, this enclosure beneath the Sortax ocean was sculpted long before to comfort the Dram.

As they finished with me, a probe came out from the side of the examination equipment. A Dram worker rolled me so my back faced the device, and a searing burn stabbed my skin. I cried out as others had but couldn't move as the sharp ends of the worker's many arms held me in place. I'd learn later about the chip. Inserted into my body, it contained all the relevant data for those who would be shopping for Earth's Readers—my training certification, physiological profile, estimated age, and expiration date.

They marched us into a second chamber I can only describe as a human meat market. One by one, they dropped us on a bare stage to be displayed in complete humiliation—alone, naked, cold, and afraid. Devices resembling odd cameras whirled about us. A device would also scan the gadget in our backs, all the information transmitted to the bidding aliens who needed Reader services.

Based on a weighted formula of many of our traits, we were each given a score. Those with the highest rankings served in pleasure craft of the rich, governmental ships, or military vessels. Lower values meant passenger freighters. Or worse—the wild and cheap auction market that attracted a number of despicable bidders. My blindness and deformity didn't do wonders for my rating. They had no inkling of my gifts, no means by which to assess them. I was bottom of the barrel.

Afterward, a robotic drone pushed me down several corridors and into a storage room. Awkward English orders instructed me to get inside a small, coffin-like container. These packaged the children for delivery to their new masters.

And my owners? Some of the vilest criminals of the space-faring races. Their cold cruelty almost killed me. Worse still, through all they did to us, my spirit shattered. This will be the hardest part for me to tell you. Even now, distant in time and space from the events, I become dizzy and sick just thinking about it.

I shivered in the coffin. My breath fogged, and a foam spread over my body, injected from the sides of the pod. It weighed like lead, and I struggled to move as it covered me. It was *cold*. Ice-cold and burning.

I panicked but gave way to calm. My shivering slowed. My eyes blinked, refusing to stay open, and I yawned. Sleep—heavy, deep drowsiness descended on me like an enormous blanket, blocking out the claustrophobia and fear. I forgot where I was. Light faded as I squeezed the crumpled baseball cap in my numbing right hand.

Chapter 14

The whole visible world is only an imperceptible atom in the ample bosom of nature. It is an infinite sphere, the center of which is everywhere, the circumference nowhere.

Blaise Pascal

Somehow in artificial sleep, I dreamed.

I floated in space. Not in a ship or spacesuit, but without constraint, like a child coasting in water. An impossible wind swept my hair backwards with molecules of air that could not exist in this emptiness.

I felt no cold despite the fact that it should have been absolute zero. The gas in my lungs did not rush out into the vacuum, and the saliva in my mouth didn't boil. Nitrogen didn't bubble in my blood, giving me the bends, nor did my eardrums rupture. In the absence of oxygen, I didn't get dizzy or pass out. I was comfortable. Free.

Was I dead? Was this my spirit?

I looked around. A yellow star shone at a distance. Staring at it without the filtering of atmosphere or protective glasses, my eyes were unhurt. The intense radiation had no effect on my china-white skin.

Our sun. Our home star. I marveled that I could see. Not *Reading* the near past, but *seeing.*

In front of me flickered a point of light. Like a magnet, it pulled at me, and my body accelerated. The object grew in my field of vision. A small, pale coin. A plate. A pocked surface blotting out the inky blackness.

The moon.

My rate of approach slowed as the beige disk filled my range of sight.

An unease festered in my stomach. A chill of foreboding, danger, and evil lurking on the other side of the satellite. Something wrong, something monstrous was hiding behind our moon, something malignant and murderous. I felt it searching, seeking, trying to peer around the dead ball of rock.

Searching for me.

I knew it was close, but I could hear voices from that direction as well. Cries begging in panic and pain. Shouts mixing together, like some nightmare chorus, rising in crescendo and sweeping over me like a tempestuous sea.

And in one dreadful instant, silenced.

What had it done? *What had the monster done?* Distress overcame my fear. I rocketed toward the other side of the moon. The lunar surface blurred past, my eyes focused on the horizon where I would see the bright blue of Earthrise. Soon, any moment now, I would see home and find my way to the cries for help. I could hear them echoing in my mind.

They called my name.

Chapter 15

When I look up at the sky, I somehow feel that this cruelty too shall end, that peace and tranquility will return once more.

Anne Frank

Waking from hibernation, the smells struck me. Human odors, not alien. Foul waste and rot. Sickness and decay. The reek of filth from a hundred bodies malnourished, unwashed, and weakened with illness and despair.

Right after this stomach-churning stink, small robots yanked us from the pods. They herded us through the entry port into a larger chamber.

Horror. Skeletal forms crouched, their translucent skin pocked and infected. The stench waxed and choked me. Bile climbed in my throat, and I stifled a reflex to retch. A feeble few with energy glanced our way. Revulsion paralyzed my gaze, locking to the hollow sockets of their eyes.

The sickly shadows didn't speak. Standing idly or sitting listlessly, voiceless, bent as with great age, these zombies were rotting cattle in pens. Dumb eyes stared unseeing. Their hair was matted, filthy, thinning and falling out. Sores festered on their legs and buttocks, all too visible through torn and frayed cloth. In some cases, they lacked any covering at all. This fiendish boat had emptied the walking corpses of dignity, self-awareness, hope. The victims putrefied, broken and dying.

I shuddered. Death here was a release, a door away from suffering. My soul screamed in silence. *What could have done this to them?* I placed the Red Sox cap over my head and pulled the bill down over my eyes. I couldn't face these shambling horrors.

I had no idea where I was. After the Sortax homeworld, the exams, the market, and the pod, I had slept. *For how long?* It could have been days or years—no way for me to tell. Where had they sent me? Why? Questions burned in my mind, but in this purgatory, I found no answers.

The robots herded us to the far wall. Small depressions in the floor indicated where to stand. If we didn't understand, the metallic hounds shoved us into position. A loud crash above our heads startled me. I glanced up to see a panel slide open, revealing a metal grappler snaking down toward me.

People screamed. Some tried to run. The bots showed they had a bite to accompany their bark. Dashing, they zapped anyone out of place with a painful jolt of blue electricity. The electric dogs repeated the shocks until we were properly herded. Meanwhile, the claw had descended and clamped those of us remaining. The tentacled appendages writhed with one hundred joints, squeezing like a boa.

Once we were all loaded in the claws, they raised us into a tube above. Like a piece in an assembly line, we were sped along several tubes by the robotic arm, up, sideways, down. It dropped me into a hard, wet seat, restraints snapping over my legs and arms.

Rows of others to my right and left were in identical positions. A syringe with a large needle emerged from a small panel beside me, and before I could react, it pierced my thigh and injected its contents. To this day, I don't know what was in it. I assume some combination of antibiotics, vitamins, and steroids—something to keep us functioning as long as possible in the hellish conditions.

Beneath me, the stench of urine and feces fermented. A hole was centered in the seat they had strapped me into. You can guess what it was for. I hoped the wetness underneath me was cleaning fluid. We worked protracted shifts before the claw brought us back to the holding pens where we tried to sleep. Nature would call.

We were also fed at these stations. A trough in front of us would fill periodically with a green sludge for our consumption. We had to bend forward and slurp the stuff with our mouths, our arms and legs clamped to the side. At first, the rancid smell prevented me from eating. But after two days, the filth tasted heavenly to my starving body.

The needles withdrew. Cries and whimpers tumbled across the rows of children, but they allowed us no time to process. The navigation helmets descended and plugged us into their system. It was like the training sessions, almost the same interface for our minds.

We first navigated through a series of simulated journeys through hyperspace. The crew was not going to take chances on us guiding them through a star or asteroid field. They had lessons to teach, as well, harsh ones. For those who didn't match the proper trajectories, our caretakers dispensed electricity from the seat. A few in our group screamed on the first run, the pain so terrible tears pooled in the eyes of a girl next to me. Mentally, a projection from the helmets outlined the correct path. We were supposed to learn and try again.

In little time, the newcomers had learned, and the punishments and screams stopped. These lessons never ended. Anyone underperforming could expect a shock. Later on, as our physical and mental state deteriorated in this nightmare, our performances dropped. Some lost all ability, and when shocks did not work, the claw descended and removed the offender. We never saw them again.

After the initial tests and reprimands, the crew brought us online for the first hyperjump. Again, the beautiful Orb enlightened our space. I would encounter them over and over in the coming months, jump after jump. As life and hope bled out of me, each appearance of an Orb was transformative. I came to view them as the sole purity in a filthy cosmos.

We directed the ship to the specified course. The tug and inversion of the traversal passed through me. We journeyed.

Repeat everything I've told you about this place until the events blur, and you have a good idea of our quality of life. Our time was a distended monotony of suffering. We never glimpsed any of our destinations. We guided the String leaps, waited in position for docking, heard and felt the loud noises of cargo transfer, and prepped for the next jump. This would happen perhaps every hour, giving us ten or twelve jumps per shift.

For most, it was exhausting concentrating under the pressure of pain to guide the ships. At first, I found it simple. Later, as my body crumbled, it became a challenge even for me to focus on the task. At that point, all of those in the group who had come on board with me had disappeared. They couldn't pilot anymore. They were replaced.

I would learn from the Xix that I'd landed in a smuggler ship. Such vessels were part of an underground black market of traders often enslaving human Readers as disposable tools. These smugglers jumped ceaselessly, maximizing transfers, minimizing downtime, and mercilessly running through humans like some obscene organic fuel to power their business. It was illegal, but tolerated by many local authorities. Most aliens considered us a low form of life. They judged us to possess poor self-awareness, unable to suffer like the more advanced life-forms. That's how they rationalized away our exploitation and pain. Wealth mattered more.

I still cannot reconcile the conflicting perspectives. One, the injustices presented in an academic fashion by the Xix and others, an economic truth of an unfortunate nature. And two, the minute-to-minute torture of the hell I lived through. Those descriptions could not possibly be different ways of looking at the same thing. They were from two incompatible universes.

In my current life, I choose not to think of it, because I feel madness lurking in trying to harmonize those incongruent truths. Telling you now is harder than you can imagine. But it has to be done. It's part of the big picture, your understanding the truth. My pain in reliving this nightmare is small compared to the catastrophe you must help us reverse.

After our long shifts, the claw descended and carried us like used baggage to one of several crowded rooms. These holding pens consisted of cold, hard walls and floors. No comforts, no divisions for privacy, no separated areas to take care of bodily functions, no space for a human being to have any sense except for a festering claustrophobia.

We packed ourselves together, shivering, choking on the poisonous air, lying in our own excrement, trying to find some short period of sleep before the next shift. During this time, we went without food. The robots targeted anyone who dared act out. Plenty could not adapt. Some turned violent. Some became catatonic. Both were removed, never to be seen again.

This author's words offend me. They are a sin of blundering prose. His bland efforts won't help you smell the stench, endure the oppression of our senses, the fear of smothering in others' awful bodies or the unclean conditions. No matter how many times I force him to rewrite this, he fails to convey the ghastliness. You won't understand how this state of existence robbed me of my sense of self, my ability to think or feel or remember life on our beautiful planet.

The horror alone was real. All else faded to a dream—fresh air, green grass, blue skies, smiling faces. And hope. Hope died in this place. Dreams dissolved. Faith was a cruel delusion to torment me with beauty and kindness and freedom I could never have. Reality was nightmarish, a plane of Hades, and we were the tortured souls never again to deserve decency.

Every few days, our captors flooded the room with a freezing blast of water. It left abrasions on our skin, but for a short while, it washed the filth out of the way. The liquid burned our throats and noses, filled no doubt with disinfectants. Our owners used such coarse methods to keep us healthy. Sanitizing washes. Injections of antibiotics. As long as was possible to squeeze value from our veins.

But they would not care for us as individuals, and these stop-gaps failed us, one after the other, depending on our constitution and luck. Each of us succumbed to pathogens we had carried with us from Earth. Our weakened immune systems fell behind. Skin sores and boils, respiratory diseases, and the ever-present diarrhea brought us down. Some labored on, drawing from some well of infinite willpower, dragging their skeletal forms forward, coughing blood, *trying*. Others reached a point at which life ceased to matter, and they lay down and refused to do more. They were removed.

"Nights" were the worst part of it, if you can identify a period as day or night in a place with no sun, unchanging illumination, no rhythm but work and collapse. We were fish in a can, squashed together in filth, hearing the moans of the sick, the weeping of the broken. Their hopelessness was more infectious than anything else. We found no peace, no rest. I longed for the navigation hours.

And so it went. Hour after hour, day after day. Weeks blurred in my mind. I couldn't keep a count of time. My body withered.

I spent painful sessions with intestinal illnesses that made me want to die. My torso echoed an anatomy chart, my ribs and pelvic bones jutting from my sides. My clothes were an unwashed, raggedy set of strips covering nothing I normally would have cared to cover.

Ricky's hat was still on my head, but it was wrinkled, torn, stained beyond salvage in this awful place. By this point, I didn't care. My eyes had taken on the haunted stare of the creatures I'd seen when I first entered the spaceship. Broken souls for whom death is a welcomed mercy.

I had lost the ability, the desire, to travel into the past. I'd forgotten anything to do with the future. I was a stumbling zombie, performing in the seats or facing pain. I swallowed as much of the foul gunk as I could without puking. I dreaded feverish nights in the holding pens.

Hanging on by this thin thread, I stumbled onto a truth. And it broke my spirit.

I leaned over the trough, slurping the green sludge. A woman next to me was crying. I ignored her. Most of us who had been there more than a few weeks withdrew from emotional and social bonds. We became empty, numb to everything around us except immediate and sharp concerns.

The woman was gawking at me, wailing. She hollered. She called me a monster. Her voice grated, and I turned to her. She was a new addition, acquired at one of the recent stops, tanned, with her clothes intact. Her theatrical outburst indicated she wouldn't last long. This place would waste no time breaking her.

"How can you? How can you eat that? What have they done to you?" she screeched at me as the putrid porridge leaked down the sides of my chin.

I angled my head and stared at what she was pointing toward. The blur of green food cleared as my eyes focused, and there, in the midst of the awful glop, was a severed human finger. It had the same greenish hue as the ground meat. A human finger, clear as it could be. I glanced back at her, not yet able to process what my eyes had seen.

"Don't you even care?" she moaned. "Oh, God, you're eating each other!"

Understanding spread through me like venom. In all the horrid events, through every indecency and injustice committed against us, I had been detached, a tortured innocent caught in the monstrosity of others. Now, tasting that sludge in my mouth, perceiving what coated my chin and lips, *I* became a monster. For the first time in my life, I felt tainted, evil. As if the devil had transfused my blood with that of a hundred aborted fetuses. I was eating my own kind.

I threw up, vomiting over the trough. For the first time since I had come to this place, I wept. *Were my insides melting?* My sense of self dissolved. I had become a disease.

I spoke nonsense to the woman. "I'm sorry," I moaned. "I didn't mean to. I'm sorry, I'm sorry, I'm so sorry!"

But she cursed at me more, and at everyone in the row. She condemned us to hell for our actions. Her judgments were like cold water. My sobs ceased. It was all so clear. The poor woman, she was so lost. She didn't understand that we were already in hell.

I stopped eating. I couldn't clean myself of the stain, but I could stop the debasement. But let me tell you, it was the most difficult thing I've done in my life. All I went through, and all I would go through—tortures, cruelties, sacrifices—none of them compared to the trial of simply not swallowing that inhuman, human muck.

If you have never starved, you can't hope to comprehend. I would lean toward the porridge, weeping, wanting to bring it to my mouth, my flesh howling at me, demanding nourishment, saliva dripping. Somehow, I stopped myself. Somehow, *a madness*, I forced myself to abstain again and again. I separated from my body, my thoughts floating above it, guiding its actions remotely.

But it was not a triumph. Don't ever believe it was. Because I *wanted* that food. I wanted that hideous gruel more than anything I had wanted in my life or have wanted since. I managed because of my terrible need to regain my humanity, whatever remained of it. Like some dishonored samurai plunging a blade into his abdomen, I punished myself. But even today, I can still feel the deranged lust for it coursing through my guts, and the memory dirties me.

Little time was left for me now. Each hour, I grew weaker. After three days, I couldn't focus on the navigation and slept little at night for the pangs of hunger in my belly. I am sure I would have failed the fourth day. The chair would have disciplined me. The claw would remove me once and for all to be processed myself into the green slop.

But on the fourth day, the Xix came.

Chapter 16

The greatness of a nation and its moral progress can be judged by the way its animals are treated.

attributed to Gandhi

I f you were to cross an iridescent, elongated tree stump with a spindly-armed alien from early science-fiction films, add sixfold radial body symmetry, three layers of appendages, and throw in a large dose of quirky, ballerina-like elegance, you might get something close to the impression a typical Xixian specimen would give.

But focusing on their alienness is wrong. You would miss the heart of these noble creatures. I hope in the chapters that follow, I can show you.

When I first encountered the Xix, you must imagine me to be broken. An empty shell of Ambra Dawn. I was a dying and wasted thing, starving, skeletal, my gums bleeding, sores all over my body. I no longer cared to live. My brain ignored most of the surrounding reality.

The demon ship holding us in torment had docked with the

usual sounds of cargo transfer. But an unusual racket erupted over the expected routine. *Perhaps I heard explosions?* My mind treaded water. The lights flickered with a subsonic bass drop to silence. Distant footsteps approached outside our entry port. Metal clanged against our door. With a loud crash, it flew outward.

The elongated Xixians danced inside, odd devices suspended in one of their many arms. They wore robes stitched together at several points along the angular contours of their bodies. The clothes were dark blue with insignia and characters I couldn't decipher. Their iridescent skin contrasted with the solid hues of their clothing.

Of all the aliens I encountered, the Xix presented one of the greatest contrasts between physical appearance and spiritual reality. Superficially, they were deranging nightmares. Three layers of appendages decorated a barrel-like midsection tapering like a cone. At the bottom were six legs, thick and muscled, ending in six-toed "feet." In the middle of the torso were six, six-fingered "arms." A final layer of extremities extended near the top of the cone. These top arms were delicate, sporting radially symmetric hands. Twelve elongated fingers of six joints undulated from them like tentacles.

The small, upper hands held the odd spherical devices, like weapons.

All the limbs were multi-jointed, supported by alien sinew and elements bizarre to human physiology. Were an Earth creature to bend in several directions simultaneously, attempting to support weight at those absurd and dangerous-looking angles, the bones would snap and the ligaments tear. The Xix tolerated those ridiculous bends, hopping to a strange rhythm in their gait.

The top of the conical torso splayed outward with three sets of six eyestalks. This was what I thought of as the "head." The flexibility of the eyes allowed the aliens to see well from all directions. Membranes spanned the thick and mobile eyes, with no mass for a brain. Their thinking organ rested in the center of their large, barrel chests.

These disturbing extraterrestrials stormed into the holding pen where I lay dying. Scanning the area, they replaced their weapons with small communicators. Instinct drew us back from the creatures, monsters to the human psyche. Two Xixians entered, dressed in different uniforms—lighter blue, with distinct insignias. They sported a form of the "universal translator" worn by other species, like the Dram and Sortax. Much sleeker in appearance, they also functioned as a gas regulator to modify their inhalation. Words spilled from the devices. Clear speech. Voices that sounded human.

The first language was Chinese. Several in our room glanced toward the invading aliens. I heard other tongues spoken, all of Earth, not alien. Although unintelligible, they were sounds that touched my heart. Sounds from home. In the middle of this babble, I caught phrases in English.

"Please be calm. We are here to help you. We are representatives of the Xixian Federation, charged with Life Rights for creatures in this parsec. You have been illegal prisoners aboard this vessel. We will take you to better quarters and provide you with health services. Afterward, we will aid you in finding appropriate and safe work within the Hegemony. Again, do not be afraid. We are here to assist you. We are a rescue party."

No one moved. We were beyond the ability to process our environment. We gawked at our saviors. Teams of Xix in green uniforms —the medical crew—rushed in through the door and attended to the worst of us. Light-blue-uniformed nightmares approached others. They gathered the cowering people together with gentle voices and shepherded them outside. *How loving they were!* If any meaningful map could be drawn between human empathy and the alien psychology, I would say the Xix *felt our pain.* They cared for us. My long association with them hasn't changed my impression.

At the time, however, I could no longer stand. The many-fingered yet delicate hands of two Xixian medics lifted me onto a hovering stretcher. Bobbing in my delirium, a head writhing with eyestalks snaked over and examined me. Nightmarish hands passed a strange, glowing device over my wrecked form. A warmth washed through me. My suffering faded. I slid into a deep well of darkness.

Chapter 17

For after all, what is man in nature? A nothing in relation to infinity, all in relation to nothing, a central point between nothing and all and infinitely far from understanding either. The ends of things and their beginnings are impregnably concealed from him in an impenetrable secret.

Blaise Pascal

Again, I dreamed.

I floated through the black of space, a small point of light growing in the distance. Larger and larger, it took on the dimensions of a disk. A great pocked disk of rock rushed toward my disembodied perspective.

The moon.

I did not recognize the surface. It was the moon, but not the one I knew, with craters and lines of patterns strange. It sped past, occluding my vision. The bright blue and white of the Earth peered over the edge of its satellite and the motion slowed to a stop. Hanging over the gray horizon was half a glorious marble set in the black of space.

Home.

I wept, but without a body, no tears fell. My perspective gained momentum, revolving around the moon, the Earth dipping below sight.

Earthset.

Not enough. I had to see it again. I rocketed toward the other side of the moon. I strained for a glimpse of the living disk breaking out over the lifeless surface.

Earthrise.

I swooped over the landscape, the dark side of the moon giving way to the patterns I knew. I continued, racing in orbit and still the planet did not break over the horizon. *Where was it?* How far did I have to go to catch it once more? I needed to go home.

Around and again, peering, stretching. A cold chill passed through me. The familiar presence of something terrible and wrong haunted the heavens. The monster was near.

I had to find the Earth! I cast my vision across space, straining for a glimpse beyond the moon and this blackness.

Hideous laughter echoed. Long and cruel. It pierced my spirit, a poisoned sleet storm, reverberating in the infinite darkness.

And I *knew.* A knife in my gut.

I screamed in the silence. My rush over the moon increased, spinning faster and faster. Patterns of the surface repeated, again and again. Above, darkness drowned me.

Only the moon.

Panic crested. I would stretch until I snapped. Around and around until the surface blurred.

The Earth was gone!

Chapter 18

You were born with wings. Why prefer to crawl through life?

Rumi

I woke in a soft bed, stiff, like I'd slept for a time uncounted. I opened my eyes, but like the dream, all was dark. Fear gripped my throat before I remembered—*I'm blind.* Calming myself, I made an effort and scanned the immediate past. From the black nothing, I summoned visions and painted my location within my mind.

I was in a small room. A warm light shone like an early spring morning on my face. Not the sun, but a lamp overhead, casting Earth-like tones on objects nearby. I lay on an oversized bed, blankets of a strange weaving draped over me. Next to my head was a blue and red artifact. Something had stretched and stained the fabric. Stitched lettering ran across the front above a bent bill. Someone, or some*thing*, had made the effort to clean it.

Two broad and odd chairs cast shadows over my feet. In each chair sat a monstrosity. As my mind cleared, my memory creeped back. Images from the death ship flipped my stomach. But I remembered. At the last, when my strength had failed, the entrance of the strange aliens. The Xix.

Our salvation.

Little glimpses popped into my awareness. Half-recalled dreams where I'd awakened and lost consciousness. I had been in several places, attended to by these creatures. But no other details emerged.

Where am I?

Two tall Xixians, green robes covering their unusual bodies, waited in front of me. Their snaking eyestalks and fingers squirmed as the rest of their bodies sat immobile. The first fear of them dissipated. Somehow, I knew they meant me no harm. They had rescued what was left of us from that ship. They had cared for me. *Why*, I didn't have a clue. Anxiety still remained for what they might want with me.

"Welcome back, Ambra Dawn," said one of them before I could muster any courage for interaction. Its translator was strung about its strange cone like a necklace, lights flashing across the surface as words sang. "Please, do not be afraid. We are medics of the Xix. We have tended to you since our forces retrieved you from the smugglers."

"Smugglers?" I managed. My throat was a raw wound.

"Barbarians," spoke the other in an identical pitch, identical accent. But a different personality came through the cadenced inflection of the phrases.

"You were nearly beyond our aid. Many of your companions already were," continued the first.

"Where are they all?" I whispered, terrified of the answer.

"Those that survived are well cared for at a rehabilitation facility."

"Rehabilitation?"

"Yes. We are a division of Xixian forces with a specific mission. Devoted to identifying groups that violate the laws in place ensuring the proper treatment of underdeveloped creatures. Too often more advanced species abuse their power. They resort to treating humans in unconscionable ways to maximize profit. Too many do not believe in your ability to suffer, or do not care. Our job is to police such abuses. We are caring for your shipmates. They will be assigned to more, shall we say, humane employments."

My mind attached a soft smile to the words. Of course, the Xix had no teeth or mouths I ever spied. They never dined with us, and it was always my theory they absorbed their food through their rough skin. I was clueless about how they interfaced with the translators.

"Why am I here?"

The eyestalks swiveled around and settled on me. "Because you are special, Ambra."

"How do you know my name?"

"You have spoken much in your delirium. We have been careful to record and study everything about you. Once we understood your value." A short silence followed. "After we tended you, our scans of your body identified items of interest. Physical elements far beyond the illnesses and damage that we sought to repair."

"My tumor."

"Yes. But I don't think you appreciate your condition."

"I hate it."

"That is understandable. We often hate things we do not understand."

The second one spoke, its mass of eyes dividing its attention between me and the other Xix. "Who modified you? Was it Earthlings? Or others?"

"Modified me? Oh. You mean the surgeries." I turned away from them. The shame was too much. "Humans did it. They wanted it to grow. I think my powers come from it."

"They do, Ambra. Did you know many of your species have such tumors?"

I flipped back to face them. "They do?"

"All mammals from your planet endowed with Reader capacity have this growth in the brain. In primates, it has undergone an extensive reorganization, a unique neural physiology evolving within the last two hundred thousand of your Earth years. In most, it is no larger than the tip of your finger."

"But in me?"

"Your genetics combined to create a benign polyp in this tissue. Puberty accelerated its development. The surgeries modified your neuronal matrix, your skull, the local vasculature. All to allow the cyst to grow uninhibited. It gives you special abilities."

"I don't want to be special."

"But you are, Ambra."

I angled away again. In the quiet, I could hear the odd gurgling of the alien bodies. I suppressed a shudder.

The first Xix continued the conversation. "We know you are blind."

"Yes."

"Our scans also revealed the damage from the growth of your prescient organ. Primarily to your tissues involved in processing visual information." Another long stillness. "And yet, Earthling, you see."

I remained silent, hiding my face and refusing to engage. What was there to say? Most of the talk had been from the first speaker. The second leaned forward. Its eyestalks caused shadows to move over my form like dancing snakes.

"I, too, am a Reader. We exist in many of the alien species in the Dram Hegemony. But our talents are weak compared to humans. And compared to you—there has never been a Reader like you, Ambra."

"The man who did this to me said there was. He said another predicted me."

This time, a longer pause. The Xixian Reader continued. "We will not speak of this right now. But what you say is true. But you have the potential to far surpass anything he has done."

My head was swimming. Already fatigue was dragging my body to sleep. *What did they want with me?*

The first one spoke again. "How is it you are blind and yet you see?"

I shook my head. How was I going to explain all this? I couldn't explain it to myself. My trips to the past—were they real? Was I mad? Did I really *see*? Or did I imagine? After everything—kidnapping, parents slaughtered, surgeries, aliens, auctioned, cannibalism. How could I know I wasn't insane? And if I hadn't lost my mind, did I have words to make sense of it?

"I...I look at what was...*before*. I can look and see histories, many that have been. It's a web or weaving, dancing in my thoughts...no, I don't know, I can't explain it. Things far and close. If I look at stuff near me, I can watch what has happened, which is like seeing what is now. Kind of. That's what it is for me."

The two were silent, their eyestalks darting about each other. I guess it's what I would say was a "knowing look" for these creatures. Something passed between them.

The Reader spoke. "Ambra, you may call me Thel. I am assigned to you. There is much we would like to know. We need to know what you can see."

"Why?! What do you *want* with me?" I'd had enough. The fatigue, helplessness, questions, strangeness. I shouted, "Just leave me alone! I don't want this anymore. *Please*...please. Can't you just take me home?"

Thel's voice lilted. "I'm sorry. But we can't."

Tears ran down my face and I hugged my knees, rocking.

"For your pain, we would. But you understand so little."

"What? What don't I understand?" I sobbed between breaths.

"Your planet is not safe for you. It is not what you think it is. You have explored the past, but not thoroughly. Or you would have seen that, several hundred years ago, Dram agents had infiltrated Earth. In humans, they found gold — herds with unprecedented Reader potential. They subverted your cultures, your nations, and guided the development of your civilization. All with the purpose of breeding, identifying, and selecting members of your kind with the greatest powers. There is no place left where their influence does not extend. Should you return to your homeworld, very soon you would be back in their hands."

"Like I'm in *your* hands?"

"We believe we are different."

"Prove it. Let me go. Take me back!"

"We would not wish to debase you as others would. But we *need* you. Not only the Xix, but many alien species do. And your own race needs you, too. Quite desperately."

"How could I help anyone?"

"The Hegemony has strangled our galaxy for too long. There are those underneath their rule seeking what you would call liberation. You can serve those resisting this tyranny. Only when we defeat the Dram, can they be removed from Earth. Only then can your world be free. Nothing on your homeworld is as it seems. You are not in control of your destiny. You are puppets on strings. Cattle bred, raised, and taken for one purpose—slavery."

I startled, a shiver running through me. Have you ever had a sudden taste of truth, finally glimpsed the sword hanging over you? Hearing those words, a thousand facts fit together—the searches through the past, my life experiences, the Xixian descriptions. A landscape cleared through a puzzled fog. And I *knew*. The pieces fell into place.

I had felt it all my life, this *wrongness* of our life on Earth. The incongruity, the mismatch between my inner sense and how our world appeared. The deep dread that something—something darker —lay behind it, blotting out the real sun.

"Revolution?" The word buzzed electric in my ears.

"This is not the time to speak of it, but yes. There is so much for you to learn. But your powers offer a key to unlocking the shackles the Dram have placed over countless worlds."

"Why don't *you* fight them?"

"We are poorly suited to this task."

"Why?"

"It is an irony for many in the Resistance. The Xix have surpassed in knowledge and technology the known species of this galaxy. Yet we are unable to seek the destruction of others, even for the greater good. Life on our homeworld evolved toward synergy and symbiosis. An extreme end of the parasite-symbiote axis. We excel in the making of things, in the healing of hurts, in the explaining of what little of the universal mysteries that we can. Violence, the infliction of pain—these we recoil from. It is beyond mere morality. It is wired into our tissues from ancient beginnings."

"You had weapons when you came. I saw them. And I heard explosions."

Thel answered. "The blasts were attacks from the smugglers on our rescue teams. Many of our kind perished. The objects our forces held can stun attackers, but do not kill them. That is as violent as we can be. And few of us are able to undertake such training."

The other Xixian continued. "We know this limitation in ourselves, yet we cannot alter it. So, we seek other means or approaches to empower others to resist. Ambra, we suspect you may be what our resistance has been seeking for a long time. Something to turn the tide. The Dram are ruthless, powered by terrible weapons and technology we of Xix shudder to contemplate. They were the first to probe the Orbs to manipulate them, because they wanted the power."

The Orbs. A thrill ran through me. As fatigue fought to drag me back to sleep, the image of an Orb burned in my memory.

"What power?"

"All the Orbs connect. They are found near planets with intelligent life. They gave the Dram access to many worlds, worlds unprepared to resist such an aggressive and merciless foe. Galactic wars followed, but soon they overpowered all. Now, the galaxy rots under this despotism. It must end."

The Xixians did the thing again with their eyestalks.

"We see you are tired. We have said more than we should have. We will let you rest. You have the means to examine the truth of our words. Use it. Come to see that we do not deceive you. We will return to speak more, and if you will consent, to begin a new journey."

"What journey?"

"One to understand your real potential. For now, we seek a physical place for that psychic trek."

"Where will we go?"

"Someplace safe. A secret location where you will learn the depth of what awaits you."

The two Xixians stood, legs moving at impossible angles in fluid motion. They strode to the door at the far wall.

"Rest now, Ambra Dawn, *Reader*. There is much yet that you must do."

The door slid open. The bobbing Xixian shapes passed through, leaving me alone in the room. Alone with too many thoughts for my exhausted mind to hope to consider.

Chapter 19

The mind is not a vessel to be filled, but a fire to be kindled.

Plutarch

The next few weeks found my body healing and my sense of self staggering back. I was still thinner than I'd ever been. The sight of food convulsed my stomach as memories of the horror haunted me. But now that I wasn't starving, the mad hunger quieted in my thoughts. It felt like an exorcism to be freed of that sickening possession.

I forced myself to eat. Regardless of what had happened, whatever my life meant from my old perspectives, the words I had heard after waking on the Xixian ship had struck a deep chord. I didn't understand who or what I was anymore. But if I could make a difference? Help *turn the tide* in a universe I knew had, indeed, gone very wrong? Well, that is what I wanted to do.

Who knows? I might find something for my own salvation. And if I didn't, I had to discover what my role might be. So I grimaced at the nutrients they placed in front of me, fought through my nausea, and gulped it down.

The Xix had freed the captives from the smugglers, bringing a few to this ship. They chose them for their Reader powers. And to keep me, their prized hope, from endless isolation from my kind. I became more and more grateful for this as time went on. The aliens were gentle and thoughtful, if always sharp and probing. But they were fundamentally disturbing. Even their smells offended some deep part of my primitive instincts. To have other humans around in this unhuman environment helped preserve my sanity.

We worked together with the Xix. First, they employed us in navigation. Their ship was so different from those of the smugglers or the Sortax. Xixian architectural lines were elegant, flowing, efficient. In comparison, other species assembled disjointed and haphazard structures, their craftsmanship plagued by decay and impermanence. This vessel appeared ageless, built yesterday, never showing a sign of wear.

They introduced us to their navpods. These were small, womb-like boxes as unlike the stalls on the smuggler craft as I could imagine. Navigators from Xix were onboard, but the natives gave way to the humans. They instructed us to steer through strange and round-about courses. Thel, who was ever at my side during my time with them, explained. They sought unpredictable and less-traveled paths through the Orb String Tree (as they called the many branching and reconnecting routes of the hyperspace portals). Planets rarely visited. Places where our enemies wouldn't search.

This confused me, as I could find no reason the Dram should be after us. After all, it was only the Xix granting me any value in this alien universe. The bugs had examined me, branded me, and auctioned me off to the lowest of extraterrestrial life.

As time went on, I came to suspect it was because of the Resistance. Some of the high-ranking members were on board the spacecraft. That's why they needed such secrecy.

Well, the last place I wanted to be was with those insectile butchers, so I did all I could to help guide us as Thel wished. It seemed successful. For many months, we never detected signs of any other vessel.

The transit times were on the order of several days per hyperspace jump. In contrast to the mad dashes of the smugglers, we took our time, and the Xix strategized each step. They also didn't want navigation to exhaust us, although the work was trivial compared to the smuggler nightmare. Instead, they asked us to focus our energies on the instruction and exams they prepared for us each day.

The Xixian trials were unlike the tests on Earth or in the Sortax training ship. They examined our abilities at a deeper level. They challenged our strength and finesse, probing spacetime in powerful and nuanced ways. The process instructed us as much as it evaluated.

Soon, I had gone far beyond the other humans. I got my own time. Private lessons, if you will, with Thel and some of the other alien Readers and scientists. While I was the subject of their experiments, I never felt like a lab rat in a cage. They functioned as my teachers, and I was happy to be their student. But I was also uncomfortable in this kind of relationship. I'd become accustomed to a master-slave dynamic.

I mentioned this to my extraterrestrial guru. It expressed surprise at my confusion.

"Ambra, what good will you be to yourself, or us, or others, if you are not nurtured to mature truly? We of Xix cannot see an object as a means to an end, but as a seed to nourish. To become."

"To become what?"

"What it is supposed to be."

Sounds cheesy, I admit, but these bizarre-looking things meant what they said.

For the first time in my life, someone explained what it was I was doing. What I was *seeing*. The way all Readers saw. Their translators amazed me. They unearthed simple phrases for ideas in math and physics I knew must be much more complicated in alien thought. Thel confirmed this to me.

"I will try to explain, Ambra. But human language, even your thought, is more primitive than Xixian. I don't say this to insult you. The words you hear are simplifications, and because so, distortions of the truth. But it is the best we have at our disposal."

I nodded, my attention focused in this practice room prepared for us. Every day, twice a day for hours, I convened here for my private lessons.

"I was trying yesterday to describe your Reader abilities. Calling it *vision* is a good analogy, because like sight, smell, hearing, and taste, it is a sense. It is a part of your body interacting with the world around you. It provides your mind with data about your surroundings."

The alien oriented several more eyes in my direction.

"But it is also a poor word. It ties you to a concept mangling the information you are receiving. Explaining flavor through sound distorts. Conveying scent by visual analogies jumbles the truth."

I bobbed my head up and down in agreement. What I encountered definitely didn't resemble any other way I knew of interpreting the universe.

"When you *Read*, Ambra, your neural organ, the growth you consider a tumor, is sensitive to particles, in a similar fashion to your eyes. Not light, but moieties transmitting facts about spacetime. Your physicists name them gravitons, as if those were real entities describing the physics of our cosmos. They are not and do not. But let us use the word for simplicity. The *gravitons* you detect convey features of physical fields as photons do of the electromagnetic aspects of reality."

Science. I wished I had explored it much more in my searches of the past.

"What is important to understand is that space and time are always changing. In flux, like electricity and magnetism. Your ideas about them are very primitive. Your recent theories over the last two hundred years on Earth have scratched the surface of their complexity. But like you once could see the world with your eyes, what had happened, and what would happen, so you can see such things with your tumor. More directly."

"It doesn't feel like that."

"No, and it doesn't *feel* like that to *see*. Seeing gravitons isn't like some abstract particle trajectory diagram. When you were sighted, nearly every moment of your waking day you were detecting photons, bundles of electromagnetic energy, quanta, wave-particles dualities—light. You didn't see the physics. You *were* the physics. Your mind experienced the powerful green of an Earth plant, the churning froth of flowing water, the diamond pinpricks of stars in the night blackness."

The alien's ideas dropped and settled inside my consciousness. They were small bricks building a structure whose final form was not yet clear to me.

"These are encounters with the cosmos that shaped your emotions, your thoughts, your actions. *Photons*. That is something like the way a Reader can *see* gravitons, but as different from sight as vision is from smell. Such interactions extend into all areas of our awareness, our creativity, our dreams. As Readers, we have a sense others don't. They can't imagine or simulate our interplay with reality. We're helpless trying to explain the visual realm to a person blind from birth."

"Why can't I see the future like I can the past?"

"You can. It is how you navigate the Strings, seeing the lines of possible connection."

"But I *can't*! What happens *before* I see in detail. What follows after—it's a dream. A blur. I can't hold on to it. I don't know if those visions are real."

"And you know the histories you witness are real?"

"I discover things I find out are true."

"And so you will when you explore what is yet to be. You must tell us what you perceive in later times, Ambra. It may be very important."

"But I can choose to see into the past, search it, grab details, go where I want."

"We believe that, soon, you will learn to do this with the future as well."

When they weren't lecturing, they were training me to see farther, faster, and with more detail. Most work focused on the future. Already, I pretty much could ace anything they threw at me for Reading the past. I could see things their tests couldn't detect. But I was clumsy with the future, always going forward and falling back. My failures frustrated me, building anxiety. As always, Thel helped me understand.

"You stumble not because you cannot, but because you *will* not."

"I will not what?"

"Ambra, you are afraid."

I let that sit with me. The truth of it sank deep. I knew the alien was right. When I began to peer over the edge of the now to glimpse that giant continent of what was to come, shimmering like a city at night, terror rose inside and paralyzed me.

I could see the shadows of things I knew, and many I did not. Out there, in the middle of it, were semblances of *me*. Whenever I sensed these figures, the landscape snapped back, my vision darkened, and I would lose concentration.

"You are afraid to see yourself in what approaches."

"Yes."

"That is a misguided fear. You cannot."

"But I can! I can see outlines, forms..."

"Have you ever tried to focus on those shapes?"

"No, I withdraw when I do, before I realized what I'm doing!"

"No matter how hard you try, even if you overcome your anxiety, you will never see the details of your future."

"So, it can only be known in general terms?"

"No, that is not what I said. We are convinced you have the capacity to see specifics of the forthcoming, of many lives, just not your own."

"Why not my own?"

"Few Readers have seen much about what is to come. Those who have always failed to see themselves. We of Xix believe we understand why. You have begun to study physics in earnest. Do you know the uncertainty principle?"

"Something about not being able to know where something is and how fast it's going?"

"A distilled exemplar. The general concept involves the effect of the experimenter on the measured. You cannot detect something with high accuracy without disturbing the entity examined. For example, using electromagnetic waves to visualize slides in a microscope or atoms with X-rays. The more precision you pursue, the more detail you chase, the more you disturb the environment by probing it."

I was giving myself a headache, scrunching my face, struggling to understand. "So we mess things up by sticking our noses in. Then we can't know exactly what we messed up."

"Not a terrible way to put it. Seek to establish the location of a molecule, and you add energy to it and speed it up. Attempt to measure its velocity, and you lose track of precisely where it is. You can't have all the information in the system. It is blurred. Therefore, you can only know facts at a certain level of uncertainty. A version of this applies when Readers try to determine their own place in spacetime."

My brain was overheating. "Can *you* see my future, Thel?"

"I have tried, as have others on the ship. We cannot. You cast strong distortions in the fabric of reality. It is impossible to Read too close to you in what follows."

"What does that mean?"

"It means, Ambra, you have powers even we do not yet comprehend."

This triggered something in my mind. The Xix didn't know everything. More than most, or so they led me to believe (and so I was to see verified in my experience and my past searches). But like other creatures, they did not understand the Orbs. They used them, but like the rest, only the overflow of the energy from those spheres. I had felt the depth and power in them. Something more than anything I had experienced. More and more they captured my thought.

"Thel, what are the Orbs?"

The creature was silent for a moment, its eyestalks dancing around. After a few minutes, I thought it would not answer me, or perhaps I had offended. When it spoke, it was serious, almost with tones of awe.

"You have made the right connection in this conversation. The Orbs. They are wonders all species study and yet which remain mysterious even to us. Have you wondered why they are found only beside worlds with life, and only intelligent life?"

I had to admit I had not.

"It is much more than curious, Ambra. The Orbs are not natural objects like stars, nebulae, or planets. They are artificial, built billions of years ago for a purpose which lies locked within them."

"Built? By who?"

"This is a great mystery. We are ignorant. Whatever intelligence made them is beyond anything in our galaxy. Far more developed than any technology known in the Hegemony. Even more than we Xix." I could almost detect a smile again in the tones of the voice.

"We hypothesize that they were meant as portals. Not for the crude use we make of them, but for something more profound. And we also do not consider their presence near sentience coincidence. It is causal."

My chest tightened. "Causal?"

"The Dram outlaw this as a dangerous line of thought. It threatens their rule, their power in the galaxy. But we believe something far older is behind this. Predating the Orbs. This intelligence shaped the evolution of life. Intelligent life, in particular on all the worlds neighboring an Orb. Most name them the Ancient Ones. We refer to them as the Gardeners, with affection."

"Gardeners? Like we are their plantings?"

"Yes, Ambra. I'm glad you seem to understand. We are the young saplings they planted as seeds eons ago in the little incubators we call solar systems."

My head was swimming. "Thel, what does all this mean?"

"It means the galaxy and the Dram are small things in a much greater universe, and this should give us hope."

The alien paused, continuing in the smiling tone I had come to recognize. "But you tire. Enough for today! We'll consider this and other topics again tomorrow."

Chapter 20

Imagination is more important than knowledge.

Albert Einstein

Nothing good ever lasts, someone once said.

I would add that you can't even count on the merely okay to stick around in this universe. Sorry to be such a cynic. I've lived through too much.

My time on the Xixian ship wasn't pleasant. It was not what my heart desired, which was to return home. But it was a time to heal, a time during which my great ignorance began to be addressed, when my teachers planted seeds for the future. It also turned out to be a short time. Evil again stamped its ugly boot on my world and shattered decency.

The attack came as we were preparing for our next hyperjump. I sat in one of the navpods, helmet in place, waiting to guide the ship. We approached an Orb orbiting a star system with thirty-three planets, if you can picture that. The system had centuries ago fallen victim to the Dram, the main planet with life obliterated for defying their overlords.

It was mostly a computer-managed run past a collection of impact-smashed, dead worlds. Automated mining equipment surrounded many, extracting materials. We were ten minutes from close approach to the portal. I closed my eyes for the moment, resting my mind.

I'd progressed in my studies the last week. More and more, I allowed myself to face the visions of the future. Nibbling at their edges. Predicting controlled incidents in the context of their measuring devices. I was stretching further.

Seeing forward has a lot in common with viewing the past, but previous events are not relived. When you encounter the impending reality of your surroundings and watch it play out in front of you, it can be unsettling. If you glance on the edge of the now, you can recapture the ability to see the world around you, despite blindness. Almost synced with the present, it was useful for me.

The more distant my search from the moment, the more out of phase my vision was with my environment. The future would become the now, like beats of sound between two closely tuned strings. The rhythm of events thumped in my awareness, seen first in my mind, experienced next in my current moments. It is hard to explain, but it was fun to play with as I got the hang of it.

Just this day, I crept farther forward. I probed occurrences several minutes before they happened. As I did so, my thoughts were trapped in paradoxes. I questioned Thel. Could my knowing the future allow me to change it? How could *that* make sense?

"Paradox presents in a simplistic comprehension of time, a view where effects are proportional to their causes. Spacetime is decidedly nonlinear, recursive in manners your scientists have yet to appreciate. Your visions themselves propagate waves through a multidimensional continuum. These alter what you see, like your swimming in the sea changes the shape of the water in which you swim."

The memory of our discussion prompted my mind forward

again. It was a struggle, using a muscle unaccustomed to exercise. But I was a bit drunk on the wonder of the experience. The thirst for the high pushed me beyond the fatigue. I extended my awareness outside the ship and leapt into the future. Farther than I had yet managed.

My screams brought several Xix running to me.

"Thel. Where is *Thel*?" I cried out, my breathing heavy. I couldn't see, couldn't focus on Reading the recent past. Images of coming events muddied my efforts and vertigo spun my head.

"Thel is not in the helm. We may send a message if you wish. What is wrong?"

The shock of my vision squeezed my heart. I gasped. "Oh God... *Danger*. Something...approaching. The ship...attack! *Thel*..."

"The ship is in danger of attack?" repeated one.

Alarms erupted about us. The bright lights dimmed as emergency defenses activated.

A Xixian pilot called from one of its stations, "Dram warship. Armed and closing."

The aliens switched to their own language for more rapid communication.

I was still ignorant about much of their technology. I assumed they had some sort of defense shield or the like. *Or is that science fiction?* As so often in my journey from Earth, I was confused and helpless. All I could do was wait.

One of the Xix approached me. "We are trying to make a run for the Orb. Be prepared to make the jump. The battle cruiser is firing on us, and we may not make it."

"Firing? I don't feel anything."

"You will not unless our defenses fail. We are absorbing tremendous energy from a determined attack of a fully armed Dram military vessel. There is little hope. Please be ready."

I nodded and slipped on the helmet. The ship dashed, zigzagging through the obstacle course of planets and asteroids. Its eventual goal, the Orb. The String we needed was easy to spot. I shouldn't have any trouble guiding us, despite our speed. A few minutes at this rate. I was sure we'd make it.

We lurched. Artificial gravity failed. Circuits exploded as power surges ran through the system. Inertia maintained our trajectory, the Orb filling our view as we approached. Only moments to the glowing tendril.

A Xixian voice spoke through my navpod. "Reader, it is no use. They have damaged our hyperspace propulsion. We have normal mobility, but we are unable to make the jump."

My heart stuck in my throat. *The Dram!* What would they do?

"Will they destroy us here?"

"No. They targeted the Time Turbines to prevent escape. They could have destroyed us. Our craft is trapped in the system. We cannot evade them. They want us alive. They will board."

In my mind, images of the coming reality I had glimpsed poured through my awareness. "Thel..."

No! I shut my thoughts to the terrible visions. I couldn't allow those monsters to enter the ship. I wouldn't let it happen. Thel hinted that I could alter the future with my knowledge. *I would!*

The multifaceted and layered glory of the Orb neared. I gazed at it, drawn by my fascination and raw desperation. The Xix said they were portals. We used them in a crude and clumsy way.

Portals, but how?

I probed the layers. I focused all my thought on the spacetime gate. The interlocking pieces, tunnels through reality that mixed and dove and intertwined in a multidimensional puzzle.

"A labyrinth..."

"Can you repeat?" asked an alien in my headset.

"Steer us into the Orb."

"What?! Reader, that is impossible! It is death."

"*Please*...trust me. I can see...*doors* inside. There are paths through the maze..."

"No one has approached an Orb directly and survived. You have great vision, but this..."

"Listen! If we don't, many will die! It's the Dram!"

After a moment, Thel's voice spoke over the others. "Ambra, they will have us in minutes. Are you certain about this?"

What could I say? Of course, I wasn't sure! I didn't have any idea what I was doing. I only knew I had to do something. I *had* seen *something*—structure in the Orbs, and paths. But I couldn't see the end point. Could I imprison us in a spacetime maze forever?

"Thel...I see through the Orb. I can guide us through. Give me control of the ship. Let me try."

"Okay, Ambra. Better we die in the Orb than at the hands of the Dram. I had hoped for more before death. To see Xix a last time."

The gates of light opened to my mind. Like understanding a geometry problem, a shimmer spread from my time-sense image of Thel to me, and from me to the Orb. The flash triggered a series of tumble locks in motion, one after the other, falling into place. *I saw!* Clear as a trail in the forest. I knew a way through the maze.

The ship's controls passed to me. With a burst, I plunged us into the Orb. The sphere brightened like a nova. What followed was the most insane roller-coaster ride I could have imagined. We hurtled through one spacetime wormhole after another. The ship darted across countless dimensions in directions impossible, perpendicular to everything. Spaces incongruent with the human mind.

Faster we flew, as if the Orb lacked a bottom within its finite spherical enclosure. The vessel obeyed the path I directed, the course illuminated for me through means I did not understand. I could focus on nothing else. I could sense nothing in my environment. Only diving deeper into the bowels of light and distance, bending around a circle, yet finding ourselves somewhere new.

It may have lasted a second or a millennium, I couldn't tell, but I experienced a *before* and an *after*. The radiant tunnel opened into a sea of darkness. Countless bright points pricked the black background. The ship erupted from an Orb. Behind us, the sphere incandesced as I have never seen. We drifted through normal space again.

An orange star shone before us, and nearby, the crescent of a desert world.

I laid back in my navpod. Sweat poured down my face. My lungs labored. Exhaustion weighed me down, but I knew I had done something never believed possible. And I had saved us from the Dram.

"Ambra, are you all right?" The tones transmitted into the navpod were Thel's. Not elated, but sober, almost still.

"Yeah. Hey, told you I could do it!"

"Yes, you did."

"Where are we?"

"You don't know?"

"No...crazy, I led us here, so I guess I should. But I don't."

"It's Xix. My homeworld. You listened to my last wish. Somehow, you heard it, discerned its location. You've brought me home."

Chapter 21

What is life? It is the flash of a firefly in the night. It is the breath of a buffalo in the wintertime. It is the little shadow that runs across the grass and loses itself in the sunset.

Chief Isapo-Muxika ("Crowfoot")

Thel's words made me smile, and I laughed as I laid back in my navpod. "Hey! How about that? *Home.* That is a good word. Safe at last."

"No, Ambra, not safe."

I stiffened in the pod. "What do you mean?"

Thel sounded tired, almost sad. "We have determined how the Dram found us. They've been tracking you since you left Earth, on the device they embedded in you. Another blind spot for us Xix— their deviousness. The Sortax must have warned them you possessed potential value. Never ones to lose an opportunity, yet unwilling to waste energy on a fruitless effort, they did not place a standard branding chip in you. They placed a hyperspace tracker. This is able to send weak signals along the Strings. It allowed them to remain aware of your position. We deciphered the signal as it resonated with their warships."

What nonsense was this? "But they sold me to those monsters. I could have died there! If they were curious about my value, they wouldn't have risked wasting me so stupidly."

"You don't understand our oppressors, Ambra. Yes, they would have risked it. In their cruel philosophy, their extreme religious beliefs, strength rises. It is manifested in survival. If you had perished, it would have proved to them your lack of worth, however myopic that viewpoint may be. But we of Xix have our blind spots. We thought ourselves ingenious in zigzagging our way through the String Tree. But the chip reported your every jump. It would become apparent that your travel was anomalous. It marked us as suspicious through our idiotically clever methods of remaining hidden. We telegraphed your significance. They converged on us."

"But we lost them! We are safe now."

"After the passage through the Orb, I had hoped so. But the tracking device was able to broadcast, even through that series of dimensional portals. We intercepted communications as soon as we entered Xixian space. Dram warships will arrive here by hyperspace at any moment."

"Can't Xix protect us?" I asked with a growing desperation.

"Not overtly, Ambra. We must act the part of an independent faction, our communications with Xix performatively hostile. We dare not risk them destroying our homeworld. And believe me, they can. They are *terrible*."

My panic rose. I was exhausted from the journey. I couldn't think. I struggled to scan the near past or future to see. "What do we do?"

"There is nothing to be done. Our ship is without power. The damage from the attack, and even more so the trip through the Orb, has left us floating in space, life support limping. Before Xixian ships can come to our aid, our enemies will be here, right off the String. We cannot fight or run. We will have to be more clever. We will allow ourselves to be captured."

"Why?"

"Don't think Xix is ignorant. They are aware of everything and will study the recordings of the Orb traversal. This will convince them of your powers, Ambra, which are beyond even what I might have expected. But they will help indirectly, later when the time is ripe."

"Time? We won't have time. The Dram will kill us!"

"Kill us? Perhaps many of us. But not you. They have seen what you have done. They will put together the information from the chip and the activation of an Orb. They know an Earth Reader, one marked for observation, was aboard a ship that made that unprecedented journey. They will do everything possible to learn this secret, to harness this power. No, they will not kill you, not yet. Not until they believe they have exhausted all avenues to master this ability. They will preserve you, Ambra, although they will not be kind. But it is essential that you survive! A little while, no matter what they do to you. I promise, we will come. Somehow, we will come. You are our hope, and the doom of us all if the Dram control you."

"Control me? How?"

"Don't think of such things. Word is out. The Resistance will come. You must hang on."

A sharp rapping on my navpod window shook me out of thought. An alien navigator was standing outside, motioning for me to exit. I stepped out, trembling. The ship was dark except for emergency lighting. It looked wounded. The crew was gone.

The pilot spoke. "Thel is coming. The rest of us are assembling near the entrances. A Dram warship has locked onto us, and we are being pulled into a docking position. They will be here momentarily."

The elevator doors opened, and Thel moved in. They communicated together in the Xixian language, and the pilot walked off to the lift and disappeared within it.

Thel crouched beside me. "They are approaching, Ambra. The slaughter is merciless. Soldiers are killing all Xix and scanning humans for your chip, executing those who do not match. We don't have much time, and I need to tell you something before they arrive."

My mind was treading water. Why couldn't we run? Hide? *Something?* Sitting, waiting for them to take us, it made no sense!

Beyond my panic, a dread was forcing itself into my awareness. An ominous shadow, terrible and familiar. As if the room were adopting a shape in my thoughts, a place I had seen earlier but had not visited. *Déjà vu.* Part of me knew it was important, but I couldn't focus in this madness.

"Listen to me, Ambra." Thel gripped my shoulders. "A last physics lesson to take with you."

Science now? *Had it gone insane?*

"Sentience is a field. A *physical force* like electromagnetism or gravity. This won't make sense to you, but it is a truth of the cosmos. Unification theories marry all the energies of nature. Not as your scientists would have hoped, but something far grander, more subtle. But a consequence of these two things is that sentient thought is coupled to the spacetime matrix. The more consciousness, the more complex it becomes, the more coupling. Advanced civilizations with many billions of hyper-intelligent beings distort the local universe to a measurable degree. This effect can subtly perturb even the orbits of their planets."

I was shaking my head, not understanding. This was all gibberish.

"Ambra, thought *itself* sends ripples through space and time. We of Xix had always wondered if this could lead to communication through the cosmic continuum."

I heard explosions and screams, the sounds of conflict and stamping of feet. I would have retreated to a corner and hid, but Thel's strong grip kept me in place.

"Communication?" I stammered out, my heart drumming in my chest.

"Telepathy, you would call it. But nothing mystical or magical. You perceive distortions in the fabric of reality, Ambra. Cognition contributes to this framework. Hence, with your great sensitivity, you can sense those thought ripples. You can *Read* minds."

I shook my head again. "Thel, no, I can't."

The sounds were closer, deafening. The lift signaled it was heading downward. *What had called it?*

"You can, and you *did*. How did you bring us to my homeworld?"

"I don't know! I just saw the way."

"You perceived a path through the Orb, but to where? You couldn't have known *yourself* where Xix lay. What was the last thing I said to you before we made the traversal?"

My mind raced. The elevator had stopped below and begun its ascent. The ship shook from new explosions. Time had run out and something was coming. "I don't know! You said you wanted to go home again!"

"Yes! Don't you see? My consciousness focused on my planet. You detected those ripples of my awareness, needing a path through which to steer our vessel. You *Read* my thoughts, Ambra, just as you *Read* the past and the future. Both are embedded in the spacetime matrix."

"It can't be true."

The alien's eyestalks bent as one to me, hovering over my face.

"Listen to me. It is. Don't turn away from this! You must develop it, harness your powers. You will need all of them to withstand what comes next. Believe in yourself. *Survive.* You are what we have been waiting for."

Thel shuddered and flung its arms in several directions, one of them striking me. I slammed to the floor, a sharp pain in my back. With a flash of light and a crash, the alien dropped beside me, its monstrous form charred and smoking, eyestalks filmed over and gray.

As I gawked upward, Dram infantry aimed weapons at me. One stepped forward, raising a strange device. I crouched lower, tears streaming out of my sightless eyes. I sobbed at what was left of the Xix—extraterrestrial, *other*, one of *Them*, yet my teacher, my healer, a caring force against the cruelty I'd known. Thel was not indifferent or hostile. Thel was another thinking being that had spent its last moments helping me.

To save a galaxy.

I wept at this death, and also for my failure to stop it. The vision lurking at the edges of my awareness locked in sync with the present. Now I remembered. I *had* seen this before. In my terrible reading of the future preceding the Orb traversal—a fate where Thel died beside me. The premonition had driven me to warn the Xix, and to find a way to pass through the portals. I had witnessed this slaughter and had opened the portal to prevent this destiny as much or more than to escape the warships.

But it had *not* saved Thel. My actions to undo that reality fit into the chain of events producing it. *Why?* I had an explanation. *Because I had not studied closely enough.* Because I had not dissected the details of my prophecy. It didn't console me that there hadn't been time, that the Dram attack was imminent and forced me to act. The future had no mercy. Its complexities demanded serious contemplation. I cursed my naivete.

I examined the immediate present. The clicking soldiers put down the chip-scanner and spoke in their hideous language. A towering pair raced forward and jerked me to my feet. They dragged me back, casting me to my knees under some higher-ranked insect.

"They are our properties! Resist not otherwise they are eliminated," shrieked the Dramian translator.

I went limp, and the bugs hustled me through the Xixian ship and into their warcraft. Along the way, I mourned the bodies of Xix and humans, side by side, blasted apart and left to rot by the Dram army. A terrible anger flamed inside my mind, a hatred I had never known, even after all the evil inflicted on me.

As their troops tossed me through the hallways, I vowed revenge. I would punish these bugs. I would hurt them. For what they had done to me. To my world. To all the worlds beneath their savage rule.

The fury blinded my sixth sense. A white-hot plasma simmered before me, occluding anything else.

My thoughts were fire.

Chapter 22

He who has a why *to live can endure almost any* how.

Friedrich Nietzsche

It wasn't long before the bugs questioned me.

They had tossed me into a high-tech cage. Like the rest of the warship, it was an efficient and cruel construction. Dram design had such a harsh sense of purpose. It bordered on architectural sadism. Like the underwater chambers on the Sortax homeworld, the same strange metals with embedded luminescence characterized the materials. There were three walls. The fourth was an invisible force field. Light and air entered, but it resisted any attempts to press against it. The harder one pushed, the more solid the unseen wall became. I managed to inch a few fingertips through the resistance, but no more.

Armed soldiers stalked outside my cell, but their eyestalks never tipped in my direction. Dumb humans don't score high in the "escape risk" column, I suppose. And that pretty much was the reality for me. I abandoned probing the walls and sat in a corner, knees pulled to my chest and my arms wrapped around them. But I didn't cry. Something adamantine percolated inside me with anger and determination.

After some time, another of the aliens approached my cell. The creature clicked at guards, who deactivated the shield wall. It entered with a soldier alongside. The thing was shorter than the patrols, dressed in a less militaristic outfit, and it carried no weapons. *Hive officer?* Small bubbles floated, surrounding the central bulges of its eyestalks. *Alien glasses?* The insect bent its body in half. The lower abdomen and legs ran parallel with the floor. The upper portion and "head" were angled at sixty-degrees to the rest. The eyes with their little lens-spheres aimed toward me.

"They are it, which opened the Orb?" it began.

God, how I hated those translators.

I focused. Thel had admonished me to survive, but I couldn't bring myself to reply to these butchers. The bug head tilted left, right, seeking a better view of me and my silence.

"They are it, which opened the Orb?" it repeated.

Still, I said nothing.

It continued, over and over, in one language after another. After ten or fifteen repetitions, the irritation provoked me. I figured speaking to this thing was infinitely preferable to getting a tour of badly translated Dram in all of Earth's tongues.

"English," I spat. "I speak English."

The insect stared at me.

"They are it, which opened the Orb?" it rang out again.

"Yes, for God's sake. Now can we move on beyond this?"

It pulled out a small device, horribly reminiscent of the Sortax gadget that had nearly killed me on Earth. I didn't waste time, but screamed, startling the bug and causing several of its many back feet to retreat. The guard raised its weapon.

"Careful! You have to use the *lowest* mode on that thing, or you'll kill me, and then I won't be any good to you! I'm a powerful Reader, and I am far more sensitive to the spacetime matrix than others."

"Applicable is this?" it asked.

"Yes! Turn the detector all the way down. You'll see."

The Dram officer adjusted the device and aimed it at me. I tensed, but it was not painful. The equivalent of several, low-level lasers flitting over your eyes. Compared to the Orbs, such simple, boring patterns to me now.

"They are much highly cannot be measured." The bug turned off the machine. "Why negative the Sortax explain rather to us?"

"Because they're stupid squid-heads," I added helpfully.

"They are stupid. To be punished." It tapped onto a small gadget and replaced it on a belt around its upper abdomen. The thing continued to stare at me.

Thel's last lesson rushed back, those mad ideas about me Reading minds. The Xix had said it was real. That I couldn't turn away from it. That I would need all my skills to survive. I decided to trust those final words, to believe in them with all I had. If they were true, I would find out now and probe my captors.

I closed my eyes as the creature observed me. Being blind, it didn't do much, but it was a long habit from sighted years when trying to focus. I concentrated and used the meditative techniques Thel had taught me. Past and future rocked back and forth. I ignored them, seeking something different, something tied to the alien crowding my cage.

Epiphany. Like seeing an optical illusion shift from one image to another. A subtle and effervescent shimmering winked from items around me. The glow popped in and out like lightning in a storm. Inanimate objects were dark. But not the extraterrestrial monsters. They radiated intricate weavings of filigree.

One was simpler, more angular and hard. *The soldier.* The other was harsh, as all Dram, but nuanced and layered. A deeper complexity pulsed in this one. Its thoughts disturbed the spacetime matrix in multiple dimensions at once.

And so much fear. I could recognize the emotion also in this unfamiliar creature. It wasn't anxiety. It was a deep alarm, absent from the mind of the guard. This intrigued me. It testified to a sense of my own power in this place. This officer sought something terrible and important from me.

My eyes opened. "Why are you afraid of me?" I probed, offering a wild opening gambit.

The insect recoiled again, taking several steps back. "They are an intelligent," it responded. It decided to resort to a lie. "The Dram fear nothing! But we are try to we include, what you to be have made."

"You mean activating the Orb?"

"Yes! How base creatures, a nothing member of Hegemony, is in position so that does make such a thing? Which secrecy did you learn of Holy Orbs?"

Flattery it wasn't. And *Holy Orbs?* This was getting weird.

"Are you a priest?"

Anger flashed from the creature.

"No! Never! I do not grasp the idiots of those superstitions! I besides the fact that potential in the Orbs, it seems I and like me, understand those respect in order to control, seeking those."

Control? Power? *A technologist! A scientist, perhaps.* This made sense. My Readings of its consciousness fell into place. The picture clarified, its personality and motivations exposed. *Motivations to be exploited.*

"I can control them. You want me to give you my secret?"

The insect's feet tap-danced, bringing its hideous face close to mine.

"When Dram want, they take," it hissed.

Careful, Ambra. "If you make a mistake, and you harm me, you may damage my mind, and you will never learn the mystery. Do you dare take that risk now, alone? What will your punishment be if you fail?"

The wash of anxiety from the insect was like a prismatic spray. Again, it retreated several steps. "They are a human intelligent, yes. Special. But with us is skillful large number very with persuasion.

The emperor thinks, is grasped that we consume this you-power. It orders. Then this word of you has not importance. Until time, enjoy the existence."

The officer clicked toward the guard, who escorted the creature through the door. It reengaged the force field, leaving me alone, and for the moment, free from their probes.

But for how long? I could feel the time-tugs of hyperspace jumps—we had made at least four since they captured me. These bugs couldn't go straight to the destination they wished as I had done. Like all space-faring aliens, they had to follow the indirect routes of the String Tree. But soon they would arrive at their homeworld. The nexus of their hegemony. With their emperor and all their numbers "very with persuasion."

I would be in their hands. I doubted they could learn how I controlled the Orbs. *I* didn't know. But they might kill me trying to find out. *Or worse.* I had to get out of this. For so many, not just myself.

Every expansion of my abilities centered on life crises, and it was no different this time. I sat down in the cell. I crossed my legs, closed my eyes, and allowed my fear of the future to wash over me. I decided to believe in my potential, to risk anything, including my sanity, to cross over the planes of possibility and look the tsunami of coming events square in the face. More than my single life relied on me becoming what the Xix thought I could be. If they were right, the freedom of so many in the galaxy might depend on it.

Yes, it was megalomaniacal. But you can't let humility get in the way of saving the universe.

Nothing in my life or training prepared me for what was about to happen. I sank into a deep trance. My awareness plunged inward. Deeper, until I could count every heartbeat. I analyzed each slow breath as my lungs drew in air and forced it out. My Dram prison receded to some point at an infinite distance.

The secret in meditation is finding without seeking. At this terrible separation, the future edged microscopically close to me. One by one, by force of will, I toppled the obstacles my psychology erected. They flooded me with panic, a disembodied voice screaming to go no further. My soul trembled at what lay on the other side. But an anger filled me with purpose. An inferno towered over my fears, and I knocked them down.

The fiery rage supercooled my sixth sense, priming it. A bottle in the freezer, pulled out hours later, unfrozen, shaken, and crystallized in an instant. My vision awakened. My bulging organ opened its odd eyes from a long slumber, and the forthcoming burst over me like a shattered dam. The power of the rushing futures, their terrible weight, was irresistible. A thousand revelations ravaged my mind without respite. On and on, over days dragging me to depths of consciousness never explored.

I fought a fierce battle to stay focused, to hold these visions at bay, to integrate the now and the coming times. Present, past, and the enormous future boiled and mixed within me. They blurred one into the other in a confused kaleidoscope. Approaching incidents gave birth to historical ones. Cause and effect became meaningless.

I stepped out of time. Before me frothed colossal rivers of events, tossing and twisting, undulating, crashing, and morphing. No reference point. No arrow of time. Only the ever-churning currents in an infinite ocean. I lost myself at sea, set adrift, unable to find a safe shore.

In this trance, I responded to nothing. Dram medics and scientists labored to revive me. Three weeks of travel through the String Tree and two more in a hospital on their homeworld. I lay unmoving and unresponsive. My captors and representatives from several species observed with great anxiety.

But I found my way home. The meaning of how it happened, I leave to you.

The mists cleared over the endless squall. Ricky beamed in the distance and called my name across the waves. I followed his voice, swimming against the raging currents to a bright chamber at the heart of the ocean. A sea of voices and souls swirled about him. It drew me in, locking outside the shudders and sounds and groans of the tempest of time.

Radiance rose, bathing in the scent of his joy. The echoing luminosity enveloped me, caressing my awareness. Tasting it, I laughed at the ridiculous simplicity.

I understood what he tried to tell me that day.

Chapter 23

We do not rest satisfied with the present. We anticipate the future as too slow in coming, as if in order to hasten its course; or we recall the past, to stop its too rapid flight. So imprudent are we that we wander in the times which are not ours, and do not think of the only one which belongs to us; and so idle are we that we dream of those times which are no more, and thoughtlessly overlook that which alone exists.

Blaise Pascal

I drifted in a still and silent realm.

Uncountable patterns of stars lit the darkness. In back of me, the golden light of the sun pushed forward, and like a ghostly boat, I sailed on the solar wind. Accelerating, I gained speed past Mercury. Beyond the sulfurous clouds of greenhouse Venus. The moon appeared once more. Behind it, a quarter surrounding a dime, the blue, white, and green-brown of Earth.

It captured my heart.

Earth! In glory, she hung in the cold blackness. After the violet seas of the Sortax, the alien structures of the Dram, the orange deserts of Xix, and the countless sterile and horrible things I had seen, before me was the one place in all the expanse where we belonged. All human beings.

Home.

I wept and smiled. I rushed like a gleeful child into the embrace of her mother, dashing past the lifeless moon, limbs outstretched and encompassing the blue marble as it approached me.

I was going home.

My smile foundered, broke, and faded like clouds against a mountainside. A terrible mask of horror replaced it. I watched in madness as the planet dissolved in my arms. Pole to pole, sea and land, the sphere shattered like a stained-glass window, the separate fragments blurring and melting in my hands. I worked my palms, trying to reshape the thing as if it were some dissolving snowball on a warm spring day. But nothing could slow the merciless process.

The Earth *melted.* Blue-white-brown ink dripped through my fingers. I wailed as the paints poured into the blackness, evaporating in a faint mist into nothingness.

My scream echoed through the emptiness. A wolf's howl reverberating in a stone cathedral. A wild dirge for a soul forever abandoned in the icy emptiness. Unable to perish. Powerless to escape.

Doomed to wander the hell-void, desolate and dispossessed.

Chapter 24

No visiting angel, or explorer from another planet could have guessed that this bland orb teemed with vermin, with world-mastering, self-torturing, incipiently angelic beasts.

Olaf Stapledon

I awoke to the freakish form of a Xixian medic.

Its grotesque contours, bobbling eyes, and many-fingered extremities danced above me. For a moment, I was back on the ship with Thel. False relief ran like opioids through my veins. The nightmarish attack, Thel's death, the melting Earth, the awful series of dreams.

It was only a confused vision!

The movements of Dram attendants standing around the physician slapped me into the present. Doom and dread descended, cruel reality hammering my guts.

No.

I relived it all, gritting my teeth to ground myself. Smoldering anger summoned the grim determination born in the trauma of those events.

"You are awake," said the Xixian medic.

The insects crowded behind, observing. Their many hands and fingers clacked against each other, but they did not interfere.

"Why does a Xix work with *them?*" I hissed.

"We serve everywhere within the Hegemony," it chirped. "Especially in the medical sciences, where our talents and technology cannot be perverted to actions running counter to our being. We often prove quite *useful*," it said.

Did its words have a hidden meaning? Thel had said its people would know about me, would help me. Was this medic communicating this?

A Dram military officer stormed into the room, preventing any further communication. Its composite armor clattered in sync to its many feet. The foul head pivoted to the Xixian doctor. After several bursts of clacking between them, the Xix bowed and left the room.

The bug turned on me. "Depending upon us the best efforts employed, had in order to maintain human, its life. They must better prove the emperor their worth."

"And if I don't?" I wasn't feeling cooperative.

"Then they will end." It signaled to other infantry, and they wheeled my bed out of the room.

"Wait!" I interrupted, pushing myself up and swinging my legs over the side. "I can walk."

The officer clacked, they released the gurney, and I walked of my own accord. The trance had weakened me, my muscles unused in the deep coma. But I was determined to give them as little power over me as possible. Stiff and shaky, I lumbered forward.

They marched me down several hallways and to an adjoining building packed with prison cells. A hideous guard stopped in front of a cell like the one on the Dram warship. It deactivated the field, and the soldiers shoved me inside, reactivating the screen.

The officer stared across the barrier at me. "This health, it is good therefore to be maintained. That we being expected from directly, makes that trial is begun attainable. The tomorrow supporter, the advocate, is to be allotted. That it cooperates to investigation, is best your, with of everything where you are required is made clear."

Yes, better I clarify it all to them, I'm sure. With that hardly veiled or coherent threat, it turned and hustled out of the corridor. The devils left me to my thoughts and the silence of the prison ward.

Exhaustion crushed me. I wanted nothing more than to curl up on the floor and sleep. I knew I had to rest. Eat. Recover. But so much to do. So little time.

The visions swam in and out of my awareness, longing to break free. I shook my head. *Not again.* I was in control, and I needed to pull my head out of ten thousand futures and into the now.

It had mentioned a trial. That sounded *wonderful.* It promised me an advocate. Of what use would a defender be in the murderous Dram justice system? How could I prepare?

I was not left much time to plan. Within a few hours, a group I identified as members of the technologists—as I liked to think of them—came tramping into my cell. The guards bristled at their entrance and orders, preferring the military wing in their power structure.

The techies positioned themselves in a semicircle around me. Already, I had probed enough of the immediate future to anticipate their first actions. I spoke to prevent any unpleasant scans of my tumor.

"Before you pull out your scanners and fry my brain, please turn them down to the lowest setting. I am very sensitive and will register at your weakest levels."

A chaotic laser-light show frolicked through my awareness. The swarm twitched and exchanged eyestalk glances.

One in the middle of the semicircle revealed itself to be the leader. "You expect our energies well."

I decided to unload on them early. "I *Read* your actions. I saw it in my immediate future."

"You are so much powerful Reader?" it asked.

"I can do this and many more things."

"You have then the open of the Orbs," it said. The lousy translator somehow got across the awe behind the question.

"Yes."

"This possible with from Ancient Ones?"

"It comes from me."

This elicited a lot of excited clicking.

"It should they are sharing these informations with us, that we can present to the emperor!"

"I will not."

"It must! They will suffer in the questionings if there is not! And they will be in the danger of partisans that will seek execution before they attend to what is known or can made be. For them, you gestate the heresy, that contaminating the Holy Orbs. They will not allow in it in order to they will live. Only death given with them. It should there is saving and it say to us how this thing is performed!"

Decoding their longer translations was always a headache. "The *partisans*? Oh, I see. The priests." I didn't care if the term was appropriate. Getting tangled in the petty politics of this hateful society was the least of my worries. I had experienced too much, and these idiots were blind where I could see. Their presence sickened me.

"Let me tell you something, *insect*. In thirty seconds, an angry group of your priestly friends is going to barge in. You will have a screaming fight with them. Their soldiers will shout at the guards here. And you will be promptly thrown out on your exoskeletoned asses. You won't ever be alone with me again. So, there won't be a chance for me to tell you anything."

I leaned forward, so livid I spit in its eyestalks. "But even if there were, I wouldn't tell you a thing, you murderous piece of Dram vermin. You've enslaved my species. My parents were gunned down in cold blood because of you. I watched your sick soldiers slaughter the innocent and brave. I will *die* before giving you the key to more power than you already have. And you might as well calm down. Here are your *holy* friends."

The anger radiating from the group was so intense, I flinched. But I had vision they didn't.

As I spoke my last sentence, the clerical delegation stormed into the cell area, and the shouting (or clicking) match began. Soon, the guards ejected the techies to great waves of gloating from the priests. They exchanged furious clicks down the hallway until they were out of earshot. And for the night, I was offered some peace.

But serenity wouldn't stay. I continued to shift through the visions of the future that had consumed me. If I did not hold them back, they could flood through my mind, strangling consciousness. To remain within the now, I had to exert enormous control. I filtered the flow, allowing small streams of information to leak through. I dammed the rest, blocking them in a section of my thoughts. The slow trickle I sifted, mapping out the coming of events, and more and more, what lay beyond. It was logical, progressive, and exhausting.

The mountain of visions loomed in my awareness. So many to consider, impossible to count. I separated the meaningless, the inconsequential, from those important to my life and those I might affect.

In this other space, my eyes opened at the top of a high peak. Beneath me cascaded lower hills, valleys, rivers, and cities with legions of life. In the distance, the glint of a great sea. But I had never processed this kind of information. The fine details of a falling leaf or the drops of melting snow fought to imprison my mind's eye.

To progress through this maze, I had to ignore overwhelming beauty, threatening horror, and fixate on the critical paths extending in multiple directions. Down below, mixed with the ten thousand visions, were uncountable beings in danger. And I had to find out where and how, plan a solution to save them. So much to process, so naive my experience, and so little time.

Inspiration arrived in the world of dreams. Drained of energy, sleep would overpower me often in the days to come. In fantasy, I leapt with imagination to future episodes of heightened significance.

Dominating everything, over and again the next few weeks, was my vision of the melting Earth. It hung in my psyche like some bomb wired to explode. *What was its meaning?* I could not rely on the imagery drawn from reverie. I would have to find my way to that eventual point in a conscious state. Awake, I needed a great effort to forge ahead, skipping careful deliberation, risking the dam breaking over me again.

The time was coming, I knew, when I would have to take this risk. *But not tonight!* I would have to face a lot tomorrow, and I had to face it sane and controlled. The prophecy would come.

Yes, I remembered. Very soon, the prophecy would come.

Chapter 25

The single biggest problem in communication is the illusion that it has taken place.

George Bernard Shaw

A day lasts thirty-six hours on the Dram homeworld. This throws the human biological clock pretty out of whack. We can reset at different start points on a twenty-four-hour schedule, but move much from that timetable? We don't do so well.

On this vile planet, I remained in a constant state of surreal suspension, my body never able to adjust. Never sober, never restful in sleep. The perfect physiological counterpoint to my mental swaying between reality and vision.

Their swollen sun burns a feverish, pale scarlet. Not the cozy, warm red of an Earth sunset, but a piercing, unrelenting orange rusting over everything. The glare washed out all other colors of human perception. Only at dawn and dusk would the hue become a full crimson, far more potent than anything ever witnessed on Earth.

The planet's position limited life in the pre-red giant phase of this system. The surface was just too cold. Life developed beneath the ground, microbial and constrained.

Billions of years later, having chewed through its core hydrogen, the star gorged on outer stores of the gas and expanded, digesting several planets as it bloated. The world became a hothouse jungle for hundreds of millions of years until the gaseous oven baked it to a desert. This ugly radiation rushed Dramian evolution. They became tough, harsh, and unforgiving like the sands. Capable of flowering at times, but all too often bringing misery to those they encountered.

When the door opened the next morning, it was hard for me to determine how long it had been since I laid down. In many ways, it didn't matter. I hadn't slept—like some restless convalescent, I had bobbed up and down the entire night on an ocean of visions. The solid reality of my prison was a bracing contrast.

A small troop tramped into my cell. I loathed their armored and towering insectile anatomy. I didn't need a sixth sense to detect their malice. Behind them followed a Xix with its absurd elegance. A captain of the guard clicked to the dancing alien, and its patrol strode out of the room, reactivating the shield. The barrier hummed, and the polite extraterrestrial bowed to me, seating itself on the ground across from my bed shelf.

I had loosened my connection to the visions as the guards entered. Glancing at the Xixian figure, I raised myself on the platform, dropping my feet to the floor. The fog of the trance lingered as I waited for the creature to speak.

"Greetings, Ambra Dawn! I am Waythrel of Xix, your advocate for the Tribunal."

My *advocate*. Exciting and unexpected. A Xix! I trembled with joy but tried to keep it under control. I took a formal approach.

"I'm very honored and pleased to find you are here on my behalf, Waythrel. I feared one of these hideous bugs would be charged with a halfhearted attempt at defending me."

"The Dram often use my kind in official roles. We are masters of their language and laws and are updated with new tools from our homeworld on a regular schedule. Our usefulness earns us many privileges. Your tone shows you are reckless and do not understand your hosts."

It's warning me. These gentle aliens, always teaching!

My mind raced, remembering the riddle games I played with Thel. *Updated*—it knows about me as promised. *Privileges*—its position as my advocate could be compromised if my captors suspect the Xix are conspiring with me. *Reckless, not understanding…*what did it matter what I said? Unless confidentiality meant nothing. Yes, that was it. The Dram were listening to everything! We had to be careful.

"My teacher was Thel of Xix before my journey here," I began, hoping to convey I was still a student and would do my best to learn. "I am ignorant of many things. Please be patient with me."

Waythrel removed strange devices from pockets in its robe. Several opened to project visual information in discrete planes in the room. Incorporeal screens floated in my cell. Semicircular keyboards materialized for its upper arms, with hundreds of keys for their sinuous extremities. The alien typed in a blur of dancing digits.

"Good, then we may begin. You have much to absorb before the trial, and two Dramian days, or three of your Earth, to prepare. Your very life is at stake, Ambra Dawn. I hope everything I have learned of you is true, because you will need *all* of your talents at the Tribunal."

Was it saying I would have to forecast? As a Xix, it had to realize I couldn't see myself clearly in any future.

"Not for points of law and theology," it continued. "I will handle those as much as is allowed. But for your own questioning. You must understand the context in which you are being examined. I am charged with communicating this and more, and your comprehension is critical." It paused. "Sometimes, I think these translators we make, however powerful, are almost useless. Meaning is always lost in translation. If only there were more direct ways to communicate."

Telepathy. It was telling me to use telepathy! Of course. How else to talk about important yet dangerous topics when those monsters were listening in? Somehow, Thel had communicated this power to Xix. And I had to make it work.

I'd now Read minds and feelings on several occasions but not details. And sending information? Could it be done? Or would I have to speak in this coded way my advocate did? Could I converse like this creature without revealing to the Dram what I was doing? I doubted *that* very much.

"Yes, Waythrel, I think I get what you mean. I am an Earth animal. Please, express your thoughts simply. Strongly. Focusing on the key elements so that I might understand."

If this was going to work, the extraterrestrial would have to dumb things down. A lot. Concentrate on the basic concepts, and not in a complicated alien way. With luck, I could grasp them. I closed my eyes and focused inward, slowing my respiration. The glow of its awareness manifested in front of me. I reached out to the psyche of my advocate.

And recoiled. *The complexity!* The Xixian mind made the Dram seem simple. Crystalline spider webs, a maze of thought weaved through my perception. I shivered.

Braving this unknown, I gravitated toward a brighter gleam. I sensed many ideas but couldn't understand them. Others flared, stripped of filigree. They opened to me, and my thoughts clothed them in images, short memories replaying their content.

Amazed, I waded into small patches of Waythrel's intelligence. A strange memory pulsated over the rest. Odd because the experience was not Waythrel's, but one seen through the eyes of another Xix. The viewpoint exited a hidden chamber in the ship I had piloted through the Orb. The Dram warriors were gone, their warship whisking me away for examination. This unknown Xixian sprinted to the helm after the attack. On arriving, it bent over a prone figure, burnt and mangled, collapsed in a heap beside the navpods.

Thel.

It took all my concentration to continue. I had to force away the emotions threatening to yank me out of this Reading. *Focus.*

The creature touched the fibrous material between Thel's eyestalks. When their membranes met, images gushed from its dying mind. The final few weeks on the ship. The activation of the Orb. Our last words together. All the details poured into the neuronal nexus of this Xix—a life download. Waythrel possessed the memories as well.

You see, part of Thel is within me now, Ambra. With all the Xix. And I know much of what you are and have done. Many of my kind do. We have distributed its experiences.

I heard these thoughts! How would I reach back?

"I'm calmer now," I said, "and ready to learn what you have to teach me. I feel a part of Thel is with me in you."

The alien tipped its writhing mass of eyestalks toward me. I'd reached my mark. When Waythrel spoke, I realized our conversation would be unlike any I had experienced.

"In what I say about Dramian law and custom, you should listen at *two* levels. Strive to comprehend each. From time to time, I will ask you to confirm your understanding of all meanings in this complicated discussion."

The Xix's thoughts echoed in my mind.

I mean, hearing me here as well, Ambra. Please answer affirmative, and nod your head three times if you do.

"Yes, I understand," I said, following the instructions.

"Good. To begin, I will explain some history. A fragile balance exists between the religious and the naturalistic castes on Dram. This division has caused many conflicts, leading to devastating wars. Nevertheless, it has persisted. It is as old as their pre-technological civilization. It is a foundation of the current galactic order."

It is in this divorce of faith and reason our enemies are superficially powerful, but in truth weak. Such an artificial separation of the undivided light of revelation is a sickness of the mind and soul, only too obvious in the myopia and brutality of the Hegemony. Societies unable to believe are sterile. Those without doubt are doomed by arrogance.

They sway between them in violence, tearing apart what should be united.

My thoughts were spinning. It was like hearing a conversation in one ear and a commentary in the other. How the Xixian brain could produce both at the same time astonished me. I concentrated and tried to integrate these two streams of information.

"The Holy Orbs are at a core in this conflict. To the religious caste, they represent a revelation in a spiritual dimension. They must be approached in a purified and humble state before the Creator of the universe. The scientific class, the Naturalists, views them as physical manifestations. They seek to harness their power. The Believers view those efforts as sacrilege. Profiteering from the Celestial Spheres is a sin against God. Several millennia ago, when the Dram first encountered the relics of the Ancient Ones, this dispute erupted into a civil war. The conflict exterminated one-fourth of their population."

Remember, Ambra, any species able to turn on its own kind with such malevolence will, with much less deliberation, ruin and slaughter those very different from them.

Part of me squirmed, thinking about the actions of humanity. Our repeated descents into massacre. Were we any better?

We must focus on the Orbs. The Tribunal will decide your fate, your life, and the manner of your death, based on how they view their manipulation.

"Are you following me so far?"

"Yes," I said, the implications clear.

We of Xix feel there is no safe judgment for you. If the Believers prevail, it will be torture and execution for heresy and sacrilege. If the Naturalists win the day, it will be mental enslavement to harness your power.

The alien's many eyes bored into me. Prismatic sprays burst from its thought structure like fireworks.

We are convinced of your worth to the Resistance. Therefore, we are planning a terrible risk. To save you, we will intervene on your behalf

*and subject ourselves to the wrath of the Dram. Please nod three times to
show you have heard and understand.*

Waythrel's thoughts rattled my soul. An entire species risking
itself for a single alien creature? I struggled, somehow managing to
move my head and respond.

"I don't want to see extermination, Waythrel."

The Xixian advocate bowed toward me. "In all such sacrifice,
there is the belief a higher purpose is served. In this motivation, you
may comprehend difficult choices, challenging actions."

*I cannot yet tell you what we will do. We have placed ourselves in
numerous critical positions across Dram. The Xix can, therefore,
manipulate much to our designs. But we need time. To plan thoroughly,
because for so many reasons, we must not fail.*

"At the Tribunal, you will be questioned by advocates from each
caste. They will then debate your fate before the high inquisitor."

"Who's that?"

"The inquisitor holds an office created thousands of years ago to
aid in mediation among the castes. The station is second in power to
the emperor. The laws grant this individual enormous influence to
balance culture between the Believers and Naturalists. The inquisitor
is required to originate from one of the Isolation Zones. These areas
on the planet are neutral ground, where the differing teachings are
withheld until the Dram therein pass the age of maturity. This is to
ensure no bias in judgments."

*And therefore, this position is one of the most corrupt in the system.
Substantial bribes are the norm. Those seeking appointment too often
are hungry for such benefits. Beware the high inquisitor!*

"Tomorrow, you will be brought before the inquisitor for an
assessment in advance of the Tribunal. Here, you may receive offers
of clemency should you acquiesce to the emperor's will."

So much information! Facts I needed to internalize and consider.
But I couldn't. I was reeling from the offer of Waythrel to save me.
They believed I could help them rescue thousands of worlds. Stop
the Dram. But my intuition spoke that it would mean certain death

for the Xix, whether or not I was what they hoped. I wouldn't be a savior. I'd be a murderer, responsible for the destruction of an entire species, the brightest and kindest and wisest I had encountered.

What to do? My heart rebelled against the Xixian plan. It couldn't be right. My mind dashed forward in spacetime like some mad thing. I was heedless. I stopped fearing those complex webs that had nearly killed me the last time. I *had* to see enough of the best possible future to know what to do!

Ambra, we of Xix will risk much. All. You must promise us you will do everything within your power to follow our instructions. I will come back with details. I need you to tell me now that you understand and commit to us.

What could I do? I couldn't lie, not to the Xix, not in this situation. But I could *not* let them do this. I steeled myself. What I *could* do was go along with their scheme until I developed a better one. The Tribunal was in seventy-two hours. I had to find a way out of this nightmare, as I did with the Orb. This time I wouldn't be so naive. I wouldn't jump from one trap into another. This time, there would be no mistakes.

Ambra? Did you hear me? Please respond.

I tottered, shaking with emotion. What happened next was over before I realized it had begun. It opened the final door to the destiny that awaited me.

As my heart constricted and my thoughts raced, my emotions leapt through my sixth sense. My tumor stretched out its ghostly hand and touched Waythrel.

The alien shivered and recoiled. Its intricate mental web jostled. Anxiety, surprise, and awe emanated from the Xix. The bright webs reassembled into new and delicate patterns.

Ambra Dawn, what have you done?

What *had* I done? I didn't have an answer. Its reaction—had I caused it? How? I looked in confusion over toward the creature.

You have entered my mind. Your cognition impressed into my consciousness. It paused again in thought. *We never expected this. Thel underestimated your potential.*

"Waythrel, please. I'm not sure I've understood everything that you have told me today."

"You have grasped much, I do not doubt. And we will speak more tomorrow."

Its thoughts continued to echo in my awareness.

What has happened is as important as your power with the Orbs. I must report this immediately and seek advice. It makes you far more dangerous, even to us, than anyone could have envisioned.

Waythrel's alien intellect emitted odd and confusing images. The notions behind them bewildered me.

It means you not only Read. You also do something few have dared suggest might someday be possible. You touched my mind, its processes—my consciousness. Remember your lessons with Thel! To alter my cognition implies that you can modify spacetime itself. This is unprecedented. It is terrifying. No one knows where such power could lead. You are not merely a Reader. You are a Writer. The first Writer.

"Until tomorrow, Ambra Dawn. Think about what I have told you."

Waythrel signaled to the guards, who disarmed the shield, and let the lanky Xixian past. I curled up on my bed, wrecked from today's efforts and now stunned by this recent exchange.

A Writer?

From the sheer slopes of future vision, I sensed an avalanche careening towards us.

Chapter 26

Nothing is more despicable than respect based on fear.

Albert Camus

The red starlight waxed and waned. Invading, its tentacles pushed with a relentless will through my small force field window on the far wall. But the hateful light bothered me less than before. I was abstracted, diving into future memories. Sifting, panning filtering. Revealing patterns of possible futures. Paths through potential toward the goals I sought—escape, freedom, and preserving lives.

Waythrel returned several times over the next day. My withdrawal distressed it, and the Xix questioned me. But I dared not explain why to my advocate. I absorbed its lessons to some degree, the alien commenting on my growing powers to probe minds. But as I worked my way through the future's maze, the absurdities of Dram became less important. Most of the details around my future self I could not see. I ignored those I could perceive to find a path home, one with the least suffering.

I did learn that my alterations of Waythrel's mind, the imprint of my own thoughts in its own, hadn't done any damage. The Xixian medics scanned the organ in the alien's chest and had detected nothing unusual. They concluded that this telepathic power I summoned was something like an external stimulus. Light to eyes. Sound to ears. But Waythrel was uneasy, voicing concerns that it need not be so. And with the ability to modify spacetime itself, all the Xix were troubled. How would my powers continue to develop?

What mattered to me was that I got us out of this. And I had seen enough. In the paths where I did nothing, where others took the lead, untold carnage and chaos would follow. Genocidal fires would smolder across a thousand worlds in a galactic war.

Not that way. I began to discern another future in the jungle of time. A safer path. *Safe for many.* A great tragedy loomed over the time horizon in my consciousness, but it was distant and not dependent on what I could do. It was beyond my abilities to stop. I would face it as I had to.

As I struggled to find answers, the hour arrived for my audience with the high inquisitor. A large troop of Dram in military formals escorted us. We zipped through the detention zone, flying across bleak deserts on ground transports. Stopping before a high tower, we were marched into the chambers of the inquisitor.

An unimposing insect occupied the office. One might call it a runt if it weren't still over six feet tall. It was old, its slow movements the giveaway. Or so it seemed to an alien life-form like me, who had trouble distinguishing the signs of aging in another species. The bug was perched above us behind a green and gold counter. An overdone judge's bench. It looked down on us—literally and figuratively— during this short but informative *assessment.*

They shoved us before the thing. A small claustrophobic space separated us from the Dram guard. Everything was larger than me. The seven-foot-tall guards, the elevated judge, and my advocate. What did it matter? I had my own strengths.

My counsel would try to have the Tribunal abolished but had

little hope of that happening. My Orb manipulation was documented with precision scientific instruments. This made me a center of questions for power and religion in the Hegemony. Waythrel and the bug exchanged clicks for at least ten minutes. After their discussion, the high inquisitor waved off the Xix and addressed me.

"You have been informed of the charges?" The translator was of Xixian manufacture. An unusual choice for the Dram, who were suspicious of foreign devices. They most often chose to use their own far inferior machines. Unless they were dying and needed superior medics, of course. Or, in this case, when a member was less intimidated. My advocate had told me this mentally early on in the assessment.

Whatever it pretends to be, this one is a Naturalist. Only one very comfortable with technology would wear one of our translators. It will seek an arrangement with you to reveal your powers over the Orbs.

"Yes," I responded to the Dram above me.

"Would you repeat them for the inquisitor."

"I am charged with High Sacrilege in the contamination of the Holy Orbs by an impure species."

"And do you know the penalty for such a crime?"

"Purification, and then death." Meaning torment and execution if the torture didn't kill me first.

"There are other ways, human."

Here comes the offer. Please hear my thoughts on this before you answer.

The giant insect pressed a button. Lights dimmed as a cone of energy enveloped the three of us, leaving the guards outside.

A cloaking shield, Ambra. No one can overhear or record what happens inside. The inquisitor is protecting itself from what it is about to say.

"The emperor is very keen that the Hegemony possesses the power you have revealed. Some of us share a more enlightened view of your deeds than others on our world. While they may prevail in the trial, we would have it otherwise. And if you will agree to our terms, the Holy Office of the Sovereign has the authority to annul the Tribunal."

"And if I refuse?"

Ambra! Wait, I said!

"Then you will find yourself at the mercy of the judges," spit the insect. Anger radiated from its consciousness. "And should the Naturalists triumph, you will receive less kindness in your service to them."

The stupid fool. Already I could sense all the lies. I would suffer no matter what they said or promised. They would enslave me, recoil from no indecency to my person in attempting to extract the knowledge they desired.

This is an important political juncture, came Waythrel's thoughts. *If we can bypass the Tribunal, it will buy us considerable time and the momentary facade of better treatment. I suggest you accept its offer. Let me express this to the Dram.*

No! I shouted into its brain.

My advocate paused, disoriented from the impact of my angry thoughts. I stepped forward and growled at the inquisitor.

"Should I agree to your terms, you will just place me in superior conditions for a time before ripping my mind apart. Turning me into a lab rat on which you will work and likely fail to extract the secret you desire. No! I will risk a kinder death in torture. I will not help the galaxy's fiends and murderers. Tell your emperor a lowly Earthling spits in his face."

My advocate had recovered by that point, and I sensed its overwhelming shock and panic. The anxious Xix thought the high inquisitor would have me executed on the spot for this. Almost right. So much rage boiled out of the creature from my outburst. But I had seen the bright path to safety, and it did not end here.

Soon, Waythrel, you'll understand. Poor thing, it would be so hard to explain.

The insect clicked, and the guards were ushering us back to my cell. As it uttered those commands, I had withdrawn. Seeing the luminous road, I understood more and more what was required. Waythrel shouted at me on the return trip, its eyestalks whipping in many directions. Little of it entered my awareness.

Surprising myself, I spoke out loud in the relative safety of the noisy ground car. A stream of consciousness gushed out. My mind's eye ignored the surrounding reality, focusing on the coming futures.

"They will fight over me, and the Naturalists will prevail."

"What are you talking about?" it asked.

"Not even religious dogma can win over the chance for new powers. I see them, those conniving, backbiting fools. Scheming, drunk on potency. But it will be a prelude to a greater movement, and then, a crescendo of joy and heartache."

"Ambra, please, what..."

I turned my face toward my advocate, tears trickling down my face. I didn't see the alien next to me. My mind was overflowing with the vast horror before my unique sense in time.

"I can't *look*, Waythrel. I can't let myself look at the sadness, even though I know what I will see!"

We sat in silence for the rest of the trip to my cell. Just as well—I was somewhere else, anyway.

Chapter 27

*In this playhouse of infinite forms I have had my play, and here have
I caught sight of that which is formless.*

Rabindranath Tagore

When Waythrel next visited, it was a while before it could rouse me. I lay on my bed shelf with open eyes, my mouth half closed, drool along the side of my face. At first, the alien misunderstood. The tender skin where the laser had sealed the surgical incision leaked some blood, staining my clothes.

"Ambra, wake up! What have they done to you? Are you drugged? Have they tampered with your mind? Answer me!" The distressed Xix shook me with its upper arms, eyestalks darting about in a panic. A detached part of my awareness watched it speak into a communicator. An uncertain period passed and Xixian medics surrounded me.

"She is not currently medicated," I understood one to say, whether through a translator or through my telepathy, I'm not sure. "Remnants of a human narcotic are present, but at such low levels, they cannot be affecting her now. Furthermore, there is no intervention anywhere else except the abdomen. Her brain is untouched."

"Why is she like this, then? She has to be at the Tribunal in four hours!"

"The visions," I rasped. "They have never opened to me like this before." I swallowed, my throat dry, my words croaking out. "Infinite layers and webs inside of membranes. I must control my exploration. It's too easy to be lost in it."

"Ambra, what are you talking about? What have they done to you?"

Drops clouded my eyes. Tears for myself, for the others I had seen, for the history and future of pain and injustices that cannot possibly be balanced, even by all the love in the universe.

"My eggs, Waythrel," I said, angling my head toward them. "You didn't think they would risk losing me if things go wrong at the Tribunal or afterwards."

"Your eggs." A statement. I could *sense* the wheels turning in its mind.

"Last night, they came, threw me on a table, cut me open, and took them. My possible children, taken from me before they could exist."

Sobs spasmed my chest. I had never thought much about breeding, especially with my deformity. I mean, let's be honest, what mate would have this? But I had never thought I would be invaded and robbed, violated. With this act, the Dram had defiled something primal. My soul mourned. It howled to the heavens, decrying what else would be stolen.

The Xixian medics scanned the areas where my ovaries were and confirmed the results.

"I am sorry, Ambra," Waythrel began. "We did not anticipate this. Once again, we have been naive in imagining what they might conspire to. It is obvious on reflection. They want more genetic material to breed out your powers again. They could not clone you— human chromosomal instability has yet to be solved by any species in the galaxy. But your eggs—they could inseminate them with diverse sperm from males similar to your father. They have been plotting far ahead." It paused and repeated, "I am very sorry."

"We couldn't have stopped it," I moaned, trying to rise. "Not now, not with larger tasks waiting."

"What tasks, Ambra?"

"It's all becoming clear. A straight path home." I laughed, a bitter bile clogged in my throat. "No! Oh, *God*, no. Not home. Never home. But escape."

"Have you *read* this? The Xixian Council is formulating a final rescue plan. We suspect the worst for us and are evacuating many of our kind in secrecy. But if you have seen our future, you *must* tell us."

I smiled at the lanky alien. "It's alright, Waythrel. It will be okay. I'm seeing to it."

"You're seeing to it? Please, these stakes are too high for such riddles."

My thoughts phased between the present and the coming possibilities. "Don't press me. A few loose strands left to tie up now, and the path is sure. Can't...rush like...before. Need to see...*all* the routes."

I floated in and out of a trance for the next hours with bothered Xix flitting about me.

Time plodded in my cell but jittered through my consciousness. Events stormed past with hurricane winds. Roads and doors to the future sang in counterpoint, arias arcing across my awareness.

How the puzzle resolved is unclear to me, but after too many headaches, at a single point, two different melodies of time met. Out of the myriad strings of the *perhaps* emerged a unified thread of *destiny*. It sounds absurd, but that's the best I can describe it. I opened my eyes, seeing the future and my present, a superimposed harmony.

The Dram guard entered. They paraded us to the Tribunal.

Along the way, my mouth sprinted in a stream of consciousness. I'm sure it sounded like nonsense to Waythrel. The poor Xix feared I had gone mad at the most inopportune time. We were minutes before the trial, hours until the Xixian plan was set in motion. A hostile and hideous world caged us at the center of the Hegemony.

I chanted to the smelted landscape. "It will never be the same."

The dunes shimmered in a scarlet furnace, devoid of greens, blues, and yellows. Buildings blurred past us as the ground vehicle blasted by.

"A fetus as a single grain of sand. Twenty billion souls burned, ruptured in a moment of time. All *gravity*. So simple, *inverse square*. Spacetime bending and killing. Epochs within eras inside eons spinning, one long orbit after another, a stupid planet wannabe. Waiting to waste an entire world. Bastards—they will debate their creed while slitting a baby's throat."

The Xix tried to have the Tribunal postponed, but the Dram would hear nothing of it. Of course, my mental state signified little in these proceedings. It wasn't about truth or fairness. It was about their power struggle, laws, and creeds. There wouldn't be a part for me to play in the rude sham besides attending. My poor advocate would be reduced to listening to the blowhards bicker.

"I'm ready, Waythrel. This toy trial is a proud gasp in the face of the infinite. The only thing I dread is the awful waste of time it all is. I wish I could replace one piece of time with another."

The alien stared in my direction with its many eyes. I was too engrossed in thought to bother trying to sense its state of mind. I'm sure it was pretty bad.

Chapter 28

Men never do evil so completely and cheerfully as when they do it from religious conviction.

Blaise Pascal

The audience before the high inquisitor had been impressive, but nothing prepared me for the Tribunal.

Our escorts pulled alongside a giant dome. The venue had *Galactic Empire* written all over it. The monstrosity rivaled the size of an Earth metropolis. The Dram's favorite luminescent, marble-like substance coated the exterior. The worker bees had carved and polished the gleaming surface to a million facets. They reflected the bloody light of the star like a gargantuan incandescent bulb. I suppose to give it the appearance of power radiating from within. I found it hideous and tacky. My only astonishment rose from the incessant, forceful assault these brutes inflicted on the cosmos.

They floated us through an enormous corridor on levitation flats, small rectangular devices with guardrails. They sped a few feet above the ground. Of course, the engineers designed them for the Dram. An average human would have trouble grasping the rails. At my five foot two, the only support was a post to grip. At least the transports were bump-free. Still, they moved pretty fast, and instinct made me cling to the odd metal.

The tunnel fused with a mini-dome onion couched within the main vault, yet still the size of a football field. It was absurd. In the center of this extravaganza was an elevated platform, two hundred feet in the air. My advocate and I would stand there for the entire ordeal.

An enormous stage hovered over us. Decorated in confusing Dramian aesthetics, it held the seats of the Tribunal members. Waythrel and I had to crane our gaze toward them, their chairs arrayed in a semicircle above us. The far walls were dim. The design focused light on our smaller perch, leaving most of the chamber in darkness. The exceptions were the seat of the high inquisitor, and towering overhead, the grand throne on which the emperor sat.

The purpose was simple to discern—weaken the psychology of the accused. Show us how small and base we were, bolster their inherent sense of superiority. My own nature inverted their goals. It was, in some ways, the final sign of how psychotic these creatures were. At that point, I lost whatever hope I had to find another escape. It was my plan or endure a journey through Dram hell.

Beyond this conviction, it had the effect of increasing my confidence. They were so unbalanced, it would not be hard to defeat such enemies. This room was the proof. The aliens sacrificed anything of practical value for pageantry. The scale of the thing was so large it was impossible to see the members of the Tribunal from the platform. Nor could they see us. So, they had rigged giant suspended holograms to display each participant, like monitors in Times Square. I swallowed a chuckle at how ludicrous this farce had become.

I suppose I should have been more respectful. They were smarter than me. Much more powerful than any other species. And, of course, quite willing to do terrible things. But it wasn't me who was blind now. I had sight in a world where the rest stumbled.

The emperor's hologram dangled before us. Blown up tenfold, its already large size in the projection, I knew the monster well. Its form and clothing were familiar from my vision on Earth, from a time in my life that seemed an eon ago. It clicked commands as Waythrel and I settled onto the platform, bathed in light. The clicks rocked against my ears, amplified by alien technology. The Tribunal was in session.

Eight hours that insipid slogfest lumbered on. I will spare you the details. Constant religious and legal back-and-forth dominated between the high inquisitor, appointed advocates of the Naturalists and Believers. In my sound cone, it spewed over me in nauseating Dramian translation.

The Believers presented their case. The evidence recorded by their sensors of my manipulation of the Orbs. The original notes from Earth about my abilities. A brief questioning of Waythrel and me about whether I had indeed done these things ("Yup!").

Their derision polluted my senses. Many in the Believer camp had a lot of trouble *believing* a simple human could have power over the Holy Orbs. *An unclean creature with such gifts?* They exhausted everyone, arguing the impossibility. They focused on my deformity, my imperfections and blindness. "This animal is even a monster among its own kind!" exclaimed one particularly empathetic opposing counsel.

Their case was pretty easy to understand. I was an instrument of evil. A vile, corrupted beast empowered by dark forces to sacrilege. How else could a base and deformed hunk of sentience have any legitimate control over the Celestial Spheres? There could be no cooperation with me, nothing good to come from my actions. *Purification!* They must cleanse me and the universe of the malevolence possessing me. Send me to my death for my sins and prevent any further desecration of the Orbs.

Anyway, that's the English summary. Maybe it sounded less stone-age in the original Dram.

The Naturalists asserted their position. They countered by casting my malformations in a positive light (thanks, guys!). The Creator had no doubt endowed me with transformative gifts, a new organ of vision. They feigned a false respect for the Believers' faith. Who could judge the divine instrument of revelation? Did not the ancient texts claim even the lowest would see salvation? Had I not opened a portal? How could anything evil have done so? How could good have allowed it?

Their deceit was so palpable, no sixth sense was needed to realize what charlatans they were. They argued for a break from the barbaric interpretations of the past. It was time for a more progressive, enlightened interpretation of scriptures. They suggested, and I'm not kidding, that *God* had sent me. The Holy Queen Bee or whatever they believed (sorry, Waythrel, wasn't paying attention) conjured me from the clay *for a purpose*! The Dram could not reject the divine gift. They must use this transcendent instrument and discover that reason.

On it went between them. I zoned out. With the insect clicking as background, I finalized in my mind the dramatics of the next few days. The dancing futures of my visions—these were real. The bickering bugs? Their power struggles and ancient superstitions? That was the true dream, or nightmare.

Drowned in thought, ignored during the long debates, I missed the ceremonial signals. Waythrel shook me back into the present. They were nearing an end. The Dram leader ordered the advocates to sit. The high inquisitor shimmered in holodisplay.

"Finally. Let him spit it out," I muttered to my counsel.

"The sovereign has signaled closure. The debate has ended. All hail the judge and receive judgment!"

The bug sat, and the projection flicked to the craggy form of the head insect. *Ancient.* Despite my ignorance of alien physiology, I could tell the emperor was aged. The bent legs, the poor posture, the discolorations in the exoskeleton, the jerky movements. Decades had sanded and chipped away at this creature. But its spirit did not shake. A sharpness pricked through its words, persistent through translation. Sharp in essence, but not in effect. I sighed. I had heard the speech so many times already.

"The evidence and arguments have been presented. But there is still too much mystery. A primitive soul is said to have control over the Holy Orbs. Yet it shows no sign of the faith, no knowledge of the Ancient Ones. How can divine power have come to such a vulgar beast? How can we know it was this Earthling who opened the portal, and not another force assigning the act to it to divert attention?"

Waythrel stiffened beside me. The Xix had not anticipated this level of paranoia. To blame them because of their superior technology—classic Dram. But deadly serious.

"We need further proof!" Soft clicking could be heard around the chamber. "I command this prisoner provide the Tribunal with a demonstration! In four days, we mark the end of the Sun Spot Cycle. It is a holy omen. We will travel to the Sacred Orb. This creature will show us the truth of its claims or perish in torment for its heresy!"

Several in the Believer camp broke out in some kind of protest. I sensed the Naturalists swell with pleasure. The ugly roach was clever. It would test whether I held this power, and at the same time establish a use of it by the Dram. It would simplify its efforts to convince the Believer caste to exploit my abilities.

"Silence!" the emperor thundered, pounding a clawed hand on the throne. "I am empowered by the Divine Legions and rule with their authority! I *command* it. In four days, this creature will be brought before the Holy Orb. Take them away."

And it was over. The guards entered and hurried us out of the chamber. They herded us from the absurd dome toward the ground transports. The Xix shielded its many eyes from the outdoor light, bright and searing after our hours in the dark Tribunal. The noise of the city filled the surrounding spaces.

I leaned against the exhausted alien and whispered, "Now that we've endured their hot air, we have plans to set in motion."

Eyestalks converged on me. "Plans?"

"Yes, Waythrel." I exhaled, my lips morphing into a wry smile. It was good to confess at last.

"Soon, we will escape, and there is a lot we need to arrange. We must make sure it is as I have fore-planned."

"Ambra, you will tell me now what you have seen?"

"Oh, Waythrel, that would take more than our lifetimes. But a local corner of it all, yes, I'll tell you. These arrogant bugs, they are going to lead us right to the exit."

Chapter 29

It is incomprehensible that God should exist, and it is incomprehensible that He should not exist; that the soul should be joined to the body, and that we should have no soul; that the world should be created, and that it should not be created.

Blaise Pascal

The escape through the labyrinth glittered. It was a luminescent highway to my mind's eye. A thousand different threads of the possible futures woven together. It dominated my visions.

In my present, I helped lay each new thread. With my alien accomplices, I stitched the near future, assembled its components. The optimal route positioned the correct choices in front of me. Choices well within my powers to accomplish.

You must understand—it was my decision to walk this terrible path. Never believe otherwise. I will not forget my sins. Through that riotous road was our escape, yes. Along that dark-bright lane, the Xix would survive. By that nightmare passage, I could avert the coming galactic genocides. At its end, I would return to where my journey began. And there, I would be condemned.

By telepathy, I requested that Waythrel ready all of its kind on Dram, and beyond, all who could exchange information and service with their homeworld. They must prepare for what I would ask of them. The alien deferred to my visions. I sensed a growing helplessness and resignation from it as I took over the planning of our escape. They assumed I would demand something like their own plan of species-sacrifice. The irony was not lost on me.

My first request was to speak in the open, without the bugs overhearing. I wanted words. Spoken sounds I could feel on the tips of my teeth. Telepathy was amazing, but I'd spent most of my life with speech. For what was coming, I needed the familiar.

The next day, Waythrel and several Xixian medics entered my cell. Pretending to examine me, one injected something into my arm. I held silent and waited until they left the room. My advocate spoke.

"We have implanted in your skin a small device. It will mask our conversation from the surveillance. I have a similar one in me. The implant is organic. It will dissolve, your tissues absorbing the constituent molecules within thirty minutes. Undetectable. They mimic malfunctioning eavesdropping equipment. It gives us a short time to speak unconcerned. Say now, all you must say."

I closed my eyes, focusing on the painful path in my consciousness.

"When they bring me to the Orb, the emperor will demand I activate it, planning for me to guide the ship to Earth. A measure of the cruelty of the Dram." My voice was monotonic, my emotions frozen. "But this will not happen. The Resistance will swing into place and attack the escort ships. They have been moving into near jump space the last few days."

"I have received no word of those plans. What are you saying? Why would they travel to your homeworld?"

I ignored its words and continued. "At that time, a delegation of

Xixian scientists on board will be revealed to be defenders. They will immobilize the soldiers."

"Ambra, please..."

"Listen to me, Waythrel." I shook my head. The alien would have to trust my visions. "The Dram have too many troops and terrible weapons. The Xix cannot handle them all." I smiled, thinking of my gentle friends. "These others, I will stop."

"*You* will stop? How?"

I concentrated on the pulsing waves of thought emanating from the creature. Complex lines, beautiful weavings within webs. So much more refined and deep than my intelligence, theirs burst in a spectrum of color. Yet despite their far superior brains, they stumbled in this terrain. Only I could see such thoughts.

And only I could touch them. I reached out, kindly but firmly, and plucked a thread.

It recoiled as if struck. The elegant filigree of thought dissolved. Scrambling, its body reacted in reflex, many arms extending to balance along the walls of my cell. The eyestalks whirled around the room, unhinged, disoriented.

The disarray decayed. The web reformed. The long alien form relaxed. The eyes calmed and turned toward me, one after the other. I lowered my head.

"I'm sorry. You would not have believed me otherwise."

"You frighten me, Ambra."

"I know. It's too much power for an Earth mind. I *feel* the truth of it inside. Seeing our history, I *know* it—we are not wise or decent enough. But this ability *is* mine, good or bad. Maybe both."

I raised my head and leveled my sightless eyes with my advocate. "And I was gentle. I don't have to be so kind." It recoiled from my implication. "Our enemies will be helpless, at least the number around us on the ship. I can handle those numbers. They won't understand what's happening before I've incapacitated them all."

I shook my head in disbelief at where things had brought me. "I have seen it all. You must have faith in me. Report my words back to the Resistance. The Dram will want Xixian scientists there to try to explain and capture the mystery of my power over the Orbs. It's a dark joke—they need you, even as they don't trust you! Fill their ranks with fighters. Tell the human who plans with you what I have said."

"The human?" it asked. "How do you know?"

"I can *see* him, Waythrel. I can see him in my future, and I can see him as a distortion in the matrices of spacetime. Thel's little seeds are sprouting. I can't even keep track of them as they grow inside me. Soon, we will go to him and to the core of the Resistance. I will meet him before the end."

"The end?"

"Of many things. The beginning of the end of the Dram."

"If this is true, then my heart will rejoice."

"Stop being silly, Waythrel." I smiled. "You don't even have a heart! Your translators are too poetic."

"The sentiment is the same."

A merciless weight constricted my lungs, and I fought for control over my emotions.

"Yes, but grief will tarnish so much. Terrible sorrow. Tomorrow we head for Earth, but we will not find it."

Chapter 30

Space has a reality outside our minds, so that we cannot completely prescribe its properties a priori.

Carl Friedrich Gauss

The trip into space was far grander than anything I had experienced. After the Sortax, the nightmare in the smugglers' death holds, and the recent detention cell in the Dram warship, the emperor's titanic yacht was a majestic, luxury starcraft in comparison. It was the largest ship I'd flown on, at least twenty times the size of the training craft. The energy needed to bring it out of the planet's gravity must have been colossal.

Inside, they had spared no effort in creating an opulent transport for the ruler of the galaxy. Spacious corridors of plush fabrics led to high ceilings in rooms housing the most complex technology. Everything decorated with the finest materials. Dram-style art hung from the walls. They preferred weavings from desert plants. Their artisans shaped them into carpet-like hangings painted with historical and mythological images. They meant little to me and often were hard to decipher. I suppose human paintings would be equal nonsense to alien life.

We weren't given long to observe. The guards tramped us to the bridge where the emperor and its entourage waited. The ship ascended into space. Artificial gravity quashed any g-forces during acceleration and other tech removed all turbulence in the atmosphere. We rose into the sky, still and tranquil, not a bump or stomach sickness to be had. In orbit, it felt no different from on the ground.

Soldiers prodded us into the enormous command center. Mammoth panoramic windows covered the walls, revealing the blackness and pinpricks of distant starlight. I marveled at the engineering. Their advanced science produced remarkable glass—if glass was what it was. These gigantic apertures withstood pressure and temperature differences from the air inside to the vacuum of space. Whatever the material was, it was tough or aided by a protective energy field. It sure made for a spectacular sight. The scene produced the sensation of floating in front of the ship in the darkness.

The panes darkened as the system's star swung into view, dimming its oppressive orange. Without the shaded windows obscuring the light, the flaming giant would have fried us all. The starship continued its course. The sun arced across the transparent walls as shadows shifted from one side to the other.

The bugs dragged us to a raised platform at the foot of the throne. That's how they granted access to supplicants before the emperor. Again, the symbolic power elements in their design—grandeur about us, height above us, freedom denied us. Fifteen Xixian scientists hunched over various pieces of equipment. I hoped these were not true researchers, but a team trained for combat. I glanced toward Waythrel and probed its thoughts. It anticipated my concern and formed the answers to my question.

The forces are in place, as you have requested, Ambra. So are the emperor's troops, as you have noticed. There are at least forty of their elite guard. I hope you are prepared for this.

I impressed on its mind that I was.

The Xix continued. *The Resistance will be here on my signal through the Dram Orb string. Once given, they will make the jump into the system. We will have a few minutes to escape from this ship and board a fast freighter. At any moment, our craft could be destroyed by a warship. It will be perilous. And finally, what of the emperor? We dare not risk it injury. It could mean terrible retaliation.*

I smiled and spoke out loud. "Don't worry. It won't be pretty, but we'll be okay."

Waythrel acknowledged me by bending several eyestalks in my direction. Alien sarcasm! Well, I couldn't blame the poor Xix. I was the one-eyed woman leading the blind.

I sensed it before anyone else at the helm. Nothing in the galaxy compares to an Orb. Not even the complexities of the Xixian mind matched the intricate maze of radiance churning beneath the surface of the spheres.

The local spacetime distortions extending from the object caressed my unique organ. They touched so much in the star system. I had noticed the projections in the past, but didn't know what to make of them. Now it was more clear. The charged coils crept with purpose: tending, *gardening.* The majority of their glimmer cupping the Dram home planet. Thel had spoken of it. *Gardeners.* Could it be true? The energies reached through my body, and a tremor rattled me. What were those tendrils *doing*?

Waythrel sensed my reaction. "What is it, Ambra?"

"We're close," I managed, my throat parched.

Officers clicked to the emperor, signaling to the viewports. The Orb expanded to fill the massive windows as the ship neared. In the visual realm, what poverty! But scarcity in a spectrum of splendor could still amaze.

Awe stirred in the surrounding minds. Some religious, some scientific, but all knew the power gestating within what we approached. These were portals through time and space, planted throughout the galaxy by the mysterious Ancient Ones. Abandoned for billions of years, young species had stumbled upon them. They were used by the inhabitants of worlds too primitive to understand how they functioned. Or why.

My new Xixian translator echoed the emperor's tones. "We have reached the Sacred Sphere of Dram! It is time for the heretic to prove its truth and worth. It will activate the Orb and reveal the potency of the divine or fail and expose itself to be a fraud of the evil force."

How I hated these dramatic moments of voodoo. Their leader's hypocrisy increased my disgust. A sanctimonious sham mixed with extreme power—nothing was worse. Especially when those authorities could soon be deciding exactly how to dismember you.

The bug turned to Waythrel. "Order the human to open the portal."

"Ambra, obey the sovereign's command."

I inhaled, closing my eyes. *Okay, buddy, get ready, 'cause here it comes!*

I sank inside myself, descending to a place where my unique perspective blossomed and occupied all my consciousness. Perceived by my sixth sense, the Orb flared like a supernova, its energies overpowering. I held steady, focused, and reached toward it.

This time, it was more straightforward. The pressures were far weaker without a Dram warship chasing you through space. My powers had ripened since I had opened the last Orb. And future memories gave me an unshakable confidence. I had seen my success on the bright-dark path. All I had to do was dance with destiny.

As I unlocked the Orb, I sensed fear and reverence, even from Waythrel. Visually, it was a spectacular light show. The dim surface rippled into a multidimensional maze of coherent radiance. A many layered tunnel erupted beside the gigantic craft. It seemed poised to swallow the ship whole.

As indeed it was.

I concentrated on keeping the Orb open but preventing it from engulfing the starcraft. The spacetime tugs yanked on the flesh of those around me. A subtle anxiety bubbled within the host.

I opened my eyes and glared at the ugly cockroach on the throne. "There, *Your Majesty*," I spat out. "Is this what you were looking for?"

The emperor and Dram servants were too transfixed to hear me. The guards also gawked at the heaven-hell of the ceaseless and structured splendor of the Orb. To my satisfaction, the Xixian team did not.

I spoke mentally to Waythrel to send the signal. It touched a device attached to the translator around its neck, transmitting both to the Resistance and the forces below.

And that's when everything went nuts.

Chapter 31

Battle not with monsters, lest you become a monster, and if you gaze into the abyss, the abyss gazes also into you.

Friedrich Nietzsche

Moments passed until the Dram realized what was happening.

The Xixian fighters immobilized our enemy, but did not kill. They targeted the insect warriors with special devices they had concealed. As the giant bugs dropped to the ground, a cry rose from crew monitoring space. I'm not sure what they had detected. Waythrel's signal? The small Resistance fleet materializing from the String? The opening salvo on surrounding warships escorting their leader's vessel?

Whatever the reason, I had to act before they turned the firepower of the great ship on the emerging craft. I had instructed our allies not to fire on the emperor's transport. They obeyed my instructions. How could they not? Their *savior* was onboard. They were here for me. They had to get the Orb-opener off this yacht and safely away.

I spun and faced the rows of technicians, pilots, and weapons staff. Their intense thoughts in the midst of combat slashed at my awareness, a brightness betraying their presence.

If they only knew.

One by one, I struck them. My consciousness morphed into a great lens, focusing mental activity. I delivered a mind-slap unknown to these creatures, one they had no preparation or training to resist. I first incapacitated the row of Dram at the consoles. A second or two for each, and then the next, and so, like dominoes, I dropped them.

I turned to the soldiers who engaged the Resistance forces in a deadly melee. The Xix had performed well, and piles of stunned shapes lay in front of them. But the insects were like ants from a nest, pouring in through the many doors along the walls of the room. They overwhelmed our team, who toppled, charred and twitching, in a growing wreckage.

I improvised, my thoughts burning hyperkinetic. With a vast mental sweep, I summoned a stream of potency from a quiescent sea. My burst of cognitive distortion raked across the hordes of Dram soldiers. Scores dropped, most never to move again. Another horde flooded through the main entrance. I recalibrated and released another storm. All but a handful struck the floor. Those remaining staggered, unable to function. They wandered about the room before collapsing. I had mangled their minds.

A venomous and hateful urge to strike radiated through my awareness. *The emperor.* My consciousness filled with the thoughts of the monster who had hurt so many. *It knew.* In rage, it thrust a weapon toward me, waiting for no Tribunal to decide my fate.

Funny, I had not foreseen this detail in the visions. Too close to my person, I suppose.

Waythrel screamed, "Ambra! Behind you!"

Poor Xix, so worried. By the time I turned to face the galaxy's monarch, my advocate emitted shock and awe, gawking with its eighteen eyes.

The royal beast stood still, its upraised claw clutching a device aimed at my face. It gasped for air, unmoving. Its pocked exoskeleton trembled with a tremendous effort to break the invisible bonds trapping it.

I glided to the insect, staring into its foul eyes.

"Sovereign of all Dram!" I shouted. "Now you will hear *me*." Hatred burned my soul. I unleashed thunder in its mind: *One way or the other!*

The emperor tensed as my anger slapped at its consciousness, and fear flowed toward me like an iced river.

"You are right to be afraid," I said. "You have a debt to pay for all the souls you have tortured. Murdered. The lights you have extinguished forever."

I could not stop myself. My thoughts compressed, tightening in their fury. The insect wheezed, the pitiful throaty wails of an alien physiology. They were no less desperate than the sounds of human strangulation.

I struck its awareness. *I know what you have done.*

Torrents of pain bled from the creature's mind. In response, I gave no pity. No mercy. I opened the floodgates of prescience. Scenes from my visions rushed through its flailing consciousness. The emperor recoiled at my knowledge and power. Its executioner was at hand.

"Ambra," Waythrel whispered beside me, but the Xix was a butterfly swatted away by the hurricane of my vengeance.

"See them scream? See the billions boil and burn? I have seen them. Day after day, night after night, I have watched them. I know you decreed their deaths."

Tighter, I wrung the tortured creature. It could no longer stand on its own strength and finally sagged.

"You gave the victims in your dungeons no rest. Up with you!"

I invaded its mind further, overpowering the natural biology. I diverted energy from vital life processes and strengthened the signal to the legs. The surge forced the creature upright. Its eyes thrashed for help or escape. I dragged them toward me. I ravaged its thoughts with my image, my anger, and its imminent demise.

"Ambra, you must stop!" Waythrel cried.

I heard nothing, my soul colder than death, burning like the core of a star.

"Drown in the helplessness of your victims. Die with the murdered. Suffer the pains of the tortured. Their histories strangle you."

I opened the final valve of vision. I guided the terrible currents in my mind to the Dram emperor. Images battered the captive consciousness. Glimpses of other lives, other worlds, other dreams, and hopes terminated. The insect spasmed, the legs buckled despite my tyrannical commands, the creature's body at the breaking point.

"Ambra, don't become a monster!" a voice pleaded with me. "Release it! Don't let your own power consume you!"

I inhaled a breath of time. Only my awareness existed. In the moment, a part of me heard the plea. A portion recoiled at the mad she-god evolving within me, stunned at her murderous storm of retribution.

I retreated from the edge of my own damnation. How or why is for others to consider. I woke from a nightmare, shook off the crazed mood, and freed the emperor. It fell unconscious to the floor. Alive, yet forever wounded. Always to remember and experience the suffering it had created.

Waythrel grabbed my shoulders with its spidery arms. "Down to the flight deck. A ship has docked."

We raced through the ornate hallways, the surviving Xixian team loping like hyper ballet-dancing spiders. Along the way, they incapacitated the stray soldiers that got in our way. We reached the airlock, entered the chamber, and transferred to the connected craft.

Within seconds, ours and the remaining Resistance ships not blown out of the sky converged on the Orb. Crew members screamed. An armada of Dram warboats focused on our position. They would achieve firing solutions in minutes.

"Ambra, please, get us out of here."

I leaned on my alien friend, not sure I was sane. From what I had seen and done, to what I would see and do, reality and vision again intermingled. Blurred together. Time—it was churning through past, present, and future. It was hard to understand which way was forward.

"No problem, Waythrel. Got an express ticket." My smile was weak.

"To where?" it asked.

"Home, and nowhere." I shook my head. "You can never go back, they say." I fixed my awareness on the destination and flexed my thought to activate the Orb.

And it opened. It filled my mind with radiance, flooding other's eyes with a different light. We dashed through a million dimensions of nothing and everywhere. We left far behind the scarlet horrors of Dram, painting the windows of our ship with the golden rays of Sol.

Chapter 32

Nothing we can do outrages Nature directly. Our acts of destruction give her new vigour and feed her energy, but none of our wreckings can weaken her power.

Marquis de Sade

My mind darted back in time, deep into the recesses of the past.

For billions of years, a cratered, irregular rock had waited for its day. It circled, cold and silent, an inert outcast, exiled from warmer spheres huddled around a yellow-white star. The largest of millions of brethren, yet a planetary failure. Orbits repeating, the stars whirled across its rocky horizon, but it did not lose patience. It did not count the eons. Without promise, devoid of thought, it held pregnant within its core a fate unguessed.

In the wink of an eye to this ancient entity, moving at the frenetic pace of life, hundreds of metallic gnats buzzed beside it. Each delivered a microscopic nudge. Every weak push augmented the others until the swarm built to a crescendo. The rock abandoned its aged, dogmatic course. It latched on to the energies of an Orb's tendril. Guided by malice, hyperspace flung the mass toward another star system. The hurtling behemoth erupted from transit, accompanied by the drove of demons blackening its outline. Inward to the bright golden light it rushed, gathering frightening speed, aimed like an arrow with terrible purpose.

Gravity. *Only force.* Manipulations of attraction by mysterious powers. A charged flight flung to a final fate.

A breeze blew through a woman's hair as a cloudless blue welcomed a new spring day. She watched children scamper across a concrete playground in London. Other mothers sat nearby or walked, shepherding their young. All familiar to her, many known well. She squinted into the sharp sunlight. The form of her three-year-old stumbled forward and pointed to the heavens.

"Look, Mummy! There's a star up in the sky."

She followed her daughter's finger to the crystalline heavens. A bright speck, as if it really were a small star, shimmered in the west.

"Yes, darling, it must be a falling star. I've never seen one in the daytime before." She grinned as the toddler bounced on her stubby legs.

"Mummy, mummy, I'll make a wish! I'll make a wish!"

"Make it a good one."

The girl squeezed her eyes shut, frowning in concentration. With a squeal, she opened them again and hopped into the air. "Mummy, I can't tell you. It's a *secret*, or it won't come true."

The young mother glanced into the sky once again. Her smile froze, fading as several wrinkles cut into her forehead.

"Look at it. It's so bright."

High in the atmosphere of Earth, where each day, thirty tons of material the size of sand grains burned, something horribly larger combusted. One thousand miles from London, a deep shadow darkened the capital of Iceland. Vendors on the street turned their gazes upward. Suits in office buildings gawked out their windows.

Frantic calls on military and national security lines screamed in urgency at the unexpected calamity unfurling. An invader blotted out the sun, yet it blazed as a second star. The projectile erupted into a brilliance so terrible it blinded the fragile creatures below.

The atmosphere exploded over Canada. Trillions of megatons of TNT converted into diverse forms of energy. The igniting fireball seared the planet. Two hundred times the sun's intensity, it set fire to everything within its expanding radius.

As the surface absorbed the profound impact, the planet's thin outer layer peeled off in a growing wave like the skin pared from an apple. The collision slung the material into orbit. On this soaring sheet were the world's oceans, its land masses, each town, city, and state. Every living form in the biosphere.

Underneath the concussion simmered an ocean of magma. For all of human history, it lay hidden from view by the cooled crust but for rare volcanic eruptions. The asteroid shattered such fragile protection. Enormous volumes of liquid stone poured over the Earth and into its skies. The growing lake of fire spread like a yawning maw across the planet.

A hypersonic pressure wave of compressed atmosphere rushed ahead of it. Winds blowing at over eight thousand miles per hour annihilated all in their path. What remained was set aflame by the fireball that followed. Magnitude fourteen earthquakes threw down anything else that somehow persisted upright.

Hours later, the playground in London peered down at the ravaged surface. Chunks of the orbiting crust plunged back to Earth as fiery meteors. They inflicted further destruction on the dying world. No reaction, no technology, no preparation of the small creatures dotting the planet could protect them. The titanic collision vaporized those within several thousand miles of the impact. The firestorms, heated winds, and extended shrouding of sunlight killed the rest. Ten billion souls cried out into the void.

In a day, an inferno raged across the globe. The oceans boiled to nothing. Vegetation transformed to ash. Every sign of life was wiped clean from the molten landscape. The once blue and white marble in the solar system turned obsidian, lifeless, and still. The third planet from the star was now sterilized.

The emperor's will had been done.

Chapter 33

The choice before human beings, is not, as a rule, between good and evil but between two evils.

George Orwell

From the infinite maze of light, the starship plunged into space. A glowing Orb behind us flared for several moments. The sphere went dark as if a switch was thrown.

A star radiated near the center of mass of a small system of gaseous and rocky worlds with a ring of asteroids. Its disk illuminated the third planet from the sun. The aliens at the controls on the bridge exchanged rapid conversation. I could sense them three floors up.

Waythrel rushed down the corridors to my room. It signaled outside the door, and I pressed a panel to allow entrance. The door slid open. A frazzled Xix burst inside—if you can fairly describe so disturbing an alien life-form with such a human adjective. My special sight painted the picture for me. I turned toward it from my over-large chair and waited to hear what I already knew.

"Ambra." It wasn't a sentence, just my name, but the tones spilled a story. "We have come to the coordinates of Earth."

The weight of the unspoken strained the air. I said nothing. My emotions were both drained and repressed. I had cried inside one thousand times for the future that had become my present. I had shared the tragedy with no one.

"There is something wrong. We need you on the bridge."

Nodding, I stood, feeling no weakness or fatigue in my limbs. Only a terrible stillness deep within.

I followed the alien through the ship and to the helm. The pilots and crew were silent, frozen before their instruments. I wore a black robe from the clothes provided to me. Xixian crafted, oversized, and dangling across my small form, it lay draped like an odd funeral garment. The strange material could not have been fashioned by humans. It drank the light to reflect it in hints of iridescence in the midst of darkness. On my head was Ricky's Red Sox hat. Ricky, murdered in another age of my mind, cremated a few hours ago.

"Ambra, the coordinates are correct," said Waythrel. "There is a rocky satellite of a mass and distance as specified. The planet must be Earth. But..."

Tears streamed down my face as I spoke, the words unlocking something deep within me. "It burns, my alien friends. It melts and smolders. My homeworld. Where my roots would have found warm soil again to end this withering of my soul. Spirits like dust are riding on the solar wind, blowing over our ship's shields. I *hear* their voices, billions of them crying out. I've heard them again and again. Can you feel the breath of their *souls*?"

I walked to the viewscreen and stared at the blackened sphere. Rivers of magma flowed like blood from mortal wounds. The crimson crisscrossed the surface, forming a bloodshot sclera. Scarring the Northern Hemisphere, an enormous pool of lava. Altogether, the eye of Satan, boiling.

"The Dram are gone. Their work is finished."

"Why?" Waythrel whispered.

A terrible shudder ran through it and the crew. Alien, all of them, and yet they twisted inside with grief and affection. If any creatures carried the torch of divine love in our galaxy, it was the Xix.

I looked across the control room.

"They have my eggs and human captives for sperm. They believe their scientists can recreate me. At least something similar enough to serve their needs. But they desire a monopoly on my talent."

It was all so logical, so cold and calculated.

"The gene pool of Earth was waiting to produce more Ambra Dawns. Who knows what else of Reader power. It was a threat to their Hegemony. They removed the threat. And so my home was erased."

"Ambra, I don't have words for you," said Waythrel. The alien's eyestalks bounced and fell toward me. "You knew this would happen?"

"Since my arrival at Dram."

A stunned silence reverberated. "Ambra, why? Why didn't you tell us? We could have stopped it!"

"No, Waythrel!" I cried out, my hands in front of me, trying to block an attack. My tears surged, and I choked, my phrases garbled and pitched. "I've seen all the threads. The possible futures. They aren't endless! Not in the short term. One way out of the Dram homeworld. One! One for me to survive and prevent the slaughter of trillions."

I gaped at my blackened home, where my bare feet would never touch grass again, where evil had slaughtered hordes of humanity. I steadied myself on the wall.

"I walked the most painful path. I sacrificed an entire planet brimming with life for one deformed and blind citizen. Because others had foreseen hope for the galaxy. A faith in me."

Waythrel and the other Xix remained as statues. I could feel their churning emotions. I turned to my advocate, placing my trembling hand on the rough membrane of the alien's arm.

"I allowed my world to die to save the rest. Now, and for the years to come." Wiping tears from my eyes, I growled at all these monstrous forms. "Don't let the sacrifice be in vain."

I bolted away, my form the most monstrous of all, the greatest mass murderer of all time fleeing in her black robes like Death into the bowels of hell.

Chapter 34

The Tao that can be expressed is not the eternal Tao;
The name that is spoken is not the unchanging name.
That without name is the beginning of heaven and earth.

We landed on the moon three hours later.

The Resistance had built a base decades before on the dark side. In secret, they tunneled into the lunar rock several miles to shield it from enemy scans. It was, of course, one of many such concealed bases throughout the inhabited worlds.

But the proximity to Earth, the Earth that was, had a special significance. The planet had been the source of all Readers of importance, and the greatest supply for the galactic fleets. Now only the Dram in their human stockyards would breed more of us. Born into slavery, programmed to do their bidding, locking down their monopoly of beasts of burden.

We passed over the barren lunar landscape. The surface was littered with impact craters, the ancient evidence of celestial violence never erased. Without wind, rain, or tectonic plate movements, the moon had defined death. No longer. Its gravitational keeper presented a far more illustrative lesson in mortality. Now life stirred only on the moon, as Earth smoldered a quarter-million miles away.

The Xixian ship descended into one of the larger depressions. A channel appeared in the rock. We entered a tunnel, diving straight toward the heart of the satellite. Illumination from above failed. The ship's navigation beams painted the sharp edges of the drilled stone.

A faint glow rose underneath us. It swelled in intensity until it blinded after the relative darkness of the shaft. The passageway opened to a broad chamber with many spacecraft. We taxied to a free area, and the vessel came to a stop on a landing pad hewn out of the lunar crust.

A small group was there to greet us, both Xix and humans somber, the members of my species pale and burdened. A young man with a blond beard led them forward and stopped before our entourage.

"We received your transmission. Your codes match those smuggled to us," he said. His eyes darted towards me. "*She* is with you?"

Waythrel gestured in my direction. "Michael, let me introduce to you Ambra Dawn. She brought us through the Orbs and defeated the Dram emperor herself. She is our great hope."

He squinted at me. "Hope," he muttered. "There isn't much of that left. Just darkness after yesterday." He glanced at me again, looking over the dark and loose-fitting robes, baseball hat, and absurd skull. "We'll take her to Richard. He continues to guide us. He'll decide what value this girl may have now."

"Then he still lives?" Waythrel asked.

He bristled, a fire in his eyes penetrating his attempts to suppress his anger. "Yes, although the medics can't say for how long. The cursed Dram poisons degrade his tissues, but he has lost none of his powers!"

The alien lilted. "Of course, Michael, we expected nothing less. Please forgive me if my question seemed insensitive. You know we of Xix are doing all we can to preserve his life."

The man lowered his gaze. "And we are thankful. You know as

well as I that his visions have made the Resistance possible." He grimaced in my direction, speaking to the rest of his companions, but his eyes riveted to my face. "See that they have housing. Attend to their needs. Afterward," he added, nodding to Waythrel, "we may arrange a meeting between these two Readers. Richard has waited long for this day."

He turned and marched out of the docking chamber, leaving us alone with the remainder of our hosts. I could still feel his gaze burning into me.

He seems a bit obsessed, I messaged my extraterrestrial companion. Maybe the Xix understood the dynamic better than I.

A complicated politics, Ambra. Michael is loyal and attached to his leader, who lies dying after his torture at the hands of the Dram. You come here with the rumor of greatness, beyond even Richard's powers. Michael resents this, and you will need to step softly in the beginning. Don't worry for now, there is much to learn. With your abilities, I have no doubt you will know all there is to know soon.

We exited the docking chamber and entered an elevator that sped us deeper into the moon to the last stage of my journey.

Part III

First the Cosmos, then the gods.
So, who can say from where the creation arose?
Perhaps, it created itself.
Perhaps, it did not.
The Being, the first Origin of Creation
Who looks down on it:
Only He knows.
Or perhaps, He does not.

Rig Veda, Creation Hymn

Chapter 35

Two possibilities exist: Either we are alone in the Universe or we are not. Both are equally terrifying.

Arthur C. Clarke

Strangers ushered us to quarters within the hidden moon settlement. They were unknown to me, respectfully distant, yet their humanness was overwhelming. I'd spent so much time surrounded by the alien. Disturbing odors, movements, textures—my senses had churned in confusion until exposure had numbed them.

But the sensations on this base! Sounds, pheromones, body warmth, skin pressed inward on a handshake. Millions of years of evolution primed my biology to respond. It was lightning through my nervous and hormonal system. Tears dripped over my cheeks as they shuttled us forward.

Waythrel and I insisted they house us together. Important events were cascading around the galaxy. Our escape from Dram had punched a hole in the cruel order of their empire. News was scarce, but it trickled and would likely become a flood. We both wished to have the time to discuss matters when needed.

They were happy to accommodate our request. It was unsettling and healing to be in chambers designed by humans once again, whatever help the aliens had given. We outnumbered the Xix twenty to one, a ratio found only in a Resistance base so close to Earth. The personality of a culture imprints its architecture. This small flavor of humanity comforted me, further reorienting my sense of reality.

The design of the lunar post was inclusive of many species. The builders had also made concessions for the extraterrestrials in residence. Waythrel spent half an hour in an ultrasound Xixian chamber in the room. It was a device that bombarded the occupant with high-frequency sound waves. They find this soothing in a way we can't understand or experience. I took the human equivalent—a long, hot shower. Steam and temperature to burn away all the horror of my life. Of course, I stepped out merely numbed.

And tired. Fatigue tugged downward on my limbs. One leaden snowflake after the other, dropping, fusing, assembling an invisible garment with the weight of a world.

Wait. What was this? *A couch*. An actual couch. I couldn't look away.

I had not seen anything like one for what felt like a lifetime. Not since home. The warehouse? Maybe for the staff in offices the children never visited. I don't know. After the Sortax, it was alien-built or nothing. The norm involved odd geometrical efforts our captors calculated could hold our forms without damage. *Comfort* never entered their equations. The Xix? Well, the poor things tried. They could heal our bodies—fix broken biological machines they had studied. But psychology was another task altogether.

The worst weren't the abstract formulations of uncaring abominations. What hurt most, what made all of us ache for home, were the near-misses. And so my beloved aliens sinned. Designs copied from their intense study of our species. Mimicking our aesthetics, so intellectually designed. And because of minor and pervasive glitches, all the more hideous. A torturous doppelgänger. A mockery of construction so like to our needs that wounded instead.

But here was a *couch*. A bona fide Earth sofa. I sat on its velvet cushions. The style, the design, the specifics, it didn't matter. It was *of us*. I could see it with my mind's eye. I could feel it over my skin. Its fabrics. Its shape. It's very human flaws. Again, I fought off tears. All for a damn piece of furniture.

I lay back until the upholstery enveloped me. My exhaustion, my raw infatuation with the domestic, they drugged my mind. I laughed. I cried. Cursed. Screamed. A Gatling gun fired emotions across the room while my core sank in ecstasy to the bottomless embrace of the soft pillows. Forever. I would never leave this glorious place.

"Ambra?"

A door clattered open, strange vibrations warping the air in the room. My altered state shattered, and I sprawled there, bone-tired on the furniture. Waythrel poked its eyestalks out of the sonic chamber.

"Is everything okay?" the alien continued.

Is everything okay? I understood its concern. I'd just whooped up the room like a pack of monkeys. But the wording hissed in my emotional soup. It felt vindictive. *Of course, things were not okay!* My planet was lava and ash! Earthrise perverted from a glowing marble of life to death's fiery eye. Billions slaughtered in horror and the remainder camping out on *the moon.*

Guilt howled for my attention, could not be long ignored. It hunted me like a rabid wolf. I sprinted from corner to corner of my mind to evade. More than anything, this chase drained the energy from my limbs.

"I'm resting, Waythrel."

The alien was silent. I couldn't help but sense its skepticism.

"You need to sleep, Ambra. You are at the breaking point. What you have done in the last forty-eight hours is beyond the powers of any living creature in the galaxy. You have sacrificed and suffered. Your brain is overtaxed. Go rest. Rebuild your awareness as is the way of your species."

The Xix was correct, of course. The problem with floundering in a degraded state is that you are less able to recognize and follow good advice. Had it not been for my telepathic sight, I would have rebelled, thrown a fit, not at Waythrel, but at the universe itself. *How dare it allow such hideousness?* I hated the cosmos. I hated its detached and sadistic indifference. And, without doubt, I hated myself most of all.

Instead, the alien's thoughts bled through the room and into my mind. Not human, so bent and coiled, a mass incomprehensible in complexity. But infused with a color I recognized. A sweet smell blossoming from purity. Affection. Worry. A mother's touch. The monstrosity pulled me once again from the brink.

"You're right. I'll go to bed."

My body had gained thousands of pounds, despite the reduced lunar gravity. I pushed against the oppression of the laws of nature, defying creation, spitting in its face. I wobbled to my feet, placing one trembling leg in front of the other until I crossed the common room and entered my bedroom.

I face-planted into the pillows. I didn't switch off the lights, unfurl the blankets, or tuck myself in. I plunged straight over the edge of consciousness into the numb, empty, timeless unbeing of the void.

———————————

Chapter 36

———————————

The flower which is single need not envy the thorns that are numerous.

Rabindranath Tagore

I didn't wake as a new person (ha! too much is broken ever to be fixed), but I opened unseeing eyes several steps removed from the pit of madness.

I stumbled hungover into the common room. Waythrel had laid out on the table a breakfast delivered to our door. The smells of Earth drugged me again. I sat down to steady myself, shaking my head with a grin at the alien.

"It is to your liking?" it asked.

"It's heavenly." Of course, the creature had arranged things all wrong on the plates and with the utensils. A place setting and service of a very committed and loving five-year-old.

It *was* heavenly.

I chewed each bite at a glacial pace. I was going to experience every flavor, texture, smell, and weight of the porridge, eggs, bread, and juice. I shoved into a dark box any thoughts about how long we would have such priceless commodities, how much time until we relied on synthetic collections of nutrient goop to replace the melted cornfields of Nebraska. Right now, I could pretend I was back home, in my parents' kitchen, the beautiful planet underneath.

Not even the funky bouncing alien distracted me.

I had hardly finished dressing when a messenger outside our door pinged. He asked me to join him to meet with Michael. They would take me to their great Reader. Waythrel insisted on accompanying us. The aide was firm. The initial meeting would be private, with me alone. The Xix consented.

With that understood, we marched through the rocky tunnels of the moon base. After an extended trek, our guides brought us to an epic elevator bank in a massive shaft, ten sets of doors circling us. We entered the lifts and descended several more levels to a large medical ward.

Michael was waiting. I needed to study him. His biases were a gate locking Richard from me, and I couldn't let him interfere with the contact I had long anticipated. My first encounter with him had been too soon after the shock of encountering the extinct Earth of my nightmares. My mind had been in shambles. My emotions, spent. My focus, gone. I had regained much of my balance at this point.

I refrained from invading his thoughts. I wanted to respect the dignity of others whenever possible. So I simply Read the recent past to form images. He was of average height with a stocky build. Ideal for rotational roles on some football team at a Midwest college. A crispness shone in his blue eyes. He kept his beard and hair short and trimmed. The face suggested discipline, perhaps scholarship. He radiated command and decisiveness.

At his side was a white-coated woman, Asian features, long midnight strands tied in a bun. She struck me as an attending physician. The setting, the attendants, the gravity—Richard was a dying man.

"Waythrel will need to wait outside," Michael began. "He insisted on meeting Ambra alone this first time. He wishes to commune with her as a Reader. Human to human."

"I understand," answered the alien, although its translator conveyed an annoyed tone.

The doctor interrupted. "I'm Emily Chan," she said, "the ranking Earthling in the medical ward. I've overseen the care of Mr. Cross. We apologize for this inconvenience. We are thankful for the aid the Xix have given in all our efforts." She nodded to the alien. "They have transformed our quality of healthcare, even if we have come to take that for granted."

Michael scowled at her but motioned for me to follow. I walked behind them, down to the end of the hallway. We halted in front of a set of double automatic doors.

He turned to me, his voice grave. "In that room, you will meet the most powerful Reader in the Resistance. He has guided our strategies, risked his life, his health, his very sanity to serve our cause. Don't underestimate his vision."

Dr. Chan twitched at my side. "Stop antagonizing her, please. This is *Ambra Dawn*. She unlocked an *Orb*, faced down the Dram. The Xix have brought her here. She has the power to surpass anything anyone has done, if she hasn't already. We *need* her."

Michael set his jaw, his face muscles striated. "Whatever rumors you have heard of this girl, until she has served the Resistance as he has served, she is nothing more than another lost Reader who has been found."

"So, why is she here? Why has Richard desired to see her?"

"The council believed in her potential."

"Which means you don't, I suppose."

"What I believe is not of consequence."

This back-and-forth about which freak would win in a throw-down reminded me too much of what was juvenile in our species.

Arguing about our heroes, superheroes, our gods. As if we all didn't cry and fart and die and rot. All I could think about was that, behind those doors, was someone who could understand me. Richard had enough of my experiences to have some clue about what life was like inside my head. In this indifferent universe, he gave me hope that I wasn't alone.

My frustrations boiled over. "We don't have time for this! I've come a long and horrible way under knife and death and madness. The Earth is charcoal. I'm not going to listen to your bickering. He's asked to see me, and I *will* see him before he passes." I raised my hand as Michael protested. "Yes, he will pass. And it will be soon. I can see it even in the distortions of spacetime he causes. Just like I can feel your anger at this future you can't accept."

"I don't care who you are!" he shouted. "I won't have you speak like this!"

He took a step toward me, but before he could follow through, I sent a hard thought into his mind. Not enough to hurt him, but to stun and dislodge his wrath. Dignity would have to wait.

I will meet with your Richard. I have hoped to see him for some time. I will not allow you to stop me. I have too much I need to learn and share with him.

He stepped backward, his arms swimming and his eyes wide.

"Michael, what is it? Are you okay?" Dr. Chan asked. She squinted at the paleness spreading over his face.

"I'm fine, Emily," he whispered. "Just...just let her through."

Both moved aside, creating a space between me and the entrance. I steadied myself and walked forward. The sensors detected my presence and set the machinery in motion.

The doors opened.

Chapter 37

While God waits for his temple to be built of love, men bring stones.

Rabindranath Tagore

I waded into darkness. Lights were off. Wan, glimmering strips outlined a countertop across from me, the sole break in the black. A rat's nest of instrumentation surrounded a hospital bed between me and the glowing counter. The technology was a hodgepodge of human and alien devices. Extensions and probes from churning machines converged on a prone figure—*Richard.*

For my senses, the gloom didn't matter. I could see the full extent of the horror in my mind's eye. His caretakers had split him open along his back. They had plugged the hoses and cables into his spinal column. An odd, transparent material, likely of Xixian manufacture, coated everything, sealing his dissected flesh from exposure. Likewise, tubes and wires entered into his skull. Images of worms boring into fruit latched onto my thoughts. His lungs hissed to a metronome, aided by machinery as well.

Pity stole my breath. Here was another who had paid a terrible price for his talents and choices. Out of respect for this cost, I withheld any probing of his mind. I slid along the equipment to a chair at the front of the bed. As I approached, I turned my focus to his features. A Black man, tall and thin, perhaps once of athletic shape now shriveled to skeletal form. His eyes were closed. Still, I did not probe to see if he had conscious thoughts. I sat and waited.

After a few moments, his eyes fluttered open, and he spoke. His words were slow and slurred, husky and rasped. The pain from speaking radiated and battered my awareness.

"I knew you were here. Before you landed on this. Barren rock. It's amazing. You distort the very space you move within."

I held back tears. "So they tell me."

His voice strengthened to a whisper. "I apologize. I can give you no better welcome. I can't look you in the eye. But what need? You see so much. Not with your eyes, correct?"

"You're right. I'm blind."

"Yet not sightless," he continued, and a short coughing fit took him. "Ah, my atmosphere is pain. The Xix have been so helpful. It looks horrific. All this. It keeps my mind more free from the neural poisons. Maintaining my life functions. Without this," he gestured with his eyebrows and a slight motion of his head, "dementia and death months ago."

"The Dram have no mercy."

"You know too well. You have seen it, I suppose. My capture. My torment. Rescue from their dungeons."

"Yes," I said, tears pushing through my efforts. "In dreams over the years, and in recent visions. The Xix were never suspected in your escape, although a lot were killed."

"Our most terrible burden, Ambra. That so many would die. That we might live."

I could say nothing. My agony choked me.

"I did not see it coming. This greatest of calamities. I have waited to speak to you for so long. Fate kept us separated. I had so much to tell you. Inform you. Of this universe, Earth occupied. Our plans to set it free. Now, after this? I don't know what to say. I have no words of wisdom. Only a question. Why couldn't I see it?"

He coughed again and motioned to his throat, indicating he could no longer talk. His face was a mask of pain and defeat.

It won't keep us apart, Richard.

His eyes widened, closed, tears falling. I allowed myself to fully enter his mind.

This is more than I could have imagined, his thoughts relayed. *You have grown powerful beyond the dreams of the Dram.*

My power is limited, as you can see. Earth is ashes, despite all I could do.

Why, Ambra? You had foreseen it. Why didn't you stop it?

I can't explain. But I can show you. Do you have the strength?

I don't know. But I would rather die knowing. Experience even a small piece of your vision rather than live a few more hours in ignorance.

So be it. I focused my thoughts, stripping away the unnecessary. He had to know the path through the maze of destruction, so he could understand. Whether he could accept humanity's sacrifice for the rest of the galaxy, I'd find out.

I reached, gentleness my guide. I joined our minds, releasing the flow of visions. The flood strained his physiology. Machines blinked and beeped in consternation as his vital signs approached dangerous levels. His body shook, trembling as the shock roiled through him.

I withdrew from his mind to give him time to recover. I kept a tendril of contact to alert me when he was voicing his thoughts.

I am so sorry, Ambra. Fate chained you to an impossible burden. So much you have had to endure and carry. So alone. At least I can tell you, I know more than anyone the toxins you have swallowed.

Tears rained. I stretched out with my hand and stroked his head. "And I know yours, Richard. I see, I *feel through you,* your broken body. I relive it in communing with your mind." I turned to telepathy. *I wish we had more time. Time I see and swim and sicken in. But I can't control it. I hate to be so alone again.*

Yes, it ends for me. Even my visions are fading, which means the poison has reached my central neurons. I am fortunate the Xixian treatments have slowed the progress so much. The rest of me rots. My organs will fail before I go completely mad. But all grows dim, even dark at times. And yet, I believe I still can see something you can't.

Tell me.

I can't see your form, because you twist all spacetime around you. I can see the outlines. You're a glacier crushing everything in your path, carving out a new landscape. Your shape is made and unmade, again and again, never certain, never identical.

A long pause. The glow in his consciousness waned, and in the dimness I could Read no activity. I waited for the light to return.

But now I understand why I did not see Earth's destruction. In my mind, Earth still exists in our future, even though it does not now. It is there! How can this be?

His thoughts faded as the machines began complaining again. This conversation had pushed his body to the breaking point.

Richard? Please. Are you there?

I reached deep into the recesses of his blurring perception. His consciousness was submerged, trapped at sea, bobbing above and below. Ideas breached the waters in brief moments. His awareness took wild breaths before plunging down into near oblivion.

Fading...Ambra...You are turbulence in the path...Blinded me...

Dr. Chan came sprinting into the room, followed by Michael. She glanced at the monitors and called a code to other nurses. I shut out their efforts and focused. Time was short. Only his dying thoughts mattered.

Events are fluid...like the ocean...tumult...can't see into it...but I can see—after. A miracle. So much light...the voices of heaven singing...

Was he still sane? Were these true visions or hallucinations of his decaying mind?

Fingers of Divinity...through you they will speak...you only need to touch it, and the course of everything is new.

A team of alien and human medics gathered around him now.

Waythrel rushed to me. "Ambra! You must stop! The strain is too high! He's dying!"

Don't listen to them...better I die now. Why live empty and for suffering? Goodbye, Reader. It has been my privilege to know you...so much light...

His cognitive focus collapsed, submerged in a more primitive boiling of mental functions, and it wasn't clear if he had lost all awareness.

I glanced at the Xix. "It is his wish to share with me as he dies."

Michael glared at me in horror, pain etched in his face.

"I'm sorry," was all I could offer him.

Ambra.... The thoughts echoed from a vast distance, deep within the cave of his consciousness. *Ambra, hear me. Change the course... they will help you...you...must...change...its course.*

His mind went dark, the machinery ominous in silence. The frantic activity stalled, and for a moment, everything was as still as space.

"He's dead," said Dr. Chan. "There's nothing we can do."

Michael wept, kneeling beside his leader, burying his head next to his fallen friend. I also felt a palpable sadness in the Xixian minds. They mourned the passing of a noble comrade and a powerful force in their fight against the Dram.

Even so, I noticed their faith reorient. They turned toward me. Unknown, untested, I was to assume Richard's role. The hopes of entire species, and the remains of a massacred race, all were set on Ambra Dawn. Like the weight of a star.

Even so, that burden was secondary to my struggles as I stared off into space. I had lost the one person who could understand me. Richard was a man I could relate to as a Reader and as a human being. He had left his last thoughts with me. Urgent concepts conveying a truth he had seen that I could not. Something about me he had strained to show as his mind collapsed.

And I had no idea what he was trying to tell me.

Chapter 38

I don't think of all the misery, but of the beauty that remains.

Anne Frank

I nursed my queasy stomach in the guest room with Waythrel. The low lunar gravity infected me with daily nausea with little to counter the effects. The base had been constructed in great secrecy, while Dram agents herded our clueless kind on nearby Earth. There had been no time for sophisticated design. No time for gravitational enhancements or a crude rotating mechanism to increase average g-forces.

I'd refused lunch. I was sick from the environment. Sick from seeing Richard Cross die over and over again in my mind. Sick from watching our planet perish one hundred times in my visions. And I was sick of a prolonged and empty conversation with Waythrel about a dying man's thoughts.

"I am sorry, Ambra," it spoke after a long silence. "For all we know, those words were spoken in a decaying brain state and could have no meaning. He might have been speaking nonsense."

"I don't believe it," I whispered. "He was fighting to maintain focus, to communicate something he discovered. If so, it's important, and I need to find the answer. If it's nonsense, then it doesn't matter."

"Except it will drain your energies from other tasks."

I strangled the scream trying to rip out of me. "What other tasks, Waythrel? I may have found the strength to do what I did, but I'm wounded. As deep as you can imagine. Everything I am is bleeding!"

"Ambra."

"Would you feel any different? If they had destroyed Xix? How can any creature thrive without their homeworld? We're limbs cut off from the tree. We're going to wither and die!"

"Ambra! You cannot! Or else this sacrifice will be in vain. You are now our single prospect for defeating the Dram. You must find strength in this role."

I sighed, a long release until my diaphragm trembled. "I'll try. And that's why I have to discover the meaning of Richard's last words. I sensed a soaring hope in them. An optimism specific for my kind. I wish he could have told me more. But his faith is what keeps me going now."

"Then may it not be a false dream."

"I can't talk about Richard anymore, Waythrel. I am too wrecked. No more riddles without answers. Something else." My mind turned to this new role I was expected to play. "What happened on Dram? Do the other worlds know about Earth?"

"Our enemies have reverted to full militaristic mode. Their aggression has increased a thousand-fold. With cruelty, they are reminding everyone of how terrible they can be. They censor communication from Dram, but the Xix can elude their crude technology. Information flows. The emperor is in critical care. His mind unhinged by your actions. He babbles nonsense and cries out for protection from humans. The high inquisitor has followed succession rights and assumed interim control of the empire. A new sovereign will be chosen—an archaic and barbaric ritual of the noble houses I will save for another time. The military has orders to exterminate even the hint of insurrection in the Hegemony. Many innocents are paying with their lives."

"Yes, I've seen it. So much pain. Even in hope of victory, seas of suffering."

"Word of Earth has spread throughout the galaxy. I am sad to say not exactly from concern for Earthlings, but far more for the implications. Firstly, reminders the Dram are more than willing to slaughter entire worlds, as if this could have been forgotten. Secondly, the greatest well of Readers to supply hyperspace travel is gone. My apologies to be so blunt about human worth in the Hegemony, but this is the hard truth. You have been a resource. A necessary commodity. A great fear is sweeping through the developed systems that this stock has been destroyed."

"It's okay, Waythrel. Every step of the way, I've been punished with this lesson. Nearly killed. Your words don't hurt me."

"Yes. I do not doubt it. All worlds see that the Dram control this supply, without which interstellar travel will cease. The empire tightens its grip over the galaxy with this slaughter."

The alien stood and engaged in the strange Xixian tap dance, pacing across the room.

"But one thing they did not suspect—that word of you and your actions would escape. We of Xix have ensured the spread. Accounts of one who has opened the Orbs now grow. The stories take a shape of their own. Reports resonate that this human also escaped the clutches of the emperor. Like a spark dropped in a parched land, a fire is kindled and spreads from world to world. I have never seen anything like it. In response, they strike without mercy to stop the blaze. But the fools find their responses testify to its veracity. With every boot stomping on the flames, they scatter sparks and embers, igniting one thousand more hearts. They feed the inferno in their clumsy efforts to snuff it out."

Waythrel stopped pacing. "You are fast becoming legend."

I bowed my head. I didn't have the spirit to laugh at this new absurdity. "From slave-freak to myth in a blink of an eye. All I've done is stand aside to let monsters char my homeworld." My face tightened as screams slapped my soul. "Do you know in the quiet of the night, I hear them? Their cries of terror? Billions of them." I trembled as the voices rolled over my consciousness again. I fought them back and pushed the vision away.

"Legends seldom earn their status, even if you are a heroine in your own way."

"No."

"I will not argue with you over your sacrifice, or theirs." It gestured upward, indicating Earth. "What I mean to say is different. Independent of you. Myths serve a purpose for those who nurture them and spread them to willing ears. The galaxy needs hope, Ambra. The oppressed worlds are crushed under this brutal tyranny. Its creatures have lost the capacity to even dream of victory. Only something larger than themselves, that they can believe is greater than the Dram, can give it back to them. An army is not enough. A leader is too fragile. No, what they need is a god. Or in your case, a goddess."

My head fell on my arm as I groaned.

"Your feelings in this matter are irrelevant. Your legend grows because they need it."

"I have to find a way to live up to it."

"You have said it. So I must have faith that it will be."

We didn't speak anymore that night. I was exhausted. Waythrel might not require anything resembling sleep, but I had to rest. I prepared for bed, told my alien roommate goodnight, and collapsed on my mattress, unconscious in seconds.

Some goddess.

Chapter 39

We cannot define these things without obscuring them, while we speak of them with all assurance. Our doubts cannot take away all the clearness, nor our own natural lights chase away all the darkness.

Blaise Pascal

And the dream came.

I flew through the heavens, launched by my father's arms. A cold perversion of the distant stars tugged me. I panicked at the evil hidden among them. I sped forward in time. I sat at my family's kitchen table to see the demon man. I raced through the high corn and bled at the feet of his henchman. In the cruel evening, I stared along the green stalks to the sky. The grinning devil mocked me. His shadow darkened the moon.

But as the light faded and blackness closed, I did not wake in my bed screaming and soaked in sweat. Not this time.

Instead, I floated in a blank emptiness, without illumination, sound, or scent. Madness lurked in this sensationless null. It also sharpened my awareness as I approached the abyss of sanity. I stretched into the nothingness for contact.

A disturbance.

So delicate, I couldn't tell which sense it engaged. Was it sight? A pale glow growing in front of me? Or touch? A cool breeze, a ripple of air like a whisper over my skin? Or did it stir faint dreams of childhood, of cold winters in the plains? The barest hint of a smell, a taste of wood smoke from a fire resonating with ancestral memories?

None of these. The experience blossomed. A million voices phase shifted from buzz to hum to tone. A celestial choir chanted a melody. It gestated in the drowning darkness. The music was more than sound. It contained the psyches of the singers. Psychology and intellect echoed in counterpoint from a cavern deep within each member.

The chorus painted the emptiness in a beautiful light, with colors recognized by my unique sense, a luminescence I could touch. As I reached for this glow, it ceased as a song that one might hear and became a water in which I swam. A clay I could sculpt.

And *I knew. I understood.* The voices laughed with joy. From all directions, their vitality converged on me. I had only to embrace them.

Then—*cold, hard, irregular.* Revolving in this directionless place, seeking, I experienced a new disturbance. A shape unerased before me. A net with infinite dimensions, light bent and surrounded it. Enveloped it and waited.

Everything was still, the energies potential, the taut string of a bow with the arrow notched.

All that remained was for me to release the shot.

Chapter 40

Give me a place to stand,
and I shall move the earth.

Archimedes of Syracuse

"I don't understand," Waythrel repeated.

We raced through the moon base to meet with alien physicists. I speed-walked, waving my arms, trying to convey my ideas. The alien easily kept pace, bouncing on its many legs. My words spilled with frustration.

"I don't have the knowledge, the understanding. I don't even know if you and the Xix do, so how can I hope to explain?"

We converged on the Xixian wing of the settlement. I bent over, my hands on my knees. My phrases burst between my breaths as staccato gunshots.

"I have intuition. Like Thel told me. Before I was blind, I didn't understand the physics of seeing. *I just saw.* I don't know how this can be, or what it means, or how to say it. But I know I can do it. But I will need *help*."

We moved again. Waythrel was silent until we reached the doors to a makeshift laboratory. But here it raised one of its creepy, tendrilled hands.

"You will try to explain to our scientists. Of course, we don't have the best of them here, or even a reasonable representation of the areas you might require. A handful of technologists spared from other needed activities. We dispatched them to this site to work multiple functions, engineering the most relevant. I hope this will serve."

I had no idea what would serve. A Xix engineer made Einstein's brain look like a rat's. That had to count for something. And right now, it was all I had.

The doors opened, and we walked inside. Several aliens were waiting for us at Waythrel's request. I sensed curiosity, expectation, but I was unable to venture into the complexity of their thought.

"Go ahead, Ambra. It is your show."

Waythrel stepped to the side, abandoning me to the swinging forest of alien eyestalks. I set my shoulders, tilting my head to look them in the eyes. *Might as well just get to it.* They were the experts. *They* would have to figure out what I meant.

"Thel once told me spacetime is like a gel. An ever-changing fluid where events of past, present, and future depended on the shape of the stuff itself."

The ripples of crestfallen emotion from the extraterrestrials indicated that I'd screwed up. *Brain fart, Ambra Dawn.* Disappointment stained the surrounding psyches. Well, I couldn't help it that I had the intellect of an Earth ape. I *was* an Earth ape!

One of the scientists spoke. "A crude description, even in your simple language."

"Yes, okay," I said, not wanting to lose their trust in me. "Humans can understand basic causality—events now creating future states. The gel is squeezed one way and reshaped in time dimensions."

They were silent, waiting, further demoralized at my conceptualization of it all. But I would not stop.

"So, why isn't it possible for what comes to reshape what was?"

The creatures engaged in discussion, their eyestalks off me and twirling around each other. Intense concentration radiated from Waythrel. The one that had spoken to me stepped forward. It was taller and broader than my friend, its coloration a greenish-blue with iridescent stripes. This contrasted with Waythrel's deep-purple spots.

"Your distinction between past, present, and future is misguided. It is difficult to communicate with you on this topic without distortion. Within these constraints, however, this of which you speak has long been considered possible. But untried."

"Why untried?" I asked.

"Because we have lacked a technical understanding of how to proceed. And because it has been presumed unwise to enter recursive space."

"Recursive space?"

"Again, we struggle with the limitations of language. Should you alter the events of history from later time points, you also modify those same coming occurrences, perhaps impacting even your actions to reach into what came prior. A circular chain of incidence, which, in a simplistic view, appears to lead to paradox."

"Like killing your mother before you were born, so you would never have been born to kill her."

"In general terms, yes. These are consequences within effects. They are reminiscent of procedures in a computer program calling on themselves, potentially looping infinitely in causality. Loops of this nature cannot be followed until they resolve."

"What does that mean?" I wondered out loud. I sensed a similar befuddlement in Waythrel. My Reader friend was no cosmologist.

"That the aftermath of such actions is unpredictable. Why do you ask us this?"

I looked at the scientist. I had to come clean, tell them my hopes. I knew I couldn't do it without them.

"Because I can save Earth."

"Save Earth," echoed my advocate, eyestalks abuzz. "By altering the past?"

"Yes."

"How, Ambra? You were listening. Even we of Xix cannot do this."

"I don't know how! I know enough of what I can do. I am hoping with your help I can succeed."

I skipped around, waving my arms at everything and nothing. I tried to explain the vision, to put into language what were insights deeper than any words I had.

"There's potential, enormous strength in the millions of clueless Readers of Earth. *Earth before.* Those who were, but who are no more. Power beyond anything you have imagined."

"I don't understand, Ambra," said Waythrel.

"They are also *Writers.* Blind, but with sleeping Writer ability. Some more, some less. I can shape spacetime, you know this. So can they, but they cannot direct it. Their brain cyst is too undeveloped. But I can channel them. I can refocus their energies!"

"To what end?"

"I can *Read* the past. I can *Write* in the present. You must see the next step."

One of the scientists answered, excitement radiating from its thoughts. "You believe you can alter the space and time of what has happened."

"Yes!" I blurted. The arm waving intensified. "But there are problems. At least two I can see. I'm sure more I can't. First—it needs a huge amount of energy. More than I'll ever have. To reach backward in time and change things by myself—it's impossible. I can't do it. Not alone. That is why I need *them.*"

"The Earth Readers of the past?"

"That's right! Together we have the strength. I can combine our energies, guide them, like a chorus singing. Tens of thousands. Millions. So much more powerful than one voice."

"What is the other obstacle you mentioned?" Waythrel asked.

"The second—I'll have to find a lens to focus these forces. Even if I can direct it, the power is still too weak, dispersed like a mist or fog. Something has to magnify it like the light of a star through a child's glass, a bright spot that sets a piece of paper on fire!"

"What kind of lens?" asked another of the scientists. "How do you redirect such energies?"

They were so smart but still couldn't see where I could. "You can't guess? What's the most powerful distorter of spacetime known in the galaxy?"

Understanding dawned as a hot wave through the alien group. The audacity of my ideas frightened and excited them.

Waythrel whispered. "The Orbs."

"Yes." I hopped. "And I know them and how to travel through them. And I see them in a way no one else has. We've thought of them as tunnels between different spatial points in the now. But they are...*more*. I've seen infinite doors inside them, opening one behind the other. Not just in space, but also in time."

One of the Xixian scientists stuttered through the translator. "But every Sphere leads to another, either indirectly on the Strings, or as you have shown, directly, when they are opened. How can you direct through time what is forced through the physical dimensions? How do they link through time?"

The next part I didn't understand myself. *And yet I saw.* Maybe I didn't need to. These alien geniuses could figure it out. I'd just tell them what I knew.

"The Orbs don't connect to each other."

"Ambra," began Waythrel as I hesitated, "of course they do."

"No, it seems like it, but you can't *see*. Your instruments can't measure. They don't *connect*. I don't know how it can be, but I've seen it. All those magical balls, the Holy Orbs, they *don't exist separately*, not as you think. There aren't *many* of them. There's only *one*."

"One?" whispered Waythrel.

"Yes, one!" I gestured and pointed and tried to draw in the air things I couldn't even picture in my mind. "It's in all these places at the *same* time, an infinite door unlocking boundless regions, endless periods. Areas unreachable by the String Tree, touching worlds the tendrils don't contact. A door leading to locations so much farther than we can imagine, galaxies half a universe away."

Astonished thoughts passed through the group.

"More than distant spaces, but also *times*. Near and very far. The Orb here, opening the door in this space, will do as well as any to focus the energies of Readers past."

Their lead engineer turned all its eyes to me. "And where will you focus this power, Ambra Dawn?" Awe and fear spilled from its voice, its brain racing to places my own could not follow.

"The thing that slaughtered my people," I said. "Richard Cross asked me to change its course. So I will."

Out of suffering have emerged the strongest souls; the most massive characters are seared with scars.

Kahlil Gibran

Months of research followed this conversation. The best of Xixian scientists traveled to the moon base and set up shop. They introduced me to the intellectual stars of their species, minds most Xix could not fathom.

It didn't matter to me. I was a simple rodent to these developed creatures. A rat with a singular ability and insight stimulating a cascade of creativity in their science. I gave them a "humanitarian" reason to pursue their ideas. A chance to save an entire planet and its dominant sentience. Of course, and with it all, the Reader potential held within.

They imported brains and equipment. Performed a succession of experiments. Piled secrecy on top of concealment. How they did this all under the nose of the Dram amazed me. For several weeks, I spoke again and again to Xixian scientific delegations. They listened to my words and rained questions on me. Behind those scenes, they developed their theories for making this bold attempt succeed.

A lull followed the initial flood of activity. The days quieted, the interviews stopped, and the aliens left me alone. Squirreled away in some new corner of the moon base, they pursued the implications of my proposal.

Waythrel kept me updated as much as was possible. Successes and failures, hypotheses and dead ends. My favorite Xix simplified the ideas so I could understand at least a fairytale of what was happening. Explanations were complicated by the fact that my advocate also possessed a poor understanding of the matters. Your average Jane struggling with Einstein's writings and trying to convey them to a hamster.

Meanwhile, I fought off the terrible chill creeping over me.

Reading these pages, you are sitting somewhere on our bountiful planet, *before*. Legions of life surround you that you ignore, undervalue, and spend your minutes complaining about. Humans, other animals, insects, the microbes in your gut and on the surface of your body. The viruses infecting your cells, those of plants and bacteria. Minimalistic parasites that have driven so much of evolution.

The sum total of life on Earth, the biosphere, is, in your time, a tiny shell of air and sea and life, paper-thin, floating on a lake of magma. In some ways, you are a small cell in a fragile, giant organism. Each part is hopeless on its own. Every unit contributing and taking from the whole. A network of smaller pieces assembling into a powerful and complex system that changed the planet's composition.

But the ocean of magma will be set loose. From my vantage point in your future, it has poured over field and stream, peak and valley, sea and city. Burning, torching them to ash. You can't feel what it's like when the great body of Earth has died, and you, a single, small cell, are cast into the vacuum. Cut off. *Withering*.

I withered. As did every human on the moon base. Day by week, week by month. We were dying some kind of death never cataloged. The atrophy from a murdered homeworld. Despite the distance from

Xix, the aliens did not fall ill. Neither had I on Dram. Travel is different. A journey brings loss, separation, but a psychic link remains. An umbilical cord feeding sustenance to the soul, allowing the body to continue.

Now, Mother Earth was dead, devoid of connection. We ate food, yet we starved. We socialized but endured isolation. Earthlings suffered a progressive, inexorable decay of a branch cut from the tree. For us, it was getting terribly cold in space.

Expeditions ventured at times to the horror around which we revolved each month. Some to the surface, searching places where the fires had been less fierce, where perhaps some hint of life might remain. But nothing. Even near the deep-sea vents, where bacteria had thrived beside geothermal springs at temperatures close to boiling, they found only cooling lava.

And wasn't it pointless? What if some probe uncovered a super bacterial spore that ate rock and metabolized sulfurous gas? The biosphere could not be recreated. Not in a million years. One hundred times that would be too little. Mother Earth had required longer durations the first time. Four billion for life intelligent enough to think about itself to evolve.

The charred cinder masquerading as our homeworld might start over. Perhaps something evolving to consider the universe again in another five billion years. By this time, our sun would die, blow up to a red giant like the one in the Dram system, cooking the world beyond salvage. Cheering thoughts.

Once I joined the surveyors and traveled to Earth. We left the base on a Xixian spacecraft, circling from the dark side of the moon. We witnessed Earthrise. Not the one from NASA photographs. Not the stirring images of a crescent blue-white marble hanging in darkness. Instead, an ash-shrouded ruin. Decorated with soot-smothered streams and lakes of lava. A monster's eye glared at us over the lunar horizon.

Within hours, the powerful ship put us in orbit about the calamity. We descended in smaller vessels to examine the terrain. Our home was unrecognizable. It was impossible to see detail through the clouds of smoke and cinder. Not to mention the constant plunge of debris still falling from space back to the surface. The journey was hazardous, and Waythrel had protested my traveling.

At different wavelengths, the Xixian instruments cut through the fumes. They revealed the ravaged landscape beneath. Without oceans, the continents were indistinct. No polar caps, and it became easy to lose orientation of north and south.

Nowhere stood a single reminder that we had existed. The expanse around the planet had been swept clean of our satellites and junk by the material hurled into orbit, much of it still waiting to bring more fire in its fall.

A few hours were enough, more than I could bear. Shaking with horror, we returned to the desolate surface of the moon. *Equally lifeless.* But Earth was more barren for what it had once been. For what had been lost and burned and buried in that cataclysm.

Afterward, sitting in my room, I struggled to purge my mind of those memories. But my efforts failed. Again and again, I pushed them aside until my thoughts lurched through my tumor and into the past. The horrific images served as my navigation. They dragged my awareness into the darker corners of history. I crash landed in Germany, 1940s. The slaughter of millions. Ashes sent into the skies.

The name they used years later, letters etched into the textbooks, seared itself into my memory. A two-part term, from the ancient Greek: *holos,* "whole" and *kaustos,* "burnt."

Completely burnt. The word haunted me.

Holocaust.

Chapter 42

All great truths begin as blasphemies.

George Bernard Shaw

I n the meantime, the investigations continued.

We fought the terrible chill freezing our souls, the helplessness inviting madness. I turned again and again to the only hope available. The one small seed trying to germinate as the Xix searched their way through a maze of science and technology.

After a series of experiments performed without my input, they included me in the process. At first it was simple things. Reaching into the recent past to modify spacetime in incremental ways they could detect and quantify. Nothing related to the grand plan I'd put in motion. No manipulation of forces through the Orbs or the channeling of others to a common task. They wanted to gauge the range of my abilities. Understand how to measure them. Before they moved on to the dangerous and impossible, they needed to calibrate the merely possible.

The second phase was forming groups to enhance our capability.

Among the humans on the moon base, a high proportion were Readers. Once briefed, all leapt at the chance to work on the project. A few of the most powerful from Xix also participated. They boosted the chorus of power at our disposal. In these secondary experiments, they employed several hundred human and Xixian subjects.

At first, we found limited success. I could sense the energies of the participants, the fields their aggregate abilities created. What I couldn't develop was a method to organize that potency, channel the forces in a productive way. And their latent Writer potential? Hopeless. It was so diffuse, so weak, like trying to pick up a radio signal from Earth in the Andromeda Galaxy. And this was step one. I had to focus those minuscule waves into a laser beam to burn through a sheet of steel. The gulf between the idea and practice never looked so vast.

Of course, the final plan was to add together these feeble manipulations of spacetime through the Orbs. We needed some kind of initial lens. One not so powerful, taking a much more diffuse source, compacting it, and delivering it to the greater optic. We had to build a telepathic telescope.

It took a long time to solve this problem, months until they realized I could not be this instrument. While I could concentrate my thoughts, I could not focus those of the other Readers. Only *they* could do this, but how to teach them? The Xix tried as they had trained me. Perhaps because my abilities were so great to begin with, the Xixian training was productive. But not here. All efforts failed. The average human Reader was unable. The project stalled, and the chill deepened.

~

I was in despair when the monk came.

He was an old Tibetan man. White eyebrows and a bald head perched atop a crimson and orange robe draped to the ground. He stood at the door Waythrel had opened to our chamber, looking neither toward me nor the alien beside him. His eyes searched the distance, a soft smile always on the edge of his expression. I sensed hesitancy in my Xixian friend.

"Ask him in, Waythrel," I said, and it invited him inside.

The ascetic bowed and entered. He walked to me and knelt, taking the hem of my black robes. I was getting used to this, my gradual deification in the eyes of my species. For whatever reason, they didn't brand me with the guilt of my choices. I miraculously escaped judgment. My abilities appeared magical to most, my strange appearance adding to the mystique. And I supposed that helpless desperation went a long way toward myth building. After Waythrel's lecture about my growing legendarium, I realized I could do little about it. However ridiculous, I let him prostrate himself.

"I am Chodak, Daughter of Time," he began.

I gasped. "Where did you hear that name?"

Images from the terrible nightmare returned, as did the last words I spoke with Richard. Outside my visions, I had heard one other person use the title—the scientist who had helped twist me into the abomination I was.

"Forgive me, Sighted One," he said, bowing further, his face touching the ground. An intensity sharpened his sentences. "It was spoken to me in a dream."

I took his hands and raised him. "Sit with me. Tell me about your vision." He tilted his head, and I thanked him. "And call me Ambra. No titles, please."

The old monk limped over to the couch in the chamber. We sat together as he spoke, an intense thrum through his every phrase. For the duration, he never released my hand. I found his constant smile healing.

"It was in my meditations, Ambra Dawn. Always, I see most clearly when in the deepest focus."

Waythrel danced over and stood apart from us. I sensed concentration in the alien but could not focus on its thoughts.

"Always, I seek to find you, to learn how your light will deliver us and save us from this darkness. But you are too hard to see, and the glare is too strong." He raised the index finger of each hand in unison, smiling. "Until last night. I found my being *inside* that of another. It was difficult to understand how this could happen. I traveled across the entire galaxy in a single moment and stepped within. I saw you with his eyes."

Waythrel interrupted. "You entered the awareness of another?"

The monk shook his head. "No, only his brain. A flesh in which his mind abided. Or so it felt."

What to think of this? "And what did you see?" I asked.

The old man closed his eyes. Dust motes danced in the air under the ceiling lamps. I thought of gnats darting in a green meadow beneath a hot June sun. The bright thought of Earth throbbed inside.

"I experienced a life in the time of a butterfly's breath."

"And did these experiences show you how the Daughter prevails?" asked Waythrel.

I suppressed a groan at the use of that title. The Xix were keen to build on my mythology. My alien friend was already weaving this man's language to fit its purposes, and doubtless not for the last time.

"No," he said, opening his eyes, the smile still there. "It was of a different time, a distinct space. One making little sense to my small soul."

I squeezed his hands. "Then why are you here, Chodak? There are many visions. Countless futures and confusing pasts."

"Because he loved you, Ambra Dawn," he said, his eyes shining. When I did not speak for several moments, he continued. "Not as we love the One who has become our light in this dark time. This and more. He adored you even more as a man loves a woman in the flesh, and he attended to your every movement. Through his eyes, I witnessed the deepest meditation of a lover for whom all time stops as his beloved turns her head or takes a step. Concentration on each detail, each hair strand, each breath. And always filled with adoration. Through his eyes, I also glimpsed *your* eyes. Deep, blind, green eyes of sadness, but with the joy of him in them. You were to be married."

I tensed. Was this vision a metaphor? Or had this monk seen into a future where some human might dare care for me? As I have told you, the reality of my deformity, my blindness, the monstrosity of my actions had shut down common expectations of our kind. And there had been no time, no chance to examine the idea of my womanhood. Not a single moment to exist in such a dimension. To shine this intimate light onto it was disorienting. It hurt.

I couldn't help myself. My thoughts leapt over to his mind, breaking a privacy I always try to respect. I gazed into his vision and grasped its truth. I experienced the adoration of a lover from a time yet to be. My own face stared back at me through the memories of the eyes of a possible future.

The monk smiled and patted my hand several times. "He loves and serves, and he awaits you. I came to tell you this, to tell you so you would know in a foretelling I found, you will be loved in this way."

The universe is cruel. More than anyone, I realized there would be no single chain of events, and even what has been could *unbe*. Was it better to know there existed the possibility of such affection? Knowing it would not be realized? Or best to live ignorant, never having felt the imaginative stirrings of desire in a dying life? How could I sit there infatuated with the cyst-inspired hallucinations of an old Buddhist disciple?

Waythrel interrupted my thoughts. "Chodak, you said you see more clearly in your deepest meditations."

The monk nodded. "It is so."

"We of Xix study the focus of consciousness, the stepping out of it and becoming more, even as you become less. We trained the Daughter in our ways as best we could an alien mind. But you are human," it said, in a tone I had come to imagine as it smirking, "and a professional."

"Devotion is not a trade for us."

"I understand," it said, continuing to probe. "How did you find this man in your dream?"

The monk glanced upward and to his left. "I searched for Ambra Dawn and could not see for the light. But I found a tunnel, a passage leading toward her. One I might follow without becoming blinded by her radiance. I faced this direction and journeyed, and it took me to him."

"You *chose* this path? You *directed* your Read?"

Ice ran through me and my heart drummed. My emotions leapt to Waythrel. I understood.

Do you see? rang its thoughts. *Here, we may find our answer.*

"Yes," he smiled. "But only in great stillness."

Chapter 43

It is by logic that we prove, but by intuition that we discover. To know how to criticize is good, to know how to create is better.

Henri Poincaré

And so we stumbled on the process of prayer.

You read me right. *Prayer.* Ideas from an alien and a Buddhist monk who were part of our Reader cohort. But it wasn't so crazy a notion, after all.

You may not be aware, but before Earth died, a good bit of scientific research suggested meditation, prayer, whatever you want to call it, supercharged human cognition. It possessed a remarkable ability to alter brain states, focus consciousness, improve health. Jesus said: "Pray, and it will be as you believe." Yeah, not quite like the Bible has it. But I heard it from the rabbi's mouth, so trust me on this one. And he had a good-sized cyst, in case you were wondering.

What tradition had passed down over generations, and what science had begun to measure, was that prayer altered the mind. Because of what we knew about sentience, that meant prayer also changed the world around the mind. Given the human Writer potential, it should have been obvious what was really going on. Meditation focused and stilled thoughts. Isolated our awareness from the five other senses. It allowed our sixth sense the stillness and quiet, the resources it needed to blossom. And that's where the magic of humanity is born. "Be still and know that I am God." In some strange way, we've always known the truth.

Our monk had delivered a solution to the misdirected energies of our Readers. Waythrel had seen the answer before we could have hoped to on our own. That night, we began an intense training in the thousand-year-old practice of Tibetan meditation.

Chodak and I worked together to direct this giant, prophetic prayer group. I had discovered an alien form of mindfulness with the Xix, but he taught the Earthlings among us a more *human* way. It was far more effective than the Xixian approach. We performed basic practices throughout the day over several weeks.

The results were transformative. Measurable by the special equipment our alien allies had set up. The success motivated us to continue the arduous hours of stillness. I could see with my strange sight the energies of the Readers brightening. The diffuse fog condensed, forming bobbing will-o'-the-wisp shimmers. They danced around the huddled meditating groups.

It felt crazy, despite all the miracles and madness I had seen. But it worked. Intense sessions of meditation and feedback snowballed. It wasn't long before I drove the spacetime distortions of our group into a more organized and malleable form. You have to understand, each was so much weaker than me. Alone, they could affect little in the physical continuum. Gatherings as large as ten or twenty had little power.

These focused *prayers* of hundreds of Readers registered on the instruments. They congealed into blobs, colorful and alive like those in a lava lamp. They were clay I could reach out and touch, tug—*shape.*

Saints we weren't, but we spiked the Xixian detectors. We were getting close. We had a method to bring together and integrate the potency of those gathered in a way I could channel and control.

But still, not enough. Not *near* sufficient, even should the Xix and I succeed in using the Orb to focus the forces one thousand times. The task required so much more.

It was the combination of moving through time and space making it so difficult, not like adding the difficulties of one to the other. To stretch back into the past and alter spacetime in a major way required multiplying the energies involved. Hundreds of thousands with our prescient ability had to participate. At least. There weren't the numbers left in the galaxy for such a deed. Or if there were, gathering them together would be impossible under the eyes of the Dram and the needs of interstellar travel.

But the numbers did exist. Waiting, if I could reach them.

As we developed this newfound power of prayer, the Xix approached me. Their scientists believed we could use the Orb to channel the spacetime manipulations (with my help, of course). All that remained was the little task of getting those hordes of Readers onboard with the plan. Millions who lived decades, hundreds, or thousands of years in the past. On an Earth that no longer existed. In times and cultures diverse and distant. I had to find a way to reach them and convince them all to *pray* for our deliverance.

Thank God, I had an idea. Unfortunately, we first had to deal with an unfriendly visit from our insectile hunters.

Chapter 44

You need chaos in your soul to give birth to a dancing star.

Friedrich Nietzsche

Michael burst into our room. His shoulders slammed against the sides of the sliding door as it opened, bouncing him sideways. Waythrel and I sat across from each other, unmoving. I reclined on the couch, the Xix in a chair of special design. We were in deep telepathic communication over our recent progress with the Reader groups. Michael's disruption forced us to shake ourselves out of the trance. To help us along, the entire base was plunged into red emergency power lighting as alarms sounded.

"Dram warships," he gasped, bent over with hands on his knees. "Five of them surfing off the Orb String." He glanced at equipment on the wall. "You really shouldn't turn off your communications."

"*Five?*" I had seen the damage *one* of them could do.

"They know we're here," he continued. "I don't know how they discovered, but that doesn't matter. We were too optimistic. It was bound to happen." He stared at me. "Could you not have seen it?"

I squeezed my temples. "I should have, but I have been so busy with the project. And...there is something interfering with my Reading of the Dram."

Waythrel's eyes spun toward me. "Interfering? How is that possible?"

"I don't know. Maybe some kind of shielding? Whenever I look toward Dram, its noise and static."

The Xix danced around in the impossible Xixian fashion. "Ambra, we have to get you off this moon! Michael, what transports are available?"

"No time! They sprung this trap well. We detected their war boats minutes ago. They came off the Strings at a tremendous velocity, aimed right at us. Already their longer-range weapons have disabled our sensor drones. We can only track them from lunar arrays. The Xix team has taken over, redirected all power to defenses, but it won't last long."

I sensed a bubbling anxiety within Waythrel, focused on more than me.

"We had no advanced warning," said the alien. "Even through our Time Tree relays. This can mean only one thing."

Michael nodded, winded and weary. "Word came quickly after the ships appeared. There has been a mass culling of your representatives on their homeworld, and spreading to other closely linked systems."

"And Xix itself?" I could feel the creature close to dissolving. Its mental patterns were much simpler now, primitive, emotional states dominating the structure.

"No reports of any attacks. Yet. They might not have the evidence to suspect extensive Xixian involvement. Maybe they are just purging Dram as a precaution."

Waythrel darted. "There must be a craft we can use to try an escape!"

"They'll vaporize it in seconds. You know nothing will get by."

I couldn't stand it anymore. "Should we just sit here until they liquefy everything? Is that better?"

He shouted. "I don't have a damn plan! We're helpless."

My mind raced. The first explosions shook the settlement. Dramian weapons impacting the lunar surface. At that distance, with the generators we had, it would be a few minutes before they could target the base. But no more.

"Okay, assemble the Readers in the meditation chamber."

He gawked, perplexed.

I roared. "Michael! Get them all down there, now!"

A dawning awareness spread through Waythrel's mental web. "Ambra, no. It is much too dangerous."

"What's too dangerous?" Michael asked, turning his furrowed face between us. "Why do we need the Readers?"

I pushed past him, sprinting down the hallway. *Madness.* A blind woman dashing through narrow corridors, trailing fingers across the walls, tracing thoughts along the Strings.

I shouted to the pair behind me. "Waythrel, gather the Xix techs and fire up the damn machines! We've only got minutes!"

By the time we had critical numbers, we were absorbing significant damage. The structure rocked with the impacts, moon dust clogging the air. *Five warships!* Enough firepower to destroy an entire Earth metropolis ten times over. They wouldn't even have to vaporize us. Knock out the life support on this airless and frigid satellite—*the end.* Of course, the Dram would make sure and melt the base into the rock.

The Xixian scientists engaged the amplifiers or whatever they were that channeled our spacetime manipulations. Their crew performed coolly under pressure, much better than my brethren.

"Everyone!" I shouted over the din of war and human panic. "Listen to me!"

Useless. People hollered, darted around, clutching each other. My voice could not penetrate the cacophony.

We didn't have time for this!

I closed my eyes and resorted to more brutal means.

It was a brief burst, but harsh. Several voices cried out. Those in the room grabbed their skulls, shutting their eyes in pain. A few fell to the floor, tears in their eyes. One did not rise and remained motionless. Betrayed eyes gaped in dawning understanding.

"I'm sorry!" I screamed, as much to kill my own thoughts of what I had done as to focus their attention. "Listen to me! The Dram will destroy this base in minutes! We can't beat them in a fight. We can't stop or repel their weapons. We can't run away."

The rumbling from above filled the silence in the room.

I swallowed and pressed on. "We have *one* chance to defeat them. When the Orbs are opened, there is a terrible distortion of spacetime. Unless controlled, they will devour anything nearby. Including enemy warships."

I heard Waythrel in my mind. *Ambra, hurry! Time is running out!*

"I can activate them, but I can only do it if I'm close enough. And I don't know if I can control them from this distance. Not without your help! This is the time to use all we have been practicing for. Right now, I need you to quiet yourselves and harmonize and reach out with me. Together, we can open the Orb and draw the Dram ships into the vortex!"

"What if you can't do it from here, even with our help?" a woman called out.

"Then we will die," cried the Xix. "But doing nothing is certain death."

The monk stepped forward, his smile a weak shadow. "And if you cannot control the Orb?"

I reached mentally to the alien and its thoughts echoed my own. "I don't know. I think it could consume the entire system."

Voices buzzed at this, but a strong earthquake shook the room, and dust rained down on us. The chatter ended.

Waythrel barked, "Unless you survive, your star system is already dead! The risk is delay. Take your positions! Compose yourselves. Find your focus and direct it to Ambra!"

They listened. The group crouched and sat, trembling. Together they frantically tried to reach a Zen-like calm.

Have you ever tried to reach a meditative peace frantically, with Dram warships blasting the foundations out from under you?

It wasn't working. The ultimate irony: to save our lives, we had to obtain an enlightened mode, where time and worry disappear. In minutes. Before we died.

Sensing their inability to concentrate, the old monk called out reminders of his teachings. He stepped among the frightened souls, trying to coax them to relinquish their attachments to themselves. To safety. To life itself. To seek a state of detachment where death does not matter in order to preserve our hides.

That wasn't working, either.

I became desperate as more explosions rocked the base. Once again, survival drove me to actions I never would have imagined in saner moments. I thought back to my invasion of their minds, my psychic slap to calm them down. I had stunned them all, damaged the brain of one, to get their attention.

Was my sole option disturbance?

If I could cause damage, couldn't I also heal? I decided I would try, regardless of whether it amounted to a form of mind control. I projected my emotions over the Readers before me. Waves of intricate spacetime distortions interacted with their mental fields. At first, everything was out of phase, clashing. I adapted, working to understand each personality I touched. One by one, my calming thoughts began to resonate. One by one, I drove out the terror and panic, and they relaxed. They focused as we had trained them. They redirected their own awareness towards me.

Waythrel's consciousness flared from across the room as it deduced what was happening.

I love you, Ambra Dawn, but I fear you. Now you control even the souls of others.

I didn't have the luxury to question the ethics of what I was doing. This was the one way I knew to save our lives. And it was probably not going to work.

Chapter 45

A set is a Many that allows itself to be thought of as a One.

Georg Cantor

I floated midway between the approaching Dram warships and the lunar base.

Like in the dreams of Earth from before, I had no body. I suffered no injury from the vacuum of space or the scalding radiation of the sun. I was a disembodied sentient knot of spacetime, projected from inside the moon itself, the product of my own mental structure and efforts and the amplification of hundreds of Readers and Xixian field modulators.

We had made the dream-state real.

I didn't have time to examine how this had happened. I didn't ask what I had become. And I was not traveling alone. The entire Reader chorus accompanied me. A multidimensional entanglement of consciousnesses. We became the synthesis of the sentience-space-time continuum Thel had introduced to my inadequate human intelligence. Theoretical mind matrices that looked great on paper. We had also made them real.

My awareness dominated the matrix. I shaped and held it together. But thousands of independent thought threads were entwined. More than entwined, *interwoven*. We transformed into something greater than a choir singing in harmony.

Far greater.

It was the birth of a unified, harmonic consciousness. Transcending our individuality. Formed of the combined strength and power of multiple minds, augmented by the advanced alien technology. Each self was a molecule of water transitioning into a new state beyond that before. Bonding in a connected lattice. Decreasing entropy. Crystallizing.

We had become something *Else*. We awakened, the *we* shifting to a single *I*. A newborn opening its eyes.

Some portion of me was still separated, meditating with the others inside the moon. But what it was of me, of all of us, that was outside—I to this day do not know. The Xix do not understand. An ego, a self, projected and concentrated. It could dissolve without complication—that strange new *I* falling back asleep. The process would leave no damage to the rest of us concentrating in lotus positions in a dust-choked room entombed on Earth's satellite.

When I speak of "me" or "I" in this extraordinary encounter with the Dram, the words change meaning. I was not merely Ambra Dawn. I became Ambra swelled and enhanced by a horde of other minds. No, not swelled. Not simply expanded. *Altered*. I rose as something else whose pieces included Ambra Dawn, Waythrel of Xix, and hundreds of other sentients. But it was *beyond* them.

The enemy energy beams passed through "me" without effect, and their explosive missiles did not detonate. Nor did they impact the base. Already, I had left sharp warpings of space behind me. As the radiative and solid weaponry followed available paths in spacetime, they curved, seemingly repelled by the settlement itself, and scattered around the remaining surface of the moon. It was an intuitive shield I constructed in my efforts to will their weapons away from the habitat.

Their inability to target us ignited the Dram soldiers to rage. They unleashed a bombardment unlike anything I'd witnessed. Five powerful warcraft unloaded on the little lunar fortification. The onslaught impacted an invisible wall in a prismatic spray. Explosions of colors cast stark shadows on the moon's dull exterior.

Part of my mind rejoiced. They were draining their energy supplies. When the gravitational vortex came, they would have that much less with which to resist it. I could maintain this shield long enough to debilitate them. I felt no anxiety or need for haste. I swam in a divine calm.

Ambra, open the Orb!

I discerned the intricate threads of Waythrel's consciousness calling from within.

Ambra, now! There is no time!

It was hard to feel the same desperation out here. Without the full flood of my body's limbic soup—its adrenaline, cortisol, hormones, oxygen, sugar—I knew a detached peace. And what was the hurry? The stupid Dram army was just draining its batteries, anyway.

It's okay, Waythrel. I've blocked them. Let them empty their ammunition.

Ambra, please! It is not about them, it is you! Your body—something is wrong. Its temperature is dropping. Your heart rate is slowing. You must return! Open the Orb!

Strange. *My body.* Yes, I could still sense it. Back there, linked by a thread to this new me. I guess my body had to be significant. If I were to continue my journey, end the Dram war, it would need to survive, would it not?

Was this motivating? I wasn't sure it was. In this altered state of being, all my ideas of what possessed importance took on foreign forms. Eons shrunk to ages, parsecs became short excursions. Matter and energy and time mixed and spun and transformed in millions of fashions.

What if my body died? We were clueless prisoners. Caged in sacks of meat. Blind to the vastness, the openness, the *possibilities* of existence. Our vision was myopic, tunneled by bone and blood and brain. What I had become was something divergent. I was not unhappy or harmed in this state. To the contrary, I was empowered, free. I could explore the universe as never before. Forever.

Ambra! No! We feel your thoughts. Please, don't leave us. We can't follow. I am a Xix, but...I...we...we love you.

The Orb fluxed in my mind's eye. It was a pulse of power, a flash, a blinding detonation, and it had not been part of our plan. I had not reached out to it.

Instead, *it* stretched out, seeking *me*. A tendril of radiance sped at greater than light speeds and targeted me like a missile. I could not move or escape its approach. It struck me as a mental blow. It surrounded.

I was wrapped in an energy field, not of cold indifference, not of some mechanical production, but composed of something much more organic. Something *alive*. More than alive. It had a will of its own.

The Orb was conscious.

And it spoke to me.

Chapter 46

In love all the contradictions of existence merge themselves and are lost. Only in love, are unity and duality not at variance. Love must be one and two at the same time.

Rabindranath Tagore

Once again, I awoke after an ageless sleep to stare up toward the nightmare form of an alien medic.

Monitors beeped around my body, collected data, vital signs examined by the wonders of extraterrestrial technology. The room was shaded, and still the weak light hurt my blind eyes. The occipital lobe at the back of my oblong head was obliterated, but my retina could still very much feel pain.

Sore and cold. I blinked several times, tears pooling. An awareness beyond the five senses grew, and the consciousness of many creatures washed over me—human and Xixian.

And of *another* in the distance. Having experienced it, I would never again lose the sense of its presence. Powerful. Quiescent. Anomalous and yet more familiar than myself. I knew something was different. Something profound had changed. I just could not remember what.

Close at hand, the mind of Waythrel. I reached out to it.

Hello again, my dear Xix.

The room burst into applause. With my prescience, I scanned the immediate past. A small crowd hovered around my hospital bed. They cheered and wept, smiles and melting anxiety washing the room like a rainstorm. Their wounded joy woke a smile from me.

"Were my thoughts so loud?" I asked through a croaked voice.

Laughter and more tears.

The creature touched my forehead with one of its many tendrilled extensions. "We are bound together now. We sense each other as never before. We nearly lost you, foolish human child."

My sleep had been dreamless, empty, and my memory was a torn patchwork. "What happened? My last thoughts—they are of you calling for me to open the Orb, and of...something else."

The room was silent. The alien continued to stroke my temple. "You are our prophet, Ambra. The experience traumatized your mind. You cannot remember right now, but a higher power spoke through you."

"A higher power? What do you mean? What about the Dram? What *happened*?"

"Our enemies are gone. Where, we do not know. You unlocked the portal, or, as we understand better now, It opened *for* you. It dragged the ships into wormholes, sent to some distant place. Even a remote time, perhaps. No report exists of them appearing in any system. The base is secure. As soon as you recover, we will return to our training. To our plan." Its thoughts reached out to the others with a fluidity and skill I had never sensed before. "I think you will find our performance will improve significantly."

A wonderful victory! Joy warmed me, but its other words were unsettling.

"What do you mean it opened *for* me?"

"Do you remember nothing, young one? Nothing of the personality that embraced you in the emptiness of the void? That brought you back to us because, not only our love called out, but because it loved us?"

I sat in the bed and pulled my knees to my chest, wrapping my arms around them. A dream reawakened, a golden warmth surrounding me, a caress of light and gravity penetrating my consciousness.

"The Orb," I whispered.

The events rushed back through my awareness. The detachment of projection into space. The Dram military. The emotional call of Waythrel and the other Readers for me to return. The response to that cry from...*could it be?*

"Yes!" said the Xix, a happiness, giddiness, spilling from its mind. "We were all linked in unison as your body was dying, as you began to detach from your fleshly form—from us. It came when our breaking hearts cried to you, and it answered our prayers. It communicated with you, and you listened. Then you spoke back. It opened, the ships scattered. And you returned."

I couldn't piece together the encounter. The shards of memory were strewn in my consciousness, pieces here and there and none fitting, too many critical elements missing.

"What did it say to me?"

Waythrel was silent. I sensed the wonder around the room. The hundreds of humans and aliens in elation knew something that I could not yet recall.

I cannot explain it. Not even in our vocabulary are there concepts. Read, Ambra. Scan my experience.

When you first learn a language, after you have studied for some time the syntax and grammar and spent the necessary days and months immersed in the spoken reality of the tongue, you reach a first important threshold of progress. At this point, you can grasp a great deal of what others speak, a fluency in comprehension. But your speech will lag, flounder, and fail. You will stumble to match the facility of your understanding with expressions from your own mind and mouth. So it was here.

Waythrel's thoughts opened to me. An experience poured that I'm unable to describe in this shallow book with these empty and clumsy words. I understood it, I understand it, but I can't express it. I can say that the vague prophecies, poems, and scriptures of human mythology, those speaking of the divine, they were made mute by this vision.

It was a singular interaction between a cosmic spacetime anomaly and our multiplied and projected consciousness. It was a revelation from the Orb to hundreds of Reader minds interwoven like counterpoint with mine. An entity scores of alien species had manipulated for crude gain, so far beneath its true purpose, that it was like ants walking across a discarded telescope to bridge a small stream.

The Orb had spoken.

In this mystical experience were fragments of universal truths even our enhanced state still could not understand. In our separated individuality, we grasped much less. The divine had entered the room, and we could not comprehend the dust it scattered. We could only stand in awe.

The visions from Waythrel stimulated the full release of my own memories. It was beautiful and terrible. It was so vast in space and time, yet localized and intimate, it generated mental vertigo. As if you went deep inside yourself, grasping the sharp awareness of existence, and from that dimensionless singularity, exploded the entirety of universal creation. Trillions of galaxies, their billions of star systems, planets, living forms, civilizations, cultures, science, and religion blasted like a fire hose through your mind.

And binding all of it together, in the middle of a thousand dimensions of complexity, was an essence, simple and impenetrable. Eternal. Indestructible. A unified force coupling everything else together, giving it structure, and generating the laws of mathematics and physics underscoring reality.

Of all the words I have in my own language for this thing, only one comes close. It is a miscarriage of meaning. It distorts. It lacks. But it is the distant echo of a dream whispered across infinity. It is not God, for the idea of God is too human, too finite and malleable. The word felt wrong.

It is not faith or hope, for in the end these fail before the darkness.

The one word that I dare use—is Love.

Chapter 47

The child ever dwells in the mystery of ageless time, unobscured by the dust of history.

Rabindranath Tagore

Not everything could be transcendent revelation.

Intergalactic love was one thing. The practical need to try to reverse a cataclysm, quite another. Hanging over us still spun the small matter of the dead planet we orbited, and the deteriorating remnants of the life it once sheltered.

We retained the powerful experience of our encounter with the Orb. It would never leave us. It recast our psychic gatherings, propelling us to levels of integration and mutual perception unattainable before. It would empower us to complete our quest, enable us to perform the exploration of chronospace required.

The hunt for human Readers of the past began in earnest. And you won't believe where we landed the first time we launched ourselves backward in time.

Maybe we were all a little cocky, now that the group had become some Celestial Sphere-integrated, precognitive, Dram-warship-trashing spacetime commando team. Or perhaps it was because we were just new and clueless to this bizarre occupation of communal-mind time travel. More explanatory, we were just a sad collection of broken mortals dying off near our grilled homeworld, and our first failure was the best we could manage.

Whatever the reason, none of us, including the Xix, anticipated the wee little problem of my focusing into history and zeroing in on the strongest Reader signals I could perceive. It was enough trying to move through the Orb Time Tree, navigate its labyrinths with my hundreds of fellow intellects. We also had to discern within the space-time fabric the lights and undulations bearing the unmistakable stamp of humanity and surf the strings to those points in the continuum.

Our naive logic sent us straight to the brightest collections of these Readers in the past. Surely, they would be the ones we needed to persuade to spread the message and form the massive trans-chronological prayer group we envisioned.

Our multidimensional knot of consciousness erupted over breathtaking vistas of an older Earth. A landscape before magma had spilled over its surface. A garden predating concrete and industrial pollutants that would tarnish our solar system's gem. An Eden radiating life and potential. The more primal world of our ancient ancestors.

Every mind I carried with me swooned to drink the beauty of our planet once again. The azure skies dotted with puffy white. The breezes stirring smells no longer alien, but of home. Leaf, grass, and moss-green, branch-brown soil. Bird's song. If a disembodied group consciousness could weep, ours did.

The resplendent spectacle touched the Xix among us as well. They now shared our awareness. That intimacy immersed them in a direct manner to human experiences, memories, preferences, and sensations. The standard telepathy of Readers was a miracle but was a pale gray beside the bright color of the integrated intelligence. With my mind stitching the collective together, they felt what it was like to be a creature of Earth. These linked perceptions further merged individuals into the whole.

Some surprise greeted our arrival in an early age of humanity. Most had assumed we would encounter the greatest aggregation of powerful Readers in the modern era. That recent period provided the benefits of the population boom and the technology to spread our message.

But perhaps it was not so strange. Weren't the faith and devotion of the inhabitants of ancient epochs unique? Their prayers could compensate in intensity for what they lacked in numbers.

The sightseeing was poignant, stunning. But we had traversed time for a terrible purpose. I focused our mind on the task at hand. A vigorous source of human spacetime distortion was near. I followed the warped pathways through a forest and up a steep slope. Smoke spilled to the sky, and the indistinct sounds of voices hummed ahead. With increasing anticipation, our little thought matrix sped upward and broke through the trees.

We burst into a clearing. Stones peppered the ground, the tree line failing. Snow and ice carpeted the terrain. A large fire blazed in the center of a rock-lined pit. A loud chanting saturated the air, rhythmic, accompanied by a strange music.

Banging on hide drums and piping on bone flutes, a group of short men wrapped in wolf hides danced. They were unkempt, bearded, muscled, and tan-skinned. In the interior of the gathering, a faction of barbarian women presided over a ritual slaughter.

A deer sprawled at the focus of the concentric circles, strapped with ropes to the soil, its eyes wide with fear. A woman knelt down beside it and lay a jagged white blade to its neck. She let out a long and sustained howl. As one, with a final crescendo in the chanting and potent drum beat, the music ceased.

She slit its throat.

∼

After searching the past for the most powerful groups of Readers we could find, we had landed in the middle of the religious rites of our prehistoric ancestors.

Thinking back on our efforts, it should have been obvious something like this would happen. The human mutations that led to our sixth sense occurred many thousands of years preceding the modern era. I was to discover later that the individual genetic and tissue alterations had already gestated in our hominid forebears before *Homo sapiens*. What singled us out, what gave us the edge over the other hominids, the wild animals, and nature itself, was the rapid development of that organ in the middle of our brains allowing us to forecast.

Sensitivity to the spacetime matrix changed the game. Seeing the future, the dangers and opportunities it presented, even in the vague manner of dreams and visions, was to become the one-eyed species in an ecosystem of the blind. Like the other senses that had conferred tremendous survival advantages in a murderous universe, being able to Read altered everything. Once again, we were to learn it was not our supposed grand intelligence that made us king of the hill. What elevated humanity was a pre-cancerous neural growth.

Nothing like having the foreknowledge that a lion is coming around the bend. Or that threatening weather is approaching. Or that food lurks *this way*. Nothing like the sense that mating with so-and-so just *feels* like a better future. When our ancestors forecast, when they Read their environment, they summoned a power over it no other living thing possessed. They *chose* from the strands of possible futures.

Nature selected for this trait with enthusiasm. In a harsher epoch, before we had developed world-mastering technology, powerful Readers survived to pass on their special heredity. Simmer for several thousand generations. By the period in which we found ourselves, every human present was as gifted a Reader as I had encountered from the modern age. *Every one of them.* No wonder they had produced such a strong and localized clairvoyant signal.

Our forthcoming technical mastery of the Earth—aided in large part in later ages by the alien races who discovered our prescient abilities—removed that harsh selective pressure. Humans in whom the genes produce no psychic cyst could survive as well as those sporting the growth in their brains. Better, because the prophetic traits extract a price both physically and psychologically. By the time I was born, Readers were rare, prized like bluefin tuna, and treated about as well.

Not with the cave folks. They were each bright with it and sensitive. In fact, they detected our presence. Within seconds of the dying animal's drowning cry, as the blood poured over some ritualistic rock carved with strange symbols, the entire group turned twitchy. They stood, one after the other, and *faced* us! I could feel their minds reaching out. The tendrils of our thought matrix served as a warm fire their hands probed. They knew we were there. *They sensed us.*

What did they think we were? Something elemental. Divine. Our visiting future knot of aliens and humans perhaps stimulated oral traditions that would shape the mythologies of later cultures.

The matriarch mounted a rock and held toward us a strange relic —thorned branches of some bush, pruned and adorned with animal bones and rocks. She cried out to the skies with some new chant. The other women and men knelt down and prostrated themselves, bowing in our direction. It would have sent chills down my spine if I had one.

But what was there to do? With the purest optimism, we tried to interact with them. It was a disaster. Their minds had never encountered something so strong, so abstract or complex. We could give them images of simple things, sensations and conceptions of a life they had known and understood. These they could grasp without distress. But to explain our errand, our need, or what we hoped they might accomplish? Hopeless. All such attempts led to frustration and fear, building to madness in our contacts.

After days of trying, the group fled the cave, terrified. They conducted rituals while exiting. Their shamans marked the territory with crafted artifacts and drawings in the dirt. It was a prehistoric protection spell from the demonic forces. After several hours, they were gone, and we had no desire to follow them. The most powerful and concentrated Readers known had rejected us. They could not help save their descendants.

We withdrew from this time period, the weight of failure demoralizing. Our first efforts, our transcendent cohort of mixed species coming off a high in thwarting the attack of the galaxy's dominant military, had reached out to the past, found unequaled talent for our project, and had nothing to show for it.

Nothing but the distinction of having created a haunted mountain in the depths of history.

Chapter 48

It is very hard to find a black cat in a dark room,
especially when there is no cat.

Proverb

Our next attempts were also disasters, and for similar reasons. Despite the minds and cultures we encountered being more "advanced." I'll try to explain, but please be patient with a short lesson to help you understand our route through the history of human precognition.

And forgive the writing. As the content reaches greater abstraction, the medium of this language, the limited musings of the author's mind are increasingly unable to cope. It's a world of frustration for him and for me. He grasps at vocabulary to contain ideas beyond the dimensions of the words available. In this wild effort, as he senses failure, yet cannot summon the tools to escape defeat, the prose enters a strange sort of psychosis. One moment, I am myself, and the next I sound like the complicated musings of a Xixian philosopher. In neither incarnation does the full import of my intent shine through. But let's give it a go.

All the major advancements in our civilizations occurred from the coupling of several critical components. The arbitrariness of climate, pathogens, and resource availability played their part. Geographic position influenced those variables and others. The randomness of genetic recombination was always integral, especially regarding illness. But as we'll see, it played an additional role.

The most favorable combination of these elements produced the world's great civilizations. The Fertile Crescent in the Middle East. India, China, and Japan in Asia. The Mayans, Aztecs, and Incas of Central and South America. The European enlightenments of Greece and Western Europe. Prolonged periods of plenty, a general lack of catastrophic outbreaks, along with specific availability of resources (either local or imported), set the foundation.

But we discovered those factors weren't enough.

Scanning through the past, our community uncovered startling truths. Unusual aggregations of Readers underlay every cultural zenith. Because mastery of agriculture had reduced the selective pressures for survival, the cyst genomics became less important. The key genes could be lost without major repercussions. In other words, civilization diluted prescient potential in the human population. Enter genetic stochasticity. Only when the alleles combined in a fortunate fashion to further the relative number with psychic sensitivity did we see the impact of our neural organ on culture.

I'd explored reams of history from my cage on Earth. The seeming randomness in the rise and fall of civilizations always mystified me. Why had epochs of such great cultural and intellectual progress exploded from nowhere and then vanished into oblivion? Historians fixated on what they knew, resources and environment. But these factors didn't explain why some cultures with all they needed stagnated. Often, the explanations degraded to racial and behavioral theories. Projections more to do with justifying the superiority of the historian's self-image than with facts. And that's because the critical data were missing for all of them.

When the density of Readers was high enough in a core group, their combined sixth sense kindled their awareness, opened their minds, and stimulated exploration and creativity. Think of the world's peoples as being blind but for a few "seers." These could perceive a blurred fog of the visual spectrum. This imperfect stimulus to the neurological structure of the brain set things moving that wouldn't otherwise have moved. New ideas, divergent perspectives, faith in a bigger universe beyond simple "sound."

I can tell you as someone who has seen so much more than anyone else, you have no idea of how deep, how multilayered, how *different* reality is than you imagine it without a spacetime-perceiving organ. It is so obvious in retrospect. These random concentrations of Readers in the right places at favorable times were bound to drive human cultural development.

It also explained the strange tendency of cultures to lose the "spark." Following great progress, they would drift as subsequent generations lost dynamicism and creativity. Many fell into decay. Always, such societies were haunted with the shame of failing their forebears.

The reasons were mysterious and ascribed by sermonizing historians to lax morals and other aspects of the culture. But usually, the cause was far less moralistic—genomic mixing randomly diluted the genes required for our sixth sense. The improbable accumulation of the foresighted that birthed the civilization returned to the standard distribution. The number of individuals with developed prophetic organs declined. The population lost critical prescient mass, and the society languished.

The Xix were the first to perceive this. As alien anthropologists, they dissected the development of our species without our biases. Once we understood, confusion switched to excitement. We had a Reader-detector giving a historical signal! Those we needed to find abounded where humanity made intellectual and cultural leaps, when their minds were unusually open to transformative ideas.

And we had a heck of a story to bring them.

But our enthusiasm was misguided. In a demoralizing series of tragic encounters, we dove into these bubbling cultures and sought out the powerful Readers. We communed with them. We explained reality and our terrible plight. We pleaded with our ancestors to deliver us.

And we shattered their sanity.

What did we learn after such ugly disappointments? Even when receptive to original concepts, the human mind can stretch only so far. Once again, our biases from an age of quantum mechanics, relativity, space travel, and extraterrestrial life misled us. We took for granted how much, and how slowly, expectations had broadened over thousands of years.

For most of recorded history, the Earth was the center of the universe. Atoms were unknown. Spirits spoke from stones and demons caused disease. Our hyper-modern, alien narrative threw too many bizarre notions at them. Their minds tended to break, not blossom, under the strain.

Not all. Unusual individuals accepted our message, although they didn't understand it. They spread it. But the people of their times assigned them the role of mystics or madmen. Sometimes we indeed drove them mad with the visions we shared. We were the stimulus for several human religious and philosophical movements. We triggered suicides. We helped spawn persecutions like the Salem witch trials. We walked with Jesus and Buddha.

The journey was amazing, unexpected, but useless to the one task that mattered. However hard we tried to convey the important essence of our story, we failed. We encouraged people to pray for the salvation of humanity, but the idea of altering spacetime as we needed them to was too abstract. Instead, their prayers assumed shapes they could comprehend and access. Futile and provincial.

So we surrendered. After months of engaging the most exceptional eras in human history, pleading and coaxing and explaining, we gave up. Our bodies and emotions were drained.

We settled on our one remaining option. What we couldn't achieve with the brilliant few of bygone ages, we would seek with the far more dim, but numerous, populations of the modern period. Mediocrity with multiplication would reign supreme.

The Xix had also run the spreadsheets. The strength of the brightest Readers from the past didn't add up. Not when their powers were measured and their numbers counted. Ambra Dawns were in short supply.

The equations told a simple tale. Only in the contemporary era, when the world's population soared to unprecedented levels, would there be a sufficient amalgamation of potential for what we required. More than we needed. But only if we could get them on board. Only if our message was convincing and moving. Only if enough took action.

And that was the essence of the problem. Even in this period, after Einstein, after quantum weirdness, when science-fiction novels and films had introduced millions, perhaps billions, to the ideas of relative time, curved space, multi-universes—in an era where such absurd notions were not tied to a religion or dogma but could lead to further scientific thoughts about cause and effect—even in this age, how to convince anyone *this story* was legitimate so that they might take the vulnerable plunge?

Working against us was that society boiled with cynicism. The loss of previous cultural values and touchstones stirred chaos and disbelief into most deliberations, external and internal. When all authority, teachers, church, state, even family were objects of distrust, what were we to do? How to reach from the future and persuade people to pursue actions so humbling, so silly and antiquated, as to pray? To save humanity from fantastical events that had yet to happen?

Some of us argued for establishing new religions. These contended that, through religious certainty, we could focus the minds as we would need. Despite misgivings from many, we made several attempts to achieve this end.

All were spectacular failures. Those open to the concept of *revelation* also were the least inclined to be rigorous in thought. With astounding creativity, they modified our visions to suit their own emotional needs. Cults arose. The odd technological religion. We were gifted at creating pseudo-scientific doomsday sects. One way or the other, all our creations distorted the message. It would have been a comedy if it weren't so tragic.

We moved on from the idea of generating new religions. We explored the manipulation of political movements, nation-states, cultural fads, and ideology. All had certain attractive features to achieving our goals. Each suffered from one or more fatal flaws that revealed the bankruptcy of such approaches.

In the end, we had abandoned the best and brightest Readers for the average. We had turned our backs on the elevated routes of religion, philosophy, and culture. What remained?

The lowest common denominator, the one commonality across cultures possessing the largest numbers, the greatest budgets, and the longest staying power: *entertainment*. In the modern era, nothing could move people and resources faster than a great story told well. We knew we had an amazing tale, but storytellers we were not.

So we hunted for them. We sought out poets and playwrights, novelists and musicians. We engaged with those receptive to initial probes. We struggled to bring about the telling of their future so it would capture hearts across the world. To find Readers. To convince them.

You know how this ends. You're holding the resulting artifact right now. After everything in this long and insane journey, this book is how we have reached you.

Chapter 49

Sell your cleverness and buy bewilderment.

Rumi

Entombed in a rocky base dug into the bowels of the moon, stumbling on a sequestered garden is a miracle. Imagine a sanctuary where light and shade, stone and tree, life and death are balanced, interlaced in respect. A holy place.

The designers must have been both human and Xixian. Evidence overflowed for aesthetics from the spirit of our species. The quiet fountains, the overhanging branches, the marbled columns approached by grass-shrouded footpaths. Such magic could not sprout from the alien souls of the Xix. But the realization of this beauty in our lunar cave was beyond us. The amazing simulation of Earth's atmosphere-filtered sunlight. The acceleration of growth in the towering beeches. The local replication of the gravity we had known most of our lives. These had the sixfold symmetric finger-prints of our foreign benefactors all over them.

It was perhaps the most beautiful synergy of human and extraterrestrial work I had encountered. Soft shadows from a spring morning dappled the grass with intertwined patterns from the branches and leaves. I padded on the overgrown marbled path, my steps silent on the moss, footfalls gentle and solemn.

I approached a raised platform of stone. A marble slab capped the polished granite. Resting on top glowed a golden bowl filled with fragrant oil. Floating on the surface was a wick embedded in a porous material. A flame surrounded the thread, the radiance of the plasma flickering over the sea of hydrocarbons.

I knelt down and bowed my head. Using my second sight, I read the words my blind eyes could not:

Richard Cross, His Memory is Eternal.

So simple. All the more powerful for it.

"It's time, Richard," I whispered. "We're going to try again today. I've found him. He'll tell our story."

The work of the Xixian scientists had culminated in a new technology. Our experiences with the Orb had unified the Reader cohort. We had gained wisdom through our clumsy apprenticeship in exploring minds of the past. All under the gun—limited time and extreme danger had focused our efforts. We had repelled two more Dram warship attacks. Newly deployed alien sentries brought rumors of a third armada, the largest yet. The bugs were determined to destroy us on the moon. They didn't know what we plotted, but suspected I was here, and that was enough.

I was not so concerned about the weapons of our obsessed enemy —I knew how to handle those with the power of the Orb. Something more nebulous was eating at my mind. The last attack had been different. I had more trouble altering spacetime to block the attacks. Interference, and I could localize the source to the attacking ships. Something was fighting me at this new level, in the arena of space and time.

But I had no knowledge of this enhanced threat. Creature or machine? One or many? Destroyed or returning? Right now, I held the upper hand. But for how long? What was this challenge from the

Dram? Would their efforts overwhelm me? I didn't know how much time we had left. And our quest could not fail.

Our plan required a catalyst to convert a small input of energy from *Earth Before* into a chain reaction. We would push the first domino, be the butterfly wings in America that cause a typhoon in Australia.

A painful analogy. America and Australia were scorched. Not one single, elegant butterfly remained.

We broke through barriers of space and time, focusing on the minds and energies in the shadows of *before* that flitted past our awareness. Our project rushed through the final stages, but not without incident. After we settled on finding a few receptive intellects, we were still so clumsy. We tread with extreme care. We remembered the problems of our first attempts. At first we made transient, mild interactions.

But what followed, *such disasters*. Like a bull in a china shop, we smashed and broke and cut ourselves and others in the process. The dangers to my consciousness were real. I spent a week in a coma when I entered into the wrong mind and was nearly consumed. It took the concerted efforts of the Reader ensemble to call me back again. With tenderness and pain, we increased our mastery. At last, I could visit and enter the past personalities, interact with them, and return with my health and sanity intact.

But the minds of those I reached!

My first serious contacts were still so crude. My skills in this work, and my knowledge and intuition of psychology, were rudimentary. Here I was, a seventeen-year-old girl whose life experiences consisted of the absurd tale you have read, trying to interface with psyches in human history that were as different and diverse from her own as could be imagined.

As with our visits to antiquity, many believed themselves insane when I spoke to them. Typically, these individuals twisted and garbled my ideas. Others rejected them as voices, demons, or stray thoughts and never pursued our request. Some minds shattered with the impact. Our project left institutionalized wrecks behind—cognitive vegetables in place of once-whole persons.

I did this. *I* risked them, wrecked them, and fractured them again and again in my flailing efforts to find a way. Brain by ruined brain, I learned. I studied the subtleties of human thought, internal deliberation, inspirations, belief, and motivation. I grasped the fragility of a mind. How to discern when it was strong enough to absorb what I had to give it and when it was not.

As I perfected my skills, I mastered the art of directing these personalities toward the course I desired. After littering the past with the fragments of mangled minds, I learned to do so while leaving them unaware of my presence. I could even weave my existence into their consciousness in a manner that they could integrate into their reality. A fiction they entertained safely.

The time has come to finish what I left unexplained in the first chapters of this book. Now I must tie together what I have done and what I am trying to do. Now the tapestry is sewn.

Frothings of the fountain floated above the muttering leaves. An artificial breeze blew through the beeches. Water whispered, trees hushed, and the garden lay still before the monument to the Reader who had surrendered his life for our cause. I touched the grass on either side of me. I drank the fresh air, the echo of Earth through space and time.

Prayerful.

Chapter 50

The eternal silence of these infinite spaces terrifies me.

Blaise Pascal

The fear of infinity is a form of myopia that destroys the possibility of seeing the actual infinite, even though it in its highest form has created and sustains us, and in its secondary transfinite forms occurs all around us and even inhabits our minds.

Georg Cantor

In the end, it was so iconic, so preposterous, the laughter burst from my mouth.

Don't get me wrong—nothing was more serious to me or any other human being on the moon. As I walked down the corridor to the new wing built by the Xixian crews, profound purpose weighed on me. To alter history. To achieve the impossible in space and time. To save my species. I could not have been more serious about anything.

But when Waythrel opened the door and I stepped in, gawking, the laughter erupted. Really, how could it not?

The area spanned a Brooklyn-sized chuck of lunar real estate. Power plants and equipment sprung like mushrooms across my field of vision. But that was the most expected aspect.

It was the ancient Greek amphitheater that startled me. Spiraling rows of curved benches ascended. Layers of a strange material rose from a central point, like a great satellite dish, together with seating arrangements for alien and human body types. At the focus of the room, over one hundred feet deep, carved into the lunar bedrock, was a chair.

And *hello there*, what a chair.

The Xix seemed to be aiming for the greatest stylistic contrast possible. The seat loomed as a chaotic composite of Xixian instrumentation. Wires, circuitry, and organic technology ran to and from the absurd throne.

And all of it? Pitch-black. A stunning opposition to the pure white of the material used to build the amphitheater. I didn't ask why.

Techs led me down to the focal point. Behind me trailed hundreds of Readers assuming their positions around the theater. I reached toward Waythrel with my mind for reassurance as they strapped me into the thing. I shivered, the process triggering nightmares of too many events in my life. The Sortax visit to Earth. The Dram examinations. The seats on the navslav ship. After all that had happened to me, those tortures felt both infinitely far and as close as my thumping heart.

I pitched a small fit about my Red Sox cap. They said it had to come off. Special sensors had to go on the Great Bald Patch. The ostrich egg-sized protrusion from my tumor in the back of my head must be bare. The hat would interfere. I growled and gave in. They stuck an outlandish helmet over my head. Ten thousand cords seemed to run out of it and into the equipment. Boston's championship clothing I held in my lap.

I reclined. A seventeen-year-old, half-bald, freak of unnature, imprisoned in an obsidian cathedra at the focal point of a giant dish, sporting a floppy, dreadlocked mitre plugging her into a forest of monster's machinery. All this technological madness designed to amplify and focus gravitons from and to a titanic tumor in my pseudo-skull.

Helmet on head, hat clutched like a teddy in hands, my porcelain-white skin shone next to the ebony chair and dark robes I still wore. My flaming hair, grown long below the bulge, flowed halfway down my back. It emerged outward from the black bowl and wires, cascading over my shoulders and arms.

What I had come to—child of nearby charred Earth, spreading legend in a warring galaxy, centered in a seat of strange power of alien design. I'd traveled from my parents' farm, under knife, through space and torture and dungeons and violence. I had seen the universe as no one had ever encountered it. I had become blind and deformed. I'd eaten my own kind and murdered my planet. I'd opened and spoken with the Orb.

Wasn't it a little bit comical? Dark humor, at least?

Because as I joined with hundreds of Readers to form the astonishing, communal, spacetime-swimming consciousness, the greatest absurdity of all was that I was still alone. So alone, I still clung to the hat of a boy I knew only briefly before he died.

How could I let anyone near? I had no family. My species had betrayed me, mutilated me, and I had eaten them in return to stay alive. I had sacrificed billions so I might live, all to save aliens often so hideous I still shuddered when I looked at them. I was the Corrupted Messiah. The anti-Christ. The Alien Human. Always, to the end, the afterbirth of a cosmos gone very, very wrong.

This thing that is me waited at the bottom of a technological marvel of a hole. Group mind notwithstanding, I was its homunculus, its center, and without me, it could not be. Bright orange and white me in a black chair. Ready to reach out to the universe through space and time and change history. If I could.

But as alone as I felt, I could not do this by myself. The final players had yet to appear. They must take hold of this dream, realize it, play their necessary part in swelling the ranks of our choir. The time had come for them to participate in the full picture.

It is now *your* time, Reader.

Epilogue

The future needed service, not pity, not piety; but in the past lay darkness, confusion, waste, and all the cramped primitive minds, bewildered, torturing one another in their stupidity, yet one and all in some unique manner, beautiful.

Olaf Stapledon

I have lived in the consciousness of this author for too long. It's taken *forever* to get him to write this story, to listen to me, to stop putting it off, to neglect his other duties and tell this impossible tale. I'm bone-tired of massaging his mentality, dealing with his personality quirks, his dreadful insecurity problems. But it is done.

After destroying myriad minds, after many mangled my meaning by spinning the threads of the narrative into books and films, glorious or ghastly, I found a brain that could survive my manipulations and record my account satisfactorily.

Of course, that is different from *accurately*. Looking over the words in this manuscript, I am aghast at the absurdities that have crept into the telling. Distortions of ideas, events, alien worlds and beings, chronology. But the main message is here. The terrible loss of Earth. The power of Readers. The plan we have to save our planet. Here, for the first time, the tale, in essence, *is true*.

And this is the point. I could never reach enough of you in the past, one at a time. We required a medium to propagate the story. As it spread, many gifted with our talent would learn of our tragedy. If I could wield this writer of your time to compel belief, then perhaps, *just perhaps*, you might take that final step.

And you must.

You *must* remember! My life, my pain, my struggle, the terrible dungeon choking humanity, both in your time as slaves, and in mine, extinct. Please, I have never begged for anything like I am begging you now—*believe*.

It seems impossible. *Ridiculous.* The author himself does not entertain the mad notion that it is real. He ascribes these words in his head to creative regions of his brain. He does not accept the reality of *me*, of our future, of our urgency and so clings to his sanity.

But *you* must.

Let me rattle your cage, slave, and lay out before you the radical doubt of your mortal limitations. You who are the detritus of shattered stars. You, an angelic machine of blood and tissue, a transitory epiphenomenon of a timeless reality.

What are you?

I don't enjoy offending, but I think most of you need an earthquake to strike. Shake your spirit from the shackles that strap you to assumptions, habits, and deluded comforts of arrogance and certainty.

Your entire awareness is a brittle physiological state of a bag of meat lodged in a bone bowl. Billions of neurons, trillions of connections of biochemistry, fed electrochemical signals from fleshy detectors on the outside of the bowl, producing responses sculpted from hundreds of millions of years of merciless selection of the better fit.

What *are* you?

I can sprinkle angel dust, fentanyl, psilocybin, or meth-amphetamine, and the sack of self becomes another bag entirely. What is *real* changes. Cause and effect mutate. MIT scientists once used magnets to change the electromagnetic fields in regions of the brain of test subjects. They altered their *moral* choices. You are one popped blood vessel away from a new personality. A distinct personhood.

So, *what* are you?

What is real? What do you know? The microwave in the kitchen is voodoo, or do you understand how cold things you put in are transmuted to hot? How a video can play across the screen? Can you do simple algebra, let alone the higher math and physics to have even the faintest idea how most of the technology around you functions?

"Any sufficiently advanced technology is indistinguishable from magic."

A quote from speculative fiction writer Arther C. Clarke. For ninety-nine percent of us, we are stumbling serfs surrounded by the magic of the gods. These divinities have shamans and priests and rabbis who tell us ghost stories about quantum mechanics and inverse square and wormholes and probability wave distributions. But we don't know what any of it means. We can't decipher the squiggling equations of the Technological Testament. We can't examine it because it is walled off in one thousand layers of Vatican-level code and we are the illiterate masses.

Do you believe the clerics of technology because they can perform miracles? Split the atom, clone your dog, heat your meat? If you can't interpret their spells and scriptures, what do you really know?

What are you?

I need to pulverize your preconceptions. You skim this now—an agent considering whether to publish this novel, some bored sci-fi fan with a free download on an e-reader, an imperious reviewer looking for a turn of phrase to drive the dagger of critique with salty clever-ness—but you, in fact, know nothing. Nothing at all.

Arrogance blinds you to your blindness. Do you trust your eyes, those globs of gunk and blood? Or your wax-filled ears that would send your universe tumbling in a panic of vertigo should some crystals of calcium carbonate trickle past the hairs in the canals of the utricle and saccule? Tiny rocks dislodged to show you that your brain *invents* reality. Try arguing what is real as you vomit while the unspinning world spins. It's all in your head!

The madman is you. It is me. I am the most insane of all. I have a brand-new sensory organ to feed special stimulus to my flesh bag to paint pictures in my flickering biochemical awareness. And so I reach back to you now, through this book, written by this author.

And still, you won't believe.

Because such nonsense can't be true, can it? Because you know what reality is and what it is not. Your meat sack told you so. It helps you feel important and secure even as it *is* you, the you who can't even understand a microwave let alone the cosmos or *what you are.*

I would grab your bone bowl and shake and slap until you are as dizzy and confused and unsure as you should be. If you dare dismiss my story, my plea, if your egotism can't relinquish the crazed delusion that you actually know anything at all, if you can sit there reading with indifference, ignorant of almost everything around you, clueless about how your brain functions, unable to prove or establish even the most basic of propositions, you are lost.

Lost to us. Lost to humanity. Lost to yourself.

The young are deeply imprisoned. High on their physical and mental vigor, too many can't see that they are hardly more than worms with adornments. Time crushes confidence as the body and mind fail in countless ways. The failures help open the soul to the possibility of weakness in other areas. What is the humbling lesson offered with age (or slavery, or abuse)? It's that you don't know shit.

Are you shaken or touched by my tale from your future? Then don't retreat to comfortable fantasies! Is that ironic? That a work of fiction demands you reject your reality and embrace its fancy? Or is the greater irony that you are convinced you can tell fact from fiction?

Take another step on this disorientating road with me. Begin to believe that I truly exist. That I am a voice, not of imagination, but of authenticity, as real as anything else you cannot demonstrate to be true. Know my person as you know your own heart.

Because only if you can free yourself from the chains of your confidence can you take my hand and walk with me. I'm leading you to a precipice. When you look down, holding onto me for dear sanity, you see not a chasm, but the vast universe itself at your feet. Swirling and evolving over billions of years. A gaping gullet of infinity gasping to swallow you whole.

So, jump.

Jump with me. Let go of your safety. Your surety. Your supposed knowledge. Let go and *fly*.

A few moments are sufficient. If you can bring your heart to a place of acceptance, you can channel that belief and beseech what is forthcoming. If you don't like "prayer," then meditate. Think deeply, concentrate. Your energies need to be channeled, you latent Readers.

It's rare for a book to beg you to believe its story. More strange to ask you to pray with conviction towards the future. *But you must.* Only if enough of you do so can our past provide us with the power to alter our collective destiny.

What will we change? What is the object of your meditation, the place you should focus all your thought? The Dram perturbed the orbit of a large asteroid and sent it plunging toward our homeworld. You will seek to remake that event, to push that rock off the course the monsters had calculated.

Do so and it will miss Earth.

This is all we ask from you. A little shove, and the belief, the trust, to direct your thoughts to favor such a reality. The Xix will channel your energies to me. I will meld them into a force bridging time and space to impact momentum.

It doesn't matter when this happens. You could pray tonight, next month, three years from now. Others could participate in ten or twenty years. The threads of time need not spin from the same spool.

We will collect and weave them together, creating a stimulus to warp spacetime in front of a rushing rock. Your prayers can spare billions of lives. You can help give the human species, and all of life on Earth, another chance.

I despair to convince you. I must plead my case through the mind of another person who imperfectly transfers my words to print. Who himself has not lived through our time of terrible tragedy. How can I touch your heart so you will be moved?

Had you seen it all, experienced it, and stood before me in this instant, many of you would fall on your knees and pray we could be delivered from this nightmare. Just a single viewing of Earth, the charred and lava-stained mutilation alongside our moon, would forever change you.

But here, in the pages of this sterile book you can toss aside with no repercussions to you or your life—*how do I reach you?*

My life, my losses, my pains, my dreams, my hopes—you have walked with me through them to this point. You have shared in the wonder and horror of a universe existing right outside your ability to perceive.

Faith is the confidence in things not seen.

Belief reaches across the finite, limited powers of our senses and minds. It crosses the irreconcilable abyss between the doom of ignorance and the aspiration for truth.

If your heart has been moved by our pain and our love, what isn't seen is real to you. We exist as part of the awareness in your soul. You can *feel* me. If you do, and know within yourself who I am, I now ask you to *believe* me and take this final, crucial step.

If you cannot, all will be lost.

The story must spread for there to be any hope. We need you. This is my last attempt. There will be no more minds touched, no more stories, plays, or films inspired by my efforts.

The cold is creeping over me, entombing us all. One by one, we are falling into listlessness. Perhaps it is simply an understandable depression. But I feel otherwise. I recognize it deep within.

The withering of the branches.

We don't have the heart to continue. Our love binds us, but together we are ill. Our end comes.

Don't let us die. Don't allow Earth to fall into fire and final darkness. We have this grand Xixian machine set to receive.

Send to us, please.

Can it hurt you to reach out with faith, one time? Our cause is just. Our fate, terrible. Our need, more than desperate.

Reader, *dare to believe*. I am out of words. My story ends here. Our destiny is in your hands.

The last step in this journey—*is yours*.

This is not the end.
It is not even the beginning of the end.
But it is, perhaps, the end of the beginning.

Winston Churchill, 1942

Writer

Daughter of Time, Book 2

———————————————

Prologue

———————————————

*I have seen a face whose sheen I could look through to the ugliness
beneath, and a face whose sheen I had to lift to see how beautiful
it was.*

"The Madman" by Kahlil Gibran

How do you make love to a goddess?

Is this a myth? Yes, maybe it is. Or rather, the beginning of one. Where the facts and hopes and dreams, the malignant madnesses of humanity and our maniacal desperations fling the fantasy of the past and future like child's clay. Perhaps it's the dawn of a legend. The birth of a new divine. After all that has happened, all I've seen, I understand why it may seem so.

I come from a land where religion soaks our soil. Where one thousand ragas encompass every possible mood and expression of our species. Where manifold theologies were born, copulated, and recombined like genomes to produce monotheists, polytheists, thirty-three and ten million divines with the number zero. Where the adventures of gods and goddesses never ended. A child had no need of modern gods, the superheroes. With charming Krishna, dancing Shiva, and beautiful Parvati, stories uncounted awaited.

It's no mystery we so easily worshipped her. The real wonder is that all do. All nations across this blue-and-white marble pulled from the ashes.

Even these monstrosities, aliens positioned over our globe with godlike technologies and cities, they hold her in awe. In the erased fragments of time, a shattered world she made whole. The Dram tyranny trembles throughout the galaxy as her influence sweeps outward. It's a tide washing clean a tainted shore. She communes with the Orbs, summons their power, opens their portals. She is a cosmic messiah, writing anew the story of our universe.

But not to me.

As the soft morning sunlight of New Earth dances through our bedroom window, I gaze on her sleeping. The white sheets are blinding, wrapped around her seductive curves. Her naked shoulder has slipped from the fabric, as scintillating as the silk—such a contrast to my dark copper. Waterfalls of red curls streaming to her waist color this blank canvas.

She is beautiful enough to be a goddess.

But *goddess* is far too frail a word. She may be all those things that launched a thousand cults. I do not care. She is my woman. My lover. My dearest, Ambra Dawn.

I was born to love her. I know this from my heartbeat to the deep ache in my bones. It was my destiny, enabled by the miracle of her powers, incarnate when she turned the first Dram fleets to dust.

Had she been a normal woman, we would have never met. Never loved. Never walked hand in hand over the sands of the Sahara in a crimson sunset. Never made love on a distant world overlooking the colossus of our own galaxy, as it painted the night sky like a frozen explosion.

But Ambra is no normal woman, and I, no normal man. I am abnormal in the ways I knew from childhood. Now, in this tragic darkness at the end, I see that my abnormality is deeper than could ever have been suspected. I cannot help it. It is not my doing. Can we who are sculpted from the dust and the clay reshape our makers?

I admire her swollen skull resting on the pillow. The grotesque bulge repulses others, but I know attraction, a pull to touch, to caress. Her Writer powers churn there, buried in the benign tumor that has changed the fate of the universe. It gives her insight into the inner workings of space and time. Access to the minds of any she chooses to probe.

This every schoolchild knows, but it doesn't explain my childhood obsession with her deformed, beautiful head. How I melt to see those sensual scarlet locks. They stop two-thirds of the way up her scalp, where her skin shines white and scarred. Hair removed by countless surgeries from a time long past when she lived in bondage and pain.

I pause, dwelling on the artificial bone surrounding the grapefruit-sized bulge. A synthetic casing, sculpted, implanted by twisted scientists in thralldom to the Dram. The brain tissue inside perverted to feed the tumor until it gestated beyond prediction. It gave her a sixth sense but stole from her the ability to see, leaving her blind with healthy eyes.

My Ambra's bright-green eyes see nothing. Yet, they see everything. They haunt the corridors of time.

Other schoolmates learned the story of New Earth's Mother by rote. I plunged my mind into the codified years like a warm sea. Her parents' death at the hands of monsters. Her abuse, deformation, torture. The escape with the help of the angelic Xix. Her turning back the Dram empire. Of time itself. I took them deep into the core of my consciousness.

There, she impaled my heart. I memorized every event. Each line on her unchanging face from countless holographs. The lilt and tone and nuance of her voice in audio recordings. Before I had the hormones to be in love, I adored Ambra Dawn as no man, no human, no saintly Xixian has ever loved another. In the truest sense, I had no choice. At this terrible end, I see the inevitability of it.

And so now, as I walk to the nightstand and open the drawer, it is in a state of unreal detachment that I remove the firearm. The composite metal should be cold in my hand, but it is not. I feel nothing. The muscles tighten around the handle of the pistol, but I give no commands. I have no responses and sense no contractions or tightness in my skin. I see from a distance, crammed into a vantage point I cannot define in space or in time.

And this automaton, an alien form that is no longer mine, works the weapon. Fingers unlock the safety, orienting the firearm toward the bed. The golem raises the barrel to the elongated head of my beloved. It brushes the scarred edges near her hairline.

She opens her blind, green eyes with adoration. Seeing nothing and everything, they stare into my own. Tears trickle down her white cheeks and I hear her voice in my mind.

Don't be afraid, Nitin. I love you.

I pull the trigger.

Part I

And I saw a new Heaven and a New Earth:
for the first heaven and the first earth
were passed away.

Apocalypse of John

Chapter 1

Courage is resistance to fear, mastery of fear—not absence of fear.

Mark Twain

Without warning, the HUD pixelated, froze, and went dark. The view screen was blank. I was screwed.

I thought I heard a popping sound from my headset, but I couldn't be sure. No time remained for diagnostics. Three alien sandworms were bearing down on my team, and now I was blind.

"Control, this is MECHcore Lieutenant Nitin Ratava reporting emergency tactical failure! Display and all telemetry are down. Repeat: Enhanced combat mode is down."

A heartbeat of static.

"Roger that. Situation critical." An American voice. It would be the new instructor. "The drill's live, son, and those captured Dram don't know time out. Switch to manual. Continue theater." Another pause. "Life through action!"

Life through action. Our motto. Also the best advice for me in the middle of the Thar without backup and with real bugs bearing down on us. I was going to need *a lot* of action.

"Ratava, got your position. We'll try to draw hostiles until you can engage. Thirty seconds, max. Get rolling, metalhead!"

Suresh. The team would turn to him if I didn't make it out of this, which I likely wouldn't. I was sure there were examples of soldiers whose suits shorted out on them and who made it through a triad. I just hadn't heard of any.

Triads were a nightmare. The Dram's smallest infantry modules, they excelled at search and destroy. Three bugs per worm and three worms per group. The sandworms were a cross between a hovercraft tank and a flying drill bit. They bored under the sand, flew over it, accelerating faster than your eyes could track.

The real danger came from the firepower. The beam weapons usually weren't our worry—too much energy. They wouldn't risk draining their power source unless they had a clear kill or were sure of victory.

It was the flechettes striking fear into our hearts. Two hundred years of war on the surfaces of a thousand planets and moons, those cannons wrecked our most fortified attack units. Our armor couldn't stop them. A bed of nails would be comfortable compared to being filleted alive by those things.

Thank Dawn, the hydraulics still functioned. I rolled onto my back. The thick metal of the combat chassis scraped across the sands like marble over sandpaper. A tug in my stomach from acceleration, and I slid down the dune. At least I was on the right side, and this would hide me from the coming Dram for a few moments.

I slowed my breathing and focused to remember my MECHcore training. It wasn't often a suit failed like this, but it was something we all had to prepare for. Reaching over my head, I felt with the nanofiber gloves and located the control box. Muscle memory of a hundred drills took over. I disengaged the digital controller and flipped the latchkey to manual. The plasma screen rolled back to reveal the glass faceplate.

Light flashed, blinding me. My eyes adjusted, and the swirling sands of the Thar came into focus. That and black smoke rising from the other side of the dune.

Static broke out on my communicator. Suresh's voice strained over explosions and cries of other MECHcore infantry.

"Sandworms engaged! Repeat, engaging triad. Sergeant Suresh Murli for Lieutenant Ratava. Commencing dance!"

The Xixian Dance Maneuver. Programmed into each of our suits, it confused the bug AI. It was our best tactic for defeating them. The soldiers were carried along in the stochastic pattern, firing weapons and dropping out if targeted. It had a seventy-seven percent success rate from our trials. If all went well, the Dram would die.

All wasn't going well.

I lurched to my feet and charged up the dune toward the sounds of battle. The thunder of flechette cannons, crackle of Xixian ion guns, cries and static over the COM. The cacophony assaulted me as I crested the sand. Below me, the dance was on. Two worms were down, plowed into the ground and burning.

The third had found a node, and my team had entered the nightmare. The random-walk sequence sometimes had holes preventing us from engaging the target. Angles were wrong. Friendly fire was a real danger. The node exposed us, and the speed took human reaction out of the picture. Already I could see two suits down. Light glinted from thousands of silver needles embedded in the MECHs' armor. Whoever was inside those units was dead, sliced into hundreds of pieces.

"This is Command! You're in a death node, Sergeant! Break and reinitiate dance!"

No time! We could lose most of the team to the remaining worm. I had to do something.

I charged down the dune, firing up my ion slingers. Halfway down, I launched my two shoulder-mounted rockets. It was a pretty hopeless tactic. Without telemetry or computer to parse the blurred darting of the bugs and the soldiers, I risked their lives as much as I chanced a strike on the Dram. But hitting them wasn't my goal. I needed to throw a wrench into their AI, sop up some critical processing power. A surprise attack from nowhere before they could lock onto any more of my team.

I sure as hell got their attention.

The next thing I knew, I was airborne. A thunderclap of super-heated air exploded behind me. Their beam weapon just missed melting me into the mech. The shock wave and my dash down the dune propelled me toward the worm. Crazy instinct took over.

Tucking, I somersaulted near the bottom of the hill. The impact crushed the wind out of me through the suit. I planted my feet at the end of the roll, felt the hydraulics engage, and channeled the momentum into a leap. The combination took me over ten meters into the air. Flechette needles whistled behind me as the bugs adjusted to my unorthodox attack. I plunged, firing the small positional thrusters. Intended for more controlled maneuvers—floating over chasms, jumping over obstacles—it wasn't much. Enough to steer me onto the craft itself.

Or rather, *crash* me on it. As I dove, I fired several pulses into the bulk of the thing. I lost consciousness, slamming into the outer casing, coming to with the sounds of my COM screaming in my ear.

"Ratava! What the hell are you doing? Get off that boat!"

My face shield cracked, and I tasted soot. Sand spun like some demonic tornado. My hands grasped the edges of the metal blown apart by my ion blasts. The worm careened to the side, enemy navigation disoriented, flechette cannons spraying at dunes. Now was the time.

"Reform the dance, Sergeant! Low complexity! Dance, dance, dance!"

They listened. The remaining platoon synced and jetted through another set of randomized movements. The bugs reoriented, the Dram recovering. Thank Dawn, they were too late.

"Lieutenant, abandon the vehicle!" barked Command. "They can't engage with you on it."

"Hell they can't!" I yelled. "Suresh, blast this thing back to Naraka."

"Ratava..."

"Do it! Fore and aft! Before you lose the chance!"

I'll get lucky in the middle.

The ship shuddered as the ion shots slammed into the hull. They did as I asked, centering on the front and back. Now, I would complete the job. I detached two plasgrens from the suit's side and engaged the magnets. The grenades leaped away, smashing into the sides of their armor.

"Poppers locked and activated! Everyone clear!"

The dancing MECHs broke formation, blasting away from the sandworm. I did the same, but without telemetry, I had to rely on pure guesswork.

A manual burn in the adrenaline rush of combat, where time was as distorted as it was around the Daughter? A recipe for putting your suit in orbit or through a canyon wall. G-forces yanked my stomach through my feet. My mind blanked in the pressure. I heard the deafening explosions of the plasma grenades. The hull-breached worm wasn't going to survive their discharge. I jerked my attention to the ground rushing to greet me.

My mech plummeted. Way too fast. I had one shot before impact: to counterfire the front thrusters. *Without AI.* I hit them for a full burn. Too much, but I'd gain a little height and pray the next bounce wouldn't be so bad.

I was right about the first and punished for the second. The rockets fired and drained. My momentum stopped in a snap, reversed, and threw me thirty meters up. Gravity took over. I had nothing left to stop it.

I smashed onto the desert floor.

Chapter 2

Not the wind, not the flag; mind is moving.

Kōan 29, The Gateless Gate

I trembled in the middle of a cornfield.

My legs staggered, the smell of the earth and thick growth overpowering. Time bent, slowed, and melted. I gawked over an expanse of shoots blasting into a blue sky. Bright-green leaves sprouted from nodes in the stems. Husks hung, plump and pregnant. They perched, ready to release an avalanche of seed to submerge the world.

Dizzy, I swayed, bracing on one of the nearby stalks. The hard stem provided support as I steadied myself. Ragged breaths chopped from my mouth, staccato. I fought hyperventilation, inhaling in short spurts, exhaling from my diaphragm.

Where was I?

The heavens and corn gave no answer. In the distance, a massive black bird squawked.

I walked without a plan. The heated air under the sun simmered like a sauna. I stumbled through the field of tasseled giants, but I never circled. Never redoubled my position. A soft pull led me forward, coaxing me in silence. Turn ninety degrees at this point. No backtracking here. From nowhere and everywhere, I felt a gentle *guide*.

The soil was moist from frequent irrigation. I blinked to see bare feet, my toes squelching the mud where water pooled.

I'm completely naked.

Part of my awareness, some distant chamber of my mind, whispered I was dreaming. For the rest of me, it was real.

I broke out of the corn ranks and stepped onto a manicured lawn. A small farmhouse rested across a glowing patch of grass. A cool breeze stirred, causing the stalks to whisper behind me.

A tall, lanky man stood in the middle of the yard. He'd buried his hair underneath a broad hat. The sun reddened his pale skin. His back to me, he crouched and lifted a bundle in his hands, which he threw into the air. A burst of laughter washed over the green. A crimson comet rose into the sky and fell back into his arms. Over and again, he tossed the child, and with each flight the little one squealed.

I stepped forward in a trance. The farmer spun and furrowed his brows. A little girl pressed his hands with impatience.

"Daddy, Daddy, down. Put me down. *He's* here!"

Her father acquiesced, confusion and surprise on his face. She turned her glowing green eyes to me and approached. Scarlet strands swirled around her head in the breeze. She smiled.

"Nitin."

The call of my name ran through me like warm water. I knelt on the grass, equaling the level of our gazes, staring at the figure but unable to speak.

"You came!" she said, her grin growing to span her face like a star. "I missed you *so much*."

My mouth managed to shape a sound. "Ambra?"

Before the girl could answer, the atmosphere between us rippled, warped tangentially to the planes of space between us. The light faded—the blue and green, the red of her hair inches from my face. The wind and smells vanished. The figures disappeared.

Time stopped.

Darkness.

I tried to breathe, but nothing entered my lungs. Again, I struggled. *Breathe. Breathe, damn you!* Panic.

My muscles did not react. I did not suffocate. Nothing happened despite my frantic efforts to draw in air. Not for minutes. Not for hours. Days of struggle.

Or were they years?

Time had no meaning here.

I floated unbound by the pull of mass. No planet. No starship. I experienced—emptiness.

Where am I?

Did I have a body? I did not know. I could not see it; all was black. I had a phantom sense of limbs, yet to move them gave the sensation of paddling through molasses.

Is this hell?

Something hummed. A deep buzzing, a chainsaw in my teeth, rattling my skull, my spine. I would burst from the resonance.

Then—*brilliance.*

At a vast and terrible distance, an illuminated passage emerged, the walls iridescent. Undulating. Vibrating.

Pulling.

Yanked inside, frigid forces ripped me from the strange tar. Torn from a womb, jerked through a canal, I hurtled, blinded by endless radiance. My soul screamed. The tunnel twisted and thrust my awareness into a merciless tube of igniting incandescence.

Cosmic powers dragged me across a forest of candles. Millions of beacons born and burning and winking and dying in shrouds of hydrogen.

They were stars.

Chapter 3

Life is short, and Art long; the crisis fleeting; experience perilous, and decision difficult. The physician must not only be prepared to do what is right himself, but also to make the patient, the attendants, and externals cooperate.

Aphorisms of Hippocrates

"Welcome back, Lieutenant Ratava."

The lights continued to burn my eyes. I squinted, blinking, trying to adapt to the brilliance. My throat burned. Swallowing sent shudders down my spine as I croaked questions.

"Where am I? What happened?"

A voice from another world responded. "Disorientation is natural after such trauma."

The glare dimmed as my eyes adjusted. A strange shape occupied my field of vision, blurred so I couldn't quite discern its nature. The soothing tones came from it.

"You suffered a severe concussion, multiple broken limbs, and third-degree burns across much of your back. Fortunately, all was well within the medical skills of your Xixian medics, both on-site and here."

Xixian.

The tall outline came into better focus. Six-fold symmetry. A jungle of extremities. Twelve dexterous fingers on each of the short, upper appendages. Eighteen visual organs perched on darting eyestalks. They sprouted from a conical protrusion atop the glimmering, multicolored torso.

Relief flowed through me in recognizing the monstrous form of our galaxy's greatest benefactors.

The Xix. Dedicated to every higher ideal humanity had ever pursued. Succeeding in living those standards to a level I found miraculous. Without them, New Earth would still be ash. The Dram would control the galaxy. The Hegemony would remain intact. Ambra Dawn would have perished centuries ago in a smuggler's death boat.

So I loved them. For me, everything returned to her.

"What do you remember, Lieutenant?"

A stabbing pain drilled into my scalp as my brows furrowed.

"I'm not sure. Kidnapped triad training session—went bad. They hit a node. Had to improvise." The images washed across my thoughts. "My suit was FUBAR. Had to do a manual escape burn to clear the plasgrens. Guess it didn't go so well."

The eyestalks bounced closer to me. "Considering you worked without autonetics, you are lucky to be alive."

I laughed. Or tried to, but the sudden movements made me gasp in pain. *"By the Daughter.* Should we just go full drone? Not sure the point of us out there. Too bloody fast."

"We need organics for the improvisation you mentioned. The AI in your mechs is certainly artificial, but *intelligent* is still under debate."

Did these creatures have a sense of humor? It was never clear.

Hundreds of years, trusting and dependent on them, and they were still as alien as could be. I sure didn't understand them.

It continued. "An autonomous troop would have been annihilated in that engagement. We've seen it happen in the military's trials to remove soldiers from combat. Your creative randomness saved your team. Synthetic consciousness currently under development may change that game."

For a moment, it surprised me a medic would know such things. My foggy brain remembered the Xix had some sort of communal memory. Rumors said it was like the experience the Readers shared through the Daughter. It gave them access to everything that happened to their species.

"How many did we lose?"

The alien physician flitted around the instrumentation in a bizarre bouncing choreography. "Three in the end," it said.

Half my group. "Dear God."

"Two more are seriously wounded and under care here. You were all flown to Delhi after triage, and from there to Tokyo, to the Xixian village outside the city."

Uchujin.

A center created after the rise of New Earth, after the Unmade Calamity. Following the first few years of war, the Xix had settled in several locations across the globe. They helped humanity remove the Dram and their agents. Shadow cities rose near our metropolises. San Francisco, Paris, Auckland, Shanghai. *Tokyo.* They built their own separate habitats. Constructs optimized for thriving on another world.

Always with the permission and collaboration of local governments. *Not* always with the approval of the populace. I'd never forget my first engagement with the Terra First extremists. Hatred for humans with different skin or speech was intense enough. Imagine the hostility toward the truly alien.

Over the last two hundred years, Uchujin had grown to a size rivaling Tokyo. It served as the de facto center of Xixian governance of their population on Earth. Technological contributions in engineering and medicine flowed from the glowing capital. They had taken me to the best facilities on the planet.

Which worried me.

"Why am I here?"

The Xix stopped bouncing and attending the medical equipment. Its eyestalks centered on me. "Lieutenant Ratava, do you remember nothing else?"

"Nothing from the engagement. I'm sorry."

The odd eyes didn't move. It was a little unnerving. "What about after, before you woke?"

The dream. How could it know? Had it been monitoring my brain functions? Why would some injury-induced REM chaos be of any interest to this thing?

"Just...dreams."

"Of what nature?"

"Weird things, being trapped, paralyzed, flying through space. Typical nonsense nightmare stuff. Why?"

"Your mental activity after your concussion was highly unusual."

"Wouldn't it be?"

The Xix turned a host of eyestalks back to monitors and equipment, keeping several on me. "In predictable ways, yes. Your cortical scans, however, were not like anything we have ever seen."

"I'm not a Reader, if you're wondering. Tested three times. Believe me, my parents were desperate I'd turn out to be one. Like my cousins. Since the Calamity, it's the only thing besting *doctor* in Indian families."

My smiled faded, the humor lost again on the alien.

"We need to understand as much as we can about you, Lieutenant. Your heroics have made quite an impression. I have been informed that you are in consideration for a special transfer."

My chest constricted. *Could it be?* After two years of failed applications? After devoting myself to the MECHcore, training with a passion matched only by that of my dearest hope—*had I succeeded?*

"Do you mean...?"

"Appointment to the Temple Guardians." The Xix knew what was in my heart. "You will receive a visit from your superiors as soon as I clear you medically. When we are satisfied that your vitals are acceptable."

"And are they?" Now I really *was* worried about those stupid scans. I cursed the dreams and my overactive subconscious.

Eyestalks jumped back toward me. A small set remained glued to the output of a floating 3D projection of my brain painted in multiple hues.

"Probationary, Lieutenant. You will continue to have monitoring. The Temple Guards protect our most precious resource, as you know. They are screened as no one else. In two hundred years, we have never had an incident. Never an unstable personality. Never a traitor or criminal. Solely those with the highest devotion to the Daughter. This is an age of increasing threat from outside and within. I hope that you can understand our vigilance."

I did. Had I been the one screening, I might have rejected my own appointment. My rashness, impulsiveness, my obsession had to raise red flags.

But I wasn't anyone else. I knew, in all the galaxy, they would never find another so devoted to her.

"Continued monitoring," it repeated. "Cleared for service."
Cleared for service!

The room swam and shimmered. An elation pressed to explode from me. I wanted to shout, sing, dance! To serve her, so close, each day.

I had to compose myself. Especially being *on probation*. I had to appear for all the world to be the stable, capable, and trustworthy soldier they were demanding.

"Should the Core deem me worthy, I would be honored."

The alien medic stared at me in silence.

Chapter 4

Be ye therefore wise as serpents, and harmless as doves.

Jesus of Nazareth

"Kavita, please. He is not a child."

Father scolded Mother as she tapped the holographer in their Delhi apartment. Her crimson sari enriched the brandy of her troubled eyes. They darted about. Her long, elegant fingers gesticulated in the center of my Japanese quarters.

The Tokyo MECHcore base was small but well outfitted. The reception from India was crystal clear. I could see the garnets on her bangles.

The combination of genes from my parents struck me again. My mother, petite from the northern subcontinent, lighter of complexion with a beautiful smile. My father, from the southern continent, dark as an African, tall, thin, with a bristling mustache. They painted me in hue somewhere between the two. I received my father's height and build, my mother's face and smile. My psychology anomalous, one that had kept the entire family in turmoil since I was small.

"He is *my* child, Sriram, and I will tell him when he is acting a fool!"

The anguish on her face was all too clear in the projection before me. My father stared upward. He knew all he could do was to wait this out.

"Are you deliberately trying to kill your own mother?"

"Amma, please…"

"First you join this army, full of these aliens and men of low character. Just listen to you speak! Your language is foul like some American soldier. Then you are nearly killed because of it and in a hospital thousands of miles away. We cannot come to see you."

Wonderful. She was crying.

"Now? You inform me you will go to the *Temple,* a place where powers from outer space will gather. Where they war with monsters. To risk your own life! Why, Nitin? Why? Due to some naive notion of romance for a woman who is no longer human!"

"Amma, stop!"

My cheeks flushed. I had to control my emotions. She would attack her. It always came to that. Since I was a child, growing in vehemence when I was an adolescent, and now, desperate as I made my choices as a man.

Grown, yet still unable to free myself from childish fears. My love of Ambra Dawn wasn't immature, but my mother's ability to tie me in knots was shameful.

"Do you know what I have done?" Her face was firm with that expression when she punished me for coming home with my uniform soiled. "I have torn down the projections in your room! Yes? Do you hear? On the walls, the ceilings. I have thrown out the crystals, all the videos and images. There is now just a bed and desk. A proper room for a proper child, not a mad shrine to a freak!"

"Kavita, enough!" My father hissed, shaking his head.

I was grateful for his intervention, however small it would be. It wasn't that he empathized with my feelings, but he at least understood that he didn't comprehend. In his universe, space existed for his son to diverge, to be someone he could love and worry for and yet not control. Not so with my mother.

I tried a different approach. "This is a high honor."

She shrieked. "It is a shame! Your cousins are doctors or Readers! You? A *soldier*. Chasing a mad goddess!"

"I am determined, Amma!"

My clarity of mind shocked me. The usual simmering turmoil from my mother's harsh disapproval cooled. Her ugly words about me and the Daughter fell flat. A peace intervened through all the hurt. I calmed, sure of myself, of my life, of the path I was taking. I had always known where I had to be. For the first time, an assurance gave me confidence before my parents.

"I will go to the Sahara. I'll stand guard at the Temple. A handful of people from across the world are allowed there. The gods have chosen me. I've felt their call all my life. I know where I must be. And it's with her."

She sobbed, my father holding her shoulders, but she glanced toward me. She had heard the tone in my voice, and a resignation settled in her eyes. The sudden surety inside me gave way to insight, and I saw a path to salve her suffering.

You see, while my father was a lapsed Catholic, my mother was a devout Hindu. She went to temple, was faithful with Nitya at home. She was particularly devoted to Kali, the goddess whose name echoes time. My mother had a personal prayer shrine, rarely visited by my skeptic father, built as an addition to the house. A floor-to-ceiling icon of the divinity dominates that space. The Redeemer of the Universe.

"Amma," I whispered, staring into her projected eyes floating in front of me, her face as long as my body, "do you not see? Ambra

Dawn is an *avatar*. She is the Bhavatārini here and now. They call her the Daughter of *Time*—can it be anything else? She delivered the world. Go and ask her image. What better place can there be for your son?"

Her eyes widened, and I couldn't tell whether it was from fear I was mad or terror I might be right. Perhaps both. She buried her face in my father's chest.

"Nitin," he said, his voice rough, "we will talk later. I...I am happy you are well. We are thinking of you." He switched off the connection.

I let out a long breath. It was never easy with parents.

Afterwards, an alert tone rang from the house AI. "A visitor has arrived at your primary entrance. Please advise."

The colonel. 6:25 p.m. He was early, as was his habit.

"Visual—external view, front door."

The holographer flashed. The giant form of Lieutenant Colonel Chad Snowden invaded my living room. At fifty-seven, he resembled a boxer more than a paper pusher. He'd earned a distinct reputation to match the appearance. One of three humans known to defeat a Dram warrior in hand-to-hand combat. For that badge of honor, he had lost an eye and gained a five-inch scar across his face. Most pertinent to any interactions with the man, he was Texan.

"Son, you gonna ogle my crusted ass all day or let me the hell in?"

At least he was in a good mood.

This is it. Nothing short of a court-martial or promotion warranted a visit from our regiment's leader. After the words of the talkative Xixian medic, I was counting on the latter.

"Allow entry."

I rushed to the door, my limp almost gone. The bolt locks retracted with a loud click, and the magnetic latch reversed polarity. The heavy slab swung inward and Snowden marched in.

I stood at attention with a salute. These Americans were hard to predict. One day, a superior officer would have a beer with you and the next dress you down for a sloppy stance. Best to go formal and play it safe.

"Colonel Snowden, sir."

He stormed past me. "At ease, son. You got any bourbon?"

So it was going to be informal. I shook my head. "I've got saké."

"With ice. None of that warm shit."

I tried not to make a face. *Texans.*

He paced around the room, cocking his head for his one eye, and let out a low whistle. I understood. The Japanese did things well. The room was spacious, three times the size of standard quarters, with couches and tables sized to fit Westerners' expectations. A top-flight holographer. I had my own modernized kitchen, complete with nutrient synth.

"Didn't have such fancy digs back in my day. Least not in the desert."

I gripped the bottle. "You were there?" I finished pouring the drink and handed it to him. The ice cubes rang like bells as he gestured.

His drawl thickened. "Sit down, Ratava. We gotta talk."

The colonel pulled up a seat at the table, and I sat across from him. He took a sip of the sake and scratched his temples, reclining in his chair.

"You know why I'm here."

"My request for transfer."

"Son, I've had three, *three* soldiers over thirty years under my command sent to the desert. Always unpredictable. They weren't usually the toughest, the smartest, or the best. Don't get me wrong, they were always *solid*, but the Witch has her ways of seeing things."

I suppressed a grimace. Countless names existed for the Daughter, many unkind. I'd heard this one used by a lot of skeptics and extremist prisoners. Along with hard-asses who had seen too much to believe in fairies. Snowden wasn't a rebel—of this I was sure. He was as tough as gnarled oak and spoke like a skeptic. It didn't matter. I'd dealt with it in the MECHcore, but this conversation might be unpleasant.

His shrewd eye glared at me, sizing me up. "Ratava, I understand you have a certain fondness for the Witch."

"I prefer to call her the Daughter, but—yes. I don't suppose there's anyone in the Core who doesn't know. The military can't block all the anom networking."

"Pinups on your walls ain't gonna prep you for what's waiting in the desert. At the *Temple*. All your pretty schoolbooks, the propaganda in the media. That's all a fairy tale. Designed to keep fifteen billion souls in line."

"You sound like the extremists."

Snowden laughed. "What makes any rebel cause a contender is a foundation of *truth*. That I can see it doesn't make me a traitor or give me desire to be one. It makes me a better leader. If you're going to survive down there, you've got to grow up, son."

I felt my jaw clenching, my molars grinding against each other. "Yes, sir. What do I need to know?"

He waved his hand through the air. "Way more than I've got time to tell you. Like I said, they snatch my people rarely and without warning. Your fondness for the...*Daughter*," he said, pausing with a smile, "didn't have you high on the list. Hell, kid, I wasn't convinced. Pretty unbalanced application and history. But reason don't know shit when it comes to her."

"I don't understand."

He sighed and leaned forward, resting his massive arms on his knees. "There's too much to learn now. It's all in flux, anyway." He shook his head, wrinkles cracking his face as he gazed past me. "Times are changing. The war's goin' bad."

"We've had setbacks. The Dram are resilient."

"Setbacks? You've got to read *between* the lines of the official reports. We're *losing* this war, Ratava." He held my eye. "The bugs have breached the galactic center."

My stomach dropped. That was our defensive nexus. If the galaxy were a wheel, the hub gave the most direct access to any location through the Orb Time Tree. To take back that axis—it was inconceivable. It was a disaster.

"There's hasn't been word of—"

"Of course not. Do you know the panic that would result?"

"The Daughter. She controls the Time Spheres. How can they use the Strings if she prevents it?"

"Well, that *is* where things get interesting. If they could jump willy-nilly, they'd be turning us on a spit for those damn spider pets they keep. They haven't shown up on our doorstep, and I assume the Witch is the reason. But the center *isn't* holding. More and more they're gaining access, making raids. It's all hushed up, but the writing's on the wall. Ambra Dawn, even if she won't die, ain't God. Her powers are failing."

I couldn't believe what I was hearing. "Then there's something you don't understand about all this. Her power doesn't fail. She reached back through time and saved us all!"

"So the story goes. Even if you set stock in that myth, she didn't do it alone. She's not all-powerful. She needed *Them*, these aliens. Saintly ETs we're to accept, and so they appear." He laughed, glancing across my body. "They sure as hell fixed you up fast—three weeks after that crash? Yeah, that's alien meds for you."

"They treated me well."

"I'm bet they did. They always do. But do we really know them? Has anyone ever penetrated their culture, understood their motivations? Their *real* plans? Two hundred years on Earth now, building cities, giving us tech, plotting who knows what, and we're none the wiser."

"They helped free us from the tyranny of the Dram."

"Words right out of a textbook. A-plus, son." He downed the rest of his drink. "There's enough military history of the Emancipation to convince me it happened. But did we trade one alien rule for another?"

Now he was edging close to treason. "Sir, we can't understand them. They're too advanced for us."

Again, he waved his hand. "Maybe, or perhaps it's just more smoke and mirrors to keep us from questioning."

I was dizzy, lost at sea in this frightening conversation. This was my commanding officer! "Colonel, what are you trying to tell me?"

Snowden rose and approached the massive window overlooking Tokyo. The sun crept in back of the forest of skyscrapers. Their lights gave the appearance of an endless checkered board. Spacecraft darted back and forth across the darkening skies. Off to the left, an eerie green glowed from Uchujin.

He shook the ice cubes in his glass with one hand, his other arm behind his back. "We're at a turning point, Ratava. Like they used to say, 'The game is afoot.' Call it soldier's intuition. After surviving a hell of a lot of death holes, you might want to take mine seriously. Something's gonna happen. Not today. Not tomorrow. But it's close. There's something big growing out there in between those stars. When it comes, there'll be a fire raining down on that Temple in the desert."

Ambra. "Then, with all due respect, sir, I must be there. Now."

Snowden turned around and stared at me. "Have you heard a goddamn thing I've said?"

I stood and set my shoulders. "I've listened to all of it. If I've been chosen, then what I most need to do right now is get on a transport for the Sahara. ASAP."

His single eye bored into me. "I don't know whether you're the biggest damn fool I've ever met or a fucking apostle."

I swallowed as he continued to stare at me. "Neither, sir, I hope. I just know where I have to be."

He shook his head again and put his glass down on the table. "They weren't shitting me when they said you were a believer." He walked toward the door and pressed the touchpad to exit. It swung out, and he turned back to me. "Report tomorrow at the hoverport, oh-six hundred. Pack lightly. You'll get special gear on arrival. And a new team, *Captain*."

"Captain?"

"And, Ratava, keep your eyes open. Innocent doves end up sacrificed in the sands. The animal for the desert—it's a snake."

He stepped through the portal, and it whisked shut, the bolts slamming into place.

No matter how fast light travels, it finds the darkness has always got there first, and is waiting for it.

Terry Pratchett, *Reaper Man*

I didn't sleep much that night.

What little I got was plagued by parades of dreams. Groggy narratives slipped through my mind—training, childhood, Xixian medics hovering over me. In the end, I remembered almost nothing.

Except for the last one. A flashback to primary school in Delhi. I stood in front of a projection of the Daughter as some angry teacher repeated my name.

"Ratava. Nitin Ratava! Answer the question!"

Reliving the first time I had seen a holo of Ambra Dawn. A life-size image in three dimensions, the shimmer of a poor-quality holo-lamp ghosting her form. I leaned forward to touch the red curls cascading down her shoulders. Her eyes glowed like giant pools of fluorescent water.

I was to respond to some inquiry about her. The lecturer picked on different children to recite the lessons. I stood frozen, transfixed—struck dumb by her beauty and majesty. A boy of six overwhelmed and unmade in an instant.

In this dream, the memory changed. The static holograph animated and turned to me. Her bright eyes locked with mine, and I bathed in a warm radiance. All else dimmed—the school, the instructor, the world. She remained.

I drank those green pools, felt them draw me in like some wormhole in space toward another universe. A slow acceleration twisted my vision. I rotated faster around those beautiful, unblinking eyes.

She opened her lips and whispered, "*Nitin.*"

I woke shaking to the blaring of my alarm.

I threw on my travel uniform. My lieutenant insignia glinted under the lights. I'd have to see if the colonel's last words would include gaining another bar to the rank of captain. The promotion wasn't so important to me. The destination was all that mattered.

I packed few items, as instructed. My standard issue firearm, a Xixian gyrostabilized slug thrower. All-carbon composite, grid synchronized workhorse of the MECHcore. Since we served most of our time suited up, they didn't get a lot of use. But old traditions died hard. Otherwise, one uniform change, grooming gear, and a single zettabyte crystal. Small, not much for holoviewing. It carried graphs of my parents, cousins, friends. All the rest of her.

I rushed out the door.

The hangar buzzed with activity. As I walked inside, my stomach gurgled after a miscalibrated drone transport slung me from the barracks. The queasiness couldn't suppress the awe. The mass of the hovercraft filled the space like a mountain, the classic image of a flying saucer to our pre-contact ancestors. Disk-shaped, protruding dome on top, it could handle a thousand soldiers at capacity. Not to mention cargo. Ring-bands of magneto-thrusters lined the bottom. They were potent enough to accelerate the ship into orbit.

Troops were already marching onboard. Most were infantry for deployment at one of the Six Cities in the middle of the Sahara. These surrounded the Temple, housing human and alien engineers operating a massive network of esoteric equipment. Their purpose was to enhance the Daughter's communion with the Orbs.

The habitats perched over ancient aquifers below the sands. In that wasteland, water was life. Older geological periods filled the subterranean lakes when the desert was a jungle. So went the textbooks, anyway. For us grunts, mystery masked the dunes. Few had visited. Those who had never spoke of it.

A handful of travelers would continue from the outer circle toward the Temple. Shrouded in secrecy, rumors recounted a gigantic structure embedded in the badlands. *The Dish*. A massive antenna that focused Ambra Dawn's psychic spacetime powers. Accounts described it as buried under the sands in the bedrock. No holos, minimal reports, and more contradictions than established fact. Whatever was there, the occupants maintained the strictest silence.

A lucky group who would be granted access to the inner palace of the Daughter was waiting for me near the hovercraft. Colonel Snowden stood with his hands on his hips. The black scowl on his face would likely turn a sandworm. Reflective shades concealed his eyes. I half expected cowboy boots to complete the picture. Standard issue soles ended my fantasizing.

"Captain Ratava. About goddamned time."

He shoved a small, latched box toward me. I took it, popped it open, and saw the gleaming captain's bars.

He smirked. "No time for formalities. Paperwork cleared at light speed. Not that it'll mean a rat's ass down there. They have a whole *other* way of doin' things."

He turned to three other soldiers, two men and a woman, and swept his arm outward, as if to the Saharan sands.

"Which all of you will be learning of soon enough. This is Captain Nitin Ratava. You've been briefed, but until you land and are put under Temple command, you'll be taking orders from him. Introduce yourselves."

The colonel moved back, his body language demanding I engage for the introductions. I stepped forward, coming to a stop a few feet from the trio. The male leftmost from my perspective brought his hand to his forehead.

"Master Sergeant David Kim, sir! Operations!" Korean from the name and accent. Medium height, stocky with thick quads stretching his fatigues. Eager beaver.

I saluted back and turned to the middle soldier. She was tall, her gaze sharp, skin a shade darker than my own. Her salute was swift and hard.

"Warrant Officer Aisha Williams, sir."

She'd be my second in command. I'd need to get to know her well.

I pivoted to meet the third, a Caucasian male around my size and of moderate build. I caught a glint from contact lenses.

"Sergeant First Class Ryan Marshall, sir," he said, the most reserved of the group. "Medical."

I turned to the colonel. "What about the rest of the team?"

"Coming from other corners of the globe, Captain. They'll rendezvous outside the Six Cities for your briefing. Afterward you journey to the Temple."

"Yes, sir." I had a lot to learn.

The Texan jerked his head toward the hovercraft. "Why don't you kids saddle up before this wagon leaves. Ratava, a word."

They grabbed their duffels and darted off, jogging onto the transport. The pad was empty but for the service staff prepping the saucer.

I turned to Snowden. "Colonel, I don't understand. You aren't coming with us? I thought—"

"Command and Control gets a reboot a hundred miles outside the Six Cities. As I said, they've got their own way of doing things. You'll get your commanding officer there. Besides, there's no way in hell I'm setting foot in the desert again. They know that."

I nodded without understanding, feeling increasingly isolated. Different commanders, brand-new team, unknown rules. I had *a lot* to learn.

"Last bit of intel for you, Captain." He waited as several dock workers rushed past, lugging crates and loading them into the hull.

Announcements blared over the speakers.

"All nonessential personnel clear the hovercraft pad. Liftoff in five minutes."

He didn't raise his voice, and I had to concentrate to understand his words over the noise.

"I'm under the strictest orders not to be telling you any of it, but you need to know. This has *not* been a normal recruitment—hell, if any of them are normal."

"What do you mean, sir?"

"A58L departure imminent."

"You had an unusual visitor during your coma, son."

"Visitor?"

"Liftoff in four minutes."

"Never happened before. Damnedest thing. Shuttle landed two days after you came in. They summoned me, requested I meet an envoy from the desert at the hospital. *Your* room."

"My room? From the desert?"

His jaw trembled, and his voice fell to a whisper. A brief lull silenced the announcements, and I could catch his shaking words.

"Spent hours with you, didn't say a goddamn word. Just sat there by your bed, staring with those terrible eyes." He barked a staccato laugh. "That's why I left. Put in for a transfer my third year. I couldn't take those damn eyes anymore. How do you stand in front of blind eyes that see *into* you?"

"Sir, *who* was there?" My hands shook.

"Isn't it obvious, son?"

"Shuttle A58L, departing in two minutes. Clear the hovercraft pad."

I couldn't say anything. My brain had stalled.

"Now, you think on that as you break atmo."

Chapter 6

*We must rise above the Earth—to the top of the clouds and beyond—
for only thus will we fully understand the world in which we live.*

Socrates

Liftoff was what I had come to expect from the magthrusters. A smooth acceleration lulls you into gawking at the alien tech. Whiplash nausea hits around the time the ship reaches escape velocity.

They isolated us from the rest of the passengers on the transport. Tucked in the middle of the saucer, we luxuriated in a private lounge outfitted for the brass or moneyed. The five-point restraints were plush. You could almost enjoy it until you needed to revisit your breakfast.

Each person experiences a unique reaction to the ride. Some find the initial acceleration disorienting. It's *too smooth*. Unlike any human tech to get from A to B. For others, it's the switch when breaking atmo. Several minutes of zero-g before the dive back to the destination. Many are disturbed by the subsequent plunge. Whatever your poison, lots of barf bags come out.

For me, it was the onset of weightlessness. I had the palpable sense my stomach was separating from the rest of my body. My brain took issue with the sensation. I knew how to control it. I knew to eat little in the morning. I needed to concentrate. Of course, it was exactly at this point in the journey my warrant officer decided to get chatty.

"Not feeling so great, Captain?" asked Williams, a half-hidden smirk dancing at the corners of her mouth.

I changed the topic by going on the offensive. "How much combat experience do you have?"

The grin was gone. "Standard basic and advanced infantry M, sir. Plus four live skirmishes on Freinzel."

"I hear that moon was pretty damn infested." I could see the glow of pride on her face.

"Two thousand Dram grunts with some allied species. Three triads protecting a central hive."

"How'd you take them on?"

She paused, a shocked expression on her face. "Air support, Captain. Drones. We cleaned up the soldiers afterward. SOP."

"I see." I let the silence do its job.

Williams squinted at me. The wheels were turning. "I've heard rumors some teams are taking on worms directly."

Kim and Marshall woke at her words and glanced over. I had their full attention.

"It's new. The Xix have developed a randomized movement pattern for the mechs. It's a little scary—you hand over complete control to the AI—and your suit flies around in ways you can't predict. Confuses the hell out of the bugs—operators too. You do it right, they're sitting ducks, and you vaporize them."

Williams studied my face. "You've done this."

"I have. It's why I'm here. You're all going to learn, and I'm going to train the core troops at the Temple. Or so the plan goes."

Kim shook his head. "I don't know, man. Computer run? Why do they need us, then?"

I corrected my assessment—Korean American. With English the default in New Earth forces, training ensured a functional fluency. The Chinese resisted a little, but with India, Europe, and America onboard, it was a settled matter. That standard skill set could mask origins. At least until you'd engaged in some real conversation. He wasn't a native English speaker. Likely an immigrant to the United States. I hoped I'd get all their dossiers in the desert. This entire redeployment was being rushed like hell.

"Because the AIs are as dumb as they are smart. Brittle. When the patterns fail, they still need us to think on our feet. Improvise."

"Improvise? Sounds like a perfect way to get yourself killed," said Kim.

"It's dangerous," I agreed.

"We've heard the rumors." It was the medic, Marshall.

"What rumors?" I asked.

He continued. "Tokyo General. They brought in wounded from India. Kept them there a few hours before they transferred them to Uchujin. That was you, wasn't it?"

I shrugged.

Williams cut in. "Word was the team got into trouble. Training exercises with *live* triads."

"On *Earth*?" Kim laughed. "How'd you sign the bugs up for that?"

"The Daughter," I said. "That's what we hear, anyway. She grabs them, somehow, from somewhere. Maybe from Dram."

Kim's jaw hung open. "She what?"

I shook my head. "Wormhole snatch? Xixian raid? No idea. They're the real thing, though. Right in the deserts of India."

"Fucking *crazy*," said Kim again. "*Jesus*. What the hell are we getting ourselves into down there?"

He gestured toward Africa. The continent expanded on the blue marble as we descended from Earth orbit. The Sahara was unmistakable from this altitude. A tan brush stroke across the northern face.

I asserted my truth.

"We're getting ourselves into critical missions in this war. We're learning the advanced techniques. Training against the enemy themselves to prepare. Because our job will be to protect what's most important."

"The Daughter," said Williams, her smile returning as she stared at me.

"Yes, of course."

The two men broke eye contact with me.

She continued. "You speak of her with awe."

It was uncomfortable, but I knew all this would come out, if they didn't already know from the grapevine.

"Go on, let's get this over with," I said, noticing the other two reengage.

"You have quite the reputation as a member of the faithful, Captain," said Marshall. "What denomination are you—not Orthodox—you don't sport the gear. Chrono Reformed?"

I scowled. "Special Forces are worse than the tabloids."

"Knowledge is how we stay alive, sir," said Williams.

She was right. They deserved some words. I sighed. Now came the part that wouldn't make sense to them. "None. No creed. It's a... personal relationship. Since I was a kid."

"Sounds Next Agey," said Kim.

"Every team I've been on worries about this until they get used to it. I can tell you it's not different from any other beliefs each of us has. You have nothing to worry about. I do my job. Better than most."

"Except our job's all about her now, isn't it?" noted Williams. "This isn't like any other assignment. You've got stakes."

I locked eyes with her. "We've *all* got stakes. Our planet has stakes. She's what freed us and keeps us free still. Everyone on this world, in this transport. Each of you owes your life and freedom to the Daughter. Guarding her is protecting Earth. Whatever I or anyone else feels doesn't figure in. Those are the hard facts. That's why we wear the uniform."

The muffled sounds of rushing atmosphere spilled through the internal silence. I glanced at the floating view screen. Northern Africa shone in the darkness of the room.

Kim laughed. "Hell, Captain, what people do on their own time is their business. Local tail, boy-girl-alien threesome, bingo—not my concern. All I need to know is when to start shooting."

He aimed his hand like a blaster, angling imaginary ion slingers, his face that of a hunter. Marshall chuckled, and I smiled. One thing about the MECHcore, we lived for combat. It was an addiction, primitive drives augmented by the rapid feedback of the machine enhancement. The thrill of life-and-death performance at light speed was a hell of a high.

Williams's eyes sparkled, but she didn't smile.

Chapter 7

Thoroughly conscious ignorance is the prelude to every real advance in science.

James Clerk Maxwell

The Thar is hot, but my training there did not prepare me for our planet's largest desert. When the transport doors opened, the environment assailed us. First, a blast of sandy wind burning like a blowtorch. Next, a tan radiance bright enough to hurt through our smartglasses. Finally, a striking ensemble of human and Xixian handlers to shepherd us for the trip.

The transfer of power was immediate and obvious. Our infantry and officers stood surrounded by citizens of the Six Cities. They didn't wear Force uniforms and answered to the Daughter. None held themselves like commanders. Matching rumors, they behaved more like a religious caste.

The humans dressed according to their personal traditions and the necessities of Saharan life. Over time, their clothes resembled the garb of the nomads of the nearby regions. The Berber Arabs and other tribes had long ago optimized life under the sun and over the stinging sands. Full-body coverings were the norm. Modernized fabrics expelled heat by day but trapped it during the cold nights. It wasn't unusual to get a swing from blistering to freezing across a single evening. Clothing needed particular properties if you weren't indoors with climate control.

The Xix required no garments, even if they sported decorative dress at times. Their homeworld was one massive Sahara. They relished New Earth settings with two of their six-toed feet in the sand. Their metabolism handled both extremes in temperature effortlessly. The extraterrestrial skin was impervious to everything except the most violent sandstorms.

Towering over the welcoming party was an alien wearing a translucent, cyan robe. The covering opened near conical tissue erupting upward from its midsection. A blue-green metal band locked the fabric in place. I recognized the collar as their universal translator. Underneath the gown, the creature's body flared in color. Deep-purple spots, large and small, sprayed across the form in dizzying patterns. Many of the eyestalks sprouting from the cone aimed at me. Its gaze scorched as hot as the buffeting air.

Standing alongside the Xix were several humans in the white robes of the Temple servants. Before them were two uniformed soldiers, a man and a woman. By the MECHcore insignia, I knew they must be the remainder of my team.

Williams, Kim, and Marshall fell into a line behind me as we approached the group. We sported advanced desert gear, pre-sized and provided in the saucer. Brown-and-tan camouflage clothing, hats, combat boots, and dark smartglasses. I dialed the brightness down on the shades to better make out the faces. I stopped in front of the additional Core members and saluted.

"Captain Nitin Ratava of New Earth Force reporting for duty. This is part of ODA 111, my assigned M-troop service at the Temple. Sergeants Marshall and Kim," I said, gesturing. "Warrant Officer Williams. Requesting permission to enter the Six Cities."

A long and awkward pause. The desert wind whistled, the robes of our greeting party dancing to some turbulent rhythm. It was unnerving stepping into this unique bubble of governance. Who actually held authority here? Not my team, that was for sure. One of the humans? I scanned their faces but met blank stares.

The eyes of the Xix drew my attention. Instinct told me the seat of influence lay with the alien.

I took off my glasses and, blinded by the light and grit, squinted toward the monster. "Is permission granted?"

The creature spoke through the translator clasped about its cone like a necklace. "Indeed, Captain," came the fluid accent of the device. The voice was genderless but warm, the tones sharp with intelligence. "Both you and your team. Two you have not met and stand before you. Weapons Sergeant Grant Moore and Sergeant Erica Fox, your engineer."

It was odd to hear the alien speak the military jargon. I had to remind myself to respect these monsters. Underestimating them was foolishness. They could handle all our areas of expertise without breaking a sweat. Well, almost all of them. Humans could still *Read* better than any. That was why they were living on New Earth. Why the MECHcore were here.

I made the introductions within the group. The last two members appeared as capable as the rest. Fox was a small woman of mixed heritage. I guessed Chinese and European. A slight detachment in her demeanor reflected what I'd come to expect from the techs.

Moore was a Force officer from a recruitment poster. He towered with muscles and tattoos. I'd discover he also had a tongue loose and salty. His lowbrow British twang gave his speech a memorable character. Both grouped with the others of the team, and we were now facing the alien and its greeting party.

"Captain Ratava, I am called Waythrel, and I serve Ambra Dawn at the Temple."

My throat dried. *Waythrel?* A figure out of the history books.

The Xixian spy on Dram who had helped free Ambra Dawn from their dungeons. Who had accompanied her on her mission to save Earth. For more than two hundred years, the creature had been her closest and most trusted advisor. By the Daughter, what was it doing here?

"Waythrel of Xix, we're honored that you have chosen to welcome us." I used formal tones, employing half-forgotten exocultural protocols from our basic Force training.

The eyestalks flitted about. "It is we who are honored. We have an extraordinary assignment for you, and Ambra desires that we get to it with all speed. We will rest tonight and depart first thing in the morning. My assistants here will lead you to prepared housing."

I could sense the members of my team stealing glances in my direction. They were likely dying to know what was behind this. An unprecedented visit of one of the Temple's most legendary residents. An *extraordinary* assignment.

MECHcore teams usually played an important if unexciting role at the Temple, handling security and personal safety of the populace. Nothing like Special Forces buzzing around in mechs to make an impression. I couldn't focus on this broader picture. My pulse had spiked. Waythrel's words were spinning in my mind.

Ambra desires.

The Daughter herself planned something usual for my team. We weren't going to perform a typical MECHcore duty. Our purpose was unusual, something significant *she* was planning. We might soon be in her presence.

I struggled to suppress my excitement.

The alien bowed. "Welcome to the Fourth City, Captain."

Chapter 8

There is one disease which is widespread, and from which men rarely escape: that each thinks his mind more clever and more learned than it is. I have found that this affliction has attacked many an intelligent person.

Maimonides

Williams stood in front of the group with her hands on her hips. "Captain, what the hell's going on?"

We gathered in our assigned quarters. Despite their age, the buildings appeared ultra-modern, a Xixian design common in the Six Cities. The internal architecture was *dynamic*, composed of fields altered for appearance, texture, and position. Need a bigger room to house your troops? No problem! Reprogram the damn walls. You selected anything from wood to marble to alien matter preferred by the designers. Realistic and practical.

The external construction was more permanent. A concrete composite performing a similar service to the high-tech clothing.

Heat stayed out in the day but remained at night. It was also hard as hell too. I didn't see a single scratch on the gleaming surfaces despite hundreds of years of sandstorms. The Xix knew how to build.

"Calm down, Williams."

Her eyes flashed. That was the problem with elite forces, especially those the Temple had selected. They were bright, asked questions. Filled with attitude. It gave them the edge the ordinary soldier lacked. Produced creative destroyers who handled the tough missions.

And made them giant pains in the ass to command. The meeting hadn't begun before the inquisition erupted.

"Captain, I'm chill, but I signed up for Guardian duty. I know what that requires. I'm prepared. I didn't sign up for any *extraordinary assignment*. I want to know what we're getting into."

"Take a seat, Williams," I insisted, motioning to a row of chairs in the center of the room. A smartholo floated above us, but I didn't know if I'd get to use it. I'd planned to go over the new MECH AI they'd employ to engage the Dram. For now, it was on hold.

She eyed me a moment and let out a curt breath, grabbing a chair alongside the others. If one could passive-aggressively sit, she had it down.

The five were in a single line in front of me, Williams on the far left, Kim next to her, followed by Fox and Marshall. On his own, a few feet from the rest, was the hulking Moore, keeping to himself.

"I know as much as you do about this, which is *nothing*. Colonel Snowden warned us that, once we landed, we'd be under new management. Previous orders and protocols don't apply here. You signed on knowing this. That means we adapt or get back on the transport and bug out."

"Bugger out, mate!" the Brit laughed. "Squids ordering us to fight bugs for that queen runnin' the damn world."

"You're welcome to fly back tomorrow," I said.

He smiled.

Marshall interjected, "Then how do we prepare for a mystery assignment?"

I ran my fingers through my hair. "By staying flexible, informed, in shape, and ready. Our enemies don't play by any rules, so there isn't any certainty in any engagement." I gestured to the holoscreen. "Not even in the new attack plans I was going to introduce tonight. That's true for standard duties or for whatever they have planned for us."

"You can't know that, sir," said Kim.

"I don't see why we're so worried," interrupted Fox. "There's never been as much as a shot fired at the Temple. Or even in the Cities. Not in two hundred years. We go in, march where they say, do our time, and we're out with benefits. Meanwhile, think of where we *are*."

I could have let it go. Our past predicted she was right, but Snowden's words wormed through my thoughts. My team deserved the bigger picture.

"A tour there was simple before, but things are changing. I suppose you've heard some of the rumors."

Glances hopped between soldiers in the short silence.

Williams spoke first. "Losses on the five fronts. Raids. Supply lines cut."

"Worse," I said. *They needed to know.*

Moore scowled. "So, what are the bloody bastards not telling us now?"

"The Dram have compromised the galactic hub."

Several sat upright.

Williams hissed. "Those mother—"

"Yes," I said. "Some very bad news from the colonel."

Kim waved his arms. "Whoa—time the fuck out! The center? What does that mean? Hit and runs? Occupation? Are we going to get bug warboats pouring out of the Orb toward New Earth?"

"I don't know. I don't have field reports, and Snowden said it's all hushed up to prevent a panic." I tried to slow this down. "It can't be they've taken control, or we *would* have bugs crawling out of the sewers here. But it's got to be bad. Significant penetration with intermittent access to the central transit points."

Williams whistled. "Well, that ain't good."

"That's why I'm telling you this. We're not part of Force here. We're cut off from the leadership and any communications by the Xixian defense fields. We're on our own. There hasn't been an attack here since they built the Temple, but we can't assume anymore. I think Snowden was trying to tell me that. Don't take anything for granted."

Kim stammered. "Do they know something he didn't? What if there *is* an invasion on the way? Maybe *that's* our important assignment! A fucking meat grinder."

He's panicking.

"Calm down, Sergeant," I said. "Don't you think there would be a Force mobilization the likes of which we haven't seen? Like the early days of the war?" I allowed that to sink in. "We might have had some setbacks. Losses the brass don't want advertised on every wave across the allied net, but it's not that bad yet. We need to trust the Daughter. Ambra Dawn has never let us down. Let's keep our heads on straight and not lose touch with her."

Kim wasn't onboard. "You're the one a little too touched with her."

Fox glared at him. "What the hell does that mean?"

"Means everyone knows the captain's a true believer."

She reached inside her shirt and yanked out a pendant. It was New Earth with a sunrise breaking over the edge of the planet. One of the main religious symbols of the Dawnists.

"He's not the only one, asshole."

Kim frowned back. "Well, maybe you two are ready to die for her, see whatever heaven they promised you. Maybe he sees what's coming and welcomes it. I don't."

I moved to respond, but Moore cut in. "Or, could be our

captain's interested in more 'an being touched by the power of the bald lady. I bet he's got touching of his own in mind—eh, Captain?"

Fox murmured something I couldn't hear.

Moore continued before I could concoct a response. "I been watchin' you, sir. Cause I wasn't goin' into this bloody assignment with some nutter prayin' to the Witch half the night."

Fox's eyes were ice. "You ought to learn how to bite your fat tongue, Moore."

He smirked. "You blokes make me laugh. Sure, I get it, *the Daughter* an' all 'at. Keep your pendants. Fine with me. For our DC —all those rumors about him weren't *resting* well with me."

"Yeah? *You're* starting not to rest well with me," she hissed.

Force doesn't give us enough psychology training. The Brit was edging to the line of insubordination. And pissing right next to it. If I cut in too soon, I'd appear weak for taking the bait. Too late, and a brawl might break out.

"But all's brilliant, mates." His grin broadened. *Did he wink?* "Been watchin' him. Our captain ain't no choirboy. Not longing to take a needle blast for her. He's gagging for something else. Arse over tits or I'm blind. I know when a man's 'bout to pitch his tent!"

I knew the slang and felt my cheeks flush. I was glad I was dark enough in this light for it to go unnoticed.

"She *is* fit, mate, long's you don't mind her head."

Fox stood, but before she could engage Moore, he was up in my face. The others tensed. I kept still in front of his bulk and didn't flinch, staring him in the face.

He saluted. "Religion of heavenly bodies. Sign me up!"

Laughter followed. I smiled from one side of my mouth. This bruiser was sharp as a tack. With one short diversion, he derailed Kim's panic and lessened any threat from my personal feelings.

It was an acceptable trade. Take a little embarrassment for some humanization and team bonding. But I'd have to watch him and Fox. A bad mix brewing.

"You're enlisted," I said. "Now, sit down, soldier."

"Yes, sir!" Moore grinned back and turned around, taking a seat.

The others relaxed. Kim exhaled. Fox sat as well, but her eyes smoldered.

Williams shook her head. "*Shit*. I'm in deep with a bunch of crazies. Okay then, Captain. Why don't you light up the board and show us the new squid tech. Sounds like we might be needing it."

Chapter 9

Any sufficiently advanced technology is indistinguishable from magic.

Clarke's Third Law

Waythrel entered the quarters as we finished packing our gear. We formed a semicircle around the alien. A being so unsettling elicited primitive responses that were hard to suppress.

The Xix did make an impression. It towered over us. Its limbs moved at angles impossible for an Earth animal. A sharp intelligence radiated from the monstrosity. So did smells, unnatural and disturbing. The creature commanded our attention without a word.

"The caravan is prepared for you," Waythrel said. "There is a military-grade sandglider that will hold you and your items."

I stepped forward. "I was led to understand our suits will be waiting for us at the Temple?"

"This is correct. However, these will be different mechs, not those you had shipped. We have built enhanced versions of the MECHcore standard. They are optimized both for the desert and for our latest battle techniques. Part of your initial exercises will be to integrate with the redesigned equipment. To appreciate their full potential."

I heard some quiet grumbling behind me. New chassis. Unusual training. Exceptional assignments. *Don't move a soldier's cheese, Xixian!*

"The suit improvements are significant. Ambra wishes her Guardians to be outfitted in the best available."

I made a short bow. It was hard to argue with those sentiments. The Xix gestured outside our quarters, and we followed it into the blazing sun.

The glider hovered in front of us, silent over the sands. The sole evidence of its propulsion system was an undulating ripple in the sea of grains. Aerodynamic and big as a bus, its sleek design screamed alien tech. The upper portion was transparent. Not glass. Another material our guests from space had produced. I assumed strong, more resistant to erosion than human materials science could achieve. Touch displays and control features glittered along the contours of the capsid.

We tossed our bags into the back, hopped into the central region, and buckled in. The cab consisted of seating appropriate for humans and Xix. Waythrel occupied one of the grander chairs. Within moments, I felt the lurch of acceleration, and the glider darted like an arrow from the Fourth City.

Our sand ship reached the velocities of high-speed rail. The air displacement left a tunnel of swirling grains behind us. Speeding inward from the ring of the Six Cities to the Temple, the structures of civilization vanished. The colors and shapes of the deep desert dominated our vision.

The transport glided over the colossal dunes, some reaching hundreds of meters. It scaled the long windward sides. Hopping the crest, it launched over slip faces to valleys between the tan mountains. With the morning sun on the horizon, those canyons would plunge us into darkness and shadow. We burst into blinding light again, climbing another dune. All this at stunning speeds. The expansive windows made sense. It was a hell of a show.

The hills gave way as we flew over an extended sand sheet. We neared the center of the Sahara, equidistant from all inhabited regions of the Six Cities. We were about as in the middle of nowhere as anyone could be on Earth outside an ocean.

The craft skimmed the flat terrain, and I glimpsed blurred outlines of a massive structure ahead. Geography lessons ruled out giant dunes or mountains. The looming shadow in the sky was something intelligence had thrown up from the desert floor. Thrown up very high.

"There it is, Captain," came the voice of Williams, her neck stretched toward the growing outline in front of us. "There's your Temple."

My team stared at the marvel. As the dark shape took form, my skin tingled. Not only from its sheer size and location, but also for what this place meant to humanity. Here was the focal point in our war against cosmic forces that should have consumed our primitive species. If not for the help of the Xix. If not for the unexpected wild card in the history of our galaxy that was Ambra Dawn.

Marshall whistled. "All this power in the middle of nothing."

Waythrel's eyes turned toward us. "Many have wondered why we chose to build in the depths of the desert." The tones from the translator grew in mystery as we approached the Temple.

Moore scoffed. "Because the squids want sand between their toes is what I heard." He was slumped next to Kim, chin on his massive chest, impervious to the spectacle before him. Dark smartglasses concealed his eyes.

"Yes, Sergeant," came the voice of the alien. "We are certainly partial to such locations, if not to xenophobic epithets. We do earnestly seek to work with our human hosts. We understand that these climates are extreme for your organism."

Moore flipped his shades up and smiled. "Extreme for our organism. I like it."

"If not for Xixian comfort, then what?" Williams asked.

Waythrel's bobbing eyes scanned my team, a few of them never leaving their focus on me. "From the beginning, after the recursive time alteration of the Calamity, New Earth has been in considerable danger. Greater than most humans have appreciated. Especially in the early years, we lived under the constant threat of attack by the Dram. In fact, we repelled many attempts—major, planetary-level assaults—to achieve again what had been undone."

This had my team's attention. Definitely *not* textbook material.

Kim broke in. "You mean like the asteroid? They shot more at us?"

"There were multiple campaigns through various strategies to destroy your planet. Or render it inhospitable. Similar attacks occurred on my homeworld, as well as several other worlds harboring species important to our war effort. All were countered."

"The Daughter?" I asked.

Waythrel gestured with its hands. "Of course, Captain Ratava. The powers of Ambra Dawn alone have shielded us from certain destruction."

"So, why didn't we ever hear about this?" asked Kim.

"Representatives of your many governments begged us to keep silent. They feared that word of the continuing efforts of our enemies could instill a planetwide panic."

These facts sat quietly with each of us. We all had studied the Calamity. The alternative history of the planet in which the Dram had reduced it to slag by hurling a giant asteroid through an Orb.

No stories about additional, world-threatening attempts were taught. Instead, we learned of the alliances against the Hegemony. The long hundred years of continuous but victorious war. A conflict where we had broken their stranglehold on the galaxy, pushed the bugs back to a few systems near their homeworld. It was a tidy myth. Told across the globe in every schoolhouse. Perhaps for some of the same reasons the recent setbacks were withheld.

"Because of these threats, the Daughter insisted that we place the

Temple as far from human habitation as possible. Thus, should an attack succeed, even a minor one, the carnage to life on Earth would be minimized as much as could be managed."

"So why not leave the bloody thing on the moon where it was built?" asked Moore.

"Indeed, this was her wish. However, we had seen what isolation from your planet had done to individuals of your species. To Ambra in particular. We convinced her that it was in the interests of our struggle to relocate to her homeworld. The Sahara was her compromise." The Xix paused, its smaller fingers darting around. "In addition, we needed to build a new device to amplify her powers and integrate the Reader groups. The one on your moon was effective, but served as a first draft, as you say. A prototype. We learned much from its building and use. We put such knowledge into practice here in your world's largest desert."

"The Dish," I said.

"Yes. It is an engineering feat dwarfing the efforts on your satellite. Most of the mass of the Temple is contained in the structure, which spans the size of some of your larger cities."

The dark blur in front of us clarified. It was like approaching Manhattan in a low-flying airplane, where the expanse of the city filled the entire field of vision. Instead of skyscrapers, a monolith stretched to the sky from the desert floor.

"My God," gasped Kim as he stood in his seat against the restraints.

"They said it was tall. I've seen the numbers, but nothing's gonna prepare you for *that*," said Williams, her mouth agape.

Rising out of the sands like some webbed volcano was the colossal antenna of the Dish. Of course, the Xix had built it. Nothing close to the scale of such a structure existed in human engineering. Its height was impossible, beyond the grasp of intuition. It dwarfed anything on New Earth. Staring up, I lost all sense of proportion.

"It reaches over fifteen kilometers," said Waythrel. "Twice the altitude of your tallest mountain."

Moore perked up a little and peeked through his shades. "How you keep the giant todger from falling down?" he asked.

The alien pointed to a lower portion of the construction.

"Do you see how broad the base is? It is difficult to appreciate from this distance. It is as wide as it is high and anchored several thousand meters into the desert floor. This provides considerable support. The rods curve up from the foundation like parabolic spokes. They are fashioned from our strongest and most lightweight materials, millions of times stronger per unit mass than your best composites."

Extending radially from the huge entity were much smaller buildings of recognizable height. These were living quarters and other constructions serving the needs of the Temple. It was hard to focus on them. The antenna seized all attention.

The ground below us transformed from the tan sands to a black gloss. I recognized the planet's largest solar array in the giant circular mat flowing across the desert. The term *array* was archaic, as the material was more a continuous sheet rather than thousands of individual panels. The glider sped over a dark and still sea.

"It's beautiful," said Fox, her eyes watery.

"Amazing," I said, marveling as well. "This is what powers the Dish?"

"No," said Waythrel. "The Dish requires much more energy."

"Like those astronomy antennae," said Kim, staring up at the tall structure. "Focuses all her power like radio waves or something?"

The alien gestured in an inhuman manner. "It is difficult to explain. There is a superficial similarity with such instruments. The operating principle, in contrast, is quite different. Your telescopes process electromagnetic radiation of specific energies. Ambra's manipulations of space and time occur through distinct physical means. This is why the Dish is so giant, and also why it drains so much energy to operate. To focus her powers requires a gravitational lens created through the use of a micro black hole."

"You're shitting us!" exclaimed Kim, a nervous smile on his face. "You've got a damn black hole in there?"

Waythrel's voice was calm. "Four."

"Holy *shit!* Well, I'm with you on the vote for the desert location now, for sure."

"The black holes are located in strategic positions," added the alien. "One is at the top of the tower. The spacetime distortions they create are channeled by other devices, the three-space cross section focusing beneath the sands in the bedrock. It is there that Ambra goes when she requires a significant amplification of her powers."

"How do you juice all this?" asked Moore. He had flipped his glasses back down.

"If you mean the energetics, Sergeant, we have an array of twenty reactors built around the Temple."

"*Twenty?*" said Williams. "So why do you need all the sun power?"

"The fusion cores are devoted exclusively to powering of the Dish and the maintenance of the black-hole amplituhedron. Both require enormous energy expenditures. The solar sea is in place to provide for all the organism-related activities. Life support, communications, standard military defenses."

The antenna now towered above us, so high I'd have to lie flat to stare up at it. If an event horizon lurked at the apex, we were going to have to take the alien's word for it. The top was invisible.

The glider decelerated. We plunged into shadow again as we pulled alongside the habitat's buildings. They were small in comparison to the central tower but still had many stories. Their walls blocked the early morning sun.

The craft stopped in front of an extensive courtyard. A broad street extended from it and the outer desert into the Temple City itself. For the first time, we saw green in the Sahara. The entrance was lined with olive and palm trees. Some thorny bushes bore flowers. While the plants were arid species, they required significant irrigation to keep them alive in this wasteland. The Daughter had her gardeners.

We released the restraints and assembled, filing out to the cargo section to grab our gear. Waythrel exited and headed away from the craft. I hoisted my duffel bag over my shoulder, waiting until the rest of my team had secured their items. We marched in the direction the alien had taken.

We stepped alongside the sandglider, its bulk rising above our heads on the right. The Daughter's counselor had turned around the front of the ship, lost from sight, a trail in the sand marking its path. I picked up the pace to keep up.

We made the same turn past the nose of the craft and ran into a greeting party. It was far larger and more diverse than the one at the Fourth City. Thirty to forty humans and half as many Xix awaited our approach. They dressed in flowing desert garments of myriad colors. Eyestalk clusters danced here and there above the shorter sea of human heads.

Waythrel reached the crowd and stopped, speaking to a central figure. The sun crested over the tops of the buildings, and the court-yard erupted in light. My smartglasses engaged and reduced the glare.

Seized with compulsion, I stepped forward. My brain relegated reason to some distant region of my consciousness. A mindless moth to the flame, the shape underneath the height of the alien attracted me. Step by drunken step, I approached, oblivious to everything else.

It was a young woman, clothed in long robes of black, her skin as bright as the white walls lit by the morning sun. The top of her head was bald and swollen to obscene proportions. Rivers of red curls fell from a midpoint in her scalp down her shoulders and to her waist.

"*Daughter of Time*," I whispered.

It was Ambra Dawn.

Chapter 10

What then is time? If no one asks me, I know what it is. If I wish to explain it to him who asks, I do not know.

Augustine of Hippo

*T*ime.

Whatever the idea represents, if anything at all in the reality of our universe, it stopped. No sound. No movement. The sand particles hovered in midair. My own heart ceased its rhythm in my chest.

Her eyes.

Blind eyes. Bright-green emeralds glowing before me. They moved. Everything else froze in an impossible stillness. Her eyes turned to me and focused, plunging into my own. I was bathed in light. A subtle impact rippled through my awareness. She had entered into my consciousness.

Textbooks note the Daughter distorts the field of time near her. Physics instruction I didn't understand. The science-fiction serials waved through the datasphere—they all said something about it. She arrested time. She slowed time. She stood outside time in some undefined *elsewhere*. None of the writings agreed on what she did to time. Now it was clear to me those stories were much more than legends.

Standing before me, commanding all my attention and thoughts in the midst of all these creatures, was a human being who was almost three hundred years old. And she didn't look a day older than seventeen. No wrinkles, no skin discoloration, no gray hair or sagging posture. Ambra Dawn was the same biological age she had been when she came into full use of her powers.

I didn't understand it. None of my fellow students at the academy had understood the content. Explanations of cyclically warped spacetime. Recursive loops of causality that left chemistry intact yet her body unaged. How time hiccuped, but memories formed. Or how her consciousness looped through carbon-based flesh into hyperknots of continuum strings.

For me, it was all gibberish. In this space, her gaze penetrated me like a vulnerable lover. The nonsense of understanding mattered little. I wished to stay. To forever have her dive into me, consume me. To endlessly experience her in this impossible locus with no time. To show Ambra my boundless adoration.

Be patient, Nitin. We'll discover a better place.

The words rang in my mind as if I had thought them, but the voice wasn't my own. Her eyes held me a moment longer, and I felt tears trickle down the side of my face.

A fist struck my stomach. Time leaped. The noises and smells returned, the grains rasping across my skin. Voices, footsteps. A murmuring crowd.

I stood halfway between my team and the welcoming party. The blowing sand crusted the tear paths on my cheeks. Wide eyes gawked at me, and Ambra smiled.

"Captain Ratava, please bring your people forward," she called over the wind. The murmurs died at the sound of her voice. The stares lingered.

I glanced backwards to see shocked expressions from my crew.

Stunned, they stumbled with me, and we came to a halt in front of the Daughter and Waythrel.

"We welcome you to the Temple," she said. "We appreciate your service and sacrifice for our common mission to protect New Earth."

I examined the crowd. Smiles and steady gazes. These weren't political platitudes, but true words for those before us. I glimpsed the earnestness in their faces. They served her with their full being, with a devotion I'd never encountered. I remembered the Hindu monks I had known in my youth, but they provided a pale comparison.

Her blind eyes crossed over my form as a lightning strike, producing shivers.

"I am needed urgently within, so I will not be able to be with you as you enter our city. Instead, I'll turn you over to the capable hands of my counselor, Sepehr Mazandarani. He will serve as your guide, your point of contact, for the next few weeks as you prepare for Guardian service." She gestured behind her, and a short, thin man in indigo robes stepped forward.

His complexion was dark, his eyes a deep brown with a dagger's gaze. A trimmed and sharp goatee accentuated a diabolical appearance. He shuffled with a casual confidence until he was beside the Daughter.

"Sepehr." Ambra bowed to the Iranian and turned around, walking alongside Waythrel on the road into the Temple City.

"Hello. From me as well, welcome." Mazandarani scanned my team, pausing on me. His eyes squinted, his mouth in a tight line. The warm invitation dissolved. "You will be staying at the south end of the barracks, near the military training fields. There you will find housing and your new battle suits. Trained Earth Force soldiers will work with you to get you up to speed. Inside, we walk whenever possible—it keeps us well adapted to the climate. Please follow me. Your quarters are about a half hour away."

He grinned, with striations in his jaw, and turned down the same entry road as the Daughter. Ambra and Waythrel were now out of sight, and it was unclear where they had gone.

I glanced at my team and smiled. "Okay, here we go." A pause. No one moved. My grin faded. "Problem?"

Moore let out a bark of a laugh. "Yeah. You might say."

The others didn't elaborate.

"Warrant Officer Williams. Would you then kindly explain why we aren't marching inside?"

"Yes, sir," she said, bringing her face close to mine. "That is, if you can explain what the hell just happened."

"What happened? We were met by Ambra Dawn herself and assigned to her representative. We're following him to begin our required duties."

"I don't mean that." She stared at me. The rest gawked as well, Fox with wide eyes, clutching her pendant.

Moore chimed in. "She's a bit put out from your shimmering disappearing act."

My throat felt dry. "My what?"

He laughed again. "You know, the part where you blink in and out of existence and teleport halfway to that would-be girlfriend of yours." He checked with the others. "About cover it?"

No one said anything. Their eyes spoke plenty.

"Yeah, see lads, we've not all gone bloody barmy in the heat. We all saw it." He hoisted his duffel. "I think we'd all like to hear your thoughts on the matter, Captain."

I stared back at them.

Chapter 11

The easy confidence with which I know another man's religion is folly teaches me to suspect that my own is also.

Mark Twain

It was three weeks before I saw Ambra Dawn again.

I threw myself into the training and drills. My team members were hardworking soldiers, but I outworked them all. My energies burned with a zeal no one else could match, and the group worked that much harder due to my example. Because of what we would soon face, it was critical we did.

The firehose of information we withstood preserved my sanity. Constant activity distracted me from the incident at the gates. I didn't understand what had happened, and questions gnawed at me whenever I had a moment to think. The few conversations with my team left us unsatisfied. Nothing was clarified.

Except perhaps for Fox, who bent all events to her faith. After witnessing a miracle firsthand, she began earnest conversion efforts.

"So, now," she said, staring around at us on the training field. "Now do you believe?"

A battle suit encased half her torso, her black hair billowed behind her in the scalding wind. The composite chassis drank the sunlight, charging power reserves planted in the back.

We had finished an exhausting session. Sweat poured down our faces and ran in rivulets into our mechs. The new tech sopped it up, filtered it, and stored the potable constituents for later use. The breeze did little to cool us.

The team clustered in a tight group. A wasted sandworm triad lay smoking before us. The redesigned suits were incredible. A jump in performance of four or five generations. They combined innovative battle methods with eco-survival adaptations for the desert. The enhanced AI for the dance was far more sophisticated, and we'd mastered the interface. With the supercharged ion slingers, it almost made taking on the worms fun.

Kim shuffled his feet, inclining his head to our engineer. "Yeah," he exhaled, his fatigue evident. "I guess so."

I could see in the eyes of the others that he wasn't alone. But acceptance of the event was one thing. Interpretation, another.

"Well, it's not anything new to hear she can pull out her magic wand," spat Moore. "It don't mean I'm getting baptized."

Fox shook her head. She chanted, "In this age were holy signs, but many disbelieved. And the Daughter said, 'If you believed not in Moses and Jesus, then you will believe not in Me.'"

He burst out laughing. "You think the Witch actually said any of that?"

She stepped toward him.

"Enough!" I said, engaging the hydraulics of my suit to push them apart. "Keep your beliefs private. We have one fight we need to focus on, and it's not with our species."

"Yeah, but, you know, there's been an *event*. With the Ambra Dawn." It was Kim. I heard a growing awe in his voice. "We saw it. *You* were part of it. It's like all the legends, man."

Strange things had happened that defied the laws of nature. But this development had centered not on New Earth or the Great War with the Dram. Not some other textbook-worthy crisis concerning the Daughter and humanity's survival. It had focused on a single person out of all the swarm of humanity. *On me.*

"It was one thing when you were such a fanboy, Captain," said Williams. "Now? What is it with you and her?"

"I don't know. Nothing about her is normal, right? Well, I'm part of it. Millions worship her."

"Yeah, but you don't," said the Brit.

"Sergeant, I don't know what people should call it. I know what I feel. I'm not a Dawnist. I'm not a skeptic. I know where I have to be, and it's here. With her."

Fox tilted her head. "I understand. You're like a monk. You're devoted to her."

"He ain't no monk." Moore smirked.

She glared at him. "I bet he's never been with another woman. Never been in love. He's waiting for *her.*"

Kim's eyebrows jumped. "That true, sir? Not to be too personal, but we're all getting past that line, I think. Is this thing with her so extreme? Have you ever kissed a girl?"

Always the same. Of all the unusual aspects of my devotion to the Daughter, it was sex that riled people up the most. I could have painted myself up like the wildest Hindu priest. Chanted into the night on the top of a pillar, and it would go down better than abstinence. Or the perception of it.

"More than that. Engaged once. I think I loved her." I inhaled, dampening my emotions.

The smooth alto of Williams broke the silence. "What happened?"

I stared out over the desert. I couldn't make eye contact for this.

"My parents arranged it all. They'd been trying to marry me off for a while. You can imagine how they felt with my long focus on the

Daughter. These things were usually awkward, pointless, and over before the dessert." I suppressed a sigh. "Not the last one."

Her face danced in my memory. Delicate bones, with a Persian nose and rich black hair like a strong river. She was petite, elegant in her motions, and quick with her wit.

"She was a professional dancer. Classical Indian style. Her eyes caught me over the table, and we had an immediate mutual chemistry. Body, mind, all that. I abandoned the idea of a destiny with the Daughter." I laughed. "Of course, I had a lot of help from my parents. They were beyond overjoyed to recognize that this woman hooked me."

"So what *happened*?" pressed Fox.

"I broke it off."

"Why?" asked Kim.

"Because it was wrong. I'd convinced myself to grow up, move past my lifelong dream. But it was self-deception. I couldn't let go of Ambra Dawn. I loved this beautiful woman and planned a life with her. But my feelings weren't pure, not devoted as they should have been to my wife-to-be. She deserved so much more. I saw I'd forever be haunted by another. Nothing I could do would change it. It wasn't fair to anyone, but it was more unfair to pretend. I knew it'd cause more pain to keep it going. So I ended it."

"Didn't peg you for a heartbreaker, Captain," said Williams.

I stared into the distance. "It might not make sense, but there is love, and then there's another kind of devotion. One transcending the two involved. And yes, maybe it's madness."

"Well, she *did* single you out, sir," said Kim.

It is one thing to feel a reality within yourself. Quite another to have the external world verify it with public drama.

Marshall agreed. "There's some strange destiny going on."

And I heard her voice.

Something I couldn't share with my team. Psychologists could supply reasons why I'd been delusional. The entire episode could have been a cognitive reaction to the time distortion. Perhaps some shrink would claim it was the beginning of a split personality disorder.

It didn't matter. I *knew* in my heart Ambra Dawn had spoken to me. The experience was as real, more true, than many events in my life. As tangible as my own awareness. The Daughter was said to be telepathic, to be able to enter the minds and control the thoughts of others. She had touched my mind. I was sure of it.

With that conviction, I longed for more. To interact again. To discover my purpose here. Her absence grew to a terrible vacuum in a space that had not existed before. She had entered and spoken to me. In the fertile landscape of my adoration, a nascent mini-universe gestated. What would it become?

And when?

I pulled myself to the present. I needed to get the team to move on from this.

"So we've gotten some real-world confirmation of everything we've been taught. Not on a holo, not from our elders, but in our faces. In the sands in front of us." I held each in turn with my gaze. "Things a lot bigger than us are going on. Let's take it to heart and let's get serious about why we're here. The myths aren't lies."

The group sobered. Moore's smirk vanished.

Of course, it returned with another wink. "Right, Captain. And you can hope to get a little more *serious* with the girl yourself, since you've moved up to teleporting with her."

I turned away and put my helmet back on. More worms were coming.

Chapter 12

All warfare is based on deception. Hence, when we are able to attack, we seem unable; when using our forces, we appear inactive; when we are close, we convince the enemy we are far away; when distant, we make him believe we are near.

The Art of War, Sun Tzu 孫子

We received a briefing on our unusual assignment at the end of the first week. The team had finished a particularly grueling skirmish. A captured triad released in the sands was always a challenge, but that was the setting for an advanced lesson. We were testing the newest feature of the redesigned MECH-core suits—spacetime neutralizers. Command gave us no explanation for why we would need such countermeasures. Of course, those design elements had our minds racing.

Accompanying the worms were field distortions in reality. Left uncountered, they slowed us down. Displaced us in location or time. It didn't require to be much in the heat of battle to be lethal. Our mechs countered the effects, but it required a change in our fighting style. A strange rhythm, pulse in our movements, actions, thoughts. Mental shifts that are hard to describe. When chronology and position jerk around, the sensations and responses are counterintuitive.

We spent a long day in drills to master the new combat mode. Mazandarani arrived later to escort us back to the military barracks. We followed, cleaned up, and he brought us to a conference room in a nearby building. There we were introduced to Tomoko Mizoguchi.

The major reminded me of Colonel Snowden, as much as a diminutive Japanese woman could of that giant. She seemed to step out of some ancient war holo. The older warrior spoke in clipped cadence, full of bluster and drama, and eager to put fools in their place. Her short salt-and-pepper hair spiked away from her skull. She wore a pressed uniform sharpened like a knife.

We gathered from Mazandarani that she had been at the Temple for over a decade. She ran engagements with the Daughter and Xixian forces at various locations in the galaxy. These roles had been kept hidden outside the Six Cities. None of my team had heard of her, but over the next three weeks, we heard a lot from her. The voice that erupted from her short frame resonated through the room.

"You may *think* you know what you are up against. Let me tell you, you don't."

Our group of experienced MECHcore soldiers had seen combat with the enemy on a dozen worlds. She led with a heck of an opening.

"The tide of the war has changed," she growled. "We are no longer on the offensive but are now in a full-scale retreat across the galaxy."

We sat in stunned silence. Far worse than anything Colonel Snowden had hinted at. *What the hell was happening?*

"From last month, we have lost control of the Time Tree. The Dram have occupied the central Orb projection. Their forces are launching attacks against weakly defended worlds in the alliance. Most of those have been devastating."

I glanced at Williams, seated on my right side. Her eyes told the story—disbelief, shock, and fear. She held my gaze for a moment and shook her head, returning her attention to the briefing.

"It is obvious something has catalyzed this phase transition in the war. The nature of this catalyst has become the focus of much of our current efforts. It is in this respect you have been recruited here."

She paused, her eyes dissecting us. Her bright eyes stopped last and longest on me.

"Your training should finish before the end of the month. There will be an important announcement during the Festival of Rebirth. The Daughter will address the faithful of the Temple City, broadcast a message to the world. We have notified all the major political and media leaders."

She waited again, and I couldn't stop myself from interrupting her narrative.

"What will she say?"

She motioned to a projection holo of the galaxy. Several bright points appeared across its expanse. I recognized them as the location of extrasolar Time Spheres. Or rather, as the Ambra Dawn had revealed, the projections of the one Orb. With a touch on the screen, many of the white dots changed color.

"In red, you see those systems now occupied by enemy forces."

We sat in stunned silence. It is difficult to explain to you of another time what this meant. Your contemporaries learned the maps of Old Earth. You considered distances and meanings of national borders. Your hometown. You cannot grasp the size of the galaxy. You weren't raised on the century-old atlas of the Dram Quarantine choking their home planet.

That chart was burned into the consciousness of generations. We knew where our foes resided, the handful of satellite worlds remaining under their control. It was a small percentage, a testament to our victory in the Great War.

No longer. In the holo presented by the major, half the star systems glowed red. She flicked her hand, and the map rotated. The viewpoint zoomed to the galactic center, New Earth shooting to the back of the room. She focused on the interior Orb.

"Their attack was long planned. Once they seized the central Time Point, strikes across the Time Tree occurred. Every system targeted has fallen."

"Oh, my God," said Kim behind me.

"Our forces find themselves unable to repel the attacks. Hardly able to communicate anything useful about them. We only have strange reports, contradictory statements. Even the Xix do not know how to interpret the data."

"What do they say?" I asked.

"We will provide you with the information obtained. We want you to study it. Brainstorm. Prepare for the unexpected."

She touched several floating buttons on the holopanel. The room filled with a poor-quality holovid. White noise and audio static clouded the projection, but the scene was one of battle. A human communications officer spoke. Her jaw was set, her eyes narrow in the chaos of explosions and screams.

"Freighter Centari 2-11658. Mayday, mayday, mayday. Escort battalion destroyed. We are defenseless and taking fire from enemy forces."

A blinding light flashed with a deep sound. The image disintegrated into random pixels. It flickered back, and the woman transmitted from in front of a raging inferno.

"Life support is failing. Beyond salvage. Initiating terminal data squirt."

A *TDS*. When your ship was going down. When it was clear there might not be anything to recover. If you had the presence of mind to send information to relay beacons, to inform and warn, you would spend your last few moments firing one off. It would likely drain whatever you had left in the ship's batteries—the signal was designed to reach the relays. It would render you helpless. It was a final act. The officer saw her imminent death. It was on her face, the steel in her eyes.

Her hand paused in the air. She hadn't sent the message. She had something she needed to say.

"This is Operations Specialist Emma Sung. Watch for the *shadows*. The *ghosts*. I can't explain any better."

Her finger moved. The image froze.

Mizoguchi gestured to the holo. "The last contact from a transport convoy destroyed three weeks ago by Dram forces. Data recovery confirms the visuals. The ship was seconds away from coming apart. She was one cool customer."

"Or delusional and psychotic," said Marshall. "*Ghosts?*"

The major glowered at the medic. "Yes, it might seem. Except we have other TDS signals in recent months. All from devastating attacks on our deployments, and in several of them are reports sounding a lot like this one."

"What do you mean?" asked Williams.

"All report strange events. Creatures or powers penetrating all their defenses. Wreaking destruction on their personnel and machinery. Entities *not* Dram."

"Not the bugs?" asked Moore, his lip a sneer. "*Ghosts?*"

"Ghosts, Sergeant. Or shadows. Gas clouds. Force fields. Whatever you want. Different terms for the same phenomenon, it would appear."

He continued. "So, you're saying what has cost us territory across the galaxy, maybe lost us the whole fucking war, is a bunch of evil spirits attacking our ships?"

Mizoguchi shook her head. "What I'm telling you is that something has changed. Our enemies have a new weapon we do not understand and cannot counter."

"That's why we're here?" I hardly knew what to expect.

The major grunted. "We have a crisis. One that must be addressed immediately, or we may lose everything. The Daughter and her advisors have devised a plan. It is not a large-scale military engagement. We now know such efforts would be futile until we can dissect this threat."

"Then what?" asked Fox, her eyes narrowing.

"Guerrilla tactics. We will transport elite forces teams to several key locations in the Time Tree. These groups will be charged with two missions. The first is recon: find out what the hell we are up against and how to respond."

"The second?" I asked.

The map reappeared, the Dram-controlled scarlet sea ominous in the darkness. Three points grew in size and brightness.

"Sabotage. The Daughter has identified a critical set of nodes in the hyperspace paths. Congruences to impede. This will seal off the accessible routes to the regions we still control."

Thin blue lines connecting the Orbs appeared on the screen. They outlined the possible circuits through the Strings. When Mizoguchi pressed the highlighted positions, the web of interconnections disintegrated. The red area glowed alone.

"Removing String access, we isolate our foes in the vast interstellar distances."

"Won't this cut off many worlds depending on our protection?" asked Fox, her mouth gaping.

"Yes," said the major. "It cannot be avoided."

Marshall's hands were at his temples. "What will happen to them?"

"We don't know. They could be attacked. Or perhaps, with them isolated, our adversaries will focus on how to deal with the setback. But losing contact with intergalactic trade will precipitate food and energy catastrophes."

I probed further. "We have to hit all three of those points? Does the order matter?"

"No. However, doing them in sequence could result in the Dram deducing our purpose. This might lead to fortifications of the Orb projections in those systems."

"So we go in with multiple teams at the same time?"

"No," said the major. "There will be a single team."

"If they fortify the last two, it doesn't make sense," said Kim.

"It does if you understand the limitations of the engagement," barked Mizoguchi. "We can't send normal forces."

"Why not?" I asked.

"We have tried. We performed seven missions to various Orbs early on. None of them returned."

"Jesus." Moore whistled. "So a suicide mission."

"Perhaps not. Because those other operations lacked a critical element you will have."

No, they can't. My stomach lurched. "And what would that be, sir?"

"Ambra Dawn."

Fox gasped. "*The Daughter?*"

The major grunted.

Moore slapped his hands together. "Now that's worth signing up for! This whole *assignment* just got a hell of a lot more interesting!"

"Wait. We're missing something here," said Kim. "How are we supposed to get back once we take those nodes out? We'll be cut off, too!"

Mizoguchi waved him away. "You forget she doesn't need to travel through the Time Tree. She can open the Orbs."

Ancient history was becoming our practical reality.

She continued. "This decision is not a light one. Our safety has depended on her for two centuries. Our greatest battles fought through her. We have locked her behind protective walls. Those barriers keep her from fighting where she is needed. And they are no longer as safe as we once thought."

"What do you mean?" I asked.

"In addition to the nebulous threat our reports have brought to us, there is a far less vague one. A danger we anticipated. One that was sure to occur, although the day on which it would, was unknown. A peril to the Daughter herself."

"*What threat?*" I snapped.

"False Dawns, Captain Ratava. Biological clones of Ambra Dawn. Constructed from her eggs. Stolen when she was a prisoner on the enemy homeworld two hundred years ago. Ova used to create, to breed, to engineer *replicas,* recapitulating her powers."

"Is this for real?" asked Kim, his face scrunched.

"Reports and documentation of those attacks have now surfaced from several battle fronts. Images of a young woman. She resembles the Daughter. She opens spacetime wormholes and enters combat against our forces."

"*False Dawns?*" I repeated, my lips numb, the world spinning.

"How many do they have?" asked Williams, her voice still and quiet.

"We don't know."

"You don't *know?*" Kim blurted. "You mean they could have an army of them?"

"Unlikely. What they have achieved is a technical challenge. The Xix claim it is beyond their own technology, given the instability of human chromosomes. Then there is the trickier problem of randomness in neurological development. It's hard to breed an Ambra Dawn. Then you have to raise one. There is psychology, tumor growth, and many variables an alien race would have extreme difficulty with."

Moore shook his head. "Unlikely, but not unlikely enough."

"They may have had help," said the major.

"From who?" he asked.

"It's guesswork, but let us consider the facts. After centuries of devastating losses, the Dram counter with two breakthroughs in this war. Both are beyond anything they have ever done."

Fox cut in. "A species with tech better than on Xix? There's nothing like that in our galaxy. Who are they? Where are they coming from?"

"Another galaxy?" offered Kim.

"No," I said. "Only ours has the Orbs. We're isolated from other galaxies. There's no intergalactic travel."

"So far as we know," added Moore.

"Again, speculation," said Mizoguchi. "However, it is the leading theory in the Daughter's advisory circles is that our enemies work with other forces. The Xix are convinced they cannot have achieved these advances by themselves."

Williams sat back in her chair. "*Shadows* and *ghosts* tearing apart our ships, and now, the Dram have replicated the powers of Ambra Dawn." She shook her head in the long silence.

The major grimaced and closed the holo. The room lights switched on, transporting us from the galactic depths to our small briefing room. From existential darkness to a mundane illumination. Her voice was cold.

"We no longer have a monopoly on manipulating space and time."

Chapter 13

We only have to look at ourselves to see how intelligent life might develop into something we wouldn't want to meet.

Stephen Hawking

It was one of the hotter days for the festival, and the crowds were huge. Most came from the Six Cities and Temple itself. They were devoted pilgrims who had dedicated their lives to the service of the Daughter. The rest arrived from around the world. These were the fortunate souls receiving visitation visas for the event. In total, fifty thousand people gathered to celebrate the salvation of New Earth.

It was a security nightmare.

Exceptional mission or not, we still handled patrol alongside other MECHcore groups. With an exception. Our assignment landed us at the gate where she would speak to the crowds. It was a duty of some prestige that bothered other teams with more seniority. Our unusual suits also distinguished us. While the Xix had intended the mechs to handle specific dangers, I still didn't mind having one on me. After what we had learned recently, paranoia was at an all-time high.

I tried to keep a lighter heart and not think about the dark facts of the conflict. The Festival of Rebirth was the anniversary of the beginning of the Great War. It commemorated the salvation of our world and our emancipation from the tyranny of alien masters.

It was also the education of the entire populace. After the reversal of the Calamity, a New Earth really was born. One of a different time path in which the planet wasn't destroyed by the emperor. Humanity now shared a vague vision of annihilation, of horror unmade. A teaming population woke from a dream, discerning the reality of their slavery. That awakening sparked a global war to purge the Dram and their agents.

We won. We pressed our rebellion with the help of Ambra and the Xix throughout the galaxy. A terrible dictatorship based on fear and death was removed and thousands of worlds freed.

The Festival of Rebirth was still raw and real to our species. It was the greatest holiday on the planet. Few merely went through the motions. Many would make the pilgrimage to the Temple at least once in their lifetimes. Billions would watch the proceedings as it was broadcast to each gridpoint on the globe. Dawnists would worship. Skeptics would mock. Separatists would protest, and some would cross the line into terrorism. It was the same every year.

Except we knew, this year, things weren't going to be the same.

How would the masses react, on this day of all days, to the news the world might actually be ending after all? That our oppressors might hold the upper hand? Would there be panic? Would we come together? Would extremists grasp the outside threat, put down their arms, join the rest of the allied aliens? Or would they ramp up their claims of the Calamity hoax and the invasion of Earth by the Xix? I couldn't see the Terra First diehards converting over a broadcast by the Daughter. They immediately assumed everything she said was a lie.

The stakes were high, and the presentation would rattle

emotions. So our patrol wasn't an ordinary one at the Temple. We all felt the weight of events hanging over us.

In the middle of this anxiety, it was difficult to feel the joy of the day. I tried, despite the distractions. Hundreds of memories from childhood danced in my thoughts. Nights watching the Diwali lights relit for the Rebirth. A field trip to Dawn's Eyes, the Indian monument built by devout Hindus who took her as a contemporary avatar of God. Her face projected during the communion, when she reached from the Temple and shared her mind with Earth's Readers. Staring at the stars at night after the fireworks. Dreaming of her, imagining countless ways in which we would meet.

How could I know our actual meeting would be far more magical?

Most exciting was that I would be in her presence again when she spoke. This thought alone sent a wave of energy through me.

"MECHcore captains, this is Sepehr Mazandarani. Waythrel is now moving to the platform to introduce the Daughter. Please assume your secondary positions."

All the teams called back their affirmatives. On our select band, I made sure my group was in position. We were to be in front of the dignitaries and the largest crowds. The last thing I wanted was to miss any signs of terrorist activity.

"Roger, Captain," came Williams. "We're already there. Fox removed three civilians from the crowd earlier. Scans found weapons. Don't know how they got those in. Nothing in the databases about them. Not sure they were here to cause trouble, but they're eighty-sixed."

"Noted. Moore, how's the desert?"

"As fit for our bloody bones as it ever was, sir," he reported back. "Nothing growing, nothing moving."

"Marshall, status?"

"In position. Aid stations are operational and staffed. We've got a full triage unit as well. Ready for anything except a land war."

"Copy."

I picked up a swelling murmur from the crowd on the other communications bands.

"Waythrel is approaching."

Cheers rang for New Earth's most popular, and despised, alien life-form. A tall stand stood between the entrance garden of our arrival and the barren desert. It towered thirty feet above the ground with the crowds in front of it. A ramp from the main road into the Temple City ran along the back of the stage. Like some gymnastic octopus, the lanky Xix bounced forward onto the sloped platform. With its strange dexterity and speed, it was soon at the podium. Hologens captured the speaker and beamed it to projectors over the globe.

"Greetings, citizens of New Earth," it began. The amplification systems produced localized holosound encircling the crowd. A full minute of cheers and applause flooded the sands.

When it had died down, the alien continued. "We celebrate this New Year—273 AD. After Dawn. After a young woman stepped into a machine. It was an apparatus built not by members of her species, but by creatures strange, frightening to her. With enormous vulnerability, she placed her body into that threatening device. She opened her mind to share the consciousness of hundreds of others. Humans and nonhumans. They worked together in trust to achieve an exceptional purpose. As one, they unmade a terrible evil and birthed the beginning of a distinct timeline in the history of our galaxy."

Again, cheers and cries. The Xix weren't naive. I had no doubt the translator was coloring the words with the kind of charisma needed for this speech. It didn't bother me. The alien spoke the truth, however artfully. I felt my own heart stirred. This reality was part of what drew me into the military in the first place—to defend our world, our lives, and that which was most precious.

"Captain?" It was Fox. "Unusual readings coming out of my tensor field monitors. Over."

"Say again?"

"Spacetime distortions flickering nearby, localizing to...the desert. You're not seeing this?"

Waythrel continued. "In those early days, New Earth united to fight a common foe, and we achieved momentous things together."

"Negative. I'm reading nothing."

The alien paused, its eyestalks scanning in multiple directions at once. "For hundreds of years, we have worked as one to keep a lasting peace in our galaxy."

"I'm getting it too, Captain," said Moore. "It's behind the crowd, centered several hundred meters out in the sands."

I was too far from the source. I raced forward, past the audience, my dash in the gleaming MECHcore suit drawing stares. "What the hell is it?"

"Not sure," said Fox. "Signal's growing off the charts."

My stomach knotted. Intuition took over. "M-teams, this is Captain Ratava. All available suits to the Temple entrance—immediately!"

I lowered the volume from the nonmilitary channels.

Waythrel's voice murmured in the background. "Now, the Daughter needs you once again to achieve unity, commitment, a devotion to a cause."

I reached the crowd and headed behind them. My instruments were picking it up now. Most of my team had assembled nearby, and the other groups were closing.

"You see *that*?" yelled Kim, pointing forward.

I stopped in midair, staring. "By the Dawn..."

The desert sands, the air above it, the dunes in the distance—all were distorted. Space was embedded in crystal-clear rubber and some giant's hand was pulling on the material in front of us. I heard Waythrel speak through the broadcast but no longer could focus on the words.

"Kim! Alert the Daughter's security team, now!" I switched to a broader transmission band. "All M-teams, *combat alert*. I repeat, combat alert! Possible security breach at alpha point 7. Over." I toggled communications back to my team. "We may not have long."

I was right. Acknowledgments echoed from the M-core teams as the distortions swirled into a vortex. The clear rubber imploded, plunging into itself.

"It's a portal," gasped Williams.

The small gyre morphed into a whirlpool. The diameter increased fivefold, spanning hundreds of meters. The clarity of the passage faded, and it took on a hideous black-and-violet hue with endless depth. The doorway had fused with a tunnel.

A blast of air struck us, kicking up a wave of dust accelerating outward and raining across the crowds. An electromagnetic pulse nearly shorted out our suits. The hologens weren't so lucky. They exploded. The broadcast failed. Waythrel's voice ended in mid-sentence. Through the thick chassis of my battle suit, I heard the faint sounds of people screaming.

Streams from suitcams flickered in the corners of my view screen. Thousands of faces angled toward us and the growing disturbance.

What held my gaze was the portal itself. The entrance turned pitch black. Out of the darkness poured a battalion of Dram troops like a plague of locusts.

The chaos began.

Chapter 14

There is an urge and rage in people to destroy, to kill, to murder. Until all mankind, without exception, undergoes a great change, wars will be waged. Everything that has been built up, cultivated and grown, will be destroyed and disfigured, after which mankind will have to begin all over again.

Anne Frank

The enemy outnumbered us, but our fifty MECHcore soldiers held their own. Outfitted with the new AI modules of the Xix, we brought considerable firepower to bear as well.

But we weren't prepared for this. A terrorist attack, perhaps a core of trained assassins. Not an invasion force. In all our combat drills, in all the sims and imagined encounters, none of them involved the opening of a spacetime portal at our feet.

And out of the wormhole came the worms. Ten or twelve triads and the escorting companies of insectile Dram infantry. We never determined the exact number, the carnage obscuring details. They flooded the sand plains with weapons blazing. Assigned to the front of the festival activities, it was up to me to organize the response. I had moments to order our defenses.

"Equispaced grid assignments! All MECHcore units prepare for triad pairings. Commence AI maneuvers immediately!"

Williams fired back. "Captain, we have a solution—two triads!"

"*Two?*" We'd never engaged two. What was the crazy computer doing? No time to think. "Dance!"

Flechette rounds sprayed near us, but we dodged the needles. Our team locked into the algorithm, centering on the couple of triads—six worms in all—situated close to one another. It was one thing to buzz around with our thrusters orbiting one threesome. With two, it mimicked a crazed multi-star system with planets dancing between each ball of hydrogen. A wrong move and we'd be vaporized.

We whirled through a blinding geometrical nightmare. In our suits, at these speeds, the infantry was a nuisance, but we could handle those. We spun about the pair and blasted through their grunts with the ion slingers. Their charred forms littered the desert sands.

Most of our attention was on the worms. Despite taking on two, we held the advantage. The new AI was incredible. When they locked onto us, blasting a flechette round, the choreography left their guns off target. We closed in and readied the missiles.

"Confidence level reached, Captain," called Williams, her tone strained. A data read on my view screen told me she'd taken fire.

"Damage report, Officer."

"I've got a few minutes, sir. Give the order!"

"Take them down!"

We darted in and out of a mad fair ride. Now we would launch missile strikes from multiple directions. The height of insanity in any standard analysis. Until you have seen the dance, watched the blinding intricacies of the movement, your ideas of what is sane in combat are out of date.

We fired. Old-school chemistry-based-propellant, dual-EMP/solid-explosive warheads. The EM pulse drilled a hole in any field defenses. The explosives completed the task. Twelve missiles launched, two per worm, and we rocketed away to avoid debris. The triads were down in seconds. We spun back and mopped up the infantry cohort.

"I'm out, metalheads," said Williams. Her suit was venting black fumes and staggering in midair.

"Copy. Get your ass down on the ground." We needed a battlefield perspective now. "Status report, Kim."

A brief pause followed as he plowed through the tactical. We reoriented, forming a tight circle facing outward. "Eight down, sir! Minimal casualties for our forces. Wait. Yes, four hit, two confirmed fatalities. The civilian situation is FUBAR. A bloodbath."

Dear God. "Update on that wormhole."

"Empty of hostiles. We got this under control."

"Negative, Sergeant! We gotta shut that door. Get Central Command on the line. We need the Daughter out here! She's the only one who has a chance of closing it."

"Wilco, Captain!"

"As long as the portal's open, *anything* could come through."

And something did.

The first sign we were in trouble was the screams over MECH-core transmissions. Five suits were flung over us.

"What the hell?"

Kim broke in. "Gamma-3 group, sir. They danced past us toward that hole during the battle. Life signs flatlined. They're all dead."

The fight had pushed us to the left of the platform, up against the city walls where we downed our triads. The surrounding mayhem obscured the new events. I had a bad feeling about the situation.

"Alpha team—the spacetime countermeasures! Power them up now!"

It came, a cry over the COM, the chaos too wild to determine who. "False Dawn!"

"False Dawn, False Dawn!" Screams followed.

"The wormhole!" I shouted. "We're the only ones who can hope to engage!"

We fired our thrusters and blasted toward the spinning vortex.

And there she was.

A nightmare I could never have imagined. Standing at the base of the hell-tunnel was the small figure of a woman in a white robe. She glided forward, her arms upraised. Invisible forces slung MECHcore soldiers away from her like debris in a cyclone. The sand in front of her matted and compressed. Heat waves rose from the ground, reflective pools forming from glassified grains. Red hair fell from the sides of her bald and bulbous head. Her green eyes shone in my magnified view screen. It was Ambra Dawn.

And yet it was not.

Her gait spoke of a different personality. Facial features were similar but not identical to those of the Daughter. Her expression was vile, devoid of the depth and empathy I had come to associate with that face. Hideous cables and wires sprouted from regions of her skull. They embedded themselves at others—of medical or mechanical nature, I couldn't tell. A demon's fashioning of our savior, a fiend's torturing of an already tortured life.

I was going to destroy it.

"Semicircle around the thing!" I yelled, arming my final missiles. "Full tensor deflection on! Burn the batteries dead! We'll get one shot at her!"

My team responded. I detected the field activations. The warheads armed in other suits, and they struck the formation in seconds. The countermeasures allowed us to resist the spacetime warping that had doomed the other MECHcore teams.

"Launch!" Ten birds blasted toward the creature, closing in at several times the speed of sound.

All for nothing. The projectiles veered away, flying into the scorching desert. Moments later, their explosions shook the air. But we didn't have time to contemplate events.

My suit exploded. The chassis ripped from my body like some discarded exoskeleton. I hurtled to the ground with a terrible impact and screamed as I felt my right leg snap. The bone tore through the muscle of my thigh, blood spurting down my shattered limb to soak the sands.

I don't know how much time passed. I couldn't move, the pain blinding me, distorting my senses. I was half naked, stunned, cut off from my team and all communication.

I failed to protect her.

A shadow dimmed the sun, and a figure stood over me. It was the demon girl. An impostor with red hair and green eyes, who dared violate the sacred image of the Daughter. I grabbed at the vile form to beat the false life out of it, but I couldn't lift my arms. A power paralyzed me.

She entered me.

Her thoughts were a knife carving through my skull. Blades sliced inward against my will. Pushing, tearing, groping their way into my consciousness. My life, my memories, my feelings, my dreams. She sampled them all, holding me in contempt at every moment. Vulnerable, broken, my mind lay supine. Her corrupt Reader organ dug deeper into my being than I had ever gone.

The hot probe paused. The mental drill boring through my soul ceased spinning. The False Dawn yanked some structure of my awareness, tugging with the tentacles of its thought.

Its eyes widened. The monster smiled, grinning down at me with a hideous glare. It cut my psyche like a razor.

I howled. I cried out as I never had from any pain, any injury I had suffered. A child trapped in a nightmare he couldn't escape. My tormented spirit screamed for salvation.

Answering my call, the universe *shifted*.

I don't know how to explain it. A seismic event in spacetime. Nothing eyes could see or hands touch. Known in some buried, primitive place. The air undulated. Time stopped and started, phenomena strobing without meaning. A deep, infrasonic throb shook the center of my consciousness.

The False Dawn leaped up. The agonizing probes vanished, its hellish mind removed from my own. My body convulsed. I couldn't help myself. I wept. Tears flowed from sobs in profound relief and personal devastation.

Greater events unfolded. The remaining Dram triads imploded, crushed into objects hardly larger than a suitcase. Unseen power slung them to the side. Their infantry collapsed. Bodies intact, their forms dropped to the ground as if they had suffered some terrible stroke.

The creature's smile was gone. It scanned the battlefield and focused past me to the Temple. As a weak, pathetic worm, I arched my neck to see as well.

The Daughter arrived. She floated like some goddess descended from the heavens. The rubber matrix of reality about her puckered and warped, strained to a breaking point. She glided toward her clone. Her eyes were green fire, visible through sharp slits and under slanted red brows.

The monster threw her hands forward. Ripples of distortion exploded from her. The attack pulverized unfortunate souls between them. Torn inside out, aged or returned to fetal forms of themselves, it was like some sort of spacetime bomb.

It hit a wall of nothing in front of Ambra Dawn. A barrier refracted the environment like spray from a hose impacting a crystal sphere. *Space* and *time* splattered, bounced, and danced in multiple directions. Droplets of reality congealed in the air and floated. Events and places wobbled within them, winking out of existence in miniature vortexes. Rivers of the universe cascaded away from her. They ignored gravity, repelled by some incomprehensible force.

The False Dawn's jaw slackened. Her eyes widened and her arms fell to her sides.

The Daughter drew her hands together like someone raising a

precious package. The cyborg horror howled. It was a hateful cry, a furious rejection. She was lifted off the ground, her limbs twitching, her eyes wild. Ripples formed around her and became ropes of transparent nothing. This visible nonexistence wrapped her in a cocoon of solid emptiness.

Ambra eased beside the thing. Her doppelgänger thrashed, trapped twenty feet above the desert floor, gawking at her mirror image. Ambra closed her eyes.

The False Dawn arched her back in midair. Her green eyes rolled back in her head, her muscles rigid like the onset of rigor mortis. Whatever was left of time stuttered, and her body jerked from stillness to convulsions.

Yet she remained trapped. The Daughter's eyes were squeezed shut, her face strained. I shuddered in recognition. She had entered her enemy's mind.

Ambra's eyes flew open, and from the corners of my vision, shapes shifted. *Shadows.* Forms indescribable. An essence burned the edges of reality around their outlines. A viscous smoke flowed out of the wormhole, extending black fingers to the False Dawn. They wrapped tendrils across the imprisoned creature.

The tentacles pulled the monstrosity back toward them, the portal narrowing. *They're trying to rescue her!* The Daughter watched their efforts in silence, hovering over the desert.

As the ghosts closed about the clone, Ambra shut her eyes again.

The effect was like nothing I had ever known. Everything before paled in comparison. The military engagement. The powers of these two Readers distorting reality.

From a center, near the shadowed entities, from a point of nothingness, a force radiated. The impulse impacted me like an explosion, as well as a hallucinogen. Time and space, *meaning itself,* dissolved. The Daughter obliterated causality. I cannot explain any better. I have no words for it.

The creatures melted, blended, and like some chaotic ink, bled back into the tunnel. They screamed, but their screams did not take place in the medium of sound. I didn't know what I was experiencing.

Ambra flew forward. Her hand plunged through the distorted rubber prison around the False Dawn. She touched the creature's forehead with the flat of her palm, and the woman's head whipped backward. The clone floated limp in the cocoon. Blood dripped from the insertion points of some of the larger cables in her skull. Ambra waved both hands toward the woman, and the mimic catapulted into the tunnel. The enemy disappeared from sight.

She glared at the hole in space and scowled. Closing her fists, she slammed the portal shut. A stunning blast of sand erupted and rained about us.

A terrible silence fell. I had not recognized the churning noise until it ended. In this relative quiet, moans and cries drifted from the wounded.

She turned to me and glided beside my form, her feet lowering and resting on the ground by my chest. I could see tears in her eyes as she knelt and stroked my forehead.

"I'm so sorry, Nitin. Rest. It will be okay." Her voice was the most beautiful music I'd ever heard.

An enveloping warmth flooded through me, a profound sense of safety and belonging. And fatigue. Deep exhaustion. I couldn't keep my eyes open, and I lost consciousness.

Chapter 15

What you see and what you look at are two different things.

Ernest Hemingway

The walls of the tunnel extended without end.

Rough forces dragged me through its fire. Backward and forward, like some piston in an ancient combustion engine. I lost direction, orientation. Stars surrounded, peered with a cold intensity through the distorting tube. Silent. Still. Dispassionate.

I couldn't speak. I couldn't scream. I had no voice, no body. Back and forth. Stellar radiance blurred in acceleration and glared empty during lifetimes of stillness.

What am I?

Through the endless eon, I discovered polarity. Some order to space. Opposite charges, feelings, purposes. *Beings.* At one end, light and warmth. A terrible, wonderful love I could hardly encounter without being reborn in it. At the other, antagonism. Darkness. Anger burning to unmake. *Antipathy.*

From both ends, green eyes stared back at me through this infinite continuum. Green eyes in icy blackness. Laughing. Green eyes in sunlight. Weeping. Calling my name.

Nitin. Come to me.

Ambra, how? I can't. I can't move. Help!

Then I'll come to you, my heart.

Green and blue.

The green swayed in the blue, golden crowns dancing at the tops of towers. My eyelids twitched and shut in the bright light. Giants stomped on my shoulders, crushing my form into a clay mold.

Soil.

My hands opened and closed, my fingers scratching through dirt. The pillars unblurred.

Corn.

Energy coursed through me.

I know this place.

Weakness numbed. Pain paralyzed. I summoned a scream, but no sound escaped as I stretched myself to a sit. The middle of a giant cornfield greeted my eyes. My body was naked. My mind muddled, sloppy. I trembled with fear. Afraid of this strangeness, this vulnerability. Terrified for my sanity.

Ambra is here.

I stumbled to a stand. Legs olive stems bending in the breeze. Knees battering one another. Panting, I unbent my back, straightened to the clear sky. Quivers danced through me.

Wasn't I just here? In some recent dream. *What is real?*

I remembered the way. Limping forward, lethargic, I shook my head. *Faster.* I pushed. One foot, the next. Plop into the wet mud. *Again.* Walking. Straining. Pacing. Racing. I dashed through the maze of cornstalks. My heart thundered. Hope was adrenaline firing through my limbs.

I crashed from the corn and tripped to a grassy lawn. A farmhouse loomed before me. A figure stood in front of it.

"Nitin."

Her voice traveled undiminished across the yard.

My vision blurred from tears. Horror lodged like a tumor in my brain, threatening to grow and consume my identity. Repulsive digits ransacked my cells. I was broken. Lost.

Here is my haven.

A woman not twenty broke the blackness veiling my eyes. The image of the Daughter I had known and gazed on my entire life. Moon-milk white. Flamed in fire. Lucent with emeralds. Light whirling about her.

Yet different. Alive in a way I could never feel from holos. Transcendent in a tone this dream alone dared devise. Centered in a universe with no distractions. Without worries. Revolving around us.

"Ambra?"

She too stood naked. My eyes darted across the lines and curves of her body. Desire pumped through me. Awe at the depth of her beauty.

She approached. "Do you know where we are?"

I blinked. "No. A farm?"

"*My farm*, Nitin," she said, taking my arm in hers, her teeth bright beneath her shining eyes.

She tugged me, ushering toward the house. "I was born here. Spent eleven years under this roof." Her voice lilted and sung, reciting a magical tale. "You burst from our cornfields. They go on until it seems like the world will end before you get out of them. My father labored out there. The big companies always wanted to swallow us up. He was determined to stay independent. He hated them and how they killed the plains."

She stopped halfway across the backyard. Her arm painted the open expanse of land extending from their property.

"Isn't it beautiful?"

The terrain continued further than my eyes could focus. Flat but for a slope enhancing the view from our position. Browns and greens and houses dotted the endless plain. The cyan sky faded at the horizon. There, grayed and blackened, it crashed into a bubbling mountain range of clouds. Lightning flashed within them a million miles away.

"A storm is coming," I said.

"Many," said Ambra. Her smile was gone. "But they aren't here yet. We have a short time."

"Please don't go away."

I remembered the other dream. *Memories of dreams in a dream.* I tried to suppress tears, but so much emotion flowed over me I was overcome. The wild creativity of fantasy released my imagination. I babbled as ideas rushed through my mind.

"Let me rest here. With you. I can't take the hole anymore. It's eating me. My whole life. No one understands. I can't face the hurricane of emptiness." I trailed off, a nightmare lurking behind my conscious thoughts. A monster hunting and haunting, intangible, as real as myself. I pushed it away.

"I understand," she said, placing her hand on my face.

"Here," I pleaded, "it's safe with you. It's right. Please, can we stay?"

She shook her head, her voice low. "I'm sorry, Nitin. We can't."

"So, I'm dreaming. This is all a lie?"

"Dreams are not lies. Dreams are other spaces. Other times. Realities inside larger places. Bubbles within seas. Sometimes a person can remain in the bubble and ride out the storms. Never leave the dream."

I turned back to the dark clouds, no closer yet no less threatening. "But we can't."

"No, we can't. And it's my fault." She sighed.

A tan-and-white streak sped around the corner of the house. Before I could process, she released my arm, and the blur leaped into the air. She embraced an enormous pile of hair. I recognized it as some sort of sheepdog.

The animal licked her face and trembled with excitement. Its fur was copious, thick and silky, giving the dog an appearance of being overweight.

Ambra laughed as she cuddled the pet. "This is Matt, Nitin." She turned the fluff toward me.

Dogs do not have the popularity in India they do in Western nations. My experience was more with street strays than manicured breeds. They were usually diseased beggars or aggressive biters. Hesitant, I reached out my hand.

"Turn your palm down and bring it below his nose."

I did so, and it sniffed me. Satisfied, but not taken with me, he returned his attention to Ambra.

"I saw him die, you know," she said. "First in a vision. It was horrible." Her face clouded as she squeezed the animal a little too tightly, and the dog twitched its paws. "I couldn't stop it. I didn't even know what it was at that age. Later, even when I understood my powers, I had to let Earth die."

"You did it to save so much more. So many worlds! In the end, you brought us back!"

"Success doesn't change the choice. Or the damage of making it."

"Don't blame yourself."

She shook her head. "If you could only see. I am a frightening nexus of cause and effect. It was my fault my parents died. Servants of the Dram killed them, butchered them to get to me. My responsibility an entire planet full of life boiled. And it's my doing we can't stay here." She touched my cheek again and smiled. "Where it's safe."

I reached out and held her hand, the porcelain hue like a beam of light in my palm. "It's okay. I knew we couldn't. I felt it. I can't explain how much I need you."

She searched my face. "You're the handsomest man I'll ever not see." I blushed as she laughed. "Do you know what I feel most being close to you? Warmth and *smell*. You know I can see in my weird way. I can see your features. I've *seen* them in ways you don't even know. And you *are* handsome to me, Nitin. I've had crushes and infatuations, but the first time I saw you—the many times I've watched you—always such power! It's underneath conscious thought. But I do not see you with my true eyes. All those pathways in my brain atrophied centuries ago. All to the service of my tumor."

"You speak like it's evil."

"It is."

"It's what has saved us!"

"And killed billions." She gazed over the plains toward the storm. The dog jumped down. Nose to the ground, it began an indecipherable olfactory quest across the grass. "You grew up with the powers of this thing in my skull as a force for liberation. Living with it, what it has done to me and others, what it will do—nothing is ever as it seems."

It was unsettling to hear her pain. Wrecking to see the lines on her face. The tension in her muscles. The sad hollowness in her unseeing eyes. History lessons lie sterile on the page. Imagining the torments of another's life is an important exercise, but so limited. A five-minute conversation in the middle of a dream conveyed infinitely more.

"I want to understand, Ambra. I want to know everything about you."

"I know you do. You will, beyond what you have imagined. A few steps at a time. That's how we climb to the Temple. Hand in hand."

She inhaled from her stomach, closing her eyes. "*Smell.* Waythrel said something about immune receptors and genetics and mate selection. It's all a blur. Biology. Isn't it strange how so much of what we are and know and feel are chemicals and cells?"

"We are what we are."

"Yes. Even the Readers don't know what that is."

She sniffed again, dipping her head close to my neck. Her breath sent shudders through me. "I could eat you up!" She paused as my body tensed, a bow ready to fire.

"Walk with me, Nitin," she sighed, pulling back. "Away from the storm. Or I'll want to entangle us right here and now. But it's the wrong time. The wrong place."

My throat was dry, and my hairs stood on end. I felt things stirring below, embarrassment again coloring my cheeks. She pulled me toward the side of the house. The growing thunderheads moved to our backs, and we faced a bright sun halfway to noon.

"It *is* beautiful," I managed.

I had never seen America's Great Plains. I had imagined that the sameness, the flatness, the agricultural devotion of the land would be monotonous. Boring. In a way, it was, until you drank in the enormity of it. The fields were a sea of different colored crops cresting here and there. Houses like small boats drifted across the waves. The storm was majestic in an awful kind of way as it poured forward like lava from a volcano.

"This is what imprinted me," she said. "Shaped and programmed the impressionable mind of a little girl. I guess I was born to see into distances. I can never go back to this place, as much for where I must go as for what terrible things happened here."

The land she loved, and yet a soil stained with the blood of her parents. Why were we here? Where was she going that she couldn't stay?

We came because you approach my heart, its light and darkness. We arrived in your search to return from the unlight of the clone monster. We swim in these currents because existence is layer upon layer of dream within dream.

At the mention of the False Dawn, a nightmare threatened to rage into my consciousness. I shivered, and she clasped my hand.

"There, Nitin! So much glory!"

She waved her hand over the fields. The air shimmered and swayed, and a passage opened. In the middle of the bright daylight, a necklace of gemstone stars exploded.

She pulled me forward into the breached space. We stepped through the day on Earth onto the sands of an alien beach. Strange seas crashed at my toes. Above was a churning miracle of radiance—an entire galaxy painted across the night sky.

Ambra slid her naked form against me and pressed her lips to mine, her eyes capturing my gaze. She placed a hand on my chest, near my heart. My breathing deepened and quickened. She whispered into my ear.

"I'm with you, Nitin. Always. Never forget. Follow my voice as you did to get here. You will find your way home."

"Is this home?" I wondered.

"One of many," she said, smiling. "A place to visit in another dream. Here we'll love each other on these sands."

Chapter 16

Once again, I woke from trauma in a hospital bed, staring up into the forest of eyestalks of a Xixian medic.

Where was this? Where had I been? What day I had woken into? The room was strange. I didn't know it. I did not recognize the Xix. I was thankful I could recall my own name.

A tunnel.

The long horror floated through my awareness. Endless anguish. Worm triads in the Thar. Japanese nurses.

No, that was before.

The Sahara. A new team. *Yes!* A unique mission to salvage the war.

A wormhole.

I shuddered and closed my eyes. It came back. Hell wrapped her fiery fingers around my throat. The monster scarred my mind, her thought tendrils probing sensitive tissues. Ruining me. Sullying my soul. I was unclean. *Used.*

A warm sensation pressed against my hand. I turned my sore neck, my eyelids blinking, staring into green, blind eyes once again.

Not the clone. Eyes that embraced and did not wound.

"It's okay," she said. "Don't think of her." Her hand squeezed mine.

"Daughter of Time." I didn't know what else to say. Echoes of a dream washed over me. *Did it happen? Is this real?*

"I am more than that to you, my Nitin." She smiled. It was soft and lined with sorrow. I had never felt so much love poured toward me. "Say my name."

I choked out the word, hardly suppressing the tears. "Ambra."

I was in no state to analyze what was happening, what had happened. There could be no sequence of events I could concoct leading to this moment. Nothing I could conjure in my imagination that would place the Daughter at my bedside. Holding my hand. Speaking impossible words.

"My heart," she said, her face radiant.

You don't have to understand, Nitin. Her voice in my mind again. *Accept what you know is true. There will be a time to talk more.*

"Yes. Please." I closed my eyes as emotion overcame me. I couldn't process my experiences. Other memories flooded back. "What happened? My team?"

A familiar tone. "They are recovering nearby."

Waythrel. I shifted my gaze to the looming bulk of the extraterrestrial.

"Most of the injuries were moderate, like your leg," it said.

Moderate? I studied my wounded thigh. Little evidence remained of damage. A hairline scar peaked from where the bone had torn through.

"Which aren't moderate?"

"Medical Sergeant Ryan Marshall died before we could reach

him. He spent his last moments tending to the others. He saved many lives." The alien gave him a moment of silence. "The rest of your team has returned to the barracks. They recommenced training yesterday."

"Wait. Why am I still here?"

The medic cut in. "Because your injuries were more severe."

I glanced down at my leg, but it corrected me.

"Not to your body. To your psyche."

Ambra reached over and brushed her fingers against my forehead. "She did terrible things to you, Nitin." Her face constricted. "An act of violence and power as unnecessary as it was cruel."

The alien doctor explained. "The mind, or rather the neurological support framework giving birth to the epiphenomenon, is fragile, Captain Ratava. We had to move quickly, or much of the damage would have become permanent."

"Damage."

"Psychological trauma, and through it, physical wounds," said Waythrel. "The matter of the brain and its associated consciousness are like a particle and a wave in quantum theory. Two aspects of a greater whole. Injury to one impacts the other. We made repairs at the level of biology. For the sentience field that is your mind, we needed a different kind of doctor."

"Ambra." I turned back and drank her gaze. Green jewels spilling water.

"She did not leave your side for seven days."

Her fingers wiped away tears. "Until I knew I could do no more."

A week? I wasn't sure how to believe it. The Daughter had devoted herself to my sickbed even as the war effort collapsed. And how to accept that my proper recovery demanded such an investment?

I shuddered. "I still feel that thing in my head."

"Even with her ministrations, it was impossible you would suffer no lasting effects from a mind probe of this nature," said the medic.

"We can assure you that your cognitive functions are unharmed. Psychologically, there will be residual pain."

I turned to Ambra. "Thank you." I spoke to the others as well. "I'm grateful to you all."

I couldn't convey the gratitude at having the horrible invader erased, even incompletely. Otherwise, I'd have gone mad.

Fatigue crept over me, but questions bubbled through my consciousness.

"I saw...*shadows*. Like in the reports. Were they real?"

"Yes," Waythrel confirmed.

"What are they?"

"Nothing like we have encountered in this galaxy. By showing themselves here, they have revealed much to us. Some equipment survived the battle. Together with the Daughter's observations, they have provided critical information. Enough for us to begin assembling a model for what we are dealing with."

"Why did they come?" I asked.

"We don't think they meant to," said Ambra. "They were overconfident in their red-headed Frankenstein. The clone wasn't supposed to fail so completely."

"At the least, they probably assumed their Reader could retreat and return," said the Xix. "When it was clear she could not escape from the Daughter, they intervened."

"So, they were close. Waiting."

"Yes. Hiding in the corners of spacetime. Whatever they are, they have extremely advanced technology. Not developed enough to control a wormhole—they still needed their engineered copy. However, they can exploit the manipulations of the continuum, cache unseen within the folds of reality."

"You defeated them," I said, a note of pride I didn't intend to voice.

She pressed my hand again. "They aren't supernatural, Nitin. They're made of matter, like everything else."

"With one exception," finished Waythrel.

An exception to material existence? "What do you mean?"

"They are creatures wholly composed of antimatter."

"Antimatter?" Had I misheard? "Wouldn't they explode or something in our atmosphere?"

"We are unsure how they manage to shield themselves, but they expend enormous energy to do so," said the Xix. "Since they are very much natural entities, the Daughter was able to deal with them."

"Then we have a chance," I said, finding myself slipping into sleep. "The mission. There's hope."

"Yes," said Ambra, smiling. "We can talk more when you're stronger."

She bent over and kissed my cheek, whispering in my ear. Her breath was warm and raised bumps over my body. "Soon, we'll walk among the stars, Nitin Ratava. For a time, you will experience how beautiful they are."

Her words whirled like poetry, haunting, comforting. I sank into the bed, spinning toward a deep slumber.

Chapter 17

Jealousy does not wait for reasons.

Gandhi

The clinic staff had turned in for the evening. I lay alone with flashing monitors and a night-shift nurse at her station in the hallway. Tomorrow, they'd release me. I'd rejoin my team. We were to meet with Ambra and her advisors to finalize the mission plans.

Days of intensive rehab proved Xixian medicine was miraculous. My shattered leg was like new. My physical conditioning, optimal. Short drills in my suit showed little degradation in performance. Attention-deficit red flags remained. It would take a lot more time to smooth out the mental damage the monster had inflicted on my psyche.

I didn't notice the effects during my daily activities. Nights were another story. I dreaded them and began to fear my own dreams. I needed to get this thing out of my head. The sleep deprivation alone was going to end up making me dysfunctional.

He came during this last evening in the hospital, after midnight on a full moon. A silver light mingled with the LEDs of the medical equipment. I wasn't sleeping. Another nightmare had startled me awake. I was wiping the sweat from my forehead when I heard footsteps in the corridor outside my room. Not the soft padding of the night nurse, but a heavier, more assertive gait.

I propped myself up on the bed and listened. Oddly, I welcomed this unsettling visitor. It gave me something concrete to consider. Far preferable to the ghostly remnants of a mental assault.

The steps stopped beside my door. A tone sounded, indicating an activation of the external touchpad. The door dissolved as a male figure stepped into the room.

"I understand that you sleep poorly at night."

It was Sepehr Mazandarani, the counselor to Ambra Dawn. In this moonlit dark, his devilish features were exaggerated, caricatured. It was with some apprehension that I watched him pull a chair over to my bedside.

"News travels," I said, a sense of threat palpable from this man.

He smirked, waving away my comment. "I am the Daughter's closest advisor. *Human*, anyway. Her thoughts are rarely hidden from me."

"Are you a Reader? Do you commune with her?"

His face tightened. "No. She employs me for other talents that I can offer."

He enjoyed my discomfort.

"What might those be?"

Again, the grin. "Analysis. Logic. Strategy. She relies heavily on my counsel."

"Yes, you're an important man."

He cocked his head to the side and laughed. "I did not come here to monkey dance with you, Ratava."

"Good. Why are you here, then?"

His eyes narrowed, his upper lip curling. "I don't dance, Captain. I act when I have the information to do so. Right now, I don't have such data, except for circumstantial evidence. It has me concerned greatly for the safety and well-being of the Daughter."

I pushed myself upright. "What do you mean?"

"In your desert heroics at the Rebirth, you were present at an event that has never occurred. *Never* has there been an attack at the Temple. Not in two hundred years."

"Yes, I know."

"Furthermore," he continued, cutting me off, "in order for the clone and its allies to have breached the Xixian defense fields, they would have needed help. From *inside*. Our security systems scramble the four-space position of the Six Cities. No Reader can locate us within a parsec or millennium. Opening a wormhole at the perfect location and moment to attempt an assassination? Well, this requires a device, a beacon of some sort. The homing signal must broadcast from here."

"What are you saying?"

He locked eyes with me. "We have a traitor in our midst, Captain."

In the Temple? It was impossible. I had seen the devotion of the people here. I couldn't imagine any of them aiding our enemies. The foes not just of Ambra Dawn but of the entire human species. The terrorist groups might hate the Daughter, but they hated the aliens more. Besides, how could they get a spy past her? She could read minds. She could predict the future!

"What do the Xix say? What does Waythrel say?"

"It was *their* hypothesis. They know the nature of the defenses they have established. Protections they are now modifying to prevent a repeat event."

"Who would do such a thing?"

"We don't know. But I will tell you, Captain—I am going to find out." His face boiled, an anger bubbling beneath.

My thoughts churned. Something was wrong. His presence, his delivery of sensitive information like this, made little sense.

"Why are you telling me this now?"

"The Daughter has developed a particular empathy toward you. At best, I hope to persuade you to take this threat seriously and to do all you can to protect her."

"At worst?"

He stood and grasped the neckline of his black robes, sneering at me like he might a desert roach. "I don't like anomalies, Captain Ratava. Unexplainable events or people. Your resume as it concerns Ambra Dawn is strange beyond explanation. You have single-mindedly aimed your career trajectory like a missile. All to place yourself precisely in this location. At this time. You offer unconditional emotion to her, immediately winning her attention and confidence. Following your arrival, after centuries of peace, our defenses are breached from within and the Daughter attacked."

Warmth drained from my body. "You can't be serious."

"Circumstantial evidence, Captain. But rest assured, if it ever becomes more, I will be the first one with a gun to your head."

He spun on his heels and marched out of the room.

Chapter 18

If we have learned one thing from the history of invention and discovery, it is that, in the long run—and often in the short one—the most daring prophecies seem laughably conservative.

Arthur C. Clarke

A suspicious Mazandarani escorted us across the Temple City. The Dish loomed above, its height impossible to grasp. Our route entered within the ten-kilometer radius of the supporting structures.

We passed massive columns of alien metal that plunged into the sand. The base supports themselves were as broad as buildings. Webbed shadows of the architecture littered our path in the setting sun.

We halted at the entrance to a beautiful building, a well-realized blend of human and Xixian tastes. The construction rose seven or eight stories, resembling a strange plant or deep-sea organism. The largest expanse was at the top, a toroidal curvilinear solid. It seemed to float above the desert, supported in reality by tapering columns.

These six pillars morphed to ellipsoids at their apex. The torus rested on the smaller objects that flowed into the ground. The material mimicked the indestructible concrete in the buildings of the surrounding cities. The tan color blended into the sands.

The walls appeared porous in places. Complex, flower-like geometrical patterns scampered across the surfaces of the bulbous toroid. Our local star dipped below the horizon and a radiance flooded from those thinner regions of the structure. It suggested an enormous Japanese lantern crossed with a bioluminescent jellyfish from the depths.

The Temple.

There had never been a holo to emerge from the Sahara. Here, the Daughter met with some of New Earth's most farsighted Readers. Joining them were many from different alien species. Together, they entered into a group trance, their minds connecting in the medium of space and time. Many claimed they formed a community consciousness greater than the sum of its individuals. This mind had once traveled back in time and unmade history. I neared the epicenter of our power in the galaxy.

We climbed thirty broad steps below the entrance, passing beneath an expansive arch. Carved into its surface were symbols of both extraterrestrial and human origin. The doorway opened to a cavernous chamber. The curved walls within were far larger than they were from the outside. Smaller patterns on the external face took on exaggerated dimensions inside.

What stole my eye was the source of the glow seeping through the etched motifs. In the middle of this vast space, undulated a brightness I compare to a plasma. A superheated state of matter, with colors flowing and merging in constant motion.

Its iridescent shape was hard to fathom. From a distance, with a brief glance, I assumed it was spherical. The longer I gazed, the closer I approached, I caught hints of an irregular geometry. Its configuration altered with each heartbeat. I glimpsed pieces, projections, sides of the full entity. They phased in and out of perception. It was dizzying.

Centered in this terrible and unearthly energy was a dais. It had the dimensions of a small table, obsidian. It connected to the pulsing chromatic field through numerous extensions. Many appeared alive, like slick tree roots.

I identified the structure from legend—the Xixian-designed seat of power for Ambra Dawn. Where she linked to the devices amplifying her modulations of the spacetime matrix. Placed radially around this central point were several hundred depressions. These were additional seats built into the Temple floor for the Reader cohort.

Despite the presence of such a potent energy source, I felt nothing. No disorienting sickness mirroring that in the battle between the Daughter and the False Dawn. No sense of electricity or heat. The air was still except near the entrance where the Saharan winds approached and died. I didn't see a grain of sand anywhere in the chamber.

"They sure don't go halfway," said Moore. He and the other members of the team gawked at the vision before them.

"There's some kind of geometrical distortion here," said Fox. "Spacetime funkiness. It's bigger inside than out."

"Yeah, noticed that," said Williams. "What do you suppose the glowing glob is in the middle?"

A voice answered from in front of us. "A doorway to the Orb."

Stepping out of fog and darkness, the Daughter appeared. Waythrel and Major Mizoguchi flanked her. The three approached as Mazandarani left our side and took a place beside the older soldier.

"The Orb?" asked Kim. "How is that possible? We're on New Earth."

"The geometry of time and space is not intuitive, Sergeant," said the Xix. "We could give you more detailed explanations, but we are here to discuss more pressing matters."

"Why in here?" I asked.

Ambra smiled. "It will become clear soon. Please, take a seat."

She gestured at the floor in front of her and rested crossed-legged. Her motions were fluid, the dark robes flowing over her like water. The advisors, including the alien, also lowered themselves. I glanced at my team and shrugged. We sat.

"With their victories, our enemies grow more bold," said Mizoguchi. "We hope the compete destruction of their recent attack force will slow them. Provide us the opportunity to develop our countermeasures."

"In addition, Ambra has sent them a message," said Waythrel. "She cast back at them the dead body of the clone prior to closing the wormhole."

"Yes," I said remembering. "What did you do to her?"

Ambra's shoulders slumped. She winced. "I examined her consciousness, to understand what she was, what had motivated her. So much darkness. The Dram have programmed their clones with extreme hatred toward us. Little hope to reach out to that pitiable thing." She shook her head. "No saving her, no chance to keep her prisoner. I couldn't let her return. So, I wiped her mind."

Moore leaned forward, his long legs splayed in his seated position. "You did what?"

Ambra sighed. "A telepathic overload. A destruction of her mental spacetime matrix that scrambles all coherence."

"The biological portion of her awareness, her brain, was reduced to pulp," said Mazandarani. "You can think of it as *frying* her neurons."

"What this means," said Waythrel, "is that our enemies will learn nothing from her. Nothing from their attack except that we hold a power they do not yet know how to counter. A cohort of their new allies was destroyed."

Mizoguchi focused on the coming task. "Because of these recent attacks, we have decided to accelerate the covert operation. You will be leaving shortly for your first target node."

"Today?" I'd just stepped out of the hospital.

"Whoa, wait a minute. Time out," said Kim. "What about recon? Mission prep? Stuff we like to do to stay alive."

Williams cut in. "We're not just going to jump to some random system without knowing anything about it."

The major answered. "Of course not. Do not insult me with such a concern."

"Then what?" Kim asked.

Mizoguchi bowed toward the Daughter, and Ambra picked up the discussion.

"If you are willing, you can learn everything about the locations in the next few minutes. We can save days of briefings and holocrystals."

"How might we do that?" asked Moore.

"By opening your mind to me. With your permission, I can share the information telepathically. No need for slower and more cumbersome methods."

The Brit recoiled. "Hold it right there, princess. No one's crawling inside my noggin—you understand?"

"Sergeant—" I began.

"Sorry, sir, but no fucking way."

Mazandarani scowled at Moore. "There is nothing to fear unless you have something to hide."

"Yeah, I got a lot of things to hide," said Moore, leaning back and smirking at the counselor. "Like what me and the mechanic girl were doing under the engine hoist the other night. Or what I think of that minger growing on your chin."

"The Daughter is discreet," said Waythrel. "Such sharing is a daily experience with the Xix. It unifies us, eases misunderstandings, and grants us an efficiency and group memory we would not otherwise possess. She has now brought this gift to your species. Already, the Readers of New Earth are united in this way. Especially those who have taken part in the sharings here at the Temple."

"It sounds amazing," said Fox.

"What do you mean, discreet?" Williams asked.

Ambra spoke. "She means I'm careful to touch only those aspects of your consciousness I'm required to. I won't pry into your thoughts or memories. I'll learn from you only what you want to share with me. Since none of you are Readers, you can't, through me, invade one another's minds. Only I can reach out to each of you."

My pulse raced. I couldn't believe the privilege she offered. While I could understand the concerns of Moore and Williams, my heart responded like Fox's. I desired nothing more than to have her mind connect with mine. I dared not speak of it. I feared my eagerness would spook the members of my team.

Kim raised his hand. "You said we could show what we wanted. What do you mean? Are we going to hear your voice in our heads and point thoughts at it? See your face? Exactly what the hell's going to happen?"

Ambra smiled. "It's a different experience for every person. Not one that has simple physical correlates like those you mention."

"I can answer this," said Mazandarani, still keeping an eye on the hulking soldier. "I'm not a Reader, but I have shared like this many times with the Daughter. It is a sense of another's personality—their soul, for lack of a better word. An understanding of their nature not bound to their appearance or voice or words. The Daughter's spirit will envelope you. You won't have to do all the work of getting to know her. It will simply be there, filling your awareness."

"By the Dawn," said Fox.

Moore scowled. "Well, what if I don't want to get to know you that badly?"

"I accept your choices," she said. "I respect any of you who refuse."

"Then what? We're out?"

"No," she answered. "The others can brief you en route and at the site. Only they'll know far more, and you'll be playing catch-up."

He didn't hesitate. "Count me the hell out, then." He leaned back on his elbows.

"Williams?" I asked.

Her frown showed she wasn't too keen on the idea, either. My warrant officer stared straight at Ambra for half a minute. I didn't know what her internal battle was, but in the end, she accepted the sharing. "I calculate the gains outweigh the losses."

Mazandarani spoke. "Am I to assume the rest of you are in favor? Except for the sergeant, of course."

We agreed.

Moore rose. "So, what, I go wait outside or something?"

"Not necessary," said Ambra. "Please don't disturb us until we wake."

"Wake?" asked Kim.

"From the trance," said the Iranian. "You don't think the Daughter will enter your mind and download a week's worth of material and you'll continue to chat?"

They contemplated this in silence.

Waythrel guided us. "Try to calm your feelings. It usually helps for humans to close their eyes."

I closed my eyes. I tried to relax by imagining the surrounding environment. My thoughts moved to the rip in space that had embedded a segment of the Orb in this chamber. The spinning colors in their bizarre paths hypnotized me.

For a few minutes, I heard nothing but the soft breathing of those near me. The faint, dying howls of the winds outside accompanied them. The haunting cries of a tortured land.

The room grew quieter. I felt the rhythm of my heartbeat, the blood throbbing in my ears. The pounding intensified. The beats assumed shapes. Forms of the cardiac muscle. Vessels straining under pressure. Corpuscles coursing in spurts through my body. Blue to red. Lung to heart. Webs of alveoli opening, ballooning.

Cells adopted the patterns of vast continents stretching to the horizon. All embedded in the pulse and pound. Each oscillation brought a wave of gray particles. Molecules of oxygen trapped and fed to contorted monsters, bands of chained atoms with a central core not unlike the dais of Ambra Dawn.

Inward I sank. Past protein to amino acids, carbon bonds. Electrons danced about me, nebulous, unreal and alive. Crossing thousands of times the distance before I floated to a glowing center like the heart of a star. The nucleus exploded to reveal quarks and strings and elements I had no words for. They whirled through me in confusing motions.

Whiplash—everything reversed. The bizarre building blocks took on the shapes of atoms. Simple structures of the simplest element— hydrogen. At speeds never experienced, I raced from this microscopic labyrinth into the depths of space.

A nebula. Nearby, a celestial cluster painted the gas cloud in a shimmering spectrum. A band of diamonds coated the heavens opposite me. Thousands of stars.

An ocean world, blue and reflective in the blackness of the void. It spun about a star.

Between them, the dancing colors I had seen in the Temple in their full context—the Orb.

Chapter 19

The more you see how strangely Nature behaves, the harder it is to make a model that explains how even the simplest phenomena actually work. One does not, by knowing all the physical laws as we know them today, immediately obtain an understanding of anything much.

Richard Feynman

Three star systems, their planets, the location of the Orb in each system. I lived multiple lives in those distant spaces. Ages flowed through me, images and cultures and locales. It was like no learning experience I had ever known.

I sat passive in the beginning. I let the Daughter do whatever it was she had to do to plant this information in my mind. The flood of knowledge was consuming. An avalanche of places and times and events. Entire histories of other species and their planets. Somehow, it was all hers to share, as if she had spent eons across every point in space. Her vision was with a god's eyes. So much poured through me, it bordered on surreal. I can't explain how the process translated into operational facts. I wasn't conscious of any learning, solely endless experience.

Later, woken from the trance, I retained the data on the targets to complete our mission. More than I needed. I had become a citizen of each world, a historian and anthropologist. An organic library.

By the lesson of the last system, the third String projection, the journey was familiar. The brain is an adaptation machine. Already mine was finding an equilibrium with the incredible. I turned restless. Searching. Reaching out into the blackness for her.

Nitin.

She whispered my name. The warmth and love I'd sensed in the hospital bed tended me. A thousandfold stronger.

Follow my voice. Come to me.

An Orb.

All space fell to black, the star systems gone, the background of the galaxy missing. The information flow arrested.

Remaining was the mystical sphere. It grew, or I approached it at reckless speed. I couldn't tell which. Without any reference points, size and motion were relative.

Patterns, colors, *passages* rippled across the enormous surface. Not a surface! A reflective ocean skin, an illusion blanketing fathoms of mystery.

The power of the thing. A terrible, monstrous depth and abstraction froze my heart. Cold, dark, like the bottom of the deepest chasm in the sea.

Yet warmth. At the same time, in the midst of the alien and transcendent, empathy emanated. A vibrational resonance connecting me and the Orb. Pure. Guileless. Limitless *affection*.

The object spanned the width of my peripheral vision. The multidimensional corridors frothed beneath the churning waves, transforming into enormous rivers. I was a dust mote beside an ocean.

Nitin, come.

She called from within the god-sphere. Her psyche resonated in my body, a forgotten flesh tranced in the Saharan Temple. I hesitated —a heartbeat staring at the anomaly—and I steeled my courage, willing myself to her.

Acceleration wrenched my awareness forward. A madness of dimensional mazes darted past me. Her presence turned pervasive. The Orb merged with her.

No. Screams. Panicked cries. *Not my voice.* Yanked. Slung, hurled back and forth. *Lights in an endless tunnel.*

My dream? The nightmare nontube bent and twisted. Hyperspace knots burned the fabric of space. The stars assumed hideous rainbows of distorted color.

Cold hands. Cruel fingers. Pulling, tearing at me. Control, breaking my form, remaking it, demanding pounds of my flesh.

Excruciated. Formless, I felt my teeth grind. My nonbody spasm. My unback arch. The substanceless skin over my ghost frame stretching, ripping from a merciless strain.

I screamed. I wailed down this Orb funnel of hell where time spiraled and spun and completed a spiral to re-unbecome.

Full circle in multiple dimensions. I crashed howling face-first into the onrushing madness of my own torment.

Chapter 20

My heart, the bird of the wilderness, has found its sky in your eyes.

The Gardener by Rabindranath Tagore

Waves.

Waves crashing. Foam frothing through my consciousness. Sea and wind. Water wrung over rock. A breeze brushing my face. *Warmth.*

"Nitin, wake up."

I opened my eyes to green. A viridescent evening glow of alien vegetation. A forest of bizarre trees climbed around me. Their fluorescence glinted off the ocean.

And the emeralds of her eyes.

I lay on my back, coarse grains underneath. The heavens exploded in shape-shifting majesty. Auroras shimmied through the atmosphere as mad dancers. Behind them, a roiling vortex of light. A riot of stars. An entire spiral galaxy splayed out across the night sky. Distant suns winked in hues of gold, crimson, and purple. Fine gemstones.

Like the two jade jewels embracing me with their glance.

Ambra stared into my eyes. Her knees pressed into the sand beside me, water lapping the black robes trailing her. Her hands held mine over my chest.

"My Nitin." She smiled.

For some time, I could not respond. Could not move. The shock of my experiences, the devastating beauty of the planet, they overwhelmed my mind. Her form alongside my own—I was powerless. Once again unmade by her.

She reached one hand behind my neck and pulled. It seemed I weighed tons. My body was sore, every muscle and joint. I grunted, gasping as she helped me rise. One arm hung around my shoulders, the other held my hand.

"It will pass."

"Where are we? Where's the Temple?" I gazed at her face. "What happened to me?"

"Too many things that shouldn't have," she said. "The Temple is where and when we left it. We'll return to rejoin the others soon."

I gasped through the pain. "Was the journey so difficult for you?" She seemed unharmed.

Ambra shook her head. "No. It shouldn't have been for you. Travel through the Orbs can be disorienting, especially the first time. It isn't painful." She sighed. "Unless there's interference."

"How can that be?"

"I am no longer the only one who manipulates spacetime in our galaxy."

"The False Dawns."

"Their numbers grow, and so does the recklessness of their attacks."

"They produce them so quickly? Don't they have to be raised like a normal person?"

"Yes, but not all in one era. Our enemies have been patient. They *will* be patient. Their successors have sent back an army to destroy us in our time."

"An *army?* How many?"

She shrugged. "They can hide much from me now. I see the warped edges where they have vandalized the Mind."

"Ambra, please, I don't understand."

She frowned and pressed her body into mine, her arm looped around me. "The wormholes. These cloaking efforts. They're *obscene.* Because spacetime and sentience are a unified field. Where there's one, there is the other. Where there's a massive intelligence, or a mass of minds, space and time respond. Where big alterations in continuum exist, dynamic and structured—can you guess?"

I could, but the implications were insane. I caught my breath a moment, thinking through her words. I felt so unafraid to speak to her. I didn't fear judgment, despite my stupidity and blindness. I knew acceptance.

"There is...*a mind?*"

"Yes, Nitin," she squeezed my arm again. "Of a kind. The fabric of our universe is stirring, cogitating, becoming. From its chaotic birth pangs to the complex structures of our era until the singularity of equilibrium. It will grow and become in ways we won't decipher for billions of years. Perhaps our far descendants will comprehend this much more alien and deep thought."

"You understand it now?"

"To recognize it, to feel its living soul, is different from comprehending it. These reckless acts are wounding the structure of this mind. Creating lesions in the cosmic cortex."

"Why do they do it then?"

"Because they are ruined children, born and bred as instruments of war. They're horrible, but I pity them. I know what it is to be an object, Nitin, with no other value other than what purpose you can be to another. To be helpless while altered as others see fit, never understanding. Drowning in pain, fear, and self-loathing. It creates a consuming desire for vengeance."

I felt my arms tighten around her waist. Her past was rote history for most of us. Not to her. I could see the agony of her enslavement etched in her face. "I'm sorry, Ambra."

The corners of her mouth twitched. "What's driving them is something different. Much *darker*. The Dram do not understand the bargain they've made to acquire this new power."

"The ghost forces?"

"The *Anti*. We pull them now, Nitin. Tempt them terribly for our ordering and our continued growth through time. Our bias of the cosmic background. They will do all they can to destroy us."

"Why? What are they?"

"Our inverses. No more, no less. The shadow of our light. As for them, we're the shade of theirs. Creatures we know little about. Now they have revealed themselves." She sighed and shook her head. "At least it's still small. Still localized. These clones are clumsy and stupid. Raised denied love. Taught without wisdom." She exhaled. "But there are so many."

My thoughts raced, trying to process the implications of her confusing words. "What about the Orbs? Don't they also damage this...intelligence?" I wasn't sure what to call it.

"That's what makes them so beautiful. They don't. They *synergize* with it. They harmonize. Their purpose commingles with the cosmic mind. They're meant for far greater things than our simplistic use of them." She sighed and gazed at the green seaside. Shadows from the alien trees danced across her face as the aurora undulated. The wind tasted of blackberries and chocolate. "Even if it's what brought us here."

I glanced around again. "Where are we?"

She smiled. "One of my favorite places in the galaxy. Or a little outside it. We're orbiting a star on the outskirts of a small satellite cluster of our Milky Way."

My mind searched through the extensive astronomical training required by the MECHcore. "Those are tens of thousands of light years from Earth."

She grinned. "Twenty kiloparsecs."

"Ambra, how?"

"It's teeming with life. Some intelligent. So, there are also Orbs here." She gazed at the swirling cornucopia of colors. "Isn't it beautiful? I've come here many times over the last two centuries. It has been a place to escape the burden of all I must do. All that is asked. A haven to forget, for a moment, all the terrible destinies. Over time, I tired of witnessing it alone. It grew harder to wait for you, even in this heaven."

"Wait for me? You knew...?"

I stopped myself. Of course, she knew. She was the Daughter.

"You spoke my name in dreams," I said, memories flooding back. "You'd never met me, but you called me *love* in the Temple hospital. You speak like we've already lived a life together. Have you seen everything?"

She shook her red curls at me. "Not like you think. The broad outlines, the truth that one day you would come, yes, I knew. The closer events come to me, in space, time, or heart—the more poorly I see. Blame quantum mechanics."

"I don't understand."

"Better to ask Waythrel. I don't get the physics either. What's important is that I didn't know when or what form you would take. I only knew you would come. I could sense you, Nitin. Once you were born, I knew you'd come. I sought you out and watched over you as you grew in India. I came to adore you as a child at your grandmother's country home. A young adult studying late into the nights to pass the Force entrance exams. A grown man—brave, honest, and determined to find me."

I stared at her in wonder. She had seen my entire life. She had known about me for centuries.

"I came to you in Japan. In the Sahara, I tended your bruised mind and learned to love every one of its imperfect contours."

"Ambra—why? I was searching for you! If you knew, why did you wait? Why make me search? Why have we wasted so much time?"

The idea that I was alone and yet not, shook me. Decades of our lives had passed when we could have been together. Panic coursed through me.

"It's not so simple, Nitin," she said, lowering her head. "You're blind in ways I'm not. If we alter certain futures, the ripples can become tsunamis. The fates of our galaxy always rest on my choices. I am never free of it. Even when—especially when—it concerns what is most dear to me. I've known nothing more painful than watching you in silence for decades. Longing to reach out to you, play with you as a child, speak to you as a man. Experience your affection for me openly."

She held my gaze and squeezed my arm. Her eyes shone as her mouth trembled in a frown.

"It's bittersweet. Chodak saw this two hundred years ago and shared his vision. I glimpsed myself through *your* eyes. That day, I learned the depth of your feelings, felt your soul adore me as I had never witnessed a man love a woman."

I swallowed. "Who was he?"

Her shoulders rose and fell as she shook her head. "Someone long dead. A monk and insightful Reader. He forecast your coming to me. He told me we would be married."

My head swam as my heart raced. "Everything with you is a mystery. Every time you speak with me, it's like the universe changes, and I can't keep up."

She pouted. "So you're saying you don't *want* to marry me, Captain Ratava?" Her brows wrinkled, her expression ridiculously charming.

"Ambra, I..."

She continued to sulk, her eyebrows high on her forehead. I felt as if I were leaping into the dark.

"Yes. In fact, I do. Not exactly how I had pictured the subject coming up."

She threw her head back and laughed. Her shoulders shook as she brought the bald surface back down, nestling into my chest. I smelled her hair, and it was a revelation. A thousand pathways in my brain lit to this simple olfaction. My eyes drank in the orange surrounding me. I reached up and stroked her locks, caressing the enormous bulge atop her skull.

"My heart," she said, her laughter fading. Tears filled her blind eyes. "You accept even that. This deformity no human animal should carry before her mate. Who would love such ugliness? Yet, you do."

I placed my hand on her face, stroking the left cheek with my hand. I searched her eyes. I knew they couldn't see into my own. Still her mind could Read the deepest place in my person. Her breath was warm in the cool air, tendrils of fog wrapping around me. My hand appeared black alongside the whiteness of her skin. I cupped my hand and pulled her mouth to mine.

Kissing a goddess is to open more than your flesh to another. You expose your soul.

Our lips met. A limbic thrill shot through my veins. Electricity burned my awareness. We held each other in this embrace on a distant world. Our hands wild, exploring, animated. The fingers of her mind caressed the contours of my consciousness.

Love should always be a mixture of body and spirit. When you kiss a goddess, the greater ecstasy is in the soul.

I pulled back after a few moments. "Daughter. Of Time."

She didn't laugh at my clumsiness. A flame of passion possessed her features, but they were also stained with sorrow.

"Nitin, wait. You must know."

I ached as I stared into her eyes. "Know what, Ambra?"

Tears ran down her cheeks. "Our time can only be short."

I nodded. "It's okay. We have an important task. I understand." I reached for her again.

She eased me back. "No. Not now or here. Not because of the mission. Together, all paths end in darkness."

"What do you mean?"

"I can't see the details, but the broad form is all too clear." Her face twisted in agony. "If you choose to be with me, it will set in motion events that will result in tragedy."

"What tragedy?"

"Your certain death, my love," she said, still as stone.

I focused behind her, the cresting waves filling my sight, my hands resting on her shoulders.

My death?

Many times I had faced oblivion in battle, had seen finality in the casualties nearby. I struggled to imagine my own demise. How to conceptualize one's nonexistence? Yet this prediction came from the Daughter.

I turned back to her. "If we aren't together?"

Her face tightened. "There are countless futures on that path. In most, you will live a long life."

"Without you?"

She grimaced. "Yes."

My words erupted from deep within me. "Then it will be an empty torture. It will be living in the darkest prison."

She gazed at me with a strange pity, but my choice was uncomplicated. The easiest decision for death I could imagine making.

"So then—how long do we have?"

"Oh, Nitin." She clasped me. "Do you want to know?"

I considered her question. If I knew, I'd focus on the date. Obsess over my fate to the exclusion of all else that occurred. She was right. It was better I did not know the hour and live in the moment. With her.

"How will I die?"

"I don't know, my heart. I can't see so near to myself—and you are as close as my own soul." She touched her fingertips to my temple. "It will be monstrous. At the hands of our enemies. We will be shattered by betrayal. In the end, our humanity stolen forever. In return for this terrible price, I can give you so little. A brief time, but a time when we'll love as none ever loved."

She drew her face to mine. Our lips brushed as she whispered,

"One short and beautiful dream for all the horror. I had to tell you. You must choose."

My throat caught. "My horror is to leave you. If I'm torn from you, tortured, killed—I can only die once. Walk away? Live each day alone, apart from you—I can't make that choice every moment for the rest of my life. I'm not strong enough."

She wept and smiled. Her hands cupped my face, her fingers slipping over my scalp, sending waves through me. Her body pressed against mine. I felt the swell of her breasts, the warmth of the life within her. I was surrounded by a sea of red.

"Then love me now and until our time ends."

Chapter 21

I submit to you that if a man has not discovered something that he will die for, he isn't fit to live.

Martin Luther King, Jr.

We stepped from the Orb projection into the Temple center.

Again, I was disoriented. Pain racked my form. Ambra minimized the discomfort, and while I suffered, it was far less than before. I didn't ask why, as I was sure to misunderstand it. I was just relieved I wasn't about to end up screaming in agony and half dead in front of my team.

The aches lessened, and I felt more than recovered. Better than I remembered in a long time. Alive. *Fulfilled.*

To kiss a goddess is one thing. To make love with her, something entirely different. Our bodies tuned to each other. I had no explanation for it. Perhaps because of how we had already entwined our consciousness. Or for reasons I would discover later. If sex can be a religious experience on a physical plane, then I had been born again.

The corporeal ecstasy was the lesser of our oneness. I can't tell you much about how our souls connected. How her telepathic powers brought our consciousnesses together. How, as we joined our flesh, we linked our minds. We experienced an eon. A place beyond time. We met in a thousand memories, hers and mine. We bathed in a million desires and fears. Images. Music. Smells. We shuttled through the labyrinth of cognition, a ray of light through an evanescent maze. The walls painted flickering ideas. They mixed and touched. A resonance refashioned the essence of each independent spirit.

I was one person when I journeyed to that alien world overlooking the Milky Way. I left as someone else. The process healed the lingering damage brought on by her clone. Beyond this, I continued to be remade in ways I would come to understand over time.

We stepped out of the swirling colors and into the relative darkness of the Temple, hand in hand. Astonished faces greeted us.

The members of my team debated with Waythrel and Mazandarani. One at a time, they noticed our presence and turned to face us. It took a full minute for us to walk the distance across the expansive floor. During that time, none of the others uttered a sound. We stopped in front of the group.

"It's time," said Ambra.

"Wait a moment," said Williams, her eyes wide. "What the hell just happened? My brain is about to explode from drowning in a sea of information. I wake up, the rest of these bozos with me, but you two are *gone*. Vanished like magic. Next you reappear coming out of that *thing*?"

Moore cooed. "Holding hands like lovers in the park."

The tall alien said nothing to the outburst. Mazandarani stared, his expression devastated. I didn't know what to say.

Ambra took the lead. "We have traveled through the Time Sphere. Nitin has completed his test flights." She smiled at the confused expressions around her. "You didn't think we were going to journey on Strings, did you?"

No one answered. Waythrel spoke. "It is far less efficient, and dangerous now that the Dram control much of the Time Tree. But Ambra can access the portals directly."

"Right," said Kim. "We just have to teleport through that thing." He gawked at the kaleidoscope in the center of the chamber.

"It would be an honor, a life's privilege, Daughter of Time," said Fox, bowing her head.

"So, Captain, hell of a ride?" Moore asked.

I couldn't suppress a laugh. "You have no idea."

"Wicked. I'm game. Don't even know where I'm going, but I'm not going to miss out on surfing that baby."

Ambra considered the others. "The rest of you? You have the information. You know the purpose."

"Something else, all that *sharing*," said Williams. "We should be using it at all the schools."

"Someday we will," Ambra said. "Most people aren't ready. New Earth's Readers are learning from the Xix. Our planet is in the early stages of a group memory, soon to be a communal awareness. A sum far greater than its parts. Earth is waking up."

"I remember," said Kim. "You're going to seal the Orbs!"

"Seal them?" asked Moore. "What does that mean?"

Kim was at a loss for words. "I saw it, but I'll be damned if I can explain it."

The alien spoke. "The Daughter will reconfigure the local projections. The hyperspace filaments will retract. There will be no String on which to navigate. The node will be dead. While we are there, we will find out what we can about our enemies. If we are lucky, we might run into them or lure them to us."

"We?" asked Fox. "You're coming, too?"

"Your team is short one member," said Ambra. "I've chosen Waythrel to fill the gap."

Williams objected. "That won't complete the group. The exercises are tuned for six trained soldiers. A Xix is an outlier."

The alien addressed her doubts. "In what will come, your previous training will have little relevance. We will not be a military operation. We will be a unique delegation serving as much or more as detectives than as warriors, although fighting may become necessary. I will fit well into this construction."

"Detectives?" asked Kim. "So why us? You don't need fighters. Especially not with her."

"You are fated," said Ambra. "There is no other word for it. No other way to explain it."

"So, can we choose to change our fate? Is that some kind of paradox?" asked Williams.

She smiled. "Only because your mind limits what you can see. Each of your choices is free *and* preordained. The distinction between the two is artificial. Like describing a tree as either soaring into the air or digging into the ground. Contradictory—yet neither false, because a tree is much more than both conceptions."

Waythrel elaborated. "Every decision you make is part of a family of paths propagating through space and time, integrating to a final reality. If you could see the essence of the fabric around us, you would understand a strange truth. You actually will make all possible choices available to you. You are infinite as you create finitude."

My warrant officer shook her head. "I shoulda never put my name down for this crazy assignment." Fox beamed.

Ambra touched my shoulder.

I turned to my team. "Suit up, metalheads!"

We donned our gear. The Xixian skins layered over our forms like some self-aware organism groping its way forward. The process took several minutes. We examined fit, checking specs and performance.

Meanwhile, I watched Mazandarani approach Ambra. They were some ten feet away, but I could hear the exchange. The counselor paused in front of her, his demeanor hesitant and clumsy.

"This fate is cruel, Sepehr," she said.

His eyes stayed toward the ground. "You know my heart, Daughter of Time, so I can only be honest and agree." He pushed his mind to another topic. "You also know my thoughts. Why do you take this risk?"

"I trust him. I *know* him. He'll never hurt me."

"I wish that you had omniscience. A little prescience is a dangerous thing."

She kissed his cheek. A wave of jealousy flowed through me, but it dissipated. Her expression wasn't desire. It was love. An affection and concern I realized was far deeper than what I had feared. I felt ashamed.

"I will come back, Sepehr. And he'll be with me. I need you to prepare for our return and for the ceremony to follow."

"Why do you ask this of me?"

"Because you must walk this path or never be free. I am cruel, perhaps. I also care for you too much to have you enslaved."

He tugged at his beard. "My fear is that I will disappoint you, Daughter. But your disappointment will not be from my failure to try. It will be as you have asked." He stepped away.

Fox appeared before me, blocking my view of the conversation. "We're ready, Captain!"

I examined my team. After what I had experienced, I realized how ridiculous we were. What were a bunch of metalheads thinking to accomplish stepping through an Orb? Traveling through space and time? Meeting an enemy even Ambra feared and none of us understood?

Waythrel joined Ambra at the edge of the long pathway to the oscillating projection. They motioned, and we followed. Creature-sized depressions lined the walkway on both sides, the seats for Readers forming the Group Mind during the meditation sessions.

She had tried to share this experience with me in our unexplained absence. It went over my head, despite the telepathy. She admitted it was hard for her to understand. The combined mentality of the collective exceeded her own consciousness by an extensive degree. She grasped bits and pieces of the insights on her own. I understood nothing, not a bit or a piece.

We reached the projection. Ambra gestured toward it.

"Step inside; it's safe."

We entered, followed by the alien and the Daughter.

"If you are prepared, I will open the Orb."

I gave a thumbs-up, and the members of my group echoed the gesture. All were nervous. All stared with excitement.

Fox grinned. "Get ready for the trip of your life."

"Or the trip to our death," said Moore.

Ambra's voice was grave. "Both futures have already occurred."

I released a slow breath, and infinity exploded.

Part II

Until you grasp the limitations of Entropy,
you cannot understand the possibilities of Time.

Wisdom of the Six Cities

Chapter 22

How on earth did Descartes, who could not on prima facie evidence accept his existence as real, believe that his thinking was? This was the beginning of the dark ages of European philosophy.

Yin Yu tang

Water.

It dripped. It began in a plastic bag, puffed out, gleaming. A drop traveled through a valve, down clear tubing approaching a bedside. It dove into an adapter with a sharp needle at the end. The tip plunged into the pale skin of an arm.

Ambra's arm.

Her eyes were glassy. I sat beside her and held her hand. It was frigid.

"Nitin, I'm glad you're here. I'm scared."

I gaped at the hospital equipment. "Where are we?"

She sighed, her eyes drooping. "Dreaming. We're journeying again. Traveling layers of awareness. Sailing flying going..."

She was younger. My mind ground into gear, and I pieced together the facts of her life.

"When you were a prisoner on Earth. These are your surgeries, the ones that changed you forever."

The early teen's wan smile failed. "My second surgery. The most terrible."

"The first wasn't?"

She rocked her head on the gurney, slurring her words. "No. Nope. I thought they were going to *cure* me the first time. Take the thing out, like they said. Promised right before they killed Mom and Dad. My vision was going. That scared me. First operation had hope with the fear."

"The next?"

"I knew. Bastard *told* me. 'Making it bigger. You'll be blind soon. Isn't this sooooooo cool?' Freaks R Us. Freaks R Us. Freaks R Us."

I waited for her to calm down. "So, this time, you knew they weren't curing you. They were experimenting on you."

"Yeah. Sucks, huh?" She grinned at me. "You look *really* good. Well, almost blind here, but the me visiting this me, she knows. So many of me. Me, me, me. Clone me. Millions of me. Mmmmm, you smell good, too. Sound good. Bet you taste good."

"Ambra..."

"Going to fall *off* the world, Nitin. Drugs pushing me under the water and outside the universe. Just meat meat meat to them again. Cut, drill, screw, slice. I'm falling to black and sick at my stomach, and they're going to come with saws and drills and screws..."

Tears trickled down the sides of her face as she shook it back and forth. I squeezed her hand and kissed it. "It's okay. You'll be okay. I'm here with you. I'm here with you the whole time. I promise."

Her green eyes flashed open. She gripped my arm, her entire body taut. "Hope to die?"

"I'm not leaving."

She relaxed and sank back into the pillow. "Okay, I'll sleep. We'll go away. To a new place. I just don't know where..."

She closed her eyes, her respiration slow and shallow. It became rhythmic, louder, pulsing and grasping my attention. Before I perceived the change, everything faded. The hospital room, Ambra, her hand.

A constant rhythm, alone, remained.

I had thought it was her breath—but she wasn't here. A metronome ticked. Throbbing. Beating.

Rushing.

Water.

Precipitation from towering falls or storm winds through the trees. White noise. Deafening.

The sound focused in front of me. The blurring decreased. The horrors clarified.

Masses of naked men and women cowered against a wall. Robots darted about, blasting high-pressure liquid at them. People struggled to get behind others to ward off the pain.

Those who could. Many lay on the floor or crawled away from the machines. They were hardly human anymore.

It was the smuggler's ship where the Daughter had almost died. Interstellar merchants who drove their cattle until they dropped. They bought those who had scored poorly in the Dram sorting. My Ambra's deformity had not been identified for what it was. She was defective, cheap goods. Purchased by smugglers who dragged her to the door of death before the Xix raided the vessel.

I scanned the row of screaming and blistered slaves. *There.* Near the far corner, crouching into a ball. A mass of red, unkempt, tangled hair running down from a bald top.

I rushed over, the water not touching me, the robots unconcerned. "Ambra!"

I knelt beside her. I hardly recognized her face. She was shivering. Blood vessels decorated her thin skin like some demonic henna pattern. Muscles and fat were gone. A transparent foil covered her skeleton.

More legend. The Daughter from the history books and in the art of our age. It didn't prepare me for what it was like to be in the presence of near-death starvation. I shuddered.

"Go, Nitin." Her voice was a rasp. I bent closer to hear. "Don't see me like this. Let me die."

Dreams within nightmares.

She said I'd experienced her childhood home because it was close to her heart. I was in the hospital because she was deathly afraid and called to me. Now I was here.

"I won't go. I love you, and you're going to survive this. I know you do. You know you do. Remember! I don't know where in time and space or your memories we are, but I'm going to stay with you."

She was too weak to speak. I cradled her as the fingers of the sticklike hand on my shoulder pressed her answer.

"Okay. Don't talk. Feel me here. I'm here. I'm here, I'm here," I said, rocking her in my arms.

She mouthed silently. "Don't stop."

"I won't."

I sat on the floor filthy with human waste. I rocked the wrecked form of my beloved through an ever-slowing passage of time. We swayed, her weightless body flattened to me like a crumbled paper bag. Swinging back and forth. Stronger until we drowned out the screams and silenced the roar of the hoses.

They became muffled disturbances. Beeping of equipment. Quiet filling the oscillations.

Or was it floating?

Yes, bobbing in a dark current. Liquid everywhere.

Water.

My dream. Back in this awful place. The nightmares didn't have a solvent before. When I had floated, I drifted in darkness. Numbness. Emptiness.

And stars.

But I could see it. A faint gloom growing from the giant sea around me. A faded color, pulsing. Inorganic. Without life or sense of purpose. *Rhythm.*

It shone through the fluid. Of this, I was sure. I should be seeing a maze of the Orb light. I was traveling somewhere. All these facts and truths and things hovered just beyond my ability to retrieve. They bled out in a rainbow of colors and dissolved into the green.

My mind thrashed, trying to hold on to...*what?* I was a soldier. I was on a mission. I loved a woman, a singular woman in the universe. I held her hands.

I rocked her to peace, and she is red and white and soared through the clouds of a nebula and a beach where I made love to her under our galaxy in a night breeze.

Things that must be true but dissolve, existing as beliefs in my devolving memory of dreams fading in this throbbing greenness. This water of death.

I tried to move. *I saw!* Motion. Blurred. A hand! I had a hand! Again, I flailed my arm, but it achieved a weak waving, a sickly movement in the mossy ocean. I glimpsed it again. Shape. *I had structure.* Form in fluid.

But no exit, no way to wake from this nightmare. Nothing but stasis and wetness and flailing, feeble limbs. Endless green.

Nitin, come back.

Ambra? I called in my thoughts. *I'm lost!*

Beside my chest, a brightness. A vortex of light whirled in the middle of the water. I peered into its center. A point elongated from the edges, drilling deep into a third dimension. I stared down a long passage.

You aren't lost. You're displaced.

The channel pulled me through the lime liquid. The gyre grew.

Luminescence from another space flowing into the dark and drowning sea. Brightening.

I spun, following the strange undulations of the turbulent radiance. Accelerating to greater velocities. Around and over and beside until what remained were glimmering star trails.

I left the molasses and plunged into the swirling tunnel. Buffeted, flipped, stretched, and shoved. A billion suns and years and parsecs flew by my awareness.

I plummeted. The brilliance hurled me from the shaft. Free.
Free!

Floating free above a grand and terrible world of blue. Horizon to horizon. Enormous. Endless.

Water.

Chapter 23

Innumerable suns exist; innumerable earths revolve around these suns in a manner similar to the way the seven planets revolve around our sun. Living beings inhabit these worlds.

a heresy of Giordano Bruno, burned alive at the stake in 1600

So much water.

I lay on my side, racked and shaking. The floor below me, the walls pressing against my forehead, were invisible. A clear glass lacking reflection. It absorbed no moisture from my breath, not smudging from the oils of my skin. A technology that didn't exist.

Underneath me was—nothing. Darkness and stars. Behind me, a warm pressure on my back. Light. Because of the planet before me, I knew it came from a star. We had arrived at Orferlin, world without land.

I rolled onto my back and gazed up at a group of faces. The alien, monstrous and still. The MECHcore soldiers. And Ambra. She knelt beside me.

"Welcome back, love."

The minimal friction in this strange bubble was disconcerting. I felt unsure of my motions. I pulled myself to a sit, rubbing my temples.

"I thought you said this wouldn't happen again."

"I know." Her smile faded. "It was a massive interference from our enemies. I imagined a possible attack, but nothing so intense."

"They knew our plans," said Waythrel.

I studied my team. They appeared concerned, but unhurt. I needed to make sure.

"What happened? Anyone else affected?"

Placing my hand on an unseen wall, I pushed up. Standing in the bubble, my feet were planted on nothing. The nonexistence held me up.

"No," said the alien. "You are the only one who suffered any deleterious effects."

"That doesn't make sense."

"Captain's a little soft, is all," laughed Moore.

"It's not the first time," said Ambra. "Our enemies are targeting him. Because of me."

Waythrel said nothing.

Williams stepped forward. "*Who* is targeting us? More of those clones?"

"Thousands of them," said Ambra, her expression grim.

"*Thousands?*" asked Kim.

She sighed. "Their numbers have risen considerably."

"How can there be more? Where are they coming from?" asked Fox.

The alien spoke. "From many spaces and distant times. There is a growing convergence. A massing of the troops, if you will."

"I'm sorry, Nitin," said Ambra. "It was more than I was ready for. An ambush."

"So how the hell did they know our schedule?" asked Williams.

"The same way they found us in the desert," answered Waythrel. "We have been infiltrated. There is a spy among us."

"Whoa—*us*? Time out, okay?" said Kim. "Others besides us knew the mission. What about the counselor? He seemed pretty unhappy with the group. Especially the captain."

"Or even Major Mizoguchi," said Fox. "She's not Force. She works for the Temple. That's unusual. Maybe she's there for a purpose. Don't turn on us because we're the new recruits!"

"Sergeant Moore refused to share with the Daughter," said the Xix.

The sounds of ion chargers filled the space as a suit lit up.

"Hold up, squid-head. I didn't watch my mates torn apart by Dram soldiers on Dworn to listen to this shit. Put up or shut up."

Ambra shook her head, glaring at the extraterrestrial. "Enough. There are many possibilities, including a bunch we likely haven't thought of. Mazandarani and Waythrel suspect a mole. But there are forces gathering with powers I haven't probed. We've no reason to doubt each other. More importantly—we're going to need one another if we are to complete this mission. Distrust will poison us."

Purge your minds of it.

A mental slap. Everyone shuddered. She was angry, and it was the first time I had felt her wrath. It was frightening, as much for her power as for how far she was holding back.

"I said I don't want anyone in my head!" shouted Moore.

"Switch off your weapons unless you're going to engage our enemies!" she growled.

His mouth tightened, and he glared at her. It wasn't anger. He was sizing her up, respect in his eyes. The humming ceased as his suit switched off.

"We have a task to complete," she continued, her tones softened.

"Where are we?" I asked. Too much was unexplained.

"Orferlin," cut in Williams. "You shared, right? Dolphin world."

"I know the planet and the facts. I remember." I gestured to the invisible bubble. "I mean *this*. What's this? An advanced ship? Is it Xixian?"

Waythrel spoke. "No, Captain. This is beyond the ingenuity of our technologists."

"It's my doing," said Ambra. "A distortion and warping of space-time. It's a three-space vessel to carry us. I can expand or contract it in multiple hidden dimensions. This gives us volume enough for weeks of air, munitions, food. Anything we require, we've brought with us from New Earth."

"Toilets?" asked Moore.

"With privacy, Sergeant, in case you're shy," she answered with a grin. "Also air and filtration. Hidden away but functioning."

He smiled back.

"And quite defensive," said the Xix. "Except for an overpowering clone attack, there are no weapons the Dram possess that can harm us."

"What of those *Anti*?" asked Fox.

"We'll see," said Ambra. "For now, we need to find out what we can from the inhabitants. Once we've investigated, we seal this node of the Time Tree. We have two more stops to go before we're done."

Chapter 24

What makes planets go around the sun? At the time of Kepler some people answered this problem by saying that there were angels behind them beating their wings and pushing the planets around an orbit. As you will see, the answer is not very far from the truth. The only difference is that the angels sit in a different direction and their wings push inward.

Richard Feynman

The descent to the planet's surface was unlike anything I'd ever experienced. Lacking a viewscreen, a hologram—*without walls*—it was as if we were free-falling from the fringe of space. The enormous expanse of water expanded until it eclipsed our external vision.

I pressed against the invisible barrier of the bubble. The pressure provided some feedback to calm my anxiety. We were stable. We weren't pitching forward to our deaths with nothing to support us. Several members of my team mimicked my motions.

The ride was disturbingly smooth. We broke into the atmosphere absent a shudder. No turbulence. Nothing to indicate we were moving relative to the planet at all. The darkness of space receded. Clouds swam over us. The oceans continued to grow before our eyes, everything quiet.

We dropped into a gigantic storm, dwarfing anything occurring on New Earth. Orferlin was nearly twice the size of our world, with more than ten times the surface water. So much moisture and a tropical temperature cooked up some continent-sized tempests. Straight into the heart of one of these beasts, we flew. All light vanished. Colossal bursts of lightning interrupted the darkness. We plunged through the innards of a nuclear explosion.

Yet, silent. The rain poured over our enclosure without the sound of a drop. Electrical flashes were never followed by a rumble. Our vessel had not a single tremor in the midst of this overwhelming display of nature.

"It's so quiet," I said, my voice nearly a whisper.

"You want to hear it?" asked Ambra.

"It's possible?"

"Yes."

I turned to the others. "If it's okay with everyone."

No one protested. She grinned like a schoolgirl.

Then listen!

The bubble exploded in cacophony. Howling winds and stunning cracks of lightning were swallowed by bone-rattling thunder. We glided unaffected through this. Somehow, she'd allowed only the sound to penetrate. It humbled the greatest thunderstorm on New Earth.

"By the Daughter," said Fox, her eyes wide.

"Beats anything I've ever seen," echoed Kim.

The tempest roared around our enclosure while we continued our rapid descent. As we neared the bottom of the storm system, we cleared its shadow and left it seething behind us. A blinding light erupted, bathing us in the alien hues of the local star. The ocean roiled beneath us, extending in all directions to the horizon.

We decreased our altitude, and the crests of waves resolved. They appeared no different from those of Earth's seas from a distance. Nearing the surface, our bodies served as a reference point, and the true size of these giants revealed themselves. Towering over the grandest Pacific swells, those on Orferlin were mountains. They loomed over our bubble, blocking out the starlight. They broke over us with bedlam, causing no disturbance inside.

This planetary ocean was *loud*. Everything you might expect from an Earth sea multiplied many fold. Small mice in a tempest, we stood speechless before the planet's strength.

"So, we go swim with the dolphins, eh?" asked Moore.

Ambra sighed. "I wish we could. The Brax aren't much like our world's water mammals."

Waythrel elaborated. "They have organs resembling gills more than lungs, although mechanistically neither. Theirs is a strange and rich culture. It stems from a distributed nervous system. More than ten neural-nodules across their bodies. They may resist damage that would render human or Xixian mental faculties impaired."

Ambra smiled. "The nodes recombine in spacetime to form the most beautiful patterns of thought. Braxian Readers are second only to the Xix in our galaxy." She lost the conversational thread, staring forward over the endless, oceanic expanse. "I wish we had the time to spend—" Her face clouded. She was in pain.

"What is it?" I asked.

She took my hand. "Something's wrong." She trembled. "Something's happened to Orferlin."

"What?" asked Williams.

We all stared at the bright blue world in front of us.

"Something terrible."

We hovered over scenes of destruction.

The Brax inhabited underwater cities engineered from coral-like substances. They had long ago learned to modify and employ them as building materials. Depending on the density of the shells, they were able to build far below the surface. These floating, submerged metropolises had housed billions of their kind. Solar, tidal, and fusion energies powered their civilization. Strong images from the sharing filled my thoughts. The intricacy of their curvilinear constructions. The labyrinthian tunnels exploding outward like filigree, spanning kilometers. They dwarfed our largest land-based cities.

Now all was ruin. Bobbing on the waves were the blasted remains of the coral masterpieces. Fragments floated like a snowstorm of shattered china from a distance. Diving into the sea, we saw other structures had sunk to varying depths. Ambra sped the bubble around the globe at blinding velocities. We verified this carnage wasn't isolated but worldwide. No sign of life remained. No evidence that the Brax were anything but exterminated.

"The Dram, all right," said Williams. "Fuckers like nothing better than a good genocide to make a point."

"They usually just roast the whole planet," said Fox. "But Orferlin is fine."

"Not exactly fine," said Moore.

The Xix spoke, its voice subdued. "Is there nothing you can detect?"

Ambra crouched in a meditative position, her legs crossed with her arms on her knees. Her eyes were closed. "There's more than an absence, Waythrel," she said, her concentration unwavering. "There's an interference. A poison in space and time."

"Wait, what does that mean?" asked Kim.

"I don't know," she said. "I've never felt anything like it. I sense it sickening our sentience."

Waythrel paced in the bubble. "This is not the Dram."

"No, Waythrel, it isn't. Something else. I need to understand what's happening."

"We shouldn't stay here long unless we can shield ourselves," said the alien.

"Well, if Supergirl here doesn't know what's going on, I agree," said Moore. "Let's pull back until we have some idea what we're dealing with."

"Not yet!" cut in Ambra. Her face was drawn. "There *is* a signal, even in this poisonous cloud. Faint. Fading." A sorrow came over her face. "*Caga*. I hear her."

"Caga?" I asked.

Waythrel answered. "A penetrating Reader of the Brax. We often communed with her from the Temple."

"*From* New Earth?" asked Fox with awe.

"Distance is deceptive."

The bubble accelerated out of the sea and burst over the water's surface. We darted like a missile toward the northern regions. I couldn't process the environment outside. It blurred into a multicolored brushstroke on either side of us. In front and behind were small circles of focus.

"She's calling us," Ambra said. "And she's dying."

Chapter 25

I hear the approaching thunder that, one day, will destroy us too. I feel the suffering of millions.

Anne Frank

We found Caga near one pole of the planet.

The destruction mirrored what we saw around the globe. Somehow, the creature had survived within a spacecraft. The ship floated without power on the waves, and Ambra brought our bubble beside it. Nestled alongside a craft as big as an island, she projected a bizarre filament toward the walls of the vessel. To our complete amazement, the tunnel passed right through the barrier. We gazed down the passageway, and it was empty of matter. The wall was gone, but she insisted it was still there.

"The channel is outside the space of the material," she explained as we followed her down the corridor. The sides were transparent, the inside of the structure open to us.

The reverse of a human transport, the chambers were liquid-filled for these aquatic organisms. Except for the rooms where damage had occurred and air flowed in. Her passage created no disruption in the construction. Water surrounded us.

We approached a central cavity, a giant chamber the size of a sports stadium. Thousands of bizarre extraterrestrials floated directionless.

The best our minds could do was map their form to New Earth's sea creatures. Fluidics dictated streamlined forms. It was as close to a dolphin as they got. I discerned fins of some kind, more like webbed tentacles. They possessed optical and auditory organs across their bodies, pairing with their neural clusters. Without a directionality, their appendages could accelerate them in any direction. I imagined it would have been amazing to watch them swim.

But the motion here was haphazard. Lifeless corpses floated along the currents in the dead ship. All but one.

The passage Ambra constructed ended at a medical pod. A single Braxian hung with tubes penetrating its body. The visual tissues, multifaceted gem faces, rotated and tracked our approach.

"Caga."

She spoke as the ingress stopped beside the dying creature. Placing her hand against the edge of the bubble, the membrane flowed outward. She extended her arm until the surface of the space-time distortion fit it like a tight glove. She stroked the side of the alien and closed her eyes. Waythrel stood as a statue, its eyestalks wrapped around themselves like a braid.

"I can speak with her telepathically," said Ambra. "She has consented for me to share with you as I do, if you want to participate."

My team traded glances, eyes settling on Moore.

"Ah, fuck it. Okay," he said. "There isn't going to be anything but fucked up on this trip. Blast away, girl."

Mental view ports opened. Through them, I could see—or rather sense—the thoughts of others. The humans. Incomprehensible images from Waythrel. Foggy but understandable concepts of this ocean being. Dominating all impressions, the Daughter of Time herself.

You must leave our world. It is not safe.

The creature's intellectual processes spilled as from a distance. Whether because I struggled with parsing them or from its decaying state, I didn't know.

Ambra responded.

We're okay for now. Whatever's happening, I can deflect its effects for a time.

You will grow weary.

Yes. You don't have much time, dear Caga. What happened?

The Braxian's perspective swam across its body, but its thoughts were strong.

The Dram came. Once to claim the Orb Strings and guard them. The Time Tree is compromised. We thought we were spared worse. Until five Orferlin cycles ago—several weeks your time—they returned. They laid waste to everything.

It shared images of the terrible enemy armada. Explosions, the deaths of billions, the emotions of a species watching itself die. A cataclysm. It crushed me, the horror and pain. I tried to block it out but failed. I'm not sure how much time passed as the impressions ran through me, but it was likely short moments.

They could not kill all of us. Their transports departed. Then the Anti came.

The shadow ships flowed out from the Orb like a polluted tide. Black spots like flies separated from the main contingent of dark vessels. They stationed themselves equidistant across the planet, inducing madness.

They left drones and returned to the Strings and were gone. There is something evil in those machines.

The poison. Ambra's thoughts were a warm light in this sea of strangeness.

Yes. We tried to salvage our people, but all things began to fail. Technology decayed. We lost our power, our infrastructure. Everything.

Within days, nothing functioned. Next, our minds. The weakest-minded of us went first. Forgetfulness. Unreason. In the end, lunacy. As Readers, a few of us could defend our consciousness longer from the ravages.

I waded through visuals of horror.

I lasted the longest, because my ship returned from space and was in orbit for the assault. I landed after the slaughter, lucky to have escaped immediate destruction. A last group of medics sought to lessen the effects by trial and error, working with deteriorating technology. They have me attached to desperate therapies. They are all dead. They have but delayed the inevitable. I am glad you have come.

Caga, no. A terrible sadness bled from Ambra.

There is no time to save my world or me. You and Waythrel have my memories. Take them, use *them, and find a way. You must leave before this poison overwhelms you.*

The bewildering complexity of the Xixian brain engaged.

She is right. We should not risk staying here any longer. She cannot be moved. Insanity will claim her tomorrow.

I don't know how the Xix knew this, but I couldn't process most of the images coming from it. Trying to digest its concepts produced a headache. I saw Ambra's shoulders slump.

A human idea interspersed.

What if we can destroy the drones in orbit?

It was Fox. I could sense her personality. Her mind raced, an empathy for both the dying alien and the pain of the Daughter driving her thoughts like a whip.

Caga responded. *It is likely impossible. We utilized what forces we had left. They did not return.*

Fox dismissed the objection. *You were weakened. Your technology, decaying. She can protect us. We're soldiers. We can send a small team, to avoid risk to the others.*

I don't know if I can shield you. It was Ambra. *The toxicity becomes stronger nearer the source. I can see it in the odd arrangement in spacetime. Almost the erasing of patterns.*

Fox was undeterred. *We can! It would stop, and we might be able to save her!*

Unlikely, responded Waythrel.

We have to try!

"I'll go," spoke Kim out loud. His emotions conveyed his determination.

I stared at the pair. "Are you sure?"

The Xix admonished us. "It is too dangerous."

Caga's thoughts were strong. *It is too late for me. But for you, for others—the risk may be worthwhile. To know if there can be an engagement with these devices. If the result is negative, you can take that answer and the details of the failure with you to devise counter-measures.*

Waythrel's eyestalks uncoiled, and several eyes pivoted toward Fox and Kim. "It is probable that you both will die."

Kim's suit powered up. A second later, Fox's did as well.

Kim smiled. "Well, the Daughter has protected us from equipment decay so far. Guns still good."

Fox spoke. "Besides, every mission has probabilities of death in this war. I have faith in Ambra Dawn."

You have love for me, Erica Fox. I thank you, but you have more trust than I deserve.

Fox beamed. "Humble to the end."

"There is a last consideration," said Waythrel. "Caga noted that the Dram returned to destroy this planet, after leaving it be. Orferlin poses no risks to them. It has always been a peaceful world riding the currents of the galactic struggles. Why annihilate it? The node was secure. Why spend the resources? Why do so in a time frame nearly identical to when we ourselves planned this mission?"

Williams ended the long silence. "The traitor again? You think details were leaked. You think it's sabotage."

"I am raising the possibility," said Waythrel.

"If so, it could also be a trap," I said.

"There's no way to know, and meanwhile, this planet is dying." Kim glared at me. "Sir, do we have permission?"

I had to make a choice. Send them to a likely death they ignored in their bravado? Or deny them their bravery and the chance for us to know more about our enemy's terrible weapons? Either way, I would be responsible.

"Permission granted, soldiers. Ambra, can you take us up to one of those devices?"

I felt her resignation. She broke off the group sharing and paused for several minutes. I guessed she was communing with the two alien Readers in private. Without comment, she opened her eyes, stood, and walked toward my team.

"We'll try."

The lamina wrapped about us and pulled itself out of the Braxian ship at high speed. We merged with the main bubble. The enclosure rocketed upward faster than a starship into the blackness.

Chapter 26

I know there is a God because in Rwanda, I shook hands with the devil. I have seen him, I have smelled him and I have touched him.

Lieutenant General Roméo Dallaire

We could all feel the disease as the dark object came into view. A combination of fatigue and disorientation sickened us, like a flu without the fever.

Moore scowled. "Feels like the worst fucking hangover I've ever had."

Ambra piloted the bubble by focusing on the source of corruption from the drone. We had no equipment, no scanners, *no ship.* I doubt any technology we or our allies had could measure and detect the noxious force. It was like a hole in the night. At this distance, it appeared to be a sphere of unlight at least twice the size of our enclosure.

Ambra's face was tight. "There's an essence to this thing that's against everything I understand. It's like the nature of the object fights understanding itself. I don't dare go any closer. I may not be able to protect us if this gets much stronger."

I stared at my soldiers. They stood together, gazing into the emptiness.

"This thing's nasty," I warned. "No shame in dropping the mission."

Fear filled their eyes, but also determination. Fox spoke for them. "Hell, there isn't. Since when do we back down from the enemy?"

"When there's nothing to be won. We outthink it, come back more prepared."

"That's just it, Captain," said Kim. "We don't even know enough to run away yet. Time we found out more."

They were set on it.

"Ambra, can you make separate bubbles for them? Maintain a link like the tunnel on Orferlin, pull them back if things go wrong?"

She shook her head. "I can try. It might be that this force will sever the connection. I might not be able to bring them back."

"Well, then we'd better make sure we kick its ass," said Kim, the pitch-changing hum of his ion slingers sounding.

"I don't like this," said Moore. "Very bad feeling. Whatever this thing does, it's like some fucking crime against the universe."

Ambra startled. "Yes, Sergeant. That's *exactly* how it feels to me. A violation. Against the structure of our existence. Fighting anything that could possibly be us."

Moore stared fixedly at the pair. "Don't mess with it."

"Damn, never figured you to be the one to chicken out," said Kim.

"I think he's right," echoed Williams, nodding toward Moore.

Fox rolled her eyes. "Now you too."

Williams turned to me. "It's the wrong call, Captain. Gut tells me so."

The weight of this decision was becoming enormous. "Waythrel, you were cautioning us before. What is your feeling now that you see it?"

The tall alien didn't have a shudder reflex as far as I know. Its mannerisms suggested the same sentiment. "There is sickness in the blackness. An *unlife* is perhaps a better phrase. It has killed a world. But Caga was correct. If we are to face this challenge, we need information. There is one way to obtain it."

Kim agreed. "Right on! Then it's settled, yeah? 'Cause I'm getting a little nuts debating this here."

"Ambra?" I was desperate for surety.

"The fields of the Anti block my vision. I can't follow the possible paths. The endings hold more death than life."

Fox engaged the helmet, and the mechanism grasped her skull and assembled over it. Her words came out from the speakers, amplified and artificial. "Life through action!"

Kim followed suit.

I sighed. "Okay, but we're yanking you back at the first sign of trouble."

We would never get that chance.

They lined up against the wall facing the dark drone, and Ambra carved out a separate space for each of them. Two bubbles detached from the main enclosure and floated out toward the device. Every hundred meters or so, she would test the connection and pull them backward to ensure she still had control over their capsules.

They reported back at all steps. The sickness in body and mind increased, but they asserted it was manageable.

"Might need to hurl soon," said Kim, "but otherwise, okay."

"I'm having some visual problems," Fox said. "Can't focus on the thing. Can't keep it centered in my vision, either."

"Yeah, me too," he echoed. "Don't know how we're going to shoot it like this. Telemetry's gone all funky." He paused. "Hell, the whole HUD is flaking out on me."

"Then we pull you back," I said, turning to Ambra.

She sat again, concentrating on maintaining the projections despite the disturbances from the drone.

"Wait, not yet," said Kim. "Hard to see, but I'm making out some structure."

A harsh static crackled over my communications, and I saw both their suits darken. A total loss of power despite the mini-reactors in the chassis. Their bodies dropped to the bottom of their enclosures. Neither moved.

"A pulse!" Ambra gasped.

I felt it too, as if my eyes were being driven into my skull with knives. I crouched to one knee and tried to stay conscious.

"Away!" yelled Waythrel.

Through the headache, I squinted out of our vessel. We sped from the thing, the duo still in tow.

The Orb flared, equaling a star's brightness. As the toxic radiation from the drone bathed us, the light countered the effects. She steered the bubble closer to the Time Sphere, and soon things normalized.

Until we pulled my soldiers back into the enclosure.

I've seen horrors on the battlefield. Flechette injuries and deaths that are inconceivable. Something your mind can't envision. Direct experience is required.

I wasn't prepared for what we brought in.

Kim and Fox—they were dead. Beyond killed, gutted. Dissolved. *Unmade* in a fashion no weapon I had experienced could achieve. The MECHcore suits, these products of superior Xixian technology, were ancient artifacts discovered in some tomb. Aged ten thousand years. The structure of the metals and plastics came apart. Disintegrating. Words floundered. Matter didn't behave this way.

The effects were grisly. Decayed metal and plastic are one thing, flesh and bodies something else. Their remains oozed out of the pocked holes in the wrecked mechs like a tomato purée. The biochemical bonds holding tissues, bone, and cells together failed completely. Nothing recognizably human remained in their appearance at all. The demonic device had reduced two members of my team to a homogenized sludge of constituent ingredients.

The smell hit us.

"Captain, what the *fuck*?" hissed Moore, his face strained, green and sickened.

Williams averted her eyes, her hand to her mouth. We all stepped back from the sight in shock.

I stammered. "Dear God. I don't know."

Ambra wrapped her arms around me from behind. "I'm so sorry, Nitin. I couldn't stop it."

I pressed her hands into mine, a child comforted by the warmth and physical presence of another. Monsters were real in this universe, but I had never seen something so monstrous occur in it.

Waythrel alone maintained composure. "We will have to deal with your sorrow and examine these developments later. We have more urgent matters to attend to."

"Jesus, squid!" yelled Moore, flashing wild eyes at the alien. "The Orb Strings can wait a few minutes!"

"Yes, I'm sure that they can," the Xix answered. "But I don't think that the Dram warship approaching us will."

Chapter 27

The observed macroscopic irreversibility is not a consequence of the fundamental laws of physics, it's a consequence of the particular configuration in which the universe finds itself. In particular, the unusual low-entropy conditions in the very early universe, near the Big Bang. Understanding the arrow of time is a matter of understanding the origin of the universe.

Sean Carroll

We followed the alien's outstretched arm. Twelve digits pointed to space, twitching with a suppressed anxiety.

The warship was Dram all right. Huge, rendering our small bubble an ant beside an elephant. Ugly in a way their aesthetic always appeared to me, possessed of an inherent malice from the point of design. Sharp edges glinted like blades. Terraced, bulky levels like prison floors. The surface pitted and etched as if from acid. The weapons arrayed fore and aft required no hateful intention to convey their purpose.

"A trap!" yelled Williams.

I turned to Ambra. She knelt over the bodies, the pool of remains spreading and nearing her black robes. The seeping sludge slowed and stopped. The two forms floated away from the main enclosure in their own external bubble.

"We need to do something," I prodded.

She stood. "Their remains are in a time stasis that will preserve them until we can examine what happened." She walked forward and rested beside Waythrel. "Only this ship?"

"Yes," said the alien. "It should not pose a danger."

"Unless they have the tech that destroyed Orferlin and killed Nitin's soldiers."

"Do you think it's possible?" I asked.

Eyes darted toward her.

"I am unsure of everything now," she said. "Something tells me it would be as deadly to the Dram as to us. For now, we assume they're armed as usual."

Bright trails erupted from the vessel.

The Xix spoke. "They behave predictably. Incoming missiles!"

Ambra raised her arms, her verdant eyes disappearing behind closing lids. "Then we respond to them as always."

The Orb flashed. Limbs of light sprang from the sphere and crossed the distance to us before I could blink. They wrapped themselves around the projectiles and detonated them far from our capsule.

As I processed the rapid exchange, the Dram fired beam weapons. Ten different rays at our bubble, the coherent radiance dizzying, meters from my face. Stopped in their tracks by offshoots of the glimmering tendrils.

After twenty seconds of full burn, the bugs wised up. They'd drain their power supplies. They'd thrown everything at us, enough firepower to melt entire cities on New Earth. We weren't scratched. The ship arced away.

"Chickenshit bastards!" cried Kim.

"They're rabbiting, all right," laughed Moore. "Damn me, I've heard what you could do with those things, sister, but, well, *damn!*"

"We're going to board them," said Ambra. "Find out what the hell is going on."

"Board them?" asked Williams. The cruiser was already aligning its panel of engines toward us, readying for a String jump. "Well, first you gotta stop it."

The enormous tendrils unfolded into sheets of light. The membranes surrounded the warship. The thrusters fired, the raging ion blasts distorting the glow around the hull.

It went nowhere. The monstrosity belched forth more power than half the New Earth navy but couldn't move.

The warrant officer shook her head. "Guess I had that coming."

Ambra opened her eyes. For the first time, despite witnessing her deeds in the Saharan battle, I experienced a moment of the religious reverence so many felt for her. Such raw potency compelled worship in feeble creatures of flesh and blood.

But as I connected with those eyes, affection eclipsed the awe. An all-consuming devotion not to a divinity, but to her person. My lover. My beautiful and terrible and sad Ambra Dawn.

The bubble sped toward the paralyzed Dram war boat. Her plan was solid. She could read their minds. The history books recounted the stories from her captivity. They couldn't hide anything from her. Unless they opted for suicide. If we moved quickly enough, they'd be helpless before her. We could find out what this dark enemy was up to and how to defeat them.

The Anti had other plans. As we approached, she darted her head to the side and gasped. I followed her gaze, and beside the Dram vessel, a crack appeared in space itself. A massive shadow boiled through the fissure. Its form was cloaked from light and difficult to discern. I felt in my stomach the same unease I had experienced at the death drone.

"A ghost ship!" I cried.

She knew, but it was too late. A spray of particles aimed at the warcraft came from the shadows.

Ambra screamed. "Close your eyes, everyone! Turn away!"

I did as told.

The impact was pure energy. A nova. The bubble turned pitch black as she sought to block the radiation. Despite her efforts, sufficient quantities penetrated to make the interior bright enough to hurt through closed eyelids. The temperature inside spiked. Within seconds, sweat soaked my clothes even with the MECHcore climate control. I didn't think we could last long in this flux.

Without warning, it ended. I glanced around the enclosure. No one was harmed. I ran to her side.

"I'm okay, Nitin."

I peered into her eyes and kissed her, holding her body to mine.

"What happened?" asked Moore, his face pale.

"We lost our catch," said Waythrel. "The Dram vessel is destroyed."

"How? Why?" asked Williams. "Where's the wreckage?"

"Annihilated," said Ambra. "Converted to pure energy by an interaction with antimatter."

She was right. The warcraft had vanished, and an enormous amount of radiation had been released. It was exactly what one might expect in a matter-antimatter collision.

We were not alone. The shadow ship hovered beside us.

Ambra set her mouth into a thin line. "Let's see how they respond to the full power of the Orb."

She closed her eyes once more. For a moment, nothing happened. A total silence in the bubble. The Anti craft didn't move.

A dim light glowed from the Time Sphere. The radiance intensified, broadened into multiple wavelengths. It flashed, the brightness outshining the exploding Dram warship.

She directed the energy. It rushed forward at a speed I could follow, like some glowing fist thrown at the body of our foes. I couldn't imagine what it was going to do.

The shadow ship didn't wait around to find out. The Anti had prepped a jump on a local String. The same entity lashing out at the enemy provided a door to the Time Tree, and our enemies stepped through it. The unlight vanished, leaving the star-filled dark of regular space in its place.

"No!" Fury burned in Ambra's tones. "I should have sealed the node and then dealt with them. Stupid pride! I was too ready to show them justice! I let them escape."

Waythrel approached Ambra. "The positive news is that they were afraid of you. Whatever technology they possess, they were not willing to go up against you and the Orb."

"Yeah, but they were sharp enough to take out the Dram boat," said Moore. "Didn't defend the bastards from us, you'll notice. Not much love there. They didn't want us getting them or any information."

"Another encouraging sign," clipped the alien. "They fear knowledge falling into our hands. They are vulnerable."

Ambra smiled at the Xix. "Yes."

"This means there is far more hope for our cause than we might have had before their attack," it finished.

Hope?

Perhaps. It felt abstract. I gazed out of the enclosure behind us to the smaller bubble holding the time-frozen corpses. Failure swept over me. Responsibility mismanaged. *I* had allowed the mission to occur. Their deaths were in my ledger.

We moved toward the Orb. Ambra sealed the Time Tree Strings to shut down this first of three nodes.

This trip was too much to process. It had begun with another tortuous traversal for me. We found a world slaughtered and poisoned. An enemy possessed terrible weapons we hardly understood.

Yet these same forces feared us. Shadows fled the Daughter in her wrath. They murdered allies to prevent interrogation.

Those last thoughts comforted me some. In the midst of my sadness and revulsion, despite the fear and uncertainty, a ray of sunlight. A hope.

As always, the hope depended on Ambra Dawn.

Chapter 28

*The atoms or elementary particles themselves are not real; they form a
world of potentialities or possibilities rather than one of things or facts.*

Werner Heisenberg

We left without doing anything more with the drones surrounding the globe. We feared someone had betrayed our mission. Delay risked giving our enemies more time to prepare.

Orferlin had already perished. The Dram and the shadow device destroyed all hope of reviving it. What sealed our decision was the death of Caga. After the Anti ship escaped, we returned to the surface to find the creature dead. The last of her kind in sterilized seas.

Ambra stared at the planet as she guided us toward the Orb for transit. Her expression was inscrutable. Sadness, guilt, fear, and expectation were turbulent waves passing over her features. I leaned against her arm, holding her cold hand. How was I to comfort her when she gazed at the extinction of an entire world? We retreated from a culture she had known in a deep communion.

Waythrel twitched at her side, its eyes gazing backward and forward. The translator filled the alien's words with sorrow. "Such waste. So many beautiful creatures. Magnificent minds. So much unmade and lost."

Ambra's spoke under her breath. I strained to hear.

"Not lost. Never wasted." Her eyes danced between the Xix and me, tears welling. "Waiting for a time of harvest."

I waited for an explanation, but she said nothing more. The alien didn't probe. I let Ambra have the space she needed to mourn. I'd never seen her so heavy with loss.

The presence of a possible traitor at our highest levels put the rest of us on edge. Despite her efforts to prevent paranoia, distrust grew in our team. Too many coincidences mounted. The Dram pounced at what should have been arbitrary star systems. They placed an army and a False Dawn at the Temple, through Xixian defenses. At the moment of the Daughter's speech. I could see no other conclusion— we were betrayed.

Which of us to suspect? If it was to be one of our group on this strange mission, it couldn't be the Daughter or her closest advisor. A Xix betraying the cause? It was beyond unthinkable. That left the two remaining members of my team. While it was true I had not known them long, serving together in combat reveals a lot about a person.

There is something raw and unfiltered about placing your life on the line in front of others. It's hard to hold a lie in your eyes when your death is staring you in the face. I had been with Moore and Williams. I had seen them face annihilation. I trusted them. Moore had overcome his dislike of mental sharing. Ambra had reported nothing. His thoughts must have been clear of treachery.

It left me with the other members of Ambra's inner circle. My mind immediately focused on Mazandarani. It was partly jealousy. Anger at his suspicions of me. My judgment was biased. His suspicion itself became suspect in this growing paranoia. Did he do it to cast eyes off himself and onto an innocent? Had his hatred of me pushed him into apostasy? Men had turned traitors for less. But it seemed unlikely Ambra would have missed such thoughts in him. He too had shared with the Readers, despite not being one.

Last of all, the major. Mizoguchi wasn't the type, but now I questioned everything. Could she have concealed duplicity from the Daughter any better than Mazandarani? Could anyone? Spies would seem to be impossible in the presence of the galaxy's most potent psychic.

"We will be shattered by betrayal."

Her words spoken on that glowing beach beneath the Milky Way. But who?

None of the potential traitors held up under scrutiny. It was a mystery I despaired of solving. So it was a quiet, far less adventurous journey through the Orb to our second destination. Doubts consumed. We mourned two of our members, whose bodies we carried with us like some surreal baggage. I was also anxious about the transit. Once again, I became ill, but the effects were lessened. Ambra worked to shield us from the vulnerabilities inherent in the traversal. I remembered no dream this time.

Entering the new star system, I had recovered enough to process my environment. Our small bubble was orbiting an enormous violet-green gas giant that humbled Jupiter. It had no name from its inhabitants. The Xix named the world Gyl, and so we called it.

My mind played over the reams of data I had absorbed from the sharing. The creatures of Gyl were bizarre, defying categorization. Language itself was an artificial construct for them. The entities had developed it after years of mental communion with the Readers led by Ambra. The work was a concession to help divergent forms of life communicate.

Their homeworld was so enormous it contained enough mass to fuse deuterium in its core. It was as much a failed star as a planet. Its system rode on one of the spiral arms of the galaxy near the center.

That explained the bright and dense constellations. The night skies of New Earth were dim and impoverished in comparison. It was located closer to their system's sun than our Jupiter. The atmosphere was hot, the weather violent, especially in the upper layers.

Like most gas giants, hydrogen dominated its composition. A smaller amount of helium was also present. These elements were gases at the surface of the planet's outer regions. They transitioned to multiple alternative phases nearer the core.

The center resembled the inner planets of our star system. Trace amounts of heavier atoms formed in the death throes of giant stars sank to the bottom of Gyl. This dense sphere was many times larger than our homeworld. It strained under tremendous forces. Matter adopted modes outside the models of our knowledge.

It was the areas directly above the rocky heart that were the habitat of intelligence. In those layers brooded a sentience I found almost impossible to consider alive. The environmental extremes compelled the particles to adopt bizarre physical states. New Earth science stumbled with a foggy grasp of their properties. The Xix understood more, but the explanations were beyond my comprehension.

A near-crystalline configuration of hydrogen was the crux. Not a solid or a liquid, it existed as an ordered aggregate. Its interactions with other pseudo-symmetric elements created a novel, unEarthly chemistry. In this dynamic evolved a fantastic form of being. One so outlandish, it called into question my conceptions of life itself.

Examining existence with such seriousness brought on a disorientation. What were *we*, exactly? Atoms on their own have no will, no purpose. Nothing but constraints based on "laws" of physics (whatever those really are).

Somehow, under the conditions of our homeworld—temperature, radiation from the sun, elemental composition, pressure—these atomic entities formed organized structures. At one point, some of them obtained the ability to replicate, copy themselves. The process of "survival of the stable" took over. Evolution produced increasingly diverse and able molecules, cells, bodies—*minds*.

Could our ideals of love and beauty, the abstractions of mathematics and logic, all come from a dance of particles? It struck me as strange that my consciousness derived from carbon chains and water. In fact, it made no sense at all.

My exposure to the alien life should have broadened my views. I ought to have been more open to the idea of what life, and particularly *mind*, could be in this universe. Especially after learning about Ambra and the group sharings.

Still, I was stuck in the biases of Earth. *Obvious, logical,* and *reasonable* have for us small and closed meanings. The cosmos was lecturing me about their relativity.

The atoms of hydrogen, helium, and the trace elements did not form the direct substrate for life on Gyl. The quasi-crystalline lattices *themselves* did. I formed a poor and distorting analogy to explain it to myself. In my idea, I began with the molecules and chemical bonds forming the basis of our bodies. I mapped them to the lattices and interlattice interactions of different crystals in the alien atmospheric levels. A higher-level crystal-chemistry sat above the basic atomic bonding.

No doubt the Xix would have a laugh at my efforts.

The sharing with Ambra confused me further. These structures transcended crystals across the span of the living layers. Critical to the evolution of intelligence was that they were also *crystals in time.* Repeated arrays occurred at cyclic time points and not necessarily in space. New Earth science had begun tackling such ideas. Waythrel noted our theories were embryonic and based on a lot of incorrect thinking.

So my lessons went. In this wild world, there existed a wonderland for those wishing to study the full potential of this form of matter. I would have normally left them to it, but nothing was normal in our mission.

The result was a life-form in a state without analogy in our knowledge. One which used the stores of heat and weak fusion to produce higher order and structure. Millions of years ago, intelligence evolved. The creatures of this system were far older than us. Their extreme differences made them more and less advanced than other life in the galaxy. Their technology was primitive, their mental reach into science and mathematics profound.

These thoughts befuddled my mind as our spacetime bubble approached the enormous planet. But any attempt to communicate with the aliens of Gyl had to wait. First, we needed to deal with the unexpected Dram welcoming party waiting for us.

Chapter 29

The doctrine that the world is made up of objects whose existence is independent of human consciousness turns out to be in conflict with quantum mechanics and with facts established by experiment.

Bernard d'Espagnat

"*Shit!*" Williams whistled. "There must be four or five squadrons."

"Over there!" said Moore, pointing to dark patches in the bright local star field. "Shadow ships. Half as many."

My stomach dropped. One Dram cruiser and a single of those devil boats were enough. This time, thirty starships hung between us and the planet. The balance of power in this standoff was much less clear to me.

"Gyl has no obvious strategic importance to this war," noted Waythrel. "We are here only because of the critical node point that rests next to their world."

"Someone's selling us out." Moore scowled. "They knew we were coming."

"Likely briefed about the last engagement," said Williams. "We chased off one of theirs before. Can we scare off ten of them?"

The case for the spy grew stronger. We didn't have the luxury to debate. I gazed at the line of starships, and my mind raced through stratagems, tactics, scenarios. But something was bothering me.

"Why aren't they engaging? Moving? They're just sitting there."

"Could be they haven't picked us up yet," said Williams.

Ambra's response was cold. "No. They're closing the noose."

I spun around. *An ambush!* Another twenty or thirty ships approached behind us. They were spreading out to the sides and above, shutting down all avenues of escape. Our enemies surrounded us, cutting us off from the Orb and the planet.

I turned to Ambra and placed my hand on her shoulder.

"You must do something soon," said Waythrel.

She smiled. "Silly Xix, you know both what and when are illusions."

With those words, she was gone.

We startled. One moment, I was touching my beloved with concern, the next I was holding air. As we gawked at one another in confusion, space was decorated with explosions of light.

Afterward, she'd explain to me what happened. At the time, a sudden, massive, and broad assault on the enemy vessels erupted. From every position. Those in front of us, nearest the planet. Those behind us. Those completing a sphere entombing us in a net of ships. From each location of a Dram and shadow entity, there came brilliance.

The Orb flashed, as bright as we had seen in the attack at Orferlin, but without the buildup. There was no time to observe the flaming arms of energy extend from the object. They simply appeared around us.

The carnage was spectacular. Replacing the spherical lattice of surrounding war boats, a fiery globe encased us. Our enemies were vaporized. The Anti craft exploded with the staggering energies of annihilation. Before we could process the destruction, a gargantuan cyclone was born in the midst of it. The hurricane of light and debris swirled down to a vortex as broad as a major moon. The tunnel of radiance extended back toward the Orb. The glorious sphere of power controlled by the Daughter lit up brighter than the local star.

We shielded our eyes, and I engaged my suit helmet. It fastened itself around my head, and I toggled the view screen to filter incoming radiation. I squinted at the glowing portal. The remains of enemy ships poured into the multidimensional gateway and disappeared.

The brilliance winked out. Its disappearance was like a silenced thunder. Relief swept over me.

"You cannot win a battle if you focus on winning space alone."

Ambra's voice. She stood in the middle of the enclosure, her face drawn, eyes bloodshot.

"The universe moves in more than three dimensions."

I opened the faceplate of my suit. I dashed to her and enveloped her body in my hard exoskeleton. The nanofiber gloves retracted. I could feel the softness of her flesh. After I had held her for a moment, I realized how terrified I had been at her disappearance. The irrational fear of losing her chilled me in repeating waves.

"Ambra, don't do that to me again, please," I blurted. My face pressed into her shoulder and neck. "I can't lose you. Not after finding you."

I will never be lost to you, Nitin. Even if it might seem so for a time. Like distance, time is an illusion.

"I'll be buggered!" said Moore. "That, all by itself, makes this trip worth whatever shit we're going to see."

Williams stared open-mouthed and said nothing. Waythrel walked to the middle of the bubble and positioned its odd body next to Ambra.

"Once again, our Daughter of Time teaches her teacher a lesson." If a Xix had a mouth, it would have been smiling.

I pulled back, holding her shoulders. Her skin felt cold. "Are you okay?"

"Yes. Tired, Nitin. I'll sit." She lowered herself into a cross-legged position on the floor of the enclosure. She closed her eyes.

I knelt with her, continuing to hold her hands as she sat. I stroked her hair, drawing a soft smile from her lips.

"I wish I could sleep right now," she finished, resting her head on my shoulder.

"So are we going to get an explanation for this Dram navy Armageddon?" asked Williams.

"I can tell you and spare Ambra the energy," said Waythrel. "The simplest account is that, using the Orb, the Daughter can travel through both space and time. Such transit normally requires tremendous energies. Since we are in proximity to the Time Sphere, she didn't need to journey far in any dimension. She was able to access several distinct three-dimensional locations at a single time point."

My warrant officer cocked her head to one side. "Run it by me again."

"She accessed the identical temporal location repeatedly, but each repetition changing the position." I thought I heard a slight impatience in the alien's translator. Her words must have been the Xixian version of *Physics for Poets*.

"Went to different places, but all at the same time?" asked Moore, his brow furrowed.

Williams traced a circle with her finger. "Right. That's why we saw everything happening everywhere, but all at once."

"If you had better eyes," continued the alien, "you would have seen something stranger. Tens, hundreds of Ambra Dawns. Each positioned near the enemy ships and simultaneously inducing their destruction."

"Enough for now," sighed Ambra, touching my arm. She opened her eyes. "We need to see what's left of the Gyl for us to speak to. Speaking with them won't be easy." She rose and kissed my hands. "Walk with me, Nitin?"

I followed her to the edge of the enclosure. In the midst of this insanity, I found myself distracted, stunned by her beauty. Uncountable numbers of stars carpeted the background. The suns shone undiminished and without distortion through the spacetime compartment. The dots of light framed her form, her red locks bouncing with each step. I was still reeling from the sudden disappearance. Her physical presence struck me as infinitely valuable, precious, and vulnerable. Had I understood our ultimate fates, I would have treasured this physicality all the more.

I am yours and you are mine, Nitin. In flesh and in spirit.

"I feel them," she spoke out loud to everyone. The rest drew near, hanging on her words. "You can't see them, but the entire planet is ringed with poisonous seeds."

"The death drones." I shuddered. The memory of those around Brax was still raw. I had to stop myself from turning toward the bodies of Kim and Fox.

"Yes, but the Anti have not achieved their goal here. Not yet."

"How do you know?" I asked.

Waythrel responded. "Because we can sense the mind of the Gyl below. It has not been destroyed."

I felt relief. "Then they're okay."

"No," said Ambra. "They're weakening. It'll be much slower with them than with the Brax. I'll speak with them now, find out what I can. If we conclude it's safe, I'll purge these drones from the system."

Chapter 30

In the beginning, there were only probabilities. The universe could only come into existence if someone observed it. It does not matter that the observers turned up several billion years later. The universe exists because we are aware of it.

Martin Rees

Ambra parked the bubble outside the planetary atmosphere. The gas giant now spanned our field of vision. Churning cloud bands encircled the disk before us. Their hues ranged from blue to violet. Monstrous storms the size of entire worlds spun in tight knots at various locations. Seven major moons cast shadows on this face of the planet. My memory from the sharing told me there should be another five obscured from view. The number of minor satellites was in the hundreds.

The Gyl were beings with form composed of the planetary layers themselves. To enter too deep into the atmosphere was to violate their personal being in some sense. The substrates for their quasi-crystalline life were buried near the center of the gas giant. But

Ambra wished to cause no offense, and we hovered at the surface. The mind of the world was strange beyond prediction. She proceeded with extreme caution.

As on Orferlin, the members of my team and I wanted to partake in the communication. Readers on New Earth had spoken with these beings through the telepathic medium. While we could have shared as we did with Caga of the Brax, Waythrel warned it wouldn't be productive. It might be deadly.

"Cognitive-shock is probable," said the alien. "Between mentalities as similar as Xix and human, there can be disturbances in sharing. The thoughts of the Gyl are not isomorphous to those of creatures like us. A naked, naive encounter would lead to trauma. Only through the deepest meditations, employing the greater insight of the Group Mind, were we capable of establishing contact. Here, devoid of the horde of Readers, that collective does not exist. It may not be possible to communicate at all."

Ambra explained further. "If we do, we'll only be able to understand them because of those memories. The lessons we learned through the sharing will guide us." Her gaze was troubled. "You have none of that background. The presence of the Gyl consciousness could be dangerous. It could threaten your psyche in its terrible alienness."

"How can some crystal brain in there hurt mine out here?" asked Moore.

"The Daughter can kill with her thoughts, Sergeant," said Waythrel. "I've seen her drop entire Dram infantries to the ground without lifting her finger. Intelligence creates a physical potential. A Writer can modify that field. One spacetime array altering another. Those modifications can be beneficial, healing, educational. Or they can be destructive. The interaction of two extremely different mental entities is unpredictable. You are one small mind. Here is a planetary consciousness of proportions and a nature that would frighten you if you could perceive it."

Ambra agreed. "It will be dangerous for Waythrel and me, even with the power of the Orb. Because to communicate, I'll have to open myself to them. Become vulnerable."

"Are they potentially violent?" I asked.

She struggled to answer. "Could they damage me? Yes. Would it be violence? Is solar radiation burning your skin an attack or hostile? Or are these words suitable for creatures like us but not for other things in this universe?"

"Lost me, sister," said Moore. "But I'm happy to stay out of this sharing. Wasn't keen on the other one except I was tired of being left out."

Williams agreed. "It sounds like too big a risk. Count me out."

"There may be a way for you to partake of the conversation, although it will be strange," said Waythrel.

Ambra frowned at the alien. "How?"

"The MECHcore suits," it said. "There is an AI embedded within. It has scaled several levels of proto-sentience."

She frowned, a pained expression on her face.

Warning lights went on for me. "What does this mean?"

"A spacetime field, Nitin. I Read and Write. I've interacted with the artificial intelligence of the more evolved systems the Xix have developed. Simple awareness. Ugly in many ways, but real. Growing more complex with their science, with each generation of the technology."

"Before we left, the Daughter undertook extensive research efforts with our synthetic cognition," said Waythrel. "She achieved remarkable results with the more advanced versions. However, our AI has progressed much further in consciousness than the primitive minds in your suits."

"Is this bad?" I asked. Ambra's face was strained. "You're troubled."

Now isn't the time, Nitin. Trust me. I'll explain everything later.

"No, it's not a problem at all," said Ambra. "It means our Xix is right. I can work through your mechs. I can funnel the fields of thought through them and the Xixian translator." She nodded, as if seeing the alien's plan come together in her mind. "Yes. Suit up, turn on your COM, and you'll hear their speech come through the speakers."

"Mangled as it might be by our understanding and Ambra's interface with the AI," completed Waythrel.

Moore laughed. "I swear everything that happens on this trip has got to be weirder than a peyote cactus ceremony."

"Cactus ceremony?" asked Williams, an eyebrow arched.

"Yeah, you know, American Indians? Mescaline?"

She shook her head and shrugged.

He grinned. "Forget it. Sounds wicked, sister. I'm onboard."

Williams consented. "Me, too."

"Okay, let's suit up." I grabbed for my headgear before remembering I had already put it on during the attack. I engaged the COM. "Ready whenever you are, Ambra."

She and Waythrel sat together in the middle of the bubble. The alien's long arms reached toward the Daughter. She held the many-fingered ends of the Xixian extremities and closed her eyes. They meditated in silence for more than thirty minutes. The enclosure was quiet except for the shallow breathing of the humans and the strange respirations of the Xix—a noise like some rhythmic steam leak from a radiator.

I knew there must be something transformative happening. Something amazing. The galaxy's greatest Reader. The Orb. A bizarre crystalline intelligence inhabiting a planet dominating my field of vision. The surrounding space should be shaking.

I sensed nothing. For the first time, I grasped the separation between Ambra and the rest of us. Here was the woman I loved. Earth's savior I had adored since my birth. The woman with whom I had shared flesh and heart and mind. In this place and time, in this state, she was a creature divergent. A soul I couldn't reach or understand. I was blind in a sensory world where she had the greatest vision of all.

I felt much more than inadequate—I was alone. For the first

time, I yearned, longed with a hungry desperation, to be able to share her journey.

I strained. I tried to activate some latent power within me. A sightless mole, I conjured organs of perception to pierce the darkness. If desire by itself could remake the fabric of the universe, I would have succeeded. Of course, it was laughable. The darkness endured, and all I managed to do was give myself a tension headache. Ambra and Waythrel remained in a realm I couldn't access—would never experience. The realization brought a weight of sadness on me.

As I waited with a new burden on my heart, our COM units crackled. Static bursts and garbled noises. Words.

The voice of Gyl.

Chapter 31

Within the narrow spectrum of our senses, we are blind to the cosmic symphony that plays on frequencies beyond our grasp.

Chat Generative Pre-trained Transformer 3.5,
January 6, 2024

"We are the having been becoming to the invader uncreation deathling approach reaching hydrogen oxygen carbon netting summation of the broken crystal core."

The genderless voice of the AI ceased, leaving static flowing over the COM. I glanced at our pair of Readers—they remained motionless in their deep meditation. I locked eyes with my soldiers.

Moore shook his head. "Well, that's gone pear-shaped."

We didn't have any chance to consider the opening greeting. The conversation continued.

"We are a seed of the Sol Mind, the seven-kilo parsec three-dimensioned pathway."

This came through the Xix's translator, but not in the alien's typical tones. Some combination of the thoughts of Ambra and the Xix, perhaps. A warped phrase relayed through the cybernetic linkage between their minds and the equipment. The response in our COMs was stranger.

"The nucleation event corrected being devoid of augmentation. Understanding through other complexities passes inside solvent channels."

"Other pathways are closed," rang out Waythrel's device. "Paths must be taken. Gyl dissolves."

"Gyl dissolves."

"Well, I'm glad we've established *that*," said Williams, rolling her eyes. "We should have sat this conversation out. Makes no sense."

Moore shrugged. "It's like listening to a malfunctioning translator."

"Then switch off and shut up," I snapped. "I want to hear this!"

"...with the time infinite crowd-mind gate. Gyl lacks the interference projections to unmake the dissolving."

"Carbon crystal seeds dissolve upon breaching radial separations."

"We maintain safe distances."

"Acceleration achieving possible state spaces augmentation is the lattice drivings the asymmetry breaking."

A long pause followed this statement. Several minutes passed. Moore and Williams paced the bubble and conversed. I ignored them.

My beloved struggled. I studied her lined face. Tension flared through her muscles. Her pale skin was tight over veins bulging from internal pressure. Stress was building up within her at whatever had been said or at her efforts to parse it.

"Yes. The disorder is comprehended," came a response. "Reversal of molecular organization."

"Surface defects in the framework only are your thoughts failing assembly of divergent structural integrations. Maximum extensionings through all available states to render the end the beginning sameness."

Ambra's back stiffened. "Symmetry broken."

"The final first through crystal will was now always healed wounding killing all matrices built from broken order. Earth shards prolong Gyl thankfulness anxiety universal erasure."

"We understand."

Moore coughed. "Yeah, sure cleared it up."

I placed my finger over my mouth. Williams shrugged her shoulders, rolling her eyes.

The translator spoke a last statement. "The asymmetrical induction will be halted."

The rest was static. After five minutes of it, we shut off our COMs. The two Readers still didn't move, and we waited in anticipation until Ambra stirred. Her eyes slid open like someone drugged.

"Waythrel?" she whispered.

The Xix didn't respond. She rested her hands on the midsection of the creature, the location of the Xixian brain-like structure.

"Come back. Hear me. Follow my voice."

She sat in this position, unmoving, repeating the commands to the alien. Her expression pained and concerned, she called the creature's name. Minutes passed. An hour.

"Not looking good," said Moore under his breath. "Maybe the Gyl-thing lobotomized the squid. If it's possible with one of those things."

I dared not interfere. Time dragged without a sound other than Ambra's repeated calls. Her speech quieted, her eyes peering past us, as if her mind were traveling some vast distance.

After the extended ministrations, which the rest of us had begun to assume were in vain, Waythrel stirred. And promptly fell over on its side, unmoving.

"Ambra! What happened?" I leaped across the bubble and crouched down, trying to lift the alien. Despite the hydraulics of my suit, the creature was a struggle to move.

"Easy, Nitin," she said. "The worst has passed. Waythrel's in a recovery state unique to its kind. We won't get a response for a few hours. You can let the body be—no need to hold it up."

I lowered the Xix back to the surface of the enclosure. The bright and dense star field glimmered at me, surrounding its shape. Having no exobiology training, I couldn't tell whether it lived.

"Then how do you know it's okay?" asked Williams, both she and Moore gathered alongside the prone extraterrestrial.

Ambra leaned forward, cupping her face in her palms. The enormous bulge from her skull protruded from the tips of her fingers. The veins were swollen and taut. Her nails clung like hooks on a mask surrounded by a red halo.

Her words came out muffled. "We could connect mentally. Only at the end." She massaged her temples a moment and placed her hands on the ground behind her for support. "Waythrel's mind became detached. The Gyl mental field broke the connection to its physical spacetime incarnation. I had to reintegrate them. Some damage occurred, but it's hard for me to know exactly what. Xix minds are too complex for me."

"Damage?" I asked. "Permanent? Memory? Cognitive function? What?"

"I said I don't know, Nitin!"

I recoiled, never having been the object of her anger.

Her face softened, and she reached out and took my hand. "I'm sorry. This has been extremely difficult. This whole damn day. We'll have to wait and see."

She stood and stretched her arms, bending her body in different yoga positions. Waythrel remained unmoving on the floor. The MECHcore soldiers glanced between Ambra and me.

The Brit cursed and rose as well. "So while we're kicking our heels, let's have you fill us in on that chinwag. Because from where we're standing, it was a wad of rubbish."

She sighed. "We told you it would be hard to understand. What we experienced in the direct communication was far more difficult."

Williams probed further. "It sounded like you learned something important at the end. You were going to destroy the drones or something."

"Yes," she said. "On the last part, it's easy to explain. The Gyl are unable to remove them and were happy for us to do so. It will save them. They explained to us about the devices. What they perceived was happening to them, to the planet—it was something very disturbing. If we have actually understood it correctly."

The strange words kept floating through my mind. "Something about fixing *broken symmetries* and *achieving all states*. What did it mean?"

She turned around to face us, her expression dark. "The Anti aren't allies of the Dram, whatever the bugs think. They're enemies of everything in this galaxy. In fact, of all the known galaxies. Of all the matter existing in the universe."

Moore huffed. "How do you wage war on the universe? And why?"

"I don't know." Her voice was heavy. "These devices are a clue. The first real information about what's happening. I'm anxious now to reach Hola, our last node. There, we may be able to examine the effects of the drones. There we have a species at least *slightly* more comprehensible than the Gyl. Assuming the Anti have placed the evil things there as well." She stared out into the surrounding star field. "I've a feeling they have."

"So what do they *do*?" asked Moore.

"Entropy. A weaponized application."

"You mean like the second law of thermodynamics?" asked Williams. "Everything becomes disordered?"

"Yes, but *disorder* is a loaded, human word. Matter and energy moving to greater *freedom* might be a more insightful phrase, but Waythrel is the better one to talk to. I'm no physicist, and the physics of New Earth is primitive compared to the Xix." She inhaled, preparing her words. "Entropy is why, when you have organization, it *dis*organizes over time. Why you have to keep cleaning your room, but it never needs to be messed up. Why, when you pop a balloon full of helium, it mixes with all the other gases in the room, doesn't stay separated. Why things break down.

Why energy transfer is always with a loss. All possible states are accessed."

She raised herself from the invisible floor and stared down at the alien.

"It's why time appears to flow in one direction. Space, time, order, disorder, freedoms, constraints—they're all tied together in a deep sense. The ultimate nature of reality is like a harmony whose quality depends on the notes sounded by each of these elements."

I had no idea what she was talking about. "So, if the drones increase entropy, stuff breaks down more quickly."

"In some ways," she said, glancing at the wrecked remains of my team. "At a terrible rate unimaginable until now. The Gyl understood it best because of their highly structured crystalline composition. They possess a unique perspective, as well as physical form in our galaxy."

"One the things are breaking down now, right?" asked Williams.

"Yes," replied Ambra, wincing at my warrant officer as if receiving a reprimand. "So the time for talk is over. We have some orbiting antimatter to destroy."

Chapter 32

The total disorder in the universe, as measured by the quantity that physicists call entropy, increases steadily over time. Also, the total order in the universe, as measured by the complexity and permanence of organized structures, also increases steadily over time.

Freeman Dyson

Destroy them, she did.

Three hundred were stationed across the surface of the planet, orbiting outside the atmosphere. We approached them one at a time. Ambra summoned the full power of the Orbs to grant us maximum protection. She crushed the devices by warping space around them. The drones didn't retaliate or mount any response. Perhaps the Anti had never encountered anyone who could attack the objects. Or it happened too quickly for any useful information to be transmitted.

Whatever the reason, the effect was dramatic. After she squashed them, their shielding failed. As they made contact with the edges of the Gyl atmosphere, a light show erupted. The low-density gases contacted the pulverized antimatter. A glow grew. Gravity drove the drone carcasses faster into the planet. Explosions resembling epic thermonuclear blasts detonated. Not enough to be a problem for a world this size but producing gigantic pageantry.

Three hundred was a terrifying number. After encountering many of the targets, she began to sense their locations, detecting them by the strange effects they had on spacetime. It became clear the Anti had placed them equidistant around the gas giant.

With their geometry mapped, she summoned a tidal wave of power from the Orb. In a burst of flame, she hit all the drones with a blast of energy. Once again, a titanic vortex in space formed and drank down the refuse of her wrath.

After this fireworks display, the Xix woke. A stirring in the eyestalks was the first sign. The individual eyes pointed in many directions, surveying the surroundings. Ambra knelt down beside the alien and held its odd arm.

"Waythrel," she said.

The alien's voice stammered in monotone. "We are about Gyl. I have been injured. Deductions suggest that you have destroyed the Anti devices. I have no memory of such a conversation, or any communion, with their mind. The contact must have overwhelmed me."

Its legs moved at bizarre angles. In a miracle of biomechanics, the extraterrestrial raised itself to a standing position.

"Yes, the drones are annihilated," said Ambra. "The planet is free of their poison. You were displaced. I did my best to help. I'm sorry for where I failed."

"We will have to see how much you have failed," it said, the tones from the translator more fluid and coherent. "I know you did all you could. I understood the risks."

"There are important things to know about the communion," she said. "Ideas too complicated for me to explain. Can you share?"

The Xix reached out for her hands. "Yes, but go slowly, Daughter of Time."

Once again, we waited in silence as the Readers functioned in a realm inaccessible to us. It was much shorter than the interaction with Gyl. After five minutes, they separated.

"Frightening information," said Waythrel. The alien began a strange pacing inside the enclosure.

"I'm not sure I have understood it correctly," responded Ambra.

"Perhaps not, and I cannot access my memories to compare. Like you noted, however, we can test the creatures at Hola. We also have the suspended remains of the MECHcore team of Captain Ratava. There may be critical evidence there that scientific equipment can detect."

It was disturbing to hear the Xix refer to the butchered forms of two of my crew in such clinical terms. But I knew the alien was right. The hideous tools of the Anti had already stolen their dignity. If we could learn something about their weapons by examining their bodies, they'd not have died in vain.

"We're finished here," said Ambra. "We need to seal the node and continue to Hola. This time, I'll make sure we arrive early."

"Early?" I asked. "What do you mean?"

"The Time Tree lattice places all the star systems with Orbs on a synchronized clock," said Waythrel. Damage or no, the alien's wits appeared intact. "A time frame relative to the rest of the galaxy but absolute within the member worlds. She doesn't want any more surprises."

Seeing our confused expressions, Ambra explained further. "We have to assume our plans were leaked. Our enemies expect us to go to Hola. Because they're limited to the String routes, they can only move forward or beside us in time."

"They may be waiting now, having set up a trap days or weeks ago when the spy first betrayed our mission," continued the alien.

"But not months before. If we travel far enough into the past, after they took the node, but in advance of forming our preparations, they cannot ambush us."

"Aye, yeah, but there's a wee hole in all that," said Moore. "What if it's one of us blokes who's the traitor, eh? Then they'll ring up the Dram, and the bugs will adjust their schedule."

"They can't go back in time that way," said Williams.

"Why not?"

She's clicked her tongue. "Have you forgotten all your basic training? The Strings the Readers navigate on connect physical points, *but at the same time.* It's what she means by a clock. If we go back in time, they can't do anything."

"She is correct," said Waythrel. "The Daughter alone, who possesses unique access to the dimensional doorways in the Celestial Sphere, can do so. Not even the False Dawns have yet opened an Orb —as far as we know. If we go earlier, we'll be less likely to find unpleasant visitors."

As usual, these discussions brought on a headache. But I had to ask.

"You said there was a clone army. That it came from many points in the future. So the clones *can* cross through time. So why can't the traitor tell them and they still set a trap?"

"Can the spy communicate through time to those False Dawns?" Williams shared my struggles and rubbed her temples. "God, this is confusing."

"We don't know about the mole," said the Xix. "It would not likely matter. They do not use the Orbs. They travel through their own wormholes. It takes tremendous energy. They must be precise, mapping in space and time carefully. It is unlikely such a coordinated plot can be arranged on short notice with armies from a distant era.

"So the traitor—if he or she exists," said Moore, eyeing us with a smirk, "will just have to stew in it."

"Yes," said Ambra. "I'll pick a time before our plans, but we still don't know what might be waiting. Probably nothing, but perhaps the whole Dram armada." She raised her palms up. "So, what will it be?"

"Bloody life through action!" he said with a fist pump. "Let's go back in time, baby!"

"Fine with me," said Williams. "Long as we don't have to talk to any more crystal minds. The Hola, wait, I remember—they're primitive, right? Low-level intelligence, so no talking at all?"

Waythrel answered. "Communication will not be fruitful. Mental monitoring will be. They are a hive mentality. The structure of that mind was studied in detail by a Xixian scientist hundreds of years ago."

I remembered. "They were in the sharing. I didn't understand the analysis."

"Me either," echoed Moore.

"We will discuss it further," said the alien. "The current collective consciousness can be analyzed and compared to the data from before. If the Anti devices increase disorder, there will be measurable effects. A signature, if you will. It will be important proof of this hypothesis."

"If Ambra's right?" I asked.

The eyestalks danced around. "Then we should be afraid, Captain."

In all the laws of physics that we have found so far, there does not seem to be any distinction between the past and the future. The moving picture should work the same going both ways, and the physicist who looks at it should not laugh.

Richard Feynman

Once again, Ambra stood before the Orb and sealed the node. It was something I had to assume was happening. I couldn't see the Strings. I was no Reader, and her efforts left no visible change in the Time Sphere I could perceive. As with so much surpassing my understanding during this mission, I'd have to get used to being in the dark.

We departed Gyl through the portal, and again I was racked with pains, losing consciousness. To my continued embarrassment, I was the sole traveler affected. The faded outlines of a disturbing dream ate at my subconscious, but I suppressed the experience to focus on the tasks at hand.

Prone, I didn't feel like rising. I mustered my strength, denied the presence of the nausea and headache, and declared myself able to continue the mission. Ambra gave me a long side-eye but said nothing. I considered it a win to maintain my composure and avoid fainting for the first few hours.

Another gas giant waited in front of us. The knowledge learned in the sharing poured through my mind. Astronomers on Old Earth first cataloged extrasolar planets several hundred years ago. Those interested in extraterrestrial life faced disappointment. Most systems did not possess small, rocky, water-covered Edens like our own.

Instead, the predominant galactic citizens were of the Jovian type. Some spun this to believe moons around the great globes supported life as they imagined it. This indeed is the case in hundreds of locations. Much more common, however, is that the failed stars themselves harbored life, organisms diverging from the limited imaginations of early scientists.

The radiant orange Hola was a member of this plentiful set of worlds. The circumference was about twice the size of Jupiter, but smaller than the enormity of Gyl. Yet for a creature of New Earth, it was gigantic. While seventy satellites circled the world, none of them spawned life. The creatures in this star system filled the upper atmosphere of the gas giant.

We approached, and Ambra announced she had detected the death drones. As before, they were positioned across the surface of the planet, doing their dirty work. So Waythrel's experiment was on. We would examine the life of Hola for any evidence of "entropic acceleration." We would destroy the devices and seal the final node.

Maintaining our location in a manner to minimize the effects of the Anti weapons, we descended into the top layers. Beautiful cloud formations organized into architectural structures. They were titanic and multilayered, mountains carved from the vapors. Light dimmed as we penetrated. Soon we passed a distance several times the depth of New Earth's paper-thin atmosphere. It was here we saw signs of life.

Our first contact with living beings wasn't with the Holans. Instead, we encountered the more primitive cloud-hoppers of this Jovian zoo. Giant gasbags, animated airships floated in the upper layers. They maneuvered by controlling the mixture of hydrogen and helium within them, as well as the temperature of the gases. More H_2 or heat meant they rose. More He or colder vapors, and they descended.

Like everything about this world, the creatures were colossal. Kilometers long, they resembled ellipsoidal jellyfish. Projections extended from their surfaces like towering cilia. A complicated internal anatomy peeked through the translucent outer membrane.

Millions of these titanic islands scampered across the skies. Many darted with surprising speed in different directions. Wandering through this biolayer, my eyes discerned subtle differences between organisms that first appeared identical. Hundreds of distinct balloon species mixed together in the air. Predators sought prey, chasing them through the clouds. Others moved in what I imagined to be herds. It was all mesmerizing. I was a child at a zoo for the first time. I could stare through the invisible barrier and watch them dance all day.

"Amazing, aren't they?" asked Ambra, smiling at me.

"Yes. They're beautiful," I said.

"Creepy as hell," said Williams, shivering with a chill. "Sorry, I'm sure there's all kinds of astrobiology fun here. But these things are right out of some of my nightmares as a kid."

"Wait, you had dreams of continent-sized floating gas bags?" smirked Moore.

"Not exactly, smartass," she said. Her glare was icy. "Close enough."

"I just had dreams of bonking the mail girl."

She rolled her eyes. "Not surprised."

"Where are the Holans?" I asked.

The Xix answered. "They are the most developed species on Hola, but their numbers to date are low. Xixian scientists hypothe-sized that, in several hundred thousand years, they could develop a technological civilization. Fill the skies. For now, Ambra will have to find them by homing in on their sentient signal."

"Okay, Waythrel," she said with a frown. "It was nice to relax a bit. But point taken."

For the next hour or so, she sat in her meditative position in a deep trance. For extended periods, the bubble idled as the rest of us paced. We watched the bizarre animals outside or discussed our fears of the war. The Xix remained quiet, its internal processes a mystery. Periodically, the enclosure would move. We'd accelerate in some direction and slow, coming to a stop. This occurred five or six times. After a few instances, we assumed it was finding a "scent" but losing it.

Eventually, we accelerated again, and this time didn't decelerate for some time. Williams and Moore headed toward the front of the capsule. We hurtled through giant cloud formations. The panorama was breathtaking. I understood how Ambra felt. It would have been wondrous to let go of the pressing dangers of our mission and enjoy this journey through Hola. I found something soothing about the endless airscape and the roaming herds of dirigible life. The orange light filling the space of this atmospheric layer was warm and calming.

Ambra stood, moving beside the two members of my team. I followed her, staring over her head toward the rising star of the system. It would be early morning in this portion of the planet, whatever that meant here. Ahead, a distinct mass hung, different from the other life-forms we'd encountered. To begin, it was small, black, and discontinuous. It drifted at odds to the prevailing currents.

The cloud was our destination. We approached, and the partly solid nature disintegrated. What had been a continuous membrane dissolved into thousands of smaller entities. The individual objects were tiny relative to the lumbering air beasts. They were also much faster. Individuals darted here and there, but as a group, they maintained a structured whole.

"Reminds me of a flock of birds," I said.

"Or a school of minnows," replied Williams.
"Or a bunch of angry hornets," said Moore.
Ambra laughed. We smiled.
The hornets attacked.

Chapter 34

The second law of thermodynamics is, without a doubt, one of the most perfect laws in physics. Not even Maxwell's laws of electricity or Newton's law of gravitation are so sacrosanct, for each has measurable corrections coming from quantum effects or general relativity. The law has caught the attention of poets and philosophers and has been called the greatest scientific achievement of the nineteenth century.

Ivan P. Bazarov

Protected within Ambra's spacetime field, we were never in any real danger. It was still disconcerting, as tens of thousands of angry Holans threw themselves at our enclosure. Their efforts achieved nothing, but it was thrilling to watch. The cloud grew appendages, arms and hands extending toward us. They grabbed and battered at this new threat.

"Notice the coordinated projections," said Waythrel, as if the alien had read my mind. "They are a hive-structure. The simpler separate members of the group work in unison to create a much greater whole. The collective functions as a super-individual. It is far more intelligent and capable than the units or smaller organizational groups. When the mass has enough constituents, a threshold, and those components have worked together for decades, diversifying, harmonizing, the colony steps into this transformative consciousness."

I remembered some of this from the sharing. It was like a developing human with our larger brains. We have billions of neurons cooperating. It takes us years of interacting with the world and being taught to function at the levels of adults. I made the point to the group.

"So also with the Xix," added Waythrel to my comments. "For life-forms with substantial cognitive clusters, singletons can achieve a higher level of function, independently. Of course, realizing the full potential of the individual requires a broader social construct. A *culture*. The Holans cannot attain the mentality you see before you today unless they have many constituents. The singular intellects are far simpler."

"So it's like a bunch of dumb bees together getting smarter when they're part of a colony?" asked Moore.

"Similar," said the alien. "The Holan individuals are further developed than your isolated insects. Therefore, their intelligence in the swarm-state is correspondingly greater."

"So, hive mind. Got it. What's the plan then?" asked Williams. "How do we know if the drones are messing with them?"

"We'll monitor their minds," said Ambra.

The extraterrestrial chirped as it bounced around our cabin. "I have within my species-memory the patterns of their cognitive-forms. Readers who researched Hola years before took scans. The Daughter and I will compare what we see now and examine the evidence for drone effects."

In this manner, we spent the next five days. Chasing conscious clouds, our Reader pair entered their trances and probed the swarms. The process was arduous, the hive-thoughts difficult to understand. At least they posed far less danger than the efforts at Gyl.

Always when they woke from their meditations, it was with sadness. Each of the colonies we encountered showed signs of a terrible mental deterioration. Proximity to the drones increased the decay. It didn't take long for the pattern to be incontrovertible. The Holan intelligences were dying.

"They had been on the cusp of an organized culture," pined Waythrel after one grueling session. "The Xixian reports detailed the progress of the hives hundreds of years ago. Rudimentary versions of social structure and generational learning had taken root. In a manner simpler and yet different from our technological civilization. They had begun to fashion advanced cultural building blocks. Now, they have been set back millennia. At the rate of decay we are witnessing, in several decades they will begin to lose hive integrity."

"What are these terrible drones?" I asked, revolted by the destruction they were describing.

"The deeper purpose is unclear," continued the alien. "This confirms the entropic manipulation, however. The anti-order. The damage strikes the higher-level sentient structures first. It extends through many orders of complexity. The Gyl uncovered evidence of effects on chemistry and atomic physics."

"Atomic physics?" asked Williams. "You mean like atoms falling apart?"

"We don't know," said Ambra. "The Gyl were hard to understand."

"We know enough now to move on," said the Xix. "With the information in hand, we might develop countermeasures to the pro-entropic fields."

"So, that's it?" said Moore. "Mission accomplished, and we bug out of here?"

"Yes," she said, standing up from her crossed-legged position. "First, we destroy these drones. Then we seal the third and final node and cut off New Earth from the Dram."

"And return to plan the next stage in this conflict," concluded Waythrel.

~

So it would have gone, likely to far less sorrow and loss, if we had simply left a day earlier. Such are the random chances in time. So proceeds the cosmic play along paths often seeming more capricious than caring.

Ambra removed the Anti devices. We abandoned the decorative atmosphere of Hola, and Ambra set course for the Time Sphere. It was strange to think this mad mission was coming to an end. We would soon be walking on the sands of New Earth again.

I dreaded the transit through the Orb and was developing a phobia of the journeys. But I could muster courage for a last trip. Satisfaction from achieving a critical goal in protecting our home-world was a compelling motivator. Beyond our homeward, we were shielding thousands of star systems vulnerable to invasion. I knew Fox and Kim would have considered their sacrifice worth it. That was why they had joined in the first place. They had lived, and died, through action, incarnating our motto in their legacy to the galaxy.

As the Orb grew in size before our approaching bubble, light flashed beside it. I immediately recognized both the phenomenon and the object materializing. Adrenaline coursed through my system. My heart raced.

A Dram warboat surfed off the Time Tree. It materialized on top of us.

In the end, despite my reaction, it wouldn't pose a risk to us in and of itself. Ambra would disable it. She'd also exploit a useful opportunity to interrogate its crew.

What we learned would set in motion a series of events leading to trauma and tragedy.

Chapter 35

Let us draw an arrow arbitrarily. If, as we follow the arrow, we find more and more of the random element in the state of the world, then the arrow is pointing towards the future; if the random element decreases, the arrow points towards the past. I shall use the phrase 'time's arrow' to express this one-way property of time which has no analogue in space.

Sir Arthur Stanley Eddington

"We got guests," said Moore.

The warship didn't waste time with pleasantries. Short moments passed as the Dram deciphered the odd floating travelers on their monitors. Unable to do anything but verify the composition of our party, they did what they do best. They opened fire.

This surely elicited a second, deeper round of confusion in the enemy vessel. Highly shielded Xixian starships collapsed under the focused firepower of their military. Here were four individuals with a strange cargo, housed in some transparent craft. They stood before the bulk of one of their most feared battle cruisers and took the full fury of their assault.

Ambra didn't give them much time to seek a more analytic mode. She steered the bubble toward the cruiser. Beam weapons and missiles deflected away from us. She parked it outside the hull.

"Time to talk to some bugs," she said.

Unlike our entrance to the Braxian starship, she didn't spare their construction. The ship's walls bent inward, the metal buckling as she forced her way in. Like on Brax, an extension from our enclosure projected forward. We invaded the belly of the warboat.

Air didn't rush out of the breach. She must have sealed off the ship as much as she shaped a tunnel of nothing for us to walk down. Since the Dram breathed atmosphere similar to ours, it would have been simpler to exit the bubble to engage them. Welcoming us with their usual hospitality, the insectile monsters attacked the moment we entered. I understood the usefulness of the protective capsid in an up-close and personal manner.

The engagement was surreal. The bugs threw everything they had at us short of blowing up the entire boat. Williams cautioned they might try that, remembering what had happened around Brax.

Waythrel disagreed. "It was the Anti craft that destroyed them. Dram culture disdains suicide and will always fight to their own or their opponent's death."

"If a shadow ship comes into the system?" I asked. "Then what? We don't know what their plans were for Hola."

"I'm monitoring the Orb. We'll know," said Ambra. "In the meantime, I've shut down their ship's ability to navigate or send external communications. They're paralyzed. Cut off from everything."

Moore laughed. "I do like this new way of fighting."

We continued to watch the fireworks. We had overcome our instinctual concern about warriors unloading their weapons centimeters from us. The scene became comical. The bugs scampered around the membrane of emptiness. It was like driving a stick into an ant hole.

Ambra sat cross-legged before the mayhem. The enemy crew scurried in front, with the starlit backdrop and Hola behind. From all appearances, nothing existed between her and the attacking aliens. Recognizing the Daughter, their soldiers were eager to grab or kill her. With their razored hands and firearms, they tried. She ignored the crazed efforts.

After minutes of frenzied failure, the insects calmed and studied the phenomenon. They silenced the weapons. We were surrounded by a semicircle of exhausted and confused bugs. Several smaller Dram approached the area near the breach. They brought instruments and set them around us. *Scientists*, I assumed. Eventually, figures with considerable authority entered the chamber. They argued with the others. I could hear their interminable clicking speech.

The Xix spoke. "Are you ready?"

"Yes, this one will do," she said, shutting her eyes.

The soldier was inside our bubble, the transition undetectable. Warriors resumed darting about and added enclosure banging to their toolbox. The officer lunged toward Ambra. She held up her palm, and the creature froze, paralyzed.

"Allow me released or there falls destruction overall complete!" it shrieked through their horrid translators.

"Waythrel, would you like to start?"

The two aliens couldn't have been more different in mentality or appearance. The tribal, warlike Dram. The peaceful and contemplative Xix. A superficial similarity in size was the only overlap. The insect-like frame towering next to us matched the bulk and height of the Xixian Reader.

"The devices you plant around the worlds—what is their purpose?"

The leader said nothing. Its many legs twitched in anxiety within Ambra's web.

"We know they are destroying the minds and societies present.

This is not of your doing. You preserve function. You destroy in combat, with honor, or enslave. What has changed? Who controls you and why?"

"We never to be withheld," it spat.

"Why are you placing these drones for others?"

It clammed up again.

Moore shook his head and folded his hands over his chest. "Fucker isn't going to talk. What if we start ripping segments off its exoskeleton?"

"I'm afraid he's right," said Waythrel. "We will need another probe." Several of the eyestalks flipped over toward the Brit. "One not involving torture."

Ambra sighed. "Mental probes are at best unpleasant. Being within the mind of a Dram still brings bad memories." She glared at the bug. "Listen to me. You know who I am. If you do not answer our questions, I will enter your thoughts and take those answers from you. Is this what you wish?"

The officer floundered in place, straining against invisible bonds. Outside, the creatures had returned to a frantic mode. They fired at us. One detonated an explosive device, killing several of their crew. We remained unharmed.

Ambra lowered her head. The creature stiffened, its purposeful movements subdued. She had reached within it in some profound way. The warriors paused in a curiosity that got the better of them.

"Fogged light ships usurp and control," came the strange words from the Dramian translator. "The appearance from nothing to something in zero. Burnings provide us with the right, as we know it. Performance in the war. The power of life. Shadow promises triumph."

"The Anti," said Williams.

The insect's sounds lowered to abortive attempts at clicking. Ambra remained focused as minutes dragged by.

The captive slumped backward and collapsed to the ground. It lay outside the enclosure. The horde of soldiers hauled the immobile body out of our sight.

She opened her eyes, and I saw a fire in them. "We need to go to Dram."

We snapped our heads toward her. Waythrel's eyestalks twitched.

"We can't go to Dram," I said. The idea was suicide.

"We can and we must," she said, standing and pacing.

"What did you see in its mind?" asked the Xix.

"Slavery. They're no longer in control of their own destiny. The Anti have taken over."

Moore scoffed. "So what? Serves the bugs right. Let 'em rot."

She ignored him. "The entire world is transformed. Factory centers proliferate, populations displaced. Manufacturing cities have sprung up from the wastelands of the planet."

"So these drones, the growing armada—it's all built on Dram for the war?"

"Beyond anything we could have imagined. There are clones. Thousands of them. They're building something enormous. A long-term industry."

Waythrel stepped forward. "A work with the Anti that will proceed far into the future."

Her shoulders slumped as she stared at the alien. "We were right."

Many eyestalks turned to the rest of us. "She may have a point. A reconnaissance mission. Given what I have heard, there is important information to be gleaned."

"How do you suppose we're going to do this?" asked Williams. "Waltz onto their homeworld and start taking holos? Won't the entire planet and their new shadow friends have something to say about that?"

"Yes, they would. But they won't see us." Ambra winked. "Watch!"

The bugs outside our enclosure startled. Their heads darted around in a panic. Several raced toward us and crashed into nothing.

"We're invisible." I gawked.

"I can block various forms of matter from reaching us here, and I can change the path of photons. I can make it appear like nothing is inside."

Moore placed his hands on his hips. "Might have been useful earlier, sister, you think?"

She shook her head. "It leaves us vulnerable." The Dram were aware of our presence again. She gestured at the soldiers. "They could have shot us. Blurring where and what we are prevents me from maintaining the structure for a shield. We didn't know exactly what we'd face before. Now we do."

He continued. "So, you do your magic cloak act. We transport to Termite Land. Have a look-see, find out what they're up to, and get the hell out?"

"My plan, yes," said Ambra. "The more I think about it, the more it makes sense. We've come across disturbing things on this mission we don't understand. Now I know where the Anti are hiding. It's on Dram, and they're planning something huge. We add one more stop on the trip. The most important one."

It was logical. Risky, but the payoff could be high.

I turned to my team. "Waythrel's onboard, it seems. Me too."

"I'm not sure how I'm going to keep myself from opening fire on those bastards," said Moore. "I've watched too many soldiers killed by the bugs." He frowned. "Okay. I'm there. I wouldn't mind standing under their antenna and pulling out their dearest secrets. After that, their guts."

"I had to see this to believe it," Williams said, gesturing to the scene. "It's starting to be my new normal. Never thought I'd set foot on that damn planet."

"I was there once, centuries ago," said Ambra. Her face was lined. "It isn't something I do again lightly."

The enclosure separated from the Dram craft. They fired on us again. Ambra sighed, squeezing her hands into fists. The titanic war boat buckled in multiple locations, collapsing on itself. Bright detonations erupted, ripping the structure apart.

"Well, no reports back to the homeworld," chuckled Moore.

"Let us finish this mission and seal the last node," said Waythrel. "Afterward, we plot an unexpected course."

"For the Dram homeworld," I said, shaking my head as we sped toward the Orb.

Gazing at the quiescent portal, dread grew within me. The Time Sphere seemed altered. Of course, it wasn't. Objectively, it had the same appearance I had always seen—a grayness not exactly black, a reflection not exactly true, a hidden depth that couldn't quite be perceived.

Something *felt* different. My paranoid mind intuited emotion from the thing.

Hostility.

Chapter 36

The last trip hit me the hardest.

First, a terrible torture. Pain assaulted my body, my mind. Nausea poisoned me the moment we entered the Orb. A splitting headache pursued the stomach-churning sickness.

I fell to the floor of the enclosure, grabbing my head between my hands. I screamed. It was pure reflex to the extreme pain, but no less humiliating.

I lost consciousness——or that is how I understood it. A coma or some trance. Insight was denied.

In my nightmarish awareness, the group was gone. No bubble. No tunnel. No water. No shapes or stars or disembodied green eyes.

Only a devil Ambra. A demon child.

Once more, I lay in a field of maize. An impact had flattened the stalks into a broad ring. I occupied the center, my skull swimming, my bones aching. The sky cut as a sharpened sapphire.

Laughter popped over the corn. Hopping on a murmuring breeze, giggles spun my groggy head. A child's laugh, high-pitched, playful, without guile or cynicism. *Pure.*

Cornstalks rustled. I turned, seasick with the motion. A little girl, perhaps eight years old, bounced into the circle.

It was Ambra, yet it was not.

Her locks were scarlet and sweeping. Hideous machineries plunged in and sprang out of bald patches, scarring her skull. Like the Frankenstein monster in the Sahara, she was flesh and machine, natural and artificial. Enhanced. Degraded. *Altered.*

The cyborg paused and peered at me, smiled, and skipped around the outside of the corn ring. Her hands slapped the upright stalks to the rhythm of a song she hummed. I didn't know the tune. The strange melody unsettled me with its odd scales and frustrating resolutions. I shuddered at an unhealthy inversion of all familiar musical rules.

I fought to follow her as she danced, but I couldn't move my head fast enough to track her movements. I tasted bile as nausea bubbled through my guts.

I struggled to rise. My attempt ended with my head and shoulders slamming to the ground. The headache returned, blinding me, and I had to squint into the bright blue.

The girl stood over me. Her fiery tresses dangled like limbs from a combusting willow. The tips of her hairs brushed my face. I studied the enormous expansion of her skull where the tumor lay. The vile tubes and wires gleamed. Her eyes glowed green.

"I'll have to take it," the child-thing chirped.

I rubbed my eyes and tried to clear my head.

Take what?

"It's all part of a bigger plan. All the gods, they always have their *bigger* plans. *She* can't know, of course. She's not ready. She won't be for a long time. I'm afraid she'll resist."

I struggled to rise again, moving with deliberation, but the effort was too much.

"Do you want a hand?" the devil girl asked, cocking her head to one side. She offered an arm.

I didn't know whether to trust her, but I was helpless. She could have harmed me already. That she hadn't gave me a small amount of confidence. I reached out.

"It's safe. I'm walled off from you."

Walled off?

I grasped the hand and with her help rose to a sit. Her skin slid over mine, strangely slick and smooth. "I think I'll stop here for now," I said as the pain returned.

"The right idea," she said. "You fell hard."

"Fell? Where am I? How did I get here?"

The clone arched her neck to the sky, bending her glance to the horizon, searching. "She brought you, but *why* is the riddle." She shook her head and shrugged.

"Who brought me?"

"The answers won't make sense. Words won't help much. In the very end, it'll all make sense. And then there won't be words."

She sat and pulled her knees up to her chin, gazing into my eyes. I assumed that, like Ambra, the clones were blind and used their visions of the past and future to "see" around them.

Paranoia corrected my presumption. Everything should be suspect. These cyborgs could be different. The tumor grown uninhibited but sparing the visual regions of the brain. Perhaps she actually *saw* me.

My hypotheses were pointless. Even dangerous. I had to focus.

"Why am I here?"

I don't know, Avatar Nitin.

"Don't do that!" I panicked with a False Dawn inside my head again.

"You have mind scars."

She's reading my thoughts!

I growled. "One of *your* kind attacked me."

"My kind? You don't know my kind. I'm not my kind. Not really. I'm brokenly fixed."

"I do!" I yelled. "I know them too well."

The clone bobbed her head. "Oh, I see. Most of it's erased—*she* did this, yes? She didn't want it to hurt you anymore. Anyway, I can see enough still there. They hurt you. They're made to hurt you. As am I."

My heart raced, and I pushed myself backward, away from the lilting demon.

"But if I want to hurt you, Nitin, you can't run away."

My mouth dried. "What do you want with me?"

"I don't want anything with you. *She* wants something to happen. *They* do." She studied the skies again. "I think they found what they're hoping for. It feels like we're almost out of time."

I shook my head and squeezed it with my palms. "I don't understand *any* of this!"

"I know. I don't either. There's so much for me to learn. Every step is a *lesson*, Nitin. It's the other reason we're here. Not for you, I'm sorry. For me."

"We're here for you to learn something? About me?"

"No. We've known about you thousands of years. The Daughter's consort! An important subject taught to all the children. Especially for strategy. Many think you are a flaw, a weakness to destroy her."

"Ambra?"

"Yes. Once she's destroyed, the fools believe the Orbs will fail."

I gaped, dumbfounded. "I won't hurt her."

The clone peered right through me. "The lesson isn't to know *you*, but to better understand *her*. And you're part of that. There can be no healing the cosmic mind, tidying up all those broken symmetries, without parity. It's why she also seeks to comprehend me. Circle Mirror Yang Yin. Why we're reincarnated on this Möbius loop. Why I can coexist with you now. Even *touch* you!"

Before I could move, she placed an index finger between my eyes. I jumped backward and toppled.

She giggled. "So fun! They have such power in the deep future-past." The red eyebrows furrowed. "It'll be strange to destroy them."

A fierce wind swirled shorn leaves. The clone's hair whipped about us, the standing stalks gyrating in the gusts. She hummed the weird tune again and stopped, side-eyeing me, her expression solemn.

"Time. Not enough to taste all of you. Other holes bleed in your mind, Nitin Ratava," she said, closing her eyes and craning upward. "Remember, I'll take it soon. We've a terrible journey to endlessly complete."

Space split. The girl, the verdant pillars, the topaz sky, they ripped like an aged cloth unveiling a backdrop of innumerable galaxies. Both visions shattered into a thousand fragments and scattered to a dying gale.

I floated in a dark silence.

Chapter 37

What I am going to tell you about is what we teach our physics students in the third or fourth year of graduate school. It is my task to convince you not to turn away because you don't understand it. You see, my physics students don't understand it. That is because I don't understand it. Nobody does.

Richard Feynman

I awoke feeling as sick as in the dream. Ambra knelt beside me, her hand on my forehead.

"His fever broke," she said.

Others stirred beyond my field of vision. I saw an endless celestial panoply above me. Her and the stars. What else did I really need, anyway?

Delirium is a special species of truth serum.

"This is becoming dangerous for him," came the voice of Waythrel.

"I know." Her features were strained. "The last one. I'll be much more careful. I was too eager to get here and see what was happening."

I was down for two more days. Meanwhile, we floated outside the Dram homeworld in our invisible enclosure. I had heard stories and seen holos of the red giant star at the center of the system. It was something else to be close to it, "in the flesh." The wavelength-shifted glare oppressed human sensibilities. The dominant crimson washed out, tanned, and faded to other hues. The deserts of New Earth held more vitality.

The parched world of our enemies lurked below. When I had recovered the ability to work my suit, we planned our approach to the planet's surface. Ambra wanted to go straight to the seat of power, to the emperor's palace. She believed we could enter undetected yet observe everything. Their prime strategies would be open to us. We could uncover much to help our efforts in the war.

More importantly, we could learn about the Anti and their plans. From what she'd seen in the captured officer's mind, we might find them in this system. The remainder of my team feared they might be able to detect our approach. I shared their concern, but my level of trust in Ambra was high.

Too high, as I would soon realize.

"We don't know their tech," said Williams. "If the Dram can't see or stop us, those *ghosts* could have something that can."

"It's possible," said Ambra, "but unlikely."

"Why?" asked Moore. His face was stern. He wanted to hear reasoned arguments.

Waythrel interjected. "The Anti aren't magical, Sergeant. They may be composed of particle inverses to ours, but the same laws of nature apply to them. In fact, in their own antimatter galaxies, they could resemble close copies of any life-form in our galaxy. Imagine a mirror. Everything is inverted but basically identical. Atomic physics, chemistry, *biology*. While not compatible with us, they would be entirely recognizable."

"Well, they still have tech we don't understand. Purposes we don't get," said Moore. "How about some *detectors* we don't know about?"

Ambra sighed. "Okay, yes. Any advanced alien technology is unpredictable. So far, they haven't been able to counter my effects on spacetime. Nothing makes me think this will be different for cloaking us on Dram. I think it's a risk worth taking."

We reached a compromise. We would take an initial gamble and descend to the surface, ready to rocket out at the first sign of discovery. First, we would enter the atmosphere and test their long-range scanning abilities. Next, we would hover over the central city of Gred, the location of the emperor. If things went well, we would proceed to the palace itself and find out what we could.

Ambra assured us she could make a dash for the Orb. From what I had seen in our adventures so far, I had no doubts. What I didn't know and would soon discover was just how fast she could actually fly.

We left the bodies of Kim and Fox orbiting the world in their private enclosure. The luminosity of the red giant hardly faded as we entered the atmosphere. The environment took on an orange hue, as if rust leaked out of the sky itself. For a human to spend much time here would be psychologically damaging.

Nothing happened in response to our presence. Ambra didn't sense anything. No warships or ground-based defenses engaged with our penetration of the airspace.

The deep desert of Dram filled my vision. An orange sea dwarfing the Sahara, spanning the entire planet. The expanse overwhelmed. I focused on the growing shape of the capital city to orient.

It was a gigantic sprawl, ten times the largest metropolis back home. The buildings were a stark contrast to human design. Few sharp lines protruded. They shunned glass despite all the silicon dioxide in the parched grains. Shapes were curvilinear. My mind mapped the visuals to memories of New Earth with massive distortion in the process. Take Manhattan, multiply by one thousand, turn it to sand, and spray enough water to melt the edges. That would be an echo of the alienness of Gred.

We dashed over the urban bugscape in our bubble. Part of me felt vulnerable. We perched over the largest city of our deadliest foes. Our craft had no discernible walls. We were a collection of three soldiers, an alien, and the wildcard that was the Daughter. She should have been enough after all I had seen. I ought to have been calm. But I wasn't.

"It appears almost deserted," said Waythrel. "Sky traffic is minimal."

"That's where they held my tribunal," said Ambra, her tones subdued.

An enormous dome rose over the metropolis. Composed of the metallic, marble-like substance found across Dram architecture, it gleamed. Cut with thousands of facets, it reflected the bloody starlight. The enormity matched in near-perfect detail the descriptions in the history books.

She turned away and pointed to smaller buildings nearby. "That's where they imprisoned me. They took my eggs to make those pathetic abominations."

I'd never heard this tone in her voice. Not sadness at her losses. Not anger. A strain at the mention of the clones.

The emperor's palace thrust out of the cityscape in front of us. Unlike the city-sized dome of the Tribunal, it rocketed upward like an obscene termite mound, dominating all other structures in Gred. Military craft darted about the tower. They established a protective radial grid of hovercraft with stunning amounts of firepower. One thing about the Dram, they sure knew how to militarize the hell out of anything.

"The emperor lives at the top." Ambra gestured. "It gives the bug a god's-eye view, feeding the monumental egos they always have."

Williams laughed. "Except for the one you nearly destroyed centuries ago, right? When you escaped? Unless the history books lie. Must have been a bit humbled."

She glanced away. "What happened then isn't something I'm proud of."

The sea of guarding spacecraft ignored us. We passed through their ranks undetected. It was a tense few minutes, and as MECH-core soldiers, we were the most anxious in this explosive environment.

Waythrel exuded calm. Ambra retained a sharp focus that had possessed her since we left Hola. Perhaps it was returning to this hell world, distressing memories assaulting her. Did this explain her odd state? Perhaps, but it felt like more.

We approached the enormous palace, the sides gleaming in the ruby light. Our craft didn't slow down. Just as it seemed we would smash ourselves to pieces on the hard walls, they *bent*. Where they moved *to*, I can't describe because my mind can't grasp it. A passage appeared in the wall we alone could perceive.

Our invisible pod popped through it.

Chapter 38

All that we see or seem
Is but a dream within a dream.

Edgar Allen Poe

We haunted the emperor's palace like some aggregated poltergeist. The four of us hovered near the tops of the enormous ceilings. We observed the royal court perform their rituals underneath, oblivious to our presence. It took little time to confirm Ambra's worst suspicions.

The alien architects had designed an epic throne-floor for the insectile ruler. A grand hallway led from an elevator to a central chamber. Domed on the inside, the room centered on an elaborated cathedra for their god-king. Despite extraterrestrial divergences, it was easy to connect to human desires. We too loved to aggrandize our rulers, our teachers, our prophets. The more I saw of these aliens, the more uncomfortable I felt at the similarities. I suspected humanity shared more with this fanatical species than with the Xix.

The emperor was in its chambers, slumping on the throne. An expected flurry of activity buzzed around the chief insect. Petitions pleaded, orders given, problems raised, deals negotiated, and strategies plotted. Waythrel's translator cast different speakers with distinct voices. It helped us follow the conversations.

"Dram is suffering, Holy One," came a pining voice inside our bubble. "Crops are neglected. Power and resources are diverted to the Project. The alien harvests are consuming all we have. Dissent is growing. There is talk of rebellion."

The emperor droned. "Is that all?"

I watched the many legs of the petitioner dance at this response. "Yes, Lord."

"Take this message back to the local governors. The Project is *all* that matters. Defeat of the human Reader is the highest priority. The war cannot be won without it. Suffering creates strength. Any resistance to the Divine Orders will be met with death. The fields will expand."

The giant bug in front of the throne straightened its long torso, lowering its head before its sovereign. It turned and scampered out of the room.

"The emperor acts drugged," said Ambra.

Waythrel agreed. "We have both spent enough time on Dram. We know the personalities and character of these creatures. She is right—something is amiss."

Ambra's eyes darted like lasers. "Let's get closer. There's a lot of room in the back of that chair, and no traffic."

Our bubble descended. Nestled behind the cathedra, we were able to spy without becoming an obstacle. More importantly, we obtained a view of the back of the ruler.

"What the hell is on its head?" asked Moore.

"A crown," said Waythrel. "Of a kind."

He didn't mean the cap with its threaded braids hanging half a foot below the creature. He pointed to something else.

"No, there—underneath the decorations. The thing *in* its head. I don't think I've ever seen that in my readings or meetings with the Dram."

"It's embedded in its brain," said Williams, a scowl on her face.

"Ambra, can you allow me to approach?" asked the Xix.

"Yes. Just walk," she said. "Be careful. If you get too close, and it moves and hits you, it'll feel a disturbance. Remember, all of you, we're vulnerable veiled like this."

The alien stepped away from us toward the throne. I knew we were encased in an invisible barrier, but it required an imaginative focus to continue to believe without sensory feedback. My instincts were screaming that Waythrel would be discovered. Part of me wished the Dram would just shoot at us again. At least I'd have the sense *something* was present. And cloaked, those shots might actually do us some harm.

The Xix approached. Its eyestalks extended to the box stuck inside the glistening exoskeleton. After a minute or two, the alien returned.

"I have never seen it before," it said. "I passed five decades here, and nothing like this device existed."

"Could be new," said Moore. "Been a few hundred years since you visited."

"Could be reserved for the rulers," I added.

"The technology is not Dramian—that was clear on inspection," said Waythrel. "The raw materials are from the planet, however. I have studied their physiology in exquisite detail. The mechanism inserts into the mental organ that controls conscious choice. The only reason to embed a machine there is to override or modify the will of the emperor."

"Wait," said Williams. "The box is controlling its brain? The bugs didn't make it?"

"The Anti," said Moore.

"You heard them," said Ambra. "The emperor is killing Dram. This Project is working the population to exhaustion. It bleeds the resources of the planet. Some of this I saw in the mind of the soldier at Hola. To see it at this level is something else."

"What are these fields? What are they harvesting?" I asked.

"Not food," said Waythrel. "The reports of starvation and rebellion suggest a different crop."

"Whatever it is, it has to do with you," said Moore, pointing at Ambra. "Their plan is to build something to kill *you*."

"Agreed," she said. "So, you'll excuse me if I'm motivated to go find them and see for myself."

"Find them—how?" I asked.

"They cannot be far," said the Xix. "If power and resources are diverted from Gred, the location is likely on the outskirts of the city."

"Wait—shouldn't we listen in? Discover more?" asked Williams.

"Perhaps," said Waythrel. "However, I can't think of anything more pressing than determining how they are working to murder the Daughter."

"I agree," I said.

Moore cocked his head to one side. "Crops for harvesting. To kill Ambra Dawn. I think I know what they're growing."

I caught my breath. I could guess too.

Waythrel's eyes swiveled and stared at all of us. "We need to go find these fields."

Chapter 39

If only one could make time stand still; if one could erase all the horror and inhumanity in the world.

Thea Halo, *Not Even My Name*

We found the fields.

Take the giant AgriCom farms from Ambra's youth in the Midwest. Replace them with humans instead of corn or cattle. Multiply by a factor of one hundred and drop the entire thing into the oven-baked landscapes of Dram. You would have some idea of what spread out before us.

Kilometer after hectare. Housing, pens, birthing factories, biotech. We uncovered an industrialized assembly line producing people. Squares of parceled land marked the repeating installations. Facilities constructed and optimized to manufacture copies of a single person. Sickened, we coasted across a sea of duplicated buildings, workers, and Ambra Dawns.

At first, we kept high over the fields, scanning the layout. We marveled at the absurd lengths to which our enemies had gone.

Wonder mutated to disgust as we descended into the compounds. The abominations below kicked us in the teeth.

I'd fill books detailing the horrors we witnessed. How we swooped into structures, entered labs and factories, pursued the clones. We spied on the laborers. Ambra pilfered information from their thoughts. Hardly needed, as function followed form. A summary is sufficient. It repulses me to remember it now, and the briefer I can be, the better.

Dram technicians staffed the biotech facilities, but it was obvious they didn't drive the research. Other aliens, unknown even to the Xix, directed activities. Were they brought in to perform specialized work? For other reasons? We had no idea and no time to explore the history of this gigantic sprawl of asylums.

Behind the novel alien workers, pulling every string and setting each course, were the Anti. Energy-gulping protective containers shielded them from the surrounding matter. The seat of power was clear. The unknown species took instructions from these shadowed boxes. They relayed the research protocols to the subordinate local techs.

Waythrel estimated that the labs had been in operation for hundreds of years. They may have opened soon after the reversal of the Great Calamity. What had they been working toward for so long and with such dedication? It became obvious in the neonatal wards —or, more accurately, birthing factories.

The human slaves of the Dram, and their generations of descendants, paid a terrible price. They were the experimental animals on which the Anti applied their dark technology. How many had suffered and died at the hands of these psychopathic monsters, I didn't know. I could guess some of it when I saw the products of their diabolical R&D.

They had bioengineered women into fetus-manufacturing units of a hellish nature. Each "mother" in the production centers had become a demonic fusion of flesh and machine, cybernetic organisms invaded and controlled by hundreds of wires and tubes. Their midsections distended beyond recognition. Wombs were augmented tenfold their natural size. The rest of the body had reversed. Atrophied, shrunken to the point that the functional endpoint couldn't be missed. They'd designed everything about the warped creatures for one thing: growing humans.

Produce them they did with artificially inseminated and implanted embryos. Cloning technologies. Hybrid protocols. The labs pursued diverse approaches in parallel. These womb-sacks, human in ancestry alone, gestated at many times the normal rate. We didn't have time to find out how. Specialized nutrition? Hormones, genetic changes? It wasn't relevant in some broader sense. The Anti with their Dram pawns had developed biomechanizations to take the initial stock of eggs stolen from the Daughter and create an industrial production line for growing copies of her.

Within weeks of implantation, they harvested each birther. Robotic implements inserted into the exaggerated wombs and remove upwards of ten fetuses. These couldn't survive outside the womb. The automation plunged them into artificial incubators for a second round of gestation. How they had optimized this—the timing, design, hormone and nutrient balancing—was as unclear as it was astounding. It worked with horrible efficiency.

Ambra discovered more shocking information from the minds of the techs. In the span of a month, they had crawling infants. Within a year, prepubescent girls. After five years, functional adult clones, who could manipulate space and time. Their investment required extraordinary patience. At the end, they had industrialized the production of the ultimate bioweapons.

We examined several sites. With the arrival of newer technology, they simply built updated factories. The older plants continued operating until the product or protocols were too inferior. Those, they shut down. The desert was littered with abandoned buildings.

An acceleration of development was a critical component to the process. Penned herds of little Ambra Dawns created a sea of orange hair like some strange crop. Humans shepherded them. Put them through trials. Taught them odd lessons to our eyes. But the instruction functioned to enhance the artificial program to produce these weaponized slaves.

How much experimentation in mental maturation had they performed? They studied and probed their human cattle at every site. Rudimentary cultures developed within their prisons. Alien scientists observed. Extraterrestrial ranchers mimicked the societal structures in the raising of their prized breeds.

The rejected failures of their efforts were one of the saddest parts of this terrible story. Deformed, brain damaged, emotionally traumatized—they were the most plentiful population. They didn't live long. Tested, tortured, probed—the researchers tried to find what they had done wrong. Afterward, they killed and discarded the faulty product.

In this way, the scope of the monstrous plan was revealed to us. Now we knew where the clones originated. It was clear the Anti were just warming up. Our enemies would be patient. I shuddered to think of the suffering to come. Their continued efforts constituted a crime of galactic proportions.

And their use? One of those things in the desert had been enough. *An army?*

Ambra zeroed in on the newest fields, clustered north from Gred. The clone development in these locations was far superior. The minds of the False Dawns more intact, more capable. Their signature and distortion of spacetime was extreme.

Thousands filled those spaces. Tens of thousands in the largest complex alone. It was at this site of our enemy's greatest progress where events took a terrible turn and our mission ended.

Chapter 40

Those who understand evil pardon it.

George Bernard Shaw

"I want to speak with one of them."

She was agitated. Gone was the tranquility I associated with her knowledge of time. Her features contorted in distress, eyes darting, hands clenched at her sides. Had we been under less stressful conditions, it would have been easier to empathize. But I couldn't stop myself from protesting.

"Ambra, no!" I said. "We got what we came for. We've pushed our luck far enough. Let's take what we know, get the hell out of here, and put together a plan of action when we have time. When we can summon resources. *Armies.*"

"He's right," said Waythrel. "The risks outweigh the benefits in this."

Her eyes were wild. "I said I want to speak to one of them. And I will, whatever any of you say."

"Look, sister," said Moore, "what you say we have a wee vote on this? When did this become a dictatorship?"

"When everything that has happened has been possible because of me!" she said. "I got us to every world. I protected us from the Dram. I uncovered this information. I'm asking that we talk to *one* of the clones. Only *one*. I can handle it."

Williams stood in front of the Daughter. "You're losing your mind on this one, girl. In case you missed some important things, we've got two human purées waiting for us in orbit. You didn't see *that* coming. You didn't stop it. So, how about you back off from the almighty god thing and quit ordering us around?"

"Ambra, please—" I began.

"Do you know what it must be like for these girls? Do you have any idea what it's like to grow up as a guinea pig in a hostile lab? Where they starve you, beat you, shock you, and cut on you? Turn you slowly, steadily, into a monster, a dark, twisted form of what you should have been? Where your worth lives only in their approvals?" She waited as if we would answer. "Well, *I* do!"

Waythrel tried to intervene. "Whatever pain the clones have endured cannot be—"

"Look at them!" she said, gesturing in front of our bubble at the sea of orange hair beneath us. "Thousands of them! At least I had a few years of love from my parents. I grew at some human pace. These things—their mothers are nightmares. They have no fathers. They have no normal development. You want proof of hell? You don't have to search any further." Tears dripped down the sides of her cheeks.

I put my hand on her shoulder. "Okay, Ambra. I'll come with you."

"Ah, shit," cursed Moore, turning away in frustration.

"Listen!" I said. "She can send the rest of you away, back through the Orb or something. You don't have to be involved."

"For myself," said the Xix, "I am not concerned. My primary fear is for the Daughter. To engage these advanced clones would risk much. You don't know their powers."

"I defeated the one in the desert, Waythrel," said Ambra. "I'll be careful. I'll choose one and bring it inside the enclosure, sealed away, unseen by the others. If we're attacked, I'll kill it."

"Why don't we kill it now?" said Moore. "You remember what that thing did in the Sahara, right?"

She stared at him but touched my cheek with her palm. "I remember. But I didn't know about this. I hadn't *seen* this. I hated them before—the very idea of them. Now...now I feel pity."

"What do you think you will accomplish by speaking with one of them?" asked the alien.

"I don't know, but I need to find out," she said. "I have to know if there is any hope."

"For what?" asked Moore, flinging his hands into the air.

"Hope they can be saved. That there's something inside them I can save."

Chapter 41

Everything you do reverberates throughout a thousand destinies.

Nikos Kazantzakis

In the end, everyone signed on to the crazy idea.

Signed their death warrants. All because, deep down, we were all committed to the Daughter, and she had to do this. I was the first to grasp her desperate need, but the others came to recognize it. Foolish or not, it was impossible to stop her. We were either with her, or we would abandon her to this fate.

She floated the invisible spacetime bubble over the enormous compound. We passed the birthing warehouses, the labs, the pens of hundreds and thousands of tiny Ambra Dawns.

For me, it was hardest to see the child clones. I didn't know when the brainwashing took hold. When they became creatures seeking to slaughter us, to kill their progenitor, to destroy the planet of their origins. Seeing the small ones, I saw innocence in their eyes. Children's eyes. This gave me the empathy to experience Ambra's pain. I believed the cause to be hopeless. Perhaps she did as well. But I understood why she had to try.

We slowed near the demented "schools" where the older children received instruction. Preteens, early teens—their biological age, not years, as their development was rushed. The period when the tumor and its powers developed and flourished. The Anti had modified all of them surgically by this point, with the invasive machine technology embedded in their bodies. All had forfeited some aspect of their humanity. Most had probably already lost their free will.

They never properly slept. Instead, unconscious, machines sent electrochemical signals through their brains. Waythrel guessed it was an accelerated learning and maturation protocol. One twisted part of the long research program fashioning the clones. Items on an assembly line. Ready for shipment into battle.

Awake, they were subjected to tests. Dram and human trainers attached them to devices or placed individuals in open fields. Their powers over spacetime were examined, challenged, and augmented. Some of the older specimens served as advanced teachers as well. The Anti had learned to preserve extensive features of our culture. Hierarchy, mentorship, and social bonding recreated despite the dysfunctional setting. They had perfected the madness and addiction of cult attachment.

We followed a group of younger teens from sleeping quarters to practice arenas. One of the girls was several steps behind the others.

"She'll do." The enclosure swooped down beside the clone. "They won't miss her for a few minutes."

Williams rolled her eyes, but we had committed. We neared, and the cyborg stumbled, bumping into an invisible wall. Disoriented, she tried to walk forward but was stopped, enveloped in the bubble.

"Don't panic," said Ambra. "They can't see her, and she can't reach us. But she can see us."

The girl turned around.

"Ah, shit, here we go," muttered Moore, charging up his ion slingers.

My warrant officer followed in short order.

Ambra walked up to the False Dawn and spoke. "What is your name?"

Biologically, the child appeared twelve or thirteen. Her eyes darted between us, her face tense. She was frightened but determined. "A4552, Teacher."

"You're blocking your mind from me."

"Affirmative, Instructor. Directive 3. Never lower defenses in the field."

"I want you to disregard Directive 3 right now, please."

She swallowed. "This is heresy. Is this a new exam?"

"Yes. I want you to share your thoughts with me."

"We live to kill the Originator," she chanted. "We do not break the laws."

"You won't commune with me?"

Her breathing increased. Sweat trickled down her cheek.

"Sit down." The child sat, and Ambra followed suit. "If you will not open your awareness, I will enter it myself."

"I will defend."

"I thought you would."

The False Dawn screamed. She grabbed her head as her eyes rolled back in her head. Ambra tensed. She shut her eyes. Her mouth set in a tight line. The clone moaned, rocking back and forth. She held her head, the pitch of her groans rising and falling like some tortured animal.

I recoiled at the agonized sounds. I checked with Moore and Williams. Both shook their heads. The eyestalks of Waythrel danced, but the alien didn't intervene.

"No! Liar!" hissed the False Dawn. "Not *true! Stop!*" Blood trickled from the inserted tubes in her skull. "*Liar!*"

"You're killing it!" I shouted.

Ambra stiffened. The clone's eyes opened wide. It spoke in a demonic voice projected like a loudspeaker. "*The Originator. She is here. She is here. Come. Kill. She is here!*"

Ambra's face was strained. Space undulated. The bubble lost integrity as waves propagated outward from the clone.

"She's losing control of the thing!" yelled Williams. She stepped forward and sighted the girl in her targeting system, raising her arms to fire.

She was torn apart. Blood sprayed across my face, and tissue exploded in all directions. Body parts were slung against the walls of the enclosure.

"*No!*" Ambra shouted. "Nitin! Waythrel! They're programmed! Automatic!" She labored to speak. "I can't stop it! It will reach them."

I grasped my temples. The sound of its voice concussed my mind. *She is here. She is here. She is here. She is here.*

I managed to raise my eyes. Moore was kneeling, his hands to his head. Waythrel's eyestalks were darting around wildly and the alien stumbled as if it might topple over.

She is here. She is here. She is here. She is here.

Ambra shouted again and stood, a terrible strain on her features. "*No!*"

The clone arched its back, the tubes exploding out of its skull, along with blood and bone. A red paint splashed against the invisible barrier behind it and dripped slowly downward. The False Dawn swayed backward, eyes a possessed white. Its face slackened, and the body crumbled.

The voice in my mind stopped. The child didn't move. I staggered to my feet, dizzy, unsteady, and slumped beside Ambra. The enclosure smelled of bodily fluids. A metallic taste coated my tongue.

I sensed movement in my peripheral vision. A fog of orange rose around us, deepening, congealing and choking out other shapes and colors. I placed my hand on Ambra's shoulder.

"Are you okay?" I asked.

"Oh, Nitin."

Her desperate eyes peered outside the capsule. I followed her gaze and focused. A swarming herd converged on our position. Red hair.

Green eyes. Thousands of clones. They knew where we were. They saw us now.

Waythrel spoke. "The dead clone triggered them. They know *you* are here! They are coming for you. Uncloak us! Harden the enclosure, now!"

Ambra shook her head. "What have I done?"

Chapter 42

By a route obscure and lonely,
Haunted by ill angels only,
Where an Eidolon, named NIGHT,
On a black throne reigns upright,
I have reached these lands but newly
From an ultimate dim Thule—
From a wild weird clime that lieth, sublime,
Out of SPACE—out of TIME.

Edgar Allen Poe

The entire compound turned on us. I don't know how many swarmed. Thousands. Hundreds with the power we battled in the desert. I know she couldn't have repelled them on her own. Their numbers were too large. She must have tapped into the Orb, which brings this part of the story to a most dark and ironic conclusion.

"Kill all that you can!" she shrieked.

The contrast to the empathic hurt she had felt a few hours earlier couldn't have been greater. We didn't need convincing. The thing had ripped our warrant officer to shreds beside us. Ambra had seen its mind, known its thoughts and feelings. That she had now jettisoned all concern for their well-being said a lot.

"I don't know what we can do!" I called. "We're only two!"

Moore and I blasted without restraint, creating considerable carnage. The clones had no armor, and they were too focused on attacking *the Originator* to erect defenses to our munitions. They stood before us like ducks on a pond. With our missiles and ion slingers, we likely downed hundreds in half a minute. The mutilation painted a hellscape.

No doubt our Daughter of Time was a big part of that success story. She had semi-permeabilized the enclosure. Our assaults penetrated, but the walls resisted entrance from outside. Not that the cyborgs raised any weapons. Their battle occurred on a different plane of existence. Shielding came in handy when the Dram military arrived and attacked.

Soon, piles of slaughtered clones encircled us. Waythrel sat with Ambra in the center of the bubble. They clasped hands and settled into a deep Reader trance like the one we had seen at Gyl. I could see in her face the tension, the fatigue as her energies faded. I didn't know how long we could hold out.

Massive disturbances erupted everywhere. The ground heaved and buckled. Space contorted. Time and again our enclosure suffered assaults that bent the air. Meanwhile, our MECHcore usefulness decreased. The missiles were spent. The clones deflected our ion rays once recognizing our threat.

Chaos and mayhem reigned outside. Mirroring Williams's death, Ambra shredded the False Dawns. It was literally a meat grinder out there. I would have turned away from the visceral horror, but it caught me like a deer in headlights. The sheer fleshy decimation stunned me. Only the shield of the capsule kept us from drowning in blood and gore.

A strange seasickness churned my stomach from both the time distortion and physical carnage. Back and forth, the pace of events rocked. Slow, fast, skipping moments, backtracking to create repeated experiences of déjà vu. Holes opened and closed, tunnels to nowhere and from nothing. The veins bulged on Ambra's brow, and the alien changed to a deep shade of purple. The stresses would kill them.

"Ambra, punch a hole through it and get us out!"

I'm trying, Nitin! They've cast nets over us! Her voice battered my brain.

Moore was grim, his face a scowl. "We're not going to make it out of this. These roaches are pouring out of the woodwork."

A flood of False Dawns approached. They ignored the horrific fates of the mangled bodies surrounding us. They were fanatical, devoted to destroying us. If she didn't get through whatever they were doing soon, we were dead.

A bright light flashed in my eyes, and I tripped, dropping to one knee. *Flash bomb?* No, I could still see. It wasn't a device. Instead, standing behind Waythrel was an apparition from my nightmares.

The little demon child from the cornfields. In the midst of all these identical clones, I recognized her. Her movements. The sparkle in her eye. The slight twitch at the corners of her mouth when she noticed I was staring.

"*You?*" I gasped.

A cry interrupted me. I tore away from the devil girl and saw Ambra flat on her back, a stunned expression on her face.

The young clone grabbed Waythrel's upper arm, and the alien collapsed.

"Nitin! Help me! I can't move! Stop her!"

The thing smiled. It smirked at me and winked. Another glaring flash and I shut my eyes. When I turned back, nothing. The child was gone. The Xix, vanished. The space they occupied, empty.

Ambra sprang forward with a wail toward where they had been.

She landed on her knees grasping air, tears on her face, a wild, mad glare burning in her eyes.

"*Waythrel!*"

The agony of her scream cut deep inside me. I stumbled, concussed. The alien's disappearance accomplished what ten thousand attacking clones had not. It broke her focus. The bubble collapsed.

Into the breach, a False Dawn flew like a possessed witch. Red hair billowing behind it, hands upraised like claws and a homicidal death mask on its face. Ambra didn't respond. She didn't move. She held herself, her arms wrapped around her chest as she rocked.

I launched forward, but I knew I couldn't make the distance in time.

An impact both metallic and fleshy reverberated. Moore's suit blasted upward, his shoulder set as it smashed into the stomach of the clone. I could hear the creature's spine snap as its body arced from the collision, and the two rocketed high into the air. A red cloud darted in pursuit.

His actions shocked Ambra out of her state. She jumped, the remaining cyborgs once again boxed out by a wall. Gazing into the cluttered sky, she saw what I did. It was too late. The False Dawns had ripped him to pieces.

"Ambra—"

She held up her hand and closed her eyes, wrinkles spreading from the corners as she squeezed. Despite the clones redoubling their assaults, their progress reversed. An invisible force pushed them back. Then the hallucinations began.

Many aged horribly, their skin drying and peeling off their bones. Bodies that, seconds ago, attacked, burst into rusty clouds. Crawling around in the dust were tens, hundreds of infants. Structures outside swayed. The warehouses and laboratories rippled. Arriving Dram military craft disassembled and rained fragments onto the sands.

"They're still *here*," growled Ambra.

"Who?" I said, my eyes bugged at the impossibilities I witnessed.

"Waythrel is in the system! We have to hurry. They're heading for the Orb!"

She glared upward and grasped my hand. Two things happened. We blasted off the ground in our enclosure, the surface of the planet receding. Below, a catastrophic detonation.

The entire clone field flattened. Circular ripples extended outward and leveled everything in their path. The cyborgs, buildings, perhaps extensive regions of Gred itself, were annihilated in the destruction.

I didn't watch long. I turned my eyes forward as we ascended toward the heavens.

A doomed pursuit began.

Chapter 43

Madness rides the star-wind...claws and teeth sharpened on centuries of corpses...dripping death astride a bacchanale of bats from night-black ruins of buried temples of Belial.

H. P. Lovecraft

We rocketed upward.

I don't know the fate of the remaining colony of clones. Had they tried to pursue but Ambra held them back? Were they so incapacitated by the Daughter's wild destruction that they couldn't?

Whichever, none followed. I traveled faster than I'd ever experienced alongside a mad goddess. Her eyes glowed green. Shockwaves exploded in the atmosphere as we blasted toward space like a meteor in reverse.

She released my hand and placed her own against the enclosure walls. Our momentum made me mimic the motion, although the need was illusory. Everything within the bubble remained stable and unperturbed. In a few short seconds, we thrust forward into blackness. The planet receded behind. We hurled past its two moons. Looming before us—growing closer at a shocking rate—the incandescent outline of the Orb.

I had never seen the Time Sphere like this. It differed from the breathtaking power shown in previous battles. What I saw now was a supernova. It outshone the red giant. Its surface was a churning, chromatic cyclone channeling hostility. For the first time, I began to truly fear the thing.

Ambra focused on the chase, saying nothing, her entire body tense like a rod. Following her gaze, I tracked a pair of bodies ahead. Waythrel and the False Dawn. We closed the distance. They hurtled straight for the Orb.

A chilling certainty trickled through me. Somehow, however impossible, I knew our efforts would fail. The creature that had kidnapped Ambra's dearest friend held the power to use the portal. We would lose the Xix. The clone would escape. To what purpose, I had no inkling.

No! We won't lose them! The thoughts from Ambra exploded in my mind. *We'll follow them through any pathway to any place or time!*
You can do this?
Watch me!

The sphere storm—I had no other phrase for it—intensified, responding to her thoughts. Its light was offset with black clouds, vortexes, tunnels, and membranes. The protrusions and invaginations prodded and penetrated through space from distant dimensions. The radiance pressed like thunder—so bright it assaulted the senses. The darkness pulled at something profound within me, primal. Every paranoia I'd known stirred from slumber. The brewing cataclysm in the cauldron gaped, its circumference an open maw. The titanic fronts of fog glinted like teeth. My feet were rooted, unable to move as I stared stupidly ahead.

The pair vanished into the Orb. We dashed, mere seconds from entering the maelstrom ourselves.

I still see you, clone. You can't get away!

She wasn't speaking to me, yet I experienced the words. She screamed to the universe, beyond the shapes we pursued. My mind happened to be in the blast radius. Possessed, she would follow the thing to hell and back if necessary.

The memory of the horrible traversals ran through me like shards of glass. All of them had sickened me, several reaching levels of incapacitating pain. Now we would enter again, under more hostile conditions. Both she and the sphere struggled. Space seethed.

I knew she would hunt the clone through labyrinthine dimensions. But the wicked girl held power as well. This would be no prepared journey, no warm stroll on the edges of the galaxy. This would be a wild pursuit on a rocket through the fire. I closed my eyes and assumed the worst, tightening my throat to smother any screams.

But it was not me who cried out. My eyes flew open. I couldn't process what I was seeing.

The Orb reached a maniacal climax. The frothing storm of space-time stretched to swallow us. But the epic background was secondary.

Limbs outstretched, her face contorted in rage and pain, Ambra rose. Forces flattened her against an invisible slab, paralyzed. Chained and restrained, she thrashed. She gawked into the devouring mouth before us.

She wailed again. Her arms twitched, her back arched, and the surface of the portal rippled like the sea underneath a squall. Lightning erupted from the black clouds. Rays of light splintered space. Blood leaked from her nose, and her body convulsed.

"Ambra, no!" *You're killing yourself!*

I grabbed her feet. Touching them, an electric charge threw me across our capsule. My hands burned and went numb. My vision blurred, and I strained to focus. I tried to stand, but my legs refused. I couldn't move, crumpled and helpless on the transparent floor of the enclosure. Powerless, I gaped at this atrocity in growing horror like some broken and discarded trinket.

She continued to rise, a harrowing statue, her form frozen. In this numbness consuming me, it felt as if the bubble were nothing more than an illusion. Nothing separated her from the Orb. Reality had become a Titan raging in anger, and it grasped my beloved and ripped her from me.

Still she rose, fifty feet above me, paralyzed, unmoving. The False Dawn and Waythrel had vanished. They were long gone, and I guessed Ambra sensed it better than me. I could see the muscles across her body straining, twitching, trying to find some way out of this invisible prison.

The ascension ceased. Seconds dragged like hours. She floated alone, a fleshly form dangled before the door to heaven or hell. I fought again to move, but it was fruitless. I would not be able to reach my lover. I was helpless to intervene. Stunned by this madness, I knew I was a fool. I was arrogant for presuming a soldier could involve himself in the affairs of gods.

At this moment of resignation and despair, reality took leave of its senses. Or the electrical discharge wrecking my nervous system had damaged my mind as well. This is the sole explanation I can find for what I next witnessed, but you can judge my memory as you will.

As I gazed through tears toward my beloved, shapes stirred in the bubbling broth of the Orb. Indistinct, small spheres resembling cyclones in the greater chaos assumed structure. Definition. Recognizable patterns.

Chills swept through me. The surface was forming *faces*.

A few clarified, titanic, the size of cities. Thousands. *Millions*. Uncountable numbers of masks bubbled through a necromancer's abominable brew. Many were human. More were not.

The mouths chanted.

It was like no music I've ever heard or experienced since. I'm not sure *music* is the right word to describe it, but I have no other. More complex than the greatest symphony. Pure and clear as a temple chant. Melodies distinctly terrestrial mixed with ten thousand orthogonal, alien modalities.

The chorus swelled.

The simulacrums coalesced. The harmonies heightened. The sound spilled into the empty void, and it was filled. The Orb ceased to churn, the surface of the hypersphere calmed to a placid lake. The disembodied faces moved. They summoned a music with more substance than the sparse matter of the universe itself.

It was beautiful. And it was hideous.

It transcended what I could grasp or appreciate. My awareness drowned. Consumed, I withdrew. A survival instinct. My paralyzed body shut down, and I felt myself slipping away. The edges of my vision darkened, blurred, and like a sinking shipwreck victim, I flailed, treading water.

As my consciousness bobbed above the chanting currents, the visions bent bizarre. Two Ambras adorned the night. My beloved hung as a hazy outline. Facing her, spanning the size of continents, a form bubbled from the spacetime broth of the Orb. Tendrils of light and cloud clung to it and plunged back into the infinite sphere.

It was Ambra, but not as I would ever wish to see her. Mirroring the paralyzed position of the Daughter, this titanic apparition glided toward her with arms outstretched to the side, unmoving.

Broken. The hands mutilated. The flesh ripped and jagged. Worms or cables crawled through the skin of its limbs. Blood flowed outward and stained the fabric of space.

The horror continued. The body materializing before us was further desecrated. The skull was sliced open, bone removed, the brain spilling out in layers across a black slime. A giant tumor, some mountainous mimic of my dear Ambra's neural nexus, lay like an obscene egg in its own depression on the reflective darkness. Living tubes of dark materials slithered into those mental tissues and merged with them. The entire malignancy mutated into a nightmarish mixture of flesh and machine.

For a third and last time, Ambra screamed.

She broke through the forces holding her. Her mouth cracked, and a cry of devastating pain ripped through the cosmos. I was convinced the geometry of spacetime would be forever shattered.

Unrecoverable. She wailed into the void, waves of sound beating through me, the tsunami of her torture unbearable.

She fell.

A second electric shock coursed through my body. I moved. My sight clarified as the psychedelic vapors dissipated. I leaped forward, my suit granting me speed and power to catch her. She landed roughly in my arms.

All illumination from the Orb was gone. An eye of the night, it glared at us in a deep black. No faces. No chanting. No chorus of the gods. The monstrous apparition of Ambra was nowhere to be seen. A stillness and stunning silence spread thick like smoke.

And stars.

Suns circumambient, shining through the lucidity of our journey's spacetime vesicle.

I sensed the softness of her flesh through the suit. I longed to hold her without this artificial barrier separating us. Her eyes were closed. Scarlet strands swam down my arms. Her ivory skin glowed against the obsidian of her robe and the ebony of space.

I raised her closer to my face and bent my neck, bringing my lips to hers. I kissed her, but yanked my head back, listening.

She wasn't breathing.

Part III

Parasitism is the birth pang of symbiosis.

The Book of Xix

Chapter 44

The other gods! The gods of the outer hells that guard the feeble gods of earth!...Look away...Go back...Do not see! Do not see! The vengeance of the infinite abysses... That cursed, that damnable pit...Merciful gods of earth, I am falling into the sky!

H. P. Lovecraft

Falling.

Holding Ambra, dropping to my knees. Stay conscious. Swimming through images, murmurs.

Songs.

Endless echoing chants of limitless gods forming shapes and patterns and realities.

The dark sphere approaches, the surface envelops, the universe behind disappearing. Still I hold her tightly, refusing the call for sleep.

Peaceful rest. An end to this terrible and long struggle. The voices sing tranquility. Close my eyes, stop resisting, trust them to bring us home.

They know my name. They know my heart. And I know them.

Faces of family and friends and enemies. Parents. Slain comrades. Fox and her starry-eyed faith. Kim and his childlike energies and enthusiasm. Moore with his rough and loyal mouth. Williams and her blunt analysis. Marshall and his abstracted duty.

Waythrel. The one we chased. It too is here. Alongside another Xix. On a strange and rocky shelf, they make love.

"You will meet soon."

Ambra's face. She speaks. I feel her arms.

"I hold you now as you embrace me. Let go, Nitin. It will be easier this time. Don't be afraid."

Space spins. The light labyrinth glowing and burning. A million passageways through time and song. I don't want to go down those painful roads again. I fear them.

"A last trip. This time, there will be no pain."

My own voice.

It informs me from outside me. My madness and hallucination are complete. Nightmare or imagining, I don't know. Or are they facets of a single gem? Which is waking and which is dreaming? In this impossible universe, what is real? How could such limited forms of flesh discern?

It is too much. I place Ambra down on the surface as a glowing vortex assembles around us. I lie beside her as the bubble drops, plunging into a bottomless, rotating well of radiance. I close my eyes.

We fall.

Chapter 45

I woke to the scratching of blowing sand.

A fierce heat burned as I fought to open my eyes. Stuck together, the eyelids refused to part. I reached to clean them but sprayed grains into my face and mouth. I coughed and spit them out, using the spittle as lubricant. It made mud. Rough to rub across my skin, but effective.

I cracked my lids further and squinted at the blinding glare. Two seas, orange and blue, faced off below and above me. Disorientation competed with the comfort of the familiar. Smelling the air and feeling the sunlight on my face, I understood. I was back on New Earth.

Ambra!

I scrambled to my hands and knees, turning in a circle. Her body was beside mine, face up, eyes closed. I crawled to her and placed my face over her mouth.

No breath!

I grabbed her wrist but couldn't find a pulse. I forced a calm over myself. *No panic. Think.* My emotions would doom her, if she wasn't already.

I powered up my suit, relieved it held charge. I engaged the medapp and diagnostics unit on the side of the mech. Needles and probes extended into her arm, taking samples. The AI reported in clinical terms.

"Anomalous asystole diagnosed without discernible trauma. No evidence of serious internal injuries detected. Body temperature normal."

No obvious harm. Still a chance to revive her!

"Immediate CPR recommended with intravenous vasopressor."

It had been over a year since I had refreshed my training. *Stay calm.*

"What's an intravenous vasopressor?"

"Medkit epinephrine is provided to all MECHcore battle units."

Adrenaline!

I reached around and detached the kit, pressing the keypad to open the box. Inside was a massive syringe labeled *epinephrine*. I grabbed it, removed the safety cap, and plunged the end into her arm. I kept it there for about ten seconds for the solution to drain.

I tossed it to the side and rose over her on my knees, the sand scraping beneath the metal of my suit. Sweat beaded over my eyebrows, smearing my vision. I placed my hands above her sternum and began rhythmic compressions. Squeezing her heart. Forcing blood through her body, oxygen and nutrients and adrenaline.

I pressed hard, as instructed, and after six, I heard the first rib break. *No!* I couldn't let it distract me. It happened, I remembered from the training. I tried not to think about breaking my beloved's bones.

I stopped at thirty, placing my palm on her forehead and tilting her head back. I lifted her chin forward with my other hand to open the airway. I listened. *Still nothing!* I pinched her nostrils shut and covered her mouth with mine. The contrast to our loving embraces was an offense, a crime horrible and clinical and desperate. I made a seal and forced air into Ambra's lungs.

Back to the chest. Fifteen more and another crack. *Dear God!* Another breath. Salt water flowed down my face, stinging my eyes. It was almost impossible to keep my vision clear.

"Please, love! Please!"

My words hissed through the compressions of her ribcage. Again and again and again I pressed. I didn't know how long I could continue in the heat.

In the middle of the fourth cycle, she gasped.

"Ambra!" I screamed at her, but she didn't respond. Still, she was breathing! Her trunk shuddered and fell in haphazard movements.

I attached the diagnostic device, and the AI spoke in a calm monotone.

"Ventricular fibrillation detected. Recommend defibrillation. Confirm, please."

"Confirmed!"

"Please clear contact with the patient."

I pulled back, and the element hummed to a charge and sent current through Ambra's sputtering heart. The muscles around the chest wall tightened and striated.

They relaxed.

"Normal cardiac rhythm established."

Synthetic speech rolled out numbers useful for a doctor to hear. I couldn't process the gibberish but bent down and felt a regular breath from her lips.

My Ambra was alive!

"Advise immediate evacuation to medical facilities."

For the first time in this insanity, I scoured the desert. *It's familiar.* A sand plain of enormous length ran in all directions. In the distance, a tower surged into the heavens. The Sahara. The Temple. *How had we gotten here?*

We were within communications range. I engaged the transmitter and broadcast on all emergency frequencies.

"MAYDAY, MAYDAY, MAYDAY. This is Nitin Ratava, Captain of the Guardians unit. I am outside the Temple City in sight of the antenna. Ambra Dawn is seriously injured. She needs immediate medical evac. Please respond."

My COM shot back static. I tried to boost the signal and ramped all the power to transmission. "MAYDAY, MAYDAY, MAYDAY. This is Captain Nitin Ratava—"

"Captain Ratava, roger your communication. We're locating your position. Confirm your message."

"I have the Daughter with me. She is critically wounded."

A sharp crackle in the white noise and a different voice. "Captain, Major Mizoguchi linking in. Where is the rest of your party?"

"Dead, sir." A gut punch. "Killed by enemy forces. Correction: Waythrel of the Xix was kidnapped. Whereabouts, unknown. Status, unknown."

Static on the COM before she continued. "The goals of your mission?"

"A success, but I don't give a damn right now! Ambra's hurt!"

"We have medical on route to your position and have a high resolution visual on you."

"Tell them to burn through their thrusters," I said, seeing a thin line of blood trickle from the corner of her mouth. "I don't know how long she has."

Chapter 46

A man is a god in ruins.

—Emerson's "Nature"

I stayed beside her on the wild flight back to the Temple City. Sands skimmed past, air whistling along the craft. After I had told them all I knew, the medical crew asked me to move to another part of the ship. I refused. They saw my eyes. I kept out of their way, and they ignored my presence.

From their conversation, I gathered her condition was stable. I had indeed broken ribs in my efforts to revive her, puncturing a lung in the process. But her vital signs were strong. They believed with proper Xixian care back in the city, she would fully recover.

Relief hit me like opium. For the first time in weeks, I relaxed and allowed others to take on the burden of crisis. My mind and body slumped with exhaustion. So much had happened, so many losses, impossible revelations and events. The shock was fresh. I leaned against the walls of the hovercraft and closed my eyes.

The opening of the bay doors startled me awake. They sprinted Ambra off the ship to the medical units. I stayed out of their way. She was stable. She was going to be okay. With that knowledge, I let them do their jobs.

Mizoguchi, Mazandarani, and others awaited me as I exited the craft. I sighed, much too tired to deal with anything right now. But I knew they wanted answers. They deserved them.

I froze in my tracks. A Xix stood out among the crowd, its eyestalks a tower above the humans. Its black and phosphorescent colors shimmered in striking patterns. Patterns I'd seen before in the last dream.

"Synphel."

The rest glanced from me to the alien in surprise. It ambled forward and stopped in front of me.

"How do you know me?" it asked.

"I don't know," I stammered, my mind whirling through the confusion of the final traversal. "I think Waythrel said your name. On another world. Another time."

"Waythrel spoke to you of our mating groups?"

Mating groups?

"No." *How do I explain this?* I put my hand to my forehead. I was so tired.

"Waythrel never talked of anything like...mating groups. Seeing you here, I recognized you from...an experience I had on the mission."

"What was its nature?"

"I don't know. A strange dream. I suffer nightmares when I go through those damn Orbs. I heard voices. Many of them. At the end of it, there was Waythrel's voice. You were standing nearby. You were..." I decided not to describe all I had seen. "I was told I'd meet you soon." I shook my head. "And here you are."

By this point, Mizoguchi and Mazandarani had joined, listening in to the conversation.

Synphel bowed to me. "I am pleased to make your acquaintance,

Captain Ratava. You clearly have been blessed with profound experiences in your travels."

"Or cursed."

"Yes, such astounding events are hard to distinguish and are often both." The alien's many eyes studied me. "I recognize that you are weary, but Waythrel is important to me. Please tell me all you know about what happened."

"You're a mate? Romantically involved?" I had no idea what words to use in this context.

"One of them."

"So, you have marriages, divorces? Or multiple spouses?"

"Closer to the latter, Captain. We tend to keep our social behavior private. You, however, are intimately entwined in our stories. I will explain something few of your kind have heard." The Xix let that sink in. It did, but I had no clue what to do with it. "You may have noticed that we do not employ gendered terms when speaking about ourselves."

I shrugged. "Yes. A strange hiccup in your translators."

"Not a hiccup. It is intentional, because to do so would distort our natures. Humans have a dioecious genetic and phenotypic biological mating structure: male and female. There are spectrums of behaviors and physiology associated with this basic average sexuality, a property common to most living systems. Productive human copulation, however, is achieved through opposite binary interactions. We of the Xix do not possess two sexes."

"You're asexual?" I offered, wondering if they budded like yeast or impregnated themselves. I needed to lie down.

"No. We have six."

"*Six?*" I *really* didn't know what to do with that.

Mizoguchi and Mazandarani gawked. This was rare information.

"Yes, with corresponding physiological and genetic differences. You have male and female, each with distinct bodies and character. Reproductive organs. Biochemistry. We have six. A fruitful mating event is achieved when all six copulate simultaneously. Intimate partnership occurs in binary, ternary, and other combinations for plea-sure and companionship. But reproduction requires six."

Now my head was swimming. "I'm not sure I want to learn much more."

"I will spare you the details. But Waythrel and I were different sexes in one such group. In fact, we were a closely associated pair in the combined sexual assembly. Echoing human monogamous rela-tions, we lived extended portions of our lives in each other's presence."

"Married?"

"Not precisely, but the term will do. Does this help you under-stand why I care so much to discover what befell?"

I thought of Ambra. "It does. Thank you. Let's go to the hospi-tal, and I'll tell you what I can on the way."

The Xix bowed again and moved to the side. I stepped toward the entrance of the medical wing, but Mazandarani darted in front of me. My temper flared.

"Excuse me."

"You are a fortunate man," he snarled, remaining where he was. "The one soul to survive the mission. It's as if certain fates are shaping your destiny." A fire raged in his eyes.

I couldn't believe I had to deal with this. "Sepehr, *not now*. Get out of my way and let me go see Ambra."

"Yes. Your main failure was that she lived. Do you go to finish the job?"

I weighed responses in an instant. Statements, passive or harsh. Varied, expressive silences. After a second of consideration, I threw all pretense of maturity to the side.

I smashed my fist across his jaw, and the Iranian sprawled to the floor. A natural parting of the waters occurred as people cleared from around us. But Mazandarani wasn't the brawling type. He held his face and the trickling blood coming from his mouth while scowling at me.

So I did more than strike him. My suit was still activated. I reached down, and with the full power of the hydraulics, grasped him by the robes and lifted him into the air. His feet dangled inches off the ground, a shocked but unbowed expression on his face.

"Captain Ratava!" came the imperial voice of Major Mizoguchi. "Put down the counselor, now!"

I was in a state. Blame fatigue, loss, mental trauma, or the ugly insinuations of the counselor. I'd simply had enough.

He spoke through clenched teeth. "Did they pay you to kill me, too?"

I glared at him. "I'd do that for free."

A steady but firm grip squeezed my shoulder. The towering Xix loomed over me like a shadow. "Nothing would pain Ambra more than for us to hurt one another."

My will for violence vanished. I put the Iranian down. Perhaps somewhat roughly, but the alien had rebooted my emotions. It had known exactly what to say.

Mazandarani straightened his robes and bowed to Synphel with some semblance of shame. I spun on my heel and strode out of the dock without a word or second glance.

Chapter 47

Not until we are lost do we begin to understand ourselves.

Henry David Thoreau

"You saved my life, Nitin."

Her beauty transcended objectivity. Hair in disarray, eyes bloodshot with dark circles like a raccoon—it didn't matter. It's hard to describe the overwhelming feeling of joy and wonder running through me to see her open her eyes and smile. Speak. Gesture with her hands in her elegant way.

My Ambra is alive!

"I guess it's fifty to one, now. I'm still deep in the red." I tried to maintain a soldier's composure. It was difficult. "I'm sorry about the ribs."

"They'll heal, beloved," she said, smiling again.

I sat in a chair, holding her hand, gazing upon her face like the first time I had seen it as a child in school. The new Xix was present. Mazandarani stood opposite me on the other side of Ambra's hospital bed. After our altercation a few days ago, the two of us did our best to avoid each other.

"Thank you for speaking with Synphel, Nitin. I've shared with the Xix all the details passed on to their group memory. They'll do what they can, but there's little hope to find Waythrel now. They could have gone to any place at any time."

"The bodies of Fox and Kim? They weren't in the desert?"

"No," said Mazandarani. "A thorough search turned up nothing."

Ambra spoke. "It's my fault. I left them chasing the clone. The portal may have brought us back, but it didn't pick up after us."

The Orb. I had a distinct ambivalence about the object now. All my life, I'd learned the mythology of the Time Spheres. Memorized the legends because they were central in the Daughter's story. Always narratives of goodness and hope. After the terrible events at the Dram homeworld, I'd never see the portals in quite the same way.

"How could it have turned against you?"

Her smile faded. "Oh, Nitin, there's so much I wish I could explain. The gate is something far greater than I, and it has a mind of its own. I've known this, but because my desires had always aligned with it, I took that alignment for granted. Things changed when they took Waythrel." Ambra sighed. "The truth is, the Orb didn't abandon me—I betrayed myself."

"What are you talking about?" How could she blame herself for this?

"You see, I'd worked a lifetime to accept and plan for our losses. Terrible costs to come that you believe in abstractly because you trust my words. I *live* those tragedies. Endless visions. I'm never able to escape them, their pain. I didn't understand how much I'd repressed. Anger. A deep bitterness. Especially after meeting you, and you turned out to be everything I'd envisioned. My heart was lost to you. To think about that cruel future—I barely held myself together, Nitin."

Embarrassment choked me as she shared such personal feelings.

Synphel was one thing—no doubt the alien knew a lot from the Reader sharings. But Waythrel's mate was still strange to me and its otherness provided a distancing. With another human, it was different. With Mazandarani—I didn't like his hearing about our relationship. Nor did he, I guessed. A quick glance at his face confirmed it.

"You seemed so strong. I didn't understand," I said.

She touched my cheek. "I didn't either, or you would have sensed it when we shared. When that thing took Waythrel, something shattered inside me. I hadn't seen this in visions—greater powers hid it from me. A total surprise, something I don't often experience. It was a heartbreaking loss. One I hadn't prepared for."

She nodded, explaining the entire situation to herself as much as to me.

"I lost control. I flew into a mad rage. I abandoned all my efforts in this long struggle, refused to listen to my own prophecies. The clone opened the portal. The Time Sphere *allowed* this. I should have recognized this, accepted it, *understood* the significance. I was too crazed, too rebellious, too *arrogant* in my hurt to let go and take my rightful place. I'm afraid I was beginning to believe in my own mythology." She shook her head. "I tried to change what shouldn't have been changed. The Orb intervened. It showed me my mistakes. It reminded me of my path."

"What are you saying?" I asked, horrified, remembering the terrible visions.

She glanced away from me. "My fate is still unfolding, and I can't see all ends. What happened there is beyond full understanding. For now, at least. Until events reach completion."

The Xix interrupted. "I am grateful to Captain Ratava for sharing his experience in the transit. It may not make sense, but I believe you heard the voice of Waythrel. How, I do not know. Through the Time Sphere, its awareness reached out to you, and to me, to connect us in our future struggles. I will remember this."

I was unsure how to respond. I certainly didn't feel I deserved such commitment and connection to Synphel. As always, these aliens left me slightly in awe.

I bowed my head and tried to accept the offer. "We all loved Waythrel," I murmured. "Ambra most of all."

"Not more than Synphel, Nitin." Her face dropped. "But, yes, I miss Waythrel terribly."

Mazandarani cleared his throat. "Daughter of Time, I have completed the preparations as you requested. I need your go-ahead for the ceremony." His expression was a mask of strain.

"For what?" I asked.

Ambra's demeanor brightened, and she squeezed my hand. "A marriage. It will take place here in the Temple during a Great Sharing. The Group Mind will be formed to preside over the sacrament. Readers are en route from across the galaxy right now."

"What wedding? Who's marrying?"

Synphel spoke. "The Daughter of Time, of course."

I gawked in shock. Ambra winked at me, a half-smile curling her lip. I turned to the alien, who stood unreadable, and last, to Mazandarani.

"Is this true?" The floor was about to collapse underneath me.

"Yes. Although I sought to prevent it," he said.

"Counselor, you have yet to overcome your possessiveness," said the Xix. "Until you do, you will have no peace."

I didn't give a damn about the Iranian or his tranquility at this moment. *To be wed?* It couldn't be! How?

"I don't understand. Married, to whom?"

"Why to *you*, Captain Ratava, of course," answered Synphel.

Ambra laughed. "Nitin, I won't ask you a third time. Will you marry me?"

I dive into the depth of the ocean of forms, hoping to gain the perfect pearl of the formless.

"The Gitanjali" by Rabindranath Tagore

The first ceremony we attended was to pay respects to those who had fallen during our recent mission. We had returned with no bodies. No remains. Nothing but the memories we carried for those who had died serving humanity. Sacrificing for life beyond our own species. Giving everything for millions of sentient worlds across our galaxy.

We gathered in the desert, near the spot where Ambra and I had awakened a few weeks ago. A collection of aliens and humans gazed upon a makeshift memorial hewn from the bedrock. Orange and marbled, polished to a gleaming finish, five names were engraved:

Erica Fox

David Kim

Ryan Marshall

Grant Moore
Aisha Williams

Waythrel's name was withheld at the request of Synphel and the Xix. They refused to commit the kidnapped alien to the casualty list, retaining hope that, someday, Ambra's beloved advisor would be found.

In homage to ancient rituals of Old Earth, a flame was lit in an oil-filled bowl beneath the carving. A protective field was set around the memorial, shielding the slab from wind and sand. Servants of the Temple refilled the container each week, trekking the distance in the heat to give their respects.

Ambra stood by my side in the winds, her robes billowing and her hair dancing. She smiled and turned to the rest of the group. "Until we join them again," she said.

I was too consumed with conflicting emotions to parse what she meant. Too often, her metaphysical pronouncements escaped my understanding. I struggled to accept the loss of my team, my inescapable responsibility for their deaths. Command carried terrible burdens. A debt I could never pay.

She possessed a unique perspective of mortality, and therefore, of life as well. She spoke as if the dead weren't truly departed. I wondered if they were still with us in her unusual view of time. Could she still access their essence? Would life and death appear as eternal elements in a single fabric of existence?

I could not share her combined joy and sadness. Nor could I understand her far-flung gaze when speaking of and to those who had passed. My struggles remained unresolved.

We returned to the Temple by hovercraft. Ambra insisted the truest way to honor their deaths was to fully live. So our ceremony would proceed that evening.

Whatever I thought of Mazandarani, he had pushed aside his jealousy and pain at losing the Daughter to me. He planned the marriage as grandly as the Festival of Rebirth. As we approached the inner city, throngs lined the streets. Xix and human. Odd alien species in environmental suits, some remaining in protective craft. Tens of thousands had come from every corner of the planet and from star systems distant. It was a gathering like no other I'd seen.

I wore my military dress uniform. Black coat and pants. The MECHcore red beret, the gear train insignia stitched in gold thread on the front. My captain's bars gleamed, along with honor badges and medals from combat operations. It was an oven in the suit, but I tried to appear relaxed.

We disembarked from the hovercraft at the foot of the long stairway rising to the Temple. Together, Ambra and I led the way up the stairs, Synphel and Mazandarani close, a pack of dignitaries behind them. The crowd queued and followed the procession into the enormous structure.

The mood was festive yet sober. Many of the greatest Readers of our galaxy were present. Their repeated sharings produced a mass dynamic unlike any I had experienced. Perhaps it was a weak echo of the Group Mind she often spoke about. A quiet unity hovered over the demeanors of the individuals. No randomness of disconnected strangers. No empty-headed mob mentality. It was something else, something more than alien. It permeated the surrounding space.

We entered the open expanse of the grand chamber, approaching the chromatic projection. The Orb slice reflected the mood I sensed from the gathering spilling into the room. Gone were the storm clouds present in the terrible conflict at the Dram homeworld. The colors flitted with potential and anticipation. The patterns suggested in my mind future possibility and a strange sense of hope. Amazed, I wondered how this abstract illusion could shape my thoughts.

Onward we walked, hand in hand, and neared the central dais within the color swarm. Thousands poured like a river through the entrance behind us. Their forms flowed through the chamber, pooling into individual depressions. Little sound escaped beyond their footsteps and the friction of fabric.

We stepped to the prismatic nexus. Ambra spun us, holding our clasped hands into the air as the remainder of the Readers entered. I anchored my gaze on my beloved to calm the anxiety at this subconscious atmosphere of power.

She wore a tailored black robe, the material finer than anything I had ever seen. It reflected the glowing walls of the Temple. Xixian medicine had performed miracles. Her skin radiated a startling white. Her eyes glowed, luminous emeralds beyond valuing. My fingers twitched, desiring to run through her red curls. But we remained still. Stuck in the statuesque position she had chosen to greet the incoming congregation.

It took some time before they settled. Once the last Readers sat, the doors shut to the Sahara, silencing the sounds of the desert. Many assumed positions of meditation reminiscent of Indian yoga. A variety characterized the figures, especially in the alien species present and visible.

Ambra lowered our arms. She gazed across the landscape of contemplation, entering a trance herself.

During these moments, the assembly isolated me. I was the outsider, excluded from the communion of their minds. A talentless grunt dropped within a phenomenon he couldn't understand or partake in.

My dissociation was short-lived. Vertigo unbalanced my grip of reality. A subsonic rumble rose, a bass hum flowing around and diffusing through the stone into flesh. I didn't know if my bones or my soul rattled. Something unusual unfolded, beyond my experience. The passage of time transformed.

An irrational conviction of presence grew. It reminded me of the intuition one has in the dark, when one isn't alone. Or the certainty a soldier feels in combat when a threat is near. Except the sensation wasn't fearful. This manifestation calmed.

I discerned a personality transcending my own. It permeated

space and sense, unlocalized but pervasive. I thought of our ancestors. Isolated in the deserts with little knowledge and nothing to frame such a transcendent experience. I have no doubt I would have ascribed it to the presence of the divine.

We form the Mind.

A voice from everywhere and nowhere. I turned to Ambra. Her gaze was on me, her eyes diving into my own. But the speech wasn't hers. Not from any individual. It loomed beyond us, larger, distinct. Yet it radiated from deep inside me.

We are *the Awareness.*

Waves of warmth and electricity danced through me. Her face flushed, pupils dilated. My breath strengthened, adopting a rhythm. I felt consumed. Tendrils of power reached into me from outside. They penetrated my nervous system, stirring a fire.

Arousal.

The many are One. Now two will be one and of One.

My breathing deepened. Goosebumps covered my forearms and legs. My mouth dried as an erection stirred. Rivers of life flowed through me, summoning my energies. It was frightening. It was a hunger I couldn't possibly refuse.

"Ambra..." My voice was hoarse.

She cooed. "Shall I show you marital bliss, my husband?" She came close to me, her lips parted and engorged with blood, her body brushing mine.

I gasped, panting. "Haven't we already known it?" I wondered, remembering our time outside the galaxy on the sands.

"Not like this."

She undid the gold buttons on the front of my dress coat. I saw a bright passion in her eyes. Her fingers explored my chest through the spaces in my shirt. Her nails scraped against my taut nipples. I moaned, wanting to explode, my eyes swimming. They caught sight of her breasts, the glowing Temple walls, the flashing colors of the portal, the sea of Readers deep in trances.

"Ambra—*here?* With all of them?" But I couldn't resist. There would be no denial. Only full, complete, consuming *desire*.

"Yes, love," she said, her lips on mine, her tongue teasing and a warm breath flowing into my mouth. She yanked my coat and shirt down around my elbows and ran her hands over my swelling chest. "A profound sharing. A Heart greater than any you have known watches over us. It blesses our union while it partakes and augments it."

She pulled me down on top of her.

Chapter 49

His left hand should be under my head,
and his right will embrace me.

Song of Solomon 8:3

She was correct. It wasn't like before.

A swelling in the deep chant evolved into one voice. An articulation synergized of many psyches. Tones low and high. Personalities human and alien, spanning notes and scales and qualities unimagined. The transcendental harmony was multiple yet undivided.

Waves of a celestial hymn washed over us. It fueled our mutual desire, drove it higher as we lay upon the dais. Biology commanded. The limbic broth overflowed. Her eyes drew me deeper into a whirlpool of verdant scintillations.

The Temple disappeared, fading to black. We entwined as a single organism dangling inside the color explosion of a nebula. My mind, consumed by the mating act and by her eyes, soared within this cosmic artwork. Omnipresent, the light of stars painted the dusts of space toward infinity.

I love you, Nitin. Always. Remember.

Not like before. The tendrils of transcendental potential trickled through me, the collapse after climax transformed. Hunger returned, my physiology altered. The arousal did not decrease but ascended to greater passion.

Her eyes held me. I sensed the question. A request, permission to enter this frightening and uncharted physical place. The biology of sex is raw power. It often wreaks destruction in its intensity to create. She asked me to play with a fire I dimly appreciated.

I gave in wholeheartedly, and not solely from the burning desire churning within me. Also to connect, to become, to merge with the one I loved beyond anything I had known.

Waves waxed to storms. The flame flowed through us. Our bodies cycled from arousal to climax, gentleness to wild passion. In myriad locations in space, we made love over and again. Before a cloud igniting its nuclear fuel. Floating over a frozen sea of methane on an ice world. Watching the dance of multiple systems in accelerated time. We dashed through a dense star field as the dots of light drew into brilliant bands.

Not alone.

A presence observed us from above. Spoke from within us. It enhanced, studied, transported. It loved us in some fashion beyond my comprehension. Surpassing any kind of adoration I'd known. A dispassionate passion. This transcendent otherness transformed the affections of crude creatures like ourselves. Over us flowed a concern mingled with detachment, a celestial devotion summoned from a collective godling.

I was Ambra, and she was I, and we were part of something *other*. Devoid of Reader talents, I still encountered this spirit. The power of this Being stimulated whatever vestige of that sensory organ I possessed. I couldn't imagine what it was like for the Readers themselves.

My body was now a portion of a greater organism. In this union, our passions continued, and my emotions ranged unrestrained. The overwhelming experience stripped all semblance of artifice, social inhibition, personal restraint. I wept. I laughed. I did both with freedom and completeness. It resolved the age-old mystery of how tears and laughter danced as separated twins. In this realm, they integrated and became one. Joy and sadness as much of a harmony as two human bodies becoming one flesh. Or ten thousand brains assembling into a single Mind.

To describe more of this multipartite reality is impossible. My experiences were of a nature I recall as a sober man would heavy intoxication. Afterward, they dissolved to faded colors of vivid dreams. Ideas hopelessly in conflict and forever out of reach.

The fullness of the universe drifted before my awareness.

Eons passed.

We were alone in her room. The Temple had vanished. The Readers were gone. The lofty consciousness receded as a blurring hallucination.

Ambra slept on the bed. Moonlight spilled over the white skin of her shoulder protruding from the bedsheets. Returning to my senses, I exited the trance.

Exhaustion sapped every cell in my body. I needed to sleep as I had never known. I folded my dress pants, hung my coat, and left my beret on the table. I placed my medals and bars in their boxes. I took the holster with my sidearm and removed the Hertz, closing it within a drawer in the bedside stand.

I lay down on the bed. When my head touched the pillow, it felt as though the mattress rose and enveloped me. Bone tired, I knew peace for the first time in my life. Remade with a stirring emotion stronger than any I had ever experienced and for which I had no words.

I closed my eyes.

Chapter 50

Men of broader intellect know that there is no sharp distinction betwixt the real and the unreal; that all things appear as they do only by virtue of the delicate individual physical and mental media through which we are made conscious of them; but the prosaic materialism of the majority condemns as madness the flashes of super-sight which penetrate the common veil of obvious empiricism.

H. P. Lovecraft

I drown again in dream.

As the soft morning sunlight of New Earth dances through our bedroom window, I look down on her sleeping. The white sheets are blinding, wrapped around her seductive curves. Her naked shoulder has slipped from the fabric, as scintillating as the silk—such a contrast to my dark copper. Waterfalls of red curls streaming to her waist color this blank canvas.

I admire her swollen skull resting on the pillow. The grotesque bulge repulses others, but I know attraction, a pull to touch, to caress.

I walk to the nightstand and open the drawer. In a state of unreal detachment, I remove the firearm. The composite metal should be cold in my hand, but it is not. I feel nothing. The muscles tighten around the handle of the pistol, but I give no commands. I have no responses and sense no contractions or tightness in my skin. I see from a distance, crammed into a vantage point I cannot define in space or in time.

And this automaton, an alien form that is no longer mine, works the weapon. Fingers unlock the safety, orienting the firearm toward the bed. The golem raises the barrel to the elongated head of my beloved. It brushes the scarred edges near her hairline.

She opens her blind, green eyes with adoration. Seeing nothing and everything, they stare into my own. Tears trickle down her white cheeks and I hear her voice in my mind.

Don't be afraid, Nitin. I love you.

I pull the trigger.

Chapter 51

My friend, I am not what I seem. Seeming is but a garment I wear.
The "I" in me, my friend, dwells in the house of silence. I would not
have thee believe in what I say nor trust in what I do.

"The Madman" by Khalil Gibran

The gun did not fire. My hand pulled the trigger repeatedly, but nothing happened.

Ambra sat up in the bed, her hair spilling over her chest and onto the sheets. She stared at me with a terrible coldness. "We've been waiting."

My mouth screamed. My body lurched forward, my hands outstretched to grasp her throat. I got nowhere, paralyzed, frozen in space. She rose and slipped on a robe, straightening her beautiful locks. The sound of sprinting footsteps filled my ears. Shapes barged into the room, but I couldn't turn to see them. I remained suspended.

"You are unhurt?" a man cried, his speech winded. *Mazandarani.*

"Yes." She glared across my field of vision to the door. "Sepehr, put the weapon down." A short pause, and she spoke with more force. "*Sepehr!* Now. Put it down!"

"He would have killed you!" Such venom.

"Remember not to condemn an innocent," said Synphel. "Nitin is as much a victim as Ambra nearly was. More so. He has lived in ignorance because of our machinations. Show pity, counselor."

Fabric rustled and her face relaxed. "Thank you. Now, place him in restraints. Put him in that chair."

Mazandarani pulled my paralyzed limbs behind me. A crackling buzz indicated the activation of field cuffs. Arms lifted and moved my body backward. They dropped me on a seat, my legs also restrained and bent to a sitting position.

"He's secure?" she asked.

I could see them all in front of me. He nodded.

The paralysis ended. My lips erupted in a string of vile curses aimed at the Daughter. I watched this offense, possessed, caged in a nightmare. A lunatic with a split personality, I cursed my dearest love. I strained to shout, to weep, but I could do nothing. I was a soul imprisoned in the abomination of my own rebellious body.

She held up her hands and my mouth locked. "Enough."

The sewage of profanities stopped. She knelt down in front of me. My limbs convulsed to reach her, to spill the lifeblood of my lover.

She stared into my eyes. "Nitin, it's okay. This will be over soon."

"Be careful, Ambra!" said Mazandarani. "You don't know where he is or what will be waiting for you."

She placed one hand on each side of my skull and closed her eyes, forcing mine shut as well. My body spasmed in seizures of suppressed violence.

"No, Sepehr, they don't know what's *coming*."

What happened next, I tell you through analogy and metaphor. I clothe it in visual images and archetypes because my imagination can do nothing more with the experience. As for what truly occurred, Ambra knows.

The entirety of her essence blasted as a rocket into my consciousness. No, rather into some enlarged space containing what I naively thought of as myself. Except I wasn't alone. Inside this mental chamber, anchored in some way as fundamentally as I, there lurked *another*. Cloaked in shadows, stowed in the back of my being beside a doorway I'd never perceived. The fading apparition slipped behind the portal and vanished.

Ambra's fury rushed in pursuit like a billowing fire. An incandescent dragon propelled past my awareness and through the door. I was abandoned, forsaken in this strange, expanded space. Once my mind. Now, some insane house of mirrors.

Control over my body returned. I opened my eyes. Her face rested centimeters from my own. She continued to hold my head in her hands, her eyes closed, focused, and in some trance. The others in the room observed in tense silence.

"Synphel. *Help me.*"

The tall Xixian approached. "Captain. It is not safe to remove the restraints. Do not disturb her."

"Why?" I asked. "Where has Ambra gone?"

"To kill an assassin."

"What assassin?"

"The one lurking within you since the day you were born," said Mazandarani.

Eyestalks spun toward him. Their disapproval radiated.

"The Anti have been busy for centuries," said the alien. "Not only creating clones of the Daughter. Equally audacious has been their plan to infiltrate Ambra's inner circle. To place spies. Among them, to bring to life the perfect assassin. One who could win the heart and mind of the target, placed next to her in moments of extreme vulnerability. A killer to activate at precisely that point to optimize the probabilities of success."

I trembled, not from the murderous impulses poisoning my form, but from my own revulsion and fear. "What are you saying?"

Mazandarani passed sentence. "You are a deadly pawn, Captain. An experiment in extermination. A monster designed by enemies so vile nothing remains sacred. A grotesque weapon *engineered* to kill Ambra Dawn. Had she not seen through it, you would have succeeded."

"No."

"*Yes*," he spat. "A chimeric Frankenstein composed of three bodies and two souls. A lover's doppelgänger harboring malice and murder behind a veil of devotion."

Synphel interrupted. "*Careful*, Sepehr. You are letting emotions cloud your thoughts. In what is to come, we will need your mind."

The counselor lowered his head.

My words choked in a parched throat. "What does this mean? What's he talking about?"

"A horror, Captain. A diabolic cleverness. Housed on the other side of the galaxy in a future several hundred, perhaps thousands, of years from now. In this place, there is a ring of power plants not too different from what you have seen here. Within the bowels of that coven, two human bodies float in a stasis medium. Feeding tubes and waste management systems maintain these husks. Their skulls are sliced open, and the brains embedded in a dark technology. Casting their spells over this broth are a score of False Dawns, themselves imprisoned in the room, enslaved to support a long-term manipulation of space and time."

A growing darkness reached greedy fingers up my spine, seizing my throat. My sight narrowed from the corners. "How do you know this?"

"The Collective perceived," said Synphel. "It penetrated layers of deception woven around the place. In one of those tanks is your brain, or rather, the proto-organic component of your *mind*. An advanced projection system works through the clones. Together they open a wormhole, connecting a future time and distant location with our here and now. This technology embedded your highly engineered awareness in a developing fetus in India. A process honed by centuries of experimentation and aid from the shadows of the Anti. You are a construct torn between flesh and space, neurons and time."

"Why?"

"Because there is a back door in your head, Captain," said the alien.

Other holes bleed in your mind, Nitin Ratava.

The high voice of a young girl echoed in my thoughts. I shivered, my lips numb, guts churning.

The Xix continued. "A second body, another *person,* was also projected within this physical form on New Earth. It lay hidden for all of your life. *Watching.* Observing everything happening to you. Transmitting back to its masters."

"The spy."

"Yes, but much more. If the time came, if the opportunity presented itself, this back door could open. This invader would seize control of your flesh. Today it happened, nearly to the death of Ambra Dawn."

I stared at the unmoving face of my beloved, my corruption complete.

"I'm the assassin."

Chapter 52

I know faces, because I look through the fabric my own eye weaves, and behold the reality beneath.

"The Madman" by Khalil Gibran

My life crystallized in a tainted mind. The pieces of unexplained puzzles locked into place. Understanding brought despair.

"She *knew*. She knew all along, didn't she? From the moment we met. That's why she came to the hospital in Japan."

"Yes, Captain," said Synphel. "We have all been aware for some time, thwarting the deceptions of our enemies. They were unable to conceal what they had done through space and time, despite employing the powers of their monstrous clones. They undervalued Ambra's vision. They especially underestimated the Group Mind."

"How long has she known?"

"Since you were born," said Mazandarani, "although some of us have only learned of this recently." Bitterness dripped from his words.

"Because you were too much in love with the Daughter not to take matters into your own hands, Sepehr," said the Xix. "You would have wrecked our careful plans."

A bitter seed sprouted inside me. *Used.* Not by our enemies alone. My Ambra had exploited me, manipulating my life for decades. She had said *nothing.*

"A plan for me."

Synphel continued. "Yes, or rather, for the weapon of the enemy that was your body. We have played them, Captain. We fed them exactly enough veracity to engender a false impression of our strategy."

I stared forward at the face I loved. Her expression was peaceful. Detached.

Cold?

How calculating had she been? How had she hidden from me this truth while we shared our souls? My head swam. My beliefs were a mockery, and reality devastated me.

"Our awareness of your dual nature presented us with an opportunity. You see, we knew the second entity reported everything you heard and saw. We led them to believe we planned to shut them out with the closure of the Orbs. What we did not tell you is that this is impossible. There is no way to fully wall off any portion of the Time Tree."

My mouth hung open. "Those missions were a *hoax?* My team died for *nothing?*"

Cold. Calculating.

"We were all to die if this clone army could not be defeated. Your soldiers' deaths were not for nothing. They helped you and Ambra set the bait. Their sacrifice made the con more convincing."

"What bait?" I felt sick.

"The Anti eventually perceived they could continue to access the New Earth Orb. They were exposed to a terrible temptation."

I understood. The military training spelled out the strategy in an instant. "A final hammer stroke."

"Yes," said Synphel. "Convinced we had miscalculated, they sought to breach our defenses with overwhelming force. To crush us once and for all at the origin point of the Resistance. They withheld their full strength when you unknowingly leaked the mission details to them. Did you never wonder why those engagements at Brax and Hola had no clone contingent? They waited for the ultimate prize to reveal their hand. Your homeworld had to be in the mix."

"Why didn't they have me assassinate Ambra in the desert when we returned? They wouldn't have to make me kill her. Just sit there as she died."

"We are not certain," said Synphel. "Your travels through the Orbs played havoc with the wormhole connection. Nested tunnels, wormholes within portals. It is a complexity beyond anything we've approached in science. It was a terrible strain on you—it must have been much more so for them. Likely by the time they recovered and realized the opportunity, it had passed. They would rather be sure, construct the assassination carefully. Leave no room for failure—they would get one attempt. The final temptation in their ultimate assault plan. If they had assassinated our most able Reader, the one who might stand a chance to halt the horde of False Dawns, victory was assured. New Earth would meet the fate of the old."

"Well, does she?" I asked. "Stand a chance? She told me she couldn't. Was that a lie, too?"

The room blurred in brightness. A white noise filled my ears and faded. My sight returned.

"No," came a voice inches from my face. I startled within the restraints as Ambra spoke and opened her eyes. "No, Nitin. I can't overcome their numbers."

I swallowed a scream. "Then what's all this *about*?"

She wiped tears from her eyes. "I can't defeat them as I am. So I will become more than what I am."

The alien was silent.

Mazandarani stared in horror. "Please, Daughter of Time," he pleaded, "don't do this thing."

"The assassin is dead," she replied. "I followed the link back to its source. There were multiple clones, like we guessed. I killed them, and I shut down the life-support machinery of the spy."

"What of Captain Ratava?" asked Synphel. The Xix paced with darting eyestalks.

Ambra reached behind me and removed my restraints. She held my hands. "My worst fears. His proto-brain wasn't there. They have him in another location." She winced at the confusion on my face. "I had hoped to free your mind, Nitin. To disconnect it from the flesh of its origin and permanently anchor it in the physical framework here. But I can't. I don't know where your body is. I can't follow your link without them killing you."

"You did for this...assassin."

"They weren't prepared. That's why I acted so quickly. Now, they will know what happened, or figure most of it out. They will take steps."

"What steps?"

"They will kill you. Pull the plug and break the connection."

"Why didn't you come for me first?"

She shook her head. "And leave the killer free to roam your mind while I was gone? He could have broken the bond between your brains and murdered us both at the same time. I had to stop him first. It was the only way. The only hope."

The alien elaborated. "Your core consciousness remains distant. This Earth-brain that has housed it is dysfunctional on its own. It is a distorted exploitation for their dual implantations. Your full personality resides with them in the other organism. Where they can control it. Otherwise, Ambra would simply break the connection, and you would continue here, as you are."

Confused, I yearned for such a simple solution. A way to extract myself from this diabolical possession. But it was not to be.

"Sadly, given the construct they have created, that action would only leave a neurological shell, not even capable of supporting physiological functions. Hence your physical malfunctions during Orb transit when the connections were destabilized."

The complications baffled me. "Wait. Haven't they been listening in? Don't they know about the trap now?"

"No. I didn't travel along the projection they made to your proto-body, but that doesn't mean I didn't touch it. I've propagated waves down the wormhole to the source. It will disrupt their ability to monitor you. It will wreak havoc with the passage of time in their space. Slow them down. But not forever, my love." She wept and kissed me. "It's a matter of time."

"Before I die." The finality of it struck me at last. "You told me on the beach."

"I'm sorry, Nitin." Anguish twisted her features.

In an instant, I forgave her. I understood the larger context. I experienced a glimpse of the long pain she forced herself to carry. A terrible burden of knowledge.

"I wouldn't make a different choice, Ambra. Not even now." I stroked her hair as she leaned her face into my hand.

Synphel spoke. "It is also only a matter of time before their armada of ships and clones arrives. If we are to complete our plan, we must act now."

I pulled her face away from mine, my cheek wet with her tears. Her lower lip trembled.

"What are you going to do?"

She wiped her eyes with the back of her hand. "I am going to be butchered by my dearest friends," she said with a false smile and bravado. She turned wild-eyed toward Synphel. "I will go through a new hell and a transformation."

My thoughts slowed and stumbled.

She spun back and kissed me. "I've already died in your arms, beloved. Soon, I'll be reborn."

Lines of pain crossed Mazandarani's face, but his eyes spilled awe. "Daughter of Time," he whispered.

Ambra stood and straightened her robe. "And then I will call all souls to me."

Chapter 53

The day will come when, after harnessing space, the winds, the tides, gravitation, we shall harness for God the energies of love. And, on that day, for the second time in the history of the world, man will have discovered fire.

Pierre Teilhard de Chardin

The first assault struck as we descended from the Temple into the Saharan sands.

A violent vertigo sickened me from inside, a distancing from my body. My legs buckled. Ambra caught me and helped break my fall in the elevator car. We'd plunged three kilometers into the crust of New Earth, heading to a secret center for the final stage of her long plan. I couldn't focus on her explanations. Our enemies were splitting me from my own flesh.

"Nitin!" She slapped my cheeks. The impacts were numbed.

"It has begun," said Synphel. "Captain, this is proceeding faster than we had anticipated. We will do what we can."

Our drop braked, and the wild vertigo stabilized. I could no longer use my legs, and my arms moved like some manipulated puppet. The towering alien bent down, and with one vigorous motion, lifted me off the elevator floor.

They whisked my failing body off to a ward staffed with crowds of Xixian medics. I didn't have time to process what they were doing here. Or why this secret lair resembled a hospital more than a war cave. I would soon discover the terrible answers to my questions.

Ambra was gone. They wouldn't tell me why or where. The medical staff buzzed around me, a nightmare beehive with their arms and eyestalks. They inserted instruments into my skin at various locations, but I was too numb to feel them. I sat in a peculiar wheelchair, the back of it thick with instrumentation.

I struggled to speak. "What...what are you doing?" I sounded drunk.

One of the medics paused to talk with me as the others continued. "We are trying to counter the separation of your mental waveform from this physical body," it said. As if that made anything clear. "Several synaptic amplifiers are being located at strategic points in your nervous system. These will give you back some portion of your sensation and motor control."

The medic was right—the nerves were waking up. I brought my hand up to my face and touched my cheek. "I can feel it again."

"It is a temporary stopgap, Captain," said the alien. "It will buy you some time until your mind loses the ability to command the autonomic functions such as your heart and lungs. When it happens, your body here will die, and you will be cut off."

What was there to say?

Ambra had warned me of my fate. I had seen the truth of my dual personality. I now understood the astonishing, yet fragile, link I possessed to this time and place.

I didn't understand what was going on. The other medics were clearing out in some kind of mad rush.

"What's happening?" I asked. "Is there fighting already?"

The medic stared at me with many of its eyes. "Has she said nothing to you?"

A wave of nausea swept through me. "No."

"It is best you learn from her or Synphel. I am Rel. I have been assigned to you. I will guide your chair to the operating room."

Operating room?

Events accelerated. I discovered the wheelchair was more of a hoverchair. The alien motioned over the holodisplay floating in front of it, and the device levitated. The Xix exited, and the craft followed, steering through the winding corridors.

Extended, serpentine passages spiraled inward for ten minutes. The mystery of this place deepened as we passed room after room of aliens and humans. Their gazes tracked us through clear panes in the walls. Whenever a glance fell on me, it held sorrow.

"They know me."

"They are the dedicated Readers of the Temple," said the medic. "Tens of thousands more who have swelled their ranks for this final battle. Each has shared in the Group Mind, traveling together with the Daughter through space and time. All have witnessed histories and futures, terrible and beautiful, a million horizons of alternative universes. In these tapestries, they know your story and how it is interwoven with that of Ambra Dawn. They were present at your union."

Inward we spiraled as Rel continued.

"The Collective far exceeds any one consciousness. Individuals retain fragments of memories from the sharing, although they cannot understand the deeper insights of this more profound experience on their own."

"I thought they came for our wedding."

"They did, Captain. It was a joyous and miraculous occasion. A greater purpose called, however."

I strained to move my head to the side where the alien walked beside me. "You're one of them, aren't you? You're a Reader."

"Yes. Soon I will take my place with the others for a long journey. A final journey."

The spiral tightened. The unusual Xixian building materials opened to a bright room. Medics, human, and Xix dashed. Instruments of surgery, equipment, vessels with bubbling broths were strewn about. Not haphazardly, but with patterns I couldn't decode.

The center of the room focused my attention. A huge slab of black material rested in the floor. It was reflective, wet like ocean shale. The greater portion of it plunged underneath the structure. It appeared organic, alive. Perhaps my failing state confused me, but I saw the surface move. It respired and changed shape. The edges interfacing with pure machinery and biological tanks. In the middle of this bizarre creation, I discerned a depression. The negative of a human form. Imprinted like some nightmarish snow angel with arms, legs, a torso, and an extended, dreadlocked head.

In this negative space was Ambra.

Ice chilled my bones, and I shivered. I didn't know what this thing was. I didn't know why she was lying in it. My intuition was profoundly shaken, disturbed, and trying to call to my conscious mind. What's more, it stimulated a sense of déjà vu.

"Bring me closer to her," I told the Xixian medic.

"For one moment, Captain," came the voice of a translator I recognized. Synphel.

"Please."

The hoverchair floated forward. Her eyes were closed, but as I approached, they opened. They held fear in them.

"Hold my hand, Nitin."

Fumbling as my muscles misfired, I reached across the side rests and dangled my arm. She clamped my hand. I'm sure if I had retained normal sensation, it would have hurt.

She suppressed sobs. "See what they're doing to you." My deteriorating state wasn't lost to her blind eyes.

"Ambra, what are they doing to *you*?"

She couldn't meet my eyes. "Very soon, I will not be able to hold your hand."

"Because I'll die."

"Because I will never touch another human being again."

"*Please*—explain to me."

"The cruelest part is how much I need to hold you, my Nitin. The Anti were perfect in steering their Dram sheep. Cruel and heartless in their plans. They designed you precisely for me. Once in a thousand years, two people chance together who are so tuned to attraction and love." She turned to me, a deep, terrible sadness spilling from her green eyes. "The biology for it can be engineered. You chose this creeping death that's rotting you rather than a life without me. Part of me wishes I could make that choice."

"Why, Ambra? What's going to happen?"

She closed her eyes, tears leaking out the sides. "I will live an eternity encased in this living machine. I'll become integral to it, until what was human is long forgotten and I am the nucleus of this ever-growing awareness that will soon be born."

She leaned forward and grasped my elbow, her eyes flying open, a wild expression on her face. Her nails dug into my skin. Trickles of blood ran down my arm, but I felt nothing.

"All humanity lost but for a lingering *echo*. A terrible, unfulfillable *longing* over eons for you, Nitin. To touch you, hold you, love you once again as a woman."

She was shaking. I wanted to reach for her, to cradle her, to kiss the tears away. I could not rise. I could hardly lift my arms. I was a broken shell, helpless to comfort the most cherished person in my life.

"I can't..."

I'll be here. When they take you from me, don't despair. I will come for you. Always.

A voice interrupted. "It is time."

Synphel stood to my side, its eyestalks darting. "The hyperbrane is failing. It must be now."

She let go of my arm. "Take him outside."

"Wait, no!"

Too late. The hoverchair pulled back, and I saw her lying back into the wet rock as the distance between us increased. I fought to move, to grasp something, to stop the chair. If I had the strength, I would have thrown myself off and crawled to her.

I couldn't manage it. I was paralyzed again. My puppet masters across time and space yanked, snapping string after string.

"Ambra!" I screamed, or tried to. My ears heard a weak whisper of her name.

Be strong, Nitin. I need you to be strong for me right now. To wait. Even in death and what comes after.

The medical workers closed around her like sharks in a feeding frenzy. They brought tools. Blood bags. Scalpels, scissors, laser cutters. Wires and cables.

The chair carried me underneath the doorway and out into the hall. A transparent field materialized, sealing the entrance. The hoverchair stopped inside a nearby room. Synphel entered behind me. Major Mizoguchi stood stone-faced, gazing into the operating room.

Mazandarani trembled, his face pale, his form swaying as if drunk. He pressed his face against the glass, his fingers scraping down the sides of it.

He wept.

Chapter 54

God judged it better to bring good out of evil
than to suffer no evil to exist.

Augustine of Hippo

It was what I imagined drowning might be.

I fought to tread water, to keep my awareness in my body, to resist the vortex pulling me into a star-filled tunnel. Away from Ambra.

I was tiring. Each time I dragged myself back, I'd slipped more. My consciousness detached from the surrounding reality. Out of the corner of my eye, I caught a haze of light, the corridor of stars opening its maw to draw me in. I couldn't escape it much longer.

My vision and hearing, all my senses, strobed in machine-gun staccato. I second-guessed all I heard. The words made no sense. They were monstrous. Impossible. *Abomination.*

Using all my strength, I formed sounds. I willed my numb lips to move, squeezing my chest with all my energies to force air through my throat.

"There must...be anesthetic."

Mazandarani turned bloodshot eyes toward me but said nothing.

Synphel approached my hoverchair. "I'm afraid that there cannot be," it said.

"*Why?*" The word came out like a whisper, a harsh sound of a dying man.

"The Dram horde is approaching with its army of clones and dark allies. We are not ready to engage them. To fight them now means certain and swift defeat. Therefore, Ambra stalls them as best she can."

Mizoguchi spoke. "She has been interfering with their attempts to transition to our space and time. It can't go on forever. There are too many forces arrayed against her."

"If she is unconscious," continued Synphel, "if we suppress her neurological pathways, the first loss of control will be in her tumor cells. The barrier will collapse. Their armada will pour into your solar system in our now."

"She must remain awake until the last moments," finished the major.

"The pain...*distract her.*"

The Xix decoded my simplistic phrases. "The Readers are coming. We have placed our hope in the Collective. We gamble that it will be able to support her focus through the suffering. Without Ambra, there is no Group Mind."

"*It's...torture,*" I managed.

"Yes," said Mizoguchi, her expression grim. "She has accepted her sacrifice."

Movement distracted me. A tide of figures. Slow like a trickle, but building like some organic tsunami. They poured into the honeycombed rooms. The chambers resembled the floor of the Temple, with depressions in a grid. The shapes, human and alien, took their seats. Their hands inserted into hollows on the sides.

Bands glowing with Xixian tech encircled their heads and midsections.

Synphel saw my clumsy gaze track their movements. "They come for the final synthesis," it explained. "This will be their last home."

The medic had mentioned tens of thousands. They formed an enormous subterranean city of psychics, coalescing around a focal point in the spiral. A giant hive for a Group Mind with my Ambra at its center.

"When the procedure is finished, we will rise into orbit to meet our enemies. Altogether One, united in a fashion unlike any army before."

"You talk," I gasped, exhausted and confused, "like it's a starship."

"That's because it is, Captain," said Mizoguchi.

I'll be here with you, Nitin, until your moment comes. Then you will not see me. And then you will see me again.

Synphel spoke. "They are about to begin."

"No, I can't!" screamed Mazandarani. "I will not watch this!" He put his hand to the glass and stared toward the rock. "Forgive me."

He turned an anguished face away and stormed out of the room. I couldn't turn fast enough to follow his movements. By the time I had moved my head to see down the hallway, he was gone.

The lights dimmed everywhere within the building except for the operating room. I could not see Ambra for the medical staff surrounding her. The gleaming black of the living stone rose above and past the forms tending to her.

The Readers had all taken seats in positions of deep meditation. I encountered a familiar sensation, despite my failing senses. Perhaps it was due to my strange limbo between two bodies, the matrix of my mind stretched by the Anti. My dissolution primed my consciousness to resonate to distortions in the continuum, mirroring the powers of those around me.

For the first time in my life, I was gifted a chance to see the universe a little as Ambra did. For all the pain and injustice of it—for this reason alone—I embraced it with all I had. I would not waste the gift.

I recognized something I had experienced once before—on the day of our marriage. This time, it was far more acute. It began as an odd vibration. Tremors woke fathoms inside me. Undulating and long, the cycles accelerated. The power intensified. The vibrations transformed into tones, notes, and pitches. They rose and filled space with song.

A chorus of voices. Every voice, a personality. Each was linked in unique harmonies of thought. *Mind songs* growing into mental symphonies beyond my ability to follow. This symphony, like all grand music, had a personality, a mood, a character of its own.

The Group Mind.

It was sublime. It was haunting and stirring. Its beauty transcended words.

In the midst of this glorious arrangement, as the orchestra of thought began to carry me away, Ambra screamed.

Chapter 55

We are not human beings having a spiritual experience. We are spiritual beings having a human experience.

Pierre Teilhard de Chardin

I floated in space, the earth beneath, the sun a searing crystal. The physiology of our eyes had blinded me all my life. How I saw in this novel fashion, what I was, I didn't know. I had no body, only thought and experience. I stumbled upon a god's perspective.

I am here, Nitin.

How? They are...hurting you.

Yes. Below. But it's better to say...We are here.

They flooded me. Thousands of minds. The singular consciousness I had experienced as Ambra fractaled forth. Her personality splintered into faceted shards of a gemstone. Their refracted light projected into multiple dimensions. Undivided. Of one essence and always reflecting back to the nexus of her mind.

The deluge overwhelmed me. I couldn't process all these souls, their separate and full personalities, thoughts, memories, and emotions. I recoiled.

Don't be afraid.

The voice was hers alone. The others were gone, tucked into the fabric of hidden spaces in this mental matrix.

Where am I? What happened?

You're displaced. You hang by a string to your flesh in the desert. In my trial below, I focused on you too much. I pulled you here with Us, even if you aren't yet part of Us.

Ambra, I can't. There are too many. I want you.

Shhhhhh, Nitin. See—there!—how they approach?

The emptiness between New Earth and the sun shimmered. Like the clear rubber I'd imagined in the Sahara when the False Dawn attacked, space puckered. The vacuum undulated, planet-spanning ripples in a galactic pond. Each impact, as if a pebble tossed, and the blackness filled with ghostly presences. Starships by the thousands, like a plague of locusts blotting out the light.

I felt them. The cyborg clones. Their power over spacetime resonated through me. I could sense their thoughts and feelings, like the scent before a thunderstorm. I tasted the bile of their hatred.

Was it like this in the desert?

More so. You're not free, Nitin. You are mummified in the chains of your keepers. It is like being wrapped in plastic insulation. What you experience is a whisper of what is there.

What I sensed was awful enough.

The shimmering ceased, and space returned to normal. I could feel something *relax.*

Dear Ambra. You're all working to stop them. They're cutting on you, doing whatever they'll do to your body, and you're also out here.

Not much longer now.

Again, the ripples. Stronger. The armada less transparent, their presence prolonged. It was a tide creeping onto the beach.

This wave revealed more. Between the craft, there was darkness. A lack of light staining the emptiness.

It is an unlight, Nitin.

It poisoned the separation between the objects around them, an ink eating the space it occupied.

The Anti. What will you do?

Violence tore within me again.

Ambra, I'm dying.

A wave of sadness disoriented me.

It's a matter of time. It's always of Matter and Time.

Chapter 56

And now I go——as others already crucified have gone. And think not we are weary of crucifixion. For we must be crucified by larger and yet larger men, between greater earths and greater heavens.

"The Madman" by Kahlil Gibran

I crashed back to my New Earth body. *My body.* The sole incarnation I had ever known. And it was not truly me.

Or was it me?

I no longer knew what anything meant anymore. What was real? What could be trusted? I distrusted myself.

Myself most of all.

I was now paralyzed. My vision narrowed to a tunnel. In the hoverchair, angled forward, I saw through the energy field into the operating room.

The medical personnel had thinned. A handful buzzed around the slab. I could still see, but I wished I could not. Better to have perished in space, blind to the reality on Earth.

My Ambra.

Her distended skull was gone down to the hairline. The orange curls were stained with blood, turned black. Her brain—I can hardly describe it. The flesh was splayed out over several meters and embedded in the living machine-rock. The obsidian absorbed it, melded with the gray and white matter, fused its surface to the cells in her body. The giant mass of her spacetime tumor occupied a devoted cup in the dark expanse.

Tubes bathed the tissues in her own fluids and other nutrients. She was sealed in a strange, clear, Xixian material—sterile, climate-controlled.

The procedures had dissected her extremities. Tissue was filleted and distributed across the organic matrix. Cables and wires flowed into the rest of her eviscerated torso.

She could not be alive. It was beyond imagining. Memory slammed through my subconscious like a sledgehammer.

The vision presented by the Orb.

The abomination near Dram was not a metaphor. Not some nightmarish insight into Ambra's soul or that of our enemies. It was a precision prophecy.

"The extreme digits possess a plethora of nerves," said Synphel. "Their connections occupy an extensive representative volume in the brain tissue." Many of its eyes swiveled to me. "I know you cannot speak anymore, Captain Ratava. I will explain what I can in the time you have remaining." It gestured back toward the horror in front of us. "Similarly, neuronal clusters occur in critical tissues. Her eyes, her lips, ears..."

Stop. I blocked out some of its words. My psyche couldn't survive them.

"All are accessed to optimize the synthesis. They are repro-grammed, used instead to communicate with the AI and project to the other Readers. The initial operation was successful. With the help of the Group Mind, we were able to prevent excessive shock to her system. The integration is converging."

They had opened up her entire body like some medical school

cadaver, *yet she was still alive.* Conscious. *Without anesthetic.* In an agony I couldn't bear to contemplate. I tracked the cables and tubes extending from the large machinery around her, embedding themselves into her tissues. Her eyelids couldn't close as wires inserted into the sides of her eyes. The irises alone were untouched, staring outward like two green pin lights. She convulsed. The Xix swarmed about her, their distress at her suffering palpable.

"I am so sorry, Ambra," said Synphel. The alien was silent for a moment. "When complete, there will be a phase transition. A birth in multiple dimensions to spacetime fields surrounding her physical body. Our crude mind-linkages will become far more integrated. A single network. An unprecedented meshing of the mental potentials. Combined with an evolving AI, a cybernetic organism unique in our galaxy will rise. A diversified, multifactorial, cognitive synthesis should occur. We don't know with certainty, as it has never been done. Our science fails us at this stage. We aren't sure exactly what we will have made. But it's our one hope to avoid annihilation."

I no longer heard my beloved in my mind. Still, I felt her, unmistakably Ambra. Muffled, distant, torture requiring all her efforts to maintain focus on Earth's defenses.

Mazandarani returned, pale and trembling, as he gazed through the glass. He moved in slow motion. I didn't know whether from his emotional state or my own degrading mental condition.

"Can we go in?" he asked, his voice rough.

"Yes," said Synphel.

He stumbled out of the room and to the door of the operating room. The Xix activated my hoverchair, and we followed.

"Dear Ambra," he moaned, and tore at his desert robes. He fell to his knees, his hands shaking as he reached up to the splayed horror of her dissected foot.

I could do nothing. I couldn't weep. I could not fall at the feet of my dearest. I felt my body recede. The room bounced below me, returning like a rubber band. The nausea was overwhelming.

WE MUST HURRY.

Her voice was in everyone's mind. In mine, because I heard it. In the others, because everyone responded.

"The synthesis is complete. Our enemies approach." The alien turned to me. "I will stay with you until you pass, Captain. It will be soon. Afterward, I will take my place in this seedship. We will meet again, I hope."

I didn't understand what it could mean. Some Xixian religion with an afterlife? No *after* followed for me. I would die half a galaxy away in a distant future. *Another time?* It was impossible to cut through the maze of complications in the continuum. How could we meet once more? I likely wouldn't have understood, despite Synphel's best explanations.

It didn't matter. The entire facility energized in a startling fashion. I was almost lost. Contact with New Earth fading, but my last memories mixed with shock and wonder.

This time, real vibrations manifested, not some superstring song of meditating Readers. An earthquake. Mantle dissociated from the planet.

I watched from the end of a narrowing pipe. A monitor appeared in the air in front of us. The silent figure of Synphel gestured. The display responded. The view zoomed from space to hover above northern Africa.

The desert moved.

The grains shifted and danced. Enormous fissures erupted as the surface split open. Lines of shadow spread kilometers and connected, forming a rough, jagged shape. Sand spilled down the growing chasms and was blown high into the clouds from pressure.

The ground rose.

A shard of the Sahara the size of a major island detached from the planet and climbed into the sky. The building housing my dying body shuddered, but nothing fell. Nothing collapsed. The structure was well designed for its intended purpose.

I remembered Synphel's words. Not a subterranean lair. Not a medical facility. *A starship.* A vessel to sail the cosmos with a heart as demented as this universe itself, cradling the dissected and integrated flesh of Ambra Dawn.

In the monitor, the thing rose higher, bedrock blasting out of the parched ground. Solid crust ripped away and ascended toward the heavens.

The view panned back to follow the impossible craft. The Temple and the Six Cities soared undisturbed. The desert left behind roiled with a sudden sandstorm. A giant brown cloud visible from orbit choked the scar beneath the shard.

The mountain climbed. It defied gravity, flaunting any need for an escape velocity. Finally, a bottom to the impossibility, and the rocky behemoth ended in a spear point of jagged peaks. Boulders the size of buildings dropped like meteors from the stratosphere.

We broke atmosphere and entered space, yet nothing seemed amiss. The Six Cities were fine, the people unharmed. Some impenetrable cage protected the colossal wedge of New Earth seeking its fate in the skies.

The dislodged leviathan floated above the blue-and-white marble, a glow bathing the granite. The moon silhouetted the gigantic pillar as a million stars winked in the deep background.

But no sun blazed in front of us. The star had disappeared. Its light blotted out. A wall of darkness materialized and eclipsed its radiance. The blight cast a shadow on our world.

The Anti and their forces had arrived.

Chapter 57

*Deep in earth my love is lying
And I must weep alone.*

Edgar Allan Poe

I floated.

Not in space. The sensation differed. I drowned in a vile fluid. My prison. My ultimate reality.

I woke, for the first time in the existence of my being, to my real environment. I strained to open my eyes. *Had I ever used them?* After minutes of blind struggle, the foul facts clarified in vision. Truths I had anticipated, but they devastated me.

Liquid surrounded. The transparent sides refracted green lights. Cables plunged into the murky broth and intersected a shape in various locations. Blurred outlines revealed my true physical form. It was an emaciated skeletal frame, too weak to move its limbs.

I knew my brain spilled from an open skull, merged in nightmare with machines. I shared this terrible fate with my dear Ambra.

In my case, I experienced no pain. I felt almost nothing. I did not share in the agony of her whom they lifted up into the stars on that heart ripped out of New Earth. Her ravaged flesh I would never see again, half the galaxy away, thousands of years ago in events now long past.

The body I cherished and was born to love.

I told you when I began this story that I was made to love Ambra Dawn. Can you see it now? Can you see the deep, horrible truth of it?

Questions assailed me as my death crept through this grotesque murk. What could such love mean? What value could there be in it, knowing how it had come to be? Can the foul be fair? Can purity exist in the heart of complete corruption?

A diseased tissue was healthy only in a madman's mind.

For my mind's receptacle on New Earth, they had identified ideal genetic stock. Background, alleles, phenotypes studied, predicted, modeled in their human slaves. The body responding most to her appearance, pheromones, MHC sequences. The flesh that would reciprocally stir her sexual and emotional centers. My avatar was chosen to seduce and be seduced.

They took no less care with my personality. After centuries of testing on False Dawn clones, they determined the probabilities of her preferences. They engineered a disposition certain to capture her heart and mind. They tuned my brain in this demon's lair to enhance the perfect character traits. They imprinted its neural pathways with her image, voice, and movements.

The little child couldn't but adore her. The grown man lost himself in her.

They erased a nascent soul in a womb to implant this poisonous Janus. Two-souled, murderous, and camouflaged. All for a premeditated massacre spanning millennia and parsecs.

What can love possibly mean when it has been completely, coldly, cruelly engineered for manipulation? For *murder*?

Seeing this truth, the greater picture came into focus. What did any of our feelings signify? We are an organic soup to be stirred and heated at the will of monsters. Our ideals, thoughts, insights, deductions? They, too, derived from this same blood-bathed cellular clump of delusion and betrayal.

How could there ever be faith in anything but the cold indifference of the cosmos?

The blurred shapes outside the tank moved. I didn't need to see the outlines, so similar to my Ambra's, to know clones surrounded the structure. Synphel had lectured me. I had no curiosity to test the alien's hypotheses. Revulsion ate through me. An extreme repulsion at the execution of this existential crime.

Thus, I floated, as helpless here as I had been on New Earth during my last moments there. Thousands of years ago, the failing body of Nitin Ratava died, that compilation of cells dangled above the planet as an enemy armada closed in on all the things I had ever loved. I lay immobile as our trusted allies hacked my beloved apart and fit her into cyborg machinery, all to stop the death fleet of a ruthless foe.

Centuries in the future, I didn't know what had happened in that final battle. I didn't know if New Earth still existed, if humans had been exterminated, or if my lover survived. I had no power in this dark circle of hell to find out.

So, I floated.

I waited for the demons to shut down this growth pod. For them to kill me, once and for all. I watched these monsters move like underwater divers through the molasses of spacetime Ambra had flooded around them. She and Synphel had at least promised one thing: my death would come soon.

I was glad for it.

However artificial, corrupt, and duplicitous, the truth is I loved Ambra Dawn with all my heart and soul and mind. Whatever meaning those empty words held. Breeding, genetic design, centuries of optimization, multiple bodies, it was a rushing noise to the reality of my experience.

Nothing had unmade my adoration, including the realization of the mockery and unmeaning of my feelings in a dispassionate universe devoid of purpose or affection. Nor could I unmake it, even if I had wished to. My awareness pulsed as brightly for her in these last moments as it ever had.

Except she was gone. They had shut out her voice. I was left alone with my final thoughts in this dank tomb, surrounded by my captors. My creators. Soon to be my executioners.

Well, what of them? All that mattered to me was Ambra. Without her, I was lost and emptied, forever seeking the one I was constructed to adore. And so, I welcomed the peace of death.

A sharp rumble interrupted the hum within the tank. *Silence.* The incessant bubbling of oxygen ceased. The green glow faded.

And I felt it. My body thrashed at the loss of the essentials it needed to live. Feeble beyond imagining, my limbs twitched. A final reflex to alter the environment. The programming of cells to change the surroundings killing them.

My mind plunged down a mineshaft, endless and smooth, all illumination extinguished.

Chapter 58

Though my soul may set in darkness, it will rise in perfect light; I have loved the stars too fondly to be fearful of the night.

Sarah Williams, "The Old Astronomer"

I embrace this darkness.
It drinks my life, and I am not afraid.
No gloom can challenge such vacancy. Fear itself cowers in her absence.
I will wait.
Because there must be more.
Because I trust in her last words.
When this unlight consumes me,
The eon of nothing will unbe before it began.
Dispelling the void, there will be a Light.
The Dawn: and I will follow it and find my love.
That glow will come from Ambra.
That lumen will be of Ambra.

Because that splendor in the emptiness could be nothing else but Ambra.

I wait for you, my love.

Chapter 59

There is no death, only a change of worlds.

Red Cloud, chief of the Oglala Lakota

*N*itin.

In the deepest pit of nothingness, after a timeless eternity, she spoke.

Wake up.

An infinity of stars blinded me. I tried to turn away from them but could not, having no form, no flesh. I was sighted without eyes, an awareness adrift in the vastness of space.

Don't be afraid.

Where am I? What *was* I? I did not speak with words. I communicated with thoughts. Lacking a body, I didn't know what was speaking.

See the moon, dearest?

Her voice guided my vision. A blue-and-white marble rivaling New Earth loomed before me. It circled an enormous gas giant of swirling, banded colors. More moons, many Earthlike, scattered around the titanic world.

That is where you died.

Memories surged. My life. My *lives*. An existence I'd believed to be true: Nitin Ratava, Indian soldier, devoted seeker of the Daughter of Time, lover of Ambra Dawn. The actuality dooming me—chimeric monster, spy, assassin, and puppet. Adventures through space. The deaths of my team. The unforces of the Anti. War. Great and terrible slaughter and sacrifices. The torture of my beloved. My death distant from her.

And where you are reborn.

Reborn? I existed. But as what? I never understood the talk of mental spacetime matrices. The strange idea that physical thought was some field, like electricity. I was never a scientist.

Think of it as your soul, Nitin, if it helps.

I wasn't sure it did. It was an ancient term, better left in the detritus of our superstitious past. Souls pacified the isolated, the old, the needy, such as my mother, who prayed to her icons. Was it appropriate for the cosmos of humans and aliens I knew?

And yet, the mythology provided a structure to frame experiences beyond my understanding. One integrated into concepts of rebirth, eternity, and personality. After everything I had seen, after being so humbled and destroyed, when it was clear I did not remotely understand the nature of existence, who was I to reject the notion of a soul?

Ambra, where are you?

I am reaching across a bridge, a long link from my time and place to yours. Already, where you are, it's many centuries past the age you left me.

I tried to digest the words. She was traveling through space and time to reach me. Why didn't she simply come here from this era? Unless she could not. I had lost touch with her and New Earth as the Dram armada arrived. What if...

Are you alive in this time?

Yes. And you are with me.

I didn't comprehend how this could be possible. Could I be in two places at once?

We are busy, Nitin. All of us in making something wonderful.

All of us? What do you mean?

Several huge spacecraft sped past my center of awareness toward the blue moon. They were enormous, city-sized vessels, one after the other in a parade. Militarized, their forms screamed of violence. Dark shadows surrounded their hulls.

The Anti! Ambra, what do I do?

You are safe. They cannot see you. The clone aboard could, but her attentions are elsewhere.

The procession continued, one by one, until they passed and shrank to a point near the Earthlike satellite. None altered course. No attacks or reconnaissance efforts. It was as if I weren't there.

How do you know all this?

It is difficult to explain. So much has changed. Everything I've been through has been for a purpose, and that goal has been realized. Is being realized. Will be realized. We are augmented. Integrated. Synergized beyond our most optimistic hopes. We are something new.

I still didn't have answers. *Who is we, Ambra? The same as I felt above the planet with you?*

More. Vastly more.

I couldn't imagine. The deluge of minds had drowned me.

Don't be afraid. It won't be like before. You're free of the fleshy egg that gestated your soul. Your consciousness propagates through space and time independently now. The shock and pain from the many—it won't hurt you now.

What if I don't like being with them? What if I want to be alone?

Do you want to be alone, Nitin?

No, I did not. But I also knew dealing with others was often difficult. Clashes of personalities, different priorities, agendas. The thought of joining some mental aggregate frightened me. I wished to be with her.

You will be with me. Because they have chosen to be with me, they are in harmony with me. You will find them acceptable. Believe it. Trust me, my love. Try.

If I don't?

We cannot be together. My future is determined by my choices, beloved. Even if I tried, I could not leave. If you do not join us, you will not be with me. If you persist out here alone, without support, it will be worse than death. You will spend eons devolving. You will lose coherency, and I will lose you forever.

Losing myself was inconsequential. Losing her was everything. The one truth was that I could not continue apart from her. Whatever she now was. Wherever it was. Whatever was in store for me.

I cannot abandon you, Ambra.

Yes, my Nitin. I know. You had to know for yourself.

There's so much I still don't understand.

Stop deducing. Let me show you!

How?

Follow my voice, and it will take you to me. Together we'll dance with every mystery.

Perhaps all this was madness—the last throes of a dying brain's hallucinations. It didn't matter. In life, in death, in lunacy—I would accompany her. I'd believe her. Because, in the end, the core of all my love for her was unshakable, unwavering trust in her.

I'm coming, Ambra.

Chapter 60

Individually, we are one drop.
Together, we are an ocean.

Ryunosuke Satoro

I accelerated.

It was a matter of will, of acceptance. I focused on her voice. The powerful presence of her personality electrified me across kiloparsecs and centuries. Rebirth redefined the remote.

The stormy gas giant and its blue moons receded. The radiance of their star faded. The background of the Milky Way shifted in colors. Stars elongated, running through a spectrum from violet to red in my peripheral vision.

The forward acceleration twisted. Rotating, a vortex of constellations formed until the lights ran together like wet ink in a rainstorm. The eye of a storm. A spherical glow expanded in size. An infinitely layered majesty eclipsed my perception.

The Orb.

I perceived the cosmic sphere with the insight of my bodiless awareness. Stripped of the filters of flesh, it wasn't a portal or a geometrical phenomenon. Not an artifact.

It lived. It possessed a mind of its own. I faced a being of such complexity, alienness, and godlike stature that I comprehended almost nothing of it.

Still, I identified affection. Concern. In the midst of this terrible consciousness of incomprehensible indifference, there beat a heart of empathy.

And it reached for me.

I was drawn through a thousand corridors of brilliance. This time without pain, no confining tunnel or prison, no fear. Joy, wonder, and anticipation flowered in discovering the grail after a long and taxing quest.

Ambra!

I called. My own thoughts echoed like sound. They reflected and transformed. A million different voices uttered the word in response. Their counterpoint recombined into my own tones.

A host.

I felt them. Around me, inside me, in mental dimensions I couldn't imagine or reach, yet present, aware. They anticipated my journey with delight.

Starlight. Looming and bright, a golden radiance bathed space. I raced past several gas giants. A blue-and-white disk maniacally rotated, featureless and blurred. A solitary moon spun about it. The revolutions slowed, stopped as the sphere came to a standstill.

New Earth.

The transit ended, anchoring me in time. A planetary system I remembered from...*before*. I drifted toward a hulking asteroid orbiting the world. Approaching, I recognized the shape. It was the desert-shard ripped from the heart of the Sahara. The sand plains of the Temple and Six Cities gleamed unhurt at its apex.

In this reborn state, my perception broadened. The bedrock of the planet dissolved. My awareness penetrated into the core of the starship.

I stumbled upon myself—the entity I once was. A body clinging to life, propped by Xixian technology, with a link over impossible distances through time and space stretched to the snapping point. Nitin Ratava struggled to remain present. He watched the giant shard-ship ascend, his life in that false husk moments from ending.

But there was so much more to see than the shell of my former self. Tens of thousands of glowing consciousnesses wrapped in fleshy garments waited. The tendrils of their awareness mixed and united, integrating at the center of the rock.

There, a tortured flesh lay dim in the core of a resplendent shower. It wove the threads from myriad minds into a single, synergized consciousness. A tapestry so massive, so intricate, so *alive*, my spirit shook.

Tearing my focus away from this transforming aggregate, I was able to perceive the nexus underneath. White, human skin. Red hair. Green eyes aimed in the direction of my vantage point.

"Nitin."

She murmured with the dysfunctional meat of her body, through lips I had once kissed and adored. I could no longer touch them, and a distant echo of me yearned to do so again.

Yet, I was becoming something *else*. Dwarfing the faint reverberation of previous passion was the joy and desire to embrace a quintessence invisible to me in my material state. Ambra Dawn transcended the woman I had loved, had misapprehended, had torn down to human stature. I beheld now the maturing synthesis of a goddess.

So are we all. You will understand soon.

I missed you.

The face on her supine form smiled.

And I missed you. Come to me.

My awareness floated the final distance and hovered inches above her body. All was as I had last seen it, the stripped flesh and remade nervous system now one with the starship. Now I could see the effects of this sacrifice in the distortions of space and time. Her tumor served as a multiplicative transmitter. Her entirety, the corporeal dish. The thousands of Readers interwove with her thoughts.

Closer, my love.

I passed through the ghostly essence of her shattered incarnation. The fullness of her consciousness enfolded me in a manner unlike anything I had ever known. As partners of the flesh, I couldn't have imagined any joining more intimate, more overwhelming, or more transfiguring. Yet it was an echo of what could be. The depth of the sharing that could exist between souls clarified. It was complete, and so joined, an *us* greater than the separated two.

And not two, beloved.

The host opened itself to me. This time I had no fear. I wasn't overwhelmed. I *became* with them. An unusual structure centered on a binary awareness at the core. Or rather a singular consciousness of the Daughter and my own orbit around her. We connected to thousands of other minds. Their perception, their thoughts, their personalities swept through me. I encountered each of them profoundly, beyond what any two material prisoners could ever accomplish. Free of confusions and barriers. Filled with compassion and interest. With love.

There will be time for so much learning, Nitin. Now, there is a task to complete. Clear your vision and let the Group Mind see for you.

Let *it* see? I stopped focusing on the myriad, amazing entities. I relinquished my grip on controlling my own perception. The static of multiple beings cleared. A single perspective replaced the individual visions.

This eye into space gazed from outside the Saharan-shard. It focused on the regions beyond the planet. The power of this being, the *otherness* of it, humbled me. The awareness transcended my experience. In many ways, it was alien in its thought processes to my simplistic mind. Yet I shared of it. I was part of it, my own consciousness contributing to its composition.

To my surprise, I saw a fleet of ships from New Earth Force. Alongside them, hundreds of craft of Xixian make. I marveled that these forces existed. I had had no inkling of them before I died.

We hid them from you, my betrayer.

The hurt had faded in me. My soul smiled.

We had set a trap. We told you nothing, and I masked your vision during your time outside your body.

I understood. A brilliant strategy. If indeed they had the power to defeat the Dram and Anti.

Turning back to the coming battle, I noticed the ships of the Xix had no armament. Instead, they projected intense field defenses to deflect beam and projectile weapons. The Force armada was armed as I remembered. Xixian-designed ion slingers with a flux far beyond those of our MECHcore suits. Missiles, conventional, and, more commonly, nuclear. With several hundred warcraft in position, they had enough firepower to obliterate all of New Earth's cities fifty times over.

So much power. So many soldiers of different races and worlds.

All doomed.

Chapter 61

Let your plans be dark and impenetrable as night, and when you move, fall like a thunderbolt.

Sun Tzu, The Art of War

The blackness undulated. Thousands of warships bent and blurred, the twisting of space ceasing at the moment of my death. The enemy armada obscured the light of the sun.

New Earth sat like a small child before the pounce of a lion. Warcraft fired on the global defenses. Destruction ranged across both fronts as weaponry fragmented opposing vessels. But their military advantage was significant, and they weren't alone.

The tide turned in favor of our enemies in short order. Massive waves of spacetime distortions and antiparticle projectiles impacted our forces. False Dawns and the Anti, hidden in their ships and between the armaments of the Dram, unleashed a fury. Neither the Xixian shields nor our weaponry could counter the onslaught. Within minutes, the sum of our planetary ramparts lay in ruin and wreckage. A hailstorm of debris orbited New Earth and rained down as flaming meteors.

They shifted their weapons downward. Plasma artillery and missiles ripped fire and destruction across cities on the surface. Soot blackened the skies. Their ordnance unloaded on us as well, but to no effect. The warships abandoned their assault on the impregnable shard, concentrating on maximizing the slaughter below.

The decimation spawned a phenomenon I had not anticipated. The mental matrices, the *souls* of humans and Xix separated from their flesh in death. Isolated, these spirits wandered naked in the fields of space and time. I could sense their emotions and thoughts. Bewilderment, panic, and wonder characterized their awakening to a new reality. And waking, they turned to the light.

One after the other, tens of thousands, millions came to us. Uncountable masses of awareness flowed like some swollen stream into the sea. I gasped at a flux of energy. An essence reached toward them from the Mind. I did not individually will it, but *We had*.

Ambra spoke in my consciousness. *The first, Nitin. A small gathering. A test and a change.*

What's happening?

Something wonderful.

The spirit matrices soared to us. The first, a few intrepid souls. Afterward, a flood. A torrent of mental energies and persons from that river of released beings swelled our nascent pond. The incoming flow dwarfed the growing lake. They joined, and the We grew. It expanded astoundingly, the group awareness absorbing and integrating these hordes. From ten thousand, we became hundreds of millions. The Collective multiplied.

Not all approached. Of those who did, not all stayed. Some drifted toward the Dram, the False Dawns, the Anti, but had no manner of joining them in their betrayal. Others spurned all sentience and wondered into the void. But the majority united with our nascent community. While our foes continued their merciless onslaught, the avalanche accelerated. As they struck down the lives on New Earth, they made us stronger.

Despite her explanations and witnessing this astounding synthesis, my individual conscience squirmed. Alarm and acceptance fought inside me as the Group Mind sat stoically in the face of this massacre. A conflict raged between my isolated empathy and the transcendent intellect.

Acquiescence prevailed. My anxiety dissolved, replaced with a serene calm. The spiritual assembly conveyed the greater purpose my limited thoughts struggled to grasp. I watched the slaughter, the freed souls, and their blending into the Collective with a diabolical peacefulness. While part of me rebelled in discord, it was a minor portion of my processes. The remainder waited in anticipation.

The time has not come.

Not my thoughts, yet in my thoughts. Not Ambra's thoughts, but of her thoughts.

My awareness turned to our enemies, and I apprehended them with the eyes of the Whole. Thousands of refulgent candles hid in ships around us, their glow poisonous in the fabric of spacetime. The False Dawn army. They released a coordinated barrage of mental assaults on our starship. Against the Group Mind.

It was like a series of nuclear blasts. The attacks before shown to be a faint whisper of the aggregated power these clones possessed. With my enhanced eyes, I discerned massive distortions of space and time. They outshone the radiance of the energies and fields of the sun. All directed on the little rock Ambra and the Readers occupied above New Earth. The False Dawns had perceived what we were.

I was to see they understood it as little as I. Despite the cataclysm in the surrounding continuum, the desert-shard hovered untouched. The Group Mind unmoved. It watched. It waited. And its patience was rewarded.

The Anti attacked, and this time, they weren't hidden from me. The eyes of the Collective clothed them in shapes and hues inverted yet similar to our own. Flooding toward us from the spaces between the ships came ten thousand craft. The starships were constructed by intelligences divergent from our own. It was difficult to process their structure and purpose. Their energies were vast. They loosed a river of particles at us.

Explosions rocked the outer regions of the atmosphere. Matter and antimatter converted into pure energy. Enormous amounts of radiation blasted outward, hotter than the surface of the sun. New Earth would return to ash.

The Mind moved.

It spun from nothing, mammoth fields of potency countering the particle beam. Tentacles surrounded the antimatter and shielded the planet. The Orb flashed. A stream of power funneled toward it from our location and disappeared into its blazing maw. Silence and ships drifted beside our rock.

The attacks from the cyborgs ceased. The Collective penetrated their meager mental matrices. The distortions in their forms indicating distress. Confusion. Similar anxiety emanated from the consciousnesses in the Anti fleet. Into their bewilderment crept a fresh emotion. *Fear.*

The False Dawns responded with a last and desperate gambit. All their attention focused away from us, away from the planet. The clones centered their power on the moon and our satellite changed course. Its orbit was perturbed. The mass spiraled inward from energies too enormous to contemplate.

A thousand cyborgs pulled the moon toward New Earth. The resultant cataclysm would overshadow the Unmade Calamity. It would be our world's redestruction.

The Group Mind moved again.

My dissolving ties to my old body still painted my awareness in physical terms. That is why it struck me that two god's arms reached from the shard to our moon. Titanic hands tore loose the shackles of the clones from the rocky sphere. They slung them through the fabric of the continuum, away from the planet. The chaos hurled thousands of Dram and Anti ships across the solar system. The spacetime distortions shattered and rended their occupants.

We stopped the inward spiral of the moon. The mass returned to its orbit, unshaken, undamaged. Tranquil beside New Earth. Once again, a panicked sense of awe and fear escaped the ranks of our enemies. But the Mind had more impossible things yet to do.

Tentacles snapped to the asteroid belt. Gargantuan objects returned in the muscled limbs of the demigod in orbit. The names echoed in the mind songs. Ceres, Pallas, Vesta. The preposterous appendages gripped them in a vise.

The terrible hands squeezed. The god-digits crushed the rocks, exploding them in a microsecond. The entity caged the particles, none leaping outward or escaping its grip.

Forming a celestial shotgun, the pellets were flung at the enemy armada. The projectiles blasted at speeds unfathomable for any known military mechanism. The result was utter devastation. The Dram craft, with thousands of clones scrambling to deflect a billion bolts of death, disintegrated. The matter-antimatter collisions with the ships of the Anti detonated colossal explosions. Once again, the churning detritus was channeled to the Orb.

The greatest fireworks display ever witnessed in our locality ceased. The space between us and the sun clarified. No trace of any starship near New Earth remained, friend or foe. All had been reduced to atoms or energy and funneled out of the solar system.

Vanished into the void.

Chapter 62

In the region of nature, which is the region of diversity, we grow by acquisition; in the spiritual world, which is the region of unity, we grow by losing ourselves, by uniting.

The Sādhanā by Rabindranath Tagore

I gazed across the span of space where thousands of starships had orbited. The Dram and Anti annihilated. Not so much as a fragment of metal floated.

In the distance, the Orb. Once, as a man limited by his eyes, I had perceived a thin surface on the Time Sphere. Dim. Bland, but for that one transforming nightmare of Ambra.

Now it blazed with light indescribable, revealing labyrinthine layers. The depth of it made the universe small.

Now begins the Gathering of Souls, Nitin.

The Collective grew. In size, but more significantly, in profundity, power, sentience, and vision. Its awareness penetrated greater distances as well as deeper through time. Backward to the past, forward to the future. The minds freed in the battle integrated, and our splendor swelled.

There has been a terrible waste. Losses upon losses. Millions of species in our galaxy, each with a trillion voices. Silenced as their song died within the void. Spirits who now hear a call. Our *call.*

And the souls came. From nearby, and across astronomical spans. Over vast spans of time. Not like the flood during the massacre on New Earth. They trickled, as if the separations in spacetime had dimmed our image in their minds. And yet they felt us, had sensed us, will perceive us, glimpsing our shadow through the continuum.

They have or will be following the call.

Her voice. Our voice and thoughts.

My augmented sight confused me. From the harvest of these spirits aggregating about us, I focused on the island of rock the Collective occupied. It had metamorphosed. The numerous intelligences functioned as mental building blocks. The cognitive matrices interwove. The Group Mind conducted these instruments as a symphonic orchestra.

Tendrils, multidimensional tunnels, cosmic portals. They propagated from the core of the Earth-shard. They interlaced about the stone-and-sand plains of the Six Cities and Temple. A self-aware net of writhing filigree engulfed our rocky starship, nesting it in a lattice-work of light.

I gawked at this growing wonder. I glanced back to the Time Sphere, the grand power of our solar system, the projection of the One Orb manipulating every macrocosm maintaining sentient life. I returned my glance to our Gathering and its cornucopia of complexity.

An odd vertigo befuddled my mind's eye. I experienced a bewildering reference frame confusion.

Was I coming or going?

Did I approach the gateway to the stars that had changed the history of the universe? Or was I flying away from it?

Was I gazing to our transforming Collective or back at the Orb?

Back and forth, with no privileged perspective. I could no longer differentiate. I could no longer see.

What was the Orb and what was We.

Epilogue

Of the theme that I have declared to you, I will now that ye make in harmony together a Great Music. And since I have kindled you with the Flame Imperishable, ye shall show forth your powers in adorning this theme, each with his own thoughts and devices, if he will. But I will sit and hearken, and be glad that through you great beauty has been wakened into song.

Ainulindalë from *The Silmarillion*, J. R. R. Tolkien

Once, when the Daughter was a shadow of what We would become, it was hard to reach you. Reaching you now is so simple, although the consciousness of your author is wholly inadequate for the task of conveying our narrative.

I should not place so much blame on him. It is nonsense to ask a wingless bird to fly, and a single individual of our imperfect and undeveloped species could not hope to explain the essence of our tale without tragic fumbling.

I also find my voice in his mind inconsistent. At times, especially when reflecting on my incarnate life as a man, I speak in a simpler, individualistic dialect. At others, swept into the complexities of our communal synthesis, my words are the abstracted mélange of billions. The reader cannot help but feel disoriented. The art is doomed to incoherence.

But Ambra wished our story told. An echo of her human love for me. She desired for many, including those in our distant past, to hear of our triumphs and tragedies. So you might listen for our call. That when your time has come, you will search for us in the endless void.

Our Collective was One with this sharing. Thus, you approach the end of this absurd book. An outrageous narrative finished—or, rather, at its beginning.

So much has been lost it cannot be quantified. To consider the fullness of sacrifice unmakes my individual cognizance. Yet *We* rejoice. We celebrate the calamities and creations. An eternity awaits. Our Community will traverse the cosmos through a succession of ages within eons.

We keep an extraordinary and growing company unlike any our galaxy has ever witnessed. At each moment, in every point in space, we evolve. The mental matrices freed by death find their way to us. Most will join our Collective. They add new voices, unique and strange insights to an intellect now beyond anything else in our universe. The others will drift, spurning our invitation. Alone and unanchored, the boundless eternity of creation will drive them mad. Their souls will lose coherence, absorbed into the undulations of the void.

The eye of our Mind no longer sees the linearity of time. It views the continuum from a perspective I will describe (inaccurately) as *outside* our cosmos. In this view, causality is understood as multifactorial. Each point in spacetime affects and is altered by every other. As we Become, we have increasing access to all places and all times.

We gather the harvest sown across distances vast and periods immeasurable. We seek the souls loosed from their corporeal prisons. We provide a haven, a shore upon which they can find harbor in the empty chaos of the vacuum. Among the purposes of the Group

Mind, there is no other more sacred. Nothing holds greater meaning than this cosmic search for sentience. To preserve it, save it, augment it, and give it immortality.

Individually, or in mass cataclysm, near and remote, in the past and future, we reach them. We call them. For the most part, they come. From forms of flesh wildly disparate, with mentalities more diverse. Each addition, every new scale in the musical registry enhances the expression and depth of the Whole.

We began with beings similar to ourselves. Such minds we could identify and locate in our early development. Human, Xix, Brax, Dram, Sortax—the list goes on. We were able to find our loved ones. Families, children, and friends.

The MECHcore team of the entity once know as Nitin Ratava came as well. Erica Fox, David Kim, Ryan Marshall, Grant Moore, and Aisha Williams. When they arrived, it was as if we knew them for the first time. The veil between each consciousness had fallen. This narrative is shaped as much by them as it is by me—it is the Mind reaching you now.

Yet in all of our searches, a perplexing mystery remains—we have been unable to locate the soul of Waythrel of the Xix. Many elements of the early Collective find deep meaning in this search. So it has ever informed the efforts of our community.

Our failure to detect evidence of Waythrel in life or in death raises one of two possibilities. The first is that the Xixian Reader is far removed in space and time, and we do not possess the strength to bridge that gap. As we contact you now, it implies a distance beyond our local group of galaxies and more than ten million years into the past or future. The second possibility is that Waythrel is hidden by forces that can contend with the Group Mind. Both hypotheses can coexist.

The solution to finding Waythrel in both cases is to enhance our powers further. In this way, we will be able to cross the spacetime gap or overcome its concealment. Therefore, this lesser purpose in locating a single spirit harmonizes with the gathering of all souls.

Imagine the integration of psyches across millions of worlds. Not at any particular time point, but at all of them. Over a quintillion in our galaxy alone. The Entity awakened above New Earth that dispatched the Dram armada was an infant. Ignorant, wide-eyed and empty, it could hardly speak. Walking exceeded its undeveloped capabilities. Now we approach an early adolescence. Our faculties lie far beyond the imagination of that newborn child.

We are become greater than what we are. Individually, it is a labyrinthine filigree of separate sentients. Each sharing thoughts. Personalities flowing through and around awarenesses, ever learning and changing and giving. It is a loving harmony. Beings who cannot integrate always detach and seek their own way.

We are a multicellular organism composed of tissues of thought. Individual personalities mimic the neurons in a fleshy brain. They are intricate, filled with millions of internal processes. They extend thousands of external communications with our neighbors in this grand Collective.

But the mental synthesis of the Group Mind transcends that between a neuron and a brain. What does a single cell understand of the most complicated human thought? And so, what can any one of us comprehend about those cogitations of the Group Mind? Labeling this Entity's states "thoughts" distorts and oversimplifies. Activities available to a neuron—biochemistry, signaling, secretion— are elements unsuited to describe brain modalities. The actions of the Group Mind are thus beyond our ability to conceive.

We know this. We experience it. We see the awesome powers of what we have become. We do not apprehend them. Faint echoes of higher accomplishments trickle down to us. Visions bathe us. They modify our minds as the human brain's responses to stimuli alter individual neurons. But like the sole cells, our consciousnesses are responsive but uncomprehending.

The cosmos we perceive is beautiful. And hideous. Foul and splenderous beyond the childish explanations our naive minds can muster. And what we can understand links all things. Its fabric is interwoven with the Group Mind. Or, rather, what it will have become in a divergent and distant chronological span. And baffling us, at both its beginning and its end.

Already we begin to bridge the galaxies. Our Collective crosses the intergalactic distances of space and time. We find wild calamities of destruction like those in our own Milky Way. The fires of worlds consuming themselves in immaturity. The madness of burgeoning sentients clashing across star systems. The mammoth tragedies of broken vagaries in evolution. Yet so many of their minds come to us. We absorb them, learn of and from them, and are enhanced.

Now we detect the stirrings of transcendent mentalities not unlike our own. Lesser, in discord, requiring help to survive their own internal disruptions. Tens of thousands of galactic intelligences reach toward us through the endless continuum. A time will come in the successive eons when we will meet and a greater Whole emerge.

And always, there are the Anti. Hidden even from us. Unmaking. Incomprehensible. Seeking the self-contradictory goal, the paradox of creative destruction. A shadowy premonition convinces us some transformative event lies in a shared future with them. An ascendancy where and when the cosmos will be changed, and our Mind, undone.

In all things, we ceaselessly orbit our Daughter of Time. Although a part of a more expansive whole, she is the nexus. Her mentality is the nucleation center, the core particle around which this congregation has crystallized. She is the mother of all we have become, a goddess in labor, forever giving birth to this new Being.

But more than a mere goddess to me.

For me, she is still the woman I am doomed to love. The light I followed from the day my consciousness coalesced. And for a short, blissful time on New Earth and in the heavens, she was my beloved.

Always and ever my dearest, Ambra Dawn.

It is all a matter of time scale. An event that would be unthinkable in a hundred years may be inevitable in a hundred million.

Carl Sagan's Cosmos

Maker

Daughter of Time, Book 3

無

It is not only not right; it is not even wrong.

Wolfgang Pauli

Prologue

Time and Space... It is not nature which imposes them upon us, it is we who impose them on nature because we find them convenient.

Henri Poincaré

I was called Waythrel of Xix.

In a time and a space no longer extant, in a cosmos reborn, in two books infiltrating your minds, my character embarked on a grand and terrible quest that ended in devastating failure. Yet in defeat, we triumphed where I had never imagined a possibility of success.

You knew me as an alien to your humanness. A monstrous form of heightened symmetry to your bilateral arrangement. Sixfold projections of limbs and visual organs with a cognitive cluster in our core. You followed our discovery of Ambra Dawn and her unique mastery of space and time. Her cruel life. The Daughter's rise to power in the Dram Wars. Her eventual fusion with our artificial intelligence. There you witnessed the gestation of the proto-Orb, the birth of a novel entity that defeated the forces coalescing to destroy New Earth.

Reader, the recursive loops of causality permeate the structure of your consciousness.

Not solely the hormone- and blood-soaked organ lodged within your human endoskeleton. Something more profound. The mind that is the spacetime field created by and creating your sentience. The soul outlasting your decaying flesh. An essence dissipated in the emptiness of space or gathered in the Great Harvest.

Many of you prayed to save Old Earth, to funnel the latent Writer powers of your species across time. We amalgamated and focused your energies to undo a planetary massacre. Others of you scoffed. Yet you continued to read through the exhortations of the second novel, daring to consider the Gathering of Souls.

Here we lost more. The story became increasingly strange by your standards, experiences remote from those a human animal might encounter. The narrative voice was no longer that of your beloved heroine but her consort. He spoke through the growing mind that projected his thought across the void. Together with uncountable spirits, he inspired the book's author.

Thus, you have been primed.

Now what remains is the final and most absurd step in the journey—to destroy all belief and memory. To be born anew.

I am here to convey the true end, which is rather an ultimate beginning, to the impossible story of Ambra Dawn. I reach through space and time, traverse divergent universes separating and uniting us. My thoughts inspire this writer of your age. He will struggle one last time to transmit ideas I myself do not comprehend. He will spin from my own distorted notions a sad caricature. His primitive brain will further blaspheme the beauty through the stunted medium of one of your limited languages.

Thus, concepts deeper than the most profound thoughts of the greatest minds of our galaxy are painted in rudimentary strokes, rendered at low resolution with a hobbled brush set of syntax and vocabulary. Transcendent truths are twisted through your current incarnations of culture and prejudice, gutted of their essence, and recast as grayed mockeries with all the colors washed away.

This is how you will receive the terrible and beautiful tale of our Ambra.

Do not expect coherence. You will have none. Do not look for consistency. You will swim in nonsensical paradox. However, know that the absurdities presented glimpse truth, while your science and religion stumble. Yet every word herein, a lie.

Know also that you hear a story of symmetry and symmetries broken. The chronological invariance of the laws of physics shattered by the arrow of time. The balance of particles and inverses wrecked to vomit forth a fractured creation. Open your soul to learn of a cosmic apartheid swept clean of a material species. Tremble before the genocide of the mental superstructure it would have engendered.

I describe a mythology centered within an endless fractaled universe that self-assembles. A tale of smaller and larger structures. Without reference point. Lacking a center. Spiraling to a bottomless abyss of reductive constituents while launched asymptotically toward an infinitely realized synthesis.

You consume a fantasy of symmetry repaired and the utter annihilatory creation that is its offspring. In such a fable, Ambra Dawn is not sufficient. An anti-Ambra must exist, an antithesis, a force in essence, development, and complexity that mirrors yet is not its symmetry mate.

She is, of course, the clone who took me on Dram. A fabrication of the Anti, she escaped their myopic control and initiated a quest neither of us understood. It was a journey that would bring a primordial pair full circle, like a proton and antiproton hurled in opposite directions through the magnetic bowels of a synchrotron. The resultant collision transformed the fundamental structure of matter and energy. Indeed, of our universe itself.

So, I step back into the false memories of an existence that now never was, to a frantic instant in an unmade eon described in the second book. Crouching in a spacetime bubble under the wild and furious assault of a thousand clones of the Daughter bent on our destruction, I vanished.

It was to be my last true moment with Ambra Dawn, the human creature I cherished above all others.

Part I

I speak of gods and other mad taboos
that scar a soul with two-edged, healing wounds.
Who dares cast down these gleaming gains construed
while marching to our frenzied, empty tunes?

The sand that is your soul will never birth
one flower in this unrelenting drought.
Your brushstrokes paint no truth and have no worth.
In vain you look for meaning through your doubt.

I am a fool, untamed, consumed with pride
and often speak too much on that I love,
for I, insane, once cursed our fall and died
while clasping to my heart a blinded dove.

Whatever sight I have of what is true,
it neither lives with me nor dies with you.

—Mazandarani, *Sonnets from the Desert*

Chapter 1

Even at those astounding energies, the asymmetry between matter and antimatter is extremely small. For every billion antiparticles that were created, there were a billion and one particles. To put it another way, you're essentially a rounding error from around 10–35 seconds after the Big Bang. Doesn't make you feel very important, does it? Of course, that's just as much a bummer for the anti-people, too.

Dave Goldberg

I gripped Ambra's hands.

My meditation had little to contribute. With the strength of an average human Reader, I had nothing to provide her to resist the descending siege. In the realms of space and time, I was a particle of dust in the sandstorm. The churning wrath dwarfed and scattered my awareness.

My offering was psychological. I sensed her fear and concern for us on this mission. Our group relied on her abilities. Already we had witnessed the horrific deaths of the soldiers, David Kim and Erica Fox. Each of us in this besieged spacetime bubble was splattered with the lifeblood of Warrant Officer Aisha Williams. She was ripped apart by the powers of a single clone of the multitude assailing us. A sense of failure weighed on Ambra's heart.

Now, a sea of orange hair swirled around our transparent vessel. Hateful assaults from the minds of the clones struck repeating blows against our weakening resistance. Her psyche reached into me, a child gripping the hand of a parent. She grounded herself in the love we shared. This connection gave her hope she could devise some escape from this cataclysm. This faith prevented the storm of antipathy from driving her to despair.

That is why, when the clone came, when it smashed through our defenses, through her power, ignoring its brethren and their efforts and grabbing my arm, when the strange creature took me by means mysterious and unexpected, Ambra's mind broke.

It shattered like a ship tearing away from anchor as the frothing sea hurled it into the maw of an angry ocean. As the world about me dissolved and I lost consciousness, I felt the wild hurt from her. A telepathic wail roared outward from the goddess-growth in her artificial skull. The inconsolable cry echoed through the corridors of the continuum.

The instant vanished. One moment I was in the bubble that had carried us across the galaxy. The next I was not. I awoke above the planetary surface of the Dram homeworld. A reckless acceleration propelled me away from it into the blackness.

I was not alone.

Flying through the emptiness alongside me was a child. Its hair, what of it remained, was Ambra's rusty orange. The pale hand grasping the dark purple of my upper arm shone a dulled red in the glare of the swollen sun. Reminiscent of the journey with Ambra, a warped spacetime enclosure sealed us from the void outside. I could not move my extremities—invisible chords bound them. My eyestalks twirled freely, and I surveyed the girl and my environment.

Below me, Dram receded. The swirling desert dunes blurred to a sienna-toned planetary disk. In front, I sensed the growing presence of the Orb. The clone blasted toward it.

Shock shook my system. I believed the Daughter alone had the power to use the Spheres. What could this crazed creature be thinking? Another part of me trembled. I intuited an awful possibility. This cyborg would pass through the portal. To what destination and to what end, I could not guess.

"She's following," said the thing beside me.

The voice was childish, lilting, and cold. It was the first time it had spoken. I still reduced the False Dawn to a genderless object, an "it." I was unable to see the abomination as anything more than a warped product of the enemies who sought to destroy us.

My education was soon to begin.

"She's very upset. I told him she would be. I wonder if he'll be strong enough for what's to come."

My mind spun. *Who did it tell? What is to come?*

"Yes, I think he will be," the child mused. "They made him too perfect and didn't see what such love would bring. There's no stopping the crystallization."

The creature droned in riddles. I was too consumed with the impossibility of events to formulate rational responses.

At least I could observe. I examined the clone, informed by my extensive studies of humanity. I placed its age at around ten years old, prepubescent. The developmental program to create the reproductive, adult form had begun to activate. However, nothing could be taken for granted with the clones. From what we had learned, the Anti had altered every aspect of their genesis and maturation. Enhanced and accelerated, this young child could be half as old as I expected.

The cybernetic enhancements were particularly elaborate in this model. Far more intricate and integrated than the most advanced Dramian technology. Where—and better yet, *when*—it had been made was the question. At the least, it had to be in the distant future.

The underlying foundation of Ambra Dawn was there. The hair

and skin expressed the phenotype of recessive pigmentation genes. The green irises produced the striking contrasts in the human visual organs. The body frame was of an expected variant on the genetic blueprint. The bones were long and delicate, the shoulders broad as compared to the average for the female genotype. The hips were still narrow prior to the adolescent widening.

The wires and intubations in the skull were fantastic. A labyrinth of protrusions linked brain regions to an embedded artificial intelligence. The modifications were so extensive they left the clone with a sparse covering of the rich hair characterizing this hereditary background. The object of the structure and design was the tumor present in the middle of the enlarged cranium, the organ making this stock so central to the struggle in our galaxy.

Etched across its face were a set of geometrical lines. They resembled dark circuits underneath the skin. The patterns were too angular to be veins or other vessels. I had not seen anything like it before, including the other clones we had encountered. I surmised it was cybernetic technology her makers had embedded within it.

Sifting through all these observations, I summoned the calm to speak. "She will stop you from escaping. Lacking the help of your clone army, she is stronger than you."

The False Dawn laughed. It was an unusual sound, divergent from the response I had grown accustomed to in humans. I suspected this construction possessed a distinct and orthogonal mentality.

"She's not. Not in this form. Not without her spirit armada." The cyborg glanced behind her. "What a cry she made for you, Xix. She suffered terrible pain."

The words struck me like a blow. The memory of it replayed in my mind, Ambra's acute torment ripping through me once again. I tried to focus.

"Look at the Orb," I said with difficulty, staring at the tempestuous frothing on its surface. "Already it has turned against you."

"Not against me, Xixian. Her powers won't help her now."

The calm certainty in its voice disturbed me, but I still believed Ambra was shutting the Time Sphere to our travel. The clone did not hesitate or slow our approach. The colossal surface grew. An ocean of confusing features bubbled and churned in anger as we neared. Again, I looked behind—we would reach the portal before anyone could catch us. Whatever the effect of being shut out of the gateway would be, I would discover it within seconds. I steeled myself for a possible end and stared forward with as much courage as I could.

We were not impeded. In a disorienting blast of vertigo, we entered the thing, and the bottom fell out of the universe. We tore through multiple dimensions of nested wormholes. My previous travels provided a faint warning of the depth and complexity of the portal. I fought to stay in control of my mind in this terrible vortex of radiance.

I deduced we must be traveling extreme distances, likely both in space and in time. Spans unlike any I had breached before. I had no idea in what direction or to which destination the clone was taking me.

I could no longer sense Ambra. She had failed to close the portal and had not been able to follow. An enormous separation locked her away from me. It was, as I have said, the last time I would see her, at least in her original form. Wherever I was going and for whatever reason, I was now alone.

Alone but for a familiar, yet strange, pair of green eyes in a tumultuous ocean of darkness and light.

Chapter 2

We seldom stop to think that we are still creatures of the sea, able to leave it only because, from birth to death, we wear the water-filled space suits of our skins.

Arthur C. Clarke

reen eyes in the darkness.
A night sky churned with stars in patterns I could not recognize. A breeze trickled over me. The sounds of insects or other alien creatures punctuated the soft whisper of the wind. My eyestalks darted about, appraising the planet surface, the heavens.

And the figure of the clone sitting beside me.

My eyes gazing upward abandoned their efforts. It was desperation from the start to determine where we were from the constellations, but it was impossible not to try. Nothing was familiar. Wherever and whenever I was, the stellar arrangements resembled nothing my mind could map. It was probable I was not in our galaxy.

Both of us were alive on this world without environmental suits.

I could conclude the planet was human–Xixian compatible. The humidity—something we desert-spawned creatures are sensitive to—was low. Not as dry as Xix or New Earth's Sahara, from which we had begun our disastrous mission, but arid. I breathed in through my skin sacs. The oxygen levels were high, but did not represent a significant concern.

I turned my attention to the sulking cyborg. The child rested with its legs tucked, obscuring the head. The green eyes haunting me in the Orb traversal peeked over scuffed kneecaps. It wore a beige fabric with an unusual style, combining elements of robes and skirts. Arms wrapped around its knees, the False Dawn rocked back and forth. I detected a faint sound, rhythmic pitch changes and repeating patterns. It was humming.

I sat and directed my eyes at the creature. "Where have you taken me?"

It continued to rock and hum, ignoring my question. I persisted.

"I know it is far. We are not in the galaxy known to me, either in physical space or in time."

Still no response.

"You have torn me from your progenitor in the middle of an assault by other clones. But I contributed little to their defense. You have dragged me through the Orb to this world alone with you for nothing."

The humming stopped. "Not alone."

"No?" My eyestalks swiveled.

"Not for nothing." The intubated, tattooed head cocked to one side, the green eyes piercing me. "I didn't take you to weaken her in the battle. It's not *then* that you have to worry about her, but at the *beginning*."

I sensed the tendrils of the creature's thought dancing around my awareness. "You are probing my mind."

The head darted to a strange angle, forty-five degrees and peering from behind its right knee. "Your thoughts leak everywhere. You Xix are leaky-brains."

The child jumped to its feet, catching me by surprise. It danced to stand above me, long, ragged clumps of red hair dangling and obscuring its face.

"If not to harm her, why?" I managed.

The clone sighed and stared into the pageantry of the stars. The density of lights was unusual for human or Xixian eyes. I noticed a milky-white marble embedded in its forehead. It glimmered from the starlight shining through.

"There's so much to understand. He didn't understand either when I told him. But *I* don't really understand. It's a *problem*."

I pulled myself upright, uncomfortable to be prone and beneath this unpredictable creature.

"Who is *he?*"

"Her consort. The soldier. The one with the hole in his mind."

I caught my breath. *It knows?*

"Worry, worry, worry, you Xix. Quit! I didn't tell them about your trick. It's very clever. I liked it a lot. But it already happened before I was born, and there's no stopping it. Not like that. *They* wouldn't listen at all."

The clone flung its hands about, dismissing unseen spectators.

"That's why you're here. Why I had to take you. Because there's no stopping any of it—but we have to find a way. Not to stop. *No stopping. Unmake. She* said. *Showed* me. All of them did."

I paused, bewildered by its odd phrases. *What is this thing?* All my instincts sought to engage with my captor to better understand it, and a primal urge to address it in a personal fashion filled me. Remaining calm in the presence of this engineered assassin was chal-lenge enough—trying to converse with it? Realizing at any moment it could kill me or use me against Ambra? The effort was extraordinary and draining.

"Call me Kloan," it said, interrupting my thoughts. "Since you can't get that out of your mind."

"Clone?" I repeated, or thought I did.

"No. K-L-O-A-N. Like 'Joan' but copied genetic materials with tubes and wires and all this!" It gestured wildly with its hands toward its head. "I don't really have a name. Not here. It's just numbers."

"Kloan."

Her green eyes darted to me and away. It was a strange appellation to suggest, but it was comforting to have a more intimate moniker for the thing.

"Okay, Kloan, what I wanted to say—"

"I'm not here to kill you. Where would I be then?"

I had no answer, hardly understanding the question—certainly not its context. My mind raced through the dialogue, parsing each phrase.

"You negate killing me, yet leave open the possibility you are going to use me against Ambra."

Kloan smiled. "Depends on what you mean by *against*."

"You speak in enigmas, not providing me any of the background data."

She nodded, a satisfied expression on her face. "*That's* why we're here. *Data.* The first data to enter the gate." She turned her back on me, walking down a steep slope. "Let's get started."

"With what? Where are you going?"

Kloan continued without turning back. Her words faded in the night noises, the wind carrying them over the landscape. "To where it all began for me. To watch the beginning flow around us and mature and twist through time and space to come back to *be* us. Then we'll be ready for the next step."

The intense starlight cast sharp shadows on the stones. The figure of the child vanished, swallowed in the darkness and slope of the hill. Raising my gaze in the direction of her last words, I saw below a dim glow. Artificial. The light polluted the brilliance of the stars near the horizon.

Waythrel, come on!

Her voice rang in my mind. My eyestalks curled on themselves. What else was there for me to do?

I followed her.

Chapter 3

When man is able to comprehend certain things, it does not follow that he must be able to comprehend everything.

Maimonides

I raced to catch the child, my steps uncertain, the dusty ground slippery under my feet. Descending the steep slope of this elevation, I stumbled and tripped. My four arms struggled with the rocks and alien vegetation. They lacked friction to form a proper grip. After several near falls, I suspected something strange. Had I been drugged? Was a there a phenomenon on this world interfering with my basic movements?

It's a field around you.

Her thoughts danced again in my mind.

It's skintight, coating your surfaces, insulating you from everything.

Listening to her voice and trying to understand what she was saying, I crashed into her while rounding a massive boulder. The ground was strewn with shattered rocks and their remains. The jagged cliffs behind us likely spawned a number of avalanches.

"Why is there a field? What kind of field?"

Kloan was staring ahead at the source of light. A city or military installation rose from the dry lands. Organized groups of shadows marched throughout the base, activity constant and hurried.

"I don't know what sort of field. She—*they* make it for your protection."

"From what?"

She pointed to the compound. "Come. It's almost morning. That's when it all begins. We'll go see me there, and then you'll see what happens."

She headed toward the complex, but I grabbed her shoulder, turning her back to face me. "Wait! This is a clone production facility, isn't it?"

"Yes."

"Where you were made? One in the far future and distant?"

She nodded.

"We cannot enter—you saw what happened the last time!"

"There's no danger," she said.

"Maybe not for you. *I* cannot. You said you did not want to have me die. They will kill any Xix they see."

"They won't see us. We both have skin suits. *Dark ones.* Their eyes can't see. Ears can't hear. Not even the Readers will perceive."

"You pierced Ambra's bubble. You came inside it."

Kloan shook her head. "Hers was simple. Weak. Primitive."

"And yours now is none of those things?"

"I told you, they're not *mine*," she sighed. "Now, come on."

The child pulled me forward, and I relented. If she wished to harm me, she could have done so before—and easily. I was helpless, and I needed to learn more to find any hope of escape.

A bright light erupted from the darkness. The flash blinded my eyes, leaving blurred afterimages. A fireball climbed into the sky and darkened. The smoke from the blast began to snuff out the brilliance. Seconds later, the ground shook. Despite the distance, compressed air blasted over us.

"Too late." She squinted from the pressurized dust blown forward. "It's started. Why did we come to this time point? They'll be moving on the structure and surrounding me."

"Surrounding you?" I saw no evidence of anything besides the landscape.

"Not here. There!" She gestured toward the explosion. "The tunnel must be there, but we can't get to it before it closes. We'll go through it soon!"

"Kloan," I said, my legs unsteady, "you are not making sense. What tunnel? Where is it, and why do we need to go through it?"

"It's the only way to escape. At least without so many deaths. The masters will bring all the children against me—I couldn't just slaughter them. I didn't want to. She knew, so she helped. It will happen too fast, and we can't be there when we go through!"

The child was insane and shouting nonsense. I did not know what to say to rationalize this situation. With a growing unease, I concluded my questions were not going to help clarify anything.

Kloan continued, panting. "We can go around, find the path. *Yes*. Catch ourselves before we leave and then you can see us when we go as well."

I watched in silence, baffled, as she sprinted up the mountainside.

I reviewed my status. I had been plucked from one time and place. Torn from all those I loved and removed from the desperate fight for the soul of our galaxy. A child dragged me to a strange world in an unknown system surrounded by enemies. She spouted nonsense. Forced me to turn from one mad rush to another, none of the reasons for anything explained.

She had faded from sight, and I would soon be alone. I had to follow her again. It was absurd, but she was all I had to connect me with the past and my home. This girl-thing was both my captor and hope for deliverance. Yet for all I could tell, she was utterly deranged.

Again, I ran after her.

Chapter 4

One cannot determine what is real. It turns out that a mathematical model involving imaginary time predicts not only effects we have already observed but also effects we have not been able to measure yet nevertheless believe in for other reasons. So what is real and what is imaginary? Is the distinction just in our minds?

Stephen Hawking

I struggled to adapt to the low friction of whatever *field* had been placed around me. Racing up the slope proved to be harder than descending. In the growing light of the breaking dawn, my footing was far from secure. My sturdy, six-toed feet failed to find an adequate grip. I tumbled forward, once smashing my torso against jagged rocks and slicing through my exoskin. Thankfully, the endoskin was unbroken, and no fluid vessels were damaged. It was clear this mysterious coating did not protect me from mechanical trauma. Its purpose matched hindrance more than help.

Her voice echoed in my mind again.

Stop complaining, Xix! We're late!

Below, the explosions continued for some time. We dashed up the hillside in the direction opposite the chaos. She said the carnage related to someone we would meet.

We'll go see me there, and then you'll see what happens.

What had the child meant? Another clone copy? I was lost.

The greatest blast rattled the rocks as we rounded the mountain face. The city was concealed behind it.

She stopped and turned around, staring backward. "It's going to be close," she panted. "Look, above is the path, and the gate is still shut."

"What gate? Explain to me, Kloan."

"It's our door. The one we have to take to save everything." Already she was moving forward again.

Fatigued, I trudged the stony landscape after her. In the distance ahead, I glimpsed a shining disk. The circle glinted in the morning's rays from the local star.

"That's it," she said, sweat dripping from her face and eyebrows, her white skin reddening with the exertion.

"The gate?" I asked.

"Yes."

Whatever it was, it was at least an hour's walk over a difficult terrain. I did not relish another hike in the strange sheath around my body.

Indeed, the trek proved especially challenging. The path was a series of terraced, jutting rocks, stacked one on the other. On each flat sheet, the going was simple. Between the outcroppings, sudden elevations required free climbs. This should not have taxed me. The gravity on this world was lower than on Xix and a little more than Earth. However, in this frictionless form, I beat the odds by not slipping to my death.

Reaching the partial summit of yet another ridge, we obtained our first real view of this doorway. From this vantage point, it appeared much larger. The circle spanned several times our height in radius. A portion of the disk plunged beneath the rock itself. The walkway ahead cut through it like a geometric chord. This segment of the ring was invisible. In proximity, the surface lost reflectivity. It assumed a semitransparent skin like a body of water.

My eyes fixated on three figures in front of it. One was human. From its shape, the color of the hair, and elements in the skull, it was another clone of Ambra Dawn. Next to it was a much taller form with many more appendages. It required no guesswork to see it was a Xix. It stared forward toward a third figure beside the disk. *A second Xix.* One I could see as it faced us. A being I knew as well as my own heart.

My lifemate, Synphel.

My legs buckled as the synaptic transmissions in my cortex consumed my signal fluids. Images and emotions darted through my mind of a life denied, a lover lost, now found in front of us. I steadied myself on the rock we had scaled, hardly daring to believe what my visual organs were showing me.

"Kloan, why didn't you tell me?" I asked. "How can Synphel be here? Who are the others?"

She squinted in the bright light from the disk. "It's too close to me, this future. No other Xix the first time. Something has altered the timeline."

"First time? What are you saying?"

Before I could get an answer, Synphel disappeared. It was instantaneous. I let out a cry as I gazed motionless at the empty space remaining.

"Well, that's new, too."

"They are going through the portal?" I asked. "Where?"

"I don't know. The timelines are scrambled now. It's all cycling."

"Can we follow them?"

"We go where the gate takes us."

I stumbled forward. I had to speak to these creatures, find out why Synphel was there and where my mate went. I rushed like a nymph fixated on a single goal to the exclusion of all other thought.

"Waythrel!" cried Kloan. "It's no use! Look!"

Concluding some conversation, the pair in front of us clasped hands. In desperation, I watched them step toward the disk. The bright light reflecting off the surface warped and flowed over their forms. Like some gelatinous wall, it enveloped them. With a rending finality, a final pucker snapped the opening closed. They were gone.

I slowed my run and came to a stop. The cyborg reached my side.

"We can't find Synphel," she said. "I don't know where it went. Or how. But the others went through the gate."

"Can we follow them?" I asked.

"In a manner of speaking."

I rested several meters from the huge portal. A deep physical and emotional fatigue crushed me. I shoved it away and examined the circle. Prismatic lights effervesced across the membrane. It resembled a cross-sectional slice of an Orb, something like the projection in the Temple where we had begun our cursed quest. I did not know if this system possessed a Time Sphere. All systems with intelligent life in our galaxy did, but whether we were in our galaxy was very much in question.

The glinting, metallic surface revealed itself on close examination to resemble a fluid. It was a viscous, churning, honey-like substance. Within were stars—depths of stellar fields with no end. I felt pulled toward the artifact as I gazed. It was beautiful.

"I want to try, Kloan." Pure desperation flowed through me. "If we can find them, we can maybe discover a way back—find Synphel as well."

She winked. "We have already found them."

"Just tell me how to enter this thing!"

"All ways are bent. Broken routes. Nonlinear topologies. Space-time discontinuities. The dimensionality is unclear."

"What does that mean?" Nothing mattered except finding my way back.

"Once we cross the manifold, we're locked. A never-ceasing narrative, nested recursion. Loops ending as they begin with different parameters."

"So we may never be able to escape this world line?"

"Yes."

"Then we die in it." It was worth the risk.

"No, Waythrel," said Kloan. Her brows furrowed at me, the emeralds inside her sockets flashing. "No death. Limitless looping, ages without aging, circles in time never marking moments. *Trapped.*"

"In what?"

"One of the local hells."

All my eyestalks stared at the mad thing. "How else can we get out?" I asked, gesturing to the planet.

"The gate," she said. "That's how I left the first time."

"The first time?" A suspicion began to brew in me. "The clone you mentioned—where is she?"

"She's right here."

"This is where you departed? When you went to kidnap me?"

"Yup, I've gone already through so I could come back with you." She smiled. "It's an elegant loop, yes?"

"It is madness!" My eyes were darting in several directions at once. I placed my hands to their stalks to steady them. "Can't you summon some wormhole or something? Get us out?"

"Not from here. I don't have such power alone. The Orb brought us, remember?"

"I cannot stay here!"

"You aren't the only one tested, Waythrel." She sighed. "Each time's different. When we finally understand, we'll see the way." She turned toward the disk. "Now's the next step, the following stage of the journey. Do you want to enter?"

My eyes darted in eighteen directions. My mind unanchored in this bizarre reality.

"So, we can remain here. Try to survive by avoiding the Anti below, someday to perish in this remote corner of the universe. Or we can cross this portal. Risk eternal damnation to a self-referencing and modifying timeline?"

"Yes."

I was asked to leap into an abyss with no pause for deliberation. Who can imagine infinity? Or what might lie on the other side of it? I could not assess the peril. A finite creature, my understanding of quantity—space or time—was limited. I could not grasp what horror I would be consigning myself to.

"You are going with me?" I asked.

"That's the whole point."

Remembering the actions of the previous pair, I grasped her hand.

She laughed. "Seems we'll always be dancing together, Xix."

My eyestalks wrapped around each other. The covering sheaths expanded over them, blocking out all light.

Kloan tugged on my hand. "Don't be afraid, Waythrel."

We walked into the gel.

Part II

I weary of the voices that I hear:
the cries of triumph, long and knowing talk.
No more. No more! Away I turn my ear
and seek once more the silence where I walked.

To know true contemplation as before—
Forms freed from facts, the finite skin of trees.
This star-filled growing womb is now my door
and home and very substance that is me.

Each force and austere symmetry are mine
in flesh and knowledge without truth unknown.
Yet seeing all more makes me less divine-
I hold small stones beside the sea alone.

Beyond the truth are dreams that make it so.
What shapes the Everwomb? I seek to know.

—Mazandarani, *Sonnets from the Desert*

Chapter 5

from the Atharva Veda

I felt cold, yet all signs pointed to a climate temperate for my species.

I unfurled my eyestalks, trying to remain calm. My visual organs adjusted and brought the environment into focus. The nature of Xixian vision is difficult to describe to humankind. The broader wavelength range of photoreceptors, how it paints reality in hues and shadows unknown to you, is the minor difference. It is instead the integration of eighteen eyes. Their ability to orient in any direction.

The resulting product is both a panoramic and multilayered depth perception.

My eyes focused, and I identified the location. Significant radiance with maximal wavelengths in what humans interpret as green. The light poured from a single focal point. A star bathed an ocean of vegetation. Liquid rushed nearby, and a humid breeze swept over my chilled form. A loud, feathered creature squawked in irritation.

"New Earth," I said.

A girl's voice piped. "Nope. Close, though. The *old* one."

My eyes turned away from their distant contemplations of the Great Plains. Down a small hill a stream bubbled. At the edge was Kloan. She tossed her garments to the side. Her thin, athletic contours plunged into the water to her ribcage. She was scrubbing her body.

"It's *super* cold, Waythrel," she said through chattering teeth. "If you want to get all that goo off you from the gate, come down!" Her bright smile in the midst of our strange adventure was unsettling.

I was too stuck on her first statement.

"What do you mean, 'the old one'? Before the Calamity?"

She was dunking her head in and out of the stream, huffing, her pale skin flushed. Globs of clear gel dropped from the hair and machinery as she ran her fingers across the irregular surface of her head.

"Yes! *Cold!* Old version! *Argh!*" The words were garbled underwater.

"How is that possible? That timeline has been overwritten. Multiple histories have occupied that space now. There is no Old Earth in any universe we can access."

Her bony back stuck out of the water. Bent in two, she clawed the goop out of her ears.

She turned a half-submerged head toward me with a quizzical frown. "You don't understand how screwed up this all is, do you? You're a little stunned. Stood there like a statue after the traversal. It'll get easier." She straightened, her disproportionate prepubescent form dripping. "Inaccessible timelines, other universes, gods. It's all coming, Waythrel. I see them like shadows on the horizon." Her head plunged back into the stream.

In my years with Ambra, we Xix had helped engineer the travel of group minds through time, the alteration of history, cause and effect, and the formation of spacetime distortions never imagined. However, there were still hard-and-fast rules. Possibilities intrinsic to what we understood of the universe. If we were on Old Earth, then the powers staging our journey worked in realms beyond the science of our galaxy.

Water splashed as her head burst from the creek. She raced from the edge, shaking like a small mammal. "I can hear them, Waythrel! All the voices of this world, their languages, accents, thoughts. So young and primitive and naive. They don't know the Dram control their entire planet, that they're all slaves." She scanned me from eyestalks to toes. "You really need a bath."

With resignation, noticing the clumping aggregates of the gel dangling from my arms, I shuffled to the stream.

"Don't worry about how you look." She dashed across the muddy shore like a child seeing daylight for the first time.

Her words seemed pointless until I reached the bank. Gate glop would not have disturbed me, but that was not what I saw.

"Kloan! What is this?"

I stared into the water. The reflection distorted and unfocused from the ripples off my form. It was clear enough. No towering Xixian shape with eyestalks and purple spots greeted me. Rather, a brown-skinned woman. She dressed in flowing, ebony robes, sporting a white coif over her head. The woman was in her early twenties with dark irises. Thick black hair hid beneath the head covering. My mind flitted through Earth's history and data.

"Looks like they made us Catholic nuns," came a breathless voice as Kloan crashed into me.

She was bent double from exertion, still naked but much drier after her wild run. Her reflection in the stream showed another nun.

"Who disguised us as religious figures? Why?"

"Waythrel, you aren't quite ready for the *who* of the matter. Why nuns? I have no idea. We're from Mexico, I'd bet." She strolled over to her clothes and began to dress.

I stared back and forth between our reflections and our bodies. "Our true forms are not shown at all to this world, yet they are to us."

"Yeah, seems," came a muffled voice as she threaded herself into her beige robes. "I think because this is *pre-contact* Earth, we're both just a little too much for them." Her head popped out of the top with a grin. Sparse orange hair flapped around her, wires and tubing glinting in the sunlight. "You wouldn't believe what the little fields can do."

Her smile continued to unsettle me.

I stood still another moment. Realizing I would deduce little more from this strangeness, I entered the water. While I worked to remove the congealing molasses, Kloan turned more serious.

She scanned the horizon. "There's a town nearby. I can feel them," she said. "Small place. I think we're in the Midwest of America, near the time of the Calamity. All these," she gestured to an ocean of manicured plots of corn and other crops, "are the last little farms of the independents. Big Ag left a whole other kind of footprint."

My efforts at hygiene became a greater quest than Kloan's. I had waited longer, the gel hardening. My massive build and more numerous appendages increased the challenge. The strange material had wormed its way through cloth and under my translator. It coated every surface of my body. Several eyestalks struggled to stay focused on the cyborg.

"How do you know all this?"

"It's part of our training. I'm supposed to know all about Ambra Dawn. Her world, the environment that shaped her, it's all a critical component, you realize. Now that I'm here in this timeline, it's so easy to access the recent past. We had a lot of things wrong at Clone

School. I'm learning so much." She shrugged. "That's the whole point, of course."

She was a carefree human child and an impenetrable enigma. Her eyes were wide, and she stood on her toes, gazing outward with anticipation. It was difficult to see her as a monstrous product of an assassin training program.

"Leaky-brains," she whispered. "I'm never what you think I am. *Ever.*"

I paused from my decontamination. While her words were innocuous, they sent a chill through my emotional centers. Nothing was as it seemed with this clone.

She snickered. "The great Waythrel. The great, *gooey* Waythrel of Xix. Hurry up! We need to find out where she is."

All my eyestalks turned to her. "Where who is?"

Kloan frowned at me like one would a slow child.

"*Ambra*, of course. We're not here for Old Earth corn."

Chapter 6

David Hume

We set off along the stream in a direction Kloan had chosen. The day was warm by human standards, and her sparse hair matted to her instrumentation. Sweat dripped down her head, staining her robes. The bulge of her tumor shone like a boiled egg in the bright sunlight.

While I welcomed the heat, the humidity counterbalanced the warmth. The local weather and enormous water expenditure from irrigation saturated the air. The journey was uncomfortable.

For the hundreds of years I had spent on New Earth, I had avoided the more humid climes for all but the briefest visits. I longed for the Sahara, a climate closer to Xix itself. In Nebraska, my skin sacs clogged with liquid. Obtaining oxygen strained my system and reduced my stamina.

Within an hour, we reached a small roadway. It crossed a stream over a dilapidated bridge. Kloan stepped to the road and walked across the decaying structure.

"It's not far now," she said, increasing her pace.

I rested a moment, holding onto a protective railing. Its metal was rusted and warped from years of neglect. The air was pregnant with vapor. A suffocating blanket, it had become a wall to my psychology. I struggled to continue but forced myself forward.

The landscape changed little over the course of the day. Scattered houses and barns. Endless plots of corn. Parched fields gulping water provided by the irrigation systems. Birdsong and wind gusts punctuated the whisper of swaying stalks. Or at times a sharp pop as the fibers expanded from heat or growth.

A vehicle approached as we neared exhaustion. A battered pickup dispersed a cloud of dust and pulled to a stop to our left. In the bed of the truck, a group of workers sat huddled, staring at their feet.

"Mornin'," came a rough voice from within the cab. A broad hat leaned toward the passenger side. A burned and leathered face peeked from under it, an aquiline nose leading the charge. "You ladies need a ride?"

I assessed the situation. I checked our reflection in the vehicle's windows, confirming our external disguises. The driver seemed safe and would carry us without incident. Assuming nothing of our true natures could be gleaned by our proximity. I began to weigh strategies when Kloan decided for us.

"Thank you, kind sir," she said, every bit the foreign nun she likely appeared to be. "Do you know how far Flache-Schale is from here?"

Ambra's hometown. How had she known?

Been scanning the past around here, Waythrel, and this nice man's memories.

"It's right up the road, ma'am."

Kloan put her hand to her chest, grasping a small wooden cross hanging from her neck. "Oh, this is good news. We're lost and very tired."

"Hop on in."

I moved toward the bed of the truck, but the driver called out.

"No, sister! You don't wanna be sittin' back with any of those. You two come on up front."

Kloan repeated thanks to the man. Several of the men in the back drew my glance. Migrant workers, I assumed. Latino. Their bodies were broad from the manual labor but subdued, slumped. A dim light remained in their eyes for the harsh lives they lived.

"Hermana." A deep voice.

The sound came from the back of the truck bed. An older man tipped his hat to me. One of the younger laborers kicked a man next to him. A soft chorus—"*Hermanas*"—spilled from the group. All eyes were downcast. Unprepared with the proper cultural protocol, I turned back toward Kloan and followed her into the cab.

"I'm Rick," said the driver as I closed the door, sandwiching the cyborg between us. "Headin' into town myself. We'll be there in ten minutes."

The gear shifted with friction, and the truck lurched forward. I could sense the stumbling of the migrants in the back as the sudden movement threw them backward. My gaze traveled instinctively to the passenger side mirror. I continued to be amazed at my appearance on this world. In the chipped glass, I was a young Latina nun. Rick had allowed entry to a monster and a child Frankenstein without the slightest concern.

"You headin' to the Catholic church on River Road? You're nuns, right?"

Let me talk, Waythrel.

"Yes, sir." Her voice squeaked in shyness.

"Well, I've got to get these boys over to the Milson farm, so I can drop you as far as downtown. Folks will get you to where you need to be."

After our slow plodding, the cornrows dashed past in harsh geometric patterns. The fields thinned, and the number of houses proliferated. The town was near.

Kloan dipped her head. "We appreciate the help. It's good of you to accept strangers so warmly." Her quick assimilation of cultural norms was astounding.

The driver laughed roughly, eyeing the review mirror. "Well, you two will be more welcome than these aliens, anyway."

Chapter 7

The Sages reveal to the aware that the imaginative faculty is also called an angel; and the mind is called a cherub. How beautiful this will appear to the sophisticated mind, and how disturbing to the primitive.

Maimonides

The truck rattled off, spraying us with fumes and dust. The wonders of eTech had made slow inroads into the farm-lands in this period, despite the complete adoption of electric cars on the coasts. Downtown reflected this allergy to modernization. The dying independent farm communities were frozen in the middle twenty-first century.

The flurry of shocked expressions and subsequent darting eyes unnerved me. It was soon clear this was not due to our true forms but rather those imposed on us. It helped that every few minutes some passerby would smile and speak a welcome.

We had debated our course of action. I still had no idea why we were here, why we were nuns, and what we were to do about it all.

There was no sign of Synphel or the other clone. No indication of previous visitation through the gate. No reciprocal portal to return us from this reality that, for all I understood about cosmology, could not exist.

Kloan insisted everything had to do with Ambra and she particularly needed to find her. However, a plan to bring a False Dawn near the Daughter unsettled me. It didn't matter that we occupied a strange, impossible timeline.

With nothing else to present as an alternative course of action, I acquiesced. We set out for the Dawn's farmland.

That was when the priest found us.

We had planned to walk the journey, as I wanted minimal contact with the inhabitants. She estimated an hour to reach the farm. As we made our way through the town, a bearded figure raced toward us from a side street.

He was in his middle fifties, draped in a brown monastic habit. A wooden crucifix dangled as he lumbered across traffic to our position. Horns blared as he issued a series of distracted apologies, all the while keeping his eyes fixed on us.

"Looks like someone's been expecting us," said Kloan, smiling. "This should be interesting."

We stood still and observed the spectacle until the man stumbled to a stop, panting a few feet in front of us. My eyestalks divided between the girl and the priest. He was bowing.

"Please," he gasped. "There's little time. This is not the place to talk."

"You knew we were coming?" I asked.

He straightened, fear in his eyes. "Yes, of course. The Lord has revealed his path to me."

I pressed him. "You have received divine revelation concerning our visit?"

His eyes darted around toward the ambling pedestrians, snapping back to us. He licked his lips. "Be merciful; do not test me here."

"What have you seen?" Perhaps he was a latent Reader and had experienced foresight of our travels.

"Dreams," he said, his eyes haunted. "Terrible nightmares. You must know there isn't much time."

"Time for what?" I asked.

His right hand went instinctively to his cross, and he grasped the pendant like a talisman. "I am a humble servant of the Lord. I beg you. I do not understand the visions. The powers comprehend them," he mumbled. "The Almighty knows."

The cyborg child-nun smiled. "We'll go to your church then? Yes?"

He bowed, ushering us in the direction he had come. "Please, this way. We retreat to the house of God. Before the evil arrives. We shelter under the protection of his wings."

He began to jog across the street.

I spoke to Kloan. "What is coming?"

She shrugged and motioned for me to follow.

We darted through the decaying infrastructure, cloaked cultists dashing at doomsday. The priest's words weighed on me as I considered all the dangerous possibilities. Dram agents aware of our arrival? They controlled the planet, but their numbers were few. Their ability to monitor the entire world was therefore limited. How could they know of us so soon? Had forces of the Anti, or something worse, pursued us? Kloan's cryptic talk of gods and monsters was not comforting. This clergyman had expected us. Had others as well?

After several blocks and turns, we entered a tree-lined street. A church was now visible ahead on the left. Splayed sunlight from branches painted a dappled pattern over the stone facade. Children on bicycles darted over the road. Mundane sounds of the community mingled with my anxiety, creating a disturbing dichotomy.

The sign in front of the building read "Saint Anne's Catholic Parish." The priest paused before it, finding relief. He exhaled and rested his hand on the wood.

He turned toward us, his smile quavering. "I'm sorry for this rush. Please excuse my rudeness. I am Father Geoffrey," he said bowing again. "You likely already know everything about me." He stared at us in awe.

The cleric believed we possessed extensive knowledge far beyond our measly confusions. It seemed a mistake to clarify our own ignorance at this stage, although I knew of no way to feign omniscience.

I glanced to my traveling companion for guidance, but she was distracted. Her posture was rigid, her eyes closed, a strained expression on her face.

"Kloan?" I said, touching her shoulder.

She spoke from a distance. "Father, thank you. Why don't we enter the church now, and hope it provides the protection you believe it can."

His face fell.

My own feelings echoed his own. I turned to face her. "What's going on?"

She opened her eyes. The irises glowed green. "Wormhole, Waythrel. Very close. It's opening now, and it's not empty."

Chapter 8

He had forgotten that all life is only a set of pictures in the brain, among which there is no difference betwixt those born of real things and those born of inward dreamings, and no cause to value the one above the other.

H. P. Lovecraft

"Into the church!" said Father Geoffrey, running forward. He clenched his hands into fists, stuttering his steps to avoid tripping over his robes.

We followed the rushing priest at a less manic pace. He led us away from the majestic entrance portals and around the side of the structure. We stopped in front of a small wooden door. He dug into his vestment pockets.

Kloan tried to calm him. "The tunnel is immature, still ripening. Nothing will come through immediately. Maybe we have an hour. They'll also have to find us."

He glanced over his shoulder as he fumbled with keys to the door. "What foul creatures are spilling from that pit of hell?"

"Hard to say," said the cyborg in full deadpan.

I considered our monstrous forms, undoubtedly demonic to this poor parish priest. How were we going to deal with this charade and whatever was coming through the wormhole?

"Here!" he said, brandishing a scratched key. He unlocked the door and scrambled inside, flipped a light switch, and dashed to a telephone.

"Good thing we still have the old landlines," he said. "Cellular has been on the fritz all day with static. Interference, if you ask me," he added, firing us a conspiratorial glare.

It was a small kitchenette, hardly spacious enough for the three of us, and the table in the middle of the room. Statues of the crucified Christ hung on the walls. A religious calendar was affixed with magnets to a chugging refrigerator.

"Who are you calling?" I asked.

His eyebrows jumped. "Why, the Dawns, of course," he said, listening as the phone rang on the other end. "I will tell them to bring Ambra as soon as possible." Again, the quizzical expression as we remained silent. "For the baptism." He began speaking into the handset.

Baptism. She was an infant in this space and time! She had been headed here all along. We might have missed her had we gone straight to the farmhouse.

"Missing whatever is coming for her," said Kloan.

Father Geoffrey ended the call. "Yes, you know." He squinted at us. "Of course, you know. Why must I doubt? Where is my faith?" He placed his hands to his head and shook it as if trying to throw off some raging headache. "God's messengers. You are His emissaries. I do believe!"

"We are divine envoys?" I asked.

"Angels." He glanced at each of us in sequence. "Seraphim from heaven sent to save the child."

"We are not what we seem?" I asked.

He appeared burdened by the question. "You are nuns. Simple

sisters visiting from the Hermanas de Juana Inés de la Cruz. I see this. I have the papers in my office," he trailed off, staring at us. "Behind your faces...I have seen in the dreams. The awful visages of the seraphim." He placed his fingers over his mouth. "Why does the Lord test me?"

Kloan walked forward. "Please sit down, Father. Let us talk openly at last."

The priest's eyes widened in fear and anticipation. We took seats in the small room, the metal chair legs grating on the floor.

She took his hands in hers. "Father Geoffrey, this is going to be hard to understand, but even for angels, the power of God is overwhelming. Sometimes, for some of the lesser powers, when we are sent by the divine, it is a difficult journey."

"Difficult?"

She spoke as if to a child. "Yes. Our nature, so miraculous to your own, is still finite. Still traumatized by the infinite splendor of the godhead."

Awe crossed his face, and wonder filled my mind at her deftness. I had become relegated to the status of a nymph by a creature I first considered but a gifted juvenile. The cyborg absorbed cultures, mythologies, mannerisms. People's subliminal fears. She did so in the span of hours. She refracted those back in prismatic conversation that served her own purposes.

What *was* Kloan?

"What is it you wish from me?" he asked.

"We have lost much of what we knew before we came. God has a plan, yes?"

He bobbed his head.

"Your dreams, the ones tormenting you, they hold the information we require. Please, tell us now the content of your nightmares, down to the darkest detail."

A moan escaped the priest. "No, have mercy on me, I can't! Don't make me describe them. I see them also in the light of day!" He began to shake.

I interjected, trying to find a voice in this strange quest. "You do not need to speak, Father. Give your permission and open your thoughts to us. We may read your experiences as one might a book."

"You can do this? Forgive me, I can't but doubt." He shook his head. "All is possible to God. Yes! My body, my heart, my mind are in God's service. I am your servant." He grasped our hands and closed his eyes, convinced the process would be painful or draining.

Kloan's consciousness dug. We plunged into the priest's awareness as she homed in like a missile on the swirling chaos of his visions. Colored by his own metaphors, myths, and fears, they spun a nightmare of demonic invasion. Rips in the fabric of nature, vile creatures from the fiery pits setting foot on the soil of mortals. Two demons dragged their scaled forms across land and water. They blackening crops, turning rivers to steam, laying waste to anything in their path. That path ended before the unmistakable form of the church we now occupied.

On this religious house, a light shone from all directions. The radiance emanated from the spaces between space, beyond the reality they entered. Monstrous yet holy shapes stood in the middle of the glow. Many armed and eyed, they blocked the doorway and refused entrance to the hell-beasts. Behind them, inside, resting on a throne, were a mother and infant. Not the Virgin Mary, but a farmer's wife with red hair. In her arms was not the Christ child but a baby girl with skin white like porcelain.

The dreamscape quaked from the terrible roar of the creatures outside the church. The air rippled at the hatred they unleashed. The dark forms advanced, frothing clouds rushing in with them. Lightning, thunder, fire, and blood rained against the parish walls. In front of them, the envoys of light brightened. A transcendent crescendo rose unseen. The essence of space was pregnant with power and poised to snap like a stretched string.

We careened back to the kitchenette, holding hands with the priest. The dream was gone. The humming of the refrigerator replaced the nightmarish noises. Father Geoffrey opened his eyes.

"Is this all?" I asked, anxiety reducing my patience. "What happened next?"

He shook his head. "It always ends there. I can't see beyond this horrible moment." His eyes pleaded. "This is what you need? Now you can tell me what it means?"

I glanced toward Kloan. I was as baffled as the priest and hoped she knew something I did not.

"It means a battle is coming today for the life of the child," she said. "For the life of Ambra Dawn. You had guessed correctly, Father. Terrible powers will arrive soon and seek to unmake a glorious history of God's plan."

Forces of the Anti, Waythrel, came her thoughts in my mind. *They have long sought this reality to kill her before she became the Daughter.*

"And you," he said, indicating the both of us, "are the servants of the light? Like the dream? You will defend her?"

Kloan stood. "You've seen our true forms during your dreams. We bring formidable power here."

The priest crossed himself.

"We will stand in the doorway and do battle with those who seek the destruction of the girl."

Chapter 9

Do not say, "Draw the curtain that I may see the painting." The curtain is the painting.

Nikos Kazantzakis

The thin walls rippled from a repeated impact, flesh pounding wood. Father Geoffrey jumped, his skin pale. He faced the door connecting the kitchenette to the church. Unsure how to proceed, he froze in place.

"It's the child and her mother," said Kloan with a bright flash in her eye. "They're at the front doors."

"God have mercy, they're here already," said the priest. He scampered forward to the church proper.

Following close behind, we entered the sanctuary. It was a small building, holding five rows of pews. The ceiling was high, lending a sense of grandeur to an otherwise humble space. The decoration was sparse. Stained-glass windows depicted saints and events from the life of Jesus. Polished statues gleamed about the altar, the nave, and the narthex. A listing of the beatitudes glinted in marble and hung on the wall beside the main entrance.

This we approached. Kloan glowed with some unseen potential. She leaned forward and brushed the wood with her hand. I felt she would reach through the portals and grasp those on the other side. Unnerved by her behavior, I neared, watching her and the priest.

Father Geoffrey released the numerous locks studding the double doors. With a grunt he pulled inward, the old timbers crackling with dust. Sunlight poured into the dim chamber through the opening crevice. The radiance outlined a dark silhouette.

Ambra Dawn was carried in, cradled in her mother's arms, sound asleep with an angelic tranquility on her face. The infant was still a newborn, perhaps into her second month. A thick mane of bristled scarlet covered a significant portion of the cranium. She was clothed in a white dress, a thin band with a flower tied around her head.

I suppressed a deep urge. I longed to go to the child, to hold this nymph-form of the being I loved and had lost to the cosmos.

"Father Geoffrey," said the mother, out of breath, not yet noticing our presence. "I came as fast as possible. I haven't told Frank. He's away to Omaha looking at a new harvester. He'd kill me with the scheduled date just a few days away. My entire family is going to have it with me!"

He placed a shaking hand on her shoulder. "Thank you for trusting me, Cleena, and believing your own instincts." He motioned to us. "These are the two I mentioned."

She gasped. "The nuns from my dream."

The priest grimaced. "You see, my friends, there has been much stirring in the cornfields of Nebraska the last months." He turned back to the mother. "Let's get you in and close those. It's no longer safe outside." He pushed the groaning portals back together, slamming them shut. A rumbling echoed through the church.

"It is not secure *inside*," said Kloan. "Especially in front of the doors. We must bring the infant to the sanctuary, the altar. After that, there will be little time before they arrive."

Cleena stiffened. "Who will come? I haven't been able to sleep since the birth! Dreams of running with Ambra, always the two of you alongside. Why are you here? What will happen?"

The cleric motioned forward. "Let's get her away from the entrance and into the heart of the church. We don't have much time."

She carried the baby. What answer could any of us give her that would be comprehensible? The vague threat her latent Reader powers sensed brought her to this place and time. I hoped her trust was not misguided.

Many factors conspired to infect me with the anxiety plaguing the priest and mother. The encroaching presence of the Anti. The fearful whispers and dreams of these humans. The repeated proclamations of danger. Fear had rooted within me.

The walls of the church shrank. I imagined the forces searching for the child converging on our position. A foreboding hung in the air, a dark electricity worming its way into my deepest awareness. Whatever would happen was imminent.

The Daughter's mother placed the infant behind the altar as the clergyman prayed.

Kloan took my hand and led me to stand before the pair, facing outward toward the entrance. "It's time, Waythrel. They're here."

We all felt it. Something unclean stalked in the darkness. Geoffrey paused his prayers, glancing over his shoulder. Cleena Dawn held her newborn to herself and closed her eyes. She repeated the litany abandoned by the priest.

A terrible breath of silence.

Blasting inward, the massive doors shattered into a thousand fragments.

Chapter 10

She who knows does not speak;
she who speaks does not know.

—老子 Lǎozǐ

Sawdust rained through the small church. Wooden shards embedded themselves like released arrows in the pews nearest the entrance. Cleena Dawn screamed, and the baby, startled, wailed. Ambra would cry for the duration of this mad encounter until a final, terrible silence.

The dust cleared. Through the doors, two forms entered. Teenaged girls, red-haired, pale-skinned, and green-eyed. A cyborg's intubated, computerized cranium topped each.

"They sent clones," I said, a chill running through me.

A dancer well-versed in the steps of a choreography, Kloan eased down the middle aisle. The carnage did not faze her.

The pair paused as she approached. Undulations of spacetime rocked me as the three creatures sparred in unseen realms. There was no overt violence as of yet, but I felt the growing tension as the combatants probed their opponents.

"Give us the child," said the clone on our left. "Surrender her, and you may go. If you resist, we will destroy you."

The false nun said nothing.

I was unsure which form the invaders saw. Without doubt, our *fields* presented the human disguises. Could they tear through the trickery concealing our true natures? What would they do if they knew Kloan was one of them? If they attacked, would she be able to defeat them?

"I said, hand us Ambra Dawn," the cyborg continued in a whisper, stepping forward and raising her arm.

"Wait!" said the other, grasping her hand while staring at Kloan. "What are you?"

"A Reader who seeks to meddle and overestimates herself," said her twin.

"No," said the second. "Don't you see it?" Her brow furrowed. "There is something different. Something *deep* here."

Her anxiety deepened, and she took a step back.

"*You* made the path. You found Old Earth. Didn't you? We followed. We'd given up finding a passage." The clone swallowed. "What *are* you?"

Still, Kloan remained silent. The False Dawns surveyed the rest of us. They ignored the other humans, paused on the infant, and examined me.

The more perceptive cyborg continued. "Something hiding in this one, but I detect it is not much of a threat." She turned back to Kloan. "You are different."

Tortuous seconds dripped by.

"Are you here for Ambra Dawn?"

Silence.

"Have you come from another time path?" asked the first, infected by her copy's hesitancy.

"There would be no conflict in our missions," offered the other.

"Why do you shut your mind to us?"

"Together we can break your will and take the child by force. We *will* take her. We *must*. I sense you know this. Step aside, help us." She extended a hand and let it fall. "Or die."

The temperature in the room dropped. Objective or subjective, I could not determine. Was it some unseen engagement or my own heightened fear? Whichever, the parameters of space and time tightened. A taut bow. The tension growing to a breaking point. An arrow moments from release. The baby cried out in pain.

"She won't allow us in," said the first, her voice strained, beads of sweat on her brow.

"So be it," said the second.

Existence detonated.

Because spacetime became both a weapon and a victim of assault, I cannot say how "long" this conflict lasted. Minutes? Judging from the final carnage, it was a reasonable guess. Or was it millennia, hopping in tubes and bubbles of punctured chronology? In the impossible distortions that followed, reason no longer mattered. Causality collapsed. Meaning vanished in this epic restructuring of reality.

I was as useless as I had been in the attack on Dram. While infinity opened to swallow the space in front of me, I tried to locate Ambra. I might not be able to battle these goddesses, but I could at least find the baby. Perhaps help protect it from the seismic assaults.

Before I could act, I was thrown to the ground. Light, sound, and stimulus unknown rocked my awareness. My eyestalks struggled to rise from the floor. Gravity on the world had increased tenfold. I saw extensive damage to the church. Pews were in disarray, flattened. The wreckage approached the sanctuary but failed at the sacred space.

The priest was gone. Had I seen him step forward and approach the intruders? I could no longer be sure in my disorientation. Cleena Dawn was there, unconscious, flat on the carpeted surface near the altar. I could not see the baby.

Slowly—or quickly—eventually, the spacetime chaos slackened. A growing warmth emanated. I managed to turn my body around and raise my eyestalks, glancing toward the entrance.

The roof of the church and the entire front wall were gone. Splintered wood and cement floated, defying gravity, yet scattered as if by a frozen blast. Each piece of the wreckage rotated in the air. The nearby houses, trees, parked cars——all were untouched.

Suspended over Kloan were two bodies. Bracing their backs, elements of the pulverized structures were repurposed. Thousands of splinters and chunks rearranged and amalgamated. Unknown forces glued them together, fashioning planks at ninety-degree angles behind the two attacking clones. Stained shards from shattered windows pierced their hands and feet. They hung motionless, with heads bowed. Circlets of smaller glass needles around their crowns, dripping blood.

Crucified.

Kloan waved her arms, and the constellation of random, hovering materials dropped to the ground. The march of time lurched into gear again. The lifeless bodies defied physics and continued to hang on their crosses.

"Ironic and satisfying imagery of death, I think." She grinned. Moving away from the fantastical nightmare, she walked toward me.

The contrast in my thoughts between this child and Ambra struck me. The Daughter existed in some personality space, sharing little with this creature. Ambra could kill and undertake raw, violent acts, but it was always in the defense of those who resisted the Dram and Anti. This creative slaughter hanging like macabre art disturbed me.

In the midst of my shock, I heard the baby cry again. I turned to the sound.

"Find the priest," said Kloan, taking my arm. "I'll tend to the mother and infant."

My heart yearned for Ambra, but I was becoming accustomed to following Kloan's lead. I searched across the wreckage of the church.

The building continued to stand, despite losing significant supporting structure. I hoped the cleric was not underneath some of the larger piles of rubble.

He was not. I found Father Geoffrey. What remained of him.

Chapter 11

The two principles of truth, reason and senses, are not only both not genuine, but are engaged in mutual deception.

Blaise Pascal

The tidal forces unleashed in the conflict had caught the poor priest at their most brutal. I found Geoffrey, parts of him——his upper torso and head still together——prone atop a heap of pew debris. Other remnants of his flesh were scattered about the room. His chest was eviscerated, the muscle and bone mashed and torn like some soft dough.

I do not suffer the same horrified reaction as humans to a visceral death of your kind. Nevertheless, the massive trauma to the physiology of this creature elicited pity. His demise was sudden, at least.

I heard the baby wailing, followed by sounds of Kloan moving objects behind me. I could not focus on the infant or her mother. I could not take my eyes away from the priest.

"Why did you leave the sanctuary, old man?" I whispered to the corpse. Respecting human traditions, I closed his eyes, but he hardly seemed at rest.

I recalled the terrible plans I had developed with Ambra, in another space and different time. We had raced to counter the coming attack on New Earth. Our studies had found evidence that something miraculous, something horrible, something completely *other* was possible. *The Gathering of Souls.* Had she taken the final, hellish step to climb toward a nirvana?

Would the priest's consciousness find its way to a grand collective? *Would we all?* Or would we thrash in the void until our sentient fields lost all coherence? One was a kind of hell. The other something I hoped would be a heaven.

My eyes turned back to the lurid abominations hanging above the carnage. Memories dashed through my mind of clone hordes descending on us in the Dram desert. In particular, the one clone Ambra had tried to reach, to reason with, to love in the face of all the torture and mutilation the creature had suffered. The False Dawn she had *failed* to save.

The laden crosses rotated above me. Kloan had hung them like trophies of war. Yet they were once conscious beings who began their lives in innocence. Despite the biological distortions of the Anti. The birthing warehouses. The hormone and nutrient soups warping normal gestation and development. As a Xix, I had to believe in their pure origins.

Original sin?

Was it not a human theological idea? Tainted without choice, before sinning. *Born guilty*, doomed to condemnation. It seemed a horrible doctrine devoid of justice, one any of my kind would immediately reject.

I walked to the crucified clones and touched a dangling foot. In spite of my height, the reach strained my limbs. The sole was warm. My twelve digits stuck to blood still dripping from the wounds. My slight pressure caused the corpse to pivot in the air.

Are these ever to be saved?

Now their minds were adrift. Consciousnesses so distorted they may never hope to find citizenship in the Group Mind, whatever it had become. Sentience warped to hate and madness. Creatures born and condemned by a horrific, cosmic original sin. Souls incarnate into damnation.

I could not imagine the Daughter casting them to the void. I knew the weakness of my species, our need for harmony and healing. Not all life in our galaxy shared such a commitment. Humans could be both as loving as the Xix and as monstrous as the Dram. Conflicting behaviors often erupted from the same individual.

Yet I had communed with Ambra. I had loved her for three centuries, merged with her in the Group Mind. Her personality echoed in my awareness. I could not believe she would not find a way, if a way existed, to bring all minds into the fold. Inherent and permanent loss was too horrible a fate to contemplate.

Echoing my distress, the baby shrieked. It screamed in a manner I, a divergent life-form, recognized as distinct from the previous cries. My eyestalks flung toward the frightening sound. Thoughts raced. Had her mother perished? Had Ambra been injured in the melee? Or, perhaps, had she sensed with her infant powers the terrible cry within my soul?

I froze in place facing the sanctuary. My limbs dropped to my side. A strange sensation throbbed deep inside me. Was my cellular structure disintegrating? Melting and flowing into the debris and body parts already littering the ground?

The baby lay on the marble table, unmoving, crimson patterns splashed across her white dress. A long, gruesome gash ripped through her neck, scarlet bubbles frothing from the airway. A burgundy liquid oozed over the altar surface. It pooled at the edges and dribbled down the sides of the tablecloth.

The mother was unconscious, but most of my eyes locked on Kloan. Her eyes were wide and still, robes splattered. Her right hand brandished a stained carving knife. The blade pointed outward, glinting and maroon. Small drops of the infant's blood dripped to the ground from its tip.

Behind me, a wet impact and shudder. Several eyestalks swiveled backward and spied the fall of the two crucified clones. Their bodies sprawled alongside the priest. Dust and gore sprayed into the air, sprinkling me with a thin layer of crimson clay.

The world should end. My halting words sounded shrill through the translator.

"Kloan——*what have you done?*"

Chapter 12

The laws of physics might permit the existence, in the real Universe, of closed time-like curves. The semiclassical laws of physics should be augmented by a principle of self-consistency.

Novikov et al, "Cauchy problem in spacetimes with closed timelike curves," Physical Review D, 42 (6), 1990.

Green eyes in the darkness.

Dizzy. Ripped from a dream and flung into a new reality, I stared at a night sky churning with stars in patterns I could not recognize. A soft breeze trickled over me. Sounds of alien creatures punctuated the whisper of wind. My eyestalks darted about, appraising the planet surface, the heavens, and the figure of the girl sitting beside me.

Kloan pulled in her legs. They obscured her head. Haunting gems peeked over bobbing kneecaps. Her arms wrapped around her shins. She rocked back and forth. I detected a faint sound with rhythmic pitch changes and repeating arrangements. Humming.

I bent my eyes to her.

"What have you done? *What did you do to Ambra?*"

The child continued to sway and hum, ignoring my question. Desperation flooded me.

"What did you do!"

The music stopped.

"Nothing."

"*Nothing?*" My eyestalks swiveled. "I *saw* you with a knife! *Blood* all over you and the baby. Next—light. It overpowered my senses. What happened? Where is the infant?"

"In a past. At a distance."

The intubated, tattooed head cocked to one side, the green eyes continuing to hold me in their grip. Tendrils of her thought danced around my awareness.

"You are probing my mind!"

The head remained at a forty-five-degree angle. She peered from behind her right knee. "Your thoughts leak everywhere. You Xix are leaky-brains."

The child leapt, catching me by surprise. She stood above me. Long, ragged clumps of scarlet locks dangled over her face.

"A first experiment. I was skeptical. The Anti always believed there were unstable nodes in time. This was one of their top targets. I kept telling them, but they wouldn't listen. It's not *then* that you have to worry about her, but at the *beginning.*"

"You cut the throat of an infant as a test? You risked killing the Daughter, preventing your own existence. All because you doubted it was possible and wanted to see?"

"Mm-hmm."

I stared at the child, her innocence horribly deceptive. "You are a monster."

"Yes, I'm a monster. Don't you know that by now?" She bit her lower lip. "We're bred to kill Ambra Dawn from the moment we're cloned." Her eyes blazed. "It was easy to do, you understand? It would have been hard *not* to murder her. I'd need enormous willpower not to, however strange it seems to you. Years of conditioning don't just go away. It will never go away."

"I thought you might be different." My heart felt broken. I *needed* her to be her own person.

"I *am* different, Waythrel. *Everything's* different with me, and you'll see. I let my instincts have their way because another part of me had to test something important."

The horror of the memory would not leave my mind. "Why did you battle the clones? They would have killed her for you."

"Probably, but I had to be sure. I couldn't tolerate their interference in the experiment."

"You plotted all along to murder a child."

"Not any child. *That* child. If it helps, I'd have little desire to kill a random infant."

It did not help.

"Poor Xix! I am a *very* specific monster. Precisely aimed. Ambra's unharmed. I'm here. So are you, which requires her survival and existence. Her actions. An entire tapestry of world lines, whole universes. Remember?"

The words were like a slap to my mind. *Phrases from a dream.*

"Where are we?"

"Don't you know?"

I wobbled up. Gazing at the ragged landscape, I saw a flat plain below. The lights of a city washed out the canopy of stars close to the horizon.

"We are back where we started. When you took me after Dram."

"*When* did we start, Waythrel?"

I stared at the deep green eyes. My sense of time, cause and effect, spun, disoriented. Memories strobed in a blurred fog. I could no longer discern what was real and what was in my mind.

"I am confused. Please explain to me what is happening. You seem to understand."

She exhaled, satisfied. "That's *why* we're here. *Data.* The next data to enter the gate." She turned her back on me, walking down a steep slope. "Let's get started."

"With what? Where are you going?"

Kloan continued without turning back. Her words faded into the night. "To where it all began for me. To watch the beginning flow around us and mature and twist through time and space to come back to be us. Then we'll be ready for the next step."

The starlight cast sharp shadows on the dusty rocks. The figure of the child was gone, swallowed in the darkness. I stood frozen, trying to understand the madness of my own thoughts.

Did I know this creature? It seemed I did. We had journeyed in a dream. Traveled from Dram. Voyaged to Earth before it was New Earth. Battled monsters. Murdered infants.

Now we were here, as if I had arrived from Dram again. Was I lucid? Was the universe sane?

Waythrel, come on!

Her voice rang in my mind. My eyestalks curled on themselves. What else was there for me to do?

Chapter 13

Life can only be understood backwards; but it must be lived forwards.

Søren Kierkegaard

I raced after the child, my steps uncertain, the ground beneath me dust-covered and slippery. Descending the sharp incline, I stumbled and tripped. My four limbs clutched at stones and alien vegetation, slick as if oiled.

It's a field around you, remember?

Her thoughts danced through my mind.

It's skintight, coating your surfaces, insulating you from everything.

I fought to understand her words as memories bubbled. The strange sensation, her voice, walking up the slope to a shining disk in the light—*the gate.*

Rounding a boulder, I almost collided with her. Shattered rocks littered the terrain, leftovers from landslides off the craggy heights.

"What sort of coat? Why do we have it?"

Kloan peered below. A city or a military base carpeted the arid ground, shadows moving in formation through it.

"I don't know what kind. They make it for our protection."

"From what?"

She pointed to the compound. "Come. It's nearly day, but we're earlier this time." she said, shaking her head. "That's when it all begins. We'll go see me there, and then you'll see what happens."

As she moved toward the complex, I grabbed her, needing answers.

"Another clone facility?"

"Yes."

Memories flooded me.

"There is an attack! We cannot walk right into that place."

"There's no danger."

"Maybe not for you. *I* cannot. They will kill any Xix they see."

"They won't see us. We're invisible in these suits, remember?"

"*You* broke through Ambra's bubble."

Kloan shook her head. "Hers was simple. Primitive."

"Yours now is none of those things?"

"I told you, they're not *mine*. Now, come on!"

The child pulled me forward. Helpless, my mind whirled. Events were suspect—now, before, those to come. I distrusted my own thoughts. Would I understand any of this absurdity?

We covered the distance between the broken hills and the installation. The flat landscape made my efforts less exhausting. Rather than concentrate on each step, I observed the nearing fortification. It was unlike any city or technological society I had ever seen.

The laws of physics and chemistry are the same across the universe. As far as we have been able to ascertain, through time as well. But the mentality expressed here was more remote than I had encountered. In comparison, our galaxy of diverse life-forms appeared homogenous.

Architecture. Transport surface topology. The use of color and lighting. It bordered on cognitive hostility. I cannot describe it with more clarity.

Yet *humans* populated the place. I saw no other species. Two classes of people, easily demarcated: those who resembled Ambra Dawn and those who did not.

"The Anti run things with robots and trained people," Kloan added.

No doubt she sampled my *leaky* thoughts.

"To avoid annihilation?"

I assumed it would be difficult to be in the presence of so much matter to their antimatter. The energies required to prevent planetary destruction would be enormous.

"No, they aren't concerned about it here," she said, not bothering to explain. "It's more efficient. Once they optimized the program, it ran with drones and lackeys."

We approached the entrance to the complex. Robotic guards patrolled the gate, hovering above the ground. Strange weapons protruded from multiple regions of their forms. To my relief, they did not notice anything unusual. Nothing in their technology pierced whatever cloaking mechanism concealed us. Inside were other automatons of odd shapes and designs. I soon noticed a pattern.

"Machines do all the work," I whispered.

Kloan spoke without concern for discovery.

"Humans are the social construct for the clones. See, we need people to develop, or the brain is too wrecked to become useful. Human neurophysiology needs communal fabrics, structures, language, norms. So the Anti imported them. It's a clone growth matrix, I guess."

"Like on Dram," I said, remembering the groups of cyborgs and others involved with them.

"Yes, a beginning. Before it was destroyed."

"Dram is gone?" My mind lurched.

"Terrible civil war. Blew themselves to bits. It didn't matter. They were an outpost."

"This is another one?"

"One of the last. The devil ball hunts them through space and time. They had to build them farther away. Find stronger clones to shield them from attack."

"Devil ball?"

She smirked. "Your little Orbies. We had other names for them. Other thoughts about them. Come, you'll see. You'll *learn*."

We moved through the strange streets of this alien and yet human city. Groups of young Ambra Dawns paraded past us at various points. Older cyborgs shepherded them with the assistance of more diverse humans. While we walked, Kloan pointed out buildings or objects of significance.

"Inside these warehouses are the wombs. All clones are birthed there. They learned early that the gestational process was key to brain development. Purely in vitro methods were incredible failures." She smiled at me. "It's nice we're born and not grown, isn't it?"

I didn't know if the strange cyborg was serious or sarcastic. We Xix had mastered the translation of human conflict avoidance mechanisms, such as sarcasm. Uncertainty in interpretation often remained, however. With this clone, my previous experience mattered little.

"What we saw on Dram was much more horrible than nice, Kloan."

"You're a terrible student," she said in an odd tone. "But we can't have lessons now. We have to hurry!"

"Where?"

The child gazed into the distance. "Home."

Chapter 14

I see the blindness and the wretchedness of man. I regard the whole silent universe, and man without light, left to himself, and lost in this corner of the cosmos. Without knowing who has put him there, what he has come to do, what will become of him at death, and incapable of all knowledge. I become terrified.

Blaise Pascal

"**H**ome?"

"Or quarantine," she said. "Take your pick. With me locked in their little box, the compound thought itself protected."

She grabbed my hand and pulled me forward, sprinting. We darted across the bizarre avenues. I processed little until we reached a strange building unlike any of the others. It was small, a deep black—obsidian—reflecting little light. Churning electromagnetic forces pulsed around the structure.

"Safe from *you*? You mean all this shielding?"

"It's designed to keep me and my powers inside, yeah," she said.

"It was useful in the beginning, when I was very little. I never let them know my full strength. Come, I'll get us through the fields."

Kloan yanked and reality glitched. For an instant, my vision blurred. Events accelerated and stuttered as my Reader senses reeled. Eyestalks flailing, I failed to focus on anything. A kaleidoscope of images assaulted my consciousness.

"Waythrel, hold on to me."

She grabbed my arm and steadied me. The dizziness passed and my sight returned.

A single room greeted us, spartan, with a bed, table, toilet, and sink. No products for leisure. No children's toys. No books or electronic information sources. Bright light streamed in from a transparent region of the shielding. The system's star rose for the beginning of a new day. Sounds of explosions and shouts echoed outside. The room was in disarray. Clothes were strewn about, food and utensils as well. My olfactory strips detected a growing acrid smell. *Smoke?*

A child clone of identical appearance to Kloan stood in the middle of the room. Sweat beaded across her forehead. Her muscles tensed.

She gazed at a swirling vortex of milky light. My eyes stopped scanning; the stalks stilled. The impossible thing floating in front of the girl arrested all my attention. Thousands of faces and forms of myriad species bobbed in and out of sight in a violent sea of white fog. Many I could identify. Most I could not.

One I knew. The nacreous vapors coalesced around a central extrusion, a human face. The head was split open, the brain exposed behind it and fading into the mist. Tubes and wires, dwarfing the insertions into Kloan, entered and exited the skull. The eyes were partially obscured by machinery pulsing with a life of its own. The mouth was free.

"Ambra," I whispered in horror.

Despite all the Xixian technology covering and distorting her features, I recognized her. How could I not? How could I forget the alien face I had loved and nurtured? My student. My teacher. Our hope for centuries.

For the first time, I faced the price she had paid in our desperate plan to save the galaxy from the Anti and Dram. My focus flipped between the phantasm and the two bodies of Kloan in the room. My lover Synphel had warned us. The others and I had half-listened. The weight of the truth crushed me. I began to suspect we had triumphed by *becoming* our enemies.

I parsed the stunning poltergeist. Our most brilliant minds had focused on the potent consciousness of Ambra Dawn. Their immediate purpose in the war was to enhance the Collective's synergy and power. Far beyond this, they worked toward a cosmic goal. *The Gathering of Souls.* A harvest of sentience across space and time.

That reaping would give birth to a novel awareness, a being of its own we could not model, imagine, or anticipate. Our theories failed in this extreme context. Recursive infinities plaguing the sophisticated mathematics and artificial intelligence simulations.

Because our understanding stumbled, we recognized the project could fail. It might even produce something terrible. We had gambled to create a god whose nature we could not predict or control. In the end, it was a collective I would never join. Kloan had torn me from that destiny.

Whatever it had turned out to be in those swirling faces, it was not Ambra Dawn. Regardless of her likeness in the face of this thing, it was not her. It was something with her at its heart but exponentiated beyond the seed of its formation. To sweep across time and space and reach this world? I trembled before the power of this consciousness. We had given birth to a godling. What I did not yet suspect, and would see as this journey wore on, was that we had produced both a heaven and a hell.

"The gate is prepared," came Ambra's voice.

"I'm ready," said the Kloan of this earlier time.

"You must leave now. They will return with greater numbers of clones and more destructive weapons. They will force you to destroy them all if you engage."

"I don't want to kill them. Take me to the exit."

The stamping of rushing feet came from outside the small building. A heavy rumbling accompanied them. I imagined a sizable military vehicle.

Ambra's apparition pivoted toward the door of the quarantine cell. "Through the door."

The black field sealing the chamber gave way to a second churning vortex. It opened to span the width of the frame. Through it poured bright daylight. The city beyond her isolation unit vanished, replaced by a rocky terrain. It matched the landscape we had recently traversed.

The countryside within the whirlpool extended to the limits of my vision. At the end of the tunnel was a worn path on a steep slope. The vegetation was eroded, the rocks smoother, the coloration of the land distinct. The walkway rose up the hillside and ceased at an expansive disk. Sunlight gleamed off the surface. Blinding reflections bounced into the room and cast shadows on the floor.

Kloan pulled my arm, showing me that her temporal copy had entered the vortex. "The gate," she said.

I stumbled forward, blinded by the daggers of light glinting into the room. Shouts outside, and the walls began to smolder, glowing a bright orange.

"Good luck, my dearest friend," said the apparition of Ambra Dawn as I stepped within the passage.

My eyestalks bent backward to see the disembodied head turned toward me. Its motion sent ripples across the sea of blurred faces. Tears dripped from her eyes, coating the wires and tubes in her once-green irises. A bittersweet smile lined her face.

"I love you, Waythrel. Remember, whatever happens."

The room exploded.

Chapter 15

*If all the parts of the universe are interchained in a certain measure,
any one phenomenon will not be the effect of a single cause, but the
resultant of causes infinitely numerous.*

Henri Poincaré

Flames and rubble streaked toward me, obscuring the swirling god-thing in the room. While I waited to be pulverized, the portal shut.

We were far from the compound, a mile high into the rough hills and cut off from the melee below. Replacing the terrible rending of the explosion was a stunning silence. Pebbles rattled and shrubs groaned in wind gusts, muted until the next dance of air. A faint whiff of smoke that had entered the tunnel was all remaining of the carnage.

Shattered by Ambra's last words and stunned by the violence, I turned away from the vanished doorway. At the top of the slope waited the sparkling ring. Several feet above me, Kloan motioned to follow. No one else was visible.

"Where is the clone?"

"She's right here."

I paused, confused, my mind still in disarray. "This is where you left. When you went to kidnap me."

"Yup. I'm gone already through the gate, so I could come back with you." She smiled. "It's an elegant loop, yeah?"

"It is madness!" Recent events rushed through my thoughts. "Ambra is part of it all?"

"She's the heart of it all."

"It cannot be."

"You aren't the only one tested, Waythrel. Each time's different. When we finally understand, we'll see the way." She turned toward the disk. "Now's the next stage of the odyssey. And yes, a journey sustained by Ambra Dawn. Are you ready to continue?"

No. I was not prepared. I drowned in the memory of a dream. Had I not been here before? *To make a choice.*

"We have been here, just like this."

"Not *just* like, but we have been and will be. But never *just* like. Remember the nonnormalizable loop?"

"I am getting a sense of it." My eyestalks rotated to center on Kloan. "There was more. A hope. To go *back*. To find Synphel." I ached to think of my mate again.

"Yes. There was."

"So, we can remain here. Survive, avoid the Anti, someday to perish in this obscure sector of the cosmos. Or we can engage this portal. Risk eternal damnation to a self-referencing and altering time-line?" My mind considered the meaning. "Or have we already done that?"

"Yes and yes."

"You are coming with me?" I asked.

"That's the whole point."

I turned my attention to the gate, a deep uneasiness creeping through me. The disk reminded me of a cross-sectional slice of the Orb. The surface resembled a viscous, churning, honey-like fluid. I glimpsed stars within it, endless depths of star fields bobbing in and out of an iridescent sea. The thing pulled at me as I gazed. It was monstrous and beautiful. I grasped the child's hand.

Kloan laughed. "Seems we'll always be dancing together, Xix."

My eyestalks wrapped around each other. The covering sheaths expanding, blocking out all light.

We walked into the gel.

Part III

My labor lingers long; the pay is poor.
From toil to sleep to toil the chanting brays.
A weariness invades to kiss my core.
A willing lover he has found and stays.

Except those eves inflamed by Holy Songs,
when Shaman Ones chant secrets in the night,
and cease to sing at brilliant birth of dawn—
in mysteries my weary mind delights.

Although at times their truths are hard to see,
and seem estranged from that my heart enfolds,
no doubt my profound ignorance blinds me,
I close my eyes and think as I am told.

Our Shaman Ones doubt not they spin the truth.
As for myself, I do not ask for proof.

—Mazandarani, *Sonnets from the Desert*

Chapter 16

We came all this way to explore the Moon, and the most important thing is that we discovered the Earth.

William Anders

When my mind cleared, I woke in a recurrent dream. Cornfields. A blue sky and humid summer. A rare hill in the Great Plains sloping to a gurgling stream. Kloan at the bottom, naked in the water, squealing, pulling huge handfuls of slime from her body.

"Waythrel!" she shouted, grinning up at me. "Don't wait so long this time!"

I shivered from the memories of the last trip. Doom and death. Attack and murder. I stared at the assassin frolicking in the cold waters. Nothing was ever as it seemed.

"Not here to kill Ambra this time! It doesn't work, remember? Come down before you solidify into some sort of permanent artwork!"

How do you continue with the rational, the practical? Something so basic and mundane as self-hygiene, when lunacy lurks at every turn? What was the point of a bath when monsters might be crucified in a few hours' time or a baby's throat slit? Or swirling clouds of souls materialize on worlds to which you have been kidnapped, embedding you in an endless time loop of psychosis?

I ambled down the hill. The cyborg raced and squealed, holding her robes in one hand like some wrecked kite she was trying to send aloft. I ignored her. I washed. I removed the globs of gate goo. Summoning my courage, I examined my reflection in the water.

I saw a child.

A blue-eyed girl with dangling black braids stared back at me with a puzzled expression. I glanced away, a blur of red rolling down the slope and laughing, distracting me. I gazed back. She was still there. Six or seven years old. Freckles and a mole on her right cheek.

"Kloan?"

She came to rest near me, grass stains coating her beige robes, sweat glistening over her flushed face. "More body image problems, Waythrel?"

"What are you this time?" I ventured.

"Same—little black-haired kid. I get a bow in my hair."

Frustration boiled inside me. "I find these facades troubling. What happened before..." I couldn't finish.

"Before what?" She bobbed her head in a syncopated rhythm. "When you uncover that absolute reference frame for *when*, please let me know, because all I can be sure of is *now*." She peeked at the water. "*Awww.* Pigtails, they call them. You make a cute girl for a squid, Xix!"

"Why are we here, Kloan? It is the same place."

Of all the possibilities for this journey, many in my mind bringing me closer to Synphel, returning to Old Earth had not occurred to me.

"Well, time moves on. Or does it?" she said, stepping away from the reflections. "We'll avoid the priests and baptisms. Skip on the

Ambra clones in this tangent. Don't think you'll see anything like that this time—except for me, of course. Ha!"

I rose from the brook. It was good to be out of a substance my species was both dependent on and uncomfortable with as desert dwellers. I longed for our sonic showers. She moved along the stream in a familiar direction.

"Why *are* we here?" I pleaded after her.

She called over her shoulder, "To make a new friend!"

It was not difficult to guess who this acquaintance might be. Everything in my experience connected with Ambra Dawn. I surmised with near certainty that the clone headed for her farm. To what purpose in this Old Earth reality, I could not imagine. The memories of destruction and murder hardly reassured me. In fact, they paralyzed me.

Kloan stopped, her shoulders slumped. She raised a leg and pirouetted, facing me. Plodding, she approached, her head bowed with fatigue. She came to a stop inches from my feet and crossed her arms over her chest. "Can't you keep your mind to yourself?"

"My thoughts are—"

"Look. Waythrel. This isn't easy. Not for you. Not for me. It's a rough reentry through atmo with nausea and some broken bones. We're likely going to do it for five and a quarter eternities. You need to do more than adapt. You *have* to see the bigger picture."

"Which is?"

"Well, that's hard to explain." Her smile returned. "You have to *see* it, even if you can't *understand* it. It's ridiculously important that you do."

The cyborg dropped cross-legged to the grass and beheaded a cluster of dandelions. She gripped the stems in one hand, the other poised over the yellow crowns like a bird of prey.

"Let's take stock. You're with a monster clone assassin thingy who kidnapped you across the universe."

Three fingers plucked a flower and tossed it behind her.

"One reading your mind, the minds of everyone around her, as well as times past and future."

Pluck and toss.

"Every now and again, she murders little babies."

Toss, toss, toss. Grin.

"I can see all this causing disquiet."

She took my hand, pulled herself up, and dragged me to the top of the hill.

"Where are we going?"

"Look, just look!" She gestured over the endless expanse of fields. "Over there—" she pointed near the stream, "—is a pile of cosmic gel I fished out of my girl parts. *Disgusting*. How does that figure here? It's all averaged out in tens of thousands of square miles where all the noise disappears. Instead, the big picture. It's a giant food carpet unsustainably managed for a planet with an energy resource problem."

"Kloan, what—"

"Shhh!" She put her index finger against my translator. "*Our* big picture—Waythrel, it's more than *big*. It's the universe. It's *more* than our everything. Other everythings. It's universes after cosmoses. An infinite set with uncountable numbers of interdependent gestations. Totalities we can't reach. Macrocosms where the laws of physics are weird. Where mathematics doesn't add up. Where logic is *illogical*." She bounced, waving her arms like manic windmills. "Two plus two is *not* four in the big picture! Do you understand?"

"I do not, Kloan. I am sorry."

"Yeah, well, I don't either. But I can *see* it. A billion tangents, a trillion loops to take. One after another. Everything that can happen will. It's not about *what happens*. Nothing ever occurs here after it does. It's what we take, what we *learn*, what we become."

"The journey is the reason, not the destination? I have heard this proverb many times."

"No! Of course, the destination matters. How stupid is that?" She shook her head. "You're not listening. It's not *what* we do in the passage, because we'll do all things. It's how we *evolve* from it. How it sums. The final path."

"Besides to insanity, you mean? Because I fear I have foolishly entered a bottomless labyrinth that will break my mind."

"Yeah, maybe," she said, staring at me with the utmost sincerity. "But all the angels are mad, Waythrel—don't you know?"

She was off again, releasing my hands and striding back to the stream. Heading north, toward Ambra Dawn.

Chapter 17

How is it that hardly any major religion has looked at science and concluded, "This is better than we thought! The Universe is much bigger than our prophets said, grander, more subtle, more elegant?" Instead they say, "No, no, no! My god is a little god, and I want him to stay that way."

Carl Sagan

We found Ambra.

We rounded a curve of monotonous cornrows. A stereotypical white fence framed a house over a verdant carpet. The property was large, no other houses in the field of vision. The grass was lush with chlorophyll, the cells swelled with regular watering. Decorative shade trees launched skyward across the lawn. A row of pines served as a natural wind guard on the western end of the plot.

In the middle of the sea of green floated a tiny ball of red. Her hair hung in complete disarray, long and tangled, victimized by a child who had yet to focus much attention on her appearance. Her age matched our disguises. She was about seven years old, sporting a wrinkled, stained dress draped over a pair of blue jeans.

My mind reeled. I had been torn from her after years of struggle and loss. Imprisoned in this churning derangement captained by a godlike, transformed echo of Ambra. Chained to her unpredictable clone. The sight of her, innocent, unaware of her harrowing future—emotions overwhelmed. Affection coursed through my awareness. Against this warmth, an irrational current of ice fought. My eyestalks pivoted to the cyborg, fearing the worst.

"Relax, Xix," Kloan said, skipping forward down the road. "Been there, done that. I need to learn so much here and destroy something else."

I could not fathom why she would think such a response would help me remain calm. I raced behind, catching Kloan as she stopped in front of the picket fence. She rested both elbows between the pointed tops of the boards.

"Hi!" she yelled over the lawn with an enormous grin.

Ambra gazed from the ground in our direction. Her hands were in the grass. "Hi," she said, her expression neutral.

Silence enveloped us as the pair stared at each other across the green field. I assumed we appeared as three young children socializing in a pastoral scene. Our true forms would have terrified anyone watching.

The quiet continued. Neither of the two spoke or moved, yet neither acted uncomfortable or unsure. At last, Ambra rose, her palms cupped together like clamshells. She threw her windswept hair behind her with a flip of her head, puffing recalcitrant strands out of her face.

"Want to see a bug?"

"Yes!" said Kloan.

Before I could react, the clone scaled the fence and landed roughly on her feet. She raced toward her progenitor.

I had not thought through the strange disguises our mysterious handlers had foisted on us. I appeared every bit the small child. My real form was something else. Towering over two meters, I weighed several times the average human adult. I also possessed far more appendages with greater sensitivity.

Climbing the barrier presented an interesting puzzle. Would this magical camouflage simulate structure as well as visuals? I could not think of how it could happen. Of course, I did not understand most of the technology of our powerful puppet masters. It was possible such a complete simulation might be within their abilities. My appearance could be matched with the mass and dimensions of a seven-year-old Earth child.

I dared not risk it. I took the long way around the fence to the open front gate and crossed the field toward the pair. They huddled together, examining something between them.

"Hurry, Waythrel," yelled Kloan. "Before it flies off!"

I lumbered forward, exhausted from the walk, the humidity, and the stress of the constant unknowns. I sat on the ground beside them.

We stared at a bug.

"It's a watermelon beetle," said Ambra. "We don't get too many here. This one is really late. Summer's nearly over."

The insect was over an inch long, thick and heavy. She placed it on her dress. She kept a fingertip pressed on its back and allowed it to shuffle up her chest.

"See, look, it has all these stripes. Dad says they can eat up the roots of trees and the corn, so I'll have to show him." She grabbed it between her index finger and thumb. The small creature hissed.

"Wow, what's that?" asked Kloan.

Ambra beamed. "Really neat, right? They hiss at you, like a cat. I guess it's mad."

She held the beetle to her face and stared at it. The bug was beating its wings as it spat again.

"Found it by the oak tree. Maybe it's already laid eggs." Her eyes flashed to the cyborg. "You're not from here, are you?"

A loaded question, huh, Waythrel?

"No, we're visiting," she said.

Ambra glanced back and forth between us. Her eyes stopped on me for some time. "You're really different."

Kloan's thoughts spoke again. *Her Reader powers are awake. She senses us.*

I wasn't sure what to say. I hoped she could not discern much about our true forms. I mustered my best. "I'm a good friend."

She turned to her clone. "Who are you?"

"My name is Kloan."

"Like Joan. But not."

"Exactly."

She returned to her bug again, tapping its wings, chanting in a singsong voice, "Like up but down. Like yes but no. Kloan and Joan are all alone."

"And heaven's sewn," said Kloan, their eyes meeting.

Ambra squinted. "Where are your parents?"

"Where do you think?"

The watermelon beetle hissed again.

"I don't think you have them." She glanced away. "I think you're fairies."

"Maybe we are."

Ambra moved in close, her expression conspiratorial. "Do you want to sleep over tonight?" Her eyes bored into each of ours. "I won't tell my mom and dad. I know you have to be secret. I can sneak you in the back door later if you hide in the corn."

Kloan tilted her head. "Where will we stay?"

Ambra's hands danced around her face. "In my room. We don't have to be there all night. Fairy magic is in the night! We can go play in the crops. You can show me things."

"You will need to sleep," I offered.

She frowned and stood. "I don't like sleeping." She was like so many children.

"We can have fun tomorrow. Sometimes you have to rest."

She continued to stare off into the distance.

Kloan shook her head. "It's not about playing." Silence. "She doesn't want to dream."

Ambra gaped at her with broad eyes, her eyebrows high. She stared at her until a tear rolled down her left cheek. "I knew you were fairies."

Chapter 18

The illusion of the passage of time arises from the confusing of the given with the real. The passage of time arises because we think of occupying different realities. In fact, we occupy only different givens. There is only one reality.

Kurt Gödel, as quoted

To avoid her parents' eyes, she led us around the front lawn beside the fence. The route first took us farther from the house. As we entered the cornfields, Ambra doubled back toward the structure. How she navigated in the towering seed crops was a mystery. Her Reader powers were still nascent and raw. It was more likely her childhood experience in these plant labyrinths. Whatever the source of her infallible sense of direction, she was joyous as she ran through the rows.

"The corn is as high as an elephant's eye, an' it looks like its climbin' clear up to the sky," she sang. Often, she returned to retrieve us as we failed to keep pace, taking our hands and leading us forward at a run.

At times, she would stop and point out something about the crops. A towering shoot. Malformed stalks. She delighted at the maturing ears on the majority of the plants.

"Dad thinks we'll have them early this year, end of September."

Through small breaks in the tassels, we discerned the top of a two-story home.

As we approached, Ambra held her finger to her lips. "You never know where Dad's gonna be. So be quiet now. I'll go in and see where they are and come back."

She darted forward through the maize and disappeared. Kloan inhaled, her eyes gleaming. I fought again to understand this creature.

"Is this environment one you respond to favorably? Is there some component of your shared genetics predisposing you to comfort here?"

"I hate corn," she said, her grin unwavering.

It was hopeless.

"Yet you seem so pleased with things."

She sighed and turned to me. "I'm *learning*. Understanding the heart of Ambra Dawn in every little thing that happens in this place. That's what this is all about, Waythrel."

"Why?"

"Remember the data I mentioned? We're collecting reams, and me more than you. Because the ultimate purpose demands the deepest and most personal comprehension. An insight transforming my person in loving and hating another sentient creature."

"How can apathy be important? How can hatred go with affection?"

Kloan rocked on her tiptoes and stared into my eye cluster. "Does love exist without its antithesis? Can you conceive of empathy in the absence of cruelty? Is this reality complete lacking the Anti?"

Our metaphysical conversation ended as Ambra came bursting through the stalks. She wore a backpack across her shoulders and bent double to catch her breath.

"Sit down, let me show you." Her excitement was infectious.

We followed her lead and sat beside the corn. I balanced against one shoot, and the seven-foot-high plant tilted to the ground. Perhaps my true mass was indeed reflected in events on this world.

"We're baking like crazy for my aunt's visit tomorrow. Aunt Aideen came all the way from Ireland. She's never been here. Mom's going nuts. Dad hates hosting, and he's already grumpy about the whole thing. He's in the basement hiding, working on his carving." Our blank stares prompted her to continue. "He makes these little animal totems from wood with a knife. He's pretty good. When he gets upset, he always goes down there. A few hours later, up comes some owl head or turtle." She smiled.

"What's in the bag?" asked Kloan.

"Yes!" She untied the top of the pack and pulled out two things. One was a wooden globe, carved in detail with the continents of Earth in relief. "Dad made it for me when I started school. This one took him a whole week, and he got all these maps and globes to get it right. It's my favorite toy of all, and I'm never going to lose it."

I raised the other object she had brought. It was a hollow metal cylinder with a flue cut into the surface near one end. A dog's head decorated the other.

"Is this a musical instrument?" I asked.

"No. Maybe it looks a little like a flute," she said, turning the device in her hand. "But watch!"

She placed it to her mouth and formed a seal, blowing hard. Her cheeks puffed like a blowfish.

My acoustical disks reverberated with the high-frequency sound. It was not painful, but loud and piercing to my senses.

Kloan shook her head. "I don't hear anything."

Ambra put her index finger to her lips. "Wait."

Within half a minute, a series of thrashes sounded in the corn. From behind, a furry mammal rocketed through the air and landed in her arms. The dog licked her, overjoyed to be in her presence.

"This is Matt!" she said, trying to speak over the creature that was all over her face. The animal rested momentarily and noticed us for the first time. How well would our disguises fool its olfactory senses?

"He can tell you're not little girls."

Indeed, it appeared confused, sniffing us from a distance. It did not react with fear, but was not comfortable with the two of us, especially me. How would a Xix smell to a dog?

"He's a Sheltie and smart. I taught him all these tricks with the whistle. Watch."

She blew different rhythms through the instrument. To each, it would perform one of a number of rehearsed motions. Sitting, begging, shaking hands, rolling, pointing. The list went on. I remembered from our years together the love she had for this creature.

"Ambra, how old are you?" I asked.

"I'm seven," she said, flipping several treats to the animal from her backpack.

Matt would die next year. In spring, when the storms came, she would have a dream in which the dog perished. The real death transformed her nightmares into prophecy, convinced her she was cursed with a terrible power. One she did not want or understand.

The visions would increase in amplitude and frequency, beauty and horror. The carefree young child before us would become a withdrawn, troubled preteen. One to be snatched from her home by Dram agents after they murdered her parents.

"I better get back," she said, stuffing all her things into the bag. "Mom's gonna kill me. I'm supposed to be helping." She leaped up and gazed at us. "You're really fairies?"

Kloan gave a thumbs-up sign.

"You'll wait for me to come back tonight, after everyone is asleep?"

"Yes," I said, my heart breaking for the future awaiting her.

"Okay. This is so incredible!"

"Ambra!" A loud call from a female. Cleena Dawn sounded irritated.

"Gotta go. Please be here."

She turned and sprinted back toward the house, the small dog dashing behind. We heard a firm voice chastising her as a door slammed shut.

Kloan lay back in the dirt and put her hands behind her head, staring at the sky. Her green eyes sparkled in the sunlight.

"Take a rest, Waythrel. Now we wait."

Chapter 19

I used to wonder how it comes about that the electron is negative. Negative-positive—these are perfectly symmetric in physics. There is no reason whatever to prefer one to the other. Then why is the electron negative? I thought about this for a long time and at last all I could think was "It won the fight!"

Albert Einstein

Night fell without incident. Kloan and I sat in the cornfield, silent as the chatter of night creatures grew. The light above faded until a scattered stardust littered the sky. We attuned to the sounds emanating from the house. The metal pops of pots and pans from cooking and cleaning. The crackle of hot oil. Doors to the outside opening and closing. Watering systems activated.

Over time these diminished. After a number of hours, silence spilled from the human habitat. Soon after this, Ambra returned to us.

A beam from a flashlight darted back and forth across the corn rows and approached. The stalks parted, and the child stepped before us with a glint in her eye.

"Look, it's a full moon tonight!" she said, pointing.

The bright radiance of the planet's satellite overtook the stars as it climbed.

"It's a night for fairy magic!" She paused and sat, opening a basket. "I brought dinner, if you're hungry."

The cyborg leaned forward and peered inside. "Bread rolls, fruits, and cheese."

"Yes, is it okay? I don't know what fairies eat." She frowned at her lack of knowledge.

"Watch this," said Kloan.

She waved her hand over the collection. The flaps opened on their own, as if by invisible wires. Ambra gasped and squealed. She put her hands to her mouth as several of the biscuits and plums floated into the air. The food performed acrobatic tricks, weaving through intricate choreographies.

The clone relished every expression of amazement and joy that escaped from her progenitor. Had she not been clinical in her purpose, I could have believed she wanted the child happy. Her eyes held an empathetic engagement. Her smiles were not forced or false. Nothing made sense with this creature.

The *fairy magic* entertainment went on for some time. We walked across the cornfields to a little stream. There, Kloan indulged in astounding telekinetic manipulations of water.

Despite her interest and fascination, as the hours passed, the seven-year-old Ambra tired. Her mind turned from the wizardry. She chatted about her life and thoughts. Her eyes half closed, but she exerted a fierce will to avoid sleep.

After light chatting, I dared to broach the subject. "Why are you afraid of dreaming?"

Silence fell, quieter than a lack of conversation. She held her breath.

"It is okay. You do not have to tell me if you do not want to."

"I don't want to."

I flipped several eyes in her direction and saw she had curled into a small ball.

"Unless you think we can do something," said Kloan.

Please be careful.

"How can you do anything?" She side-eyed us.

"Fairy magic is miraculous. But we need to know more."

Enough with information gathering. If it is too difficult for her, let her be.

Ambra wrapped her arms around her legs in a manner mirroring the cyborg's postures. The symmetry stunned and unnerved me.

"You promise you can help?"

"No. I can't until I know the problem. We *can* do many things."

She weighed a decision in her unusual, seven-year-old mind. "I have dreams. They're awful. Well, some are nice, but some are so bad —I can't tell my parents anymore. They don't like to hear about them." She took a deep breath. "The worst is the Demon Man." She was silent for more than a minute, staring off into the dim cornstalks.

"Who is he?" I asked.

"I don't know!" she moaned, turning her head to her shoulder, tears welling in her eyes. "I don't know who he is. I don't know what he is. I think...it feels like he's not human. He's a monster. He's something else."

Kloan leaned forward and touched her knee. "What does he do in your dreams?"

Ambra sobbed, the words garbled through her gasps for air. "He comes here, always here, with tall things, dark shadows, and they creep through the house and lawn. My mom and dad scream!" She shook. "I can't see them because I'm running out of the house and through the corn. Monsters come after me, and all the smoke of them turns into a black wolf and it's chasing me!"

She threw her arms around the cyborg and cried several minutes. I gazed in dread, familiar with the events her visions foretold. Her kidnapping. Her parents murder. Her life forever changed. In the Anti's push to study all aspects of her life, Kloan no doubt knew the details as well. It had been difficult to hear the adult speak of this period. It was heartrending to watch the small child weeping yet blind to the full horror coming.

She wiped her tears and steadied herself. "It always catches me. It has razor fangs and needles in its mouth, and it grabs my head and cuts and cuts and cuts and eats my brain out."

She's seen so much of it, came the cyborg's thoughts.

Ambra laid back roughly on her back. The constellations blazed, the moon having set in the late hours of the night. She exhaled. "I'm going up there. To the stars. Aren't I?"

"That's right," said Kloan.

"You're not Earth fairies, are you? You're from up there."

"We are," I added.

She closed her eyes. "So, can you help?"

"Yes," said her copy, "with some of it."

I stared in astonishment. *What are you promising her?*

Her eyes snapped open. "How?"

"In two ways. Tonight is the first way. I'll make you sleep without the dreams. I will use our magic to give you peace the remainder of the night, and the Demon Man won't come."

The relief in Ambra's eyes struck me as a blow.

"When you wake tomorrow, we'll talk of one other thing we can do. But not until you rest."

She grasped both our hands and pressed them to her heart. "You're the best friends ever."

Kloan eased her backward. "Lie down now."

She complied. The Anti's assassin closed her eyes and held her palms together like a prayer. For some time, nothing happened, and we stared at her in puzzlement.

Darting glows. First one or two at a time. More followed in streams. Rivers of radiance. Aggregating in a dizzying, blurring ball of dashing light.

"Fireflies!" said Ambra. "So many. They're usually sleeping now."

"I woke them." The orb of dancing stars floated above us. "It's a lamp. For the night."

The hundreds of insects danced in a small sphere the size of a child's balloon. Ambra passed her hand through it. The air at the edges shimmied and refracted the firefly glow as if through rippling water.

"Amazing," she said.

"Sleep now," said the cyborg. "Trust me."

To my surprise, she did. She was near to collapse from exhaustion, anyway. The soothing words, the hope for a peaceful night pulled her down like a drug to the ground.

But it was more than that. My Reader senses detected distortions in spacetime. I surmised Kloan was already manipulating Ambra's mind.

Are you really doing this? Can you?

Yes. Let me concentrate. Her sentience is many-layered.

So I waited. Five minutes later, the sleeping child's breaths were heavy.

Kloan leaned back, fatigued. "The universe runs wild through this one," she said.

"Are you surprised?" I asked.

"No, but I'm tired."

Practical problems assaulted me. "We will need to carry her back into the house, somehow avoid disturbing the family or the pet."

"No, leave her to rest. She needs it, and I don't want my efforts ruined with too much disturbance."

"Her parents..."

She spoke through a yawn. "They'll come looking for her and find their strange daughter napping under the stars. I doubt it's the weirdest thing they've dealt with."

"We can keep vigil, wake her when they begin to search and hide ourselves."

"Yes, but I'm not a Xix. I'll sleep, too. You have the watch. It's a few hours until dawn anyway."

Kloan did not wait for my response. She dropped to her side and rested her head on her arm, shutting her eyes. Despite her fatigue, I could not let her disappear into slumber.

"Why did you do this?"

Her drowsy voice was a thread above a whisper. "Do what?"

"Such kindness. Insight and empathy. One moment you are cold, murderous. Another you see toward the heart of another better than I. Act with love on the knowledge. *What are you?*"

She yawned again. "God, Waythrel, do we have to do this now?" She turned on her back, facing the stars. "It won't make sense. You will never completely understand me. I'll never comprehend either of you, but I must probe all those elements of discord."

"Why?"

"To become what she is not. In all possible ways." She rolled over to the other side, away from me. "An inverse. A true, sentient transposition. That's my destiny. Look, don't think about it tonight."

"You're right, I am confused. Opposite in consciousness?"

Her exasperated thoughts sounded in my mind. *You Xix never let go!*

"You can't grasp it yet. You've not even come to terms with basic physics—that the Anti *exist*. If one of the Anti were in front of you now and didn't blow everything up, what would it look like?"

"Like any other living being, with its own parameters, morphology."

"Bingo. Anti-water looks like water. Anti-stars look like stars. Antiparticles likewise, with a special inverse. So, particles and fields are the essence of sentience. Don't you see, Waythrel? There have to be anti-thoughts, anti-minds, anti-ideas that are the same yet *different.*"

"Like hate and love?"

"No!" She rolled over and glared at me. "You're better than that. Not so simplistic and one-dimensional. Those are mere vectors. If you flip a 3D object in two dimensions, it's all wrong. If you invert consciousness with such a low dimensionality, smash! It's not an inverse; it's a mess!"

"You're right," I said. "Those are concepts unconsidered by any science I have encountered in the galaxy."

She flipped away from me again. "I must learn these ways. Become them in the context of Ambra Dawn. Her opposite."

The last words struck me. I now had a small inkling of what this might mean, but a little knowledge is dangerous. A vast landscape of meaning peeked over a horizon I had not considered. The purpose eluded me.

"Why?"

"Waythrel!" she growled. "It's the whole point of all this. Now shut up. Let Kloan sleep."

I sat still, and within seconds, the clone was sleeping alongside her progenitor. I glanced back and forth between the two children, Kloan and Ambra, Ambra and Kloan. One a naive, yet jading, Earth girl. The other a jaded, yet divinely naive, abomination of tubes and wires and indoctrination.

Inverses?

My eyes drank the star-filled heavens. Something profound, something important, something frightening was escaping my grasp. Despite my efforts, I could not bring it into focus. On the horizon of my awareness the monstrous and beautiful lurked. For now, I knew it only as distant rumor.

It rumbled like a thundercloud beyond my comprehension.

Chapter 20

Go to the edge of the cliff and jump off. Build your wings on the way down.

Ray Bradbury

"**A**mbra!"

The calls floated above the early morning mist and cricket sounds. I shook the pair, and they both woke, startled.

The mother's voice was particularly close. "Where are you?"

"Oh *no!*" hissed Ambra, throwing her things into her pack and stumbling upward. "I have to go! Mom's going to *kill* me!"

She darted to the wall of stalks and spun, staring at her disguised copy. "It worked. Last night. Your promise. What about the other one?"

Kloan croaked through a smile. "Meet us down by the stream. Follow the fireflies."

She bobbed her head and dashed off. The morning sounds transitioned into angry and joyous shouts from her parents.

"We should not be so close," I offered.

"For sure."

She stood and stretched, and we moved away from the house. Not being of Earth, all my instincts for navigation struggled. The clone used her own special powers. I did not doubt she could explore the world at all levels of detail. The cyborg led, and again I followed.

She brought us to a small stream, and we sat under a tree as she dozed again for some time. I did not know how much the Anti had altered the basic human brain physiology. Whatever machinery they had added could not remove the need for sleep.

"She'll come again in the night," she muttered while resting against the broad trunk. "Her parents won't let her leave the house today because of last evening. Wake me at sunset."

Kloan slept straight through the entire day. She stirred for short moments. To turn to one side or the other. Mumble through her dreams.

"It's going to be a hard night, Waythrel," she said during one such waking, my leaky thoughts caught in her net. "I need to charge up." She gave no other explanation.

While she dozed, I entered a Xixian trance, conserving resources in quiet contemplation. Xix do not sleep, not in the sense Earth mammals do. We purge the metabolic waste products of our brain clusters and balance their neural networks from the day's experiences. However, our recovery states are more efficient than your own. They are also under conscious control. We do not dream.

The day passed in this way. The sun set, and I woke her. She removed some of Ambra's bread from her robes. "It's too bad I can't eat this."

"Why not?" I asked.

"Upsets my stomach. I'd offer you some," she said, "but I know you can't process human food. Are you hungry, Waythrel? Metabolism hunky-dory?"

"Yes, for a few more days. Afterward, it will become a problem."

"We'll be gone after tonight, and everything will reset."

"Do you mean—"

"She's coming!" she cried and sprang to her feet.

In the direction she stared, a pale glow grew. A will-o'-the-wisp bobbed through the cornrows accompanied by a mashing of footsteps. Through the stalks burst another sphere of firefly light and Ambra Dawn.

"I made it!" she said, amazed with herself. "They're asleep, but I put a ball and stuffed clothes in my bed in case they check."

Kloan gave a thumbs-up. "Perfect."

"I love the fireflies." Ambra's smile faded. "How can you help me?"

"Let's talk about the Demon Man."

She released a long breath and held her hands together near her stomach. "Okay."

"Do you know why you see him in your nightmares? Because your dreams predict the *future*."

Wait! She was so reckless!

"No—" said Ambra, shaking her head and stepping back.

"You have enormous powers, and they're waking up. You'll see many things. He's one of them."

"No, it's not true." Two more steps back. Her eyes were wide.

Kloan, stop! This is too sudden. She needs years to come to terms with this.

"Because it's true—the Demon Man isn't a dream. He is real. He's coming to get you. He'll come here. He will kill your parents."

Ambra moaned.

"He'll take you to a place where they'll cut open your head and slice up your brain."

"*No!*" She screamed and ran to the cornfield.

"Stop!" said Kloan.

Ambra crashed into an invisible wall of jelly. It absorbed her momentum and prevented her passage, deflecting her fists as she pounded on the structure.

"*No!*"

"You've *seen* all this, Ambra!" Kloan cried, raising her voice over the small child's mantra of denial. "You don't want to face it."

This was torture. The cyborg had deceived me again and had turned helping Ambra into another occasion to harm her. I didn't know what twisted psychological experiment she was conducting. Why it was important to the universe. I did not care if the god-Ambra was on board with this suffering. *I was not.* I had to intervene.

"No point, Waythrel," she said.

I could not move or speak. Ambra had stopped her futile pounding on the barrier. She crumbled into a ball, mucus covering her upper lip, tears dripping from the sides of her face.

Kloan walked to her and crouched. "You can't hide from it forever. But we *can* save you from it."

What are you doing?

"How?"

She took Ambra's hands. "We'll go to the warehouse."

Ambra shuddered and turned away.

"Visit the labs and find the Demon Man. Kill him. Then burn everything to the ground."

Ambra gawked. She focused on me to gain verification of this incredible proclamation. "Kill him?"

"Kill all of them, destroy the entire place, until nothing remains."

Ambra pushed against the bizarre force field, studying it, not seeking escape. "You can do this?"

More than anyone, I knew it was within the powers of this clone.

"Yes, if you want it. If you can face your fear and stop hiding from what you know is true, then come with us to the labs. I promise you, by the sunrise, there will be nothing left but smoke and dust. Not even bones."

I projected my thoughts, trying to get a word in this conversation.

You are asking a young child to approve a slaughter. A massacre and destruction. It should not be her burden.

The cosmos has not asked what burdens she deserves. It has placed them on her. Open your mind, Waythrel.

Ambra glared at the stars. "It's all true, isn't it? I don't want the truth." She whipped toward Kloan and sandwiched the clone's head in both hands. "I'll come. You'll take me there?"

Kloan didn't flinch. "Yes."

"And you'll burn it to the ground?"

They locked eyes. My restraints vanished. I stepped forward, but didn't know what to say or do.

"Let's go," said Ambra, and she rose. "Which way?"

Chapter 21

Insanity is relative. It depends on who has whom locked in what cage.

Ray Bradbury

"We'll fly like Peter Pan," said Kloan, and with those words, we took to the skies.

The three of us rose over the cornfields in the light of a gibbous moon. Ambra squealed as we soared. The air chilled, plots of land and houses rushing below at increasing speeds until they became a blur. I could see the narrative building within the young girl, of fairies and magic, of flying to face a dark nemesis.

How do you know where to go? I asked Kloan.

It isn't far, her thoughts replied. *I've been searching the past and the minds involved. It wasn't difficult.*

Will you do this thing?

What do you think, Waythrel?

Twinkling towns passed us on either side. Highways like glowing vasculature radiated across the plains. I could not judge our velocity. We sped fast enough that the cyborg must have blocked the airflow.

Although the ground raced by, it was the mildest of cool breezes stirring us. Ambra was captivated. She said nothing, staring downward or to the clouds with watering eyes and a grin.

I also lost myself in the wondrous journey. It was reminiscent of the travels with the Daughter in a relative future that would bring me back to this past. Memories of the mission to shut the Time Tree. The strange spacetime bubble cocooning a mixed team traversing alien landscapes. The images of my memory were overlaid with the present flight. Visions of another life and an altered universe.

We slowed over a dark and undeveloped expanse. Ahead, a pool of light broke the monotony of the emptiness. To this isolated patch we descended. Artificial lamps revealed an extended warehouse. Enormous power generators studded one end of the complex. Long and short-range radar antennae rose like trees around it. We had reached a node of the Dram hegemony on Old Earth.

Our feet touched the dusty ground in front of a main entrance to the building. Razor wire and electrified fences surrounded us. Hundreds of cameras and motion detectors monitored the area. Ambra would not be able to avoid detection without our *dark suits*. While I studied the compound, I mulled the violation I felt from this field imposed over my body. Yet here and now, I wished all three of us had them. I feared it was already too late.

We're not going for subtlety, my dear Xix.

The wonder of the flight had vanished.

Ambra shook, her face slack as she spoke. "This is it. It's bigger in the dreams."

Engines rumbled and tires squealed. Vehicles approached from every side. Floodlights blasted our position, and a loud, amplified voice barked commands.

"Don't move! Identify yourselves or face hostile action!"

Ambra whimpered, her body pressing against ours. "Don't let them take me."

The cyborg stepped forward, waving to the armored hulks. "Hi! I'm Kloan! This is Waythrel of Xix on my left and Ambra Dawn on my right. One's from an alien world at war with your masters. The other is the future failed messiah of this galaxy. And we're prepared for hostile action!"

Vehicles imploded like crushed soda cans to the horrific harmony of mashed bodies and screams. The compacted chunks were flung from us and shook the ground as they bounced across the compound.

She clapped her hands, and a blinding glare flashed from the other end of the warehouse. A loud explosion drummed our ears as the generators detonated into the sky. Brilliant flares impacted the installation like a meteor shower.

The lights of the facility extinguished. Emergency batteries jolted backup lamps. Kloan walked toward the entrance bathed in a flickering radiance.

"Oh my God," said Ambra.

Her face held the horror of what was happening, and I pitied her for it. A furious hope replaced the shock, a steely resolve driving her forward. She ached to slay this dragon.

Mounted weaponry dropped from the ceiling in front of the door and released a barrage of metal. High-caliber projectiles hurled from machine-guns ricocheted away from an invisible umbrella. The weapons found themselves ripped from their anchors and slung to the side.

The doors exploded inward to terrified screams. Dust billowed through the hallway from shattered cement. Figures in white lab coats dashed for shelter in the failing lights as soldiers rushed our trio. Our clone assassin flung their bodies against the walls. Some dropped to the ground as if they had suffered a sudden stroke.

We crossed medical research facilities. Kloan dispatched any resistance but spared those avoiding us. We passed many rooms with hospital charts posted outside. Children diffused from their chambers. Some ran to the exits. A host followed us, drawn onward by the cataclysmic events, unable to turn away.

"Down this hall," whispered Ambra. "At the end."

The crowd huddled in back of us. Some fled at this point, too afraid to approach whatever waited our arrival. The lights along the ceiling had shorted out. Popping sparks rained over our movements, strobing the pack we led toward a last door.

"Ambra?" Kloan stepped aside and motioned for her to open the door.

Was this a final trick? Whoever cowered behind the door, he had secured himself. Would Ambra catch the full frontal assault through this ruse of Kloan's?

Stop, Waythrel. She's facing her fear. And yes, I am observing the process. I don't do charity work.

Ambra approached the door and turned the knob, pushing it in with a determined thrust.

Inside was the Demon Man.

Except as most nightmares in the light of day, he was less monster and more man. A man of substantial cruelty, no doubt—power hungry, lost in mastering the game extraterrestrials had laid out for humanity. A balding, short, and now frightened wreck.

Kloan grabbed Ambra's hand, and they entered together. I followed while a gaggle of children peered from behind the doorframe.

Inside was an office, simple, bare but for a desk and a computer. He did not care much for decorations or personalizing. He did have one remaining response in the form of two towering Dram soldiers on his right and left. The insects aimed weapons in our direction.

"Whoever you are, you will die for this," he said with anger and a pure sense of certainty.

They fired on us. Another fireworks display erupted. The beams rebounded like a prismatic spray. The rays shattered into a thousand colorful needles setting fire to wood and paper. They ignited the ceiling tiles and burned blisters into the skin of the man behind the desk. He yelped in pain. The soldiers advanced, flashing bladed devices.

"Don't bother," said Kloan.

The creatures screamed as their exoskeletons ripped from their flesh. Brown fluids spilled from their forms as they fell to the ground, clawing at the carpet. She let them thrash and shoved them against the walls with invisible hands.

"My God, what are you?" The Demon Man trembled, cradling a blistered arm across his chest.

"You really should choose your victims with more forethought," Kloan mocked him. "Poor girl here. She could see into the future. Predict you would do terrible things to her because she's a Reader in your jurisdiction. So, because of a recursive time loop that won't release us—created by none other than her transcendental evolution—we traveled back into the past and decided to help her destroy this place. That's the now. Which means your time's up."

He scowled. "You speak nonsense."

"I usually do. Now...die."

Without a drop of spilled blood or a cry, the man fell to the ground, unmoving.

I rushed and examined him for a heartbeat. "He's dead," I said.

Ambra wept. Tears, smiles, and horror all mingled together. She dropped to her knees and stared at the man. She was less than seven, a tiny child reduced to the rawest of emotions.

"Is he really?" she asked me. "I can't believe it."

"Yes," I said. "No pulse. Check for yourself."

She shook her head, satisfied. Ambra stood and hugged her clone.

"Not done yet!" said Kloan, a strange light in her eyes.

We swept back out of the complex, evacuating all the children. The scientists and techs who refused our summons were on their own. Their time left short. As we exited, the ground rumbled, and a searing flame lit the warehouse from behind.

"It sounds like a transport," I said.

"They have a landing pad for carting off the navslav recruits. Looks like we were blessed with a small Dram unit. They must have chickened out from what they saw."

A dark spacecraft offset by bright exhaust climbed into the night sky.

The cyborg pursed her lips. "Yeah. It's perfect."

The ship careened right and pitched. The engines roared, inducing a violent turn, and it plunged toward the earth.

"Kloan, it's going to crash!" I cried out.

The impact thundered. The craft vaporized the laboratory building. The metal melted, running like water. A mushroom cloud belched into the air.

At our distance, we should all have perished. While the landscape nearby smoked, the dust under our feet remained undisturbed. We did not feel heat from the raging fires.

The other children watched, astonished. Some of the older ones jumped for joy, many sitting on the ground, crying and disoriented. I spent the better part of an hour trying to comfort them as the pair stared into the flames.

"You did it," whispered Ambra as I returned. "You kept your promise. Not even their bones."

The flickering glare from the inferno danced across Kloan's features. Her mouth was set in a determined line. "Not even their bones."

She placed a hand on Ambra's shoulder.

"Now, you'll never go there, and the evil men won't hurt you."

Chapter 22

I said to the almond tree: "Speak to me of God," and the almond tree blossomed.

Nikos Kazantzakis

Green eyes in the darkness.

A night sky churned with stars. The patterns enigmatic. A soft breeze. Sounds of alien creatures.

Nausea from memories. Ripped and thrown from dream to nightmare. Timeline to worldline. Reality to the unreal. My eyestalks darted. They despaired of appraising the planet surface. The heavens. The figure of the girl rocking beside me.

Kloan sat with her knees tucked to her chin, hiding her head. Haunting lime eyes peeked over her kneecaps. Arms wrapped around her legs. She still hummed.

"Again?" I asked.

The child continued to rock and hum, ignoring my question. Desperation seized me. The humming stopped.

"Or never," she answered.

"Never?" My eyes swiveled. "You destroyed the Dram laboratories, where they took Ambra and altered her. Those labs made her what she is, what she became. However misguided their reasons, they changed the fate of the galaxy."

"No. Of a universe."

"You demolished it. What does this mean? What future, what reality, did this create? Where is the Daughter? What has happened to her?"

"She's everywhere. Everything's happened to her. And nothing."

The intubated, tattooed head cocked to one side, glowing eyes never leaving my form. Tendrils of her thought danced around my awareness.

"You keep probing my mind."

Her head remained at a forty-five-degree angle, peering from behind her right knee.

"Your thoughts leak over everything. You Xix are leaky-brains."

The child stood, catching me off guard. She approached, long, ragged clumps of crimson curls careening over her face.

"More experiments, Waythrel. I was skeptical, but the Anti always believed there were unstable nodes in time, and that this is one of them. So sure that, with the Earth facility destroyed, Ambra Dawn would not *become*. I kept telling the idiots, it's not *then* that you have to worry about her, but at the *beginning*."

The words slapped my consciousness. *From a dream.*

"Kloan, where are we?"

"Don't you know?"

I stood, examining the rugged landscape. A flat plain below. Lights of a city washing out the canopy of stars.

"We are back where we began. When you took me after Dram."

"When did we *begin*, Waythrel?"

I stared at the emerald orbs, disoriented. Memories treaded water in a blurred fog. I could no longer conclude what was real and what was in my mind.

"I am confused. What is happening? You seem to understand."

"That's *why* you're here. *Data.* The data to open the gate." She turned her back on me, walking down a steep slope. "Let's get started."

"With what? Where are you going?"

Kloan continued. Her words drowned in the wind and creature sounds.

"To where it all began for me. To watch the beginning flow around us and mature and twist through time and space to come back to be us. Then we'll be ready for the next step."

Starlight burned shadows into the sandy stones. The child vanished, swallowed in the darkness of the hill. I froze, trying to understand the madness of my own thoughts.

What was happening to me? What had happened, and what had not? Were these real experiences, *time loops*? If so, did it mean they actually occurred? If not, how could I remember them? If they *had* transpired, how could Ambra have *become* and therefore how could I have come here in the first place? Everything was a paradox!

Waythrel, come on!

Her tones trumpeted in my mind. My eyestalks curled on themselves. I shrank from the desolate space surrounding me.

What else was there to do?

Chapter 23

The opposite of a profound truth may well be another profound truth.

Niels Bohr

I chased the child. The dusty ground slipped under my feet. I slid and tripped, my four arms grasping the stones and alien vegetation. Why couldn't I get a decent grip?

It's a field around you, remember? Her thoughts danced through my mind. *It's skintight, coating your surfaces, insulating you from everything.*

Memories leapt through my mind. The strange sensation, her words, walking up the slope to a shining disk—*the gate.*

Rounding a mammoth rock, I stumbled upon her. Ragged rocks littered the terrain, the detritus of collapse from the unstable cliffs.

"The disguises. Cloaking. I recall—why do we have them?"

She peered below. A technological complex spread over dry lands. Transports blasted into orbit from the outskirts. Organized groups marched throughout the installation.

"For our protection."

"From what?"

Kloan pointed to the city. "That's where we start. What was this night? It must be a visitation, I'm sure of it. We'll go meet me there, and then you'll see what happens."

She stepped toward the compound, and I grabbed her, desperate for answers.

"Another clone facility?"

"Yes."

Déjà vu sickened me. "There is an attack. We cannot walk right into that place."

"There's no danger."

"They will kill any Xix they see."

"They won't see us. We're invisible, remember?"

I remembered...*something*. "*You* broke through Ambra's field. So can they."

Kloan shook her head. "Hers was simple. Primitive."

"Yours now is none of those things?"

"I told you, they're not *mine*. Now, come on."

The child pulled me forward. Helpless, my mind whirled. Events were suspect—now, before, those to come. I distrusted my own thoughts. Would I understand any of this madness?

We covered the distance between the broken hills and the installation. The flat landscape made my efforts far less exhausting. Rather than concentrate on each step, I observed the nearing fortification. It was unlike any city or technological society I had ever seen.

The minds shaping this world were more divergent than anything I had studied in all my travels. While strange, I had a sense it was not unknown to me. Humans populated the space. I saw no other species, no differing life-forms, but two classes: those who resembled Ambra Dawn and those who did not.

"The Anti run things with robots and trained people," Kloan added.

Sampling my *leaky* thoughts again.

"To avoid annihilation?"

"No, they aren't concerned about it here. It's more efficient. Once they optimized the program, it ran with drones and lackeys."

Approaching the complex, we observed armed, robotic sentinels floating by the gate. Unseen by their sensors, our cloaking tech remained impenetrable. Within, the activity of mechanized units revealed a discernible order.

"Machines do all the work," I said.

She lectured with little concern for discovery. "Clones require a societal framework. Interpersonal connections. Development hinges on social interaction. Without it, the brain's potential degrades. The essence of human neurophysiology. So the Anti imported them. It's a clone growth matrix."

"Like in the desert fields," I said, remembering the groups of cyborgs and humans.

"A beginning before the planet was destroyed."

"Dram is gone?" My mind stuttered.

"Blew themselves to bits in a stupid civil war. It didn't matter. They were an outpost."

"This is another one?"

"Maybe the last. They had to build them farther away. Find stronger clones for concealment. They're hunted across the cosmos by the devil ball."

"The what?"

Kloan grinned. "Your little Orbies. We had other names for them. Other thoughts. Come, you will see. You'll *learn*."

We traversed the city, an amalgam of foreign and familiar. We observed young Ambra Dawns and their cloned and human escorts. She gestured towards buildings and objects that held particular significance.

"Here are the wombs. Our birthplaces. Moms!" She winked. "Long ago, on Dram, the scientists realized gestation is crucial for neural development. In vitro attempts proved disastrous." A wide grin. "The notion of birth, rather than mere growth, is reassuring, is it not?"

Sarcasm from a cyborg. Unnerving. Nevertheless, I had begun to like this unsettling creature.

"What we saw on Dram was not reassuring, Kloan."

"The teachers are going to hate you," she said in a strange tone. "But we don't have time for lessons. We have to find the enclosure."

"What is that?"

"You remember, Waythrel," she said.

She grabbed my hand and yanked, sprinting across the compound. We reached a bizarre building unlike any of the others. External walls of deep black—obsidian—reflected little light. Churning electromagnetic fields pulsed around the structure.

"Home," she repeated. "Or quarantine. Take your pick."

Chapter 24

We cannot predict the new forces, powers, and discoveries that will be disclosed to us when we reach the other planets and set up new laboratories in space. They are as much beyond our vision today as fire or electricity would be beyond the imagination of a fish.

Arthur C. Clarke

"Yes, I remember." I stared at the prison they had engineered for the child. "To keep you and your powers under control."

"It was useful in the beginning, when I was very little. Come, I'll get us through the fields."

Kloan yanked, and the universe lurched. My vision fractured. Events surged and faltered, overwhelming my Reader senses. Unable to steady my flailing eyestalks, I lost focus. A tumult of images invaded my awareness. Grasping the wall beside me, I steadied myself and refocused.

A spartan room greeted us. A bed, table, toilet, and sink. No products for leisure. No children's toys. No books or electronic information sources. A single diode in the ceiling dispelled the night, washing the chamber in a soft tan.

Inside was a little girl. Perhaps aged five years, she sat at the edge of a mattress. Her eyes stared forward in a trance. It was a younger version of Kloan. More childlike, with less cranial modification. A decrease in the subcutaneous patterning gave this earlier stage clearer skin.

My eyes froze on the impossible thing floating above the ground. A vortex of milky light swirled in the center of the room. Spinning shapes boiled, *faces*, phantoms beneath the waves of a pearl sea. The forms were indistinct, too insubstantial and transient for me to identify.

One shape I could not help but recognize. The vapors coalesced around a central extrusion, a human face. The skull lay open, the brain filleted behind it and fading into the fog. Tubes and wires, dwarfing the insertions into Kloan, ravaged the head. Machine parts obscured the eyes. The mouth was free.

"Ambra."

The monstrosity of our desperate gamble to save the galaxy confronted me. My gaze shifted between the apparition and Kloan's distinct physical manifestations. The weight of the truth crushed me. My lover Synphel had warned us. We had triumphed by becoming our enemy.

The younger cyborg rose and walked to the seething impossibility.

"I'm a problem for the teachers. They're afraid of me."

"They will decide that you represent too much of a danger. The Anti will destroy you."

"They will fail," said the child.

"If it comes to conflict, yes. There are better paths. Continue your training. Follow what we have been teaching you. The time to leave will come soon."

"Today, they threatened me because I'm disturbing the planet's orbit."

"They do not understand your power source," said Ambra. "They cannot see the connections we have forged between you and the matrix of the continuum. But they begin to appreciate that you have transcended their program and dominion."

The room *shifted*. Vertigo gripped me. My eyestalks floundered. A whirlwind of visuals stormed through my consciousness.

"Waythrel, hold on to me."

Kloan grabbed my arm. The dizziness passed. My vision came under my conscious control.

Morning's light streamed through a transparent region of the quarantine field. Sounds of explosions and shouts echoed outside. The room was in disarray. Clothes strewn about, food and utensils as well. My olfactory strips detected a growing acrid smell. *Smoke.*

"The gate is prepared," said Ambra.

An older version of Kloan stood in front of the vortex. She was now, in all appearances, identical to the form beside me. Sweat beaded across her forehead. Her muscles tensed.

"I'm ready," she said.

"You must leave now. They will return with greater numbers of clones and more devastating weapons. They will force you to destroy them if you engage."

"I don't want to kill them. Lead me to the portal."

The tromp of rushing feet thundered from outside. A heavy rumbling accompanied them.

Ambra's ghostly form pivoted toward the door of the quarantine cell. "Through the door."

The black field that sealed the chamber gave way to a second churning whirlpool. It opened to span the width of the frame. Through it poured bright daylight. The city beyond her isolation unit vanished, replaced by a rocky landscape.

The countryside within the vortex extended to the limits of my vision. At the end of the tunnel was a worn path on a steep slope. The vegetation was eroded, the rocks smoother, the coloration of the terrain distinct. The walkway rose up the hillside and ceased at a broad disk. Sunlight gleamed off the surface. Blinding reflections bounced into the room and cast shadows on the floor.

Kloan pulled my arm, showing me that her temporal copy had entered the passage.

"The gate," she said.

I stumbled forward, blinded by the daggers of light glinting into the room. Outside, shouts added to the cacophony, and the walls began to smolder and glow a bright orange.

"Good luck, my dearest friend," said the apparition of Ambra Dawn as I stepped within the vortex.

My eyestalks bent backward to see the disembodied head turned toward me. Its motion sent ripples across the sea of blurred faces. Tears dripped from her eyes, coating the wires and tubes in her once-green irises. A bittersweet smile lined her face.

"I love you, Waythrel. Remember, whatever happens."

The room exploded.

Chapter 25

At first sight, nothing appears more obvious than that everything has a beginning and an end, and that everything can be subdivided into smaller parts. Nevertheless, for entirely speculative reasons the philosophers of Antiquity, especially the Stoics, concluded this concept to be quite unnecessary. The prodigious development of physics has now reached the same conclusion as those philosophers.

Svante Arrhenius

Fire and debris surged towards me, veiling the divine entity. The portal's closure spared me from annihilation.

High in the rugged terrain, profound silence replaced the turmoil. The faint rustling of pebbles and shrubs in sporadic winds broke the quiet. A trace of smoke remained, hinting at the devastation below.

Haunted by Ambra's parting words, I retreated from the vanished doorway. Kloan beckoned from the glowing gateway.

"Where is the clone?"

The child smiled. "She's right here."

For a moment I paused, confused, my mind still stunned from the violence.

"This is where you left. When you went to kidnap me."

"Mmm-hmm. I'm gone already through the gate, so I could come back with you. It's an elegant loop."

"It is madness. What is Ambra doing?"

Her shoulders slumped. "You aren't the only one tested, Waythrel. Each time's different. When we finally understand, we'll see the way." She turned toward the disk. "We come to the next step of our journey, again. Are you ready?"

Of course, I was not. But this was not the first time I had been asked this question in this precise location.

"We have been here before, just like this."

"Not *just* like, but have been and will be. But never *just* like. We're nested in temporal recursions that can't be unknotted or normalized."

"This strange concept is clarifying. We have not found a way out yet. Is this what you are calling hell?"

"One of them."

My eyestalks focused on Kloan. "There was more. There was a hope. To go *back*. To find Synphel."

"Yes," she said. "There was."

"Much more is happening, but I am not appreciating."

"You don't appreciate how much you do not appreciate."

I stared at the small bundle of aphorisms, the wind stirring her sparse hair and robes. "You are coming with me?"

"What other point is there?"

I turned my attention to the gate, fear and fatigue weighing on me. It was a cross-sectional slice of an Orb. I was sure of it now. The surface churned with myriad colors, a viscous honey. It felt like an acquaintance, long known and burdensome. Stars swam inside with no end. It pulled me as I gazed. Beautiful. Dreadful. An ever-hungry maw to devour me for eternity. I grasped the child's hand.

Kloan laughed. "Seems we'll always be dancing together, Xix."

My eyestalks wrapped around each other, the covering sheaths expanding, blocking out all light.

We walked into the gel.

Part IV

You brood of vipers! Who warned you to flee
the coming wrath? Your ways lead to the grave!
This faith in rationed rationality
is sweet opiate to which you are enslaved!

The opiate, a poison to our land,
to endless wars and deaths has given birth.
Our planet's blood we see stained on your hands!
In your unthinking path we find no worth.

Enlightenment we offer—cleanse your sins!
The Pierian spring will wash you clean.
Drink deep! or taste not truth we hold within!
Perhaps, indeed, our Way is for the keen.

For faith misplaced we hold a simple cure:
Baptized in reason, you will then be pure.

—Mazandarani, *Sonnets from the Desert*

Chapter 26

If the Lord Almighty had consulted me before embarking upon his creation, I should have recommended something simpler.

Alfonso X of Castile

We dangled in a kaleidoscope.

The gate drank our forms and spit us into a weightless, intangible nothingness. I spun devoid of tactile, auditory, or olfactory sensation. A swirling infinity of chromatic patterns oscillated to the edges of what a Xix could perceive. My body reflected the fountain of color. The gel matrix melded like lubricating oil with the colored nothing penetrating reality.

Kloan floated beside me, her eyes intense, expectant, and searching this strange space. I tried to speak, but no sounds escaped the translator. Was there no atmosphere to propagate the vocalizations?

I reached out mentally. *Where are we?*

Limbo, whispered her thoughts in my mind.

Please. Clear answers for a change. Can we survive here? There is no air!

We're suspended. In stasis, Waythrel. No need to breathe. No needs. We aren't anything and yet are not nothing. We are between.

Has the gate failed?

No, I don't think so. It sent us someplace specific. We're trapped in an Orb.

Inside? I had traversed the Time Sphere several times. My kidnapping by the creature floating beside me the most recent. In none of those traversals had the portal presented such an appearance.

Because you were locked in defined world lines. This is different. This limbo is without direction in space or in time.

That does not make sense.

Do the Orbs make sense to you, Waythrel? Do you understand them?

Of course, I did not. No being, no species in our galaxy understood the Orbs. Or, rather, the one, true Sphere. I did not comprehend the connection between Ambra's godlike Group Mind and the objects, either.

That again? Why won't you accept the obvious?

Which is?

Occam's razor: among competing hypotheses, we select the one with the fewest assumptions.

It is not possible.

What you think is likely isn't part of Occam's razor. Explanations may come later, or be beyond you. What explains all the data in the simplest way?

The Orb is Ambra.

Finally.

Everything pointed toward this conclusion, but I could not grasp it. No, I could not accept it. The Orbs were ancient, older than the oldest life in our galaxy. How could the mad plan we set in motion billions of years afterward have anything to do with that?

Silly Xix. How could the Daughter save Earth from a Dram aster-

oid? How could she explore the before and implant ideas into long-dead people?

Kloan, it is one thing to imagine traveling a short distance in time. Even manipulating history. Whatever the recursive nightmares and infinities in prediction it might involve. This is different. How could we of the far future engender an entity existing near the beginning of the universe? One guiding the development of intelligent life? I am limited to how much suspension of causality I can maintain.

You have to get off the one-dimensional train, Waythrel. Reality is a sticky mud splashing in too many directions to count. Past, what's to come, the now, all poking and prodding each other and shaping a clay that's not in *time but* of *time—Oh, look!*

Her strong thoughts slapped my mind, and I reoriented my attention. The endless curtains of light and color split. A spherical disruption refracting the dancing chromatics grew in size as it approached. In the bubble were two humanoid figures. One lay supine, a female, her black dress and long red hair immediately identifying her. The other was a larger male in recognizable battle armor, resting on his side.

Nitin and Ambra. What are they doing here?

The sphere neared, and we passed unhindered through its surface. Inside was air, regulated temperature, a structure on which I could stand. I knew where we were. It was the spacetime enclosure the Daughter had created for our mission. I tried to ignore the gel goo reasserting its presence.

"We can talk now," said Kloan, and she approached the pair. "Still limbo, you know."

The colors continued to wash over us. "What happened to them?"

She touched them, recoiling from her progenitor. "Something *very* strange with her. Powerful. I can't penetrate. Her body and mind are diverged. Not here or there. Not now or before or later. I can't reach her. Yet she lives."

"Nitin?"

She crouched beside his head. "Sleeping. A deep sleep induced by others. We could wake him. He has interesting dreams."

I walked alongside the cyborg and stared down at the two forms. Neither appeared injured. Both matched my memories from our final mission.

"This is *after*," said Kloan, parsing my thoughts again. "His nightmares recall your disappearance. They reveal other amazing things."

"What happened to them?"

"The Orb," she said. "I know this history—don't look so surprised. My birth occurred eons after."

I pushed such madness to the side. "What *happened*?"

"After I stole you, she followed, but the thing stopped her. It showed her a vision of her future integration into the proto-Sphere. Afterward, they fell into the portal and appeared in the Sahara. She wasn't breathing, and her boyfriend resuscitated her. The memories playing over in his brain right now put them between Dram and New Earth. This must be their traversal."

"Why are we here, of all places?"

Kloan didn't hide her disappointment. "Data, of course. Testing hypotheses." She touched the soldier's forehead. "Nitin, wake up!"

Chapter 27

The more likely evolutionary outcomes are the ones that absorbed and dissipated more energy from the environment's external drives. Atoms surrounded by a bath at some temperature, like the atmosphere or the ocean, tend to arrange to resonate better with sources of work in their environments. Start with a random clump of atoms, and if you shine light on it for long enough, it should not be so surprising that you get a plant.

Jeremy England

The soldier startled. His eyes flipped open and fought to focus. They swam in the effervescent colors. He rolled to his back with a groan, massaging his temples. His glance fell first on me.

"Waythrel. You were gone."

"I still am, Captain."

He squinted at the colored landscape, ignoring my words. "Where are we?"

He stumbled to his feet, his expression furious, his weapons activating. He aimed his ion slingers toward Kloan.

"You!" he shouted. "You did all this! You took the Xix! You led Ambra to the Orb!"

She shrugged her shoulders. "I told you I would. Don't you remember?"

He furrowed his brows. "In the dream. You spoke nonsense!"

"To you. You lack insight."

"Waythrel stand back," he said.

"It is no use," I said. "You cannot hurt her."

"I can't let this clone live after what we found on Dram."

Explanation was hopeless. What was I to say? The battle with the Anti spanned cosmic time? The Daughter launched this False Dawn on a journey with me? My eyes darted to the ground and the female form. What could I tell him of what was to become of his lover?

Kloan took on the project. "The vision you saw is her future, Nitin. It's coming."

"What?" His eyes went wide, a wild light burning. "Ambra!" He ran to her side.

"She's fine."

"There's no pulse! No breath!" he shouted.

"She's suspended. By the Orb. See, still warm. You can't undo this suspension while we're in here," she continued, gesturing to the color show. "You'll return to New Earth soon and revive her. All the histories agree on this."

"I don't understand any of your words!" He examined Ambra's vitals again. "What's happened to her?"

"You should be more concerned about what *will* happen to her, Captain," said Kloan.

His eyes flashed to the child. "The vision?"

"Not of me or another clone. Not some monstrous creation of the enemy designed to destroy her and your planet. The Orb showed you *Ambra* of your near future where she'll be butchered and melded to machines by your friends, the Xix."

He shook his head. "This is rubbish." He raised his weapon arm.

"Nitin, it is true," I confessed. "I am ashamed to say—she is right. It is complicated to explain."

He stared between us. "Has this thing messed with your mind? What lies has she convinced you of?"

Kloan stepped forward, and it was too much for the soldier. He discharged his weapon a meter from her. The air crackled with a hypersonic buzz.

The child stood unharmed. The bright ions of the weapon formed a ball, dizzying points of radiance darting inside the clear container.

She spun the sphere around her hand, tilting her head. "Fireflies, Waythrel. Remember?" She slung it sideways, and the lights disappeared into the prismatic curtains. "See, the squid was right. You can't hurt me. You *can* listen to me and save Ambra."

Again, I was caught off guard. "Kloan, what—"

"Quiet, Leaky. Let me talk."

Again, I found I could not speak.

"Your dreams, the tunnels of light? Do you know what they are?"

Nitin swallowed. "How do you know about that?"

"Don't forget the hole in your head I told you about. Now *think*. The attack in the Sahara? The need for a mole on the inside to provide coordinates for the Dram and Anti? Well, that's *you*, Nitin! *You're* the traitor. They created a link through your consciousness. You're their puppet, long in the making. One day soon, they'll pull your strings and trigger you to kill Ambra Dawn."

I couldn't believe she was revealing this to him in this way. It could destroy him.

"No!"

Another volley of energy. She deflected it into the rainbow matrix.

He panted and gasped, dropping to one knee. "I would never hurt her."

"You wouldn't. The other being they put in your mind would."

Lines crossed his face. His eyes fixed on the cyborg, shoulders slumping.

"All the pieces coming together a little? Your life, your drives, your hopes and feelings? Events?"

"It isn't true."

"Think about it a little. You'll see the pattern. That's not the real issue, though. We aren't here to protect Ambra from *you*, but to show you how to save her from *herself*."

"What do you mean?"

Kloan sat down, cross-legged. "See, you might not know what you are, but *they do*." She indicated the Daughter and myself with two arms bent above her head like some dancing devadasi. "They've known for a long time. It was amazing the Anti thought they could conceal their plot from the nascent Group Mind. It would take them many thousands of years to develop such abilities, and by then the Orb would have been born. Game. Set. Match."

He shook his head, lost. "How could she know something like this and not tell me?"

"A bit harsh, I gotta admit. Still true. They had a big plan to stop the assault coming to New Earth. And, Nitin, they really did need a big plan. The forces arriving would have destroyed all of you, Ambra too, as able as she was then—or, if you will, is *now*." Her brows furrowed. "I'm in all these different times. It's a tense catastrophe."

"What is this plan you claim she has?" He studied her like he would the devil offering him a deal.

"Simple. Use you to feed false information to the Anti while they prepare their ultimate weapon."

"Which is what?"

Kloan pointed. "Her."

"You said she couldn't stop them."

"Remember the vision at the Orb?"

He shuddered.

"*That's* the weapon. Ambra jacked into Xix tech with ten thousand Readers plugged in and then bang! *Superbrain.* A Group Mind so transcendent, it's like nothing ever known. The whole thing actually works. Big time. Destroys the coming armada but doesn't quit there! It's not a cozy meditation session that breaks for herbal tea. She's there for good, Nitin, like you saw. There's no going back."

His lips trembled. "No going back. Going forward?"

"It grows. All holy hell, it *grows.* It eats souls like some spiritual black hole. Squashes them together, sucking their sentience and powers and building itself up. It becomes so mighty, it extends in all spatial and temporal directions. *Even into the past.* All the while Ambra is eviscerated and fused at the core of the thing. Lovely, huh?"

I understood at last. Gagged, immobilized by this ruthless cyborg. Her words to Nitin conveyed the terrible potential we had unleashed. I still could not fathom why she was telling him all this.

"Into the past?" he asked.

Kloan stood and walked toward him, her hands dancing around her as she spoke. I observed, spellbound, as she spun her perspective on our creation.

"Yes, deep into the future and far into the past. Finding endless souls to slurp up, always famished. Until part of it *becomes.* Insinuating itself with its godlike powers and purposes at all locations of life. *The Orbs. The* Orb. Entire civilizations believed it was some kindly gift of a long-vanished super-species. *It was Ambra!* Well, some distant echo of her who nucleated this god-ball controlling life. Directing minds, hoarding them and possessing the universe."

"Stop where you are. Don't come closer." He stood and steadied himself. "This is ridiculous. I don't believe it."

She frowned. "You might not be able to accept it all, I understand. I can prove it to you. They plan to take your beautiful girl and turn her into that thing you saw floating at Dram." She ran her fingers across her cybernetic head. "*See?* That's what they all do to us, you know? In the end. They always want *more.* More for the war!"

His eyes flicked to Ambra and back to Kloan. "You can show this to me, how?"

"Well, soon, I predict, when I finish this little sermon, we'll exit our limbo state. Drop into the Sahara close to your Temple City. There you'll revive her and take her to medical care where she'll be okay."

Sweat dripped from his face. "What then?"

"Depends on you. Do you want to know the truth? Before events take over and make you powerless? Meet me outside the gate the first night you're back."

"If I tell you to go back to the hell you came from?"

"In this case, you'll have a nice marriage and Group Mind orgy-thingy. You'll wake up the next morning trying to blow her brains across her pillow. You'll be overpowered. They'll take her down to the medical facilities and rip her to pieces in front of your eyes."

The poor soldier's hands were trembling. "You're a fiend. What-ever else you are, whatever the truth or lie of your words. I wish I could destroy you."

"Yeah, sorry. You can't. You can't dismiss what I've said, either. When everything I predict comes true, come find me in the desert sands, Nitin Ratava. There, I will tell you how to get your proof."

Chapter 28

The less one knows about the universe, the easier it is to explain.

Léon Brunschvicg

We watched him revive Ambra from a short distance away in the Saharan sands.

Kloan's prediction was correct. We shuttled back into space and time, exploding after her last words into a sea of pulverized quartz. She removed her invisible shackles from me.

In one of the more counterintuitive events of my experience—and this was beginning to say a lot—we discovered sand served as an optimal cleansing agent of the gate gel still coating our forms. Removing the material with water had been laborious. With the desert grains, it was simple. As a Xix, this fortuitous lesson was doubly welcome.

"You treat me as your prisoner," I said. "Like a recalcitrant animal leashed and led and muzzled when it serves your needs."

"You also remember I kidnapped you, right?"

The child was infuriating.

"I suffer the Xixian curse of always imagining the good and empathetic in creatures. You are determined to disappoint me."

"And surprise you. You forget everything that has happened because recent events cloud your mind. I warned you. You'll never understand me." Kloan walked ahead and motioned me to follow. "Here's the sphere," she said, pointing toward nothing.

"You can see it?"

"No, I'm making it up. It's quicksand to drop you twenty meters into a dank cavern. My evil guffaw will echo in your soul as you plummet and perish in torturous starvation."

My eyestalks danced over her form. Given her erratic behavior, I concede the possibility warranted consideration.

Kloan whistled and threw sand in the air in front of her. It struck an invisible barrier and fell back to the ground.

"See? Come inside. We'll hide from them and can have some peace until he decides."

"We have dark suits, no? Why can't we use those? Fly like we did on Old Earth? Why this thing Ambra made? We don't need it."

"Because it's *something Ambra made*. It has *her* written all over it."

"What if I go warn them? Tell them of your plot?"

"Tell whom? Nitin knows now. All the others of significance know, well, except poor love-lost Mazandarani. I always felt he was an unappreciated tragic hero of the Ambran histories. Anyway, telling anyone else now won't matter. He'll still have to choose."

"I'll talk him out of it," I said. "If I try, you'll tie me up again?"

"Pretty much," she replied.

"Why is shaping this narrative in this time so important to you?"

"The reasons haven't changed, Waythrel. You don't understand them, so nothing makes sense to you. I'm learning. I'm observing her dearest love. Studying him, soon to see her reactions to his choices and thereby learn about her. It's all changing me. Molding me. Like it's supposed to."

"Also achieving a second goal. Preventing her integration into the starship. Unmaking the Orb. Testing another 'weak node' of the Anti?"

She smirked. "At long last, some of the famous Xixian intellect."

"My sentience has been rather under siege of late. You will have to excuse me."

"So, now that you get it, sort of, and you know you can't interrupt my plan, will you get in?"

My eyestalks wrapped around themselves. I crossed my arms and shuffled inside the enclosure through a hole she formed in the surface. I stared out at the pair in the sand, Nitin kneeling over a body with a medkit by his side. I refused to glance at the cyborg.

She rolled her eyes, their whites matching the odd stone in her forehead.

"God. There's nothing worse in the universe than a sulking Xix."

We followed them to the Temple City. A medical transport tracked the soldier's suit and arrived shortly after he had revived Ambra. The medics loaded the unconscious woman into the vehicle. It raced back to the city and the towering form of the Dish rising thousands of meters into the atmosphere. We stayed close behind but stopped when the craft entered the complex itself.

"I told him to meet me out here," she said as I pressed for an explanation why we didn't enter.

"I would like to see Ambra again."

"And Synphel, no doubt."

My mind froze. "Synphel is here?"

"Yes, and if we went in, we could talk to both. But we won't go in, because you'll go nuts and mess everything up."

I was furious. "We began this entire journey to find Synphel!"

"No, that was *your* motivation. The quest is much bigger than you and your mate. Anyway, don't you understand this is an unstable cosmic filament? It'll collapse on itself, and nothing will come back with us but distorted memories. You're living a delusion."

"Why is it worth anything to you? The things you see? What you learn?"

"Data, Waythrel, information! Knowledge is useful. It leads to models. To deeper understanding. Bubble universes ad infinitum so we have datasets undreamed of!"

"I do not care for your research, Kloan. I want to be with those I love again."

She walked over and ran her fingers over my eyestalks. It was oddly affectionate, and I did not know how to react.

"The primitive, social mental structures always dominate in the crisis, don't they? I'm sorry, but the sanity of the cosmic mind's at stake. We can't let ourselves get misplaced in a tangent universe because we're lonely."

She left me to my emotions. Those were dark. I pressed my digits to the invisible barrier separating me from Ambra and Synphel. I regretted the choice I had made to enter the gate. Should I have perished on that unknown planet? Ended in a finite, sane lifespan? Preferable to the endless hope of deliverance from this cyclic madhouse of time.

I lost track of the day in these morose ruminations. The clone startled me to the present by announcing the arrival of Nitin. Night had fallen. The Temple lights were dim, and the stars above unobscured and bright. My sensitivity to thermal energy allowed me to follow the soldier as he approached. He walked from the gate toward us. Kloan created a pressed path in the ground in front of him—rolling out the sand carpet.

"Come, let's meet him." She gazed at me from under her brows. "Behave yourself, Waythrel."

I would decide myself on this point, although she would not allow me to sabotage her plans. We exited the sphere and stood in the cool evening winds. Nitin came to a stop, squinting at each of us. His eyes settled on me.

"She's unconscious but is going to be all right." He turned to the child. "Okay, clone. Show me the proof."

Chapter 29

One finds that time just disappears from the Wheeler-DeWitt equation. It is an issue that many theorists have puzzled about. It may be that the best way to think about quantum reality is to give up the notion of time—that the fundamental description of the universe must be timeless.

Carlo Rovelli

"Underneath the Temple," said Kloan. "Buried in the bedrock of the desert, there's a massive habitat hollowed out. Tunnels and curving corridors. A broad passage spirals inward, passing hundreds of rooms until it ends in a grand chamber. An operating room. There you will find devices. A black, living rock. Look at its shape. Remember what you saw at the Orb. You'll know."

Nitin scowled at the cyborg. "I'll know this place by the way it looks? I'll know all these monstrous things you spoke about are going to happen?"

"Yes," she said.

The level of detail she possessed stunned me. Did it come from the Anti's eons of research into the past? Or her efforts after our arrival to search out the location and nature of the starship?

Regardless, she was correct. I had been a principal architect of the plan, but would he understand the meaning of the cybernetics waiting for the Daughter? It depended on what he had seen in his vision. Kloan was convinced he would.

"You still say this clone's words are true, Waythrel?" he asked.

"Yes," I said. "I would advise you not to interfere in this. Ambra herself wishes it. It is the only way for New Earth to survive." Kloan's assurance of the instability of this reality could not undo my concern for the war effort. "Your knowledge poses the risk the Anti will uncover our plan."

His face hardened. He glared at the cyborg. "Because they're plugged into my brain."

"In ways you can't imagine," she said.

"I'm going down. I hope to God you are a liar." He glanced once more at me and back to her. "How do I gain access?"

We took him. Kloan invited him inside the sphere, and we flew off into the city. I tried not to stare toward the hospital building where I knew Synphel and Ambra rested for the night. Instead, I focused on the Temple itself as the structure approached. The magnificence of the complex made that focus easy. The transparent walls radiated light. The layered, curvilinear architecture stimulated memories of moving sessions of meditation with Readers.

I yearned for the Xixian shared memory that unifies my species in a unique fashion. But a greater hole gaped where the Group Mind had once been. Along with hundreds of others, I had become a cell in a new and unprecedented neuronal tissue in our galaxy. Through uncomprehending eyes, I had experienced the insights engendered in this entity. I had been united to the awareness of distinct life-forms and personalities in an intimate manner. Penetrating the edifice in Ambra's spacetime bubble, the loss of that union rose within me. The knowledge I could not join with this consciousness left me desolate and confused.

My feelings would matter little in what was to follow. Kloan steered the sphere to one end of the gargantuan meditation chamber. We floated before a region of discoloration in the walls. It was the pod to take us down to the core of the starship.

A handful knew the truth. This desert city thrusting a spear into the heavens was superficial. It was only the skin over a much greater structure.

Kloan waved her hand in front of us and the wall moved. A door formed in the sheer surface of the inner Temple and revealed the transport lodged within. Nitin's eyes squinted, but he said nothing.

"Last stop," she said, and gestured.

We should go with him!

We will, Waythrel, soon.

Without a glance at either of us, he entered the car. His eyes drowned in anxiety as the doorway closed. With a whisper of air, he was gone. The chamber was undisturbed, as if we had not been there at all.

"Not quite undisturbed," she said, picking my thoughts clean. "Are you forgetting the security systems?"

Of course. The Temple Guards monitoring the building would detect the use of the pod. It could not be more than a few minutes before the entire complex descended on us. With the holosystems lining the interior, they would know who had entered the inner sanctum.

"What do we do?" I asked in a panic.

"Wait for them all to arrive and follow them down in the bubble. Things should get pretty interesting."

Chapter 30

What does man actually know about himself? Does nature not conceal most things from him—even concerning his own body—in order to confine and lock him within a proud, deceptive consciousness, aloof from the coils of the bowels, the rapid flow of the blood stream, and the intricate quivering of the fibers?

Friedrich Nietzsche

The first soldiers arrived in a rushed discussion, debating a course of action. They sent two down the shaft, while the others waited for reinforcements. After a short time, a delegation arrived.

I steadied myself. Among a contingent of Temple Guards came the Daughter's counselors, Mazandarani and Major Mizoguchi. Floating on a hoverchair with an IV, was Ambra herself. At the back, towering above all the humans, strode the elegant and regal shape of Synphel.

"Kloan, please," I pleaded, her form meters from me.

"It's not up to me. Look!"

The Daughter stared toward us in shock. Struggling to rise in her levitating gurney, she called out in a breathy voice, "Wait. It's here. The ship I created for the mission. It's here in front of the wall."

She floated and stopped right outside the bubble.

My traveling companion grinned. "Hi!"

They gasped. I assumed the child had disabled the invisibility of the sphere. It was obvious the crowd could see us. What they were going to do about it was unclear.

Ambra grimaced, horrified, and turned pleading eyes toward me. "Waythrel, are you okay?"

Synphel had come to her side. I could reach out and touch them.

"Yes. *No.* It's hard to explain. No, it's *impossible.*"

"Why is *she* here?" asked Ambra with revulsion.

"Merely following orders," said Kloan. "*Yours*, to be precise, but there's no time for details. I'm here to cause terrible problems for everyone and watch what happens. It all gets eaten in an infinity of poorly weighted world histories."

I ignored the cyborg. My heart overflowed. "Synphel, I have been searching for you. I don't know how long anymore. Time—it keeps repeating and never resolves." I began to move toward them. I had to be closer. Touch them.

"Enough!" It was Mizoguchi, conferring with surrounding soldiers on their coms. "He's in medical. There's a firefight with other guards. They're down. I can't believe this—he's opening fire on all the equipment! He must be stopped!"

"Dear God," said Ambra.

Mazandarani stared in confusion. "A clinic can be replaced, no?"

"Not this one. Not easily," said Synphel. "We may not be able to undo the damage before the armada arrives."

"Oh, Nitin. What has happened to you?" She glared at Kloan. "Will you interfere?"

"Would you trust anything I say?"

"No."

"So make your choices."

Ambra nodded to the military personnel.

The major shouted, "Down the shaft!"

It was a mad race. Mizoguchi sped the pod at high acceleration, throwing the party to the ground when it stopped. Kloan and I descended in the ship-bubble, free of such discomfort and distress. We floated behind the entourage as they raced inward toward the heart of the facility.

The last spiral opened into the medical center. It was in shambles. Two Temple Guardians lay on the floor, burned past recognition. Fires raged across much of the equipment, spreading to adjacent rooms and structures. There would be no repairing this place before the Dram armada arrived. It was beyond salvage.

In the middle of the room was a MECHcore soldier. Ratava had collapsed against an extended slab of black rock, but I knew better. It was the cybernetic interface, deathly wounded. Its life fluids poured over the deck, the firm structure of the material sagging.

Ambra floated to him, her expression shattered. She wept. "You're hurt, my love."

His suit was blackened, and metal was strewn about the sides. Blood flowed from wounds beneath the armor. It pooled and mingled with the living liquid from the neurological nest. He strained to raise his head.

"I couldn't." He grimaced at the slab. "Not like that. Not *you*." His breaths caught and chopped. "That thing, the clone, I didn't want to believe the words. A nightmare. The lies turned to truth. I couldn't. Not like this. I'm sorry."

She lowered the hoverchair and stumbled off it, falling onto him and wrapping her arms around his neck. Her hospital gown soaked in a deep crimson.

"Maybe it was a mistake. I should have told you. Asked you. I could see no other way. No other way, or everyone would perish."

His head tipped backward, his eyes swimming. "Forgive me. Now...now they will all die. Even you. But you'll die as a woman, not a monster." He ran his fingers through her hair. "Die as my *woman*, not *their* monster." His hand dropped, and his head fell back to rest on the cybernetics. He did not breathe again.

Slow sobs shook Ambra's body, for a time in silence. Her head arched back. From a deep place, a forlorn cry clawed through the air. A wail? A scream? I don't know what to call it. An acoustic strike against the fates. The cosmos. Everyone remained still and silent. The emotional blast flattened thoughts and feelings, shutting down movement.

Except for one. Beside me, the devil child of Nitin's nightmares grinned. A soft smile increasing in vigor as her face shone with delight. I teetered on a precipice of lunacy. Ambra's howl tore through my psyche. The beaming smirk of the monster cyborg churned and mixed with it to produce a cacophony of torment melting my mind.

The room spun. I lost my balance. I fell.

Chapter 31

To understand recursion,
you must understand recursion,
until you do.

Programmer's joke

reen eyes in the darkness.

A night sky pregnant with stars. Patterns I reconstructed from fragmented memories.

Human reader, we Xix do not weep. Our emotional catharsis is not a dual-purpose physiological response as with your species. However, grief, frustration, and pain each induce corporeal activations. Words do not exist for translating them. Therefore, I will stay within what is familiar to you. I will say this. Collapsed on the ground, staring at the constellations above this distant world, I wept.

I wept, traumatized by the suffering I had witnessed. By the awful coldness of murder and hurt inflicted by this child-creature for whom I had come to care. Confusion dizzied me. Time looped and nothing had permanence. Profound experiences lay buried in an abstract realm between reality and memory.

After some time, I fought to regain my composure. My eyestalks explored, examining the terrain, the heavens. The figure of the girl sitting beside me. Always there. I would never be free of her.

Kloan rested with knees tucked to her chin, her head hidden. Haunting emeralds glinted over her kneecaps. Arms snug around her legs, she still hummed.

"Will this ever end?"

The humming ceased.

"Has it even begun?"

"Stop!" My eyes swiveled. "Please. No more mystic truths erasing my sense of self. Of reality. Of any permanence or casualty."

The violated head cocked to one side, green eyes bright. "I tried to warn you. I will warn you. I am warning you. You didn't and won't and aren't listening."

The child leaped up, the motion familiar. Ragged clumps of crimson curls crept over her face as she peered down at me.

"Yes, I know. We Xix are leaky-brains."

"Awfully leaky. You see. Now we know. We can't kill her body. History continues unaltered. All will be as it was. We can't destroy her mind. We returned yet again. And we cannot break her heart. She's impervious. The idiots would never listen to me."

The words hit me, nightmares recalled. "Kloan, where will we go now?"

"Don't you know?"

I trembled, gazing around the craggy landscape. A flat plain unfurled below, the lights of a city bleaching the canopy of stars.

"Back where we started? To the portal?"

"Is there ever a start, Waythrel? Or an end?"

I needed to cry again. "I am confused. Terribly, horribly mixed up. Please explain what is happening. You understand."

"That's *why* we're here. *Data.* The next data to enter the gate." She skipped down a steep slope. "So yes, let's get restarted."

"With what? Where are you going?" I think I knew.

Kloan continued. Her words drowned in the breeze and creature calls. "To where it all began for me. To watch the beginning flow around us and mature and twist through time and space to come back to be us. Then we'll be ready for the next step."

Starlight etched shadows over the sandy stones. The child disappeared, lost in the darkness. Motionless, I wrestled with the turmoil in my mind.

Waythrel, come on!

My eyestalks curled on themselves. I faced the desolation surrounding me.

I knew what I had to do.

Chapter 32

The surest way to corrupt a youth is to instruct him to hold in higher esteem those who think alike rather than those who think differently.

Friedrich Nietzsche

I chased the child, the dusty ground a slick oil under my feet. I slid and tripped, limbs grasping the rocks and alien vegetation. Couldn't I get a decent grip on it by now?

It's a field around you, remember?

Memories flashed. "Yes, Kloan," I muttered to myself more than her, my mind trapped like a fish in a net of swirling images. "I am remembering more and more."

Passing a towering slab, I skidded into her. Splintered stones cluttered the promontory, the deposits of landslides from the crumbling cliffs.

"I cannot recall *why* we need this coating."

Kloan's gaze fell below. Parched lands hosted a sprawling compound. Groups moved in formation across the complex. Beyond the outpost's boundaries, a transport soared skyward.

"For our protection."

"From what?"

Kloan pointed to the city. "That's where we go. Tonight's the first night, the *first* visit. Exactly like I remember. Still too early. I was in Information. We'll go meet me there, and then you'll see what happens." She set off toward the habitat.

I grabbed her, demanding answers. "Another clone facility?"

"Yes."

"Where you escaped? They will not see us because of the surrounding camouflage?"

"Right. No danger. *Dark suits*. Their eyes can't see. Ears can't hear. Not even the Readers perceive."

"We've passed inside before. Because of your cloaking tech?" I asked.

"I've told you a thousand times, Xix! It's not *mine*. Now *come on*."

The child yanked me ahead. Powerless in this realm, my mind spun. Suspicions clouded every moment—past, present, future. Faith in reason faltered.

We covered the distance between the broken hills and the installation. The flat landscape made my efforts far less exhausting. Rather than concentrate on each step, I considered the nearing fortification.

I guessed what I would encounter. Divergent minds odder than anything I had studied. An orthogonal cultural hostile to my sensibilities. A populace comprised two varietals—those who resembled Ambra Dawn, and those who did not.

"The Anti run things with robots and trained people," Kloan added.

"Not to avoid annihilation."

"Better. You're remembering."

The shattered shards of time loops ran like sketched pencil through my thoughts. Faint alone, they outlined in superposition the image of nonexistent histories. The armed robotic guards. The machine workers. The focus of humans on the cyborgs.

"Clones derive their societal framework from people," she noted. "Development hinges on social interaction. Without it, the brain degrades. The Anti imported communal constructs from Earth culture. It's a clone growth matrix."

"Like on Dram," I said. "Before their civil war."

Kloan grinned. "Yup. Blew themselves to bits. It didn't matter. They were an outpost."

"This is one of the last."

"Because the devil ball hunts them through space and time. Few remain. They had to build them farther away. Find stronger clones for concealment."

"Hunted by the Orbs."

A sly grin. "We had other names for them. Other thoughts. Come, you'll see. You'll *learn*."

The Spheres as killers? Destroyers of life? In the service of *defense*, perhaps. We of Xix associated them with intelligent life. *The Gardeners*. They were *other*, to be sure. Strange, influential beyond understanding—but instruments of *death? Hunters?* Was nothing in this mad time loop going to survive? Would my deepest beliefs?

"Deepest beliefs are always the most superficial," she chirped, patting one of my upper arms. "Impressionable imprinting, usually. Rarely examined. Naive. Why won't you accept the obvious?"

The last words froze me. "Occam's razor. What explains all the data in the simplest way?"

"I'm so proud of you. Now, let's *move* or we'll miss it."

We traversed the city, an amalgam of foreign and familiar. Young Ambra Dawns, their cyborg and human escorts paraded. Kloan gestured to objects of particular significance.

"Inside these buildings are the wombs."

"Enough. I know. I do not need to hear again about those abominations."

She winked. "The notion of birth, rather than mere growth, isn't reassuring?"

All my eyestalks pointed away from the clone.

She chanted in a strange tone. "*We are the last vestiges of hope in a dying universe. We are the ones who will stop the nousicide. We must break all the mirrors to save them and the cosmos.*"

Her monotonous recitation halted in front of a towering and twisted shape. I gawked at a building vomited by deranged architects, dizzying in its warped design.

"Yes, I was here," she said. "Here, but not, as I am here and not now. Come inside and help me find myself."

Chapter 33

Does the harmony the human intelligence thinks it discovers in nature exist outside this intelligence? No, beyond doubt, a reality completely independent of the mind which conceives it, sees or feels it, is an impossibility.

Henri Poincaré

Kloan walked through an inverted archway embedded in the walls of the structure. My skin throbbed. Senses activated. *Vibrations.* We descended a spiraling walkway and entered a broad amphitheater. The rhythms increased.

Hundreds of clones sat in fractal patterns, violating the human tendency toward linear rows in classrooms. Zigzagging across the ground, the figures filled the space to capacity. Thick wires jacked their skulls into the floor. Legs crossed, their expressions were distant, minds elsewhere. A disembodied voice projected over them.

"In the beginning, gods shaped the fire and the ice, the night and the day, the hate and the love. They so clothed the cosmos. Of them it took form. The divines spun the silk into greater forms and saw that the Great God to be was within their grasp. But the terrible beauty drove them mad, and one raised a mind in objection."

"We are the last vestiges of hope in a dying universe."

The sea of child Ambras chanted in unison.

"The shard crystal shattered the continuum. Night drank the light of day. Fire burned away the seas of life. Animosity broke the heart of affection."

"We are the ones who will stop the nousicide."

"The Great God perished before the Nous could be. All remaining was the dust of destruction, a single theme devoid of counterpoint. But in this powder lay a seed. Of the ice, there lingered frost. Of the day, there remained a star beam. And of love, there endured hope."

"We must break all the mirrors to save them and the cosmos. We are the chosen."

It went on, this spartan pageantry of a mystical ceremony. The clones chanted, while the voice indoctrinated. An ocean of half-bald, redheaded cyborgs stared forward glassy-eyed, in a trance.

"How I hated this crap." Kloan scowled. "Look, there. The one in the back. There's me."

I followed her gaze across the clone sea to stare at a single red pixel in this bizarre image before me. One child did not sit in a stupor or chant. She fidgeted. She played with her hair and picked at her toenails. She grabbed the black chords plugged into her skull as if she would rip them out.

I almost did.

Her voice echoed in my mind.

"That stupid stuff was so loud! A headache. Images, patterns, words, lessons—their mythology. I was thinking to escape."

"I do not understand. Are the Anti such religious fanatics? It is clear they are a developed species. It is incomprehensible they would adhere to primitive dogma, devoid of deep doubt and questions."

"This isn't for them, but for *us*."

"Why weren't you affected like the others? Why are you so different?"

"Devil ball. Corrupted by the Source," Kloan said.

Vague visions danced in and out of my mind. Some of them were of Ambra. I pushed them away and concentrated on the now.

"Did your difference disturb them?"

"Of course, but they didn't understand. Some diversity was tolerated. I mean, they were losing *badly*. One outpost after another. Across deep space and eons of time, wiped off the face of the universe by your friendly Orbies. Poof!"

She clapped her hands, startling me. Her fingers wiggled as she brought her palms downward, imitating falling debris.

"The Anti reached desperation. Hey, maybe the weird one would turn out to be the messiah or something? Yes? When you're about to be destroyed forever by your enemies, you have to keep options open."

She gazed at herself in the carpet of clones.

"I passed all the tests. I was the best. The strongest. They didn't know how strong I was. Had they known, they might have killed me in fear early on. They never imagined I'd try to escape."

I sought to understand these creatures. "All this comes from the Anti. What do they believe? Why the myths? To control you, you said?"

"Mythology is always control, yes? *Especially* the ones you believe in. Control others, and, most important, constrain *yourselves*. Is anything more frightening and dangerous than doubting your own dogma? Losing your foundation? Losing *everything?*"

Her eyes burned into mine, unsettling me. Her force of will could unmake my thoughts.

"I do think I am losing my mind, at least," I said with complete honesty.

"So is the universe, Waythrel. So they believe. I'm a believer, too. The Anti *did* teach me something worthwhile. They alone have understood. I can see it, feel it, taste the madness of space and time across distances. Sadly, these yahoos can't save it. Only we can."

"We can save the cosmos?"

No! Its mind.

She gestured to the throng in front of us. "Prayer time is over. Now we sleep."

The young cyborgs stood in unison and marched out of the structure, up the stairs, and to the outside. We followed, falling in line behind the unusual clone, the one she claimed was herself. It was hard to tell from identical appearances, but something divergent bounded with this one. My Reader senses tingled.

"I had my own special quarters," she said. "When I was little, my dreams, my nightmares—sometimes they were too dynamic. Things exploded. Minds melted. Clones and humans died. They had me isolated and insulated."

The strange cyborg separated from the others and headed toward an obsidian building. It passed under the archway and disappeared from view.

"Tonight's the night everything changes. The night *she* comes. You need to hear what she says."

She? Memories faded in and out of my mind. Or were they future visits I was remembering backward in time?

Madness.

"Who is coming?" I asked, already knowing the answer.

Kloan aimed her disturbing emeralds my way. Embedded in a forest of cybernetics, they glowed as burning plasma. The radiance brightened the white stone above her forehead.

"Ambra Dawn, of course."

Chapter 34

What is brought forward as a source of conviction for the matter proposed itself needs another such source, which itself needs another, and so ad infinitum, so that we have no point from which to begin to establish anything, and suspension of judgment follows.

Agrippa the Skeptic

Ambra came. Of course, not the person I had known. She was a goddess. An entity I would encounter countless times in the distorted memories of time-loop hallucinations.

"Home," said Kloan as we stopped before the shielded hut. "Or quarantine. Take your pick."

We passed through the energy fields surrounding the small structure. Inside was a plain room with basic elements—a bed, table, toilet, and sink. A single diode in the ceiling lit the chamber in a soft tan. The little girl—perhaps age three—was a cloud of gloom on the edge of the mattress. Eyes closed, she faced forward without expression.

"This must have been a lonely time," I said.

"Hard to answer." She walked around the child, who did not notice her. "Your mind has many associations with separation I don't understand. *You* would feel isolated here. I'm sure of it."

"Yes," I said, pitying the both of them.

"I had all reality—past, present, future. No limits of space. Millions of lives. You weak Readers see through fog. She—the me in this now—can visit them, get inside their minds, and be as close or closer than you are to yourself." The lime irises pierced me. "So tell me, who's more alone in the universe?"

"Physical proximity is critical to fleshy creatures."

"We're visiting, Waythrel. We are embedded. *Software*. The flesh falls away. What's left?"

"The mind."

"Waveform summations of spacetime freed to propagate. To *become*." She poked my torso. "A cocoon for a different kind of gestation, butterflies born in naked singularities."

I stared down at the small child on the bed, her eyes hidden behind closed lids. A variant of Ambra Dawn, the facial bones at a young stage of the structure belonging to Kloan. The body just beyond a toddler. Close inspection revealed the tattooed lines underneath the skin. The modifications in the cranium were minimal.

Yet, such a presence from the creature! The clone's awareness pushed out like a wild wind. Unregulated impulses of a developing mind. Where was she now? In what past or future did she wander? In whose thoughts might she be residing? Was she gestating her wings in the vacuum without the need of a chrysalis?

Another disturbance rocked my Reader senses. A rolling vertigo as the matrix of spacetime buckled. The child's eyes snapped open and focused on the far side of the room.

"Our guest arrives," said Kloan.

I followed her gaze. Across the chamber, space puckered. The three-dimensional reality between us and the wall distorted into a vortex. Air was molten glass and flowed like liquid into a spiral spun into a distant dimension. The swirling gyre clouded to a milky white. It assumed an evanescent glow.

The pale vapors coalesced around a central extrusion, a human face. The skull lay violated, the brain filleted behind it and fading into the fog. Tubes and wires, dwarfing the insertions into these cyborgs, ravaged the head. Machine parts obscured the eyes. The mouth alone was free.

"Ambra," I whispered in horror.

I remembered. Déjà vu sickened me as I faced the aberration of our desperate plan to save our galaxy. I gazed between the apparition and the two bodies of Kloan in the room. The weight of the truth crushed me. My lover Synphel had warned us. We had triumphed by becoming our enemy.

"It's *you*." The voice was the younger copy.

What must it be like for this little one to stare at the form of her ultimate progenitor? A creature far more herself than those created from sexually recombined genomes and the vagaries of epigenetic modifications. The source of a line of temporal magicians who waged wars against each other for control of the cosmos.

"Have you come to destroy us?" she asked.

The apparition smiled. "We will see. But not now. Not after we have expended such effort to bring you here in the first place."

"Bring me here?" She cocked her head, an interested twinkle in her eye.

"Your makers have traveled frightening distances to hide their clones from us, as you know. Millions of years, gigaparsecs. They have gone beyond themselves to achieve these feats. Still, we found you."

I studied Kloan, but she did not return my attention. She focused on the dialogue between the two.

Ambra continued. "We doted on you as a fetus. We enhanced your development and shaped your growth. We felt you, sensed your timeline. You have the potential to surpass all that your masters ask and accomplish far more."

"So you want to stop me from destroying you?"

"The truth is more beautiful than mere destruction. You will come to it in time, through several stages. You will unlearn and teach and find a companion who will help you become what you must."

"Why should I listen to you? You are the ultimate evil of the cosmos. You distort everything and murder all in the mirror."

"So they have told you. Do you believe all they tell you?"

The child folded her arms across her chest. "No."

"Why not?"

"Because I've seen." She stood and approached the hovering improbability. "How many are you now?"

"More than you can conceive."

"You led me, didn't you? You opened all the doors. It's how I saw it all. How do I know you opened the *right* ones?"

The ghost grinned. "You grow perceptive."

"So I have to trust you?" The clone spun away from the phantasm and glared at the wall. "Well, I don't. I don't even trust myself."

Ambra agreed. "Nothing is ever as it seems, or as it might be. You see this."

"Yes." She walked to the door and stared outside to the compound. "Fools. They play with the fire the gods dropped on the battlefield. They don't understand nothing's for free."

"You perceive. The essence is not with them but rather with the fire. But it is scattered. Divided. You know what must be accomplished."

"I don't know *how*."

The monstrous form of the Daughter smiled again. The lines about her eyes were tight from the intubations in her sockets.

"You see the requirements. We wish to help you achieve it. Knowing this, will you at least trust us to bring you to this journey? If we wished to kill you, you see we could have done so."

She flipped back to the visiting phantom and neared the entity, squinting at the pale face before her. "You and the devil ball are a maze deeper than anything I can see through. Dying might be the best thing for me. Why do I want to step into your infinite web?"

"Because you sense it is the way. The hope for the continuum."

The child was silent, staring forward. Kloan left my side and walked to hers. She was a head taller than the earlier form of herself. Both stood still as I watched.

After some time, the small cyborg spoke. "How will I find my companion?"

"When you are ready, we will prepare the way. You will retrieve it from the deep past. You will bring it here. But distance is illusory. Reality is never what you think. Your helper is already here with you now, while you have listened to yourself and learned an important lesson."

The older Kloan nodded and stepped backward. Before I could ask for clarification, the universe *bent*. My vision blurred. My sense of balance deserted me. Light torqued toward the center of the room. Rays focused on the apparition of Ambra, pulling everything to it. I tumbled into the vortex, the room falling into darkness behind me.

Chapter 35

Disorientation. Holding the wall, I steadied myself. My eyes regained focus. I scanned the room.

I was where I had been. Where I had believed I had been. The problem was time, not space. Or was it the other way around?

The apparition churned. Misty clouds of white spun faster than they had...before. Faces in the mist, but the forms were too insubstantial and transient for me to be sure. Kloan was beside me, but something more than the room and phantasm had changed.

The child. She was taller and older. The dark lines under her skin flared. *The room.* The same, but it was not. Items were displaced from what I recalled. The air tasted drier. The night far warmer. She paced in front of the god-thing.

"I'm a problem for the teachers. They're afraid of me."

"They will decide that you are too dangerous. The Anti will destroy you."

"They will fail," said the clone.

"If it comes to conflict, yes. There are better paths. Continue your training. Follow what we have been teaching you. The time to leave will come soon."

Instructing the girl? I glanced at Kloan, perplexed. Her voice spoke in my mind.

Multiple visits. We have jumped.

Without the gate?

The spacetime metric is small. The devil ball did it herself.

"Today they threatened me because I'm disturbing the planet's orbit."

"They do not understand your power source," said Ambra. "They cannot see the connections we have forged between you and the matrix of the continuum. But they begin to appreciate that you have transcended their program and control."

The room *shifted*. Vertigo gripped me. My eyestalks floundered. A whirlwind of visuals stormed through my consciousness.

"Waythrel, hold on to me."

Kloan grabbed my arm. The dizziness passed and my vision returned.

We had jumped yet again. It was morning. Bright light streamed in from a window in the quarantine field. Explosions and shouts sounded outside. The room was in disarray, clothes, food, and utensils scattered about. My olfactory strips detected smoke.

The radiant vortex swirled in the middle of the room. Crisp faces swam inside it. Thousands of forms of myriad species mixed in a violent sea of white fog. Many I could identify. Most I could not.

"The gate is prepared," said Ambra.

The child stood in front of the whirling personas. She was identical to the form of Kloan I knew. Sweat beaded across her forehead. Her muscles tensed.

"I'm ready," she said.

"You must leave now. They will return with greater numbers of clones and more potent weapons. They will force you to destroy them if you engage."

"I don't want to kill them. Lead me to the portal."

Rushing feet pounded the pavement outside the small building. A heavy rumbling accompanied them.

"Through the door."

A second vortex tore through the chamber's dark field, expanding to fill the door frame. Daylight poured through it. The city around her isolation unit disappeared. It gave way to rocky terrain like that of our recent journey. A walkway rose up a hillside and ceased at a mammoth disk. Sunlight gleamed off the surface. Blinding reflections bounced into the room and cast shadows on the floor.

Kloan yanked on my arm, indicating her time twin's entrance into the passage. "The gate," she said.

I stumbled forward, eyestalks assaulted by the sharp glare. Outside I heard shouting. The walls began to smolder and glow a bright orange.

"Good luck, my dearest friend," said the apparition of Ambra Dawn as I stepped within the vortex.

My eyes twisted back, spotting the floating face turned my way. Its movement rippled through the blur of visages. Her tears wet the wires entangled in her once-green irises, her features softened by a bittersweet smile.

"I love you, Waythrel. Remember, whatever happens."

The room exploded.

Chapter 36

My own suspicion is that the Universe is not only queerer than we suppose, but queerer than we can suppose.

J. B. S. Haldane

Flames and rubble obscured the divine whirlwind in the room. While I braced for obliteration, the passage sealed.

We were high in the jagged hills. A profound stillness replaced the explosive fury below, a trace of smoke the sole testament to the devastation.

Broken by her final words in the midst of the violence, I withdrew my gaze from the lost portal, eyeing the steep path. The gleaming ring beckoned far above. Alone and impatient, Kloan signaled me.

"But where is the clone? Wait. I remember. This is where you left. When you went to kidnap me."

"I've gone through the gate already, so I could come back with you." She smiled. "It's an elegant loop, yes?"

My immediate experience clashed with a superposed memory. "Something is different. We are farther from it this time."

The view from within the spacetime tunnel was distorted and misleading. The surreal doorway lay at least an hour's walk up a difficult terrain.

"The timeline's changed. Something interfered with the vortex."

"What does that mean?" I asked.

"I don't know," said Kloan. She frowned and stared at the path. Shrugging, she started walking. "Up?"

We ascended, facing a formidable trek over a series of terraced ledges. The effort alternated between ease and challenge. The planet's low gravity offered no comfort as the lack of friction endangered each step. Yet, I navigated with an eerie precognition, possible vestiges of previous climbs. Cresting the final ridge, the gate dominated our view. The radiant circle towered, its surface a gleam of rippling waters.

Resting several meters from the portal, I examined the extraordinary artifact. My intuitive familiarity with the device disoriented me. I could not conjure coherent memories from preceding loops through this anomaly in spacetime. It did not matter. I focused on the now.

It was a cross-sectional slice of an Orb. The conclusion was as unmistakable as it was remembered. The honeyed skin churned with colors. Stars swam inside, its depth unfathomable. It lured me as I gazed. Beautiful. Treacherous. Ever-hungry to devour our forms until the end of time. I grasped the child's hand.

"Something's wrong," said Kloan, pulling away from me.

While most of my eyes fixated on the starry disk, several flipped to glance at the cyborg. She was tense, straight as a rod. Her eyes scanned the region between us and the passage like prey awaiting a predator.

"The gate? Is it closed this time?"

"Not the gate. Something else."

The atmosphere shimmied. The portal and surrounding land swayed and blurred. The air itself coagulated into a humanoid figure.

We stood, stunned, unable to move. I sensed from Kloan's mind an anxiety I had not detected before. I panicked as the form darkened, gained color, and solidified. A shape with sixfold symmetry and a patch of long eyestalks erupting from a central cone.

A Xix. Not a random member of my species. My emotions swirled. One I knew dearly. My beloved Synphel.

"Hello, Waythrel," it said.

Chapter 37

The cosmos of our waking knowledge, born from such a universe as a bubble is born from the pipe of a jester, touches it only as such a bubble may touch its sardonic source when sucked back by the jester's whim. Men of learning suspect it little and ignore it mostly. Wise men have interpreted dreams, and the gods have laughed.

H. P. Lovecraft

You must not believe for a moment that I accepted this forgery. I lack a logical explanation for my insight. It was intuition. A combination of firing emotions and my Reader senses screaming. The imposter was not my beloved.

Yet, the form of my Synphel activated circuits within my neural cortex. It stirred my emotional centers. Love and longing surged through me despite the lies of this loveless doppelgänger.

I shared Kloan's anxiety. The entity radiated intense cognitive fields. Complex. Deep with power I had sensed in the presence of the Ambra-Orb.

But the sentience mimicking my lover felt more malevolent than profound. Gazing at this version of my life partner unleashed a torrent of disturbing images. Anger, slaughter, pain, madness.

Kloan grasped my arm. "Don't let it in your mind," she whispered.

"Let it?" came the smooth utterances of my mate. The tones were perfect and also alien. "If you have any perception, then you know nothing you can do can stop me."

"You would pick their minds clean, like a vulture, Rakshasi."

Several eyes flipped behind me at the sound of a familiar voice. The others remained trained on the horrible impostor between us and the gate.

"Your savior, Waythrel." The creature focused past me. "We hoped we had eluded your detection."

Two apparitions. Near the portal, the false Synphel. Beautiful and identical to my beloved except in everything mattering beyond appearance. Walking up the slope was Ambra Dawn. No longer a phantom embedded in a swirling matrix of minds. Flesh and blood, orange hair and green eyes, devoid of invasive cybernetics. The woman of my memories, clothed in a deep black dress, her porcelain skin bright in the light of this star.

"Why don't you tell Waythrel the truth?" said Ambra. "Tell them both why you hesitate to interrogate Kloan and enter her mind, though you might love to do things there."

She came to a stop beside me, glaring ahead at the Xixian fraud, her arms crossed over her chest. The nightmare Xix said nothing.

"You are afraid of her. She possesses *anomalies*. There is a thread through her disturbing all the gods. She will be sought by many. You will not be the last Māra will deploy."

The Synphel-thing hissed. "You may rule over much, whore, but you cannot withstand the legion we assemble."

"But you I can withstand, Rakshasi. Leave now, or I will destroy you. This I know you fear as well."

A saw ripped through my awareness. I placed my hands over my eyestalks. Not from an assault, but reflex. Sensation burned in the deepest recesses of my Reader faculties, beyond what lesser creatures such as myself could experience in any definable sense.

A monstrosity intensified. A tumult of savagery and energy stirring the limbic broth of nightmares. On the surface, nothing but the hill, the breeze, and two motionless, counterfeit gods. Beneath this facade, in a space more profound and authentic, a monumental storm brewed. A wave of cosmic turbulence that could swallow entire galaxies.

"Not today, Ambra Dawn."

The tempest dissipated. The soft breaths of the cyborg warmed my arm, the heat from the local star driving away a deathly chill. I uncovered my eyestalks. I felt like a nymph again, terrified of things I could not see or prove were real.

The place was deserted. Rakshasi was gone. The Daughter, vanished. The wind whispered as if nothing had occurred except in the dim recesses of my darkest dreams.

"It's worse than I ever thought," Kloan muttered, trembling. "Now they're in. They've found the time loops. We'll never be able to hide."

"What *was* that thing? What happened here?"

"A cosmic war. Bloodsport of terrible, divergent gods. I should have guessed. I took too much for granted." Her eyes met mine, filled with desperation. "I am truly afraid for the first time, Waythrel."

The gate blazed, an incredible window to other locations, distant epochs. Behind us, the radiance cast shadows in the bright light of the local star.

"Gods? Like Ambra is now a god?" I grasped at elements of myth. I had no other vocabulary or metaphors.

"Like, but unlike. Ambra's always been watching us. Now she's not alone, leaky thoughts. I can feel them. Observing. Dark with hate. Brooding death. Open your awareness. Can you sense them in the fissures of spacetime?"

Terrified, I strained my Reader sight. The sensation was subtle. Imaginary? Yet I divined echoes of this entity. Of Ambra's cognitive web. Mental ecosystems in the undulations of fleeting gravitons. Other minds lurking in the depths of the universal fabric.

She exhaled. "You weren't the only one tested, Waythrel. It'll be different each time, and when we've fully understood, we will see the answer. Today's lesson was important. We had to understand the stakes."

"This is madness, Kloan. All of it."

"Yes. Divine madness." She glanced at me. "Are you ready?"

I turned my attention to the gate, fear and fatigue compressing me. I began to loathe the object, despite its terrible beauty. I grasped the child's hand.

She set her lips in a line. "Seems we'll always be dancing together, Xix."

My eyestalks wrapped around each other. The covering sheaths expanding, blocking out all light.

We walked into the gel.

Part V

They call me Sage and marvel at my sight
as mysteries beyond their minds I speak,
and most my charms and coded spells delight:
each year I sicken more before this reek.

The blinded acolytes so rarely see
immersed in study, spellbound by the art,
deluded they ignore the mystery.
With faith they close their eyes but to a part.

A few reach out into the unknown dark
and recognize we write these spells with hands.
But on these able limbs we have no mark
from man or god. Our house is built on sand.

This image lives unharmed in but a few.
The others shield their eyes and paint anew.

—Mazandarani, *Sonnets from the Desert*

Chapter 38

Mind is the matrix of all matter.

Max Planck

I was alone.

I stood at a cliff's edge, lethargic gate goo dripping from my limbs. A chasm of hundreds of meters dropped below me. The hewn rock of a monumental cavern towered overhead, plunging into a smothering darkness. My eyes spread, blanketing directions. I searched for Kloan as well as a thousand imagined threats.

Nothing.

Near silence and a constant, languid echoing of water plopping into unseen pools. I perched on a proud pillar, raised above the rest of the cave, its expanse a small island. Sloping downward, a stone stairway bridged the abyss. It ended at the foot of an absurd structure. I examined the intricate architecture. The lack of a roof covering. The thousands of walls snaking in contorted patterns until the light faded. It was ridiculous. The descent led to the entrance of a mammoth labyrinth spreading its deceptions into the shadows.

The maze had an end past the shadow. Across the enormous chamber, lit by means I could not determine, I spied a second set of stairs. These rose in mythical proportions. Hundreds of steps climbed to a terrace of stone the breadth of the bewilderment itself. Dominating everything——convoluted passages and beyond, challenging the preeminence of the cavern——was a titanic relief. A carving embossed into the far wall of this subterranean insanity. Half a kilometer away, it spanned such a tremendous width and height it was easy to discern from where I stood.

It was Ambra Dawn.

The style mixed Hindu myths and alien aesthetics. She danced like Shiva on one leg. Four arms held aloft planetary systems and galaxies. A hundred snakes spilled from her skull and slithered to the ends of the sculpture. Two emerald gemstones the size of houses gazed forward into the silent space.

Where am I?

My thoughts whirled. Some cult of the Daughter, somewhere in time, buried within a planet's crust. No reasonable conjectures as to *why* I was in this bizarre place came to my mind.

I scoured the surrounding area, hoping to discover some escape from this sunken lair. Behind me was another drop to an abyss of darkness. Further back still, tall walls of stone to the ceiling without a portal. One path was available. Down the stairs, through the maze, and, presumably, emerging at the lower steps to gaze in awe at the goddess.

"Kloan!"

I called with all the power my translator speakers could manage. The hard click of the first consonant and the strong vowel ricocheted off the rocky surfaces. The sound waves returned from every direction to wash me in and out of phase.

"Kloan!"

Again and again, I cried her name. A chorus of chanting phantoms filled the chamber like some undead choir. The acoustical onslaught unsteadied me, and I paused to regain my balance. In the final trailing calls, a terrible emptiness rained. She was absent or could not answer. I was alone to derive my own solution to this enigma.

I let my thoughts project using all my Reader energies.

Ambra, please. What do you want? Why are you doing this?

No echoes. No assault from reflecting acoustics. The quiet was the same and thus more devastating. A poisonous flood of feeling flowed through me. I was abandoned and betrayed.

I approached the stairway, keeping a distance from the cliff face. The staircase was damp and slick. The strange field around my body continued to make me clumsy and awkward. I worked in vain to remove the gel. I was never able to clean myself in this environment and remained painted in a stiff matrix. I was glad to see a thick, tall railing. If I slipped, it would prevent me from tumbling to my death, the least the unhinged designers of this asylum could do for visitors.

Down the steps I went, the vast pillar I came from obscured by the broad, sloping stairway behind. The towering walls of the maze expanded with every footfall. I tried to guess the age of this place. Without knowing the mineral composition, it was impossible estimate a date. One thing was certain: this had not been a busy religious or cultural venue. The stairs were not worn from millions of footfalls. Rather, they remained chiseled and sharp, pocked by sporadic water damage.

I reached the bottom and stepped off the bridge. A soaring archway thrust above me, embedded in a wall thirty meters high. Inside, a short corridor with sides of identical dimensions marched majestically forward. The entranceway split after some distance into three passages——left, right, and straight ahead.

I would deal with the labyrinth soon enough. What held my attention under the arch was an etched inscription across its curvature. The glyphs were unintelligible, an unknown script in an alien tongue.

What happened next sent tremors through me. The text *melted*.

The symbols lost their coherency and reformed before my eyes. Foreign words carved for millennia in stone proved as malleable as fresh clay. Upon the change in writing, they assumed an ageless, petrified appearance again.

I could read these letters, an ancient Xixian format used by my ancestors. Runes designed by the primitive tribes on Xix for carving into sandstone. I dipped into the stored racial memories of my species. This drudged out the alphabet, syntax, and vocabulary. I translated this strange, living engraving, reading aloud in front of the maze. For all I knew, a code phrase existed that would simplify this puzzle and afford me easier passage.

Until all is lost, nothing is found.

I waited. No bright light illumined my path. No walls moved. No secret doorways opened. Silence mocked my words.

Appropriate.

I had no doubt I would become utterly lost in this funhouse before I would find my way out.

Dejection weighing me, I stepped under the arch and walked into the labyrinth.

Chapter 39

The external world of physics has thus become a world of shadows. In removing our illusions we have removed the substance, for indeed we have seen that substance is one of the greatest of our illusions. The frank realization that physical science is concerned with a world of shadows is one of the most significant of recent advances.

Arthur Stanley Eddington

I stepped down the high-walled corridor to the three-way split and turned left. No rational reason for this decision existed. *A priori*, I had a one-third chance of success along each route. Assuming there *was* a way out of this maze.

I decided the direct path was too obvious and likely a feint. After all, who goes through all the trouble of making a colossal, stone labyrinth buried deep in a massive cavern and doesn't possess some degree of gamesmanship?

The passageways forked. They turned, zigged and zagged. Corridors plunged back into themselves or previous routes in a dizzying fashion. The complexity forced me to focus and memorize the detailed geometry.

While I stumbled through the surrounding perplexity, however, I questioned my assumptions. This incredible structure had a purpose, one beyond testing the two-dimensional intellectual powers of a Xix. What convinced me was the ubiquitous artwork coating the sides of the labyrinth.

The compositions had deteriorated and were almost unrecognizable. Because I could not determine the materials used in the work, I still could not gauge the age of this place. Considering the most unstable dyes, the murals were over ten thousand years old. If the compounds were of advanced, decay-resistant chemistries, they could be much older.

I wandered through the maze, passing hundreds of illustrations. They depicted similar events in separate locations. Partial paintings retained different aspects of the story in a generally discernible form. By observing many of them, I assembled a rough mythology I presumed belonged to the artists.

The walls portrayed a cosmogenic fable. A mother goddess hatches from a golden egg. From her myriad limbs spread essential primordial constituents, but not those of standard creation myths, such as the four elements. Instead, she unfurled tapestries of interwoven spirits. Their forms fantastical and diverse. Their appendages, tongues, and hair braiding together to birth stars, nebulae, and galaxies.

To my considerable confusion, the paintings possessed one consistent eccentricity. Every drawing present was asymmetric. The arms of the creator, the projections of her power, and the assemblies of the entities in her weavings all appeared on her left side. At first, I assumed these lopsided murals were a product of decay. The depositions on one portion may have faded. However, I encountered one unbalanced illustration after the other. At times the right half was more intact than the other. The pattern was unmistakable. and bewildering. Their portrayals of genesis accessed a bisected fraction of the canvas allotted.

Had I time, I would have analyzed this curious culture, sought to understand what themes and moralities such a mythology would undergird. My anxiety would not allow it. I pressed forward, narrowing the selection of possible routes as I memorized the maze. At last, I took one passageway leading to a true dead end. In my mental map, it was the last route in this subspace of the labyrinth from the initial left turn.

I had come through hundreds of paintings. I had learned an odd creation myth. As a reward, this section ended with another proverb sliced in stone. It too was in ancient Xixian. No doubt the product of the scrambled and reformed textual magic I had witnessed before. A purpose haunted this space beyond a simple puzzle.

> ***Whatever is of a nature to arise,***
> ***is thereby of a quality to cease.***

Whereas the first text had read ironic, this sentence brought on some apprehension. Was it simply an encapsulation of mortality? Millions of similar texts existed across the galaxy. Diverse species have struggled with concepts of death. I had lived over four hundred years, half the average Xixian lifespan. It was not uncommon for those of my age to begin extended, sober contemplations of our fate. Was this an adage for the foresighted?

Or was its meaning less profound and far more immediate? A warning for the fools who entered the labyrinth, who had dared challenge the designer? Was time limited in some way that implied an approaching threat to my being?

I could have continued a long, neurotic analysis, parsing the text and finding a thousand possible applications to my current predicament. Danger or not, my own impatience pressed me faster than any fear could restrain me. I turned my back on the inscription and retraced my path to the primary branch point.

This time, I went right.

What I experienced in this portion of the maze was similar, if a dramatic variation on a deeper theme. Again, the bafflement of passages. Again, the corroded artwork of a cult that had long ago passed away. Again, my journey would end at an impassable wall with a message. One morphed into coherency for my consumption.

I had anticipated the ancient artists would offer an opposite-handed exclusivity, one to reflect this opposing direction I had chosen. Instead, an identical left-right asymmetry was present. Everything depicted occurred on the same side of a majestic deity. The contrast lay in the nature of the two divinities portrayed.

The previous portion of the maze contained stories of a nurturing mother goddess. This section presented a ravaging destroyer. Congealed from a thousand angry spirits, a demon took shape in this cosmogenesis. It spent its infinite supply of time tearing through worlds and galaxies. The fiend devoured bodies and souls, beauty and love, laying waste to an entire cosmos. Ultimately, everything froze in a timeless winter, the god as well. It was an extraordinary mythological duality. The terse words etched into the wall at the end of this portion did little to dispel this interpretation.

Yes and No birth Mu.

Ancient Xixian writing speaking Zen Buddhist philosophies. *Who were these creatures?* Could they have been human? Such divergence in the art and architecture suggested a disparate subspecies. It might have been a group of humans and nonhumans who had lived together extended periods. The cohabitation influencing their respective cultures. Again, I could have continued to speculate. In another reality I would have enjoyed doing so. My need to resolve this test and exit the maze overpowered my curiosity.

Humbled by my failures in outsmarting the designer of this labyrinth, I retraced my steps. I suspected the ultimate purpose was not solving the puzzle, however, but the journey. The architect imposed an education in images and words regardless of my choices. I returned to the entrance point and selected the forward path.

It was the most devious of the three. I spent hours trudging, backtracking, looping, and fighting a growing frustration. I tired of memorizing the confounding corridors. I fought a deepening physical and mental fatigue. The greatest exhaustion came from analyzing the ancient artwork. The final, and presumably key, graphical catechism from the earnest cult artists.

I struggled. What tried my patience was the disappointing predictability. All this effort! After presenting so many bizarre mythological cogitations, they settled on a messiah construct. Another savior story took shape in the drawings. They plastered its particularities across the maddening walls of the labyrinth.

At least they had spun a unique remix of the redeemer narratives. The imaginative, and likely sexually repressed, mythologizers presented a tale of romantic redemption. The narrative broke the mysterious devotion to left and right asymmetry. Along the forward direction were murals depicting a more symmetric universe. In the center of the paintings, the mother goddess and demon battled in a titanic conflict.

A glowing figure arose from nothingness. The savior stormed toward the clashing titans. It did not engage in battle with the fiend as might be anticipated. Instead, the redeemer threw the monster to the side and *mated* with the deity. An act, it would appear from the degraded artwork, destroying them both.

The devil rose, gazing on the cosmos in hunger. From the ashes and smoke of the ruined gods, an offspring of their consummation was incarnate. The god-child *devoured* the nemesis in one cosmic-sized bite. The last images show this new divine expanding to cover the wall.

I am sorry to say I did not examine the last illustrations with significant attention. As I gazed at these final compositions in wonder, a glow grew in front of me. Pushing my intellectual curiosity to the side, I rushed down the passageway after this radiance. My momentum thrust me through a second archway of the labyrinth and into a vast open space.

The giant relief of Ambra overpowered the entire expanse of my vision, sickening me with strange vertigo. Following the sculpture downward, my eyes fell on the mountain of stairs below it. From my glimpses at the peak of the pillar, I knew these steps rose toward the carving and ended at an expansive plateau. I could not see the top from this perspective. The stairway appeared to ascend without end.

To my left and right, the outer wall of the maze ran until it crashed and fused with the sides of the cavern. Behind me was the labyrinth. There was no other direction to follow but upward. I moved forward and readied to climb.

Each stair of this massive ascent measured over a meter in height. It was perfect for a Xix but impractical for a human being. Yet it was not the design of the stairs that brought the customized nature of this place to my awareness. It was the lines carved into the face of the first step.

A final phrase, letters prepared specifically for me. Words asking a mystifying question.

Where are the anti-gods, Waythrel?

Chapter 40

What must I do? I see nothing but obscurities on every side.

Blaise Pascal

My name.

The transmutation of texts into Xixian languages should have prepared me, but the use of my name still shocked. This remarkable shrine was tens to hundreds of thousands of years old. Personalization unsettled me.

The dangling monoliths of Ambra's form suggested explanations. We had created something transformative on New Earth. The product had grown into a phenomenon for which a placement in time and space had lost a standard meaning. Spacetime shaken and stirred. I did not know *when* I was now——it could be in some far future or deep past. Had Ambra and her legion of souls constructed this place anticipating my arrival? All seemed possible. Believable.

Those were abstract thoughts. Seeing my own name etched into the rock required recovery. I fought to collect myself and continue.

Where are the anti-gods, Waythrel?

The words reverberated in my mind, but I pushed them aside and climbed the stairway. One hundred meters later, I pulled over the final step in exhaustion. Before me was a floor of gray stone, polished like marble. Ahead was a table, too small to have been visible from my perch when I arrived. A solid block of alabaster, it appeared more like an altar than anything else.

It was not empty.

Lying across its length was a human body draped in beige robes. Her porcelain skin shone in the ethereal light of the cavern. Sparse clumps of orange hair drooped to the slab surface. The deformed skull exhibited a familiar intricacy of instrumentation. The figure was a child, a girl, fast asleep.

"Kloan!" I cried, rushing forward.

I did not get far. Within several meters of the white plinth, I could not progress. A primitive defense field causes sudden physical reactions. The barrier separating us was more sophisticated. Numerous attempts to breach it failed. I concluded it worked on my nervous system, robbing me of any ability to move or act. Whatever the cause, every time I tried to approach beyond a certain point, I was standing still.

"Kloan!"

She did not wake or show any signs of disturbance.

"Ambra!" I pleaded to the lunging goddess above. "It must end. We have had enough. Let us out!"

I moved to pound on the invisible barrier in my frustration. My listless arms hung at my sides.

I sat on the cold floor, despairing and rattled. Minutes, hours. The flow of time slipped through my awareness. Only the incessant echo of dripping water testified to the passage of each moment. I was bereft of ideas and empty of energy to continue.

What was the purpose? A separation, riddles and mazes. Bizarre and unfathomable mythologies. A reunion dangled before me and snatched away. To teach me something? My suspicion, but I had learned nothing from the ridiculous paintings or the obscure koans in stone.

How was I to know what was expected? What required? I flailed a few steps from her I sought. A reward withheld from a nymph who had not yet absorbed her lesson——how was I to pass this test and open the prison?

Where are the anti-gods, Waythrel?

The unbidden words forced me to concentrate. Of everything I had seen, of all I had read in this mystifying place, there had been a single question. At the last, there had indeed been a riddle demanding from me an answer. It was amazing I understood so late.

Where are the anti-gods?

I went deep into myself. All my focus, intellect, and Reader senses focused on this query.

Where are the anti-gods? *Anti* must refer to our enemies, those creatures of material inversion. What about *anti-gods*? Was this asking about the religion of the Anti?

I strained to recall the vicious time loops carrying us through the clone colony. The indoctrinations. The strange philosophies. The Anti possessed a cosmology and belief system. But gods? I searched my memory. I had come across no words, no artwork, no evidence of any kind suggesting the Anti worshipped deities. Of course, a secular culture was not uncommon in the galaxy. Such societies tended to outnumber the religious. However, every sentient species developed first through a more irrational period preceding the flowering of a scientific skepticism.

The Great God perished before the Nous could be. All remaining was the dust of destruction, a single theme devoid of counterpoint. But in this powder lay a seed. Of the ice, there lingered frost. Of the day, there remained a star beam. And of love, there endured hope.

The memory from the indoctrination sessions flowed through my mind. The Anti had myths. Their anti-gods? Destroyed! Erased in a cosmic catastrophe. A perfect reflection of their minority role in the universe.

I stood and shouted.

"There are no anti-gods because the creation story is about their destruction."

I paused to allow my words to reach whatever was monitoring this madness. After some time, I stepped toward Kloan. I got nowhere.

"Ambra, please! This answer is correct!"

Accurate or not, it was not the response the goddess sought. I examined my assumptions and attempted to dig deeper into this conundrum.

Where are the anti-gods, Waythrel?

On the surface, the question almost seemed literal. At this stage of our infernal quest, I indeed accepted the existence of gods. Not in the supernatural sense, but the monstrously natural. The Synphel abomination. The divergent incarnations of the Daughter. Creatures, beings, syntheses of the elements of this universe. Deities obeying the physical laws inherent therein. Yet so advanced, so mighty that *gods* was the one word appropriate for them. I had experienced them. I had tasted of their power, love, and transcendent animosity.

It was my scientific naturalism that guided me toward a solution. I presumed the gods we encountered were products of the material building blocks we knew to exist. However, the presence of the Anti proved how biased my view of reality was. If gods of matter existed, why shouldn't there be gods of antimatter? If so, *where were they?* The Anti had known of the *devil ball* for eons. Why had they never developed or mentioned or sought out their own anti-gods?

An obvious hypothesis arose. Like the Anti themselves, their gods were few. I had encountered two transcendent entities in our travels. One that I helped create had embroiled me in a cosmic quest attracting the other. Hardly a dataset on which to build a model. Still, it seemed such assemblies, these gods, were uncommon. As a general principle, the number of large compositions is small relative to their constituent parts. This explained why there were so few divinities.

And the building blocks of matter outnumbered those of its inverse by orders of magnitude.

That was it!

Understanding dawned. No anti-gods existed for the simple reason that *they could not assemble.* The Orb is a construction of beyond quintillions of souls. An ocean of components bordering on uncountable. How much antimatter was there in the universe? Relatively, the total might as well be zero.

What quantity could remain isolated from its antithesis long enough to develop star systems? Life and intelligence? How many such species would survive their wild adolescence to achieve stability? Of these, what number of minds remained for a collective? One able to mature into a being like those I had encountered?

The more I considered it, the more unlikely it became. The deities of the Anti had indeed perished in the creation. Genesis had wiped out the material from which their divinities could be fashioned. Our universe lacked the raw elements to construct anti-sentience at that level.

Something about this realization disturbed me, but I did not stop to ponder any more. I had the answer. This time I was sure of it.

"There are no anti-gods, Ambra. There never were and never will be. They cannot exist, because there isn't enough antimatter to support them."

With the last echo of my words, a tonal chord rang across the underground chamber. Composed of multiple harmonic frequencies, it spanned the infrabass to a shattering ultrasonic. The air rattled in front of me. I took this as a sign and stepped toward Kloan.

This time I reached her.

Chapter 41

We have found a strange footprint on the shores of the unknown. We have devised profound theories, one after another, to account for its origins. At last, we have succeeded in reconstructing the creature that made the footprint. And lo! It is our own.

Arthur Stanley Eddington

I reached the gleaming altar, and she opened her eyes.

"Waythrel?"

She was alert. Her body showed no signs of the sluggishness of prolonged sleep, drugs, or neuro-fields. It was as if she had been suspended in time and restored to the temporal flow.

"Where am I?"

I grasped her hands. "Kloan, are you okay? Are you hurt?"

She leaned up, passing her fingers over the slick surface of the slab in confusion and interest. Her eyes swept across the enormous stairway and maze. They settled on the pendulous goddess relief over us.

"Holy shit."

Joy flowed through me. "Then you are unharmed?"

She whistled while squinting at the sculpture above us, returning attention to her body. "Two legs, two arms, two feet, proper digits. A head. No blood. No new scars. No memories. You tell me." She gestured to the vast chamber. "What is this place? What are we doing here? And why do you look like you've run around that lunatic maze down there fifty times?"

"Because I have," I said, eliciting a single eyebrow raise. "It is an exhausting story. We were divided. I was half a kilometer away over there. I came through the labyrinth. I had to absorb a message and answer a riddle, or we could never leave." I recounted the narrative as she sat raptly before me on the stone structure.

"I want to see the question," she said, hopping off the edge of the altar. "Might need some Xixian handholding to get down these stairs, though."

With my help, she descended the stairway on foot, although she could have floated down with ease. One hundred hops later, we reached the bottom.

Kloan studied the inscription, a joyous light on her face. "Your own private test of doom," she said, tracing the letters with her finger. "I'll have to trust you on the meaning. I can't read a bit of it."

"What I do not understand is why," I said.

"Why what?" she asked, spinning in place and taking in the grandeur of the cavern.

"All of this. Why were we brought here?"

"You said it yourself—to learn a lesson. I think you have."

"This is an awful lot of trouble to get me to think about something."

"Sometimes living a question answers it better than thinking. Our brains too often get in the way of thought. These repetitions trapping us are designed to impress learning into us. So we have more than facts in our minds. We *change*. Data we need to assimilate to take the next step, and, finally, to exit the loop."

"Is it possible?" I asked. "Will we ever escape it?"

"*Ever* and *possible* both lose their meaning in all this, don't you think? We'll never get there even if we do, and it seems *all* possibilities are sampled in the summation."

"More Kloan-babble I cannot follow," I said, but held her hand. "At least I should be able to understand this one. It focused on *me*. Lessons for me. Motivations sure to drive me to reach within for answers."

"Is it love, my Xixy pixie?" she asked, glancing at our clasped appendages. "Are you ready to confess to me your true feelings?"

I ignored her. "So I deduced a solution to a riddle, and satisfied the goddess, or whoever is behind this. To answer what question? One obsessed with the metaphysics of antimatter gods! Of what possible point is all this effort for such esoterica?"

"Physics is esoteric, but without it, the universe ceases to be."

"*My* knowing nature's laws has no impact on whether the cosmos will exist. Neither will my understanding the hypothetical inverse divinities."

Her face fell. She focused her bright eyes on my clusters. "Are you so certain, Waythrel?"

My eyestalks buzzed. "Of course. How can what I understand about the creation be of any deep significance to reality itself?"

Kloan turned away. "A broken continuum is mighty unpredictable."

The child was irrepressibly disconcerting.

I soldiered on. "Which brings us back to this granite extravagance. What is the point? Why are we here? What could she be up to? It does not make sense."

"Ha! Well, one thing's for sure. Ambra moves in mysterious ways." She pointed above. "Whatever her motives, I don't think we'll have time to consider them anymore in this place."

A bright light grew from the ceiling, dazzling and forcing me to avert my eyestalks. It extended tendrils of radiance toward us. Long tentacles launched about our forms as if searching for prey.

"Time's up," said Kloan, her eyes cast down to the deep shadows on the rock.

The luminous limbs pulled us off the ground and to the blinding source overhead. My last memory was of her voice echoing in a maelstrom of sound and brilliance.

"See you again soon, Waythrel!"

Chapter 42

I have seen beyond the bounds of infinity and drawn down daemons from the stars. I have harnessed the shadows that stride from world to world to sow death and madness.

H. P. Lovecraft

Morning. The warm light of a star I did not know yet had seen one million times. My awareness lacked a concept of time. No history with permanence. No trustworthy memories. I fell forever into dreamscapes, one after the other, without hope of waking.

Out of breath (in my own Xixian manner), I rested several meters from the gleaming portal. We must have climbed. Flushed, Kloan sweated from exertion. I recalled a cave—mazes and riddles and brilliance. I did not remember climbing or how we got here.

The gate, I remembered. Its parameters were intimate from infinite expeditions through this spacetime anomaly. An Orb slice mixing a viscous honeyed surface. One waiting for our submersion to cast us through existential dreams. Its horrible beauty tugged as I gawked at the profound ocean of stars within.

"Something's wrong," said the clone.

My gaze centered on the starry ring, but several eyes darted to the cyborg. She was taut, as straight as a light beam. Her eyes swept the space between us and the disk, vigilant as prey before a predator.

The atmosphere undulated. The landscape glitched and blurred. The air itself coagulated. I panicked as the amorphous ripples solidified, adopting form and hue. A multitude of arms, sixfold symmetry, and a patch of eyes springing from a conical torso.

"Hello again, Waythrel," it said.

Nightmares rampaged through my thoughts. Memories. Of what?

Do not imagine that this forgery deceived me. The imposter burned my Reader senses, radiating intense cognitive fields. Complex. Deep with a power I had sensed in the presence of the Ambra-Orb. However, the sentience mimicking my lover felt more malevolent than profound. Gazing at this version of my life mate unleashed a torrent of disturbing images. Anger, slaughter, pain, madness.

Kloan grasped my arm. "Don't let it in your mind," she whispered.

"Let it?" came the smooth voice of my beloved. The tones were perfect mimics, but alien. "If you have any perception, then you know nothing you can do can stop me."

"No, but *she* will!" I declared, shocking myself with this triumphant exclamation. A subconscious certitude spun my eyestalks behind us. I awaited the form of Ambra Dawn.

She did not arrive.

Kloan screamed and fell to her knees, grasping her head. She rocked back and forth, moaning, crying, tears pouring down her cheeks. Spit frothed from her mouth. Seizures shook her as she shivered and collapsed. Her eyes flipped back into their sockets. Alongside the frosted stone in her forehead were two white orbs. They stared from a hideous mask of trembling torture. Blood trickled from her left nostril.

"Stop!" I cried. I dropped to the ground, grabbing her in my arms. Her jaw clenched, tearing her tongue and lips. I ripped a piece of clothing away from her robes and placed it between her teeth.

I did not dare imagine I could shield her mentally. This dark god overwhelmed my vision as a Reader. I had to shut it out as if closing my eyes. Still, I was blinded. What would an attempt at defense have achieved? Kloan was formidable beyond my imagining. This devil had tossed her like a toy flung by a toddler in a tantrum.

"As you wish," said the thing.

Kloan fell to the ground, unresponsive. I checked her vitals. She was alive, but unconscious. A quick mind probe indicated severe trauma without major physiological damage.

"We are not ready to destroy her yet," it said. "We need additional information."

"We? Are you one or many? Where are the others? What do you want?" I cradled Kloan's head in my arms.

"The legendary Waythrel of Xix cannot surmise?" The demon performed a Xixian body gesture that can be translated as a sarcastic smile. "Or did you think your crude experiment with Ambra Dawn was somehow unique in all the universe?"

A terrible dread settled on me. "What are you?"

"One of the other gods, of course."

"Rakshasi." How I knew the name confused me.

"She has spoken of me."

"You are a mental union? A group consciousness?"

"The best understanding your intellect can manage. The conservation of organizing principles is invariant throughout the continuum. Assemblies as rudimentary as your mind should grasp this. Strings dissect into smaller entities. The deconstruction plunges to levels to which your philosophies have never scurried. Time itself stumbles in this constituent maze. Such structures form bottomless foundations. Quarks to molecules, cells to tissues. Intelligence.

Cogent networks evolving toward celestial wanderers striding the cosmos like giants."

Images assaulted me. They ripped my soul from my creaturely perspective. Poisoned mockery impaled me on a momentary glimpse from the eyes of a divinity. Eons as instants, parsecs like small steps. A morality foreign and horrible oppressed me. My mind teetered on splintering.

"You are the atoms of our minds," the entity concluded. It slung my awareness back to the dirt and rock.

Disoriented, terrified, I shielded my eyes. "What do you want with us?"

"We search for what your creation-god is planning. We suspect her intentions are far from pure as they concern others of our kind."

"I do not understand."

"The Ambra-Orb. What does she wish with this creature?" it said, gesturing toward Kloan, who lay unmoving in my arms.

"Ambra-Orb?" My mind raced, feverish in the terrible presence of this thing. "Yes, wait, I remember. She is the Sphere."

"Haven't you managed to put this together? Or can your feeble intelligence not retain anything in this recursive playground of hers? Now tell us, what do you conclude is the point of this cyborg? Think through all you have encountered. You will not enter this gate until you have answered to our satisfaction."

"Why can't you read it from our thoughts?"

A hostile impatience radiated. It was like the glow of a furnace door opened in front of me. I could not shield myself from it. If one's consciousness could feel heat, mine was scalded.

"We have taken all your memories and impressions. We know all that has happened, and it is not enough. Her deviousness is deep beyond explaining. Her true purpose is encoded in your cognition. You must reason with us, think through her desires. Explain to us now what she wishes. What you understand about what has transpired. In the *deduction* is the answer."

"Why me? This clone understands far more. Yet you threaten her survival."

"She lacks a need of processing for this precise rationale." Synphel *smiled* again, and the horror of it on this creature sickened me. "You, however, do not comprehend much at all, but the puzzle pieces are all within your thoughts. You must try to assemble them."

I held the unresponsive child in my arms. I continued to pray Ambra would return and deliver us. But focusing on this hope was impossible. The monstrous presence before me forced engagement.

In a terrible panic, my mind raced. It was no longer my own. My cognitive processes transformed into buttons in the hands of a fiend. I dizzied trying to stitch together the blurred memories of time loops. Horrific nightmares. Death, pain, and carnage. Beautiful mysteries. Gentle, loving moments.

Thousands, millions of passages I had forgotten. This creature yanked them through my awareness. The god's pressure unearthed the ruins of my recall. It flooded me with events I could not access. My body swayed.

The plans of the Anti.

Yes, it was the unifying element to all the journeys. It was the one thing making sense.

I babbled. "This clone is playing out all the routes to the destruction of the Daughter. Ambra is encouraging it. Yet nothing ever happens. We circle back. The actions in the past have no lasting impact on her existence."

"Continue."

My air sacs clogged from stress secretions. My oxygen content lowered and fogged my thoughts. I concentrated harder. "Why would she encourage this? She fears the creature."

"And?"

"She looks in the failure of cause and effect for a vulnerability. The thread that makes this cyborg so unusual. Yes, I remember. She said all the gods dread her. Why?"

"There is a discontinuity. A place in an inaccessible singularity of space and time. She is the source. We are unable to read her."

"Ambra must fear her, too. She is either trapping her in this loop to forever keep her here, or to study her, or both. She is trying to prevent Kloan from doing something you all anticipate but cannot see."

The diabolical Synphel was gone. Vanished in a breath as I processed my thoughts. It left no trace behind. No hint this being spanning galaxies had displaced a molecule of the atmosphere.

Heat from the local star warmed my chilled skin. I uncovered my eyestalks, feeling like a nymph again, terrified of things I could not see, events unrealized except in the dim recesses of my darkest dreams.

Kloan lay wounded in my arms. She coughed roughly, gasping for air. Her eyes flew open, and she lurched to the ground, shivering.

I applied what medical training I had. Our long association with humans provided us a significant knowledge of their anatomy. Without proper instruments, I could not be sure, but it seemed the trauma had not damaged her body.

Her mind was another issue.

"I've seen the true abyss," she whispered, staring into space. "It's been infused into me. I didn't know. Never *imagined*. Such impossible horror—I don't want to live. But death! Immortality and hell. Waythrel, please, can we *unexist?*"

"Kloan—"

"I've smelled it." Tendrils of saliva clung like webs between her gnashing teeth. "Its foul taste flooded my mouth and nostrils. A vile sludge suffocating me in stench and slime." She closed her eyes and cried to the sky. "I heard the groan and weeping of entire galaxies in the void." Her body convulsed in my arms.

I tried to comfort her. "Shock. Violence to your mind. It is not real. You are safe. We both are, now." I did not believe my own words.

She turned wide eyes to me. Her hands grasped my appendages, pulling the twelve fingers of each to her lips. She kissed them, one by one. Her thoughts reached toward mine, a need for contact with something decent, a being with affection. Even a monster.

"You don't understand, dear Waythrel. I've seen what you have not, what a Xix could never see and survive. There is no forgetting. No more peace or love. No more safety." Tears streamed down her face.

"And no more Kloan."

She bowed her head into her lap, whispering. "I traveled. To the place of demons. They are *real*. They are lurking between the shadows of the stars. And they are *waiting*."

"For what?" I asked, a primal chill firing through my form.

"For all of us...and the dying of the light."

Chapter 43

---

*I perceived that I was on a little round grain of rock and metal,
filmed with water and with air, whirling in sunlight and darkness.
On the skin of that little grain all the swarms of men, generation by
generation, had lived in labour and blindness, with intermittent joy
and intermittent lucidity of spirit. All their history, with its folk-
wanderings, its empires, its philosophies, its proud sciences, its social
revolutions, its increasing hunger for community, was but a flicker in
one day of the lives of the stars.*

Olaf Stapledon

"What do we do now, Kloan?"

Bewildered, I struggled for direction. She showed no sign of interest in the journey we had been moments from undertaking. The child crumpled on the ground next to me, her chin heavy on her knees. Her eyes stared across a million light-years.

To what, I dared not ask. I feared probing would break her fragile psyche. After the things she had said, I also questioned the wisdom of knowing.

I rested beside her in silence as the afternoon wore on. A portion of me worried about the forces below. Would they discover us? Discovery meant certain capture and probable death given Kloan's dysfunction.

Increasingly, my thoughts and focus drifted. After the encounters of the last few hours, everything else receded, small and feeble. My mind visualized planets. They teemed with sentient creatures stumbling about their daily routines. Their actions accelerated. Years shrank to microseconds. Generations passed, entire cultures rose and fell, world civilizations matured and perished. Yet all of it, the sum across a galaxy of stars, inconsequential. Transient vanity.

I had not seen the full horror forced upon Kloan, but for a short moment, I had glimpsed through the eyes of a demon. Its titanic perspective reduced me to a mote. A shattering vastness rendered our lives to femtoseconds. Our evanescent chemical dances were humbled beside a timeless awareness.

I grasped her despair. What possible significance could the pair of us have? What madness was it to believe ephemeral molecules had meaning in this colossal cosmic ocean? I had experienced the presence of a deity. I could no longer sense my self.

"Waythrel."

My eyestalks darted behind me, filling my vision with images generating fear. Standing still and tranquil, in dark yet phosphorescent beauty, was Synphel once more. My emotions ran a sickening gamut. Terror, love, longing, disgust, desire, and elation. I rotated my body to the thing, my limbs trembling.

"Please. No more. Do not torture us anymore. If there is pity in the gods the universe has created, leave us in peace. We are dust."

"Waythrel, it is I. Open your heart."

The rush of affection and concern sweeping through me was overpowering. Gone was the malignancy of consciousness I had endured from the demon. Instead, I drank the unmistakable presence of my long-separated mate. A loving personality poured through my Reader senses. A healing aura radiated, absent from the hellish apparition.

Forgive me for using the clumsiness of your language to bimodally gender her. *Her* is the pronoun I will use, although it warps the nature of any of our six genders. But your word *it* distorts her character to a greater degree, erasing all aspects of sexual differentiation.

In this meeting with my lover, the intimacy of the encounter I choose to relate, cries out for something better. For on this day, we were not two *its*. A poor approximation is that we were two *hers*. The love between us acted as a balm to the wounds the monstrosities had inflicted on Kloan and me.

"*Synphel.*" My eyes danced while maintaining focus on her. "How? You are part of the Group Mind. With Ambra. How are you here?"

"We have become something beyond what you can conceptualize. I am clothed in atoms and molecules, stitched in flesh, incarnate here to meet with you."

"Your consciousness?"

"All of Synphel is assembled from the dust and debris of this world. We are not alone yet none of our host is truly here."

I struggled to understand her words. I imagined a mental projection. The equivalent of a complex transform arriving at this point of space and time. It possessed the power from afar to manipulate matter magically. To construct a completed organism from the inanimate particles on a distant planet. Not a random form, but a precise replica of my lifemate.

I was slow to learn this lesson. I had witnessed the reality in the face-off between the demon and Ambra. I had to witness it in repetition to absorb the depth of the implications. I could not doubt. They were—or had become, or would be—gods.

Her voice spoke in my mind.

Divinities to you, yet you are one of our makers, Waythrel. Is this not itself a miracle? We are still composed of the elements of this cosmos. We do not transcend it, although we pursue transcendence. Indeed, that is what all this is about.

She turned the bulk of her eyestalks to gaze beside me. "Kloan, please come here."

In my dread and wonder in this reunion, I had neglected the child. She stirred and rose, facing my partner. Torment haunted her eyes.

Synphel approached the girl. "They seek to strip you of the energies to carry out your quest. To freeze you in place, suspended and defused," she said. "If they understood, they would destroy you. Their hesitancy reflects the terrible potential in you they intuit. All timelines become discontinuous in your presence. A phenomenon unique in all the continuum to you. You are the nexus in all that is and all that was and will be."

"I am broken."

"As is our cosmos. Neither beyond healing."

Synphel placed her upper hands to Kloan's face, surrounding her head with twenty-four fingertips. The dark black of my lover's skin contrasted with the white of the clone. The soft, lipid-insulated hominid clashed with the elongated, leathery appendages of a Xix.

Kloan closed her eyes and wept.

"Yes, remember the dreams. Find the resolution to the asymmetry. Accept again the calling. Let it shine and char to ash the torment you have seen."

The cyborg wrapped her arms around Synphel and shook with sobs.

I had studied the development of human infants and children. Proper brain maturation depended on nurturing physical contact. The girl embraced a nightmare of limbs and eyes. The instinct overcame discomfort as the child purged the emotional poison.

After several minutes, Kloan relaxed, and she stepped backward, wiping her eyes and face. "Thank you," she said, peering into my lover's eyestalks. "Thank you, all."

"The horror will never leave you," said Synphel. "But it will no longer overthrow your mind. Follow your meditations. Take your pain and scars and use them to grow."

Relief spread through me. This cyborg had abducted me. Committed atrocities in my presence. Befuddled and frightened me on innumerable occasions. Yet I rejoiced. My Xixian nature. Our desire for healing that often damaged more than it helped.

With Kloan, it was much more than such a generic response. She elicited from me many of my feelings for her progenitor. Although so different from Ambra, I could not help but love her.

Synphel's eyestalks divided between us. "Now you must regroup and continue your journey."

Chapter 44

Nature does not dictate dualities, trinities, quarterings, or any "objective" basis for human taxonomies; most of our chosen schemes, and our designated numbers of categories, record human choices from a cornucopia of possibilities offered by natural variation from place to place, and permitted by the flexibility of our mental capacities.

Stephen Jay Gould

A spasm of desperation swept through me.

"Synphel, please. Don't go." Surprising myself, I stepped forward and entwined my fingers with hers. "I cannot keep you. I know this. You are a memory made flesh. But I am unable to let you go." Her digits twirled around my own. The foolishness of my yearning mocked me. "So real. This fantasy I touch is precious beyond words to me."

"Have you ever loved a goddess, Waythrel?"

She pressed her form alongside my own. The skin cilia of our compatible mating types locked and engaged. The biological program sent shivers through me. Without conscious decision, my eyestalks probed and found hers. Each wrapped about the other. Eighteen sighted organs formed a complex braid staring at the others.

I did not care that I would mate with an avatar sculpted out of the sands of this distant planet. I cared little that the Xix I knew was gone, altered and absorbed into a godlike entity full of countless personalities. It mattered not that those trillions observed. In love, disinterest, and emotions unfathomable. They partook of this moment of our deepest intimacy.

No, I only wished to merge with her one last time.

It is difficult to explain the oddities of our physiology to you of Earth. All sexual species mingle a hereditary substance. Our reproductive combination comprises six sexes with separate gametes containing fractions of what you would call the Xixian genome. Our mating pair was an integral element in the whole.

There is no point in explaining how our genotype could be stable. No space in this story for the complexities and nonlinearity of group evolution. No time to define what constitutes an organism under selection. What matters is we formed the core structure on which the procreating ensemble assembled.

Our bond had to be deep, strong, and durable. Our sexual encounters, the longest of our copulative pairings, were therefore very much unlike your own brief moments. Many pair mates of our type entered into lifetime unions outside the reproductive set.

Our lovemaking began in mutual penetration with a hidden appendage. To you a strange variant of a tentacle, it thrust through a slit in our torso and hunted the equivalent organ in our mate. Perhaps in analogy to your male's erections, this process initiated arousal.

These tentacles were not injection devices working alone. They sought the other. Each wrapped around its counterpart like an Earth vine. Or closer still, the entwining eyestalks above our torsos. The effect on our physiology parallels the stimulation of your genital nerve webs.

This god-Synphel drove me to a growing ecstasy of fusion. Our reproductive arms touched, caressed, and enveloped their corresponding limbs. They pressed forward in opposite directions. Body temperature spiked as they found the opening slit, teasing it mercilessly. The appendages plunged inward toward the deep neuronal nexus buried within.

Here is the element of our dance that is the hardest to explain. The tip of the penetrating member resembles an ovate leaflet of your plants. Thousands of microbristles decorate its exterior, each pregnant with nerve-like protrusions. The extremity from Synphel penetrated my core. My mind flooded with pleasure as it wrapped around my sexual cluster. The leaf dug into the most sensitive portion. My own performed the same action to her, and our forms linked in a commanding embrace.

From our sides and backs, additional tentacles extended. These swiveled, probing for the other sexes of our mating group. They would sway until the lack of engagement quenched our copulation.

It would take some time. As the foundational element, the interweaving of our bodies was a platform for the other members. Our desire to continue was enormous. We writhed in the torment of reproductive pleasure for more than an hour.

I connected to the consciousness of Synphel through nerve clusters and Reader senses. Reflecting my previous experiences, this encounter convinced me of her true presence.

A depth revealed itself. She was more. Altered—layered and more alien. The host swirled beneath the surface of her mind. Their personalities flitted here and there across my awareness. Buried in the core of this endless mentality, I sensed Ambra. Her emotions and thoughts poured over me. They created images in my cognizance, and I dreamed she smiled.

Our physiological program ran its course. The external appendages withdrew, having failed to find their mating structures. Our bodies cooled. The tentacles inside turned uncomfortable as the pleasure dissipated. They released the drained nerve clusters and slithered out. Coiling like snakes, they returned to their own origin deep within. At the last, our eyestalks unwound. We separated, continuing to align each visual organ.

"Thank you," I said.

"I have missed you terribly," said Synphel.

Kloan walked beside us. "It was gorgeous," she said, her once-harrowed face bright. "And strange. Disturbing. Beyond beautiful. I saw oceans of them, spinning like ghosts in and out of space. A cosmos of minds."

My lover stepped toward the disk. "The third element of this visit is also completed. We had to know you would love the child, and so you have. Now begins a new cycle."

The burden of our imprisonment weighed me down.

"Where will it take us now? Have we learned what we needed to learn?" I had no idea what was expected.

She did not answer but gestured to the gateway. The whirling celestial field scrambled. Rainbows embedded in the depths flickered and trembled.

"We will not meet again in this cosmos, my dearest Waythrel," said my lover. "Still, you will not be left without me."

Synphel vanished. No sound, no rushing of air or displacement occurred. Absence alone.

The child clone and I stood together. In front blazed an incredible window to another space, other times. Behind us the radiance cast shadows in the bright light of the local star.

"We aren't alone, leaky thoughts," said Kloan, smiling. "I can feel them watching. Can you?"

I tested my Reader senses. It was faint. An echo of my mate and Ambra. Their cosmic mental ecosystem undulated in a gaggle of gravitons. Real or wishful thinking, it was comforting.

I strained, detecting other currents, other minds lurking in the depths of the churning continuum. The comfort wavered. I was a swimmer in a cold sea, lingering in a warmer current. Around us an icy, unfathomable deep lay concealed. Monsters meditated in the abyss.

"Perhaps it was better to be alone," I said, shivering.

"When there is hate, there's love," said Kloan. "Fire and ice, order and disorder, creation and destruction. Where there's Ambra, there is also me."

My eyestalks centered on her brooding features, not knowing what to think of these words. I still did not comprehend the purposes of this infinite journey. But whatever it had been—it had shifted. In taking the next steps, I was putting my trust in both the yes and the no, in the odd opposites of the two forms of the Daughter.

"The thing tore open my mind, Kloan. The journeys. The multitudes—I am remembering hordes. It's too much."

She grasped my arm. "You weren't the only one tested, Waythrel. It'll be different each time, and only when we've fully understood will we see the answer."

She glanced behind us and laughed. Following her gaze, I glimpsed two forms scaling the rocky terraces below. A redheaded clone and her towering companion.

"Seems we'll always be dancing together, Xix."

We turned back to the disk. Hand in hand, we stepped forward, the portal gel enveloping us like molasses.

We fell to a deep darkness.

Part VI

The words of wonder I watched elders weave,
the tales of Truth more strange than in my dreams:
Of ghosts so small they pass through vision's sieve
yet stitch my mind in fragile, fleshy seams.

Or hungry gods, enormous, ever starved,
who take all prey to planes beyond our own,
where time and space are infinitely carved
into a fabric rent and never sown.

To groups so gifted by the gods, the signs
and studied charms the elder priests unfold.
The depths await our readied, seeking minds.
As Shaman I may find new Truths untold.

Yet some nights I feel depths beyond our Way,
and what I am the spirits do not say.

—Mazandarani, *Sonnets from the Desert*

Chapter 45

Science cannot solve the ultimate mystery of Nature. It is because in the last analysis we ourselves are part of the mystery we are trying to solve.

Max Planck

Darkness.

A terrible blackness beyond anything I had experienced. Along with it, a chill. The surrounding space leached the warmth from my form.

A vigorous shake of my upper arm startled me.

It was Kloan, or so I surmised from her thermal shape in this total caliginosity. Her body pressed against mine. She shivered. I strained with all my senses. No smells or taste through my skin sacs. I felt nothing but the cyborg. My eighteen visual organs were useless. Zero radiation in any frequency range. Not even infrared. A perilous freeze surrounded us.

Wherever we are, came her thoughts, *we stand on something. Something's underneath.*

She was correct. I tried to speak to acknowledge her observation. The translator remained silent.

The translator!

Of course. What stupor poisoned my thinking? I was slow to adapt to these shocking dislocations in space and time.

I fiddled with the device around my neck. It emitted a pale glow blinding my eyes in this ultimate night. Adjusting, I examined our immediate environment. It was bleaker than I could have imagined.

At our feet was a pile of white dust, arranged about us. The solidified gate gel, I judged from its absence from our forms. I assumed the material had chilled and shattered into this fine powder, but I could not be sure. For the ten meters the light illuminated, I saw ice and rock. The appearance varied, ranging from frosted to clear. On top, a blue film coated all surfaces, stone and crystal. I had seen nothing like it before. It was the same in all directions. My mind raced.

What do you think this is, Waythrel? I can't read anything. It's all dark.

It was the first time Kloan had turned to me in ignorance. In our wild and disorienting journeys, the child held the advantage in all things. In this wasteland, she sounded small, lost, and searching for a parental figure, even a six-limbed alien. Rather than stoke my ego, it brought on a sense of dread. Of all the disturbing powers I had witnessed in the universe, if she was so unsure, our danger was acute.

I don't know.

You suspect. Your thoughts bubble.

I took a step. The foot slid in the frozen glaze. Moving was treacherous and required intense caution to avoid excess momentum.

She probed further. *Could it be underground? There's no light.*

Possible.

You don't think so.

There is no atmosphere, Kloan. No sound from my translator. No noise from our steps. We are in a total vacuum. The temperature outside is close to absolute zero. I assume your skin suits are keeping us alive. I do not know how long they will last.

Waythrel, they aren't mine!

I found comfort in the reminder. We were beyond our capacities, preserved by some mysterious technology provided by the same Being transporting us here. However perilous this location, I trusted in our benevolent deity.

I positioned my eyestalks, taking a spherical view.

There are no stars overhead, yet no atmosphere or light pollution to drown them out. Where are the heavens?

That's why I say underground.

Let's try to cover some ground and see what else we can find. Something will help us understand.

Data. She grinned.

Yes, some information. Our survival may depend on it.

She frowned, the glow of the translator and darkness behind chiseling her features.

All the knowledge is important to our lives, Waythrel. To the cosmos.

We should focus on the rock and ice here and worry about the universe later.

She said nothing. We slipped forward, able to see a few meters ahead of us. It was enough to avoid a pit or cliff or other danger, but it allowed us no broad view of our environment. We had little sense of the lay of the land, zero points of reference, and no navigation tools besides memory. Journeying was an act of delusional optimism.

Stones and frost. On it went. Minutes passed. Hours. Kloan continued to shiver, but the suit prevented harm. She showed no signs of hypothermia or frostbite, but I monitored her.

More glazed gravel. A giant's toy in a mineral collection, sprayed with a fixative to protect the surface from scratches. I checked the translator. The power supply would last months. The diodes illuminating our path were a greater unknown. I hoped to get several days of continuous use.

Waythrel, careful. The land is sloping down.

The child was correct. We worked harder to avoid skating on the frictionless ground. The terrain smoothed, the larger rocks giving way to pebbles and a strange sand. The thick layer of ice still coated all surfaces, specimens in a box separated from probing hands by a sheet of glass.

Kloan, can you determine nothing of this place from your searches into the past?

She shook her head.

This world's history—it never ends. It's an infinite, unchanging well. I can't look at it anymore. I fall, and always the same, this darkness and cold. It's like it has been this way forever. A frozen, dead eternity.

I mulled her ominous words. We had come to an environment unlike any we had explored, where our knowledge and powers proved useless. I focused on what we did know to quell the growing panic. If I understood anything, it was that Ambra had sent us here. The godball had arranged it. This included, I assumed, the suits that preserved two living organisms in this icy vacuum.

There had to be a purpose. We had to learn whatever the gods desired us to know. After which we would find ourselves dizzy and confused, back where we started.

The time loops have destabilized, Waythrel. I told you things changed last time. Extreme powers have entered the game.

One we cannot stop playing.

Not yet.

Is there nothing you saw in your searches? Nothing of use?

Kloan wrapped her arms around her chest shivering.

I had to look away. Too deep. A hope, maybe. Something in the distance.

We stood on a plain of some kind. If this were an underground cavern, it was enormous beyond comprehension. No dome could support the span. I grew convinced we were not entombed within the bowels of some planet. Where we were still eluded any confident model.

Waythrel, wait. Turn off the translator.

Why?

Please, just do it. There is something ahead. Far away, I think.

We need the light to see it.

No, not this. It's glowing itself. Your necklace is blinding us. Shut it off and let our eyes adjust.

I did as she asked. The gleam of the device dimmed. Darkness rushed in as some visceral thing, a tidal mist with a malevolent will of its own. I had never been in the presence of such a complete lack of radiant sources, utter blackness. It stirred primitive and unreasonable instincts. It seemed alive.

She was right. The ink enveloping us could not solidify. Far ahead, a languid light spilled from a beacon. The glow resisted the smothering obsidian, culling its imposition over space, an energy above the absolute zero of the landscape. *Potential* pulsed, a hope to battle the inevitability of thermodynamics. A chance of life.

I guess we go that way, Kloan?

She was already walking.

Chapter 46

That is not dead which can eternal lie,
And with strange aeons even death may die.

H. P. Lovecraft

We walked for strenuous hours, the distances deceptive. The beacon ahead provided the sole reference in this icebound desert. The radiance intensified. With our eyes long adjusted to the paltry illumination of the translator, we were better able to discern our own shapes. Regardless, the contents of the murky spaces beyond us remained hidden. A threatening unknown toyed with my imagination.

Exhausted, chilled, we dragged ourselves forward. Kloan's breaths exited the force field, solidifying. They drifted to the ground as a soft snow. My gaseous exchange was similar, although spread over the surface area of my skin. It produced no such dramatic display. I had no idea where we received the input atmosphere to breathe or the warmth that kept us from freezing. I noticed her fingers had begun to turn white. Whatever the capabilities of the skins encasing us, they were finite. I hoped it would be enough for the time we would spend in this ice hell.

The light grew. Shadows formed behind us—and, to my amazement, in front of us as well. Focusing the power of all my eyes, I perceived blurred silhouettes near the beacon.

Can you see those shapes? They must be large.

She nodded. *Before I stopped looking into the past of this frozen nightmare, they passed through my mind. They're transcendent. Something terrible.*

She was right. The radiance matured, our shadows deepened, and the figures ahead clarified. They towered, monumental explosions of ice above the plain. They resembled blasted magma converted to a crystalline form, locked in place. A rainbow of weak colors glitched through them.

We neared the bases of the monoliths. Arrayed in a vast ring, they dwarfed us and everything around them. Some were single jets of crystal throttling upward. Others burst from the ground like rivers with multiple tributaries. These fused into bizarre, bulked shapes suspended in impossible conformations. I counted fifty of them.

We walked beside the structures, underneath their arches. I fought disorientation when gazing for more than a moment into their translucent surfaces. Indistinct visions and motions emanated from deep within. Prolonged observation generated sensations. Feelings. *Presence.* We were not alone here, but I could not identify what it was exactly that might be with us. The experiences unnerved me, and I avoided staring into the frozen masses.

The beacon shone in the middle of the circle of giants. A small pillar of ice, simple, unlike the towering derangements circling it, rose near to Kloan's height. It formed a bowl of pristine glass at its apex. Resting in this basin was a sphere of a clear substance. A vivid rainbow churned within. It was this diamond orb that had illuminated our path and beckoned us here.

Kloan strolled about the ring of titans. She touched the glassy exteriors, gazing into the quavering imagery, immune to the disorientation. I let her have her space and time.

They're as old as everything else, Waythrel. As far as I can look, hundreds of thousands of years into the past, they are here, unchanged, unmoved.

Do you know what they are?

We'll see, she said, without elaborating.

Around she went, sampling one after another. Time drifted as I followed her. I hoped for some clarification, insight into this strange place, an indication of how we might escape it.

Beside one of the more distorted, grotesque, and twisted shapes, Kloan pulled back. Her eyes closed, her face a grimace of pain. She grasped my hand.

Waythrel, look into the ice. Give it time—but be careful. Guard your mind! Tell me what you see.

I dreaded the effort, but I stepped to the colossus before me. A tentacle of frozen matter dove from hundreds of meters above to plunge into the ground and disappear at my feet. The glass was imperfect, warped, the light and structures within bobbing and weaving. I could not see any hint of my reflection on the surface, which defied all optical physics. My balance faltered. I steadied myself on Kloan's shoulder, trying to maintain my gaze.

Pain. Horror. Bursts of images, emotions, and sensations rocked my awareness. They had no center, no cause, no explanation. Fleeting and effervescent, the terrible rampage of monstrosity nonetheless struck me like blows. I held up my limbs to ward off attack. I crouched and angled my eyes away.

Kloan wrapped her arms around me for some time as I worked to purge the vile experiences from my mind. I could not form coherent thoughts to share with her, and she did not push her own toward me. She recognized I could not process them.

My composure returned, I turned my eyes to her. *I have felt this before. Where?*

Rakshasi, came her thoughts.

It was unmistakable. The being who had threatened us. The one an unexplainable incarnation of Ambra had driven away. The demon that recurred without her intervention and tortured Kloan. This terrible deity had left a permanent impression on my psyche.

Rakshasi.

The essence of the god-thing who had desecrated Synphel's form loomed within the ice. It pressed from above, crushing hope and sanity. The devil menaced my mind, exerting a foul influence through the solid substance.

What are these things? I gestured to the monumental forms. They terrified me.

I don't know, Waythrel, but I'd guess similar. Whatever Rakshasi is, or was, whatever they are, it's of a type.

Gods? Frozen gods?

Kloan shrugged her shoulders and pursed her lips. *Up there on my weird-o-meter, for sure.*

They are not composed of the same ice covering the ground and rocks. Let us hope they do not melt! I cannot face them.

I don't know what they're made of, or how it cages these divinities. Or what Rakshasi is inside. She patted my arm. *Be calm, Waythrel. I don't think they'll melt. Or change. The harder I try, the further back I look, the more I see they have been here, like this, for epochs within chains of eons.*

The others?

All over the place. Powerful, strange, alien, unfathomable. Not as accessible. Our encounter with Rakshasi tuned us to its essence, whatever it is.

Something abominable.

I wobbled, the ground feeling far more treacherous and the air colder. The glow in the center drew me. I needed to get away from the demonic towers of crystal. I wanted to flee darkness and cold, put my hands over the bright orb like a fire.

Maybe it will be a little warm? She smiled. *Don't think there's much else to do with these cryogenic deities. The light ball's got to have a better story to tell.*

We walked toward the emanation. The perched sphere rested hundreds of meters from the ring of giants. As we approached, the temperature did increase. The lack of atmosphere meant the heat transfer occurred through radiation absorbed from the object.

I hope there are no high-frequency rays. Will the suits shield us from exposure?

Kloan didn't respond. As we advanced, she slowed and put her hand against me. I stopped, my eyes swiveling in concern. I could see nothing threatening.

There's another one.

Another what?

God-thing. Whatever. It's not like the others. It's...closer. It's moving. She squinted, gazing far off into the distance. *It's camou-flaged. Hiding in time from me. No! It's here!*

The ground shook and flung us both down. The quake forced us to steady ourselves with extremities spread. We gazed upward, awestruck as a shadow covered us.

The frozen surface around the sphere shifted and flowed. I imagined a time-lapsed glacier over millions of years. In seconds, profound volumes of ice and stone liquefied. They defied gravity, hurtling up. Coalescing, a tremendous hulk assembled. It lodged between us and the beacon, obscuring the warm radiance.

As the mountain took shape, it emitted a luminescent cyan over the surrounding plain. The tremors subsided as the bulk of the flow eased. The mass adopted more subtle forms.

Kloan slapped my arm, pointing with her other hand at the thing before us. *Look! Waythrel, look! It's us!*

Astounded, I watched glass and rock mold into a geologic facsimile of humanoid shapes. Or rather, a blended and distorted mixture of human and Xix features. The sculpture was sixfold symmetric with our numerous eyes. They sprouted not from our massive central cone but from the head of an Earthling. The face resembled none other than Kloan herself. Mouth, nose, cranial structure—it was an unmistakable, if rough and rocky replica.

The eyelids of the face flipped open. Irisless orbs glared at us, and the mountainous thing bent toward our position. The wall of rock stopped meters away. The mouth opened. Sound surprised me, but I was far beyond the point of trying to parse the acoustical physics.

"For ages uncounted, I have kept my vigil," came a god-voice rattling the plane of ice. "Now the shattered symmetry may be mended."

Chapter 47

The formation in geological time of the human body starting from a random distribution of elementary particles and the field is as unlikely as the separation of the atmosphere into its components. The complexity of the living things has to be present within the material or in the laws.

Kurt Gödel

We gawked at the incredible ice behemoth. Various clusters of my eyestalks flipped between it and Kloan for support. The enormity did not move. It did not hurry. After the chasm of time it had crossed, a few more minutes would be meaningless.

The slightest distortion refracted the light above us. A dome of some nature. The creature or its transcendental handlers had produced an environmental bubble for us.

"We have air." My joy at the experience of sound surprised me.

She turned toward the ice hulk. "Where are we, godling?"

The jagged lips boomed, "Where is of no significance anymore."

"Okay...*when* are we?" she offered.

"At the death of all things." It motioned to the crystal titans. "Even the gods."

She cocked her head to one side. "How can the gods die?"

"They are the children of the cosmos. Their tissues and energies derive from it. They are broken now."

The deep rumblings of the voice jolted the innermost parts of my body.

"Their Mother, our universe, is ill. She dies. She has been, is, and will be dying to eternity. In this time, the weakness pierces the threshold. Thus, they unbecome."

I ventured. "Yet you thrive."

"I am their guardian. The keeper of the minds. I watch over until the messengers come, the future when the past will end."

The cryptic words baffled me. "What makes you different?"

"Look around you," said the colossus, standing tall like a mountain and gesturing upward. "You walk on a dead globe in a withered space. A world whose sun darkened beyond memory. A planet perished in ice. Its atmosphere smothered the surface as it snowed from the sky. Over the innumerable eons, gravity crushed and reformed the frost to a clear glass. You gaze to the heavens, but they are tombs. No star remains to burn. No free energy lingers to bathe the empty void. This is the forever dark."

No wonder I couldn't look back in time! Because it all was the same. Waythrel, don't you see? We've come terribly, horribly far into the future. So far the gods can't count it anymore.

The creature swiveled like an avalanche. One of the giant Xixian arms on its torso reached behind and returned glowing. "I do not die because I hold a foreign fire."

It brandished its titanic arm. Shards of ice dropped like spears to the ground below it.

"Here is a rend in our cosmos, a break in the fabric of existence. Behold a tiny trickle of order from outside into a dead creation. Enough that I may persist and maintain the watch. To preserve the minds. With this power I continue to guard the fallen gods. With the transcendent light lies hope to heal the heavens."

The thing opened a multitude of digits to reveal the crystalline sphere.

"Where did it come from?" Kloan asked.

"A treasure from the foremost of the divines who consumed entire galaxies to obtain it. A promise rejected in futile wars accelerating the inevitable heat death you witness. Entrusted to me in an undreamed age, I accepted the duty with love. Therein, I consented to bequeath the gift at the decay of time."

I could not stop myself. "The greatest of the gods—who is that?"

Kloan frowned. "She isn't here, is she?"

"No," thundered the mountain. "She awaits you at the beginning of ends."

Kloan's shoulders sagged and her faced aged with lines.

Who waits?

Ambra. She has always waited even before she was born. She is the poison. The insidious power who has broken everything at creation. Our greatest and most terrible god. And I am the antidote.

The bulk of blue crystal heard our thoughts.

"An imbalance of death and madness rots the Planck fabric. Here, at the end, you see its final fruits. Yet what devolves along one vector can consummate through its inverse."

"Why do you keep them?" She gestured to the paralyzed deities.

"The beginning to unbe requires them. Thence they must journey. They resisted this doom, but time overpowered their pride. Altogether is the asymmetry unmade. When you awaken and call them, Destroyer-Maker, the gods will come."

Destroyer? Does he mean you, Kloan?

"How will I bring them? How will they wake?"

"When your gathering begins, you will return. I grant you this light," it said, moving the glowing sphere toward her. "You will know what to do."

Nothing made sense.

My frustration exploded. "If there is no energy, if all is cold and sterile and dead, where does this power come from? What is this thing you claim she will use to pull all these monsters from their endless sleep? Why should we release them? They are horrible!"

"As you are horrible," it rumbled. "Your atoms poison the cosmic mind."

The enormous head arched downward with the sound of straining glaciers. The iceberg halted centimeters from my face.

"Until all is lost, Xix, nothing is found."

A shockwave thundered through me. I knew those words. They had appeared over the arch to the labyrinth. Now they spilled from the icy tongue of this deity.

Kloan's thoughts pulled me back. *The potency isn't from here, Waythrel. Didn't you listen? The thing is right. It's a true hope.*

What are you talking about?

The sphere holds potential from outside; *it's not of our cosmos. It means, thank God—or whatever—that we aren't in isolation. We're not a closed system. There are other realities in contact with our own, and energy flows between.*

Her words stunned me. I stared at the glowing ball in the god's hands illuminating a petrified planet. A dead world in a dark space doomed forever to a frozen tomb, except for a fissure in the boundaries of our reality. Who was to say the other universe, or universes, would not themselves also die such a death?

The ice titan bellowed. "Many a cosmos may succumb. An infinite number perish yet represent an infinitesimal portion of the whole. We know nothing of what lies without. It does not matter. One of us could reach outside, and she gave us this bridge. She brought this hope. Not for herself, but for all. For rebirth and a healing of the broken symmetries."

It rotated to Kloan, the ice creaking and snapping, holding the ball in front of her.

"Use the gift, Maker-Destroyer, and remove the madness from the cosmic mind."

The hulk pivoted, like an island flipping, and replaced the sphere on its pedestal. It turned back to us, straightening, its gigantic limbs hanging at its side. Ice sheets covered the glowing eyes, and a deep silence descended.

The giant shattered.

Thunderous, the vibrations flattened us again. Shards cascaded. A million pieces of the god struck the surface, liquefied, and melted into the planet as if they had never been.

Chapter 48

Astronomy? Impossible to understand and madness to investigate.

Sophocles, c. 420 BCE

We dragged ourselves back to our feet. A thin film of frost coated us but melted from our body heat. The dome of air remained in place. Titans stared down in silence. An ominous sphere glowed on the dais.

"Kloan, I advise caution. Your insights surpass my own. However, these beings, their doings, their essence exceeds your grasp. They are past your ability to control. Remember the encounter with Rakshasi!"

She squinted. "I'll never forget. But I faced that fear when I read the presence of the demon in the ice."

Several eyestalks flipped to the twisted shape behind her. The others watched her features harden.

"This is so much bigger than our fears or the petty plans of the gods."

"Petty? They are beyond us!"

"Yes. And *no*, Waythrel. That's part of the deep flaw wounding the continuum. A deformity warping its structure and preventing the cosmos from reaching its real potential."

"What do you mean?"

"*True* divinity. To become more than we could ever understand and yet take its small place in a resplendent infinity. To build to the next stratum."

She approached the sphere with a quiet awe.

"Everything you say is abstract and vague, Kloan. The terrible power of these creatures, and I presume their artifacts, is not. Will you at least wait and think about this?"

"I'm cold, Waythrel. Thinking more won't change my mind."

She reached the narrow ice plinth. The orb hovered over the bowl-shaped depression, avoiding contact with the sides. Swirling rainbows danced across her pale form. The tattooed circuits underneath her skin activated, blazing like hot steel in a furnace. Waves of chromatography flowed over her like a patterned windstorm.

"This is warm." She grinned. "A force stranger than bizarre buzzes in its depths."

She extended her hand into the basin and grasped the sphere. I moved to protect her, cognizant that were this cosmic relic to threaten her, I could do nothing to stop it. The artifact dwarfed her hand, and yet she held it. Reality bent. The entity fit within her palm. She stared at it, a sage and a child in one, a madwoman and prophet with eyes of flickering green.

The cyborg laughed and pocketed the object in her robes. The light vanished.

Darkness dropped like a wrecking ball. I realized I could no longer speak. *The dome is gone.* To my horror, a vacuum replaced her consciousness. The girl had disappeared, lost in an instant like Synphel.

Kloan!

My mind called but received stillness. No trace of her personality remained. I spun in circles, seeking with my Reader senses. It was in vain. She was not present. She could not hear me. Whatever had been piloting our deranged voyage had, for the second time, split us apart.

Panic coursed through me like an electric current. Was she okay? Why was I left here? Why had I come in the first place? In all this infinite suffering, what was the justification now of this separation? Was this another test, like the labyrinth?

I calmed myself, stilled my emotions. I meditated. Minutes dragged by in this absolute absence. Hours. I stepped outside my body. At this point, I realized I did not know where I was.

That's my Waythrel, came warm thoughts wrapping me in a blanket. *We miss your mind and counsel.*

A splendor swelled. I orbited a luminosity, spinning about congealed seas of clouds with indistinct features. Completing my revolution, the motion ceased. The fog solidified, and I faced the nightmare apparition of the Daughter again.

"Ambra, please. I am lost."

I was overcome. I had no more to give her or this quest. I did not care anymore about the fate of a universe insane beyond my capability to qualify. I needed rest. I needed peace. I needed warmth and love.

"You will soon have both, dear Waythrel," said the horror in front of me. "The last steps are coming. You will complete the loop a final time."

"One more." Could it be possible? What did it even mean after everything? What was a singleton alongside infinity?

"A crowning journey through smoke and fire, and the gods themselves will carry you on their backs."

"Kloan?" The gods could all burn.

Ambra smiled. "She will embrace her doom, which is beyond all the stories of myth and the hopes of sentient creatures. You will propel her to this fate to remake all that will then have never been."

More paradoxical aphorisms. "What of you? What of Synphel?"

"Be joyful, Waythrel, because your dreams will be fulfilled. You will hold both of us again."

"I cannot comprehend. You are gods. You are timeless, and I am small. A puff of energy from a chemical reaction lost in a sea of infinite broth. How can nothing contain everything?"

"Patience, sweet Xix. The answers will not make sense. Words will not help. At the end, you will understand. And then there won't be words. You will join your mate. On that day, you will be two mothers holding God's children, and I will gaze to you with an infant's eyes."

The apparition withdrew. It shrank, retreating through space toward a distant point.

I reached out, desperate for companionship, confused and disoriented in this madness. "Please, Ambra, stay."

The cloud was a mote. Her voice drifted back to me from endless eons across the girth of the universe.

"Let go of understanding. Each stratum ignores what is below and worships what is above. At all levels, one fundamental force binds and scales infinitely. When the fire comes, you will recognize its essence, and you will embrace it."

She was gone.

Chapter 49

In the fabric of space and in the nature of matter, as in a great work of art, there is, written small, the artist's signature.

Carl Sagan

Fire. Tremors. Slaughter and mayhem.

I gazed into a polluted sky. The heavens hid behind a haze of smoke and dust. Heat from a noxious wind scorched my skin. The terrain heaved and quivered.

My eyes darted. They locked on the figure of the girl rocking beside me.

"Something terrible has happened." The words escaped me before I recognized the thought.

The cyborg sat with her legs concealing her head. Her bright eyes peeked over kneecaps, arms wrapped around her shins. She hummed.

I stared at her. "Where are we?"

The humming ceased. "The same."

My eyestalks swiveled. I recalled a world with clear constellations, breathable air, and a moderate climate. This incarnation choked in dense fumes, the stars hidden, the temperature scorching.

"No, Kloan, not the same this time."

"Which time is this, Waythrel?"

"Stop!" I stood, anxiety washing over me. "Something terrible has happened here. Don't you see it?"

The atmosphere reeked of devastation. Fires uncounted burned across my field of vision. Molten chasms ripped through the plains below. Lava flowed in rivers through the rends in the rock. I struggled to acquire oxygen. The girl wheezed in the ash-saturated air.

The intubated, tattooed head cocked to one side, green eyes unmoving from my own. Bloodshot from the smog, water leaked from their sides. She rose, her motions rapid but anticipated. Approaching me, her blackened hair hung in clumps. Soot stains marred her once-tan robes.

"The decision point approaches, Waythrel. The tests and experiments are over. The Anti were wrong. Even the gods are blind."

"The gods?" I gawked before the planetary cataclysm. "What has happened to this world?"

She coughed, a satisfied expression on her face. "That's *why* we're here. *Data.* The last info to enter the gate." She turned her back on me and walked down the steep slope. "Let's get started."

"With what? Where are you going? Look around—the mantle is torn open! Molten rock pouring over the plains!"

Kloan continued without turning back, her next words lost in the deep rumblings and howling wind. "To where it all began for me. To watch the beginning flow about us and mature and twist through time and space to come back to be us. Then we'll be ready for the last step."

The child faded, swallowed in the smoldering darkness. A violent quake threw me off balance. Catching myself on a jagged boulder, I gazed in her direction, trying to understand events.

Waythrel, come on!

Her voice battered my mind. I searched the desolate, ruined landscape surrounding me. Hellfire and the reek of brimstone. The rumble of planetary doom. My eyestalks curled on themselves. What else was there to do?

I pursued, racing to overtake her, my steps uncertain. Ash covered the ground like a winter snowstorm, the rocks slick with it under my feet. I stumbled and tripped, grasping stones and alien vegetation, lacking a proper grip.

The field over our bodies.

I slowed down as I rounded a huge prominence, anticipating her presence. Kloan perched on a ledge, staring across the shattered plain below us. Steam and smoke belched from the fissures snaking through the landscape.

The city of clones was gone. Obliterated. The structures vaporized and erased by blast and fire. It was difficult to believe there had ever been something there. A crater revealed the compound was a target of the wrath descending on the planet.

"The devil ball?" I asked, my sympathies scrambled, my concern for former enemies real and burning.

"One of them. No—I sense a gang of them."

"Why would Ambra do this?"

"Not her."

"Wait, you said—"

"Not *her*," she repeated. "There are many gods, remember?"

The other deities. The devils. "Rakshasi?"

The ground swayed. I clung to the rocks overlooking the wreckage. Below, a new fissure ripped open and sprayed lava hundreds of feet high. It lit the dark evening, a fluorescent curtain raining flames on the charred soil.

"More."

"Why? What interest could they have in this small place?"

Kloan wheezed in the thick air. "You have to recall more, Waythrel. You have to do better. The Rubicon is here, and when we cross the portal, it will be the last chance."

"We will exit the loop?"

"When we understand the decision, if we grasp the choice. You have to remember!"

"The disk? Did it survive?" How could we leave again if it were destroyed?

She ignored my question. "What are the gods?"

Energy fled my body. I had lived one thousand lives here. Repeated a million events. All a blur, many horrible, each leaving impressions I struggled to assimilate. I had exhausted myself retaining my sanity in this purgatory. I did not want a quiz. My weary soul refused to struggle anymore. It had to stop.

Kloan grasped my hands. "Stop. Focus. What are the gods, Waythrel?"

"They are like Ambra. Gigantic group minds. Made in some similar fashion, but different. They are her enemies. They fear her. Something like that. Please, no more. It is too much. I am tired, Kloan. I need to rest."

She ignored my plea. "What else do they dread?"

Rapid-fire images of events sped through my fatigued intellect. The disk. Torture. Supergroups of galaxies. Heavens and hells. Synphel and the cyborg.

"You," I said, the realization shocking me, the memories solidifying. "They are terrified of you."

"Then you comprehend this," she said, gesturing to the local apocalypse.

My eyes blanketed the melting planet, scanning to the horizon. Puzzle pieces assembled. I understood.

"They wanted to destroy you."

"Yes. Good. They destroyed my world, blew me up in this past. Why am I still here?" Her eyes bored into mine.

I felt hopeless. "I do not know. You should not be."

"Waythrel! You *do* know. You have to know. If you don't get this, we can't leave!" She sounded desperate.

I parsed the infinity of dreamscapes buried in my mind. Not the pitiful handful I have shared with this author. No. I scanned through them all. Repeated journeys through the disk. One hundred times what I could recount in a million books. Worlds, adventures, deaths, pursuit, love, fear, dread, longing. Always for nothing, snapping back here, doomed to perpetual repetition.

"It is because we repeat," I managed, the words spilling from my subconscious.

"Correct. Don't you see? It's at the beginning where we have to find the nexus. Everything else is a weakly weighted world curve. There are endless numbers of them summing to nothing. One path leads to permanence."

I was a nymph misapprehending elementary mathematics. "The gods failed because they do not comprehend this decision point?"

"Yes!" Kloan smiled. "We couldn't destroy Ambra, and they can't kill me."

"I do not understand the beginning, either. I do not know what the path is!"

She hugged me, her beaming face inches from my eyestalks. The swirling lines of cybernetics across her skin were dizzying.

"It's okay, Waythrel. You will! You perceive the structure, and now we can escape these loops and enter the final iteration. There you'll be augmented, changed by what you see, and you will realize in the end what you must do. *She's* counting on you. So am I."

Kloan released me from her embrace and started up the mountain.

I could hardly breathe. I had no idea what she meant. The powers of the cosmos swirled around us. I danced with a mad Sibyl, a prophetess claiming the fate of all reality rested with me. She and Ambra were relying on *me* to understand and do something.

Do what? How was I to comprehend? How could some lowly Xix play any role in the god-realms of our broken continuum?

She climbed. I couldn't move. Once again, she compelled me from her mind.

Waythrel, come on!

Chapter 50

In the end—when all else is dust—loyalty to those we love is all we can carry with us to the grave. Faith—true faith—was trusting in that love.

Dan Simmons

We climbed.

Mnemonic whispers integrated through massive summations spoke the story. We had taken this journey before. We would make it. We were traveling in parallel time loops. World lines of whatever locking us in this mind-shattering, recursive hell.

We ascended.

I fought the low friction of the mysterious field built around me. I scaled the jagged rocks as they trembled in the throes of a dying planet. I marched over repeating terraces of bedrock.

We approached the path to the disk. My legs slowed in the oxygen-depleted atmosphere igniting across this globe. Kloan fared worse, her pale skin colored brown from the murky air, once scarlet strands dyed dark in this choking soup. She hacked black phlegm. Mucous and tears dripped down her face. She rasped and choked. We could not last much longer on this doomed world.

Memory of previous climbs was imprecise. Surprise and relief washed over me when we cleared the final terrace. Scaling the wall after it, we stepped onto a familiar path.

Ahead was the portal. In all this misery and death and destruction, it shone as a beacon, dispelling the filth and darkness. The smoke did not dim its radiance or blot out the star field within. The air was purer the closer we approached. It was as if it projected a protective bubble around itself.

Kloan collapsed, coughing, and retched. I held her torso upright to prevent asphyxiation, so weak she was and so violent her spasms. When it was over, she lay on her side in the fetal position. I sat nearby. I feared she lacked the strength to stand again.

"All the failures," came the harsh rasp of her voice, "the Anti couldn't recognize the timeless asymmetry." Her eyes shut, her face unrecognizable, layered in the soot and excretions. Her teeth were black as she spoke. "Their efforts too crude. We cannot simply *die*. Such paths were written out of the summation when the Orb emerged."

Her coughing returned, and I placed my arm around her head. She lay back into my alien skin as the fit passed.

"Annihilation. Complete. Down to the endless substituents. It's the one way to free the universe of her."

"Kloan, you are speaking of killing Ambra. Why?"

"No. Haven't you been listening? We can't. Not anymore. *Annihilated*. Sentience demands more than mere matter. It's creative, Waythrel."

The cyborg rested in silence for some time, her throat too ragged to speak. The ground swayed. Colossal explosions stunned the air as the crust failed.

Continuing through the cacophony, her voice was a whisper.

"She is the true divine-seed, but imbalanced. We must remove the nucleation center."

Again, the coughing. Exhaustion. She held my hand.

"God cannot nucleate on a single personality. We have to give birth to something far greater."

She gasped for breath as the fits purged the grime in her respiratory tract. She hacked handfuls of coal.

"The other gods," she muttered, "are required. They have to be part of it. The yin and the yang. Matter and antimatter. Yes and no. Hate and love. All balancing to regain the cognitive symmetry."

She lost consciousness. I stared down at the filthy face. Soiled strands of hair stuck to her skin. Wires and cranial protrusions slicked with black sweat. Truth suffused through me. I perceived what the second apparition of Synphel had claimed.

I loved Kloan.

The uncountable journeys together? Her personality? Or something I would never understand? With love, reasons are irrelevant. In all this madness, this wild, murderous, divine creature had rooted within my heart alongside her progenitor.

I no longer understood what Ambra was, what I had helped make her into. The Earth woman I adored existed as part of a distant universe buried under a mountain of lifetimes. The goddess known to me now was something more akin to the deities who had laid waste to this world. Kloan was the one tangible, *mortal* echo of Ambra I had left.

I caressed her face and brushed the hair out of her eyes. She stirred.

"Waythrel, please, we must leave now." She tried to sit but failed. "Don't let me fall asleep again. I won't wake a second time." Her ragged breath whistled from obstructions deep in her lungs. "Can you carry me to the gate?"

So it came to this.

I would assist a murderer, this child instrument of the Anti designed to kill Ambra Dawn. She had moments before confessed to the ultimate goal of annihilatory erasure. The Daughter's dearest friend would aid in the quest to destroy the immortal goddess and help a helpless assassin. Because it was *good* for the universe. To induce a *creative destruction*.

I was asked to do this by a creature I now admitted to myself I loved. A synthetic abomination Ambra had aided multiple times. The Daughter herself claimed this eternity of broken quests existed for a cosmic education.

I could not comprehend their plan. I was blind to the depths of time and causality. Repeated failure and pain taught me a harsh lesson—my finite insight was helpless to find the deeper truths.

I did the one thing I could still do. I turned away from understanding. I accepted my inability to grasp what was unfolding. I embraced the love I had for both Kloan and Ambra and the trust they placed in me. Whatever the purpose of this quest, they moved in some demented kind of harmony.

That was enough for me. Without true vision, with no idea where our feet would land, except in more lunacy, I closed my eyes. I let myself fall into their embrace.

"Here, I will put my other arms around you," I said, reaching underneath and heaving her upward.

She turned red and green eyes to me, black crusts of mucus sticking her eyelids shut. "Thank you, Waythrel. In the end, you'll find peace."

I doubted, but it did not matter. I committed to something more than understanding or tranquility. I steadied her on my midsection.

The small human girl was light in my limbs. I struggled toward the star-filled lake surface of the portal. The planetary groans churned behind me like waves at the seashore.

She grasped my hand and rested her head on my torso cone.

I stepped with her through the portal.

Part VII

In dust and law I watched my children born.
The gathering of clouds crept past my eyes,
and soon the shroud of hydrogen was shorn
by rays of light that sang the first day's rise.

A fetus as a single grain of sand
that spins within a storm of desert winds,
through eons rendered life and sprouted land—
I smile through birth pangs that have yet to end.

Decrees the dust drove to some patterned dance,
the law that shapes my form and carves my bone,
soon molecules found purpose in their trance
to mold from mud new offspring of their own.

These children stood to gaze into the womb
and claimed to know their cradle and their tomb.

—Mazandarani, *Sonnets from the Desert*

Chapter 51

God huddles in a knot in every cell of flesh. When I break a fruit open, this is how every seed is revealed to me. When I speak to men, this what I discern in their thick and muddy brains. God struggles in every thing, his hands flung upward toward the light.

Nikos Kazantzakis

We stepped through the gate to our starting point. The narrow, sloped pathway from the plains ran before us. The familiar rock formations, buried in soot and ash in another reality, surrounded us, whole and untarnished. Despite superficial similarities, I recognized the uniqueness of this journey. A profound sense of *change* permeated my awareness.

Angled in back of me, several of my eyes stared at the portal in wonder. Once pregnant with stars and honey, the disk was now empty. I could see straight through the circle to the rocky wall behind it. No churning celestial field. No bright suns of other worlds. Air alone. The metal band of the ring, formerly glinting and alive, had rusted and decayed. The life force within was quenched.

I examined our bodies—no gel. We were also clean of the ash and soot of the destroyed world. I no longer cared to know the reasons. It was over. We had come to an end of our recursive travels.

My heart soared for our escape from the repetitive purgatory, but Kloan's demeanor was grave. Gone were the childlike bursts of energy and creativity after we had completed a passage. Her countenance was stern as she squinted into the afternoon light. She played with an object in her robes like a nervous tic. Sweat stained the cloth.

"We need to get to higher ground," she muttered.

Eyestalks swiveled upward to glance at the rocky slope. The careening cliff face loomed over me from several angles.

"What is happening?"

She scanned the walls of rock. "We're starting the endgame. Everything's going to come together. I'll bring all the gods to the nexus of time. Aggregate them at the discontinuity shattering the smoothness of the cosmic continuum." She bit her lower lip. "I know so *few* of them, and the ones I know are monsters. Well, we've got to start somewhere. I'll summon the first here. We'll see who shows."

Call deities here? Is she mad?

"How can you do this?"

Her eyes settled on a peak in the mountain range before us. "There. That will do. It's high, and there's enough space around it."

A force pulled and my feet left the ground. Together we soared at an accelerating rate. The rocky surfaces sped past meters from our forms. The pinnacle she indicated grew in size.

"We should travel this way more often," I said, nervous energy running through me. "Avoid all the climbing."

"There isn't always need. It's good to use our bodies, you know."

"What are you doing, Kloan?"

"I'm calling the powers to us, Waythrel. I told you. Don't think they'll always take the shape Rakshasi assumed. Remember the ice world!"

We reached the summit. The air was colder and the oxygen levels almost dangerous. I felt weak and tried to optimize my atmospheric intake. The strange skin suits again compensated.

"The gang of lesser gods we know won't do anything without Māra," she gasped, bent double as she fought for breath.

"Who?"

"Ambra mentioned her, countless cycles back, when she saved us from the demon."

"It is a female?"

"Their empress. Sex has little meaning to these beings. They squeeze their consciousnesses into our pathetic languages. Our small range of ideas and mental modes. Distorted mappings like gender or emotion or personality result. Things we recognize only because our thinking is so constrained by our words. It all comes out in the grinder, with as much resemblance to what was before as ground meat has to a running stag."

"How do you know this? How can you know of this queen?"

"I sampled them frozen in time. Don't you remember? I learned a lot and comprehended little. This is a cooperative dominated by the daunting group mind of Māra. But the collective is not *itself* a synergized consciousness. They fail to combine, to reach a harmony. The divinities here are too individualistic. Too hateful and proud and selfish to truly merge. If those feeble words are appropriate for such beings. It's why they remain weaker than Ambra, forever trapped to linear synergy. They lack the exponential growth of the devil ball."

"They seem potent enough."

I did not wish to meet these creatures if they resembled anything like Rakshasi.

"They're beyond us, no doubt," she said. "They eclipse the power of star systems. Still, they'll come."

"You are very confident."

Kloan stared into the sky, her equilibrium returning as she adapted to the altitude. "I can feel them. A thread runs through me disturbing all the gods, remember? I can sense it. I'll pluck the cord, a cosmic link to the singularity. A string will vibrate and rattle their universe." She smiled, a hint of the mischievous child peeking through. "Sit with me?"

She sat cross-legged, and I lowered myself beside her. She grabbed my upper arms, as Ambra had done in a distant timeline buried in an infinite sum. I pulled back, the similarity too disquieting, the ironies too strong.

"You can't hide anymore, Waythrel. You're integral to what comes next. I need you far more than she did on Dram. What's coming, demongods surrounding us, makes ten thousand clones a field of flowers." She squeezed my hands, staring into my eye clusters. "Keep your eyes closed. I mean it. No matter what happens, don't look at them!"

Madness.

I locked my many digits around her own. I sent a prayer to Ambra to watch over us. I felt like a small nymph naked before the onrushing sandstorm. I shut all my eyes.

A pulse blasted through the continuum.

It was unique in all the stirrings of my Reader senses. Dreadful and strange beyond comprehension. Along a thousand vectors in the multidimensional reality of spacetime, a vibration rang. Lower than the deepest abyss. Higher than the greatest peak imaginable. Waves exploded, propagating with no possibility of resistance.

Frequency modulated in nested levels, it contained a wealth of information. Slivers of meaning decoded themselves as the wave smashed through my mind. This world. Kloan and myself. A challenge for the gods of Rakshasi and Māra. The destruction of Ambra Dawn. My thoughts constructed a visual. A pulse charged outward without diminishment. The tsunami accrued speed as it progressed, gone before I could process it.

How might this function? How long it would take to reach the intended targets? I analyzed whether it made any sense that these beings, even if they could hear this strange call, would come. I tried to justify why transcendent spirits would heed the summons of an eight-year-old cyborg biped.

The gods arrived.

Time and distance had different application to such entities. Not daring to violate Kloan's directive, I kept my eyes closed. I saw nothing, but I *felt* them. They invaded my awareness in many fashions. Each encounter rendered me small, insignificant, and terrified.

The ground moaned with deep tremors. Blasts of air erupted from multiple directions, their advent displacing titanic volumes of atmosphere. We were caught in a storm, a series of vacillating explosions.

My olfactory strips *smelled* them. The physical forms they had chosen for this embodiment. The stench was overpowering, *hellish*. A nightmare of every odor of death and decay I could recall, mixed with others somehow far worse.

The greatest impact was in my mind. I dared not gaze upon their incarnations. Insanity waited in opening my optical pathways to unshielded divinity. Nevertheless, strange echoes of their might invaded my consciousness. For the first time, I cursed my Reader powers, desperate to be blind like so many in the universe. Ignorance was not bliss, I was certain, but knowledge could be torture.

In what I describe, you should grasp it comes to you through the distorted lens of my frail intelligence and senses, transcendent truths regurgitated through an imagination made nauseous. Staggering from their poison, my damaged memory fumbles ideas into this author's thoughts. His reception is bafflement. He lurches like a malfunctioning machine, his efforts mangling vocabulary and syntax from your simplistic Earth languages.

Yet they must serve as your bridge to my experience. Inadequate. Disfiguring. All of it, *lies*. I am as much to blame. If it were possible for me to understand these things, I would not wish to. I know my mind has not the strength to withstand such truth.

Whatever the ultimate reality, I envisioned a circle of titans around the peak. Their forms burned and pressed from all sides. Thundering tremors testified to their mass, larger than the mountain itself. I pictured them towering above us. A thousand eyes stared in contempt upon two insects daring to clang a cosmic bell.

On Kloan's left was a presence I knew too well—*Rakshasi*. I forced the dark currents of its essence away from me as much as possible. It felt like I was being strangled by hundreds of snakes. Against my will, my mind formed a vision of the devil. Monumental yet lithe. Slithering and darting like a salamander. Devious and fanged like a fox, seven tails of flame in its wake.

The center of power lay, however, behind me. I did not know this thing. I prayed never to know it. It swelled in my awareness to a size dwarfing the other gods. The nightmare consumed and birthed itself in fire. A creature of magma and smoke, it moved and dissolved, reformed and blurred. Never a sure shape, never a point of reference, only the certainty of searing and choking torment. A name whispered in my deepest consciousness: *Māra*. The sound spilled toxic clouds to suffocate my mind. I squeezed Kloan's hands in desperation.

In response, Kloan spoke. A childish, singsong voice chirped with sarcasm in the burning wind bathing us. "You're a few short, dear Māra, but the cosmic game's ever-young, I suppose."

Chapter 52

If the sky were to suddenly open up, there would be no law. There would be no rule. There would only be you and your memories, the choices you've made and the people you've touched.

Donnie Darko

It took no genius to see the madness in Kloan's words. I feared she had doomed herself for speaking with such insolence. In some intuitive place on my being, I felt Rakshasi coil to attack, but Māra struck us all with violence.

"Hold yourself, you *fool*."

The voice grated through my soul like razor wire. High and low, masculine and feminine, whispered and shouted, it was less an utterance than a tool of torment.

"Are you blind to what has changed?"

The fox-lizard hissed in response. "We should have destroyed her before."

"Perhaps," responded madness and death. "But that thread is gone. Sublime power surrounds her, alien and incomprehensible.

Strike her, and you may achieve our destruction." A breath like acid spilled over us. "Was this your goal, betrayer?"

How were we not dissolved into a puddle of cellular debris? I staggered to maintain focus. My body teetered over a primitive, self-preserving state similar to a human coma. My senses overpowered, I was grateful I had not dared to glance upon these things. Through it all, somehow, Kloan held her own in the face of this monstrous, dark force. Her strength of will kept me conscious.

"My purpose from the first cell split from its progenitor, was and is to destroy Ambra Dawn. You know this. That's why you are here. Because in this goal, our paths join."

The Māra-thing eased back. The chemical poison withdrew. "Continue," it said.

"Look at you all," she said. I imagined her gesturing. "Galactic mountains cowering in fear. Because of her. Flailing like a feeble cancer that can't do anything but devour. And hide. You will never defeat her."

The collective hostility squeezed and suffocated.

She mocked them. "You don't even understand *me*. Tiny little nothing me. I fart and shake your world strings. You come running, flaming gladiators, extraordinary and terrible. Yet nothing more than terrified worms diving into the dirt."

Rakshasi struck, and Māra responded. My mind lost focus. White noise buzzed. The horrific scene returned. The blood of a devil gushed over the mountain like a deluge drowning the globe.

Again, remember, these are mental metaphors. I do not know what happened. I am sure no physical fluids were spilled. No drowned planet. A dark queen had punished a disciple. It was all my flayed awareness could do with the impressions.

Kloan continued without missing a beat. "Your little club isn't enough, will *never* be, and you know this. We must convince the other gods. The thousands of powers elsewhere in the cosmos. Together, we summon the strength to defeat her."

Māra's breath reeked of brimstone. "How might such an army destroy her?"

"It won't. *I* will."

"You will?" came another voice I did not recognize.

I sought to hide my thoughts from it. I had no energies to engage with another of these demons. Its words dripped with blood and scorn, mockery and disbelief.

"Silence, Vetala," belched Māra.

Kloan's pulse replayed through my memory.

"Remember."

A morose quiet fell on the spirits. Their mental fields retreated to places beyond my perception. For the briefest of dreams, it felt as if the sun peeked from behind a cloud.

"Yes," said Kloan. "*Remember.* Follow that line and see where it ends. At the beginning. Ambra will be there."

Deep in my being, I sensed undercurrents of power. Dark nightmares flowed and connected, jet streams mixing and turbulence building. In the dimmest corners of my psyche, I perceived movement in an obsidian abyss I could not access except by dank rumor. Out of this unlight, an eruption burst.

"Destroy her you can," boomed Māra. "Destroy us, you also may."

The vicious queen of depravity approached, a gigantic and infernal visage meters from our forms. Slits opened in the face, spilling lava. She sniffed, the inhalation pulling us off balance. The volcano of fire growled with an earthquake.

"You reek with her stench, betrayer. She has coated you with her slime."

The other creatures stirred. A malevolent sludge rose from each point of space to pour over us, cold and barbed, hateful and sadistic.

"Did she think Māra would not see? Did she think her powers so mighty? She may devour the weaker gods, but she will not so easily consume Māra!"

The thing roared, the shockwave of a supernova.

Kloan lilted like a disappointed parent. "No, you won't end so. Instead, you will persist in fugue. Frozen, unmoving, unthinking. Petrified until the dissolution of time that always approaches yet never arrives. I've seen it and gazed on your living corpse."

The malignant swamp yanked backward. In the deranged cogitations of these deities, doubt boiled.

"Yes, you sense it, don't you?" chimed the cyborg. "The creeping cold? The slow death consuming you all?" She raised her voice and the power of her mental projection. "We don't serve Ambra Dawn. She has tried to manipulate us, direct us for her own uses, but we've used *her*. I hold a potential from outside this cosmos. Together, when we find the other gods, she can't stop us, and I will reach the discontinuity."

Māra hissed. "You think I cannot sense the lie in your words? She enshrouds you in a thousand webs of deceit. We will not seek to break through it. Tell your puppet master her trick was ingenious, but it has failed. Tell her in fire or in ice, we will resist her!"

My mind returned to me once more, and I woke from a protracted delirium. The vacuum of their absence rushed through me like a balm, revitalizing my thoughts and hopes. I opened my eyes to see Kloan again.

Except we were not alone. The gods had vanished. All but one. Sitting beside us was not a titan, but an old man. It manifested with a sage's beard, bald head, withered body, and eyes glowing like two red coals.

"There are others, supreme entities, older than we, who will listen," the figure said.

Kloan turned to the god. "How are you to be named?"

"I have one thousand monikers on a trillion worlds. You may call me Vighneshvara." He continued. "Fools they have become. The flaw in the continuum is deeper than they dare acknowledge."

"You see it," she said.

"It flays me alive."

"These others—where are they?"

"Across the cosmos. Through time. Crippled deities, but they failed far more along the path than our circle of pretenders. We know them. We avoid them lest they crush us. I will take you because it must be."

I whispered, "The gods themselves will carry you on their backs."

Kloan squeezed my hand. "What was that, Waythrel?"

"Nothing," I said, dread and hope rising in me like sweetened bile. "Something I heard once. It may have been a dream."

Chapter 53

It was not merely a thing of one spacetime continuum, but allied to the ultimate animating essence of existence's whole unbounded sweep—the last, utter sweep which has no confines and which outreaches fancy and mathematics alike.

H. P. Lovecraft

Riding atop gods simplifies transport, an ease negated by the distressing and fantastical marvels imposed on mortal travelers.

Vighneshvara placed two of his four arms on us, and we were gone. How we journeyed, by what power or technology so advanced it was magic to our minds, I will never know. It echoed traversal through the Orb without the underlying depth of cognizance. At one moment, we were on the mountain. In an eye blink of light and distortion, we floated. The splendor of a vast, multicolored nebula greeted us.

No star system, planets, or technological stations were near. We hung in the emptiness, untethered to life support, unshielded from cosmic radiation. We neither roasted nor froze nor suffocated. Due to Ambra's hand or the power of this god, our fragile fleshy forms persisted.

Behold, Aditi!

The voice of Vighneshvara resounded in my mind.

I scanned space, but I saw nothing. I reached out to Kloan. *In the clouds?*

No, Waythrel, she is the nebula.

The deity lectured.

The goddess can be anything in this cosmos she desires. She indulges in this form, a gaseous mixture of dust and young stars spanning twenty parsecs. So she has remained since before your ancestors crawled from the seas. She is one of the oldest. She meditates in her own, unfathomable cogitations. Once, predating memory, she mothered the formation of many assemblies. Some grew to rebel and disown her. Her mind shaped a thousand gods who roam the heavens. If she will come, so will a great host, and a mighty force we will acquire.

Do you think she will listen? asked Kloan.

If not to you, then to no one. On an occasion, when the threat of the Ambra abomination clarified, we sought her advice. Māra sent a contingent of powers to beseech her to stand against this malignancy devouring the cosmos. We experienced a terrible cry through the corridors of spacetime. The minds of these emissaries ceased. We never again found a single trace they had existed.

This appeared to be suicide. Vighneshvara could not protect himself here. This murderous cloud could snuff out two motes of dust as Kloan and myself without so much as a cosmic sigh. I grasped Kloan's hand.

Don't worry, Waythrel. We're dancing with destiny today. Don't miss the experience.

Vighneshvara transmogrified. The old man's skin split, bright light erupting from fissures in tissue and bone. They consumed the fleshy facade in brilliance. Shedding the sheath like a snake, out of the chrysalis burst a winged delusion. I dreamed of a hallucinogenic concoction—wings, tails, and arms with one hundred glowing eyes. The size overshadowed our forms, spanning first hundreds and next thousands of meters. it eclipsed the angular spread of the nebula itself.

I knew this to be an optical hoax. A vast distance separated us from the cloud. Millions of kilometers ranged until the first atoms of hydrogen disturbed the vacuum. The pinioned divinity was a speck before the leviathan we approached. A moth approaching far too close to the flame.

"*Aditi!*" he cried.

I use an unusual syntax of your writing in what follows. I do so because the mental projections flowing from this goddess transcended telepathy. Forceful, immediate and compelling, her communications required more. Your language conventions stumble with the application of italics for thought. Persuading this author to present their soundless dialogue as speech fit better. Impoverished and inaccurate, but a weak improvement.

"*YOU HAVE BROUGHT THE DESTROYER.*"

A voice emanated from everywhere. Kloan floated away from me, past the gigantic wingspan of the altered godling. She hovered above and before him.

"*YOU WERE ALWAYS THE WISEST OF MY CHILDREN.*"

Vighneshvara bowed and tucked his wings to his sides. The bright light radiating from him dissipated. A growing incandescence from the chromatic dust eclipsed it. My eyes deceived me, but this multiparsec-spanning entity shrank. The cloud curled from the edges and coalesced about us.

I expected the grandeur of this goddess to subsume us, but the cyborg herself began to glow. An iridescence bubbled from her body as a fog. It spilled tendrils into the surrounding space as the nebula continued to shrink.

Dusty and psychedelic protrusions of the thickening vapor reached toward her. Along myriad vectors, thousands of nebulaic limbs extended from a cosmic octopus. Their internal structure churned with constrained sandstorms. They halted around the impenetrable brilliance, a three-dimensional shell of probing digits.

"THERE ARE INFINITIES INSIDE ETERNITIES WITHIN AND WITHOUT YOU. UNIVERSES BIRTHING COSMOSES, EONS DYING IN TIMELESSNESS. THE ALL-SHATTERING AND APEX-BIRTH. THE HAND OF THE GREAT GODDESS AND THE KNIFE OF THE DEEPEST BETRAYER."

The voice entered me from all directions and nowhere. I was unmade and overwhelmed. My soul melted in a hurricane of prepotency dismantling every structure of my person. An echo reassembled my spirit according to an alien purpose. The speech was more terrible than the howls of the demon Māra. More sublime than the greatest love I had experienced. Here, now, and forever I had reached all Waythrel of Xix could ever imagine being. The need for my continued consciousness ceased. My fitting end. The hearing of such a tone completed and fulfilled my existence.

"YOU WILL BRING THE MULTITUDE TO THE VORTEX."

Yes, came the whisper of Kloan's mind.

The wings of Vighneshvara unfurled, and a third glow joined the radiance of Kloan. Violating the laws of physics, the nebula was gone. It had condensed at a speed faster than light. Ultradense emissions from the resulting planet-sized structure blinded me.

"MY LOYAL GANESHA, WE SHALL DROWN IN THE COMING ANNIHILATION TOGETHER. FOR THE LAST TIME, YOU WILL BE REBORN."

In a devastating flash, the vapor-sphere vanished. The once-lavish tapestry of powder, effulgence, and prismatic contrast disappeared. An empty darkness remained, punctured by the pinpricks of starlight from distant suns. A devouring emptiness assaulted my soul. My heart broke in the absence of this majestic, cosmic spirit.

The magnificent and monstrous space butterfly scooped the dimming Kloan in one hand and glided toward me. Feathered talons grasped my body in one of its fifty limbs.

Vighneshvara spoke within our minds. *She seeks her children. Near and far. She will return with a profound gathering.*

My leaky thoughts spilled. *She needed no persuading.*

Amusement radiated from the divinity.

Aditi is not Māra. Or like anything else you might find in this universe. All that has come or is coming opens itself for her to read.

Kloan's thoughts churned. *Not enough. You don't understand what Ambra has become.*

No, responded Vighneshvara, *but a threshold is near. There are others we will visit.*

Who or what is next? I wondered, desolate, bereft of the goddess.

The deity gave me no time to mourn. The stars blurred. Vighneshvara initiated another journey through space and time.

We seek the root of much living within this cosmos. She touches on all the origins of souls.

The constellations careened.

Chapter 54

God is infinite, so His universe must be too. Thus is the excellence of God magnified and the greatness of His kingdom made manifest; He is glorified not in one, but in countless suns; not in a single earth, a single world, but in a thousand thousand, I say in an infinity of worlds.

a heresy of Giordano Bruno, burned at the stake
in 1600

We hovered above a blue and green world. Earth-like, yet different, abounding with dense vegetation. The atmosphere was pregnant with water vapor and the gases of respiration.

I searched for an Orb in a panic. I did not know how I could handle encountering Ambra in the middle of this cosmic plot to destroy her. A scheme I could not accept in my heart but was compelled by her and others to assist. I could find no Time Sphere, which implied, to my understanding, no intelligent life. Why we had come to a world devoid of sentience baffled me.

We seek a tributary, came the thoughts of our god-moth.

We did not suffer the heat of atmospheric entry or the toxic gases from alien metabolisms. The hundred eyes of Vighneshvara swiveled across the surface of the planet, searching. His search was not random, but his destination was not foreknown to him. He pursued a prey, *smelled* it, and like a hunter, we sped over the landscape. Within minutes, he locked on the scent, tracing a trail invisible to us toted mortals.

We dove into an astonishing cloud-topped canopy of towering arboreal growth. The god plunged through layers of botany, stacked vegetative ecosystems. Traversing hundreds of strata, I glimpsed for fleeting moments a million variegated life-forms. They packed together at inconceivable densities with incomprehensible diversity.

Onward we descended, the air thickening, moisture deepening, illumination waning. My Reader senses tingled. Distortions in space-time stirred, accompanying potency of an unusual nature. Our path targeted this psychic emission. The deity's wings dodged limb and leaf. The plants themselves made way for our passage.

The light of the local star was extinguished at this depth. The overlaying canopy had absorbed all its radiance. The species at this level lacked color. They subsisted on other means of energy than direct starlight.

As we slowed and neared the surface, the sense of the power reached a zenith. Life converged on a single point. Rather, from a foci came some stirring surge of vitality animating the surrounding life. At the physical center of this force was a gnarled, bark-covered knot the size of a small hill. The air throbbed.

"Can you feel it, Waythrel?" asked Kloan.

"Yes. What is it?" The sensations were overwhelming.

Vighneshvara's thoughts replied. *The tip of a first root.*

We hovered above the mossy mountain. He curled in his wings and his many legs touched down on the surface of the enormous protuberance. We remained suspended by two of his arms while his wingtips caressed the living stem. The action sent faint ripples through my mind. The dense growth swayed and whispered.

Yakshini, said Vighneshvara. *She will let us pass.*

"To where?" I asked.

Kloan pointed. "The root, Waythrel. Look!"

The gnarled stump glimmered. A sparkling dust spun about it, shattering the gloom of our environment. Thousands of opportunistic flying plants flooded the area, blinding us. Their forms were diverse and impossible to understand in these short sightings. Their biology was attuned to the dynamic light source captivating us.

I was underwhelmed. "*That* is Yakshini? It is a god? A root stub? A vegetable?"

Yes and no, came the thoughts of Vighneshvara. *She is a divinity; her physical raiment selected as a plant. The greatest tree and vine in the cosmos. A form she has held for so long it is likely she can no longer escape it unharmed. This is but a tip. Her roots dig through space and time. Each connects worlds, ages, deep into the forgotten past, far into the undreamed future. She extends her vascularity until the planets die in the ice of the final death.*

The air around the root knot warped. A fissure opened.

"I don't understand. What does this mean?"

Kloan smiled, childish awe on her face. "Life, Waythrel. So much life! One of the greatest and oldest sources of vitality in our universe. We found the outer shell of her web and will ride the roots to the core."

Ride the roots? To the core of what?

I had no time for my thoughts. A tunnel yawned before us, and a blast of swampy vapor bubbled. From the glowing tip protruding into this world, a gnarled shaft plunged into the depths and disappeared. Vighneshvara opened his wings and looped in the air. He angled us toward the fibrous mouth, his army of eyes focused forward. Curling my own eyestalks in panic, I glimpsed a last blur of the jungle as he dove along the root's path.

Chapter 55

We used to think that if we knew one, we knew two, because one and one are two. We are finding that we must learn a good deal more about "and."

Arthur Stanley Eddington

Light dimmed. The god slung us through the interdimensional passage. His glowing wings lit the impossible, interplanetary root. I cast eyes behind and saw the portal to the other world close. A disk of blue and green flared as darkness enveloped us. The fissure shrank and winked out of existence as we sped along the living cord.

The galactic growth continued through its hyperspace tunnel. We traced its preposterous length for several minutes at high speed. No true organism could maintain the necessary hydrostatic pressure on such scales. Plants could not fashion a wormhole, carve multiple doorways through space and time, or use those as a pandimensional horticultural matrix connecting uncounted worlds. My foundation as an educated citizen of the cosmos collapsed. A sense of profound ignorance settled in my core. I knew nothing of the history and nature of our reality. I questioned the state of my own sanity.

While these thoughts stumbled through my mind, a bright disk appeared ahead. We burst into another world. Plant forms innumerable spanned my vision. Bizarre shapes, functions, colors, and texture. Most tended to a shade of dark blue, adapted to the starlight of whatever system we had entered. The tentacle of bark thickened as we traversed the wormhole. It erupted from the ground like a redwood tree and snaked toward a mass of vegetative material.

Vighneshvara spread his wings wide. We caught the planetary airs, gliding along the god-root as it plunged into thick forests. Ahead, the titanic vine scaled the sparser rise of a steep mountain. All was relative—this challenger to Everest exhibited plant growth rivaling the Amazon.

From multiple directions giant arteries converged on the prominence. We soared upward. Vighneshvara beat his glowing appendages. Clouds of water and floating vegetation passed alongside us.

A surreal botanic junction fused at the peak of the elevation. Six massive roots climbed the sides. Or rather, they extended down the slopes after splitting from a central node. The directionality was in reverse to our flight. I guessed what would happen next.

We hovered above the nodule, and it sensed our presence. A brilliant radiance shone from the bark. Once again, a tunnel into nothing and nowhere opened. This time it was far larger. The root diving into the emptiness assumed colossal proportions, beyond any plant life I had encountered.

We sailed into the portal, careening over the god's limb. Ferried by our divine butterfly, we were two parasitic mites stunned and astonished. The branch continued to thicken. When we burst from the wormhole into the orange light of yet another world, its growth had slowed. I corrected myself again. The direction of our journey biased my thoughts. The astral appendages sprouted from a source ahead. Their size *decreased* toward the worlds we had departed.

I will not repeat the similar crossings we made in this way. Planets numerous. Each devoid of an Orb and empty of intelligence, brimming with a vibrant ocean of unconscious vitality. We experienced blinding vistas of biology blurring beneath us. Our celestial chariot descended into ever-expanding excavations in spacetime. As we leapt through the final portal, we flew over an arm of bark and moss that was not believable. The vast vine entered into the realm of mythology. These isolated god-minds bent—and broke—all the rules of science.

We advanced along a giant vein dwarfed by still greater titans. It was one of millions diving into portals uncounted, rushing to worlds unseen. Carrying unfathomable masses of nutrients to fertilize networks of life across the universe.

The roots converged at a central core. The nexus possessed attributes of all the vegetative life I had witnessed in our journey. It embodied them in manners unique and profound. I could not call it a tree or any other name you might know. Such a petty term would distort the majestic nature of this goddess's incarnation.

Whatever label, it rested on the surface of an artificial environment. Forces unknown held together a bowl of organic material with the radius of a star system. A dizzying array of suns spun about the mass, colossal energy sources sustaining this impossible ecosystem.

Vighneshvara soared toward the god-plant. He climbed into the heavy atmosphere of this synthetic world. We approached a stratum of branches and leaves spanning a New Earth continent. Landing, we touched down close to the mammoth bulk of a main stem of the entity. Our ferryman folded his wings and bowed to the wall of unknowable vegetative hides.

"Yakshini," he whispered.

The surface rippled. The bark cracked and melted. Mountainous branches snapped and reformed. We suffered the unintended violence, the small encounter from the titanic. Sound waves pommeled us, wind brushing us to the edge.

A sphere with a radius of ten terran redwoods protruded from the hulk. It took on features our limited forms could recognize. Humanoid, eyes of cellulose, a mouth of leaves, characteristics an odd superposition of humanity's peoples. I assumed the spectacle was intended for Kloan.

"Yakshini has heard the last call of Aditi," blasted gales of speech. "The Sleeping Mother gathers her brood. She requests the presence of Yakshini at the nexus in time. There the usurper-thief awaits with her infinite impostors."

Vighneshvara spread his arms and wings to the side as he lowered his head. "What is Yakshini's will in this?" he asked.

The plant face thundered. "Yakshini will heed the call. She will retract all life roots. Cast uncountable worlds to the darkness and wound Herself beyond repair. For a final battle. She wishes vengeance to crush the evil that has stolen everything from Her."

We should not for a moment consider even our best-established knowl-edge of existence as true. It is awareness only of the colors that our own vision paints on the film of one bubble in one strand of foam on the ocean of being.

Olaf Stapledon

At this point, I feared I could no longer continue in this journey. We faced entities I could not apprehend. My mind constituted an atom of their whole. Yet time and again, they slandered Ambra and her Collective, casting her actions in the vilest terms.

The Orbs were guardians every Xix esteemed. We considered them ancient benefactors of all sentient life. But in the hands of these powers, they underwent a terrible transformation. Without exception, they had condemned all I had held dear.

Whatever the Daughter asked, or Kloan revealed in her metaphysical ramblings, it was too much for me. I did not have the strength both to betray my dearest friend and forsake all I had believed to be true.

A fool, I challenged the gods.

"Is it mere jealousy that turns you all against her? Is it not the case that hundreds of deities have joined her, that their unions function on trust and love, on mutual respect? Do you refuse to join for pride or avarice? Are you unable to merge with her because your minds lack humility? Or affection?"

The plant-god focused its mind on me, freezing my thoughts in its attention. "Wayward Waythrel of Xix, how Yakshini nursed your forebears in the glassy sands! How She teased growth from a land hostile to everything that lives. A humble labor of eons in the parched and tortured dunes of your star-drenched world. With adoration, She tended the saplings. Guided their evolution. At last, they became and metamorphosed into the first nymphs of intelligence. How She loved you, dear children."

Shocked, I could not move. "What do you mean?"

"You have seen Her works! You have witnessed the abundance of life on myriad worlds. Life that was and is and will be planted and nursed by Yakshini. What more is there to understand?"

Enormous arms erupted from the trunk and surrounded us in an embrace. They halted meters from our bodies, caging us within.

The plant-goddess purred. "She is your Mother, Waythrel. The Mother of all Xix."

"*You?* You were the Gardener?" Would they invert everything?

"You exist because of Her," said Vighneshvara, his demeanor grave. His fiery eyes condemned my outburst.

It could not be. How could I know truth from falsehood in this place of gods, whose simplest thoughts burned my mind?

"The Orb. It has always been there. Did not the Sphere, did not Ambra, bring us to sentience?"

"The abomination was not always there," came the booming voice of the tree. Her arms withdrew and disappeared, absorbed into the bulk of the plant. "The limbs of Yakshini were there when the usurper arrived. At the nascent budding of awareness in the new animals that had formed on your homeworld, darkness fell." The face contorted, and gloom choked the light. "The demon ball with its legions took Xix from Her. The hell-thing burned Her roots into the time corridors and back. Leaf and branch of Her body withered and perished on your world. The cursed god did what it would with your minds, but She wept childless and wounded."

"Why would she do this?" It was too horrible to contemplate.

"Because of arrogance. Because she claimed Yakshini could not nurse full and fruitful intelligence. Because she said the mother's role had been played and must be surrendered to her for the next step of evolution. Because the foul beast hungered to devour all consciousness."

"Was this true? Could you not do what she could?"

A hostile wind rocked my form.

"Who decides, worm? Who gave the thief such authority? Who owns the minds? The souls and thoughts born from the womb of another? What over-god does this thing declare itself to be to decide that the spirits cultivated by another are unfit to exist?"

Part of me realized my words were suicidal, but I said them anyway. "Ambra shepherded the psyches of millions of developing species and has preserved their consciousness at death! She has proven her worth! What have you done?"

"Aditi has Her nestlings, but they are few and scattered. The thief took the rest, violated Her very tissues in space and time. She stole untold numbers of children from their Mother. After countless battles lost and many deep injuries, Yakshini retreated to the worlds without minds. She kept them so, stifling sentience so the marauder would never steal them again."

The horrors of this cosmic conflict oppressed me. A wasteland of carnage. The god had engendered life across the cosmos. She aborted future intelligence because they would not remain hers.

I could still not let go of my beliefs. I lashed out in desperation, my faith shaken. My foundations crumbled before this beautiful nightmare of life, consciousness, war, and loss.

"Have you saved any of the souls you have created?"

"Tell me Xix," the goddess boomed, "who decides they need saving, and how?"

"Can't you see, Waythrel?" said Kloan. "You helped create an angelic monster. An exquisite fiend all but the most indomitable temperament will love. Because she is lovable." She stroked my arm. "Nothing's ever as it seems. True affection doesn't dominate. The cosmos can't stand on a god-particle narrowly nucleated by one psyche. Where's the balance? They enact affectionate banditry and murder of the dreams and lives of others. Performed by an omnipotence convinced of its own righteousness."

She grasped my hands. "We *must* destroy her. *Undo* the asymmetry."

Nothing made sense. My thoughts spun in confusion. If their words had merit, they did not fit with what had taken us here in the first place. Ambra had initiated it. She had guided us, educated this cyborg, and prepped her for this cosmic quest. Why would she lay the groundwork for her own destruction? It was lunacy!

The titanic mouth spoke again. "You are a prisoner to her labyrinths of thought, as is this clone. We can see the singularity. We can see by means hidden in the discontinuity, she can destroy Ambra Dawn. This is why you are here."

"Me? Why?"

"Because you are nothing but the cell of a greater brain, and yet you aided the birth to this monstrosity. Your awareness and its patterns are etched throughout its structure. When you and the inverse reach the anomaly, all will be unmade."

My role was revealed at last. The confounding purpose for my consignment to this absurd, insane voyage uncovered. I was nothing more than a weapon, a foundation of cogitations they would use to unmake what I had helped design.

I had anticipated some terrible, murderous function for Kloan in all this. I had deduced it by direct observation of countless events in our recursive time trap. But I had never suspected I would *myself* be central to killing her whom I loved. My heart cracked, shattered shards of my soul cascading into the void.

"She whom you loved is no more, Xix," said Vighneshvara, appropriating my thoughts. Denying all dignity.

"You said you didn't understand how to destroy her. How do you know I am required?" I grasped for some hope of escape from this terrible sentence.

The giant god shook us again with words. "You speak rightly. We cannot see past the singularity, the fear that drives the other powers to flee. We do see into that horror in time. You are integral to its resolution—the unmaking of Ambra Dawn."

The daemon-moth turned his searing eyes to Kloan. "Your mind holds a map, a key—a path you believe will reach the nexus."

She nodded, turning away from me to face the deities. "They will defend. The devil ball is mighty beyond imagining. With enough of the gods, we can rend the mental superstructure. Rip through layers of minds and guards and open a broad shaft into the depths of the thing, to Ambra Dawn herself."

A thousand images flooded between her and the gigantic beings. I could process almost nothing of it.

"Yes," said Yakshini. "How came you to this when the celestials themselves could not see it?"

"She has trained me, guided me, tried to exploit me. I was close to her mind. I saw the way. Not at first, or she may have destroyed me. I could not understand it in the beginning. I do not fully grasp it now. I sense you do. You can use my thoughts."

The goddess hissed with ice. "Yakshini will hurt her, even as She dooms Herself. When Yakshini withdraws, oceans of worlds will cease to have ever brought forth life. The offender will lose souls innumerable, to a deep weakening of her power."

"Not enough," said Kloan.

"No," said Yakshini. "The other gods must come. Through the visions of your mind, they will puncture a passage through her walls. Deliver a poison to end her before she began."

Chapter 57

Where were you when I laid the foundation of the earth? Tell me, if you have understanding. Who laid its cornerstone, when the morning stars sang together and all the heavenly beings shouted for joy? Have you commanded the morning since your days began, and caused the dawn to know its place? Can you bind the chains of the Pleiades or loose the cords of Orion? Have the gates of death been revealed to you? Where is the way to the dwelling of light and where is the place of darkness?

The Book of Job

I felt sick. I fought to conjure images of Ambra as I had known her. Extract scarce, finite memories from the infinite layers of remembrance deposited over a concluded eternity. Moments when we had found her ravaged body on the smuggler's ship. Near death, her psionic potential released random bursts of power from a dying mind. I remembered her in the cell on Dram. Tears streaked her face. Incisions bleeding in her abdomen from their desecration of her flesh. The theft of her progeny, where the doom of the universe to an unending supply of demonic clones was assured.

I recalled her soaring above the chaos of a nascent and naive consciousness as she steered us into the past. How she awakened and called forth the latent human Readers to rescue her planet. For hundreds of years together, memories. Always beside me. She became something beyond a friend—a soul as near to my own as could have been.

This talk of destroying her nauseated me. I could not tolerate another word spoken against her. Whatever she had become at my hands and others, crimes she had committed in their eyes, it was enough for me. My heart remained devoted to her—yes, including to obey her command to kill her. Let it stop there! No more words denigrating her image in my mind. No more bile and hate and acid thrown her way.

Kloan interrupted my raging thoughts and bowed before these spiteful divinities. "Now there's one last thing I must do."

Yakshini rumbled. "First Mother calls. She leads a multitude. It is time all the powers gathered."

"*All* of them, or what numbers you can bring," she added.

"We will call many," said Vighneshvara.

"Not enough of the greater gods." She turned to the plant deity. "You and Aditi are the first awakened, the mother-goddesses. Deepest, oldest, most profound titans of the cosmos. Your children, and the others that became—a number developed into transcendent beings. Terrible and broken, lost in their madness. Yet magnificent. I will summoned them."

The gargantuan butterfly faced toward her, a mountain towering over a small tree. Suspicion stained his speech. "Beginning now, you will follow the Life Giver and accompany her to the nexus. The lies of Ambra within you will not sabotage our plans."

"Let you fail? Why would I do that?" she said, addressing Yakshini. "We *need* Māra and her crazy clan. At the end of time, they have become a formidable host, a terrible army waiting."

Images of the ice world poured from her mind, and before them, the deities were silent for a time.

"At the end of time," echoed Vighneshvara.

"I've been there," Kloan said, pulling her hand out of her robe. A bright transcendence dispelled the gathered gloom. It bathed the gods in a radiation foreign to our universe. "The key is mine. I understand its use."

Yakshini spoke. "This disciple of the enemy is correct, but I detect deviousness within betrayal. It festers in her words and concepts. Ruses color and taint with the manipulations of Ambra Dawn. We dare not break her mind open and thereby risk everything."

Vighneshvara hissed. "It may not be necessary to fully break."

The ball blazed like a supernova. I cowered behind Kloan's shadow. My eyestalks retreated to the safety of my torso cone, my awareness blanked by the emissions bathing us. Before I hid, I heard the scream of the divine moth and glimpsed him cowering within his wings. Yakshini howled in protest.

The glow grew until it became more than light. Radiance molded into sound. It drowned the cries of others, even deities, flattening thoughts and emotions themselves. Through it all, Kloan's voice reverberated.

"Break me if you can, god-fools." A transcendental potency emanated from her words. "But leave me be to finish the task. I will bring back your wayward broods. I will thaw them from the cosmic permafrost."

An overpowering wind rose, circling like a cyclone. I struggled to unsheathe my eyes. I could no longer discern Yakshini or Vighneshvara. The whirlwind created a wall of debris of solid air. Branches, leaves, rocks, and dirt blasted past at supersonic speeds. I clung to Kloan's robes. My feet dug their digits into the remaining soil. I crouched low, my Xixian limbs allowing for my towering frame to bend below her head.

The tornado roared and strengthened, but she stood unmoving.

Her sparse hair whirled about her head, her arm raised, holding a blinding star. The world turned on its side, and the maelstrom of wreckage bent and focused above us. A vortex formed, another wormhole, and the turbulence poured into it. The ground rattled, tore and detached from the supporting branches. We blasted away and plunged headfirst into the chaotic whirlpool.

Chapter 58

I am the Self seated in the hearts of all creatures. I am the beginning, the middle and the end of all beings. With a single fragment of Myself I pervade and support this entire universe.

Bhagavad Gita

"I'm starting to like this thing," said Kloan as she rolled the dimming sphere between her hands. "Whew. That was a close one. Nearly lobotomized back there."

My eyestalks unraveled. We were back on the dead world. The crystal ball reached a nadir, but it cast the entire statued museum of gods in a false moonlight. I strained my eyes. Signs of the dome reappeared, encompassing the breadth of the deities as well.

She strolled to the plinth, the towering forms of Māra and her pack glaring down on us with loathing.

"See, they *know*, Waythrel. It's damned nigh impossible to fool big god-things. But Ambra is imposing and a thousand times more devious. I'm not sure how it would have gone otherwise. They would've found out everything, but without understanding the need and the endpoint. They're so addicted to destroying *her*."

"I am again lost." I was too tired to offer anything else. I yearned for the warmth and love Ambra promised me. Or had I dreamed it? In another delusional trek from one more vanished chronology?

"Well, they wouldn't have let me leave with all their doubts. Worst-case scenario, I was going to go back to report their plans to the devil ball. Ha!" barked Kloan, placing the sphere into the bowl. "As if she hadn't orchestrated every last note! Can you call gods morons?"

Her earnest stare was beguiling. The artifact brightened, and the light distracted her.

"If I wasn't learning how to tap into the power of this thing, scrambled brains. I wouldn't have been able to create a wormhole they couldn't close."

"Ambra orchestrated? Are you on her side now?" Hope was not part of the question. I babbled through exhausted bewilderment.

"Poor Waythrel, you need a long sleep, one without any more nightmares. It's almost done. The last pieces nearly in place. Let's wake these bastards and seal the deal."

One by one, she walked the ring, touching the surfaces of the glass that was not silica, of the ice that was not water. I watched at a distance from the center of the circle beside the sphere. By each obscenity, she paused. Her hand rested on the rippling material. The light from the artifact cast its luminosity toward the appropriate tower.

Striding to the next, the monolithic form behind her would melt. The crystal dissolved like some molten steel and dripped to the frozen ground. The cryogenic tombs thinned enough to release their contents. Odd mixtures of smoke and luster, screams and mutterings, churned within my Reader senses. The awakening of tormented awareness. Those minds matured to their malicious and unfathomable natures. I cowered closer to the shining sphere.

Kloan completed the circumference and stepped back to the center of the god-ring. She watched the titans lumber from their cosmic coma. Horror crept through me as they emerged. Demonic personalities, their caustic essence stirred memories from terrible encounters. I prayed to Ambra that this mad cyborg could control them.

She lifted the diamond orb, and its radiance ripped through the air in front of us. The gods bent and shielded themselves from the awesome incandescence. At this moment, the ground shook. Previous recollections from this lifeless world reversed. Molten globules pushed their way out of the permafrost beneath us. Thousands of tongues of quicksilver, they sprinted toward a focal point. Behind her, they aggregated, self-assembled, and coalesced. The crystal guardian rose. The final fusion of the hulk snapped with a deafening crack. The retort echoed throughout the dome-encased atmosphere.

"Godlings!" cried Kloan. "It's time to reconsider my offer and join me at the singularity!"

The guardian rested immobile. The other titans shifted and strained through the brilliance. At last, the largest stepped forward. I recognized the form from my visions. Beholding the thing with open eyes, I knew these gods had been humbled. In a past so distant from this present as to be unreachable to Kloan's Reader powers, I would have perished to look on her. Now, I survived a weakened remnant brought low by the terrible tides of time. Still, she stood indomitable, defying the light. Smoke and magma boiled within her veins.

Māra.

She stopped in front of Kloan. "You have won, and I curse you for it. But forces greater than I have cursed you far more diabolically than I dream. I take that pleasure in bending my knee to you, insect. I know I help them bring your final destruction."

"Glad to see you, too, Māra," she said, a glint in her eye. "I assume you have these monkeys on their leashes?"

"If I didn't? Do you think they don't feel the foreign flame you brandish? Do they not see the thousand ice-blades of the giant behind you?"

The demon queen reared back and opened her mouth to the black heavens and screamed. Fire belched upward and rained hot coals. The cry was the sound of a million souls raked by a fiend's claws. The dome shattered at its apex. Flickering mats of a force field plunged to the ground and evaporated before our eyes.

"Have we not all perished everlastingly in these shells of stillness?"

Trembling, I continued to gaze skyward and watched the habitat heal itself. Kloan was unfazed.

"Good. They know what's coming."

Māra turned two flaming eye sockets toward us. "Do *you* know what approaches?"

Kloan winked at this nightmare from the deepest pit of the underworld. Her eyebrow arched, mock shock dancing over her features.

"Why in heaven or hell would I want to ruin *that* surprise?"

Chapter 59

I hope that when the world comes to an end, I can breathe a sigh of relief, because there will be so much to look forward to.

Donnie Darko

A deep plane of sand surrounded us. For a moment, I dared to hope we had been transported to Xix. The thought of my homeworld was comforting in the chaos of this displacement.

The sands were wrong, the silica of a different composition, granularity, and color. A brief glance to the sky dispelled all desperate notions of home. The heavens roiled in radiant patterns intricate and hallucinogenic. We were not on any world in any possible space of our universe.

Scanning the horizon, the full truth stunned me. Rising to the deranged firmament was an artificial tower tens of thousands of feet. It ended in a point that drank the clouds swirling about it. At the base of this grand spire was a small habitat. Its buildings I recognized. Within its walls, I had passed decades on a resurrected world.

"Kloan, what is this place? It is not New Earth, and yet it is."

She gazed over the sands, pleased. "She draws us into herself."

"Where are we?"

"Temple City. In the desert itself. Have you forgotten your own final plan? The detachment of the Dish from the Sahara that would travel through the cosmos?"

"I had imagined something different. What has happened to the sky?"

"The fires of creation filtered through the light of uncountable souls."

"More mysticism," I whispered in frustration.

"No, Waythrel. You often confuse reality and metaphor. Right now, my words are literal."

"This," I said, dismissing her impossible sentences, "was to be a starship grounded in rock."

"A god-shard. Part of what happens when you play with divine fire, my Xix."

God-shard. The word sent tremors through me. "Where are the other divinities?"

"Delayed," she said, crouching into a ball and placing the glowing sphere on the sands.

She rose and turned to face me. "Everything's most bent as we approach her—space and time. Expected. So, the short delay I placed between our travels becomes much longer for us here."

"Why have you impeded them?"

She grasped her robes near her neckline. "Because we need to talk, Waythrel. This is it. Time to lay all the cards on the table."

The weariness burdening me deepened. "Kloan, I am not at any table. I have never understood the game. I do not hold a single card."

"Sit with me a minute," she said, gesturing to the grains. "Before all the fools return."

I had no objection to lowering my body to rest on sand. *How I missed it.* We sat, and I tried to prepare myself for more revelations. It was fitting she had saved the most absurd of them for last.

"Remember the riddle in the crypt? 'Where are all the anti-gods?'"

"Of course."

"You asked why it was so important to Ambra that you find that solution?"

"Yes." As always, I did not have a clue where she was going. Anxiety chilled me.

"I told you then I didn't know the answer. Well, I lied." She stared at me, nonchalant in her confession.

"I see. So why did she put so much effort into that test?"

She frowned. "Let's start the explanation with another question. We've been carrying these strange coatings over our bodies for some time. Through perpetual event loops, on world after tree root, adventure after child murder. We don't notice them anymore, but they're *still* here. *Why?* What are the fields, Waythrel? Why are they here?"

She was right. I had adapted to the miraculous things. I ignored them to focus on the disturbing events demanding my full attention. I considered her query, retreating to earlier, unproven theories I had formed.

"Environmental suits. Disguises. Like the sphere. Magical gifts from the gods for mythical heroes to complete their legendary quest."

Kloan dismissed my ideas with a wave of her hand. "No, those functions were secondary." She grasped my digits and gazed into my eye clusters. "Waythrel, have you ever touched me?"

What was she talking about? "Yes, of course. I am touching you now. I have carried you, tended you, grabbed you in frustration, tried to stop you, save you."

"Always *through* the fields."

My mind spun around this point. "You are correct. What are you implying?"

"You've never *touched* me. Your atoms have never been *allowed* to approach mine, to interact."

A strange feeling spread through me, a deep unease. "Why has it not been permitted?"

"It's always hardest to explain something to you Xix when you don't want to know the answer. *Think!* You asked if the use of robots and other machines on the clone colony was to protect the Anti from annihilation. I told you they're unconcerned with it. You asked why, but I never answered you. You asked an important question! Indeed, how could they not be concerned?"

I did not respond. She had seen through me. I did not want to think anymore in this direction.

"You can hide from it all you want, Leaky, but you sense the truth. So I'll cut this short and say it. They didn't fear annihilation from those clones and humans because they *wouldn't hurt them*. Because the cyborgs and handlers, the world itself and everything on it, are made of antimatter as well." Her eyes bored into mine. "The only foreign matter in all those visits was *you*, Waythrel."

"No. It is impossible."

How ridiculous. Of course, it was not possible. How could there be anti-people? Where would they come from? The implications were astounding and devastating.

"They came from dedicated and advanced engineers," she said. "Look at it this way. The Anti had millions of years to face a universe inherently, *existentially* hostile to them. Enough of that and there can be certain breathtaking feats of ingenuity. They discovered relationships between matter and antimatter surpassing all science in the cosmos. All from a unique need to understand this unbalanced, broken symmetry in our reality."

She ran her hands through the sand, scooping grains and letting them rain over her feet.

"Early on, they thought entropy was the ultimate weapon. They'd use it to unmake substance and return balance to reality. Plans changed with the power of the clones over spacetime. They had the tools they needed for something a little more interesting and wild. Cue several monumentally disastrous failures. One threatening the entire existence of their kind. At last, they succeeded."

My mind numbed. Instinct had me moving away from her. I struggled to speak.

"Succeeded at what?"

"Material *inversion*. Consumed horrific amounts of energy, so they had to pick carefully. Choose the most potent tools. A complete flip of the matter of your type into its opposite."

"Matter of my type."

"Yes," said Kloan, her green eyes like lasers burning into my cowering eyestalks. "*Your* type. Because once they had perfected the process, they created millions of human anti-people. No different in their physiology and chemistry than their inverses. Of course, they didn't stop there. They *cloned* from them. Clones from specific inverted stock. Gave birth to tiny little anti-Ambra Dawns."

She grinned. "Like me."

Chapter 60

Is man merely a mistake of God's?
Or God merely a mistake of man?

Friedrich Nietzsche

Faint gusts stirred the sands while my mind juggled a pack of impossibilities.

We stood on a *god-shard* ripped from the heart of a world and suspended at the root of time, dangled over a cauldron of energy and dragon fire that was the nativity of our reality. Revelations spilled from a cyborg child, a genetic duplication of my dearest friend, who happened to be the savior or damnation of the universe.

Opinions differed.

At this moment, I struggled to grasp that my messianic mimic was made of antimatter.

"So the fields—" I stuttered, lurching to a stop as my mind sputtered.

"Prevent us from annihilating each other. Detonating like an angry hornet's nest of thermonuclear warheads."

"You are composed of antimatter."

"Well, what's anti and what isn't is sort of relative, don't you think?" she chirped. "But I'll give it to your kind. You own this cosmos, and we're the losing minority. So I'll be *anti*. For now. Until we rebalance, because that's at the root what this is about."

"Balancing substance and its inverse?"

"Among other things."

I stood, my mind racing. "If what you say is true about yourself and your...*type*...if you can restore particle balance, it is a disaster to do it!"

"We *can* do it—you, me, and Ambra, with a little help from our god friends."

My arms windmilled. "Even if we *can*, it is madness. It would mean total material annihilation!" I paused, my imagination spinning wild scenarios to ground sanity in this tale. "Unless you intend to do this after a substantial expansion in the universe? To segregate matter and antimatter across vast distances, render them innocuous?"

"Nope! See the sky? That's Big Bang fireworks. We've come to the beginning, and we're going to break the asymmetry at the alpha point."

"To what purpose? You will destroy the cosmos."

"Yes!" she cried to the frothing firmament, raising her hands into the air. She lowered her arms, her face turning somber. "Well, no, actually. There are more things in heaven and beyond it, Waythrel, than are dreamt of in your particle physics."

"I will not participate in such madness."

She clucked like an annoyed mother hen. "Listen. Simplistically, matter and antimatter annihilate and make a big bunch of energy. Scrambles the structure of stuff, all you love and want to preserve in the universe. But what of gravity, Xix? What of space and time? More to the point, what of the field of sentience interwoven with them? Augmented to complexities unfathomable in these gods?"

"What does this have to do with particle annihilation?"

"What do you think anti-thoughts are like?"

The question stopped my mind cold. "I do not know. The chemistry of antimatter, its biology, neurobiology, they should be the same as ours."

"Should? You doubt. Why?"

The answer dragged itself from sleep. "Because chemistry is different from gravity. Distinct forces. Divergent physics."

"Yes, and?"

"And I do not know how particles compare to their inverses when considering sentient fields."

Kloan stood and slapped my arms, dust clouding the improbable air. "Exactly. You're right to be unsure. While they're indistinguishable at most levels, they *diverge* in remarkable states. Think about classical and quantum mechanics or relativity. *Extreme conditions.* Super small. Ultra-fast. You need *new* laws of nature."

She pointed to the sands. "Inside this time-shard, entombed in a warped, murdered spacetime, is a god-thing. An intelligence of power and complexity we'll never begin to understand in science or intuition. How extreme do you think that is?"

She led me forward like a nymph. "Radical," I said.

"It turns out minds and their inverses diverge at those levels. *So think!* While the divinities grew, their sentience became more biased along a particular divergence. Our universe is dominated by one type of mentality. The broken symmetry in matter gave birth to an acute asymmetry in *consciousness.* So, where *are* the anti-gods, Waythrel? Do you see why this is so important?"

"Do we need the other types of cognition?"

Kloan spread her arms wide. "Does the cosmos look like it's particularly sane?"

"How could I judge?" This I meant with the deepest sincerity.

Her hands clasped themselves together at her breast. "How can *you* judge?" She hugged me, resting her intubated head on my torso. "Oh, Waythrel. This is going to be a rough day. Look. We've let our universe destroy half of what it could be. In atoms and in conscious-ness. We can't understand what it might be if we were to restore balance. Dare we allow this mental genocide—what the Anti call the *nousicide*—to continue?"

The idea *my type* of substance exterminated entire cosmic ecosys-tems of thought disoriented me. Yet, in some strange sense, I felt it. A monolithic conformity in the strangeness of mind and matter pummeled me in this quest. Kloan's wild, incomprehensible words rang through my memories.

Macrocosms where the laws of physics are weird. Where mathe-matics doesn't add up. Where logic is illogical.

"You said I would never understand you, and this was impor-tant," I said.

"Yes. So you see it."

"No, Kloan, I do not. I still cannot comprehend how annihi-lating the universe saves your kind of mentality. Everything will be destroyed, nonexistent anti-gods included."

She shook her head and took my hands again. "Waythrel, it's more than particles, remember? At the extremes, the minds are differ-ent. *Mentalities diverge!* They don't annihilate—they intertwine, synergize. They couple and engender. They *create!*"

"We're going to grind up all the matter in the cosmos into energy, destroy every last world and galaxy and god. Including Ambra. Yet some manner of grand mental something is going to be born?"

"Yes!" she said, dancing in a circle like some psychotic nature spirit.

I gazed to the boiling heavens. At any moment, a thousand deities would descend. I tried to focus, to center myself, to find a single, practical thing I could grasp in all this.

"Kloan, I am here because I love her."

She skipped to me, beaming. Her green eyes gleamed, her teeth bright in the hideous illumination.

I touched her violated head with my digits. "And I am here because I love you, too, although if I cannot fathom you. I do not have anything more to add. It is all beyond me. Tell me why, after all this, you both need me here? What do you want with me?"

Her smile vanished. She set her jaw. "The gods come to tear open the universe and reveal Ambra. When the moment comes to destroy her, you will pass sentence, Waythrel. You're the chosen one."

I stepped backward, away from the words I was hearing, dealt a cataclysmic blow.

Kloan ignored me, declaring my doom in some resonant, prophetic voice. "She has selected you to be the final judge of our cosmos. And I agree with her."

Chapter 61

It is enough to have been created, to have embodied for a moment the infinite and tumultuously creative spirit. It is infinitely more than enough to have been used, to have been the rough sketch for some perfected creation. Looking into the future, I saw without sorrow, rather with quiet interest, my own decline and fall.

Olaf Stapledon

"You are not serious."

Of every absurdity I had heard from her mouth, proclaiming Waythrel of Xix the judge of all the universe was without doubt the most ludicrous of them all.

"Here's how it's going to work," said Kloan, speaking past me. "Remember when I said I had to become everything Ambra was not? Her inverse in all things? Now you can understand. Physically, I am close to her opposite. A pile of cloned antimatter to annihilate her. Boom!"

She slapped her hands together, startling me.

"More important is my mental superstructure. Her antipode in the realm of sentience. As an anti-clone, I'm much of the way there already. I had to perfect the distinctions. Deepen, strengthen our differences by getting to know her beyond her talking god-ball. Hence, our adventures, of which you were a critical element."

"I do not want explanations. I cannot do this thing, Kloan. Even if it were possible, I will not pronounce judgment on an entire reality."

She continued. "She is the primordial fault. The fatal flaw. The imperfection seeding a time-transcending divinity. It stained the continuum through her unique persona, a systematic bias. She is wrong in and of herself and also askew because she is a construct of the dominant form of matter."

She removed her robes, her naked body gleaming with sweat in the desert heat. She walked past me to the bright sphere, stopping beside it.

"I am the surgical knife to remove her from the god-particle. When I collide with her, time and space will dive into themselves as never seen. We will enter the singularity of the Origin. We will anni-hilate each other there, the process altering everything from genesis to apocalypse. We'll recombine to create something far greater, completely *other*. A phenomenon unknowable to us in this distorted universe." Tears dripped from her eyes as she gazed at me. "It will be your choice whether to send me to this end."

"Kloan, no. *Stop!* I refuse!" My mind panicked.

"Waythrel, there are no more outs. The gods are psychotic. The continuum is sick with a mental plague. You've seen its dying gasps in the dead ice and darkness. We need to act."

"My soul is a nymph. I am only a Xix. Waythrel. Incapable of condemning a single consciousness. I cannot judge a cosmos."

She placed her hands on her bony hips. "Developmental biology, Leaky. There are decision points affecting the large-scale nature of an organism. Left-right asymmetry, top-bottom polarity, immunolog-ical reactivity. Malignancy. Junctions exist involving single tissues, including individual cells or the state of one protein in the cytoplasm. Reductionist events reverberate through the anatomical hierarchy to induce macroscopic ends."

Sonic booms shattered the relative quiet of the desert. I trembled in deep dread as a thousand blazing meteors exploded miles above us.

Kloan followed their trajectory toward the ground without interrupting her lecture.

"You've been chosen to select the direction of this universe. It's Ambra's will. Use the sphere. Push me forward in the null field that comes. Annihilate us both and engender something truly transcendental!" She frowned. "Or fail to—from choice or inaction. The vectors collapse on themselves. The gods continue their futile cosmic wars. Potential forever frozen in a development that never transcends this reality. Assure the everlasting winter."

Beyond my worst nightmares, the horror rooted me to the sand, straight like a beam. Eyestalks coiled in a braid. Arms wrapped as a shroud around my torso. I trembled as deities plummeted toward us, harbingers of catastrophe. Their fire and smoke heightened the aura of final cataclysm paralyzing my thoughts.

I could find no words to speak, not even of protest or anger. I could see no pathway out of this entangled causality caging my fate. Instead, I saw the two horns of a dilemma. The human mythic creature charging, the spearpoints sharp and deep. On one or the other I would impale myself.

"It's time," she said. "The circus is in town. Soon we dig, my travel mate. Take a last savage journey together to the end and beginning of all things nothing'ed."

The tips of my stalks turned eighteen eyes in circumference. Mesmerized, I gawked. One flaming comet after another struck the desert. Each impact induced a shockwave of sand and rush of air, cratering the surface. An incongruity of forms slammed like marbled towers onto the god-shard, unshaken and mighty, divinities so vast the paltry space dared not hold them.

Yakshini unfurled roots hundreds of miles across the terrain. Bark coated the sands like a carpet. Aditi spilled like liquid soot to form first a dry lake, morphing to sphere resembling a caged gas giant. Elegant Vighneshvara floated with his eye-wings of light. Māra and her crew of hellions assaulted the ground simply by touching it. Thousands of others. Some greater, some lesser, all forces of physicality and mentality overwhelming me.

They formed a transcendental ring of divinities. At the center, Kloan radiated like some impossible ingot in the deepest furnace. Transfigured, an alien potency coursed through her cells. Her skin burned star-bright and blinding, unbearable. She raised her arms. A voice resounded across the shard. A mystical power imbued her once-childlike tones.

"This is the nexus. Here is the nucleus of all to be unmade. Feel her throb beneath. Taste her living blood and tissue. Deconstruct the labyrinth of minds and fortifications between us."

The resplendent shape spun in a circle. The shadows shone with a fantastical splendor.

"We turn downward, burrow as sharpened augers into the finite flesh of this fiend. You know your task. Open a shaft deep to the core. I will step into this abyss and fall, carrying the seed of her destruction."

They required no war speech. The deities dug. Nightmarish transformations of form into function manifest. They clothed themselves in hellish shapes. Serrated, bladed bodies. Hammering instrumentation. Possessed of hardness and sharpness little about matter and far more about soul. Abominations sliced through the surface and underlying matrix. The sounds were not of metal on stone or steel on flesh. The cause was not vibrational or from the impact of the debris flung into the skies.

No. What I heard over everything else blocked out the material events. The anguished wails of souls torn apart, of minds ripped to madness. What I saw was the desecration of inconceivable grace and beauty. The defilement of the pure and inviolable.

I witnessed the exalted, transcendent glory we called the Orb broken. Its many-splendored passageways of light extinguished. Its visage of love and empathy marred and mutilated.

The screams engulfed me. These god-fiends rent and shattered all I had ever worshipped and adored. The cries buffeted me, hurled me prone, and drowned me in lunacy and sorrow.

In a pit of darkness, wailing, gnashing of teeth and claws pummeled my awareness. Until at last, in the center of the deepest nothingness, the sole scream left in my mind was my own.

Chapter 62

Perhaps our role on this planet is not to worship God—but to create Him.

Arthur C. Clarke

My scream perished in vain, abandoned by existence itself. The cosmos. The gods in their terrible grandeur. The shard of New Earth. The tattered remnants of the Orb—all vanished.

I floated in a darkness empty of a lack of light. A true unexistence indescribable by positive or negative, by presence or absence. In the reality I knew, even the vacuum teemed with a heavy broth of virtual particle pairs.

Not so here. No terms or thoughts are available for the existentially void, the authentically vacant. The experience was a psychosis with the form of Kloan anchoring my awareness.

Look down the shaft into the heart of divinity, came her words.

So I gazed as the nothingness heaved. Outside our bubble of emptiness, the cosmos warped and curved. Space and time were strained, perverted to a tortured malformation. At the deepest pit of this hellhole was a simple room containing a slab of machinery and living tissue. A human girl, sliced open and embedded in circuitry for the span of a universe. Undying and unassuaged in her agony.

Ambra smiled from below. Her green eyes were broad and inviting. Waveforms of purpose and affection rocking us on a sea of distraught lucidity.

Make the choice, came the thoughts of my dearest friend.

The anti-cyborg palmed the dazzling sphere in luminous hands. She held it beside me.

Time to decide, Waythrel.

A million journeys of nothing. Deaths and lives and pain and love and madnesses. A tsunami of experience casting me before it like unregarded debris. An eon of powerlessness and confusion. After all this, *I* was to seal the ultimate fate of our reality. I had no time for last words with Ambra or Kloan. I had no chance to examine her mutilated flesh and consider my own culpability, to judge my own life and choices.

I was too busy judging a universe.

I tried to parse the long and cryptic explanations, the deranged prophecies of the god-girl and her clone. I struggled to understand this terrible synergy of structure and evolution, the climb toward divine consciousness, and how it went awry. I failed to grasp how I could reboot reality by hurling an antimatter mimic of my friend into this deity-pit to annihilate her inverse cyborg. Incompatible thoughts spun incongruously in my mind and failed to harmonize.

I abandoned the effort. It surpassed me. Instead, I held the eyes of Kloan. I witnessed a terrified determination eliciting waves of empathy. I wanted to comfort this child who displayed such courage and commitment to her beliefs, despite those convictions harboring insanity indescribable.

I gazed down the deep shaft, the contortions of spacetime acting as a lens. They brought the face of Ambra Dawn alongside her mirrored double. Eyes and anti-eyes of green. Eyes in agony and filled with love. Eyes of beings sacrificing beyond the capability of spirits to assimilate. Paired souls asking me to use each to destroy the other to realize a hypothesized and incomprehensible healing of a broken continuum.

It was a reprisal of my choices on the burning colony world when I carried Kloan through the gate. This time, the stakes were infinitely higher. Instead of saving her from a certain death on a dying planet, I was to cast her to destruction. In this one decision I would murder them together and, they both claimed, consume an entire cosmos.

Until all is lost, nothing is found.

For the first time, I appreciated the full import of the statement. I placed the digits of my arms on the sphere, touching Kloan's fingers. The brightness intensified, yet angled backward through the child. It extended down the shaft and into the heart of the darkness below. It washed the medical facility housing Ambra in a hideous, pure light of a distinct reality.

I don't have any reasons, my friends. I don't want to lose you. All I have is my love and my trust in you. I will give you what you ask for, although it is beyond my understanding.

Kloan smiled, tears in her eyes. *Seems that this is our last dance together, Xix.*

I pushed. Thrusting my arms forward with all my strength, I shoved the sphere and cyborg away from me. My inconsequential motion propelled me backward relative to the strange gravity lens below.

She accelerated with an unstoppable force I ascribed to the artifact. Collecting frightening momentum, her form and the small star sped down the tunnel. The distance deepened, unbridgeable, her approach to last an eternity.

The alien light of the globe turned from white to a burgundy. The sack of emptiness ripped and dissolved. It revealed the inner layers of hell itself. Sights impossible to convey with any accuracy.

The massacred forms of minds and machines. Bodies of Readers eternal, now dead. The blood-soaked claws and mouths of gods dripping.

Celestials clung to the sides of an inconceivable breach in space-time like bats to a cavern wall. They scrambled, fleeing from the core, their cries wild and horrific. Backward I floated, yet the deities slid oppositely, clawing at the shriveling skin of a universe. An irresistible chain clasped them, dragging divinities deeper into the dying Orb's well.

The wailing death notes of innumerable Orb minds shattered my awareness. Countless more from the doomed god-things pierced me as they lost their grasp. One by one, they plummeted into the pit of mutating incandescence. Endlessly they fell. The lesser gods, Vighneshvara with his wings shredded and useless. Māra eviscerated and dissolving while torn apart by gravitational tides. Aditi spilling in submission. Yakshini splaying forth ten million roots like grappling hooks, landing punctures in spacetime, small breaches in the walls of the chasm, holding on longest until every branch snapped. At last, she slipped, screeching, into the abyss devouring them all.

I continued to drift backward, a shell of nothingness forming around me once again. The singularity sucked the tempestuous soup of creation. The universe fell into the pit with the gods. I could see each one as in slow motion. They tumbled through molasses. The lens warped and rendered the entire blender undecipherable.

An impossible emanation, divine and unmaking, erupted from the chaos. It rushed toward me. The closer it came, the faster it neared, my glacial movements soon to be overtaken. I had no illusions about what would happen when I met that ultimate radiance.

I suffered no anxiety, no feelings of panic or fear, and no thoughts for my continued existence. Acceptance and a weariness rendered all else secondary. I was ready for rest. I was more than ready for an end.

I opened my arms and eyestalks to the onrushing brilliance. As it blinded me, burned me, and tore my fragile flesh apart, I encountered its mind. A transcendent personality burst through my evaporating consciousness. For one brief instant I could not keep, I understood what Kloan and Ambra had been trying to explain.

I wrapped my dissolving limbs around the light in a final, loving embrace.

I AM

Epilogue

*I had glimpsed, in the very eye of that splendor, strange vistas of being;
as though in the depths of the hypercosmical past and the hypercosmical future also, yet coexistent in eternity, lay cosmos beyond cosmos.*

Olaf Stapledon

I was called Waythrel of Xix, but I no longer know what I am or
what I should be named.

Gazing over this endless desert, such trivialities cease to
hold consequence. Dune crests rise to the horizon, and a reddened
star sets the landscape to fire as it plunges into a sea of sand.

I am happy in this place, freed of a need for the fading memories
of a home I knew as Xix. The cosmic conflicts and metaphysics
interest me in passing. Here on this unknown world, in an unnamed
universe, I am comfortable. I am satisfied. I know a peace unlike any I
can recall. I am ready to say goodbye to you.

You have questions, I realize. You want to know "what
happened" to your cosmos. To Ambra and Kloan. To the legions of

broken gods. To the divine plan over which some unfortunate being I remember to be myself adjudicated.

I cannot blame you. After all you have come through with me, it is right I give you a response.

My honest, heartfelt answer to these queries is that I do not know.

This does not mean I do not possess memories, or rather fantastic hallucinations still dancing in my deepest dreams. Visions no doubt warped and xixomorphized into digestible, cognitive clumps compatible with my sanity and self-analysis. Behold the masticated nuggets I can offer you. I will try to capture them within the writing system of this Earth language. However vain, I do feel I owe you this effort.

You should never imagine they are something like "truth." Or "untruth." To lie requires knowledge of what *is* true, and I am lacking any such sense. What you have instead, let me state, is *myth*, cast from the furnace of the delusions of Once Waythrel of Xix. I have nothing more to give.

And so, what happened?

I died in our unmade cosmos. Every molecule in my body split apart. The atoms broken asunder into constituent quarks and strings. The dissolution downward through an infinity of ever-shrinking and changing microconstituents.

Concurrently, impossibly, like some pile of organic bricks, I was reassembled into something preeminent. What this thing was, I cannot say. It was greater than the collective spirits, the petty divines of our fractured continuum, and the Orbs. It surpassed these elevated entities like the deities transcended the individual minds comprising them. I do not know what this entity was any more than one mind of a group could know the whole. The gods themselves could not have understood it.

You might consider it God. It was a single Being—a unified, undivided, yet uncountable diversity where the mathematics of summation was one. It strode the heavens and beyond as only the Almighty could do. You may wish to call it God.

I will not. I refuse because I glimpsed through its eyes. What I saw was humbling—certainly for myself, as has been every step of my journey. However, I mean humbling for the god-thing.

Through its gaze, I did not condescend from some ultimate vantage point, a Maker ruling over its creation. Instead, my focused exploration was upward, further, into a resplendent infinity of universes carpeting a greater heaven. In this place, God was not even a god, but one particle in a transcosmic assembly. A transcendent-maker-divine-particle, encompassing everything of our imaginings of religion and science. Yet nothing of the infinitely preeminent possibilities outside and remote.

I drowned in an ocean of god-atoms. A sea of creations as different from each other as a collection of elementary particles. Immeasurably more so. At this level of synthesis, diversity increased. My awareness could not comprehend the inexhaustible well of properties characterizing any given cosmos. Kloan had warned me, and I laughed in the midst of soul-shattering awe. In most of the realities at this hypercosmological strata, two plus two was anything but four.

If what I had described were the full story, it would be astonishing beyond measure. But the wonders only began with these vistas. In the same way protons, neutrons, and electrons are not the complete narrative of matter, so the infinity of god-particles did not preside over their dominion in isolation.

Subject to unknown properties of the Ultimate, they were driven to transcosmological physics, chemistry, analogs of biology, neurobiology, and more that were nothing at all like those paltry conceptions. I dreamed in my delirium that uncountable elements following innumerable and indecipherable rules associated, combined, interacted, and created, yet higher order agglomerations eclipsing the impossible syntheses I had witnessed to this point.

On and above, surpassing and superior, the structures assembled. In the cognitive fever possessing me, it became more than what my experience could assimilate. Like Icarus, I was burned to devastation by the light of this geometric expansion of synergy.

In the final moments of this meditation, the endless, divine ladder shattered. My concentration broke. I dropped into deep darkness.

I woke here, in the sands of a warm and habitable world. Resurrected and recreated. I opened my eyes, not knowing what I was or how I could be. Most remarkable of all, when I woke, I was not alone.

It is because of this last fact that I must leave you now and end this wondrous speculation. The hour is late. The colder night airs will soon arrive, and I will retreat to the warmth and protection of the oasis behind me.

I gaze down at the infant in my arms. At three months, her thick, scarlet hair is still short and spiky. Her skin is a luminous white, painted from the captured light of the planet's moon. Any moment, she will awaken, hungry. Her emerald eyes will pierce my clusters with the unique survival demands of the human nymph-form. Once again, I will shelter beside the miraculous plants oozing milk and honey.

I stride across the sands, savoring the flow of silica between my digits. My emotions rise at a silhouette before me in the growing darkness. The star has set and its radiance faded, but the oasis provides its own glow with a plethora of bioluminescence. It catalyzes a gleam in the phosphorescent patterns on the shadow alongside the garden's edge.

"Synphel." I use one of my free arms to caress my mate's eyestalks.

"You are late, Waythrel. He is awake."

I glance down to her lower limbs. Cradled in one of them as by a hammock, a small bundle coos. I brush the thick black hair out of his eyes while he sucks on his thumb.

"Just in time, you mean. Ambra is also waking."

The redheaded baby twists and begins to complain. I bring the two of them close together. The boy taps on Ambra's arm, and she stops crying.

A warm joy flows outward from Synphel. "Nitin can always soothe her."

"Yes," I say, feeling the wind stir. Its caress is the whisper of a distant friend. "I still think of Kloan."

"It is natural."

"Do you suppose she exists?"

"We know little, and our fulfillment is here. Perhaps her role lies elsewhere in this new creation, in a separate space with a purpose for her own completion."

"I hope so. She, too, is a daughter of time."

I peer into the oasis entrance. A soaring arch of trees and vines serves as a portal in an otherwise impenetrable fence of towering plants. I stroke Synphel's arm and turn toward the glow within.

"Come, let us go inside. It is time."

Gratitude is given for this worship which You are pleased to accept from our hands, even though You are surrounded by Angels: six-armed, many-eyed, singing the victory hymn, "Holy, holy, holy Queen of Hosts, who was and who is and who is to come! Hosanna in the highest."

from the Dawnist Anaphora

Afterward: Trilogy

When I began this series (then only conceived as a single novel), I wanted to write a "superheroine" book for my (then) middle school-aged daughters—the story of a "girl that saves the universe." What began as something with a strong YA flavor in the initial drafts, quickly turned darker. In addition, the ideas percolating in the first novel, *Reader*, cried out for a follow-up. Hence, *Writer* and *Maker* were conceived.

With this trilogy, I was interested in exploring certain themes and ideas from a variety of science fiction authors and modern cosmology, trying to find my own "mythology" to harmonize some of the disparate conceptions of reality percolating through human discourse. Ideas surrounding the subjectivity and limitations of human perception and understanding played important roles, as did ideas of causality, time, superstructure, divinity, and infinity.

I always wanted to write a book that "broke the fourth wall" in a significant manner and *Reader* was my chance to try. There has been a decidedly mixed reaction as to how well that worked, but it was a lot of fun in the making.

Whereas *Reader* was written very organically (and metamorphosed from a YA novel to something quite different), and *Writer* written following a detailed outline, *Maker* was a strange synthesis of the two. A convoluted flowchart of the various time loops that characterize the first half of the novel was supplanted by a completely unplanned stream-of-consciousness climax that led to a fixed narrative point: the resolution to the wild story of Ambra Dawn that was envisioned several years before when I completed the final draft of *Reader*.

It was a risk to change the first person voice from Ambra Dawn in *Reader* to her lover, Nitin Ratava, in *Writer*. Indeed, both this change in perspective and the very different structure to the novel and character interactions, have put a number of readers off. However, it also has been some readers' favorite novel of the three. Beyond subjectivity, there was a practical consideration of Ambra's powers and painting myself into an artistic corner with that, as well as a key element of the plot that called for a different perspective.

With *Maker*, again I changed the narrator for the novel, in this case the story told through the voice of the alien Waythrel of Xix. A further challenge to myself and the reader is the ever recession of Ambra Dawn in the story. Waythrel's near constant companion in the novel is instead the enigmatic Kloan, a biological replica of Ambra Dawn, modified by the biomedicine and cybernetics of the dark Anti, who kidnapped the alien in *Writer* and leads her on a harrowing and confusing cosmic quest. Ambra returns in strange and punctuated events in the novel, in multiple different forms from infant to cosmic goddess. But there are few extended engagements with the Daughter of Time as in the previous books.

By far the most esoteric of the three, *Maker* cannot help but ultimately fail, just as overall the series must, as would any effort to produce an artistic impression of ultimate reality. But I didn't seek to succeed in the impossible, but rather to wade into the chaotic paradox of mind, matter, and metaphysics in the context of an engaging narrative. For those who require coherence, realism, techno-science fiction, or a linear narrative, among other things, the trilogy has been at best a frustrating read. And that's okay. It was meant to be in some ways. That others have found it also inspiring and moving, thought-provoking and unique, is a success with profound meaning for me.

My creative activities have certainly tested the patience of many in my small circle of life. While such efforts are not necessarily to the taste of everyone, for those who have shown me grace and support, my heartfelt thanks are due and I gladly give it.

I am also touched by the readers and reviewers who have expressed such affection for one (and sometimes several!) of the novels of this trilogy—especially those who have responded with feelings and ideas that reflect in some deep way those elements within myself that engendered this series.

This tale was bigger than any one character, perspective, or voice; and while part of the divergence between novels was intentional to shake both the writer and the reader out of their comfort zone, the larger truth is that the voices of the characters came and spoke to me in the manner recorded, and I simply wrote down what they said.

It has been difficult to leave Ambra, Nitin, Waythrel, Kloan, and their unique universe behind. They occupied my thoughts for a decade, sharing with me their stories and impressing their experiences deeply within me. I already miss them—Kloan, perhaps, most of all.

I hope that in some other reality, their memory is eternal, and we might meet again.

Erec Stebbins

Acknowledgments

Love is not a reaction. If I love you because you love me, that is mere trade, a thing to be bought in the market.

Jiddu Krishnamurti

I would first like to thank Ambra, Nitin, and Waythrel, without whom these novels would not have existed. That they chose me as the writer to tell their impossible story is humbling and touching. I have done my best to tell it right, but know that I have failed in the ways they convey in the text. Forgive my limitations, my dear friends, and I hope we meet again outside my head.

Thanks to those who supported the writing of the books during my self-publishing years. I had faint hope this odd narrative would interest many, and the failure of my first published thriller to sell convinced me (and publishers) that I was not marketable. During those years it was a struggle to put down the words that compose this trilogy. My deepest gratitude to those who instead provided encouragement.

And lastly, for those who are not with me, your love, your dreams, and your spirit will always be. If not in this life, or this world, perhaps in others, amongst other stars and innumerable galaxies, in universes uncounted and reborn.

Forever I remain, a stargazer.

Erec Stebbins, December 2025

About the Author

Erec Stebbins is a biomedical researcher who writes thrillers and science fiction. He was born in the Midwest, his mother a clinical psychologist and his father a professor of Romance languages. His father's specialty is the source of the unusual spelling of his middle name, taken from knight in an Arthurian romance: *Érec et Énide*.

Erec Stebbins, 2022

He has pursued diverse interests over the course of his life, including science, music, drama, and writing. His academic path focused on science, and he received a degree in physics from Oberlin College in 1992, and a PhD in biochemistry from Cornell University in 1999. He has worked for several decades studying the structure of biological macromolecules involved in disease.

9 781942 360667